# Forbidden Hearts

A Forbidden Love Romance Collection

Alison Reid

Forbidden Hearts - A Forbidden Love Romance Collection

by Alison Reid



ISBN: 978-1-7644837-4-2

First edition

Independently published

Introduction to...

# Forbidden Hearts

## A Forbidden Love Romance Collection

**Secrets. Desire. Forbidden love.**

Welcome to **Forbidden Hearts**—a collection of emotionally charged romances where attraction defies the rules, and love comes with a price. From glittering holiday soirées to high-stakes family dramas and secret pregnancies, these stories follow men and women whose hearts refuse to obey reason.

Each novel in this collection is a complete standalone romance, written in the spirit of classic Mills & Boon with a modern edge. You'll find alpha heroes, slow-burning tension, enemies-to-lovers sparks, and situations where love feels impossible—but irresistible.

Inside these pages, passion collides with secrets, loyalties are tested, and hearts are challenged to choose love against the odds. There is no cheating, and every story delivers a guaranteed happily-ever-after.

Whether you're discovering these characters for the first time or returning to favourite heroines and heroes, **Forbidden Hearts** invites you to immerse yourself in a binge-worthy collection where temptation is irresistible, and love refuses to stay forbidden.

Enjoy the journey.

# Table of Contents

# New Year's Eve Kiss

## Alison Reid

A complete standalone romance

Previously published individually

# Chapter One

At twenty-six, Emily Sinclair carried herself with a quiet, unspoken grace that drew attention without her ever seeking it. Her beauty was the kind that revealed itself slowly—subtle, refined, all the more striking because she never tried to showcase it. Delicate features framed by honey-brown hair that fell in soft, effortless waves down her back gave her an air of classic elegance. And her eyes—deep, shimmering blue— were soft with warmth yet shadowed by an introspective depth that hinted at stories she rarely voiced.

When she spoke, her voice was gentle and measured, touched by a natural shyness that made her words feel achingly sincere. Compliments tended to bring a pink flush to her cheeks, and she'd lower her gaze, tucking a strand of hair behind her ear—a modest gesture that only magnified her quiet charm. Her presence was like a calm breeze on a warm day: soothing, unassuming, yet impossible to dismiss.

Emily had inherited a substantial fortune after her mother's tragic death in a car accident when she was just a child. The money was life-changing by any measure, but it had never become the axis of her identity. To Emily, wealth was a utility, not a destination—a way to build a secure life and support the few causes that mattered to her. She found far more satisfaction in the grounded simplicity of hard work, of purpose, of doing things that felt meaningful.

Yet her inheritance was a shadow she could never quite shake. It distorted people's intentions. It made friendships complicated. It made love nearly impossible. Far too often, others saw the heiress before they saw Emily—the thoughtful, yearning woman behind the veneer of privilege. And so, she lived with a quiet ache, wondering if she would ever find someone who loved her for the woman she was, not the wealth she owned.

With a steady hand, she slid the keycard into the penthouse lock. The light blinked red once—then green. A soft beep. A click. The door drifted open.

She stepped inside, her heels tapping lightly against polished timber floors. The suite was dark, illuminated only by the spill of city lights through the towering glass windows. Sydney glittered below—New Year's Eve crowds surging, fireworks warming the horizon—but the silence inside felt cavernous.

"William?" she called softly, her voice swallowed by the stillness. No reply.

Downstairs, the party had been a haze of champagne, laughter, and clinking glasses. She'd been smiling, engaged in a lively conversation with the hostess, when she realised William had slipped away. Vanished without a word. Typical. The evening had begun with promise—a chance to represent her father's firm, to enjoy the celebratory energy of the night—but her date's disappearance had already soured the festivities, leaving her wandering the ballroom with a mix of frustration and rising anxiety.

The penthouse itself was the crown of the hotel—sleek, modern, perched high above the harbour with a panoramic view that felt almost unreal. The lounge, bathed in natural light by day, now glowed faintly from the cityscape beyond. Clean lines, bold art, and plush furniture created a perfect blend of comfort and sophistication. The hardwood floors gleamed, the air faintly scented with eucalyptus from the suite's diffuser.

On either side of the lounge, private suites branched off—two spacious bedrooms, each a sanctuary. William's room faced the pulsating skyline; hers overlooked the serene waters of the harbour, where reflections shimmered in gentle waves. Marble ensuites, deep soaking tubs, rainfall showers—luxury at every turn, though none of it mattered in this moment.

Emily felt her irritation shift into something tighter, sharper. She walked further in, her pulse quickening. Perhaps he was lounging on the sofa. Or standing by the windows with a drink, watching the crowds below. But the room was undisturbed—the cushions still perfectly aligned, the bar untouched, the air heavy with stillness.

Her breath caught as she reached for the handle of his bedroom door. She pushed, slowly, gently, bracing herself against a growing sense of dread.

The door opened.

And her world stilled.

William was on the bed—completely naked—with a woman straddling him. They were mid-movement, her breathy moan snapping into silence as both froze at the sight of Emily in the doorway.

"Emily!" William shoved the woman aside and lurched upright, scrambling for the sheet. "This—this isn't—" He was babbling, frantic, entirely exposed.

Emily turned her face away, teeth clenched, bile rising in her throat. She heard him step toward her, feet padding across the carpet.

"Please, Emily, wait—"

She lifted her hand, stepping back. "Stop. Don't come near me." Her voice was steady, cool, almost eerily calm. "Get your things and leave."

"Emily, I'm sorry. It didn't mean anything," he said desperately, grabbing for discarded clothes.

Her gaze drifted, unbidden, to the woman curled awkwardly on the bed, hastily clutching a sheet around herself. Only moments ago, William had been inside her. The humiliation burned hot in Emily's chest, but beneath it was something unexpected—relief.

She had been planning to break up with him after New Year's anyway. The spark had long faded, replaced by boredom, annoyance, and the dawning realisation that he was more interested in her bank account than in her heart. She hadn't even wanted him at the event tonight. But when her father suggested she bring him—for appearances—she hadn't had the energy to argue.

This, at least, made things simple.

Emily pivoted on her heel and walked out of the room, out of the penthouse, and into the cool corridor beyond. Her heart pounded, but her steps were steady. Certain. Free.

For the first time that night, she felt oddly, beautifully clear.


In the elevator, Emily took a long, steadying breath and shook her head sharply, as if the motion could fling off the last remnants of humiliation clinging to her. No. She wasn't going to dwell on what she'd seen upstairs. It was finished—dead, buried, done. In her mind, the door had slammed shut on William long before she'd actually walked out of that suite.

She still had a couple of hours before the party wound down, and she refused to spend them sulking. She was twenty-six, attractive, and—when she allowed herself to be—confident. Surely, she could find someone charming to talk to. Someone to dance with. Someone who didn't see dollar signs when they looked at her.

Tonight, she decided, she would shed her usual shyness like an old skin and see where the night carried her. No expectations. No fears. No self-imposed boundaries. She'd never see these people again anyway. *Why not be bold? Why not be reckless? Why not, for once, have a little fun?*

The elevator doors slid open, spilling light and sound into the confined space. The ballroom stretched before her—alive with sparkling gowns, tuxedos, and the effervescent glow of the approaching New Year. Music thrummed through the air, a sultry rhythm that vibrated in her chest. Laughter rose and swirled among the glittering chandeliers.

Emily stepped out, her heels clicking with more purpose than she felt. But determination—new, fragile, and exhilarating—carried her forward.

Her usually modest demeanour was tucked beneath an elegant, daring dress that hugged her figure with quiet but unmistakable sensuality. The fabric shimmered as she moved, catching the golden light and tracing the graceful lines of her body. For once, she didn't shrink from the attention. She let it brush over her, warming her, awakening something bold and unfamiliar within her.

At the bar, she ordered a whisky—something she rarely touched. But tonight, she needed a spark of courage, a liquid reminder that she wasn't as fragile as she felt. When the bartender slid the glass toward her, she nodded, thanked him softly, and tossed it back in one swift, decisive swallow.

Heat spread through her instantly—warm, fierce, almost dizzying.

Probably not her smartest choice. She hadn't eaten since breakfast, and it was nearing ten-thirty. The room tilted a degree before steadying again.

Emily leaned her elbows on the bar, exhaling a long breath. She was tired—tired of dating, tired of men who saw her as a prize or a bank account, tired of pretending she didn't want more than empty compliments and veiled intentions.

Maybe it was time to stop waiting for the perfect man or the perfect moment. Time to embrace the kind of freedom other women her age seemed to enjoy without question. Time to choose pleasure for pleasure's sake. Time to lose her virginity on her own terms.

People often mistook her silence for simplicity, assuming the beautiful heiress must be naïve or easily dazzled. But Emily was far more than that—wealthy, yes, but also bright, capable, compassionate. She cared deeply. She gave generously. She loved fiercely.

And nearly every man she'd dated had loved her money more.

Her mind flicked briefly—annoyingly—to James Fraser. Sinfully handsome, charming to the point of danger, her father's business partner. He had made his interest very clear on more than one occasion. The idea had always left her uneasy, though not entirely immune. James had a reputation: he enjoyed women the way others enjoyed wine—savouring, indulging, then moving on to the next bottle.

Emily wasn't built for heartbreak, which was why she still carried her innocence. Still, she couldn't deny the thought had crossed her mind. A man with such experience surely knew exactly how to please a woman. If she'd ever wanted a physical education, he would have been a tempting choice. At least she would've known what it felt like to be deeply, hungrily desired, even if only for a night.

Her thoughts were interrupted by a quiet, uncertain voice.

"Emily?"

She stiffened. The fragile bubble around her burst.

*William.*

She didn't turn. She simply stared at her empty glass, jaw clenched, pulse ticking with irritation rather than pain.

"Emily, she means nothing to me. It was a mistake." His hand brushed hers, seeking forgiveness he had no right to.

Emily slid her hand away, the rejection sharp and clean. "Just go, William. I'm not interested in anything you have to say."

He opened his mouth, but she turned to face him fully, lifting her palm to silence him.

"You cannot possibly expect me to forgive you after walking in on you having sex with another woman." Her voice was ice—steady, calm, lethal. "There is no excuse you could give me that would make any difference. Pack your things. Leave my suite. And do not come back."

"But—!"

"I'm not discussing this further." Her eyes hardened. "Go."

He deflated with a slow exhale, shoulders slumping. Realising the futility of arguing, he walked away—finally, mercifully gone.

Emily let out her own breath, this one shaky but liberating. The whisky hummed through her blood, loosening her inhibitions, granting her a boldness she barely recognised. A small, unexpected laugh escaped her—a giggle at the memory of William's wide-eyed shock when she'd caught him earlier. Served him right.

Her amusement faded when a strange sensation prickled down her spine.

A presence. A gaze.

She looked up. And found him.

The most devastatingly handsome man she had ever seen.

Her breath hitched.

He stood across the room—tall, commanding, the kind of man who stole air from a space simply by existing. At least six-foot-four, built with powerful, broad shoulders beneath a perfectly tailored suit that hinted at strong, sculpted muscle. His jet-black hair, slightly tousled as if he'd run his fingers through it moments before, gave him a dangerously seductive edge.

But it was his face—God, his face—that unhinged her. High cheekbones, a sharp jaw, a mouth carved in sensual lines, and eyes—a piercing, hypnotic green—that seemed to look straight through her, stripping her bare in a way that sent heat rushing to her skin.

He radiated something dark, magnetic, almost predatory. Confidence. Power. A simmering danger wrapped in elegance.

Emily's pulse kicked hard in her throat.

Her imagination spiralled.

Images—wicked, bold, uncharacteristically reckless—stormed her mind in a rush that made her toes curl inside her heels.

He was exactly the kind of man who could test the limits of her newfound courage.

A slow, subtle smile curved her lips—soft but edged with challenge. She let her gaze lock with his, holding him there, refusing to look away.

A silent dare.

A spark thrown across the room.

*Your move.*

# Chapter Two

Marcus Winters was the embodiment of corporate sophistication, the kind of man whose presence commanded attention without effort. His black tuxedo—tailored with flawless precision—fit him like it had been crafted directly onto his body. The crisp white shirt beneath was immaculate, the stiff collar framing the strong line of his jaw. Platinum cufflinks glinted under the ballroom chandeliers, and his polished leather shoes gleamed with a mirror-like finish. Every detail spoke of discipline, of a man who never let anything slip—not in his appearance, not in his work, not in his life.

In the corporate world, Marcus was a name people invoked with a mix of respect and fear. He was the lawyer businesses sought out when the stakes were sky-high—millions, sometimes billions, hanging in the balance. Specialising in mergers, acquisitions, and high-pressure contract law, he'd earned a reputation for his icy calm and razor-sharp mind. He was the man you hired when you couldn't afford to lose.

But beneath that composed exterior was a mind constantly in motion. Marcus lived in strategy. Every conversation, every negotiation, every room—he assessed it like a board he was already three moves ahead on. Yet his brilliance wasn't just in calculation. He possessed an intuitive understanding of people, of corporate dynamics, of the subtle balance between power and persuasion. He could read motives the way others read headlines. Clients didn't just trust him—they depended on him, often far more than they admitted.


At the bar of the Sydney hotel ballroom, Marcus surveyed the New Year's Eve festivities with cool detachment. Laughter, clinking glasses, and the low pulse of music filled the air. His date, Selina Ellis, had stormed off after his polite refusal to dance—her dramatic hair flip and pointed comment about "finding someone who actually cared" still lingering like perfume. Marcus hadn't bothered to watch her go. He knew exactly what she meant: she intended to leave with someone else.

Fine. Let her.

He'd already fulfilled his obligations for the evening—charm the host, a key client; endure Selina's theatrics; put in a respectable appearance. All that remained was to finish his drink and make a quiet exit.

Then he saw her.

She didn't simply walk into the ballroom—she transformed it. Every head subtly shifted, every conversation paused for a fraction of a second. She moved like someone unaware of her own impact, which only made her more irresistible. Tall, elegant, effortlessly statuesque, she glided through the room with a mixture of grace and intention that captivated him instantly.

Her strapless, floor-length gown—royal blue silk—clung to her with an understated sensuality. The fabric shimmered under the lights, the high slit offering glimpses of a long, toned leg with every step. The fitted bodice hugged her slender waist, highlighting her curves with tasteful sophistication. A sapphire-and-diamond necklace rested against her graceful throat, the gemstones catching the light like captured stars.

Her golden-brown hair cascaded in soft waves, framing a face that looked almost too beautiful to be real—smooth, luminous skin; high cheekbones flushed with natural colour; a delicate nose; and lips shaped for temptation. But it was her eyes that held him—deep blue, startlingly expressive, brimming with warmth, intelligence, and something else he couldn't quite name.

He didn't know her. But she had his absolute attention.

She approached the bar, ordered a drink, and downed it in one swift, confident motion—though Marcus noticed the faint tremor beneath her composure. Something had rattled her.

Moments later, a man appeared beside her, tense, and earnest. Marcus heard her name in the exchange: Emily. And it was immediately clear the man was her ex—or about to be. The pleading tone, the desperate eyes, the faint slur of alcohol. Marcus watched as Emily handled him with poise and precision that rivalled a seasoned diplomat. Her voice was cool, controlled, cutting without ever raising in volume. She dismissed the man with a mixture of strength and grace that made Marcus's admiration sharpen into something deeper.

This woman wasn't just beautiful. She was formidable.

Then, as if she felt him watching, Emily turned her head.

Their gazes collided.

Her lips curved—not shy, not polite—but warm, knowing, subtly provocative. A smile that slid under his skin like a spark. A smile that said she had noticed him long before he realised he had been watching her.

Heat shot through him. Controlled, measured Marcus felt his pulse shift.

Setting his glass down, he crossed the room toward her with slow, deliberate strides. People stepped aside without knowing why; Marcus had always carried an aura of command. But now, his entire focus narrowed to the woman waiting at the bar.

When he reached her, he extended his hand, his voice low, smooth, warm.

"Hi," he said. "I'm Marcus."

She placed her hand in his, her skin soft, warm, sending a jolt up his arm that he felt far too deeply. "Hello," she replied, her voice a gentle melody with an undercurrent of confidence. "I'm Emily."

"Pleasure to meet you, Emily," he said, his thumb brushing lightly—intentionally—against her hand as he held it just a moment longer than necessary.

Her smile deepened.

And Marcus, a man who planned everything, suddenly knew one thing with startling certainty:

*He wasn't leaving this party anytime soon.*

Emily slid onto the barstool, the silky fall of her gown settling around her legs. Marcus took the seat beside her, turning his entire body toward her as though she'd become the only thing in the room worth looking at. When his thigh brushed the warm, exposed skin revealed by the slit of her dress, the contact was brief—accidental—but it sent a quick, undeniable jolt through him.

She caught the flicker in his eyes and gave him a rueful, slightly embarrassed smile. "Sorry about that scene," she murmured, tucking a strand of hair behind her ear. "I didn't mean to provide the hotel with entertainment."

"Are you okay?" Marcus asked, his voice low, warm, and edged with concern that felt startlingly genuine.

"I'll be fine." She gave a small, self-deprecating smile. "He's not worth worrying about."

Marcus studied her for a beat, tilting his head as though trying to read more in the set of her shoulders, the steadiness of her breath. "Was that your husband?"

Emily laughed—light, melodic, a sound that made his chest tighten. "Oh God, no. Thank goodness. Just a boyfriend—now ex-boyfriend."

Her eyes lifted to his, sapphire bright and slightly searching. "Are you waiting for someone?"

"Yes," he said without hesitation, a cheeky, irresistible grin breaking across his face. "You."

Emily raised an eyebrow, feigning surprise even as her lips curved. "Were you now?"

Marcus leaned in, the scent of his cologne—clean, masculine, a hint of amber—slipping around her. His voice dropped to a low murmur. "You're absolutely gorgeous."

Heat rushed to her cheeks, but she didn't look away. "Mmm. I was just about to say the same thing to you."

He laughed, a deep, rich sound that slid over her skin like silk, leaving a shiver in its wake.

"Can I call you Marc?" she asked, tilting her head. "Or do you prefer Marcus?"

"You can call me anything you like, beautiful." He lifted his hand, brushing his thumb lightly across her bottom lip.

Emily's breath caught. Then—bold, wicked—she extended her tongue and grazed the pad of his thumb, never breaking eye contact. A slow, burning tension coiled between them. Marcus's breath hitched audibly, heat flaring in his chest—and lower.

She slid her hand over his, fingertips tracing idle, teasing patterns across his knuckles. "Well then, Marc… you can call me Em."

"Em," he repeated, tasting the name, letting it linger on his tongue. A slow smile unfurled. "I like that."

Their gazes held—smouldering, deliberate—until the rest of the bar blurred into nothingness.

But then reality nudged her spine. William. Her suite. The last loose thread she needed to cut.

Breaking eye contact with effort, Emily turned to the bartender. "Could I use the phone, please?" she asked politely. He pointed her toward one at the far end of the bar. "I won't be long." She gave Marcus a quick smile—a promise—and slipped off her stool.

At the phone, the bartender dialled for her, then handed her the receiver.

"Hi, this is Emily Sinclair. May I speak with the manager, please?"

A moment later, a smooth, confident voice answered, "This is Mr. Giovanni. How can I assist you, Miss Sinclair?"

"I need security sent to my suite to escort Mr. William Hamilton out and retrieve his room keycard. And… please have his belongings removed."

"Of course. Consider it done," the manager replied without hesitation.

"Thank you. I appreciate it." Emily ended the call, releasing a long, quiet breath as the last of her tension slid away.

Returning to Marcus, she deliberately let her bare leg brush his as she settled back onto the stool. He noticed—oh, he definitely noticed. His warm hand slid onto her thigh, fingers curling gently but possessively against her skin, sending a pulse of heat shooting through her.

"Everything alright?" he asked, searching her eyes.

"Yes," she replied softly, confidence blooming. "I just needed to have someone cleared out of my suite."

"Oh," he said with a knowing glint. "The gentleman you dismissed earlier, I assume?"

She nodded. "Exactly. And honestly? I'm relieved to be rid of him."

Marcus's mouth curved. "I'm glad you are too." His voice dropped to a low, teasing rumble. "How about a drink?"

"No, thank you," Emily said sweetly, leaning a little closer. "I think I've had enough for one night. But…" Her lips brushed the barest smile. "I would love to dance."

Marcus stood immediately, offering his arm with a warmth that melted straight into her. His expression softened into something intimate, protective, almost reverent.

"It would be my honour," he said.

And the way he said it made her pulse skip—and made her wonder just how many more moments tonight would steal her breath completely.

Taking his arm, Emily let him guide her toward the dance floor. His hand brushed hers, warm and certain, sending a flutter of anticipation spiralling through her. The moment they stepped into the soft glow of the ballroom lights, Marcus turned to face her fully. With a slow, deliberate motion, he pulled her into his arms—closer than she expected, closer than she'd ever let a man hold her on a first dance.

The intimacy stole her breath.

His hand settled confidently on the small of her back, his palm hot through the delicate fabric of her gown. With his other hand, he lifted hers and placed it over his broad chest, right above the steady, powerful thrum of his heartbeat. She felt every rise and fall of his breath, every shift of the muscles beneath her fingertips.

Marcus began to move, leading her effortlessly. His steps were firm, sure, almost possessive in their certainty, and she followed him as though her body had been waiting for his guidance. Their eyes locked, and the crowded ballroom instantly blurred into insignificance—there was no music, no people, no world beyond the quiet furnace of their shared gaze.

"Where have you been all my life?" he asked, his teasing smile curved with charm and something deeper.

"In Brisbane," she replied, laughing softly, the sound lilting like a warm breeze.

His brows lifted, genuine interest sparking. "Oh? So that's where you're from?"

"Maybe." She tilted her head, her lips tugging into a coy, mischievous smile. "Maybe not."

A slow, appreciative grin spread across his mouth as he leaned in, lowering his voice to a delicious murmur. "You like to play, don't you?"

"Only with worthy opponents," she countered, her tone light but edged in challenge—flirtatious, confident, daring.

The spark between them flared.

Marcus dipped his head and brushed a featherlight kiss against the side of her neck—soft, teasing, devastating. Emily inhaled sharply, her lips parting as a quiet moan escaped her. Heat pooled low in her stomach, spreading through her limbs with dizzying sweetness.

"Do you know how beautiful you are?" he whispered against her ear, his breath warm, his voice reverent in a way that made her heart stutter.

"I do now," she whispered back, blushing, her eyes drifting closed for a moment.

They moved together, their bodies slipping into a rhythm so natural it felt choreographed by fate itself. Each sway brought her closer; each turn wrapped her deeper into his heat, his scent, his presence. Desire, excitement, and a new, glowing confidence coursed through her. For the first time, Emily understood what it meant to be wanted not for convenience—not for comfort—but simply because a man couldn't look away.

Marcus was equally undone. Holding her like this awakened a hunger he hadn't felt in years—deep, primal, undeniable. He wanted her in every sense: in his arms, in his bed, beneath him, around him. And yet beyond that raw desire lay something gentler, something startlingly rare. A reverence for the quiet innocence she carried, for the sweetness she didn't hide, for the trust she offered so easily. That softness only made her more intoxicating.

As she leaned into him, her tall frame aligning perfectly with his, he felt a surge of exhilaration. Her body moulded against his as though created for him alone.

"You feel like you were made for me," he murmured, his voice low, rough with the wanting he could no longer mask.

Before she could respond, he guided her into a graceful dip. Their faces hovered inches apart, breaths mingling, warmth merging. Then he brushed his lips across hers—a quick, teasing kiss that ignited a spark so vivid it left them both breathless.

Emily laughed softly, the musical sound curling around his heart. "You're incorrigible."

"You have no idea," Marcus replied, his voice a velvety whisper loaded with promise.

She felt the effect she had on him—felt the strength of his body, the tension coiled beneath his elegant control—and the knowledge sent a thrill through her veins. For the first time in her life, she revelled in her own power as a woman, as a desirable, irresistible force.

"It's almost midnight," Marcus murmured, his voice softer, though no less charged.

"Mmm," Emily breathed, resting her head against his shoulder. Her cheek brushed his jaw, her lips dangerously close to his neck.

The warm exhale of her breath on his skin made Marcus's entire body tighten. The coil of desire pulled taut, need pulsing through him with unrestrained force. He realised, with a clarity that shook him:

He didn't merely want this woman.

He needed her.

And he needed her soon.

# Chapter Three

The countdown to midnight reverberated through the ballroom, the collective voices building in unison:

"Ten... nine... eight... seven... six... five... four... three... two... one... Happy New Year!"

Time seemed to slow. In that instant, Marc's fingers threaded into the soft waves of Emily's hair at the nape of her neck, his touch gentle, deliberate, electric. He leaned closer, giving her the chance to pull away—but she didn't. Her wide eyes, shimmering with anticipation, held him captive.

His other hand cupped her face with exquisite care, his thumb grazing her cheek as he tilted her head slightly.

When their lips met, the world fell away. The kiss began tender, exploratory, but it quickly deepened, igniting a surge of raw, consuming desire neither of them had anticipated. Marc's arms drew her firmly against him, moulding her to his body as though he could erase all space between them.

Emily responded instinctively, heat flaring through her veins, every nerve alight. His kiss was urgent, persuasive, a promise and a challenge rolled into one. Her knees weakened slightly, but she clung to him, hands sliding over his chest, winding up around his neck. She tangled her fingers in the thick black strands at his nape, eliciting a low, unrestrained shiver from him. She had been kissed before, but never with such intensity—never with a passion that left her breathless, trembling, craving more.

Marc's tongue teased her lips, coaxing them open, exploring with insatiable need. She was intoxicating—a perfect storm of sweetness, fire, and raw magnetism. Her scent, the subtle warmth of her skin, the way she moved instinctively against him—it overwhelmed him, consumed him.

His hands slid down to her hips, drawing her impossibly close, as though even the smallest space between them was unbearable. Emily's body responded instinctively, moving with his, arcing into him, leaning in as her desire spiked with every brush of his fingers. When his lips left hers to trail along the column of her neck, she tilted her head back, granting him access. Each kiss, each whisper of his mouth against her skin, sent jolts of pleasure coursing through her, fire igniting in a place deeper than mere desire.

Marc lifted her slightly, holding her close, the intensity between them unbearable—but then, with a slow, deliberate restraint, he softened, his lips brushing hers in a tender, almost reverent retreat. His chest heaved, his breath ragged. Emily blinked up at him, lips swollen, body trembling. The sudden absence of his touch stung, but deep down, she understood the restraint—the dangerous ground they were treading.

Their foreheads pressed together, breath mingling, hearts hammering in parallel. Marc's hands lingered at her waist, as though letting go would shatter him.

"Emily," he murmured, voice thick with longing, "you're driving me insane."

She smiled softly; cheeks flushed with heat and embarrassment. "I could say the same about you."

A crooked grin tugged at his lips. "This isn't over," he promised, voice low, resolute, certain.

Her pulse leapt, heart fluttering, but she merely nodded, knowing—both of them knowing—this was far from finished.

Then a sharp, cutting voice shredded the intimate bubble around them. "Well, you obviously wanted to dance—just not with me," Selina spat, her words dripping with venom. "Who is this… whore?"

Emily froze, shock and embarrassment blooming hot in her chest. She pulled back from Marc instinctively, suddenly aware of the crowded ballroom, the glittering chandeliers, the eyes upon them. Marc's jaw tightened, a controlled storm behind his calm green eyes.

"You left me, Selina," he snapped, voice low but sharp as steel. "And what you just said was completely out of line."

Turning to Emily, his expression softened immediately. "Emily… I'm so sorry."

Mortified, Emily managed a shaky smile. "It's okay. Thank you for the dance." She stepped back, ready to retreat—but Marc's hand caught hers gently, a tether she didn't want to ignore.

"Emily, wait—" he began, voice pleading, desperate.

She glanced at his hand, the intensity in his eyes, then back to his face, conflicted. "Goodnight, Marc," she whispered softly, freeing herself.

Marc's hand lingered in the air, unwilling to let her go.

"Who the hell is she, Marc?" Selina demanded, stepping closer, her tone rising with faux sweetness.

Marc's patience snapped like a taut wire. "Selina, go away," he said, steel threading through his voice.

Ignoring him, she draped her arms around his neck, attempting a seductive recovery. "Darling, I'm sorry. I didn't mean what I said. Can't we just forget it?"

Emily's heels clicked softly across the marble floor as she walked away, chest tight, face burning, resisting the urge to look back.

Marc wrenched Selina's arms from him with deliberate force, his tone final, cutting. "Well, I did," he said, icy and precise. Without another glance, he strode after Emily.

"Emily, wait!" he called, urgency threading his words.

She stopped at the lift, turning slightly to face him. Calm, composed, but resolute. "I don't think so, Marc. Thank you for the dance. Goodnight."

The lift doors slid open, and she stepped inside. Marc reached the threshold just as the doors began to close, his gaze locked on her, silent and desperate. "Emily—" he started, but she shook her head.

Inside the lift, she leaned back against the cool metal wall, catching one last glimpse of Selina trailing after him. Emily's chest tightened, pulse racing—not just from the confrontation but from the undeniable pull toward Marc, a magnetism she knew she had to resist… for now.

Outside, Marc stood frozen, staring at the closing doors, a hollow ache settling in his chest. Something vital had just slipped through his fingers, something he couldn't yet name, but instinctively knew he wasn't ready to let go.

And in that frozen moment, with the echo of the New Year's cheer fading around him, he realised one truth: Emily had already claimed him, whether he was willing to admit it or not.


It was late March when Marcus sat back in his Sydney office chair, the polished wood of his desk cool beneath his palms. He stared at the phone, debating whether to make the call. He needed to ring James Fraser, his best friend, to tell him he couldn't attend the five-day house party at the private Whitsundays retreat owned by James's business partner. The event marked the twenty-fifth anniversary of the wealth management firm where James had been a partner for the past decade.

Marcus had been planning to use the trip not only to celebrate but to explore a potential career shift—joining the firm as their corporate lawyer. A permanent move to Queensland had been tempting, especially now that his sister Mary was supposedly settled into her married life. But life, as it often did, had other plans.

Her recent engagement had collapsed, leaving the wedding abruptly cancelled. Marcus couldn't ignore her heartbreak—nor could he leave her untended. Their parents had died in a boating accident when Marcus was just nineteen, leaving him to care for twelve-year-old Mary. Since then, it had always been the two of them against the world. While their parents' wealth provided financial security, Marcus had grown it significantly through careful investments—and with the help of James's financial acumen, he was now comfortably wealthy, a multimillionaire with both freedom and influence.

At thirty-two, Marcus embodied the archetype of the charming playboy. Chiselled features, sharp green eyes, a jawline that could cut glass, and an effortlessly athletic physique made him the centre of attention wherever he went. He had always relished his bachelor lifestyle—fleeting romances, glamorous women, no commitments, no responsibilities beyond work and family. Life had been uncomplicated and thrilling.

But since that fateful New Year's Eve, everything had shifted. The night Emily had slipped away from him—Selina's drama inadvertently driving her from his arms—had left an unshakable ache. He hadn't been with anyone since, an unfamiliar emptiness pressing at the edges of his carefully controlled existence. Something had been lost that night, something vital.

Marcus finally lifted the receiver and dialled James's number, leaning back in his chair, stretching his long legs beneath the desk. The line clicked, then rang.

"Hello, Marcus," James's upbeat voice came through, warm and familiar.

"Hey, James! How's it going?" Marcus asked, genuinely curious.

"Good! And you?"

"Great—living the dream," Marcus replied, the corners of his mouth tugging into a grin.

James chuckled. "Oh, what's that? Fast cars and even faster women?"

"You know it," Marcus laughed. "And you're no better than me."

"Not anymore," James said, a note of pride threading through his tone.

Marcus frowned, momentarily caught off guard. "Wait... what? Are you telling me you've got a steady girl now?"

"I'm hoping to have a fiancée very soon," James admitted, voice softening with a boyish excitement that Marcus rarely heard in him.

"Oh my God," Marcus said, leaning back, running a hand through his dark hair, feeling a weight in his chest. "How the mighty have fallen. Are you serious?"

"Dead serious," James replied, his tone practically vibrating with enthusiasm. "And I don't mind admitting it. You'll love her, Marc—she's the sweetest, most genuine woman I've ever met. She's got this warmth… and yeah, she's absolutely stunning. A total knockout."

Marcus paused, the words hanging in the air. James—his high school, university, and career partner in crime—wasn't supposed to be the settling-down type. He'd always been the unflinching bachelor, the one who laughed in the face of commitment. And now… he sounded like a man on the verge of falling headfirst.

"So, who is she?" Marcus asked, curiosity sharpening, a subtle edge of incredulity in his voice.

"Emily Sinclair," James said, light and almost playful, like he was testing Marcus's reaction. "My partner's daughter."

Marcus blinked, his eyebrows lifting. "The boss's daughter, huh?" He let out a low whistle, amusement, and surprise mingling. "She must be incredible in bed for you to be this… head over heels."

There was a pause on the line, and Marcus caught a note of hesitation in James's voice—unusual, almost shy. "Well… that's not it, actually. It's not like that with her. She's… special."

Marcus leaned forward, resting his elbows on the desk, sensing the shift in his friend's tone. "You haven't slept with her yet, have you?"

James hesitated, then admitted reluctantly, "Well, no."

Marcus laughed, disbelief lacing the deep timbre of his voice. "What? Are you serious? James, the great womaniser hasn't sealed the deal. This is unreal."

James sighed, frustration and vulnerability threading his voice. "Emily's a 'good girl', Marc. I'm done with gold diggers. She's different—marriage material."

"Marriage material?" Marcus echoed, shaking his head in disbelief, a low chuckle escaping him. "And you haven't even slept with her? Man… you really are serious about this one, huh?"

"Completely," James admitted, the grin audible even over the phone. "And I've never been happier."

Marcus leaned back in his chair, the leather creaking under him, and stared at the ceiling. Happiness, contentment… it wasn't a feeling he was used to associating with people like James. And yet, he couldn't deny the flicker of something else—something quietly unsettling—stirring in his chest.

Emily. The name lingered, unbidden, in his mind. He pushed it away, scolding himself, but the memory of her sapphire eyes, the brush of her skin, the heat that had flared between them that New Year's Eve… it refused to fade.

"So, what makes this one so special?" Marcus asked, trying—and failing—to mask the disbelief threading through his voice. Curiosity, sharp and unwelcome, coiled in his chest.

"As soon as you meet her, you'll understand. Trust me," James said, sincerity softening his usually confident tone. "I've known her for ten years, but we've only been dating for two months. When it's right, you just know. I'd been trying to get her to go out with me for ages, but she was with a loser boyfriend at the time."

Marcus arched a brow. "What happened to him?" Despite the casualness of his voice, he felt himself leaning forward, interest sparked.

"He cheated on her. She caught him in the act in her penthouse suite on New Year's Eve."

Marcus stilled, his breath faltering for half a second. "On New Year's Eve? Where?"

"In Sydney," James answered, confusion creeping into his tone. "Why?"

A cold ripple travelled down Marcus's spine. His fingers tightened instinctively around the edge of his desk. No. There was no way. It couldn't be her.

But his mind betrayed him—flashing with vivid clarity to midnight on the dance floor: her sapphire-blue eyes, luminous and startled; the soft fullness of her lips under his; the way she'd melted into him like she'd been made to fit there. The taste of champagne and something sweet on her tongue. The way he'd burned for her—still burned for her.

Heat rose up his chest, quick and unwelcome. He tried to brush it aside, but the thought dug deeper, relentless. *Was James's Emily the same woman he'd been unable to forget?*

Oblivious to Marcus's spiralling thoughts, James continued talking. "I've had my eye on her for years, but she was too young when we met. Now she's older, and... I don't know. I just know she's the one. I don't want to let her slip away."

Marcus forced a laugh, the sound brittle. "Well, good luck with that, mate. She sounds... special."

James chuckled. "She is. I can't wait for you to meet her. You'll see exactly what I mean."

Marcus managed a faint smile, but his mind churned violently. *I already have.*

And the thought of James with her—touching her, claiming her—sat like a hot coal in his chest.

# Chapter Four

That night had ended in chaos. Selina's venomous outburst had shattered something fragile and new. After Emily fled, Selina had launched into an endless tirade—excuses, tears, manipulations. Marcus had felt nothing but irritation, then revulsion. Every shrill word from her underscored just how far beneath Emily she was—Emily, with her quiet elegance and steady grace. Selina was noise; Emily was calm.

The moment Emily walked away from him, something inside Marcus had shifted—something he hadn't wanted to examine too closely.

Months had passed, yet she lingered in his mind like a melody he couldn't stop humming. He'd tried to move on—dates, casual flings that went nowhere—but everything felt hollow. Mechanical. Wrong. He hadn't slept with anyone since that night. The longest celibate stretch of his adult life, and it wasn't intentional.

*Emily had ruined him without even trying.*

Her warmth. Her scent. The way she had looked at him like she felt that same sudden, undeniable spark. The way her body had moulded to his on the dance floor as if it already knew him.

*And now she might be James's Emily.*

His stomach twisted painfully.

He tried to focus on James's voice, but his thoughts were a roaring blur.

"Marc, I'm not proud of this, but I set it up," James confessed suddenly, guilt colouring his words.

Marcus's attention snapped into sharp focus. "Wait, what? Set what up? What are you talking about?"

"I didn't like the guy she was dating," James said, clearing his throat. "William Hamilton. He used to work here—a complete jerk. Treated her terribly. Pawing at her in public. You could tell she hated it, and he was only using her for her money."

*William.* The name slammed into Marcus's memory like a jolt.

He sat forward. "What did you do, James?"

"I paid a woman to hit on him," James admitted, almost casually. "It was at a party her father asked her to attend on his behalf. I wanted to prove William was trash. Took five minutes before he suggested they go up to his room. She told me everything."

Marcus stared at the wall, stunned. "And Emily doesn't know?"

"No. And she can't. I'm only telling you because I trust you. You've got to promise me you won't say a word."

"So let me get this straight," Marcus said slowly. "You sabotaged her relationship... and now you're dating her?"

"In a nutshell, yes," James replied without apology.

There was a beat of silence before James added, lightly, "It's not like you've never manipulated a woman before, Marc."

"True," Marcus said, blunt and honest. "But I've never planned on marrying any of them."

"When you meet Emily, you'll understand," James insisted. "Men chase her constantly, but she's not vain. She doesn't trade on her looks. She's incredible. But listen—"

His tone hardened. "Keep your hands to yourself. She's mine."

The words hit Marcus like a punch. His pulse spiked, something hot and possessive flaring in his chest before he shut it down.

He cleared his throat. "Actually, that's why I'm calling. I don't think I can make it. Mary's a mess after the breakup with her fiancé, and I don't want to leave her alone."

James sighed. "Bring her. Seriously. She's about Emily's age. They might even become friends. And honestly, Marc, it might be good for all of us. Just... come. I want you to meet Emily."

Marcus hesitated, torn between dread and an undeniable, magnetic pull.

"I'll speak to Mary," he said quietly. "I'll let you know."


After ending the call, Marcus leaned back in his chair, letting out a long, slow breath. His mind refused to rest, a storm of conflicting thoughts and desires tearing at him. He hadn't explicitly promised James that he would keep his hands off Emily, but the unspoken understanding was clear. James was his best friend, practically a brother, and the idea of betraying him—of taking what rightfully belonged to James—was unbearable.

And yet... the doubt persisted, gnawing at him like a quiet, insistent ache. *If she turns out to be my Emily... what then?* The thought sent a shiver down his spine. She had haunted him since that fateful New Year's Eve—the shock of her lips on his, the heat of her body pressed against his, the way her eyes had looked at him, wide and bold, yet vulnerable. He'd searched for her afterward, desperate to see her again, but the hotel staff had refused to give him her name. He had waited in the lobby the next morning, nursing a faint hope that she might appear, but she never did.

Now, all he had was her first name—and James's glowing, almost reverent descriptions. Too many details aligned: her name, her ex-boyfriend, the cheating incident in Sydney. He couldn't ignore the nagging certainty settling in his chest. *It had to be the same woman.*

Marcus ran a hand over his face, rubbing his jaw as he leaned forward, elbows on the desk. He felt that familiar ache in his chest—the one that had taken hold that night, after Selina's outburst drove Emily away. Desire, longing, frustration—it was all tangled up together, impossible to untangle. Every other woman he had been with since had felt hollow, empty, meaningless. Emily had set a standard no one else could reach.

He needed answers. He needed to see her again, to confirm that the woman who had invaded his thoughts, his dreams, and every idle fantasy of late, was indeed James's Emily. That meant convincing Mary to come with him to the party. It was a simple plan on paper—but Marcus knew nothing about this would be simple.

*Because if she was Emily, if those sapphire eyes were hers, what then? Could he really stay away? Could he resist her pull, her magnetism, the way she made him feel like he was on fire from the inside out? And if he couldn't... what would that mean for his friendship with James? Could he betray him, even with the truth glaring him in the face?*

Marcus sat in the quiet of his office, tension coiling in his chest, and knew one thing with absolute clarity: he was walking toward a storm, and nothing—neither loyalty, nor desire, nor reason—was going to make it any less dangerous.


"Good morning, Jeremy," Emily greeted warmly as she stepped into her father's personal assistant's office, her bright smile lighting up the room and infusing it with energy. "How are you this morning?"

"Good morning, Miss Sinclair," Jeremy Saunders replied, looking up from his desk with a cheerful smile. "I'm doing very well, thank you. And you?"

Stopping in front of him, Emily tilted her head playfully and pouted. "Jeremy, it's Emily, not 'Miss Sinclair'. I've told you countless times—there's no need for the formality."

Jeremy flushed slightly, a sheepish smile tugging at his lips. "Sorry, Emily. Force of habit."

She grinned, her eyes sparkling. "I'm wonderful! It's such a lovely day, and I've finally finished all the preparations for the house party. You're coming, right?"

"Oh yes, I wouldn't miss it," Jeremy said, a hint of shyness creeping into his tone.

"Excellent. I look forward to seeing you there," Emily said, giving him a quick wink. Her gaze then drifted to the closed door of her father's office. "Is he available?"

Jeremy leaned back in his chair, a knowing smile on his face. "You know he's always available for you."

"Yes, but is he on the phone?"

Jeremy glanced at the switchboard on his desk and shook his head. "Clear."

"Thanks, Jeremy," Emily said, offering a warm parting smile before moving to the door. She knocked softly.

"Come in," came her father's familiar voice from the other side.

Emily entered, her smile widening. "Good morning, Dad. How are you?" She circled the large mahogany desk and kissed him lightly on the cheek.

John Sinclair, 51, exuded the quiet authority of a man who had built an empire with his own two hands. Salt-and-pepper hair neatly combed, sharp grey eyes that seemed to pierce right through to the truth, he carried himself with a presence that commanded attention. Owner of seventy percent of a highly successful wealth management firm, he was a multimillionaire—but wealth alone never defined him. His greatest pride and joy had always been Emily, the daughter he had raised single-handedly after the tragic loss of his wife in a car accident ten years earlier.

Though his sharp suits and polished demeanour made him a formidable figure in any boardroom, his softer side was reserved entirely for his daughter. John admired her independence, her determination to carve out her own path, and the way she balanced strength with kindness. Watching Emily flourish into a confident, capable woman was a pride that far outshone any corporate triumph.

"Good morning, sweetheart. You look happy," he said, the affection in his voice softening his normally commanding tone.

"I am," Emily replied, settling into the chair across from him. "I've finished all the preparations for the anniversary celebration. I hope you're happy with everything."

"You know I'm always proud of you," John said warmly, leaning back in his chair. "So, what do you have planned for the guests?"

Emily's eyes gleamed as she flipped open her notebook. "Plenty! There's a fishing trip for the men, a shopping outing for the women, whale watching, movie nights, picnics, archery, and, of course, the ball, where the rest of the staff will join us. I've tried to make sure there's something for everyone."

John's face lit up with a proud smile. "You've outdone yourself, as always. I can already picture the look on everyone's faces when they arrive."

"Thanks, Dad." She scribbled a quick note in the margins of her planner before adding, "I should have the final headcount by tomorrow. Couples will have the cabins, and singles will stay in the main house. So far, it looks like a full house! Oh, and I believe Marcus Winters is coming—with his sister. I just need to double-check with James." She crossed her fingers playfully.

"Good. I'm looking forward to speaking with Marcus about the position. Paul's departure is coming up quickly."

Emily nodded. "I know. Marcus wasn't planning to come at first—his sister's engagement was called off, and she's understandably upset—but James suggested she join him." She grinned, lifting her fingers in a victory sign. "Crisis averted."

John chuckled softly, shaking his head. "Excellent. I knew I could count on you to make everything run smoothly. You always find a way."

Emily stood, leaning over to place a gentle kiss on his cheek. "Don't forget to thank Jeremy and Karen—they've been a huge help." She paused at the door, turning back to him with a warm smile. "I love you, Dad. Have a wonderful day."

"I love you too, Emily," John called after her, his tone filled with genuine affection.


As Emily stepped back into the hallway, she offered Jeremy a cheerful wave before moving to the next office. Her heels clicked lightly on the polished floor, the soft sound matching the buoyancy in her step.

"Good morning, Karen! Isn't it a beautiful day?" she said brightly as she entered.

Karen—James's long-time personal assistant and the unofficial keeper of every secret in the building—turned from the filing cabinet, her warm smile creasing the corners of her eyes. "Hello, sweetie. He's in," she replied, nodding toward the connecting door.

"Perfect. Thanks, Karen." Emily knocked softly, waited for the familiar, deep "Enter," and stepped inside.

James Fraser looked up from his desk, and every part of him seemed to sharpen at the sight of her. At six foot three, he carried himself with an effortless, athletic grace that made heads turn without him ever noticing—or caring. Sun-touched blonde hair fell in artful disarray over his brow, framing features that were all sharp lines and masculine elegance. His piercing blue eyes—eyes that saw everything and missed nothing—lit up with a warmth reserved exclusively for her.

The combination made him impossible to ignore. And dangerously easy to fall for.

He rose instantly, crossing the room in two long, unhurried strides. Wrapping his arms around her waist, he pulled her close and kissed her deeply, his mouth warm, familiar, and far too tempting for a workday morning. "Good morning, sweetheart. I've missed you."

Emily laughed against his chest, her heart doing an unhelpful little flutter. "You saw me last night," she teased lightly. "How could you possibly miss me already?"

James's grin was slow and devastating, his voice dropping into that husky register that always turned her spine to warm honey. "I miss you whenever you're not with me."

Another kiss followed—just as lingering, just as persuasive—before Emily gently pushed at his chest. "If you keep that up, you'll get nothing done today."

"Ah," he murmured, brushing his thumb over her jaw. "Worth it."

She glowed under his attention before finally slipping into the chair across from his desk. James sat reluctantly, his eyes still devouring her in that quiet, appreciative way that made her toes curl.

"What's on your mind?" he asked.

"I'm just double-checking numbers for the anniversary celebration. Have you heard from Marcus?" Emily asked, flipping open her notebook.

James nodded. "He called last night. He and his sister are coming."

Emily's smile blossomed. "Wonderful! I'm really looking forward to meeting her. She might be the only woman close to my age attending. I hope we get along."

The corners of James's mouth softened. "You're sweet for including her. Marc said she's been struggling—her engagement ended recently."

Emily's expression softened with genuine empathy. "Oh, poor thing. I'll make sure she feels welcome." She paused, reflecting for a moment. Although Emily had dated, no relationship had ever reached the intensity or depth her friends spoke of—not until now, not until James. With him, everything felt…different. Safer. More real.

James watched her thoughtfully, his gaze warming. "She's going to adore you, Emily. Everyone does."

Emily laughed softly, though her cheeks flushed with that familiar, traitorous warmth. There was only one person whose affection mattered right now—only one man whose approval, admiration, and love she found herself craving more and more with each passing day.

Without overthinking it—because if she did, she'd lose her nerve—Emily rose from her chair. She walked around the desk, and James immediately leaned back, making room for her. She settled onto his lap, slipping her arms around his neck. His hands settled instinctively at her waist, fingers curling as though they belonged there.

Her heart hammered so loudly she feared he might hear it.

She drew in a steadying breath, her voice trembling just enough to betray how much this moment meant. "I love you, James Fraser," she whispered, words feather-soft but irrevocably true. Heat rushed to her cheeks; vulnerability tightened her throat.

For a heartbeat, James stilled. Surprise flickered across his face—and then, just as quickly, melted into something warm, steady, and profoundly gentle. Lifting one hand, he tucked a stray strand of hair behind her ear, his fingers tracing down her cheek with exquisite tenderness.

"I love you, Emily Sinclair," he said quietly, the sincerity in his tone wrapping around her like a warm embrace.

His lips met hers in a soft, reverent kiss—one that felt like a promise.

Tears welled in her eyes, blurring the edges of his beautiful face. James immediately noticed, brushing them away with his thumb. "Why the tears, sweetheart?"

"You just make me so happy," she breathed, her voice cracking with emotion.

A slow, heartfelt smile spread across his features. "And you make me happy. More than you know."

Reluctantly, Emily eased off his lap, smoothing her dress with trembling hands. "I should go before I distract you any more than I already have."

"Impossible," James said with a chuckle, leaning back as he watched her head toward the door. "Have a wonderful day, Emily."

She paused, her hand on the handle, turning back with a soft, radiant smile. "I will— now that I know you love me."

James's eyes gleamed, full of affection. "Always."

Emily stepped into the hallway, feeling almost weightless, as if the floor had softened beneath her feet. She couldn't stop smiling, couldn't stop replaying the morning's intimate moment with James in her mind. Her chest felt light, yet full, and warmth radiated through her in a way that made her heart ache with happiness.

He loves me, she thought, the words blooming inside her like sunlight through morning mist, gentle yet undeniable.

Yet, even as a smile lingered on her lips, a flicker of memory tugged at her—sharp, insistent, impossible to ignore. That unforgettable kiss on New Year's Eve, with the stranger whose green eyes had ignited something deep and thrilling within her… Marc.

The thought sent a shiver racing down her spine, a reminder of a heat and longing that James's tender affection had never sparked.

Emily shook her head, chastising herself. No—she couldn't linger there. James made her feel safe. He made her feel cared for. *And hadn't that always been what she wanted?* Stability, trust, someone who saw her beyond the surface, beyond the allure that so often drew shallow attention. *That was what mattered, wasn't it?*

Still, deep down, a tiny, mischievous part of her couldn't help but remember the intensity of that fleeting, dangerous connection—the fire she had felt with Marc. And for just a heartbeat, she wondered what might happen if fate ever allowed their paths to cross again.

# Chapter Five

The day flew by as Emily finalised the numbers and sorted the sleeping arrangements for the five-night stay. She cherished every moment on the island her father had owned for nearly thirty years—a place born from her mother's dream and gifted to her by her new husband.

Nestled in the heart of the Great Barrier Reef, the privately owned island was a hidden gem. Two beaches framed its shores, each with a distinct personality. One curved in soft, white sand, meeting crystal-clear turquoise waters where gentle waves lapped in soothing rhythm—a perfect haven for sun-soaked relaxation. The other was wilder, jagged rocks forming natural pools at low tide, though at high tide the waves crashed with raw, untamed power, a reminder of nature's force.

At the island's centre, a dense jungle thrived. Vines dangled from towering trees, ferns and shrubs carpeted the undergrowth, and the air pulsed with birdsong and the subtle rustle of wildlife. The earthy scent of jungle mingled with the salty breeze drifting from the beaches.

Perched at the highest point stood a grand mansion—a luxurious sanctuary blending modern comfort with timeless elegance. The polished marble floors of the foyer gleamed in the filtered light streaming through expansive windows, while a sweeping staircase with a dark wooden banister curved gracefully to the upper levels. Ten spacious bedrooms offered private havens with floor-to-ceiling windows framing either the beach or jungle, each with marble-topped ensuites, freestanding tubs, and rain showers designed to soothe and indulge.

The mansion's chef's kitchen was a dream, with state-of-the-art appliances, vast countertops, and a large island that flowed seamlessly into the dining room, where a long, polished table sat beneath a grand chandelier. Several sitting rooms offered a mix of intimate corners and airy lounges for quiet conversation or reading, while a study/library, lined with leather-bound volumes and overlooking the greenery, provided a tranquil retreat.

For entertainment, a billiard room with dark wood panelling and a bar invited playful competition, while the ballroom, with gleaming floors and intricate ceiling mouldings, promised grand celebrations. Outside, the terrace offered cushioned loungers, alfresco dining, and a garden bursting with tropical flowers, winding stone paths, and the scent of jasmine and frangipani. Beyond it, an infinity pool shimmered, its waters blending seamlessly with the horizon, casting a serene glow at sunset.

Four small cabins dotted the coastline, each offering a private retreat. Sunset Hideaway boasted unobstructed ocean views; Jungle Retreat was nestled deep in foliage; Ocean

Breeze sat closest to the shore with a wrap-around deck; and Seaside Sanctuary promised an intimate, romantic escape. Every cabin allowed guests to immerse themselves in the island's natural beauty while enjoying modern comforts.

Since her mother's tragic death, her father had visited less often, and the vibrant island that once pulsed with family laughter had become a bittersweet reminder of the life they had shared. Yet for Emily, it remained a place of solace—a blend of luxury and nature, where memories lingered and new ones could be made.

Late in the afternoon, Emily had just stepped out of a relaxing bath when her phone rang. Wrapped in a soft, white bathrobe, she answered with a smile.

"Hello?"

"Hi, sweetheart," James' warm voice greeted her.

"Hi, James. How was your day?" she asked, her lips curving into a smile.

"Good. And yours?"

"I just finished arranging the accommodations for the house party and making sure the staff were ready. Then I had a bath and—well, I just got out."

"Oh, really?" His voice carried a teasing edge.

"Yes," she giggled, enjoying his tone. "I'm standing here in nothing but a bathrobe."

"Don't tempt me, witch," he shot back playfully.

"I'm not tempting anyone," she replied, feigning innocence with a sassy tilt in her voice.

"You tempt me every time I see you," he said, his tone softening with sincerity.

Emily's laughter faded into a quiet smile as she noticed the weariness in his voice. "Are you done for the day?"

He groaned. "Yes, thankfully. I'm exhausted."

"You should go home and rest," she suggested gently.

"How can I rest knowing you're just in a bathrobe?" he teased. "I wouldn't be able to stop thinking about you."

"Oh, my apologies," she said with a playful smirk.

"Don't apologise for that, Emily. I love your playfulness… and your sense of humour," he said sincerely.

Her heart warmed. "You always know exactly what to say, don't you?"

"I try," he murmured, pausing for a beat. "I just wanted to make sure everything is set for tomorrow night."

"I'll be ready at five, just for you. How should I dress?" she asked, her curiosity piqued.

"In a bathrobe would be perfect," he joked.

"You wish," she laughed, shaking her head.

"Yes, yes, I do," he said dreamily, and she could hear the longing in his voice.

"James?" she teased, letting a hint of sternness slip in.

"Alright, alright," he said with a laugh. "Dress formally. It's going to be a special night."

"Why?" she asked, a flutter of anticipation in her stomach.

"You'll have to wait and see," he replied, keeping his voice low and mysterious.

Emily smiled softly. "Okay, I'll try," she said, her pulse quickening. Then, her voice softened even further, barely above a whisper: "I love you."

"I love you too, sweetheart," he said lovingly. "I'd better go now. I'll see you tomorrow night. Sleep well, my darling."

"You too… good night," Emily whispered, a dreamy smile lingering on her lips.

"Good night," he replied, and the line went silent.


After dinner, Emily settled on the couch, intending to relax with some television, but her mind refused to cooperate. Thoughts of the next evening kept intruding. *What did James mean by a "special night"?* He had always taken her to wonderful places, yet something about tomorrow felt different, charged with a tension she couldn't name.

Determined to be prepared, she pulled her black dress from the wardrobe, holding it against herself and imagining how she might style her hair. Her fingers brushed over the fabric as excitement and curiosity mingled, making it impossible to focus on the flickering images on the screen.

With a soft sigh, she turned off the TV and headed to bed, her mind still buzzing with possibilities. Sleep came reluctantly, each thought of James and tomorrow's promise sending a thrill through her that left her heart racing long after the lights were out.

Emily slept soundly and woke around seven, refreshed and ready for the day. She stretched languidly before slipping out of bed and reaching for the robe she'd left draped over a chair. In the kitchen, she started the coffee machine and put together a simple breakfast. She had just sat down with her meal when her phone rang.

"Hello?" she answered.

"Hi, darling," her father said warmly.

"Hi, Dad. How are you? Is everything alright?" She frowned—he rarely called this early.

"Yes, sweetheart, everything's fine," he assured her. "I was just talking to James, and he mentioned he's taking you out tonight?"

Emily blinked. Her father almost never brought up her relationship unless she did first. He was supportive, but he kept his distance, something she'd always appreciated.

"Yes, he is," she said slowly. "Why?"

"Oh, no reason." His tone shifted—gentle, but strangely earnest. "I just wanted to tell you how proud I am of you… and that I love you."

Emily felt her stomach tighten. "I love you too, Dad. You're the best father I could ask for." She hesitated. "But… are you sure everything's okay? You'd tell me if something was wrong?"

"Of course, darling. Everything's fine—more than fine," he said lightly, trying to smooth over her concern.

"Alright," she murmured, unconvinced.

They chatted for another moment before ending the call, but the odd note in his voice stayed with her long after she put the phone down.

Unable to shake the feeling, she called Jeremy.

"John Sinclair's office, good morning," his assistant answered crisply.

"Hi, Jeremy, it's Emily."

"Oh! Emily—good morning. How are you?" His voice instantly brightened.

"I'm fine, thanks. Have you seen my dad today?"

"Yes, he's in. Do you want me to transfer you?"

"No, it's actually you I wanted to speak to." Her tone dropped, more serious now.

Jeremy paused. "Of course. What's going on?"

"My dad called me earlier… and he sounded a bit off."

"Well, he seemed perfectly normal when he arrived," Jeremy said thoughtfully. "Mr. Fraser was with him for a while—they both looked pleased about something. Your dad even walked him out, shaking his hand like he'd won the lottery. Maybe they landed a big client."

"Maybe," she agreed, though uncertainty still tugged at her. "Can you just… keep an eye on him today? For me?"

"Absolutely. Anything you need," Jeremy said quickly, a little breathless.

"Thank you, Jeremy. Really."

# Chapter Six

After the call, Emily set her phone down and stepped onto the balcony of her three-bedroom penthouse in Brisbane. The view was one of her favourite things about the apartment her father had gifted her on her twenty-first birthday. High above the city, she could see the Brisbane River winding between skyscrapers and lush green parks—a peaceful escape suspended in the sky.

She breathed in the warm afternoon air, but her thoughts drifted restlessly. Whatever James had planned, it was beginning to feel bigger than she'd expected.

By two o'clock, a knock sounded at the door.

"Hi, Sarah! How've you been?" Emily greeted, pulling it open.

"Great! Busy, but the good kind of busy," Sarah said with a bright smile.

Their familiar, easy chatter filled the apartment as Sarah worked her magic, brushing and pinning Emily's long waves into a graceful up-do. Soft tendrils framed Emily's face, the rest swept elegantly back.

When Sarah handed her a mirror, Emily's breath caught. "Sarah, it's gorgeous. Truly."

"You look beautiful," Sarah said warmly.

As she helped Emily into her gown, Emily felt excitement flutter through her. The black dress flowed like liquid midnight, hugging her curves before drifting into a soft flare. The off-the-shoulder neckline left her collarbones bare, and her black heels added height and elegance.

"You're stunning," Sarah said, admiration shining.

Emily laughed lightly. "Not done yet—I need makeup."

Sarah got to work, adding a radiant glow to Emily's skin, a soft warmth to her cheeks, and just enough mascara to make her eyes sparkle. A whisper of colour on her lips completed the look. Natural. Polished. Captivating.

When Sarah fastened a simple strand of pearls around her neck, Emily smiled. "You're a gem, you know that?"

"Anytime," Sarah replied before gathering her things and heading out.

Once alone, Emily glanced at the clock. Almost five. Butterflies erupted in her stomach. Excitement. Nerves. Anticipation. She smoothed her hands over her dress and tried to steady her breathing.

A knock echoed through the penthouse.

Emily exhaled slowly, grabbed her small black purse, and opened the door.

For a moment, James simply stared.

His breath stilled, his blue eyes widening as if he'd never seen anything quite like her. He looked devastatingly handsome himself—tall, powerful, wrapped in a sleek tuxedo that fit like it had been made for him. His blonde hair was neatly styled, catching the light, and there was a warmth in his gaze that made her heart lift.

"James, you look very handsome," she said softly.

He swallowed, still taking her in. "Wow," he murmured, voice low. "You look… breathtaking. I've never seen anyone so beautiful."

He stepped closer and gently took her hands, his touch warm, grounding.

Emily felt heat bloom across her cheeks. "Thank you. I was hoping you'd like it."

"Like it?" His brows lifted as though the idea was absurd. "Emily, you're incredible."

Her smile softened—not from vanity, but from the tenderness in his voice, the way he looked at her as if the world had narrowed to this moment alone.

He lifted her hands to his lips, brushing them lightly. "Are you ready to go?"

She picked up her purse. "Yes."

"Then let's go," he said, still looking at her as if he'd just witnessed something extraordinary.

With that, they headed out, James locking her door behind them. In the elevator, he never once released her hand, his thumb brushing lightly over her knuckles as if he couldn't help touching her.

Outside, he opened the door of a sleek black limousine and helped her inside. Once the door closed and the hum of the engine settled around them, Emily turned to him, both shy and curious.

"Where are we going?" she asked, voice soft.

"It's a surprise," he replied, his smile warm and just a little mischievous.

Before she could respond, he reached over and traced a fingertip down her cheek. Heat blossomed beneath her skin.

"I love the way you blush," he murmured. "It's absolutely enchanting."

She laughed shyly. "Honestly, I'm not a fan."

He only smiled, leaning back with an admiring look that made her heart flutter.

A few moments passed before she remembered. "Oh—did you land a new client or something? Jeremy said this morning that Dad was very pleased with you."

James's jaw tightened almost imperceptibly. "Did he?"

"Yes…" She frowned, sensing something off. "Is everything okay?"

He smoothed a hand over her thigh, reassuring but evasive. "Everything's fine, sweetheart."

She didn't entirely believe him, but before she could press further, the limousine curved toward the marina. Emily's eyes brightened.

"Are we going on a boat? You know how much I love being on the water!"

His lips curved into a secretive smile. "I know. But you'll have to wait."

She pouted playfully. James swooped in, kissing her lightly, and she giggled.

"You're incorrigible," she said.

"Yes, I know. But you love me."

"Yes," she whispered, lost in the way he looked at her.

When the limousine rolled to a stop, James stepped out first, offering his hand. They walked toward a wharf lined with a red carpet that reflected the marina lights. Emily blinked in surprise.

James bowed theatrically. "For my princess."

"Oh, James… you're unbelievable," she said, touched.

At the end of the carpet waited a magnificent yacht, its polished exterior gleaming under the evening sky. James helped her aboard, guiding her to the upper deck where a beautifully set table awaited—crystal glasses, soft candlelight, a view of the river like scattered diamonds.

Emily turned to him, breathless. "This is… incredible."

"So, you like it?" he teased.

She laughed, throwing her arms around him. "I love it. It's perfect."

He lifted her chin gently, his eyes softening. "You're perfect."

Then he kissed her—slowly, reverently, as though the whole night had been created just for her.

As the yacht eased away from the wharf, Emily drifted toward the railing, watching the water ripple and break beneath them. The night breeze lifted the hem of her dress, carrying the faint scent of the sea. James slipped behind her, wrapping his arms around her waist and pulling her back against the solid warmth of his chest.

She exhaled softly, sinking into him.

"We're going to watch the sunset and then have dinner," he murmured against her ear, his breath warm on her skin. A shiver ran through her, and he smiled against her neck before pressing a tender kiss there. They stayed like that for what felt like forever—silent, content, wrapped in the unfolding beauty of a burning gold sunset sinking into the horizon.

When the last light faded, James guided her to the table and helped her into her seat. The four-course dinner was exquisite—lobster, fresh fish, crisp vegetables, delicate desserts—but it was James's laughter, the way he watched her, the way their fingers brushed and lingered, that made the meal unforgettable.

After dessert, the waitstaff disappeared, leaving them alone with soft music drifting through hidden speakers. James rose, extended his hand, and whispered, "Dance with me."

She stepped into his arms, and they swayed on the deck as though the world had narrowed to the two of them. Emily rested her head on his shoulder; he pressed quiet kisses to her cheek, her lips—small, reverent touches that made her heart flutter.

"Mmm," she breathed, dreamy. "Tonight, has been wonderful, James."

His hand tightened at her waist. "I'm glad. Because… I wanted to ask you something."

Emily lifted her head, brows knitting together—then froze as James lowered to one knee.

Her hand flew to her mouth.

"Emily," he began, voice thick with emotion, "you are the most caring, compassionate, loving, and beautiful person I've ever known." He reached into his jacket and produced a small box. Inside, an emerald-cut diamond caught the soft deck lights, throwing shards of brilliance across the night. "Would you make me the happiest man alive… and marry me?"

Tears spilled down her cheeks. She nodded, breathless. "Yes, James. Yes—of course yes."

He rose, slid the ring onto her finger, and kissed it before capturing her mouth in a deep, aching kiss. They held each other for a long time, wrapped in joy, in love, in the promise of everything still ahead.

Later, as the yacht drifted toward a different wharf, Emily gave James a questioning look. He smiled.

"I knew you'd want to share this moment with your father."

And then she saw him—her father—stepping aboard, eyes already misty with happiness. Emily rushed into his arms.

"Oh, Dad," she whispered through tears, "I'm so happy."

He kissed her forehead. "You deserve that happiness, sweetheart. James loves you—and you love him. That's all a father can hope for."

After champagne and celebration, the limousine took her father home. On the way back to her apartment, Emily squeezed James's hand. "Thank you for including him."

"I wouldn't have done it any other way," he said softly. "I asked him for your hand this morning."

She smiled, understanding suddenly lighting her eyes. "So that's why he called."

Admiring the ring, she turned her hand, so it caught the light. Elegant. Understated. Perfect.

"If you'd prefer something bigger," James offered gently, "I can—"

"No," she interrupted, stunned. "This is perfect. I love it just the way it is."

Relief softened his features, and he pulled her close, his arm warm around her shoulders.

At her door, Emily hesitated. "Would you… like to come in?"

For a moment, desire flickered in his eyes—hot, immediate—but he cupped her chin gently. "Believe me, I'd love nothing more than to spend all night making love to you. But I want to honour what you asked for when we started dating. You matter too much to me. And when the moment comes… it will be worth the wait."

Her heart melted. She kissed him softly. "I love you."

"I love you too."

They said goodnight, and as Emily closed the door behind him, she leaned back against it, her heart full to overflowing—her future glittering as brightly as the ring on her finger.

# Chapter Seven

Marcus Winters stepped into James Fraser's office with the casual confidence of a man who knew he was welcome. James rose the moment he appeared, his expression brightening into a warm, genuine smile.

"Good to see you, Marc," he said, reaching out to shake his hand.

"Good to see you too," Marc replied, gripping his hand firmly.

"Take a seat," James offered, gesturing to the chair opposite his desk.

"Thanks." Marc settled in, leaning back comfortably as James resumed his place behind the sleek mahogany desk.

"So," James began, leaning forward slightly, "when did you get in? How was the flight?"

Marc exhaled slowly. "Got in last night. Long, but good. I thought I'd stop by a little early before the meeting—hope that's alright?"

"More than alright," James said with a grin. "Actually, I'm glad you did. I've got some news."

Marc arched a brow, curiosity instantly lit. "Oh? You're already starting with the suspense?"

James chuckled but didn't answer immediately. "Before I get to that—how's Mary?"

Marc's shoulders eased, but his voice softened. "She's… getting better. She still has her bad days, but she tries to hide them."

James nodded slowly, concern clouding his usually sharp gaze. "Do you know what happened?"

"She hasn't told me yet," Marc said, emphasising yet with quiet determination. "I liked Eric. Thought they were solid. Then one morning she just comes home with her bags and says it's over."

James let out a low laugh. "She's probably worried you're going to knock the poor guy's lights out."

Marc smirked. "Wouldn't be the first time I've been tempted."

Then he leaned forward, interest sharpening his tone. "Alright, enough about my sister. What's your news?"

James leaned back, pride warming his entire expression. "Well… you're looking at a very happily engaged man."

Marc blinked. Froze. Then his jaw dropped so suddenly he looked almost comical. "Engaged? To who? Don't tell me—wait." His eyes widened. "The boss's daughter?"

James burst out laughing. "Yes, the boss's daughter. Who else did you think I meant?"

Marc lifted a brow knowingly. "I don't know—maybe one of the five women you were juggling back in the day?"

James shook his head with dramatic, self-deprecating resignation. "Those days are over, thank God. And I'm looking forward to what's ahead."

Marc stood, genuinely happy now, and extended his hand. "Congratulations, mate. If you're happy, then I'm happy."

James shook his hand firmly. "I am. She's… she's incredible."

Marc sat back down, watching the unmistakable glow on James's face. "So, when did this all happen?"

"Last Friday night," James said, his eyes softening with the memory.

Marc's curiosity sharpened. The way James smiled—damn, it was real. "You're really in deep, huh?"

"Yes," James said without hesitation. "You'll understand when you meet her. I was hoping you could today, but she's already gone to the island to organise things for the week."

"Ah, that's too bad," Marc said casually—but something tugged at him. A flicker of unease. He pushed it down. *She can't be the woman from New Year's Eve,* he told himself. *She can't be.* "So, when's the wedding?"

"As soon as humanly possible," James said with a grin.

Marc laughed. "Wow. The great James Fraser ready to sprint down the aisle. Never thought I'd see the day."

James pointed at him. "No, you've got it backwards—I'm the lucky one. Truly."

Marc felt something twist in his chest—an unexpected, unwelcome pang. *Envy? Longing? No. Ridiculous.* "Well," he said lightly, forcing the odd feeling aside, "she must be something extraordinary if she got you of all people to fall this hard."

Before James could respond, his phone buzzed. He tapped the intercom button.

"Yes, Karen?"

"Mr. Sinclair is here for your meeting," came the assistant's voice. "Shall I send him in?"

"Yes, thank you."

James released the button and shot Marc a quick grin. "Showtime."

Marc smiled back—but inside, one thought echoed like a warning:

Please don't let her be the woman from New Year's Eve…

The office door opened, and John Sinclair stepped in, a warm smile on his face as he extended a hand toward Marc. "You must be Marc," he said, his voice friendly. "James has told me a lot about you."

"I hope it's all positive," Marc replied with a grin, shaking his hand firmly.

"Of course," John said with a chuckle. "Did James share his big news with you already?"

"Yes, he did. Congratulations! Your daughter, I believe?"

John's expression softened, pride radiating from his features. "Yes, Emily. You'll meet her tomorrow. She's already at our island, getting everything ready for the upcoming week."

Marc raised an eyebrow, impressed. "That's quite a responsibility."

"Oh, she handles it beautifully," John said, his tone warm. "She loves it. Since my wife passed, she's been my rock—a wonderful source of joy and support." His eyes glimmered with emotion.

Marc's voice softened. "I'm sorry for your loss, sir."

John waved a hand dismissively. "No, no—it was ten years ago. I miss her every day, of course, but life moves forward." He paused, thoughtful. "Her passing is exactly why I brought in a partner—so I could dedicate more time to Emily. And now… well, he's taking her away from me," he said, glancing affectionately at James.

James smiled reassuringly. "Emily would never let that happen, sir. She's devoted to you, and she'll always be there whenever you need her."

John's gaze softened, emotion thick in his voice. "Yes, yes, I know. She truly is the best of daughters. But one good thing—maybe I'll be seeing some grandchildren soon," he added, his eyes twinkling with hope.

James returned the smile, the thought of starting a family with Emily filling him with quiet happiness. "Let's hope so," he said.

Curious to keep the conversation professional, Marc shifted slightly. "Does Emily work here as well?"

John shook his head with a small smile. "Not officially. She helps with the social side of things—dinner parties, entertaining clients, and sometimes translating for us. She's fluent in Italian, French, and Japanese, both spoken and written."

"Impressive," Marc said, nodding in genuine admiration.

"Yes, indeed," John said proudly. "She's remarkable."

James rose from behind his desk and gestured toward the round table across the room. "Why don't we all sit and go over the details?"

Marc and John moved to the table, settling into the chairs as James joined them. John leaned forward, clearly energised as he outlined Marc's prospective role.

As the discussion unfolded, Marc asked thoughtful questions, and both John and James elaborated with patience and precision. The conversation moved smoothly, punctuated with clarifications, professional anecdotes, and a shared sense of purpose.

An hour later, the meeting concluded, and the three men stood. James and Marc shook John's hand, expressing their gratitude for his time and insights.

On his way out, John paused at the doorway, turning to Marc. "Thank you for coming today. If you'd like, James can introduce you to Paul and his team for another perspective on the role. Paul's retiring in four weeks, so we'd appreciate it if you could let us know your decision soon."

Marc nodded appreciatively. "Absolutely. Thank you, sir."

With a final nod, John left, leaving Marc and James alone in the office, the weight of the conversation settling comfortably between them as they prepared for the next step.

James turned to Marc with a casual smile. "How about we grab a drink?"

"Sounds good," Marc agreed, rising from his chair.

Marc had to admit he was genuinely impressed by the job offer. He'd decided some time ago that it was time for a change—not because of money, which he had plenty of, but because of a restless energy he could no longer ignore. A new challenge, new people, a new direction—he was ready.

They arrived at the bar, a sophisticated lounge with soft amber lighting that reflected off polished wood and glass. James ordered two whiskeys and carried them back to the table Marc had already scoped out, the air between them easy and familiar.

Sitting down, James handed Marc the tumbler with a grin. "Here you go."

"Congrats, James," Marc said, lifting his glass in a toast.

James clinked his glass gently against Marc's. "Thanks, mate. Means a lot."

Marc took a sip, letting the warmth of the whiskey settle. "So, Emily… she sounds quite impressive. Fluent in four languages, organised, well-educated. And from what you said, she's also charitable?"

"Yes," James said, pride evident in his tone. "She's invaluable—especially with clients who speak those languages. And beyond that, she has a heart of gold. She's been my anchor in more ways than one. Bachelor's degree in social work, actively involved in charity, and she's always thinking of others."

Marc raised an eyebrow. "A paragon?"

James laughed softly. "I haven't found a fault yet. And I've known her for ten years." His eyes gleamed with affection.

"I'm really looking forward to meeting her tomorrow," Marc said, swirling his drink. He tried to keep his tone light, but there was a faint curiosity in his voice.

"She'll get along with Mary," James added. "Emily's excited to meet her—she's hoping they can become friends."

Marc nodded thoughtfully. "Let's hope so. Mary could use a friend right now."

For the next hour, their conversation drifted between work, old memories, and light-hearted banter. Marc found himself enjoying the easy rhythm with James, appreciating the steadiness of their friendship. When the time came to part ways, he shook James's hand outside the bar.

"Good seeing you, mate," James said.

"You too," Marc replied, though his thoughts were already drifting elsewhere.

As he walked back to his hotel, he couldn't stop thinking about James's fiancée. Emily. He hoped she wasn't the same Emily he'd encountered on New Year's Eve. James's happiness with her was clear, and the last thing Marc wanted was to complicate that. Yet if it was her… he knew sticking to his 'hands-off' rule would be harder than he imagined.

Well, it would all be revealed tomorrow, he told himself. Marc genuinely wanted James to be happy—he had earned it—but he couldn't ignore the nagging curiosity, the flicker of unease at the thought that Emily might remember him. The memory of that night lingered, teasing, and unresolved, leaving him unsettled as he made his way through the city streets.

Emily entered the kitchen, her face lighting up as she greeted Rosa with a warm smile. "Rosa Del Mattino," she said, planting a quick kiss on her cheek.

Rosa, their cook and housekeeper for nearly fifteen years and a cherished member of the household, beamed. "Mattina, Emily," she replied, her voice rich with affection.

"Is everything ready for tonight? Have you briefed the caterers?" Emily asked, scanning the kitchen with a practiced eye.

"Si, si, tutto è organizzato," Rosa assured her, her hands busy arranging a tray of freshly baked pastries.

"Thank you, Rosa. You're a gem," Emily said sincerely. "I'm going to check with the cleaning staff when they arrive; they'll need to give the cabins a final once-over."

As Emily turned to leave, Rosa called after her, "Devi fare colazione?"

"Oh, Rosa, I'll get something to eat soon. Do not worry," Emily replied, laughing softly. "And please, when everyone arrives, try to speak English," she added with a playful smile.

"Of course, Miss Emily," Rosa promised, her thick Italian accent charming as ever.

"Grazie," Emily said before briskly heading out to meet the launch ferrying the cleaners in.

The morning passed in a flurry of activity. Emily oversaw the final preparations with meticulous care, coordinating with cleaners and caterers to ensure every detail was perfect. After lunch, she bid farewell to the staff as they departed on the launch, their tasks complete. The guests were scheduled to arrive on the return ferry at 5:30 p.m.

Next, Emily met with Daisy and Darren, the friendly middle-aged couple she had hired as guest liaisons. Her father had insisted on the extra help so she could enjoy herself rather than being tied to every minor detail. Together, they reviewed room assignments, guest arrival procedures, and any special dietary or accessibility requests. By mid-afternoon, Emily felt confident that everything was in place.


At four o'clock, she retreated to her room to shower and dress. Once ready, she examined herself in the mirror. Her golden-brown hair had been swept into a high ponytail that shimmered in the light, while her red dress hugged her figure perfectly. The fitted bodice and delicate straps highlighted her graceful shoulders, and the skirt flared just above her knees, swinging playfully with every movement. Small-heeled sandals, long dangling gold earrings, and a matching bracelet completed the ensemble. She smiled, pleased with her reflection—youthful, sophisticated, and ready for the evening.

Guests began arriving promptly, trickling into the ballroom in small groups. With her father and James still absent, Emily took it upon herself to welcome everyone. She circulated among the guests, offering warm greetings and handing out cocktails—or mocktails for those who preferred them. Emily sipped a mocktail herself, realising she had not eaten all day, and tried to stay composed despite the flurry of activity.

When James finally arrived, his eyes immediately found her across the room. He weaved through the crowd and took her hand. Emily excused herself from her conversation and turned to him. He grinned, kissed her softly on the lips, and playfully traced kisses down her neck. "You look good enough to eat," he whispered.

Emily laughed softly, her cheeks flushing.

James's eyes sparkled with pride as he said, "Sweetheart, I want you to meet Marcus Winters." He gently guided her attention to the man standing behind her.

Emily's heart skipped a beat. Her breath caught in her throat as she saw the stranger from the New Year's Eve party standing there, tall, dark, and impossibly familiar. A wave of dizziness swept over her, her vision blurring. Her knees buckled, and she felt herself crumpling.

Before she could hit the floor, strong arms caught her. James's voice was urgent, filled with concern. "Emily!"

Her father's voice joined his, equally anxious. "Emily!"

Everything spun around her, and the room seemed to dissolve into shadows and light as her mind struggled to focus. She felt the warmth and strength of James holding her, grounding her even as darkness threatened to take her away.

# Chapter Eight

When Emily slowly regained her senses, she opened her eyes to find herself reclining on a plush couch in the library. Sunlight filtered through the tall windows, catching dust motes that drifted lazily in the warm air. James knelt beside her, his face etched with worry, one hand gently holding hers, the other brushing a stray strand of hair from her forehead.

Behind him stood her father, Jeremy, and Marc. Her father's gaze was heavy with concern, Jeremy's calm but vigilant, and Marc's expression was an intriguing mixture of curiosity, care, and something else Emily couldn't quite place. She understood their concern, but it was Jeremy's sharp, almost angry glance at James that made her pause.

"Emily, sweetheart, are you okay?" James asked, his voice thick with worry as he pressed soft kisses to her knuckles. "Please… be okay."

Emily tried to sit up, her head spinning slightly. "What happened?" she murmured, her voice barely above a whisper.

Her father leaned closer, his tone firm yet tender. "Emily, are you alright? I've never known you to faint before."

Rosa appeared at the doorway, her face a mix of worry and exasperation. "Non hai mangiato tutto il giorno!" she scolded, her thick Italian accent sharp.

Emily sighed, embarrassed. "Ero occupata… me ne sono dimenticata."

Rosa turned to her father, explaining with fervent concern, "Miss Emily, she hasn't eaten all day, Mr. Sinclair."

James' brow furrowed, and he looked at her intently. "Is that true, Emily? You haven't eaten all day?"

Frustrated at the attention but wanting to ease their worry, Emily forced herself to stand, her legs trembling slightly. "Sorry," she said softly, offering James a small, reassuring smile. "I just… forgot. I've been busy. Really, I'm fine."

She steadied herself, taking a deep breath as she felt the familiar flutter of nervous energy in her stomach. Turning her attention to Marc, she extended her hand, her voice calm but careful. "I'm so sorry about that. I must have spun around too quickly. You must be Marc. It's a pleasure to meet you."

Marc's smile widened, and Emily's stomach skipped a beat. He took her hand with deliberate gentleness, bringing it to his lips for a brief, courteous kiss. "The pleasure's mine, Emily. May I call you Em?"

Recognition sparked in her eyes, and she returned his smile, a flicker of warmth and hesitation mingling. "If you wish," she said softly.

James, blissfully unaware of the undercurrent between Emily and Marc, chuckled. "Be careful, Marc. Emily is spoken for."

Marc's gaze lingered on her with an almost imperceptible smirk. "More's the pity," he murmured, his tone low, teasing, and filled with subtle challenge.

Emily felt her cheeks heat and quickly redirected the conversation. "We should return to the ballroom; we have guests to attend to. I'm perfectly fine now."

Marc extended his arm in a gentlemanly gesture, his eyes sparkling with playful insistence. "Come, Emily. I'd like you to meet my sister."

James shot her a questioning glance, but she smiled reassuringly, subtly signalling that she was okay. Emily allowed Marc to guide her from the library, her heart still racing, her pulse quickened by the electric tension of the encounter.

As they walked toward the ballroom, Marc leaned in slightly, his voice low and teasing, brushing against her ear. "So… you do remember me?" he murmured, the mischievous undertone impossible to ignore.

Emily felt a shiver run down her spine at his closeness. She managed a composed laugh, keeping her voice light. "Of course," she replied, her mind whirling. *This is going to be a very interesting evening…*

She held her composure, carefully masking any flicker of recognition, but Marc noticed the faint tension in her posture. "Yes, Marcus, I remember you," she said, her voice steady, controlled.

He offered a small, knowing smile, his eyes never leaving hers. "I'm glad," he murmured, the weight behind the words barely perceptible but there nonetheless.

Marc then gestured toward a petite woman of around twenty-five. Her delicate frame was softened by the gentle drape of a green summer dress, the light fabric moving gracefully with each step. Shoulder-length black hair framed her face in soft waves, and her vivid green eyes, striking and luminous, mirrored Marc's own. There was an air of warmth and approachability about her that instantly put Emily at ease.

The young woman looked from Marc to Emily, curiosity lighting her features. Marc spoke first. "Mary, this is Emily, James's fiancée."

Mary's eyes brightened, and she extended her hand with a genuine, welcoming smile. "Oh, I'm so happy to meet you, Emily. I hope we can get to know each other better this week."

Emily returned the gesture, squeezing her hand warmly. "I'd love that," she said, feeling an immediate connection with Mary's cheerful openness.

With Emily's arm lightly linked in his, Marc suggested a casual stroll through the room. "You could point out the other guests for me," he suggested, his tone easy yet carrying a subtle undertone of intent.

Emily agreed politely, offering a nod toward Mary. "You'll be seated near me at dinner. We can talk more then," she said, her voice smooth and unhurried. Mary's smile widened, and she added that she was eager to catch up with James, whom she hadn't seen in years.

As they moved through the ballroom, Marc leaned just enough to lower his voice. "So... have you told James about New Year's Eve?" he asked casually, though his green eyes held a quiet intensity.

Emily glanced up at him, her smile sweet yet carefully measured. "James and I weren't a couple at the time," she said. "I don't dwell on his past relationships, so I see no reason to bring up my experiences."

Marc nodded slowly, digesting her words. "Based on your reaction, I take it you'd prefer I keep quiet about it?"

Her gaze met his directly, steady, and unwavering. "Marcus, you must do what you think is right. I won't try to sway you either way. But if you believe revealing it is in James's best interest, then by all means, tell him. Just know this—he can be far more protective than you realise when it comes to me."

Marc studied her, a flicker of admiration passing through his eyes. She's sharp... confident... and completely aware of her own power. A smirk tugged at his lips as he considered her words. She's right. If James ever found out about our little interlude, I'd be barred from even breathing in her direction. Best to let that detail remain buried.

Emily's voice cut through his thoughts, sweet yet mischievous. "By the way," she said, tilting her head, "how is Selina?"

Marc blinked, momentarily caught off guard. "I don't know. I haven't seen her since New Year's Eve."

Her cheeky smile widened, teasing. "She must be disappointed."

Marc chuckled despite himself, shaking his head at her audacity. "You're a cheeky one," he admitted, a trace of fondness in his tone.

Her grin deepened, but then his expression shifted, serious and earnest. "I should apologise again for her outburst that night," he said, his voice low, sincere.

Emily tilted her head, amusement flickering in her eyes. "I must admit, no one's ever called me a—"

"Please," Marc interrupted quickly, his jaw tightening, "don't repeat it. She had no right to say that."

Emily's smile softened, warmth replacing her playful air. "It's fine. You didn't say it."

"And I never would," Marc replied firmly, his voice resolute, the intensity in his gaze lingering just a fraction too long.

A brief silence followed, charged with unspoken understanding, each of them aware of the history between them and the delicate balance of the present. Emily felt her pulse quicken, while Marc found himself reluctant to break the connection. And yet, civility demanded they step back into the social dance surrounding them.

Before either of them could continue, a tall, impeccably dressed gentleman approached, his posture flawless, his every movement exuding confidence. He stopped in front of Emily and inclined his head slightly. "Bonjour, Emily, c'est un plaisir de te revoir," he greeted, his French smooth and polished, with a warmth that suggested familiarity.

Emily's face lit up instantly at the sight of him, her eyes sparkling with recognition. She responded effortlessly, her French flowing naturally, the cadence and tone betraying her comfort with the language. "Bonjour, Louis. J'espère que tu vas bien."

Marc watched the exchange, even though he didn't understand the words. The ease with which Emily conversed, the subtle grace in her gestures, and the warmth in her expression made her presence undeniably magnetic. Whoever this Louis was, it was clear he held her in high regard—and Marc felt an unfamiliar twinge of jealousy, sharp and unsettling, creeping into his chest.

Emily turned to Marc, seamlessly switching back to English. "Marc, allow me to introduce Louis Barbier. Louis, this is Marcus Winters. My father is hoping to recruit him as our corporate lawyer. Louis here is our Chief Investment Officer."

Marc extended his hand, and Louis greeted him with a firm, confident shake. "A pleasure, Marcus," he said with a charming smile, his French accent rolling off his tongue even in English.

Emily tilted her head slightly, her tone teasing as she asked, "And where is your lovely wife, Helena?"

Louis chuckled, a rich, warm sound. "She's probably chasing James," he said, eyes glinting with amusement. "I'd better go save him and let her know he's taken now." With that, he leaned in and placed a quick, affectionate kiss on each of Emily's cheeks. She giggled softly as he departed, striding confidently toward the other guests.

Emily resumed guiding Marc through the room, pointing out other attendees with a practiced ease that left him both impressed and slightly overwhelmed.

"Those two over there are Ryan Ridding, our Chief Financial Officer, and his wife, Irene," she said, nodding toward a lively couple whose linked arms betrayed a strong, protective partnership. "She's very protective of me, so watch out," she added with a playful laugh.

Marc followed her gaze as she continued, pointing toward a platinum blonde beside a muscular man. "That's Selena Hyde, our Chief Compliance Officer, with her husband, Stan. He doesn't like anyone getting too chummy with her, so perhaps keep your distance," she said with a mischievous grin.

A little further along, Emily indicated a tall, dark-haired woman standing next to a shorter, dark-skinned man. "That's Maria Lopez, our Chief Marketing Officer, and her husband, Mateo. He's full of energy—always a delight to talk to."

Her eyes softened as they moved toward an older couple. "And that's Paul Vines, our current Corporate Lawyer, and his wife, Helen. Paul's retiring in four weeks, as you know. He'll be sorely missed; both are wonderful people."

Finally, Emily gestured toward a sharp-looking woman with black hair. "You met Karen King at the office yesterday. She's James's personal assistant."

She glanced at Marc with a small, teasing smile. "And of course, you know the Chief Executive Officer, my father—and the Chief Operating Officer, my fiancé." She felt the subtle stiffening of Marc's arm at the mention of James, and though it puzzled her, she chose to ignore it, focusing instead on her role as host.

Marc regarded her with an approving look, the corner of his mouth tilting in a faint smile. "You're quite adept at being a hostess. Do you enjoy it?"

Emily considered the question, her expression thoughtful yet poised. "I do," she admitted softly, brushing a stray lock of hair behind her ear. "It's a way to make everyone feel welcome, to see people enjoying themselves… and I love ensuring that everything runs smoothly. There's a certain satisfaction in orchestrating a perfect evening."

Marc's gaze lingered on her, impressed. "It's clear you take pride in it. You have a natural elegance about you, Emily. I can see why everyone responds to you so well."

Emily felt a faint warmth creep up her neck at his compliment but smiled graciously. "Thank you, Marcus. That's very kind of you to say."

She gestured around the grand ballroom with her free hand. "I enjoy helping my father. After my mother passed away, he struggled to balance the business and raising me alone, which is why he brought James on board. I started hosting at sixteen, observing my mother carefully at every gathering. By eighteen, I had become quite proficient at it—though I never expected it would become second nature."

"Why did you learn all those languages?" Marc asked, his curiosity sharpening. He wanted to understand this remarkable woman more fully.

Emily smiled, recalling her early motivation. "About seven years ago, my father started doing business with Italians, so I decided to learn Italian to help with translations. Then I picked up French because of Louis—he really helped me with my pronunciation. Later, I learnt Japanese, mostly out of interest. I don't have a full-time job, so I had the time to devote to it."

Marc gestured around the ballroom, his voice teasing. "I'd say this counts as a job. James also mentioned you have a bachelor's degree, yes?"

Emily laughed softly, a melodic sound that made Marc shift his focus entirely to her. "Yes, in Social Work. I wanted to focus on charity work, and the degree gave me a deeper understanding of what's involved. I really enjoyed it."

"Has anyone ever told you that you're quite amazing?" Marc asked, a flicker of admiration in his eyes. It was clear why both James and her father thought so highly of her.

Emily blushed, shyly averting her gaze. "Thank you, but you really shouldn't say things like that to me."

Marc's smirk widened. "Is that a blush I see? Humble, too. But why shouldn't I say it?"

"Because I'm an engaged woman," Emily replied, discomfort tugging at her composure.

"Yes, that is a pity," Marc said softly, deliberately, letting his words hang.

Emily flushed deeper, her pulse quickening. She hesitated, then asked carefully, "Why did you say that?"

Marc's voice lowered, serious, almost intimate. "You have to ask? That kiss we shared is imprinted in my mind." His eyes darkened slightly, memory vivid.

Emily's cheeks flamed crimson. Before she could respond, Jeremy's familiar presence interrupted, placing a hand on her shoulder in a familiarity that made Marc bristle.

"Hello, Emily. The place looks wonderful; you've outdone yourself this time," Jeremy said warmly, admiration in his tone.

Marc's jaw tightened, and he asked directly, "And you are?"

"I..." Jeremy faltered, clearly caught off guard by Marc's intensity.

Emily quickly interjected. "This is Jeremy Saunders, my father's personal assistant."

Marc's smile turned cold but polite. "Okay," he said curtly, letting his protective instincts simmer just beneath the surface.

Jeremy glanced at Marc with a fleeting flash of distaste before returning his attention to Emily. "I hope you'll save a dance for me at the ball later this week?"

"Of course," Emily replied, smiling politely.

Marc, uninterested in further pleasantries, moved them along. Emily, surprised by his forwardness, said, "That was rude, Mr. Winters."

He arched an eyebrow. "He's a bit too familiar for my liking," Marc said, a low edge in his voice. There was something in the way Jeremy had looked at her that unsettled him, a silent alarm that pricked his protective instincts.

Emily shook her head, a faint laugh escaping. "You don't even know him. I've known Jeremy for six years. He's a great guy."

"Be careful, Emily," Marc warned, his tone dropping, serious and measured. "I sense he has too much interest in you."

"You're being ridiculous," Emily said, brushing off his concern with a playful wave. "No one has any interest in me except James," she added with absolute conviction.

Marc froze, stunned. "Excuse me?" His voice was incredulous. "You really believe that?"

Emily blinked, caught off guard by his intensity. "Yes, of course I do," she replied earnestly. "I haven't encouraged anyone else's attention—only James."

Marc shook his head slowly, trying to wrap his mind around her genuine innocence. "Let me give you a little insight into the opposite sex, my dear Emily," he said, stepping closer, voice steady but edged with frustration. "You are—without exaggeration—the epitome of sex on legs. Whether you realise it or not, you don't have to encourage anyone. They're not blind or deaf."

Emily's eyes widened, her cheeks blazing crimson. She glanced around as if hoping someone might step in to rescue her from his frankness. "Mr. Winters, please… that's simply not true."

"Yes, it is," Marc insisted, unwavering. His piercing gaze held hers, a curious mix of exasperation and admiration. "And please, call me Marc."

Emily opened her mouth to protest again, but his sincerity left her faltering. Her heart fluttered in a way that was both unnerving and thrilling. "I… think you're exaggerating," she murmured, gaze dropping.

Marc leaned in slightly, voice softening yet deliberate. "Emily, it's not just your looks—though you're undeniably stunning. It's how you carry yourself, the way you smile, how you can light up a room without even trying. One day, you'll see yourself the way the rest of us do… and when you do, you'll understand—it's not just James who notices."

Her breath caught, and she instinctively pressed a hand to her chest, overwhelmed by the intensity in his words. "I… I think you're mistaken," she whispered, almost afraid to meet his eyes.

"I'm not," Marc said firmly, stepping back to give her space, though his gaze never wavered. "One day, you'll realise just how remarkable you are—and that the world will take notice, whether you're ready or not."

Emily stared at him, mind spinning, heart pounding. She wanted to laugh it off, to brush away the unease fluttering in her stomach—but somewhere deep down, she wondered if perhaps she had underestimated her own allure… or at least the effect she had on men who truly saw her.

# Chapter Nine

Before Emily could respond, James approached, his presence calm but commanding. He gently took her arm from Marc's, guiding it onto his own. "I think you've monopolised my fiancée long enough," he said, his voice both firm and playful, noting the delicate flush on Emily's cheeks. "It seems you've been saying things you probably shouldn't have. Emily looks… a little embarrassed."

Marc's lips curved into a knowing smile. "She gets that lovely blush every time she's complimented. She's very modest, you know."

"She is," James agreed, offering Emily a warm, protective smile that made her heart flutter.

Realising it was time to change for dinner and wanting to shift the conversation, Emily suggested softly, "Let's all get ready and meet in the library at 7:30 p.m."

Everyone nodded in agreement, and the group began to disperse, the soft clatter of footsteps fading down the hall. James lingered behind, his hand lightly resting on Emily's as he escorted her toward her room. The hallway felt quieter now, the soft glow of sconces casting a warm light over them.

When they reached her door, Emily leaned lightly against it, gazing up at him. "Did Marc upset you? Or say anything inappropriate?" James asked, his tone serious but not accusatory.

Emily let out a soft laugh that didn't quite reach her eyes. "No, he just gave me a few too many compliments. You know how I get when people say things like that."

James nodded, a small smile tugging at his lips. "Yes, I know. But you are amazing."

Emily's cheeks warmed once more, and she lowered her eyes briefly before lifting them to meet his gaze, her lips parting in a quiet, unspoken invitation. "Please don't," she whispered.

Unable to resist, James pulled her gently into his arms, pressing a soft, lingering kiss to her lips. "I'm sorry, sweetheart," he murmured, brushing his lips against hers once more. "I love teasing you. I'll see you at dinner."

He stepped back, leaving a charged stillness in his wake, and turned toward his room, closing the door with a gentle click. Emily watched him go, a frown creasing her forehead. *Why did Marc call me 'sex on legs'?* she wondered, the words echoing in her mind. *Was there something about her that made her seem… flirtatious or provocative?* A flicker of unease stirred, but she shook it off, determined not to dwell.

Once inside her room, Emily decided against a full change for dinner; the affair was meant to be casual. Instead, she freshened up, smoothing her hair and switching her jewellery to a ruby set that perfectly complemented her red dress. A delicate string of small rubies encircled her neck, paired with matching stud earrings and a bracelet that caught the light with every subtle movement. The set elevated her outfit gracefully, adding understated elegance without appearing ostentatious.

At 7:25 p.m., a knock at the door made her pause. Expecting James, she was surprised to find Jeremy standing there instead. He looked slightly hesitant, a subtle tension in his posture.

"I was hoping to escort you down to dinner," he said, his voice quieter than usual, almost shy.

Emily smiled, the unease from earlier softening. "That would be lovely," she replied, stepping into the hall. She took Jeremy's offered arm, and together they made their way toward the library, their steps echoing softly on the polished floors.

As they walked, Emily's mind drifted back to Marc's words and James's protective presence. A mix of embarrassment, curiosity, and a small thrill tugged at her, though she pushed the feelings aside, focusing instead on the evening ahead. The library, bathed in warm light and lined with books that gave it a quiet elegance, awaited them. Dinner promised laughter, conversation, and the comforting presence of friends and family.

They arrived first, each taking a cocktail from the tray offered by a poised waiter. Emily chose a light mocktail, savouring the subtle sweetness as she tried to settle her racing thoughts. Wanting to keep the conversation neutral, she commented on the weather, prompting Jeremy to launch into an enthusiastic—but safe—discussion about the unusually mild evening breeze and the clear skies over the marina. Emily listened with polite interest, grateful for the opportunity to gather her composure.

A short while later, Marc and Mary entered the room. Emily immediately noticed a fleeting flash of tension cross Marc's face when he spotted her walking arm-in-arm with Jeremy. She couldn't understand the cause, though a small unease settled in her stomach.

Mary's eyes, however, brightened the moment they landed on Emily's ruby necklace. "Oh, that necklace is lovely. It looks so delicate," she said warmly, lifting Emily's hand gently to admire it more closely. "And the matching bracelet, too!"

Emily's lips curved in a soft, proud smile. "Thank you. It was my mother's. She loved jewellery that wasn't too showy, just like me. I was lucky James knew that when he chose my engagement ring."

"Oh! I forgot to ask—may I see it?" Mary's enthusiasm was genuine and endearing.

Emily lifted her hand, and Mary's fingers brushed lightly over the smooth metal and sparkling stone. "It's beautiful," Mary said, her eyes shining. Marc glanced at the ring too, lips tightening just slightly, a flash of something Emily couldn't quite read.

"I've never understood why anyone would want a huge rock on their hand," Emily added casually, a note of amusement in her voice.

At that moment, James appeared, his expression softening as he took her hand in his and kissed the ringed knuckles. "I'm glad I got it right," he murmured, a proud smile tugging at his lips.

"You always do, James," Emily replied, laughing softly.

Another shadow of annoyance crossed Marc's face, leaving Emily more puzzled than ever. *What's his problem?* she wondered, though she said nothing.

"Dinner is served," a waiter announced, the soft clatter of silverware and muted conversation signalling it was time.

James guided Emily into the dining room, while Marc led Mary and Jeremy followed behind. The long table, set for seventeen, gleamed with polished silver, crystal glasses catching the warm candlelight. Emily took her seat to the left of her father, James settling beside her. Mary was placed to John Sinclair's right, with Marc beside her.

John tapped his glass gently, and the room hushed, all eyes turning toward him. His presence was commanding yet infused with warmth, a man used to leading in business but equally capable of tenderness as a father.

"Thank you all for being here tonight," he began, his voice steady but rich with emotion. "It means the world to have so many colleagues together in one place. I've had the privilege of building something special alongside all of you—but tonight is not about business. Tonight is about my daughter."

His gaze softened as he looked directly at Emily. "For those who may not know, Emily has always been the light of my life. I've watched her grow into a remarkable woman— intelligent, compassionate, and determined. I couldn't be prouder of her accomplishments."

He paused, smiling as he shifted his gaze toward James. "And tonight, I have the immense pleasure of sharing some incredibly special news. I am proud to announce that my beautiful daughter Emily is engaged to a wonderful man, James Fraser."

The room erupted in applause, glasses clinking, smiles spreading as the news settled over the guests. John continued, his voice thick with pride and affection.

"James, I've seen firsthand how deeply you care for Emily, and I couldn't ask for a better partner for her. You are now part of this family, and I know that together, you will build a future as bright as your love for one another."

Raising his glass higher, he added, "So let us toast to Emily and James—may their lives be filled with love, joy, and every happiness the world can offer. To the happy couple!"

A chorus of cheers followed, the warmth of celebration filling the room. Yet, despite the joyful energy, Emily noticed that Jeremy and Marc remained unusually quiet, their expressions neutral, almost contemplative.

Blushing, Emily squeezed James's hand, drawing strength from his steady presence. She smiled at her father, mouthing a silent, heartfelt "thank you" for his words and for the pride he radiated.

Even as the festivities carried on around her, Emily's thoughts flickered back to Marc, and the faint tension his silence suggested lingered at the edge of her mind. But for now, she allowed herself to sink into the warmth of James's touch, resting her hand lightly on his arm and letting the familiar comfort of his presence ground her. Laughter and conversation rippled around the room, and for a moment, the world narrowed to the glow of candlelight, the clink of glasses, and the steady reassurance of the man beside her.

As dinner began, the table came alive with animated discussion. The narrow arrangement allowed Emily and Mary to chat easily, sharing small observations and gentle laughter, while Marc and James engaged in their own conversation about business strategy and market trends. Yet, Marc's gaze kept drifting toward Emily, subtle but intent, always careful to avoid being noticed by James. It wasn't difficult; James was entirely absorbed in ensuring Emily was comfortable, laughing softly at her comments and leaning in whenever she spoke.

Before Emily had become James's fiancée, Marc had seriously considered taking a position with her father's company. But now, the thought of working alongside James while harbouring feelings for Emily felt impossible to reconcile. He was torn—between the desire to be near her, the thrill of just observing her, and the loyalty he owed his best friend. James's trust weighed heavily on him, and Mary had hinted that she might relocate with him if he took the position. But how could he justify putting himself in a situation that might jeopardise everything?

Marc observed Emily as she laughed softly at something Mary said, the delicate curl of her lips, the way her eyes sparkled with genuine amusement. Her modesty, her complete unawareness of her own magnetic charm, was refreshing, almost disarming. And yet… she was also undeniably intoxicating. Even in her casual elegance, Marc's mind betrayed him, wandering to forbidden imaginings: what it would feel like to have those long legs wrapped around him, to taste the sweetness of her lips again. He bit the inside of his cheek, forcing the thought away. He had never allowed himself to desire a friend's partner before. He couldn't now.

Emily, meanwhile, felt the weight of Marc's gaze without fully admitting it to herself. Every time their eyes met, a subtle heat crept across her cheeks, and her pulse picked up despite her conscious efforts to focus on James. She was painfully aware of her engagement ring, of the man sitting beside her, steady and loving, whose mere presence should have been enough. And yet… her mind betrayed her, drifting back to that fleeting moment on New Year's Eve, the taste and warmth of Marc's kiss, the shock of closeness. A shiver ran down her spine at the memory.

"Are you cold, sweetheart?" James asked, leaning closer and draping his arm gently around her shoulders, pulling her slightly into him. His eyes were filled with quiet concern.

Emily smiled up at him, brushing a stray curl from her face. "No, I'm fine," she whispered, though her fingers instinctively tightened around his arm.

Marc, watching the subtle interplay, smiled inwardly, though a pang of guilt accompanied it. He realised she was not entirely unaware of his attention—there was a flicker of recognition, a momentary tension whenever their eyes met. His thoughts momentarily wandered to a dangerous place, imagining how she might react if he kissed her again, if he tested the magnetic pull that lingered between them. But he quickly pushed the fantasy aside. James would kill him—and rightly so. He had never considered jeopardising a friendship for a woman before, and yet, sitting here, watching her laugh softly, feeling her warmth even across the table, he knew that tonight, in some small way, he already was.

Marc exhaled slowly, his expression carefully neutral as he refocused on his conversation with James, though his mind remained stubbornly preoccupied. Across the table, Emily leaned a little closer to James, unaware of the storm of emotions her presence stirred, her heart beating steadily with love and a faint, inexplicable flutter she couldn't quite name.

# Chapter Ten

After dinner, the guests dispersed in various directions. Some drifted toward the billiards room, laughing and challenging one another to games, while James, Mary, and a few others headed to the home cinema. Others, invigorated by the warm evening, stripped down and dove into the pool, their laughter echoing across the terrace.

Marc, Emily, Jeremy, and John lingered on the terrace, the cool night air brushing against their skin as they strolled among the potted plants and twinkling lights. Conversation flowed easily, light and teasing at first, then deeper as the hour passed. They laughed, shared stories, and enjoyed the ease of each other's company, the warmth of the terrace lanterns casting a golden glow over their faces.

Eventually, her father yawned and announced he was tired, planting a soft kiss on Emily's cheek before heading to bed. "Goodnight, my darling," he said warmly.

Marc turned to Emily with a subtle smirk. "Shall we take that walk I asked for?" he said, his tone light but his eyes carrying something heavier.

Emily nodded, slipping her arm through his. As Jeremy moved to join them, Marc tilted his head slightly and said, "Have a good night," with a polite but firm finality that made it clear Jeremy wasn't welcome.

"Oh… yes, goodnight," Jeremy said, forcing a smile at Emily, then casting a sharp glance at Marc before heading to his room.

Once Jeremy was out of earshot, Marc's voice dropped to a low murmur. "Be careful, Emily. There's something about that guy when it comes to you."

Emily shrugged lightly, a small smile on her lips. "Jeremy is harmless; he's just a friend."

Marc's lips pressed into a thin line, but he didn't press the matter further. Instead, he fell into step beside her as they wandered slowly through the garden, the night alive with the soft murmurs of laughter from the pool and distant conversation from the billiards room. Emily gestured at the carefully curated flowerbeds and towering hedges.

"This is my favourite place," she said softly. "Mum planted most of this before she… before she passed."

Marc's expression softened. "That must have been hard, being so young."

Emily's gaze dropped to her hands. "I was devastated. But Dad… he was worse. My parents loved each other deeply. Mum was his world."

Marc's voice was gentle. "What happened?"

"She was on her way to pick me up from school. A drunk driver came out of a side street and T-boned her car. She held on for two days," Emily said, her voice quiet, a single tear escaping down her cheek.

Instinctively, Marc stopped walking. He gently lifted her chin, brushing the tear away with his thumb, then pulled her into his arms. She leaned against him, letting herself be held, finding comfort in the solid warmth of his body.

"You still miss her," he murmured, his voice low and soft.

Emily rested her head on his shoulder. "Yes. I know it's silly, it's been ten years… I shouldn't still feel this way."

"It's not silly," Marc said, sliding his hands down her back, his touch both protective and intimate.

Suddenly, Emily stiffened, pulling back slightly. Marc noted the subtle hesitation—the fleeting mix of longing and caution. She tried to compose herself and continued walking.

"Dad was a mess, and I was finishing high school. One day, I suggested he might need someone to help at work," she explained lightly, her voice tinged with nostalgia.

Marc's brows rose in understanding. "Ah, so that's when James joined the firm?"

Emily nodded. "Yes. Dad was extremely impressed by James. He told me James was a genius with numbers."

Marc smiled. "And the rest is history."

"Definitely," Emily said, returning his smile. "Recruiting James was one of the best decisions Dad ever made."

They had wandered to the far end of the garden, where the tall hedge formed a private sanctuary. The only sounds were the soft rustle of leaves in the night breeze and the distant hum of conversation from the house. Marc stopped and turned Emily to face him. His expression was unreadable, magnetic.

"Marc?" she asked softly, uncertainty knitting her brows.

"Em," he began, his voice low, carrying weight that made her heart flutter. "I can't stop thinking about our kiss."

Her cheeks flushed a deep pink, and she averted her gaze. "I… I'm sorry."

Marc's lips quirked into a faint smile, though there was no humour in it. Slowly, he slid his hands down her arms, sending tiny shivers through her, then captured her hands in his, lifting them to his lips to place a tender kiss on her knuckles.

Emily's breath caught, her pulse quickening. "You shouldn't do that," she whispered, barely audible.

"I know," Marc admitted, his voice low and rough, as though he was battling a war within himself. Yet he didn't let go. He stepped closer, their bodies mere inches apart, his gaze fixed firmly on hers, laden with unspoken desire.

Emily's resolve wavered. Her eyes flickered to his lips, her heart pounding, her mind screaming that this was dangerous territory. Yet, she didn't pull away. The air between them thrummed with tension, charged with everything they hadn't allowed themselves to say.

Marc tilted his head slightly, closing the distance almost imperceptibly. The world seemed to slow, the night air thick with anticipation. Her breath hitched, her pulse racing—until—

"Marc!" Mary's voice rang out, sharp and startled.

"Emily!" James's call followed, commanding and unmistakable.

Marc swore softly under his breath, the fragile moment shattering like glass. His hands reluctantly released hers, the warmth of her touch lingering longer than he wanted to admit. He straightened, jaw clenched, a storm of frustration and desire warring behind his composed exterior. Yet his eyes never left Emily, frozen there, cheeks flushed, a mixture of embarrassment, confusion, and something unspoken that made his chest tighten.

Without a word, he offered his arm, his touch light but steady. "We should go," he said quietly, the calm in his tone a thin veneer over the turmoil raging inside him.

Emily nodded, her voice caught somewhere between relief and disorientation. She allowed him to guide her back toward the sounds of the house, toward James and Mary. Her thoughts swirled in chaos, each step weighed down by the ghost of what had almost happened. Her fingers brushed against his arm occasionally, and each contact sent an electric thrill through her, a confusing reminder of the fire she had tried so hard to suppress.

As they rounded the corner, James and Mary spotted them and approached with friendly smiles. "Ah, there you are," James said warmly, oblivious to the tension lingering between Marc and Emily.

"Emily was showing me her mother's garden," Marc explained, his voice casual, carefully neutral, belying the storm beneath his calm exterior.

Mary's eyes lit up. "Oh, did your mother plant this garden? What a wonderful gift she left you," she said, her tone full of admiration.

"Yes, I love this garden," Emily said, forcing a small, polite yawn and covering her mouth with her free hand. "She was passionate about gardening." She tilted her head just slightly at Marc, a silent signal, a small shield against the vulnerability still thrumming through her.

James noticed the yawn, his protective instincts kicking in. "Sweetheart, you're tired. I'll walk you to your room."

Emily released Marc's arm, letting her hand slip into James's. "Thank you. Goodnight," she said softly, glancing at both Mary and Marc, masking the lingering flutter in her chest.

They all exchanged courteous goodnights, and James led her inside, his hand firm and comforting around hers. Marc watched them walk away, the pull of desire and frustration stronger than ever. He couldn't deny the effect she had on him; the fake yawn, the subtle playfulness—it was genius. He allowed himself a wry smile. Well played, Emily.

Inside the house, James guided Emily down the softly lit hallway, their footsteps echoing quietly. They reached her bedroom door, and Emily turned, capturing him with a bold yet tentative motion. She wrapped her arms around his neck, pulling him close, their lips meeting in a passionate kiss.

James responded eagerly, wrapping his arms around her waist, deepening the kiss. Yet, as she kissed him, Emily felt a subtle difference—the butterflies that had erupted when Marc kissed her on New Year's Eve were absent. The warmth was comforting, familiar, but it lacked the spark that had jolted through her that night.

James gently pulled away, breath unsteady, his forehead brushing against hers. "Emily… if we don't stop now, I won't be able to," he murmured, his eyes searching hers, filled with desire but restrained by respect.

Emily froze, her heart hammering in her chest. When she and James first started dating, she had been honest with him—telling him she had no intention of rushing intimacy, that she was still a virgin. Now, engaged and so close to taking that step, they had agreed to wait until their wedding night. James had always been patient, never pressuring her, and she had trusted him completely.

But tonight, uncertainty gnawed at her. The memory of Marc's kiss months ago—the warmth, the audacity, the way it had made her pulse race—stirred something inside her she hadn't expected. Suddenly, the certainty she had always felt about waiting wavered, leaving her breathless and unsettled.

Flustered, she stepped back, dropping her arms from around James's neck. "I'm sorry," she murmured, forcing a soft smile, her cheeks still warm. "Goodnight."

James's brow furrowed, concern flickering across his face as he watched her retreat. "Goodnight, Emily," he said quietly, his voice tinged with unease.

She disappeared into her bedroom, the soft click of the door echoing in the hallway. James remained standing there, his gaze fixed on the closed door, his mind a storm of thoughts. He replayed the moment in his head—her hesitation, the way she had pulled back—and a knot of worry tightened in his chest. Was she truly tired, or was something else troubling her?

He ran a hand through his hair, exhaling slowly, trying to quell the unease that churned within him. James had always been patient, confident in their mutual respect and love, but tonight, for the first time, he couldn't shake the fear that something—some lingering doubt—was unsettling her.

Meanwhile, outside, Marc lingered near the terrace door, hands in his pockets, the night air heavy with unsaid words. His jaw clenched as he replayed every second of their walk, every fleeting glance, every whisper of touch. Desire, frustration, and a reluctant respect warred inside him. She was James's fiancée, untouchable—and yet, the thought of her, of her warmth pressed against him, refused to leave his mind.

# Chapter Eleven

The first day passed smoothly. Guests moved about the island freely—some swimming in the crystalline waters, others lounging with books, playing billiards, testing their aim at the archery range, or simply soaking up the sun. Lunch was served either as a casual picnic on the beach or in the dining room for those who preferred a more traditional setting.

Emily and Mary spent the morning together, their laughter carrying across the sand as they explored the shoreline and swapped stories. By the time noon arrived, they were laughing like old friends, their bond strengthened by the ease of their conversation and the carefree rhythm of the day.

Deciding to join the other guests on the beach for a picnic, they found a shaded area where blankets and chairs were arranged near a table piled high with fresh fruit, sandwiches, pastries, and chilled beverages. They selected a checkered blanket, spreading it over the soft golden sand. The gentle rhythm of the waves lapping the shore created a soothing soundtrack, while the sun cast a warm, golden glow across the scene.

Emily, in a flowing white sundress, brushed a strand of hair behind her ear, letting the breeze lift it playfully, while Mary's vibrant yellow dress swayed around her as she settled onto the blanket. Seagulls circled above, curious but keeping their distance. Emily picked up a plump strawberry, closing her eyes briefly to savour its sweetness and the quiet comfort of the moment.

"I've missed days like this," Emily murmured, her voice soft, almost reverent.

Mary nodded, smiling. "It's perfect out here. Just the sea, the sun… no expectations, no worries."

After their meal, they leaned back on the blanket, letting the sun warm them as they watched clouds drift lazily across the sky. Their conversation shifted naturally, flowing between dreams, laughter, and memories. There was a calm intimacy in the quiet that stretched between them, an unspoken understanding forming in the warmth of the afternoon.

Emily took a breath, curiosity edging her words. "Tell me if I'm being nosy, but… what happened with your engagement?" she asked cautiously.

Mary looked down at her hands, her fingers fidgeting with the edge of her sleeve. When she spoke, her voice was quiet, threaded with sorrow and something sharper—frustration, maybe even shame. "It was bad," she admitted, letting out a trembling breath. "At first, Eric was charming, attentive… everything I thought I wanted. But over time he became someone else. More possessive. More controlling. I kept thinking it was just stress, that it was a phase he'd grow out of. But it didn't stop."

A shudder rippled through her, subtle but unmistakable. "And I never told Marc because I know exactly how he would've reacted. He's always been so protective of me. I didn't want to drag him into something that wasn't his fight."

Emily's heart tightened painfully as she listened, her mind spinning with questions and disbelief. "But Mary… what exactly happened? Why didn't you just leave him?" she asked gently, trying to piece together how someone like Mary—warm, kind, confident—could have endured something so dark alone.

Mary hesitated, her gaze drifting toward the horizon as though the ocean might give her strength. She took a long, steadying breath before speaking. "I didn't leave because… I kept hoping it would get better," she said, her voice barely above a whisper. "I didn't want to believe someone I loved could change so drastically. We had just gotten engaged—he proposed, and I thought we were building a future together."

She paused, closing her eyes as if bracing herself. "Then one night, we ran into an ex-boyfriend of mine at a bar. Completely innocent—we talked for maybe five minutes. Just catching up. Everything was fine. But when Eric and I got to the car…" Mary's voice faltered. A tear escaped, sliding down her cheek.

Emily leaned forward immediately, resting her hand over Mary's in a quiet gesture of support. "What happened?" she asked softly. Her heart pounded, already sensing the gravity of the memory Mary was about to relive.

Mary inhaled shakily. "The minute we got to the car, he snapped. He grabbed me by the hair—hard—and yanked me toward him. Called me a whore."

Emily gasped, horrified.

"I was so shocked I couldn't even react," Mary continued, her voice trembling. "I tried to push him away, but he kept yelling at me, accusing me of things that weren't true. He forced me into the car, slammed the door, and as we were driving… he started hitting me."

Emily's stomach twisted. "Oh my God, Mary…"

"I thought he was going to kill me," Mary whispered, tears spilling freely now. "I honestly thought that was it."

Emily squeezed her hand tightly, grounding her. "Couldn't you scream? Try to get help?"

"I was in shock," Mary said miserably. "I didn't know what to do. I didn't want to make it worse. I thought maybe if I stayed quiet, he'd eventually calm down." She swallowed, her throat working. "We drove the rest of the way in silence. When we got to his apartment… he dragged me upstairs. I was numb. Completely numb."

Emily felt her own breath stutter, imagining the terror Mary must have felt, alone and hurt and trapped. "Didn't anyone see? No one helped?"

Mary shook her head. "We were parked on a quiet street. No cars, no people. It was late. But once we got inside…" She hugged her arms around herself. "It got worse. He threw me onto the living room floor. I honestly thought he was going to rape me."

Emily's heart broke a little. She reached out, brushing a tear from Mary's cheek.

"But then," Mary whispered, as if still unable to believe it, "he just… stopped. Out of nowhere. He dropped to the floor beside me and started crying. Sobbing. Apologising over and over." She gave a small, strangled laugh—one with no humour at all. "It felt surreal, Emily. Like I was stuck in someone else's nightmare."

Emily shook her head slowly, anger burning hot under her skin. "He hurt you, and then he expected you to just forgive him because he cried?"

Mary's lips trembled. "He helped me clean up. Made me dinner. Tried to act like nothing had happened. But I could feel it in my bones—this was who he truly was. And I knew… if I stayed, it would happen again."

"So, I left," Mary finished softly. "The next morning, while he was still asleep. I packed what I could, left my engagement ring on the counter, and walked out. I didn't look back."

Emily exhaled shakily, overwhelmed with grief and admiration all at once. "Mary… I am so proud of you," she whispered. "I can't even imagine how hard that was. But you did the bravest thing you could have done. You got out.

Mary wiped at her eyes with trembling fingers. "You're the first person I've told. All my friends are still friends with Eric. And Marc…" Her voice cracked. "If Marc knew, he'd kill him. I know he would."

Silence settled over them, thick with pain and relief and the fragile beginnings of healing. Emily didn't hesitate—she leaned in and wrapped Mary tightly in her arms. Mary collapsed into her, sobbing softly, her body shaking with the release of long-buried fear.

They stayed like that for a long time, two women clinging to each other in the warm ocean breeze, united by trust and the unspoken promise that Mary would never have to carry this alone again.

It wasn't until the sound of footsteps approached through the sand that they both stiffened—

"Mary?" Marc asked, his face filled with concern.

"Emily?" James asked, looking just as worried.

Emily looked up at the two men, tears streaming openly down her cheeks. Mary tensed in her arms, her entire body going rigid with the realisation that Marc—her fiercely protective brother—was now only a few steps away. She wasn't ready. Not yet.

Sensing Mary's hesitation, Emily lifted her gaze to the men and spoke softly, her voice trembling. "Could you please give us a few minutes?" Her eyes pleaded with them.

Marc and James exchanged a worried glance but nodded without argument. They stepped back toward the picnic tables, lingering close enough to watch, but far enough to give the women space.

Emily turned to Mary again. Mary's sobs had quieted, but tears still shimmered in her eyes, clinging thickly to her lashes.

"Mary," Emily whispered gently, brushing a hand along her friend's arm, "you know Marc needs to know."

Mary nodded, though her face twisted in dread.

"Do you want me to leave you alone so you can tell him?" Emily asked softly.

But Mary immediately grabbed her hand, her fingers tightening in panic. "I can't," she breathed, shaking her head, her voice breaking. "Emily, I can't tell him myself."

Emily hesitated. "Do you want me to? Are you sure?"

"Yes," Mary whispered, desperation raw in her eyes. "Please."

Emily's expression softened, a sigh escaping her chest. She squeezed Mary's hands. "Alright," she said gently. "If that's what you want, I'll do it."

Relief flooded Mary's face. "Thank you," she murmured, gripping Emily's hands like a lifeline.

Emily signalled Marc and James to return. When they reached the blanket, Emily inhaled deeply and said, "James, could you take Mary back to the house? She needs a moment to freshen up."

James nodded immediately, sensing the gravity of the situation. He helped Mary to her feet, slipping an arm around her shoulders. Mary managed the smallest grateful glance at Emily before letting James guide her up the sandy path toward the house.

Once they were out of sight, Marc stepped forward. Without a word, he extended a hand and helped Emily stand. She accepted it, and they began walking slowly along the shoreline, the waves whispering at their feet.

Marc broke the silence first, his voice low and sharp with intuition. "This is about Eric, isn't it?"

Emily nodded, wiping her damp cheeks. She placed her hand in his, needing the steadiness. Marc didn't hesitate—he clasped her hand tightly, his concern written across every line of his face.

"Marc," she began carefully, "Mary's been through something terrible." Her voice shook. Marc's brows tightened, but he remained silent. "She asked me to tell you because she's too scared to do it herself."

He exhaled hard through his nose, fury already simmering. Emily squeezed his hand.

"She's terrified of how you'll react," Emily continued softly. "She doesn't want revenge. She doesn't want a fight. She just wants you to know—and to move on. Can you do that for her?"

Marc clenched his jaw so hard the muscle twitched. "I can't promise that," he admitted, his voice rough. "But I'll try."

Emily gave him a small, encouraging smile before she began recounting Mary's story—the possessiveness, the confrontation, the violence, the terror. Every word seemed to hit Marc like a physical blow.

His grip on her hand tightened… and tightened… and tightened.

"Marc!" Emily gasped, trying to pry her fingers free.

He looked down, startled, instantly releasing enough pressure so he wasn't hurting her—but he still didn't let go. His chest rose and fell rapidly, fury radiating off him like heat.

"Sorry," he muttered, though the apology was strained, barely controlled. His voice was low and lethal when he added, "I'm going to kill him."

Emily nodded, not dismissing his anger. "I know. And honestly? I understand why you feel that way. Anyone would."

Marc's eyes snapped toward her, burning with protective rage.

"But," Emily continued gently, "you need to stay calm—for Mary's sake. She told me she didn't want you to fix anything. She just needs you to be there for her."

Marc shook his head, frustration spilling out in a harsh exhale. "How am I supposed to stay calm when someone hurt her like that?"

"Because she needs you steady," Emily said softly, stepping closer. "Not explosive. Not dangerous. Just… safe. She doesn't need a hero—she needs her brother."

Marc swallowed hard, the muscles in his throat working. He looked out at the waves, fists trembling, breathing deeply as he tried to leash the storm inside him.

Emily kept hold of his hand, grounding him.

And slowly, the fury in his posture shifted—not disappearing but focusing. Sharpening.

Protective, not destructive.

"I'll be there for her," he said finally, voice hoarse. "Whatever she needs."

Emily nodded, relief washing through her. "That's all she wants."

Marc exhaled shakily, squeezing Emily's hand once more. "Thank you for telling me," he murmured. "I know that wasn't easy."

"No," Emily whispered, "but she needs you."

Marc stopped walking and turned to look at her, his eyes unnaturally bright, a storm of emotion swirling behind them. Emily couldn't resist the pull any longer; she wrapped her arms around him, feeling the familiar flutter of butterflies in her stomach—a reaction she both feared and craved. The warmth of his body against hers, the subtle scent of him, the steady thrum of his heartbeat—it was intoxicating.

For a suspended moment, the world seemed to vanish. The laughter of guests in the distance, the gentle lapping of the waves, even her own thoughts faded, leaving only the heat between them. Stop, she reminded herself, a whisper in her mind. You're engaged to another man.

Marc pulled back slightly, just enough to look into her eyes. His gaze softened yet held a tension that made her stomach clench. He gave her hand a gentle squeeze, grounding her. "Thank you," he said quietly, almost reluctantly, and they resumed walking in silence, the evening air thick with unspoken words.

After a while, he spoke again, his voice low and edged with frustration. "I actually liked the guy... I can't believe I didn't see it," he admitted, anger and regret mixing in his tone. "I should have noticed."

Emily shook her head, her voice soft, trying to calm him. "No, Marc. Don't blame yourself. It's not your fault."

He stopped, turning to face her fully, and for a heartbeat, Emily was lost in the intensity of his gaze. There was a hunger there, a raw longing that pulled at her own desires. His fingers lifted slowly, brushing against her jaw, tracing the line down to her lips. The touch sent a jolt through her, her breath catching, her body betraying her reason.

As if drawn by a magnetic force, she leaned toward him, the space between them charged and heavy with unsaid emotions. She bit her lip nervously, feeling the pull of want and fear.

Marc didn't hesitate. His hands tangled in her hair, drawing her closer, and when their lips met, the world exploded. The kiss was slow and deliberate at first, tender and searching, then deepened with a heat that left her dizzy. Every press of his lips, every brush of his hands, seemed to call out to something primal within her, igniting a longing she had tried to suppress for months.

He pressed her body against his, and she leaned into him, every nerve alight, every beat of her heart thrumming in rhythm with his. It was intoxicating, terrifying, and overwhelming all at once. She wanted it, wanted him—more than she had ever allowed herself to admit.

Then, as quickly as it began, he pulled back. His chest rose and fell rapidly; his eyes shadowed with regret and conflict.

"Em… I'm sorry," he whispered, his voice strained, heavy with the weight of restraint.

Emily's chest tightened, her heart still racing from the kiss, leaving a raw ache in its wake. She touched her lips, tingling and sensitive, and stepped back, forcing the distance between them. Her body ached, her mind whirled, and confusion battled with desire.

She turned away without a word, her steps deliberate and heavy, each one echoing the unspoken feelings left in their wake. The ache of what could have been, and yet never would be, weighed down her shoulders, and the air between them felt impossibly wide, a chasm she didn't know how to bridge.

Marc remained frozen where he stood, watching her retreat. His chest felt tight, his mind a storm of frustration, longing, and guilt. The silence stretched, heavy and suffocating, as he realised that the moment had passed—but the tension, the electricity, and the unspoken desire remained, lingering like a phantom between them.

# Chapter Twelve

Marc must have followed Emily, as they arrived back at the house at the same time. James and Mary were seated on the terrace, sipping drinks in the soft glow of the evening. Emily paused in front of their table; her brow furrowed with concern.

"Are you okay, Mary?" she asked gently, her voice carrying a note of genuine care.

Mary's face was flushed, but she managed a grateful smile. "Yes, thanks to you. I feel… lighter now that I've talked about it," she admitted, her voice soft but steady.

"I'm glad," Emily said warmly, squeezing her friend's hand briefly before letting go.

James rose, offering Emily his hand, and she took it, allowing him to guide her away from the terrace. As they walked, Emily's gaze flickered back, catching sight of Marc enveloping Mary in a comforting hug. Her heart skipped an unexpected beat, a pang of unease—or something else entirely—curling in her chest. Hastily, she turned back to James, trying to push the feeling aside.

James led her to her room, but once inside, Emily closed the door behind them with a soft click, shutting out the rest of the house. Without hesitation, she wrapped her arms around him and kissed him deeply, searching for the spark she had felt with Marc, hoping it would ignite that familiar thrill.

James responded eagerly, his hands holding her close, but as the kiss deepened, Emily felt… nothing. The butterflies she had anticipated, the warmth and rush she associated with desire, were absent. It was pleasant, safe even, but a hollow emptiness lingered beneath it, leaving her unsteady.

James pulled back, confusion and concern flickering across his face. "Emily… what's going on?" His voice was low, tentative, tinged with worry. "Why did that feel so… urgent?"

Emily's chest tightened painfully. She swallowed hard, voice trembling. "Aren't you attracted to me?"

"Of course I am!" James replied quickly, almost defensively, though a flicker of unease shadowed his expression. "What are you talking about?"

Her throat tightened, the words choking her. The spark she had been searching for— the fire she had just felt with Marc—was missing. She felt adrift, untethered, and the emptiness gnawed at her. She wanted something more, something raw and real, though she didn't fully understand it herself.

Before she could stop herself, the words tumbled out, raw and impulsive: "Make love to me." Her voice was a whisper, hoarse with confusion and emotion, carrying the weight of longing she couldn't name.

James froze, his face paling slightly, his body tensing. "Emily… you're upset," he said softly, reaching for her, concern deepening in his eyes.

"No, I'm not," she protested too quickly, shaking her head, though a small, hesitant part of her wondered if that was true. *Was she upset, or was it something else entirely?* Something complicated and messy she hadn't yet put a name to.

"Sweetheart…" he began, stepping closer, his hand hovering near her cheek, intent on comforting her. But before he could speak further, a sharp knock echoed through the room, slicing through the tension like a knife.

The intrusion startled them both. Emily's face flushed, the fragile intimacy of the moment shattered. She opened the door to find Daisy standing there, clipboard in hand, and remembered with a pang that she had a meeting with Daisy and Darren to discuss the next few days' plans.

"I'm so sorry, Daisy," Emily said quickly, flustered. "Give me a couple of minutes, and I'll meet you in the library."

Daisy nodded, smiling politely, and retreated. Emily closed the door and exhaled, pressing her hand to her chest as if to steady her racing heart.

James approached from behind, resting his hands lightly on her shoulders. He leaned down, kissing the curve of her shoulder, and whispered, "I'll see you at dinner," his eyes lingering on her face, searching for reassurance.

Emily offered a hesitant smile. "Okay… sorry, James," she murmured, her voice small.

He pulled her into a gentle embrace, kissing her softly on the lips. "You have nothing to apologise for," he murmured. After a pause, he added, "And if I made you feel like I wasn't attracted to you… I'm sorry. That couldn't be further from the truth."

They left the room together, walking down the hall. As Emily closed the door behind them, she noticed Jeremy standing there, his expression flickering between curiosity and unease. He lingered for a moment, then scurried off toward his room. Emily frowned slightly at his odd behaviour but didn't dwell; her mind was elsewhere.

As they continued down the hall, hand in hand, Emily's thoughts kept drifting back to Marc—the kiss, the heat, the intensity she couldn't ignore. A quiet, gnawing tension settled in her chest, leaving her unsettled despite James's presence. The night stretched ahead, but her heart felt caught between loyalty, desire, and confusion, and she couldn't shake the feeling that nothing would feel simple ever again.

Marc had just finished a long, honest conversation with his sister on the terrace. After Mary left, he remained seated, his beer untouched, the cool liquid forgotten in his hand. His thoughts kept circling back to what had happened with Emily. He shouldn't have kissed her. That thought echoed relentlessly in his mind, each replay sharper than the last.

"Hey, Marc," a familiar voice broke through his reverie. James slid into the seat across from him, his eyes holding a mixture of curiosity, confusion, and something unspoken that made Marc's chest tighten.

"Hey," Marc replied, glancing up and nodding for James to sit. He took a slow breath, steeling himself for whatever was coming. "What's wrong?" he asked, trying to keep his voice steady despite the anxiety gnawing at his chest.

"Emily?" James's voice faltered slightly, uncertain, as though he were trying to put the words into some logical order.

Marc's heart skipped. She had told him. The thought made his pulse quicken, a mixture of dread and anticipation coursing through him. "What's wrong with her?" he asked, forcing calm into his tone.

James hesitated, his brow furrowing as he searched for the right words. "You won't believe what she just asked me," he admitted, stopping mid-sentence as if the request itself was surreal.

"Well, don't keep me in suspense," Marc urged, leaning forward, every muscle taut with a strange mix of curiosity and apprehension.

"She… she asked me if I was attracted to her," James said, a bewildered laugh escaping his lips as he shook his head in disbelief.

Marc froze, nearly choking on his beer as the words hit him like a hammer. Disbelief, panic, and a jolt of something dangerously close to jealousy settled over him in one wave. "What?" he asked sharply, then cleared his throat. "And… are you?" The words slipped out before he could stop them, almost as if he needed to hear the confirmation. Of course, James was attracted to her. Who wouldn't be?

"Of course I am," James said, his tone thick with astonishment. "Look at her!"

Marc let out a long, quiet sigh, a twinge of jealousy flaring, but he pushed forward, desperate to understand the situation. "What would make her think you aren't?" he asked, his curiosity and concern mingling. Something about her behaviour, her hesitation, the way she'd seemed so unsettled… it gnawed at him.

James shook his head, frustration creeping into his voice. "I have no idea. I'm not sure what's going on with her, Marc. She seems… off. It's like she thinks I don't care, or that my feelings aren't genuine." His shoulders slumped slightly, a rare vulnerability flickering across his face.

Marc leaned back, processing the words. He ran a hand through his hair, gaze dropping to his empty beer. "She really doesn't realise how attractive she is, does she?" His voice was low, almost thoughtful, tinged with an ache he couldn't quite mask. His mind drifted to the night on New Year's Eve, to the memory of Emily in that stunning blue gown, more beautiful than anyone he had ever seen, radiating a mix of innocence and allure that left him breathless.

"No, she doesn't," James said softly, sadness creeping into his voice. "She genuinely believes that when men are nice to her, it's just… politeness. She's sharp, intelligent in every other way, but when it comes to herself, she's completely naive. It's part of what makes her… captivating." He shook his head with a faint smile, lost for a moment in thought. "She doesn't seek attention, doesn't ask for compliments, and when she gets them… she blushes, almost like she doesn't know how to react."

"Yeah," Marc said quietly, a small, bitter smile tugging at the corner of his lips. "I've noticed that too."

James leaned back in his chair, staring down into his drink. "How's Mary?" he asked, trying to shift the subject, though the tension in the air remained thick. "She told me what happened while we were walking back… what are you planning to do?"

Marc's expression darkened, thoughtful. "She begged me not to get involved, and I think that's wise. He's left her alone since they split, and if I step in now, it could just stir things up again. But… if he had crossed the line…" His voice faltered slightly, heavy with the weight of what could have been.

"I think that's smart," James said. "I've read too many stories of people intervening and making things worse. Best to let sleeping dogs lie."

Marc nodded, but his mind was already shifting elsewhere. "By the way, I've decided to take the position. Mary mentioned she'd really like to relocate, so it all fits."

James's face lit up, a genuine smile breaking across his features. "That's great news! I'm really happy for you. John will be too."

Marc returned the smile, but it faded quickly, replaced by a pensive shadow. *Had he made the right choice? How could he work so closely with Emily and resist the pull he felt?* He knew the only way to protect everyone—and himself—was to keep his distance. Yet even as he thought it, he realised how impossible that would be. The question wasn't whether he could stay away—it was whether he wanted to.

Dinner arrived quickly, and the seating arrangement was as unconventional as expected. Partners weren't allowed to sit together, encouraging mingling. Emily found herself seated between Marc on her left and Louis on her right, while James sat across from her, flanked by Mary and Irene.

"This should be interesting," Emily whispered with a playful smile, catching James's eye. He winked back, unfazed.

"Yes, it should," Marc murmured in her ear, his voice low and intimate, sending a shiver down her spine.

The dining room buzzed with conversation, laughter spilling across the polished table. James leaned forward, engrossed in a discussion with Mary about a book, his face animated as he gestured. Emily tried to engage Louis in conversation, though his eyes continually flicked toward Helen, who laughed at his jokes with easy familiarity. Mary, meanwhile, seemed lighter, more relaxed, as she seized the chance to recount stories from her past without judgment.

Marc, sitting a little too close, occasionally brushed against Emily as he reached for his wine. She tried to dismiss it, focusing on her plate, but a more deliberate touch on her knee under the table made her heart skip. She glanced at him, and though his face remained neutral, his fingers traced slow, casual circles that lingered just a moment too long.

By the time dinner ended, Emily's pulse was a mix of unease and anticipation, her stomach fluttering with the memory of Marc's proximity. The next day's whale-watching trip promised adventure, with an optional afternoon snorkelling excursion. Mary practically begged Emily to join, and despite not planning on it, Emily agreed with a smile. James and Marc chose to stay on dry land, which suited the girls perfectly.

# Chapter Thirteen

Most guests turned in early, and Emily followed suit. James, as always, walked her to her door, kissed her deeply, and whispered goodnight, the warmth of his lips lingering in her mind.

Once inside her room, Emily slipped into a sheer silk nightie and pulled back the covers—only to freeze. Her breath caught, and a scream tore from her throat. She bolted for the door, throwing it open and fleeing into the hallway, heart pounding wildly.

James was the first to reach her, followed closely by Marc. James wrapped his arms around her; his face etched with concern.

"What's wrong? What happened?" he asked urgently, his voice tight with worry.

Emily could barely speak, trembling violently. "Snake…" she managed to whisper.

Marc's eyes snapped toward her. "Where?"

"Bed," she replied, shivering.

The silk nightie offered no comfort; Emily's only thought was distance from the creature curled in her sheets. Her father appeared in the doorway; concern etched into every line of his face. Without hesitation, he gathered her into a tight hug, murmuring softly, "It's okay, sweetheart. I've got you."

Other guests, including Mary and Jeremy, clustered nearby, their eyes wide with concern and curiosity.

"What happened, sweetheart? Tell me," her father asked gently.

"There's a snake in my bed," Emily repeated, voice trembling, clinging to him.

Her father's brow furrowed. "What? How? How did a snake get in there?"

Marc and James exchanged a tense glance before cautiously approaching the bed. The room seemed impossibly still, every heartbeat echoing. Then, sure enough, a snake, sleek and dark, was curled up among the soft sheets, its tongue flicking in and out as it stirred.

Marc's voice was a low growl, a mixture of anger and concern. "How the hell did that get there?" His eyes darted toward the coiled snake, then back at James.

James ran a hand through his hair, equally bewildered. "I… I have no idea." His voice faltered, betraying a rare edge of uncertainty.

Marc's mind raced. Someone had to have put it there. *Was it a prank? Or something more sinister?* "Someone put that there," he muttered, his tone tight with suspicion.

James stared at him; disbelief etched across his face. "What? Who would want to hurt Emily?"

Marc's gaze hardened as he pointed at the snake. "I don't know, but there's no way that thing got there on its own." His chest tightened, protective instincts flaring.

Mary entered the room just then, and both men instinctively turned toward her, eyes sharp.

"Get out," they said in unison, their tone leaving no room for argument.

She held up her hands defensively. "I need to get a robe for Emily. She's practically naked out there!"

Marc and James's expressions shifted as reality hit—they both realised how little Emily had been wearing. They exchanged a quick, embarrassed glance, then nodded. "Okay, fine," Marc muttered.

James grabbed a soft, warm bathrobe from the bathroom and handed it to Mary. She smiled gratefully and hurried to Emily's side.

Emily let out a shaky breath as Mary helped her slip into the robe, the familiar warmth and soft fabric offering a small measure of comfort. Her father gently adjusted the robe, pulling it snug around her.

"I think we'd better go downstairs. You need a stiff drink," John said softly, his tone both comforting and authoritative.

Emily didn't resist. She allowed him to guide her carefully down the stairs. John turned to the other guests, his voice calm but firm. "Everything's okay—she just had a fright. Please go back to bed."

The guests, reassured, returned to their rooms. Only Mary remained, standing close to Emily's side like a guardian angel.

John settled Emily onto the lounge in the library and poured her a generous glass of whiskey. She lifted it to her lips and downed it in a single gulp, feeling the warmth spread through her chest.

A small, nervous laugh escaped her. "It must have slithered in and... liked my bed," she said, trying to sound light-hearted, unaware of the more sinister possibilities Marc had already considered.

Mary's arm tightened around her in silent support. They sat in the quiet, the library bathed in soft lamplight, until footsteps echoed from the hallway. Ten minutes later, James and Marc entered.

James went straight to Emily, pulling her into his arms. His embrace was firm, protective, and trembling with emotion. "Are you okay?" he asked, his voice low and worried as he rubbed her back in slow, calming circles.

Emily nodded, leaning into him. "Yes… I think so," she murmured, grateful for the safety of his presence. "Where is it?"

James met her gaze. "Marc and I managed to wrap it in a bedsheet. Rosa's upstairs now, changing the linen on your bed." He held her tighter, the tension in his body betraying his anger and relief. "This should never have happened."

Emily managed a weak smile, the corners of her lips tugging upward. "You can't control where nature wants to be," she said softly.

Over her shoulder, James exchanged a brief, meaningful glance with Marc—a silent acknowledgment of their shared concern and the underlying tension that had been simmering between them.

Rosa appeared moments later, giving Emily a warm hug and a quick kiss on the cheek. "All ready, Emily. Everything's clean and fresh now," she said reassuringly.

Marc's voice softened as he addressed Mary. "Can you take Emily upstairs to her room? She needs to rest."

"Of course," Mary replied, gently guiding Emily toward the staircase, her hands steady and reassuring.

Before they left, Marc stepped closer, brushing a strand of hair from Emily's face. His eyes softened, and his voice carried a rare tenderness. "Try to get some sleep, okay, Em?"

Emily nodded, letting herself be guided by Mary. She cast one last glance at Marc, catching the mixture of concern and something unspoken in his gaze, before the library door closed softly behind them.

James and Marc poured themselves generous glasses of whiskey, the amber liquid catching the dim light of the library. They sank into the chairs, each lost in thought, the weight of the night pressing down on them. Silence stretched between them until John, observing their tense expressions, broke it.

"What's wrong? I can see something's not right with you, James," he asked, concern lining his features.

James let out a dry, bitter laugh. "Ha! That's an understatement." His hand clenched around the glass as he ran a finger along the rim, still staring into the amber depths.

Marc turned sharply to John, his voice taut with urgency. "Has anyone threatened Emily?"

John's eyes widened in disbelief, the colour draining from his face. "What? Why would anyone want to hurt Emily?"

James walked to the library door, closing it with a soft but firm click, then returned to face John. "That snake didn't end up in her bed by accident."

John stared at both men, incredulous, as if they had just spoken another language. "That... that can't be," he whispered, his voice trembling.

"She's the sweetest person I know," John continued, his voice thick with emotion. "She's never hurt anyone. How could someone want to harm her?" Tears welled in his eyes, threatening to spill over.

Marc's jaw tightened, his expression resolute. "I agree, John. But James and I can't accept that the snake was there by accident. It just doesn't make sense."

John shook his head, a mix of fear and disbelief. "She doesn't think that," he countered. "She believes it got there by accident. You heard her."

James leaned forward, voice firm yet gentle. "Emily would never think poorly of anyone. She'd never believe anyone would want to hurt her."

John buried his face in his hands, his voice breaking. "They can't take my baby from me."

James rested a steady hand on his shoulder. "That's not going to happen. I won't let it."

Marc's voice joined in, resolute and unwavering. "Neither will I. We need to keep a close eye on her."

"Agreed," the two men said in unison, the gravity of their shared promise hanging heavy in the room.

John drew in a deep breath, trying to steady his racing heart, and rose from his chair. "I'm going to see my daughter before turning in for the night." After exchanging solemn goodnights, he left Marc and James alone, the quiet settling around them like a weight.

James studied Marc, concern etched across his face. "You've only known Emily for a few days, but... you've got a good sense of character. Can you imagine anyone wanting to hurt her?"

Marc leaned back, eyes dark with thought. "James… everything you've told me about Emily is spot on. I can't imagine her doing anything to deserve harm. And I can't imagine anyone wanting to hurt her. But…" His jaw tightened. "…we can't take chances."

James nodded grimly. "We need to keep her safe, without her knowing. If it were up to me, she'd already be back on the mainland, staying at my apartment."

Marc's brows knit in concern. "She'd never leave her father, especially after everything she's put into this trip. And she'd hate being cooped up somewhere she doesn't belong."

"You're right," James admitted. He paused, choosing his next words carefully. "Marc… I know she's not your responsibility. But will you help me keep her safe?"

Marc didn't hesitate. "Yes. Of course. I'll do whatever it takes." His voice carried conviction.

James let out a breath he hadn't realised he'd been holding. "Thank you. Truly."

They spent the next few minutes quietly discussing their plan—checking doors, maintaining a presence nearby without alarming Emily, and making sure staff were on alert—before rising to head upstairs.

As they reached the landing, Mary appeared, emerging quietly from Emily's room. She paused when she saw them, her face serious.

"How is she?" Marc asked immediately, stepping closer.

"She's asleep now," Mary replied. "She believes the snake got there by accident. But it didn't, did it? Someone's trying to scare her—or worse, hurt her."

Marc and James exchanged a brief, loaded glance. James exhaled slowly. "You can't let her know."

Mary's expression fell, the weight of reality settling over her. "I won't," she said quietly. "But shouldn't she go home? Get out of here?"

James smiled faintly, a touch of wry humour in his eyes. "She wouldn't go."

Mary considered this, then a small, knowing smile tugged at her lips. "Well, it looks like you two are going snorkelling tomorrow," she said, teasing, before turning and sauntering off to her own room.

Marc and James shared grimaces, the tension between worry and determination heavy in the air. As they continued to their own rooms, the weight of their responsibility for Emily pressed on their minds, unspoken but undeniable.

Emily woke several times during the night, each time startled by the faint creaks of the house or the wind rustling through the trees outside. The soft glow of the light she'd left on offered a small measure of comfort, a tether to the familiar. By seven o'clock, sleep had abandoned her entirely. She rose, feeling both restless and alert, and headed to the shower, letting the warm water wash away the lingering unease from the previous night.

After slipping into her white bikini and pulling a flowing blue sundress over it, Emily felt a spark of excitement for the day ahead. She made her way downstairs, the smell of fresh coffee and pastries greeting her, and found a handful of early-rising guests already at breakfast.

"Good morning!" she said brightly, offering a warm smile to those nearby. Her gaze fell on Jeremy, who approached with a tentative, concerned expression.

"Are you okay this morning?" he asked quietly, his voice carrying genuine worry.

Emily placed her hand gently over his. "Yes, I'm fine. It was just a little scare last night. Nothing to worry about. Thank you for checking." Her touch was light, reassuring, and she thought she'd seen some relief in his eyes—until Marc entered the room.

His presence immediately shifted the air. His gaze flicked to Emily's hand in Jeremy's, and she pulled back instinctively, heat rising in her cheeks. Marc's steps were measured, deliberate, and when he reached them, he ignored Jeremy entirely, taking both of Emily's hands in his own and bringing them to his lips.

"Morning, Saunders," he said dismissively, a flicker of a smirk on his face, before turning back to Emily and guiding her to a seat slightly further down the table, away from the others.

Emily, caught up in the intensity of his attention, felt her pulse quicken. "Good morning, Marc. Did you sleep well?"

"No," he replied simply, his voice low and steady. "I spent the night thinking about you."

The words sent a shiver down Emily's spine, her cheeks warming. She tried to play it off casually. "Why?"

Marc's mind churned with thoughts he could never voice aloud. *Because I want to feel you beneath me, to pleasure you in ways you've never known.* Instead, he said, voice measured and calm, "Because you had a scare last night."

Emily waved her hand lightly, forcing a casual tone. "Oh, I'm fine. Just a freak occurrence. It won't happen again."

Marc's gaze lingered on her, doubt, and concern evident in his eyes. "Mmm. How are you this morning? Did you get plenty of sleep?"

"Yes, thank you," Emily said, forcing a smile. Marc could see straight through it—he always did.

He allowed himself a small, gentle smile in response. "Good."

Trying to shift the conversation, Emily asked, "So, what are you and James doing today? Mary mentioned you weren't going snorkelling."

At that moment, James entered the room, his presence smooth and unassuming, but he couldn't hide the flicker of curiosity in his eyes as he noticed Marc and Emily together.

"Actually," James interjected, a subtle note of amusement in his voice, "Marc and I have decided to go after all."

Emily's face lit up, the sunlight catching her hair, and a smile spread across her face. "Oh really? That's great!"

Marc's heart skipped a beat at the sight of her smiling at him like that. *If she looked like that every time she got her way...* His thoughts threatened to spiral, but he forced himself to shake it off. *She's my best friend's fiancée. I don't want to—just...* His mind twisted itself in knots as he tried to regain composure.

Mary approached, a brow raised in mild curiosity. "What's so great?"

"Marc and James are joining us for snorkelling today," Emily replied warmly, her voice light, almost triumphant.

Mary's gaze flicked between the two men, confusion briefly crossing her features. "I thought you two weren't planning to go?"

James, casual and unbothered, picked up a croissant from the table. "We changed our minds."

Mary laughed softly, her eyes twinkling with amusement. Emily, slightly puzzled by the exchange but choosing not to dwell on it, shrugged, feeling a small surge of anticipation for the day ahead.

Marc, seated beside her, stole a subtle glance at Emily's profile, the sunlight illuminating her skin and making her hair shimmer. He forced himself to focus on breakfast instead of the intoxicating pull he felt toward her. The day had only just begun, and he knew already that keeping his distance was going to be a battle.

Emily, blissfully unaware of the storm she stirred in both men, took a bite of her fruit, feeling the warmth of the morning and the promise of adventure in the air.

# Chapter Fourteen

The group finished breakfast, gathered their belongings, and made their way to the wharf by nine o'clock. The morning air was crisp, carrying the briny tang of saltwater and the distant cries of seabirds wheeling overhead. The dock hummed with excited chatter, boots clattering against the wooden planks as guests jostled for a better view of the boats bobbing in the harbour.

Once everyone was aboard, the crew began untying the ropes, and the boat's engine rumbled to life. Slowly, it pulled away from the dock, leaving behind the gentle slap of water against pilings and the fading clamour of well-wishers. Guests crowded the rails, eyes scanning the endless expanse of cerulean sea, each whispering and pointing, waiting for that first awe-inspiring glimpse of a whale breaking the surface.

Excitement rippled through the passengers as dolphins arced gracefully beside the hull, a dugong lazily surfaced, and sea turtles bobbed among the gentle swells. Then, the real spectacle appeared: a mother whale and her calf, their massive forms gliding through the waves, sending sprays of saltwater into the air. Laughter and exclamations of delight carried across the deck. The weather was perfect—sunlight warm against their skin, softened by a light sea breeze that ruffled hair and stirred laughter. After a light lunch on deck, the boat glided toward a pontoon where snorkelling gear was laid out for the afternoon adventure.

Emily unzipped her sundress and folded it neatly into her bag, relieved she'd chosen a style that wouldn't wrinkle. She stepped onto the pontoon in her white bikini, the sun highlighting the gentle curve of her shoulders and the lean strength of her legs.

"Oh my, Emily!" Mary exclaimed, her eyes wide with admiration.

"What?" Emily asked, a flicker of worry in her voice.

Mary grinned broadly. "My goodness, you look stunning. Absolutely gorgeous. You could be a model!"

Emily's cheeks flamed a deep pink, and she fidgeted with the strap of her bikini top. Marc, standing nearby, felt heat rise to his face as he took in the sight of her—so effortlessly beautiful, radiant in the sunlight, every curve and contour accentuated. He tried to look away, but it was impossible; she was breathtaking.

"Don't be silly," Emily said, her voice low and embarrassed. "I'd blush every time someone looked at me."

One of the crew members whistled audibly, clearly catching Mary's compliment. "You could model for me any day, love. I'd die a happy man," he called out with a cheeky grin.

Emily's face turned crimson, and James, standing just a few steps away, shot the man a sharp, commanding look. The crewman's grin faltered, and he quickly diverted his attention elsewhere.

Marc clenched his jaw, trying not to let his eyes linger, though the sight of Emily in her bikini—so confident yet so self-conscious—was hard to resist. Clothes or no clothes, she left him struggling for composure.

Sensing the tension, Irene, one of the executives' wives, stepped gracefully in front of Emily, shielding her from the unwanted attention. "Stop embarrassing the poor girl," she said firmly, offering Emily a reassuring smile as she guided her a step away.

"Thank you, Irene," Emily whispered, relief washing over her.

"You're welcome, love," Irene said warmly. "Though I must admit, I'd die for a figure like that."

Her husband, Ryan, chuckled from behind her. "So would I!"

Irene playfully swatted him on the chest. "You wish, Ryan."

Ryan laughed, shrugging innocently. "Isn't that exactly what I just said?"

Emily allowed herself a small smile, amused by their banter, but her gaze inevitably flicked to James and Marc. Both men were standing nearby, their expressions taut and serious, their eyes fixed on the pontoon like guardians ready to defend their territory. The tension radiating from them left her puzzled—and a little flustered.

Guests had the choice of stepping off the pontoon or plunging down the bright orange slide into the sparkling water below. Emily and Mary exchanged a mischievous glance before choosing the slide, waiting their turn as sunlight danced over the rippling surface.

Mary leaned in with a sly grin. "Mind if I pair off with James? Marc's a bit of a bore," she whispered, mischief lighting her eyes.

Emily let out a soft laugh, glancing over her shoulder at Marc and James, who were preparing to dive into the water. She turned to Marc, her voice light but edged with something warmer. "Are you okay to pair off with me?"

Marc's chest tightened, a spark of anticipation shooting through him. "Yeah… yeah, I'm okay," he said, aiming for casual but failing to hide the thrill pulsing beneath his words.

Marc and James floated near the bottom of the slide, waiting. Then, with a splash and a delighted squeal, the two women shot down into the water. James and Mary immediately swam off together, laughing and teasing each other, leaving Emily and Marc alone in their own pocket of sunlit sea.

Emily paddled toward him, her gaze flicking up to meet his. Marc answered with a small, knowing smile—one that said more than words could—and together they swam toward a quieter stretch of reef, the water warm and inviting around them.

For the next hour, they explored the underwater world. Brightly coloured fish flitted past swaying corals, starfish clung to rocks, and curious sea urchins dotted the ocean floor. Every so often, Marc tapped her shoulder to point out a particularly striking fish or an intricate coral formation. They surfaced frequently, their laughter echoing across the water as they compared discoveries, revelling in the freedom and beauty of the sea.

As the hour wore on, Emily surfaced and waited for Marc. He appeared behind her, suddenly slipping his arms around her waist and pressing her close. She gasped in surprise, a startled laugh breaking free.

"Stop it!" she giggled, splashing water lightly against his chest. "You scared me!"

"I'm sorry," Marc murmured, his voice low and teasing. "Let me kiss it better."

Before Emily could protest or even breathe, Marc turned her gently in his arms, his hands firm but reverent as they guided her. His lips brushed hers in a kiss so soft it stole the air from her lungs. She stiffened, startled, but the warmth of his body, the steady strength of his hold, the patient, sensual pressure of his mouth against hers—slow and deliberate—melted every last thread of resistance.

His kiss deepened gradually, coaxing her open, tasting her with a hunger he could no longer hide. His hands slid down the curve of her back, pulling her closer until her chest pressed against the hard lines of his body. When their tongues finally met, a molten wave of heat surged through her, sharp and overwhelming.

Her legs moved without thought—wrapping around his waist, drawing him tighter between her thighs, needing him, needing more.

A breathy moan escaped her, swallowed by his mouth, and Marc answered with a low, guttural sound that vibrated through her. His grip tightened as if he could fuse her body to his. She felt him—hot, hard, unyielding—pressing into her, and desire rushed through her so fast her knees trembled.

"You're not close enough," he whispered, voice raw and ragged, his breath brushing her lips.

"Marc…" she breathed, clinging to his shoulders, her fingers digging into his skin as her body trembled with wanting.

His lips trailed along her cheek, then lower, grazing the shell of her ear. A shiver raced through her.

"I want you so badly, Em," he murmured, the confession torn straight from his chest. "You have no idea how much."

Heat pooled low inside her as his hands roamed—wide palms tracing her waist, her hips, her ribs. Her pulse throbbed beneath her skin, every nerve ending awake and aching.

"Marc…" she whispered again, her voice barely forming the word, but heavy with desire, confusion… and something deeper.

He tightened his hold just enough to pull a helpless sigh from her. "I love hearing you say my name," he breathed against her temple. "I want to hear you say it when I'm inside you, when I make love to you."

Then his mouth claimed hers again—harder, deeper, searing—his kiss a brand she could feel down to her bones. One of his hands slid up to cup her breast, his thumb brushing over her nipple. It hardened instantly under his touch, and she gasped against his mouth.

His other arm crushed her closer, pressing her flush to the thick, insistent heat straining against her softness. He rolled his hips, grinding into her, drawing a broken moan from her lips.

Her body arched instinctively, craving him.

And then—

A sharp whistle sliced through the air.

Emily jolted, the spell shattering. Marc cursed under his breath, jaw tightening as he reluctantly eased his hold, though his hands lingered, his heat clinging to her even as he released her.

The desire between them didn't dissipate—it only simmered, hotter and more dangerous, waiting.

Emily floated, dazed, and flushed, the water cooling her wet skin but doing nothing to quell the fire in her veins. She couldn't stop the thoughts swirling in her mind, the echo of his lips, the pressure of his body, the intoxicating warmth of his hands. *How does he make me feel like this?*

Marc smirked, the shadow of mischief in his dark eyes softening with a hint of warning. "Don't look at me like that, or we'll never make it back to the boat," he teased, releasing her completely.

Heat crept up her cheeks as she swam toward the pontoon, her heart still racing. By the time she climbed back aboard, James and Mary were already there, drying off and laughing. James extended a hand to help her up, his easy smile warm and confident, but Emily felt frayed, her emotions tangled.

"Enjoy yourself?" he asked lightly, leaning slightly closer.

Emily forced a nod, unable to trust her voice. She wrapped her arms around herself, trying to steady her racing heart, all the while aware that the memory of Marc's kiss was etched indelibly into her mind—and it had left her wanting far more than she could admit.

Marc climbed out of the water after her, gripping a towel and shaking droplets from his hair. James stepped forward, draping another towel around Emily's shoulders to ward off the chill. She shivered, but it wasn't just the sea spray or the breeze—her body still thrummed with the echoes of her stolen moments with Marc.

As the boat began its slow journey back to the island, the other guests chattered excitedly about the snorkelling—the brilliant fish, the swaying corals, the occasional dolphin sighting—but Emily hardly registered their words. Her gaze drifted over the endless blue; her mind trapped in a whirl of sensation and memory. Every brush of Marc's hand, every whisper of his lips, replayed in vivid detail, warming and simultaneously torturing her.

Exhaustion weighed heavily on her, not just from the physical effort but from the storm inside her. Her sleep the previous night had been fitful, broken repeatedly by the memory of the snake curled in her bed, the fear and adrenaline still lingering in her system. And now, layered on top of that lingering unease, was the memory of Marc's kiss—sharp, electric, and maddeningly intoxicating.

She hated how much it had affected her. She hated the way her pulse had spiked, the way heat had pooled low in her stomach, the way her body had responded instinctively to him. And yet… she couldn't deny it. She had wanted it. Wanted him.

But the guilt was immediate and suffocating. Every heartbeat whispered reminders of James—James, who had been nothing but patient, kind, and faithful. Her hands tightened around the towel wrapped around her, knuckles blanching, as a sick twist of shame settled in her stomach. How could a fleeting, reckless moment with Marc— someone she shouldn't even be thinking about in that way—leave her feeling both exhilarated and horrified?

She tried to steady her breathing, forcing herself to focus on the horizon, the boat, anything other than the memory of him. But it was impossible. Marc's presence beside her, quiet yet unwavering, seemed to magnify every sensation. Every time he glanced her way, even casually, it made her stomach leap, and her heart betray her resolve.

By the time the island came into view, Emily felt both drained and unsettled, trapped between desire, guilt, and a growing sense of confusion she wasn't ready to face. She knew she needed to regain control of herself, but the thought of doing so while Marc remained nearby made it almost laughably impossible.

Emily rose early the next morning, the soft golden light of dawn spilling through her window and illuminating the room. She dressed in a comfortable sundress, its light fabric brushing against her skin, hoping the simple routine of getting ready would help lift the lingering weight of the previous evening's confusion. The men had planned a fishing trip, while the women were set for a shopping excursion on the mainland. It was supposed to be a carefree, enjoyable day, but try as she might, Emily couldn't shake the persistent thoughts of Marc—and the kiss they had shared.

After a quick breakfast with the group, the women gathered at the wharf, the fresh scent of saltwater mingling with the soft breeze. Emily tried to anchor herself in the moment, letting her gaze wander across the sparkling water and the distant horizon, but every flash of sunlight on the waves seemed to pull her thoughts back to Marc. The stirrings she felt when he crossed her mind made her chest tighten, a mix of exhilaration and guilt that refused to be ignored.

The first stop was a luxurious indulgence: a visit to a local spa for manicures and pedicures. The women were ushered into a serene space, the air thick with the soothing scent of lavender and eucalyptus. Emily let herself sink into the calm, the gentle hum of conversation and soft music wrapping around her like a warm blanket. As the nail technicians transformed her nails into a delicate shade of rose pink, she felt a rare lightness, allowing herself to forget, if only briefly, the tangled emotions churning inside her.

Laughter and chatter flowed easily among the group, a comforting rhythm that carried Emily through the morning. Stories of favourite books, travel adventures, and amusing anecdotes filled the air, and she found herself genuinely smiling, the tension in her shoulders softening. For the first time in days, the weight on her chest seemed to lift.

After the spa, the women wandered through charming boutiques, the vibrant colours of handcrafted scarves, delicate jewellery, and unique clothing captivating her. Emily marvelled at the exquisite pieces, revelling in the escape they offered from her inner turmoil. Each shop felt like a small adventure, the thrill of discovery mingling with the indulgence of treating herself to something special.

Lunch was at a tucked-away Italian restaurant, warm and rustic, its wooden beams and soft light creating a cozy haven. Emily savoured every bite of her pasta, the rich tomato sauce comforting her senses. Conversation flowed effortlessly over glasses of wine, and for a few hours, she laughed with the women, letting the joy of the moment replace the conflict in her mind.

The afternoon brought more shopping, small gifts and trinkets filling their bags. Emily's eyes lingered on a display of diamond earrings at a local jeweller, their sparkle catching the light and calling to her. With Mary's gentle encouragement, she treated herself, the small indulgence bringing a bright, genuine smile to her face. As the clerk wrapped the earrings, Emily caught her reflection in the glass, pausing to appreciate the moment—a tiny victory of self-care and joy amidst the undercurrent of emotional unrest.

As the launch returned to the island, the sun hung low, casting a golden shimmer across the water. For a few fleeting hours, Emily had managed to push thoughts of Marc—and of James—into the background, fully immersed in the beauty and camaraderie around her. But as the mainland receded in the distance, the quiet hum of the boat and the rhythmic lapping of waves brought her mind crashing back to the kiss she could not forget.

She felt the ghost of Marc's touch, the memory of his lips pressing against hers, the heat that had flared through her body. The exhilaration clashed violently with guilt, reminding her of James—his patience, his devotion, and the loyalty she had pledged. The tug-of-war in her chest left her restless, heart fluttering and stomach knotted, a storm of desire, remorse, and confusion she could neither deny nor resolve.

Emily pressed her palms to her thighs, trying to steady herself, as the boat glided over the water. For all the fun and beauty of the day, the truth remained unavoidable: her heart—and her body—had been irrevocably stirred, leaving her caught between what she wanted and what she knew she should honour.

# Chapter Fifteen

Meanwhile, Marc had joined the fishing party with the other eight men, the morning air crisp and salty as the boat cut through the calm waters. The men laughed and bantered, casting their lines with practiced ease, the sun climbing higher and warming their backs. They landed a handful of sizeable fish, exchanging proud grins and playful boasts. The camaraderie was refreshing, a welcome distraction from his usual routines, yet Marc found that no matter how hard he tried, his mind kept drifting back to Emily.

He replayed her laughter, the sparkle in her eyes, and—most dangerously—the taste and warmth of her lips from the kiss they had shared. Each memory made his chest tighten, a mixture of exhilaration and guilt twisting through him. He knew he was treading dangerous waters, and yet the temptation was impossible to resist.

During a break for lunch, the men gathered in the shade of the cabin roof, passing around sandwiches and cold drinks. John's voice cut through the casual chatter, tinged with genuine concern.

"Marc, James… is Emily going to be safe while we're out here?" His eyes searched theirs, reflecting the protective worry of a father.

Marc set down his sandwich and gave a reassuring nod. "I've hired a private security firm to keep an eye on things while we're on the water," he said calmly. "They'll be watching over Emily and the other women while they're on the mainland."

James and John exchanged a glance, surprise flickering across their faces, but both appreciated the precaution. Marc, however, felt a twinge of unease gnawing at him. He knew that if Emily discovered the security detail, she would likely bristle at the thought of being watched. Fiercely independent, she hated the idea of being treated as someone who needed protection. Yet after the snake incident, Marc could not ignore the nagging sense of danger. Better safe than sorry, he reasoned, even if it meant earning her ire.

As the afternoon sun began its slow descent toward the horizon, painting the sky in streaks of gold and rose, Marc's thoughts turned once again to Emily. He imagined her on the mainland, exploring shops, laughing, perhaps teasing Mary or glancing at the sparkling jewellery with that infectious smile. *Did she think about him the way he thought about her? Did she feel the same tug of desire that had nearly undone them both during the snorkelling trip?*

He shook his head, trying to dispel the thought, but it clung stubbornly, making him restless despite the success of the day's fishing. The boat rocked gently beneath him, the scent of salt and the tang of fish in the air, yet none of it could anchor his mind. The questions remained, a relentless undertow beneath the surface of his thoughts: *Is she thinking of me? Does she even realise what she does to me?*

Marc exhaled slowly, forcing himself to focus on the simple pleasures of the trip—the feel of the rod in his hands, the sun on his face, the laughter of the men around him. Still, he couldn't ignore the pull of Emily's presence in his mind, a constant, unyielding current that threatened to sweep him away.

At seven, all the guests gathered for pre-dinner drinks at the house. The living room was filled with soft chatter, clinking glasses, and the warm glow of candlelight reflecting off the polished wood floors. Emily arrived with the other women, her steps light, her spirits buoyed by the day's pleasures—the spa, the shopping, and the fleeting freedom she had felt exploring the mainland. Yet beneath the surface, a heavier undercurrent of emotion tugged at her, threatening to unsettle the ease she tried to project.

Marc spotted her the moment she entered, her sundress swaying gently with her movements. His gaze lingered, drinking in the sight of her, the way the soft light kissed her hair, highlighting the faint blush on her cheeks. A smile tugged at his lips when Emily's eyes met his across the room, a spark of recognition and unspoken understanding passing between them.

"Hello, Em. Did you have a good day?" His voice was warm and casual, carefully measured, yet his eyes betrayed the intensity he struggled to conceal.

Emily returned his smile, though it faltered slightly under the weight of her thoughts. "Yes… it was lovely. How was your fishing trip?" Her tone was light, but her fingers flexed slightly at her side, betraying her inner tension.

"It was good," Marc replied, letting a playful lilt creep into his voice. "I even managed to catch a fish." He winked, the teasing edge barely masking the pull he felt toward her.

"I'm glad," Emily murmured, beginning to turn away, as though moving on would ease the tension thrumming between them.

Marc caught her arm gently, his touch firm but not forceful, stopping her mid-step. She froze, her breath catching at the contact. Leaning close, his warm breath brushing against her ear, he whispered, "You can't avoid me forever, you know."

Emily's eyes widened, a swirl of fear, guilt, and desire clouding their depths. "Please, Marc," she whispered, her voice trembling, almost breaking. "It was a mistake. James doesn't deserve any of this. I… I feel so ashamed."

Her words struck him harder than she could have imagined. He blinked, the warmth of his expression softening as he dropped his hand from her arm, stepping back to give her space. The hurt and conflict in her eyes mirrored the turmoil in his chest, and for a moment, Marc was caught between wanting to pull her close again and respecting the boundaries she had set.

Emily exhaled shakily, grateful for the distance, and attempted a small, nervous smile before turning her attention to the others. The soft clink of glasses and murmured conversation resumed around them, but the charged silence between Marc and Emily lingered like a taut wire.

Soon, James arrived, his presence anchoring Emily in the reality she desperately wanted to maintain. They slipped into conversation, leaning toward one another, their words low and intimate, forming a small, protective bubble amidst the lively room. Marc watched from a distance, his heart heavy with unspoken desire and the weight of restraint. Every laugh, every glance Emily shared with James tightened the knot of longing in his chest. He looked away at last, his jaw clenched, forcing himself to focus on anything else—the warm glow of the candles, the soft laughter of the other guests, even the faint aroma of the hors d'oeuvres—anything to distract him from the ache of what could not be.

Dinner was a lively affair, the room alive with the hum of animated conversations, clinking silverware, and bursts of laughter. The dining room radiated warmth, the soft glow of candlelight reflecting off polished wood and crystal glasses, while the fading light of dusk filtered through the large windows, painting everything in golden hues. The scent of freshly cooked food mingled with faint traces of lavender from the floral centrepiece, creating a comforting, almost intoxicating atmosphere.

Emily found herself mostly engaged in conversation with her father, John, and Mary. They moved seamlessly between topics—family news, reflections on the day's adventures, and little anecdotes that drew peals of laughter from the table. Mary, brimming with energy, recounted the day's indulgences with an enthusiasm that was impossible to ignore.

"We were practically spoiled!" Mary exclaimed, leaning forward, eyes sparkling. "The spa alone—manicures, pedicures, the works! And the shopping—oh, Em, I swear those boutiques were magical. You practically glowed when you picked out those earrings." She glanced at Emily, her grin mischievous. "I had to drag you into the shop, practically kicking and screaming. But then… when you saw those diamonds, it was like watching magic. You're going to look absolutely stunning tomorrow night."

Emily felt a warmth spread through her chest, her cheeks flushing with both embarrassment and delight. She had been captivated by the earrings' delicate sparkle, the way they seemed to catch the light and hold it, reflecting a brilliance that felt almost like a promise. A small thrill ran through her at the thought of wearing them, a personal indulgence that somehow also felt like a tribute.

Her father, noticing the light in her eyes, turned to her with a tender smile. "I'd love to see them, Emily," he said, his voice soft, warm, threaded with affection.

Emily smiled back, her heart swelling with a quiet joy. "You will, Dad—but not until tomorrow night at the ball," she replied, her voice carrying an edge of excitement. "I want them to complement Mum's necklace. It feels like the perfect way to carry her memory with me."

At the mention of her late mother, John's expression softened, a deep, wistful warmth spreading across his features. His eyes glimmered with both pride and sorrow, the weight of memory settling like a gentle presence in the room. "Your mother would have loved that," he murmured quietly, his gaze lingering on Emily with an almost tangible tenderness. "It's a beautiful way to keep her close."

Marc, seated nearby, felt a pang of something he hadn't expected. Watching the gentle, unspoken bond between father and daughter—the quiet reverence Emily carried for her mother's memory—stirred a mixture of admiration and longing in him. He caught James's glance across the table, and they shared a silent acknowledgment: this was more than mere sentiment; it was the foundation of Emily's strength, her warmth, her resilience.

Marc's eyes softened as he observed the subtle gestures—the way Emily's fingers brushed against her father's hand, the tilt of her head as she listened to his words, the reverent attention in her gaze. It was a delicate, intimate display of love and loss, a sacred connection that grounded her in ways neither time nor grief could sever.

"That sounds like a beautiful pairing," Marc murmured, almost to himself, his voice low, carrying just enough for Emily to hear. His gaze met hers briefly, acknowledging her reverence without intruding, silently honouring the moment.

Emily's lips curved into a small, grateful smile. Memories of her mother, of simpler days filled with laughter and warmth, surfaced in her mind. She realised how much she had missed these quiet, tender moments with her father—the soft comfort of family, the unspoken understanding that no matter what storms raged in the world, some things remained steadfast.

Her father nodded, eyes glistening, clearly moved by the thought of sharing this tradition with his daughter. "Tomorrow will be a special night, then," he said, his voice thick with emotion. "I'm looking forward to it."

The conversation slowly shifted to lighter topics, and the room buzzed once more with laughter and easy chatter. Yet Emily remained slightly adrift in thought, her gaze distant for a moment, lost in the quiet, luminous connection that tied her to her mother's legacy. It was a tether, a promise, a reminder that no matter the chaos or confusion around her, there was a place of unwavering love and belonging she could always return to—a sanctuary that belonged to her alone, held in the heart of her family.

After dinner, the guests gradually dispersed, leaving the familiar group—Emily, Marc, John, James, and Mary—on the terrace to enjoy the cool night air. The soft rustling of leaves in the evening breeze mingled with the distant hum of quiet conversation, creating a serene backdrop. They lingered together, each absorbed in thought, yet sharing the comfort of one another's presence.

Her father, ever thoughtful, turned toward Emily. "Are all the preparations for the ball tomorrow night complete?" he asked, his tone gentle but curious.

Emily felt a small surge of pride at the question. She smiled, nodding confidently. "Yes, everything's sorted," she replied, the satisfaction evident in her voice.

Mary, bubbling with excitement, leaned forward. "I'm so looking forward to it! I'm wearing a green gown. What about you, Emily?" Her eyes sparkled with anticipation.

Emily's lips curved into a mischievous smile. "You'll just have to wait and see," she teased, delighting in Mary's playful frustration.

"Oh, come on," Mary pouted, crossing her arms dramatically.

Emily laughed, feeling the tension of the day lift slightly. "Trust me, it'll be worth the wait."

James, standing nearby, couldn't hide his admiration. He leaned in, his smile warm, eyes fixed on Emily. "I bet it will. If you look even half as stunning as the night I proposed, it'll be unforgettable." His words carried a quiet pride, and Emily felt herself blush under his gaze.

Mary, insatiable in her curiosity, pressed, "Oh, please tell me!"

James obliged, recounting the night of his proposal with vivid detail—how Emily had looked, how her eyes had shone, the way her laughter had filled the room. Emily listened, cheeks flushed with a mix of embarrassment and pleasure, her heart swelling at his words.

Feeling a touch restless, Emily excused herself and strolled along the terrace's edge. The night was calm, the stars overhead sparkling like diamonds in the ink-black sky. She traced the intricate patterns of the tiled floor beneath her feet, hoping the motion would calm the uneasy flutter in her chest. Yet, despite the peaceful night, her mind remained restless, replaying moments from the day and the tangle of emotions she still carried.

Suddenly, a sharp scraping noise shattered the quiet. Her head jerked up just in time to see a massive concrete potted plant teetering on the balcony's edge. The sound of shifting weight intensified, and Emily's stomach lurched as she realised the plant was moments from toppling over.

"Watch out, Emily!" Mary's frantic scream pierced the night, sharp and urgent.

Before Emily could react, Marc's reflexes kicked in. He lunged forward, his arms snaking around her waist, pulling her forcefully out of harm's way. The next instant, they both went sprawling to the terrace floor as the heavy pot crashed with a deafening bang. Shards of concrete and clumps of soil scattered, bouncing dangerously close. Emily's heart hammered in her chest, adrenaline surging as she tried to process the near disaster.

For a suspended moment, the world seemed to hold its breath. Emily lay against Marc, the warmth of his body grounding her as her mind raced to catch up. Her pulse thundered in her ears, nearly drowning out all else.

# Chapter Sixteen

Marc was the first to move, his hands steadying her as he scanned the terrace for additional hazards. "Are you okay?" he asked, voice low but tense, the concern clear in every syllable. His hands trembled slightly, a reflection of his own shock at how close they had come to disaster.

Emily nodded, breath uneven, brushing dust and soil from her dress. "Yes… thanks to you," she murmured, her voice still shaky. Her gaze fell on the shattered remnants of the pot, the debris scattered across the terrace like jagged teeth, a stark reminder of their narrow escape.

Marc exhaled slowly, relief flooding his features. He pulled Emily into a tight embrace, his arms firm and protective, unwilling to let go until he was certain she was unharmed. "Thank God you're okay," he whispered, pressing his forehead lightly against hers.

Emily rested against him for a moment longer, her racing heart gradually calming. There was a grounding warmth in his embrace, a tether to reality after the shock. The strength radiating from him, the subtle reassurance in the firmness of his hold, made the turmoil of the past days—the confusion, the guilt, the lingering tension—fade just enough for her to breathe.

Even as she pulled back slightly, Marc's hands lingered, brushing a stray strand of hair from her face. His dark eyes searched hers, intense and unflinching, silently conveying concern—and something more. An emotion Emily couldn't name yet, but that sent a flutter through her chest, a mixture of fear, exhilaration, and a hint of desire she didn't want to admit.

The tense calm broke as the others hurried over, their voices rising in alarm. Mary's eyes widened when she noticed blood on Emily's arm.

"Emily! You're bleeding!" Mary exclaimed, rushing forward, panic in her tone.

Marc instinctively tightened his hold on Emily, his jaw set, while James crouched beside her, examining the small cut with careful attention. His face mirrored Marc's worry, furrowed brows and clenched jaw revealing a protective anger that didn't need words. Emily, still in shock, barely registered their silent exchange, her focus fixed on the remnants of the pot and the adrenaline still coursing through her.

Mary returned quickly with the first aid kit, John close behind, offering his quiet, reassuring presence. Marc reluctantly released Emily, supporting her as she lowered onto a chair, careful not to let her move too suddenly. Mary worked quickly, cleaning the cut, her gentle touch making Emily wince only slightly.

"It's not too deep," Mary reassured her, though her voice carried a tremor of concern.

John handed Emily a glass of whiskey, the warmth of the liquid burning as it went down. She swallowed it in one gulp, hoping the sting would steady her nerves. Her legs felt like jelly as the adrenaline drained from her body, leaving a lingering tremor in its wake.

Finally, Emily found her voice, weak and uncertain. "How… how did that fall?"

Her father's face hardened with determination. "We don't know yet, but we'll find out," he said firmly, his protective instincts flaring.

Emily turned to Marc, eyes wide, a mixture of gratitude, lingering shock, and awe shining through. "Thank you. You… you saved my life," she whispered, her voice barely audible.

Marc's lips pressed into a thin line, and he offered her a small, shaky smile. His protective instincts remained taut, his fingers lingering on her arm as if he could anchor her in place and shield her from all harm.

"I think I need to lie down," Emily said softly, her voice frail. When she tried to stand, her legs gave way beneath her. James reacted immediately, scooping her into his arms with careful ease.

"Easy, sweetheart," he murmured, his voice low and reassuring. Emily wrapped her arms around his neck, resting her head against his shoulder, feeling the steady beat of his heart beneath her cheek. Marc's voice drifted from behind, instructing Mary to stay with her, his tone filled with concern that only deepened the intimacy of the moment.

James carried her up the stairs, Mary holding the door open for them. Inside her room, he gently laid her on the bed, brushing a loose strand of hair from her face. Every movement spoke of his tenderness and devotion, the quiet care of a man determined to protect her.

"Rest, sweetheart," James whispered, leaning down to press a soft kiss to her lips. Emily offered a faint, tired smile in return, her eyes fluttering closed as exhaustion finally claimed her.

Mary settled quietly in a chair nearby, keeping vigil without interruption. The room was calm, the faint rustle of leaves outside the window the only sound.

James lingered for a moment at the door, hand resting lightly on the doorknob. He gazed at Emily, her chest rising and falling with steady breaths, and his eyes softened. With a final, lingering look, he stepped into the hallway and closed the door gently, leaving her to find a fragile sense of peace and safety within the quiet cocoon of her room.

As James stepped out of Emily's room and eased the door shut behind him, he found Marc striding in from the balcony, jaw tight, eyes hard.

"Well?" James demanded.

Marc's reply was clipped. "Not here."

They made their way to the library, where John sat hunched forward, his elbows on his knees, his head buried in his hands. When he finally looked up, his face was blotched with worry and barely contained fear.

"Marc, I can't thank you enough," John said hoarsely. "You saved my little girl's life." A lone tear slid down his cheek.

Marc gave a simple nod, accepting both the gratitude and the gravity of what had happened.

James poured drinks with stiff hands and passed them around. "So," he said, voice tight with impatience, "what did you find?"

Marc's tone turned icy. "It wasn't an accident. Someone pushed it over. There are deep scrape marks on the balustrade—fresh ones."

"Bloody hell!" James exploded, fury flashing through him.

John's voice broke as he whispered, "Why? Why would anyone do this?"

Marc exhaled sharply. "I don't know. But someone wanted that thing to hit Emily. Someone's trying to hurt her—or kill her."

The three men exchanged stunned looks, the weight of the truth settling over the room like a suffocating fog.

Mary stepped inside then, quietly closing the library door behind her. Her face was pale, eyes wide with disbelief. John immediately asked, voice trembling, "How is she?"

"She woke up," Mary said, swallowing hard. "I helped her into her nightie, and she took a sleeping pill. She's out again now." Her voice wavered. "But someone tried to kill her."

"We know," James said softly, his jaw clenching.

"Why?" Mary asked again, as if saying it aloud would somehow make it make sense.

"We don't know," Marc replied, his gaze fixed on a distant point. "But whoever it is—they're getting bold."

John straightened, urgency in his voice. "How do we keep her safe?"

"I've already called my security team," Marc said, all business now. "They'll send three bodyguards tomorrow with the rest of the guests. Just tell me what time the launch is leaving the dock."

"I'll let you know first thing in the morning," John said.

Marc gave a curt nod. "Good."

"She's dancing with no one but the three of us tomorrow night," James declared.

"I agree," John murmured, though he looked exhausted saying it.

Mary shook her head. "She's not going to like that. You know Emily. And men have already been asking her to save them a dance."

"Too bad," Marc snapped, harsher than he intended.

Mary flinched, startled by his vehemence, but said nothing more.

The conversation dragged on a few minutes longer—low voices, tense words, unspoken fears—before they finally decided to call it a night. One by one they drifted away, each of them carrying the heavy, chilling truth of what had nearly happened.


Marc paced his room for hours, the silence of the house pressing in on him like a vice. Every time he closed his eyes, he saw it again—the sickening drop, the shattering impact, the split-second where Emily's life hung by a thread. The thought of how close they'd come to losing her made his stomach twist.

Finally, unable to bear it any longer, he left his room. Consequences be damned. His bare feet made no sound on the polished wooden floor as he moved through the dim hallway, drawn to her like a tide he couldn't fight. At her door, he hesitated only a heartbeat before turning the handle and slipping inside.

A soft bedside lamp cast a warm, fragile glow across the room. Emily was sitting upright against her pillows, her face pale and tight with unease. At the sound of the door, her eyes flashed wide with fear—but when she saw him, her shoulders sagged with visible relief.

"Marc," she breathed, her voice trembling with confusion and something softer. "What are you doing here?"

"I couldn't stay away," he confessed, the words tumbling out, raw and unfiltered. "I couldn't sleep. Not after tonight. I just—" He exhaled shakily. "I needed to see you. I needed to know you were okay."

Her lips parted, her expression softening, though fear still flickered beneath the surface. "Why is someone trying to kill me?" she whispered, clutching the bedsheet a little tighter around her. "Why would anyone want me dead?"

The vulnerability in her voice sliced straight through him. Marc stepped closer, sinking to one knee beside the bed. He took her trembling hand gently in his own and lifted it to his lips, pressing a soft, reverent kiss to her skin.

"I don't know," he said quietly, his voice thick with helplessness and fury at his own lack of answers.

Her eyes shimmered with unshed tears. "Why would anyone hate me that much?" Her voice cracked. "I haven't done anything to anyone."

Seeing her like this—fragile, frightened, breaking—shattered something inside him.

"I wish I had answers," he whispered, brushing his thumb along her knuckles. "I wish I could promise you this will all stop tomorrow. But all I can do—the only thing I can do—is be here for you and protect you."

Her lip trembled, a tear spilling over. "Will you… will you hold me?" she asked, barely above a breath.

He didn't hesitate. Marc sat beside her on the bed and gathered her into his arms. She folded into him instantly, trembling against his chest, her fingers curling into his shirt as if anchoring herself. Marc held her tightly, one hand smoothing through her hair, the other steady on her back—solid, warm, unwavering.

Time blurred as he held her through her quiet sobs, letting her release every ounce of fear and panic she'd kept bottled inside. Slowly, her breathing evened out. Her shivers eased. When she finally pulled back, her face was flushed and tear-streaked, her expression exhausted but open.

"Thank you," she whispered, her voice hoarse but full of sincerity.

Marc looked into her eyes, something fierce and tender twisting inside him. Before he could second-guess it, he leaned forward and brushed his lips gently against hers—soft, tentative, a fragile promise in the making.

"I was terrified tonight," he murmured against her mouth. "I never want to feel that again. Never."

A weak, tired smile tugged at her lips. "You didn't want to feel that way?" she teased faintly. "Imagine how I felt."

Despite everything, he laughed softly—only for her. He lifted a hand, tucking a stray lock of hair behind her ear, his fingers lingering on her cheek. His gaze deepened, darkened.

"You're beautiful, Emily," he whispered. "Inside and out. I can't understand why anyone would want to hurt you."

Her smile faltered, her eyes dropping. "But someone does," she said, barely audible.

He gently tilted her chin back up with his fingertips, his touch trembling with restraint. "Emily," he breathed, voice low and rough, "I need to kiss you."

Her breath caught, heat blooming in her eyes. She nodded, slow and helpless.

"Okay," she whispered. Because right now, she needed to feel anything other than fear.

This time, the kiss wasn't tentative or gentle—it was deep and consuming. Marc's lips lingered on hers, pouring every emotion he'd been holding back into the connection: fear, protectiveness, longing… and something far more dangerous. It wasn't just a kiss. It was a confession. A surrender.

Emily stiffened for a heartbeat, startled by the intensity—but then she melted into him, her arms sliding around his neck as though she'd been waiting for this, for him, without even knowing it. A soft, broken moan slipped from her lips, swallowed instantly by his.

"Em…" he murmured against her mouth, breath unsteady. "I want you. So damn much."

Her pulse throbbed in her throat. Her voice trembled when she tried to speak. "Marc, you make me feel—"

But she never finished. His lips claimed hers again, deeper, hotter, silencing her with need he could no longer hide.

His hands traced down her sides, slow and reverent, then slid back up to cup her breasts through the thin fabric of her nightgown. Emily gasped—a sharp, helpless sound—as heat surged through her, her body arching into his touch.

"Oh, Marc… please…" she whispered, breathless, desperate.

His thumbs brushed over her hardened nipples, and her head fell back, a shiver running through her as pleasure curled low in her belly. In the warm glow of the bedside lamp, her skin looked flushed and luminous, the thin silk of her nightgown clinging to every soft curve. Marc's breath hitched at the sight—raw desire flickering across his face.

But beneath that desire, something else stirred. Conflict. Pain. A brutal restraint.

"I can't…" he muttered suddenly, voice fractured. His hands stilled, then slipped away from her as though the contact scorched him. His whole body trembled with the effort to pull back.

Emily's heart squeezed. "Marc," she whispered, reaching up to touch his cheek, her thumb brushing gently along his jaw. "Please… I need you."

He closed his eyes, leaning into her touch for a fleeting moment—like a starving man savouring his last taste of something forbidden. But then he stepped back, the loss of warmth hitting her like a blow.

"I'm sorry," he said, voice raw. "God, Em… I'm so sorry."

Tears blurred her vision. "Marc, please don't leave me," she whispered, her voice breaking around the plea.

His eyes snapped to hers—dark, tormented, overflowing with everything he couldn't let himself have. "You have no idea how much I want you," he rasped. "But I can't. Not like this."

He stood abruptly, tension radiating from him, every muscle locked tight as though holding himself back took everything he had left. Emily reached for him again, but he took another step away, jaw clenched, breath shaking.

He turned slightly, shoulders bowed beneath the weight of everything he wouldn't say—want, fear, restraint all pressing down on him. Then he walked to the door, each step heavy with conflict.

"Marc," she whispered, a last fragile plea that trembled in the space between them.

He froze—just for a heartbeat. She saw it: the tension in his spine, the way his fingers curled against his thigh, the silent war raging inside him. But he didn't turn around.

With a soft, agonising click, the door closed behind him.

Silence swallowed the room.

Emily sagged back against the pillows, curling in on herself as the weight of the moment crashed over her. Her chest ached, her heart splintering in sharp, quiet pieces she had no strength to gather. Hot tears slid down her cheeks, soaking into the pillow.

Exhaustion tugged at her, but sleep was a merciless stranger—hovering close yet refusing to claim her. She lay there in the dim glow of the bedside lamp, lost in the hollow ache of longing, the echo of his touch, and the agonising sense of what might have been.

# Chapter Seventeen

Emily came down to breakfast late, hoping she could slip in unnoticed—and slip out again even faster. The last thing she wanted was to see Marc. Her humiliation from the night before still burned hot beneath her skin, mixed with guilt she couldn't shake.

But fate wasn't on her side.

He was there. Alone. And looking up at her the moment she stepped into the dining room.

Her heart lurched. She froze. Then turned on her heel, desperate to escape before he—

"Emily!"

His voice caught her, but it was his hand around her arm that spun her back toward him.

"Don't touch me!" she snapped, the sting of humiliation flaring all over again.

"Em, please," he said softly, urgently. "Just listen—"

"No!" Her voice cracked. "You didn't want to touch me last night, so why now?"

The pain in her words hit him like a blow. He flinched. "It wasn't that. I couldn't—"

"Yes, I know. I'm repulsive." She tore her arm from his grasp. "Don't ever come near me again."

Tears blurred her vision before she even reached the door—and collided with someone solid.

"Emily." James's hands steadied her instantly. "Are you okay? What's wrong?"

Her laugh was sharp and brittle. "Someone is trying to kill me, that's what's wrong."

James's expression softened with concern, not judgment. "I will keep you safe. You know that, don't you?"

Her shoulders sagged, remorse replacing the raw edge of her voice. "I'm sorry. I didn't mean to snap. I know you will, James."

He nodded gently. "Have you eaten?"

"No."

"Then come on." He took her hand, guiding her back toward the dining room with quiet insistence.

Marc was still inside, elbows braced on the table, his head in his hands. He looked up as they entered, startled—almost haunted.

"Oh, Marc, did you get up late too?" James asked lightly, oblivious to the tension.

Marc blinked. "Uh… yeah."

"Help me get Emily to eat," James said cheerfully.

Emily let out a soft laugh. "I am eating, James. No one needs to force me."

"Good." He kissed her quickly, affectionately, before pulling out a chair for her. "Sit."

She obeyed with a small smile as he filled a plate and set it in front of her. "Eat."

"Yes, sir," she said playfully, picking up her fork.

James turned toward Marc. "Aren't you going to have something?"

Marc shook his head, pushing back from the table. "No. I'm… not hungry." Without waiting for a response, he strode out of the room.

James watched him leave, eyebrows pulling together. "That was strange."

But his focus returned to Emily almost immediately. "There's something I need you to do tonight."

She paused mid-bite. "What's that?"

He hesitated. "I don't want you to dance with anyone except your father, Marc, and me."

"No," she said simply.

"Emily?"

"I'll dance with you and my father. That's it."

James stared at her, confused. "Why not Marc?"

She swallowed hard. "Because he's not my fiancé. You are. And my father… well, that's obvious."

"You don't want to dance with Marc?" he asked gently.

"I do," she admitted. Then lied. "But people are talking."

James's brows knit. "Talking? About what?"

"About how much time we spend together," she said, avoiding his eyes. "They're getting the wrong idea."

"Oh. I... I haven't heard anything."

"Do you really think they'd say it in front of you?" she asked softly.

Realisation dawned in his expression. Then guilt. He knelt beside her, taking her hand. "I'm sorry, Emily. I didn't realise."

Her chest tightened at the sight of him apologising for a lie she told. "It's okay. I just don't want to start rumours."

"Of course." He kissed her hand tenderly. "I understand."

"I need to speak to John. I'll see you later?" he asked, brushing a kiss across her forehead before standing.

"Okay," she replied, forcing a smile.

The moment he left, she pushed her plate away. Appetite gone. Resolve crumbling.

She walked out of the dining room, the weight of guilt, heartbreak, and fear pressing down on her like a storm she couldn't outrun.


Marc paced the library, the polished wooden floors echoing beneath his steps, frustration mounting with each turn. He couldn't stop replaying the moment he'd seen the pain in Emily's eyes—the mixture of fear, guilt, and longing that had nearly broken him. Every movement, every glance he'd given her, now felt like a betrayal he couldn't undo.

"Ah, there you are, Marc," John's voice broke through his spiralling thoughts, followed by James's quieter, more controlled presence.

Marc stopped mid-step and turned, forcing a neutral expression. "Good morning, John," he said, his tone clipped, betraying the tension coiling in his chest.

"I'm glad you're here," James said, his eyes serious, unwavering as they met Marc's. "We need to talk about Emily."

Marc's stomach tightened. "What about her?" he asked cautiously, though a part of him already feared the answer.

James's gaze didn't waver. "She knows someone is trying to hurt her."

John's brow furrowed in surprise, his voice tight. "She does?"

"Your daughter's smart, John," James said, a hint of admiration threading through his words. "She puts the pieces together."

"Yes," John replied, pride and worry intertwining in his expression. "She always has been."

There was a brief pause, the weight of unspoken fears filling the space. James's eyes shifted to Marc, steady and deliberate. "Since she knows, I asked her to dance with only three people tonight."

Marc frowned, his mind resisting the logic. "And...?"

"She said no," James replied simply.

Marc froze. "No?" His voice betrayed both disbelief and a quiet hurt.

"She refuses to dance with you," James clarified, letting the words hang in the air like a tangible weight.

"What?" Marc's voice rose, tinged with confusion, though part of him already suspected this outcome.

John's expression darkened, shock giving way to protective instinct. "Why would she—?"

James inhaled slowly before explaining, his voice measured but firm. "She said people are talking about you two."

Marc's eyes narrowed, disbelief mixing with anger. "Talking about us? What—what are they saying?"

John's concern sharpened. "What do you mean, talking? Are they accusing her?"

James shook his head. "No, not accusing her... but they're noticing how much time you spend together. And Emily... she doesn't want anyone thinking she might be unfaithful to me."

Marc's jaw tightened, and for a moment, he struggled to process the words. A sharp edge of frustration laced his voice. "That's absurd. It's ridiculous."

John's hand rested on his shoulder, grounding him. "Marc, she's trying to protect herself from judgment. From scandal. She wouldn't do anything to betray James."

"I know that," Marc muttered, his voice quieter now, tinged with resignation. "I get it... I just—" He let the sentence trail off, unwilling to voice the bitter disappointment curling in his chest.

James stepped closer, placing a reassuring hand on Marc's arm. "I trust both of you completely. But Emily... she hates the idea of people misjudging her. She can't bear it. That's all this is about."

John nodded in agreement. "Yes. She values her reputation and the people she loves. She wouldn't risk either for anything."

Marc exhaled slowly, a heavy, controlled breath that barely masked the turmoil churning inside him. Guilt settled low in his gut, tightening his shoulders, making his chest feel too small for the breath he'd just taken. He stared at the floor, jaw working as he fought the truth he could never say aloud—the fierce, aching desire he held for Emily.

"Okay," he said at last, his voice low and strained, threaded with disappointment he couldn't hide and understanding he couldn't deny. "I'll stay away. If it gives her peace of mind... I'll do it."

James offered him a small, earnest smile. "Thanks, Marc. That means more than you know."

Marc didn't answer. He couldn't. His thoughts roiled like a gathering storm—wanting her, needing her, the heat of longing still burning under his skin—but none of that mattered. Whatever he felt, whatever pulled him helplessly toward her, Emily's safety— her comfort, her sense of control—had to come first.

And he would sacrifice every unspoken desire to protect that.

The day flew by in a blur of excitement and anticipation. After lunch, most of the women retreated to their rooms to prepare for the ball, slipping into gowns and perfecting their hair and makeup. Meanwhile, the guests arriving from the mainland began to gather in the grand ballroom, their laughter and chatter filling the air with a growing sense of expectation.

Marc met with the three bodyguards hired for the night, briefing them meticulously on their duties. "Keep a close eye on her," he said, his tone firm, "and as soon as Emily appears, I'll point her out. No one gets close without my say-so." The men nodded in unison, their expressions serious.

Satisfied with the plan, Marc excused himself and went to his room. A quick shower washed away the tension of the day, and soon he was slipping into his tuxedo, adjusting his cufflinks with a practiced eye. He examined his reflection, running a hand through his hair, mentally preparing for the long night ahead.

Once ready, he headed to pick up his sister. Knocking on Mary's door, he wished, briefly, that it were Emily instead. The door opened to reveal Mary, radiant in her gown.

"Mary, you look stunning," he said, his eyes taking in every detail.

Mary's petite frame was accentuated by the emerald-green gown that hugged her waist and flared dramatically at the skirt. Her jet-black hair fell in soft waves around her shoulders, perfectly framing her porcelain skin and sparkling green eyes. She smiled warmly, taking his arm.

"Thank you, Marc. I feel beautiful," she replied.

As they descended the stairs, a thought tugged at Marc hard enough to slow his steps. "Mary?"

She glanced over, immediately attuned to the seriousness in his voice. "Yes, Marc?"

"Emily told James that people have been gossiping about her and me—implying she might be unfaithful." His jaw tightened. "Have you heard anything like that?"

Mary stopped short, eyes widening with alarm. "No. Absolutely not. And if I had, I'd shut it down before the words even finished leaving someone's mouth. Emily is far too wonderful for anyone to smear her like that."

Relief flickered through him. Marc gave her hand a grateful squeeze. "Thank you, sis."

He never truly believed there were rumours—Emily's claim had carried a certain... convenience. A gentle excuse to avoid dancing with him without revealing to James just how powerfully he affected her.

Still, he had to be sure. Emily meant too much to him to leave even the shadow of doubt hanging over her name.


Meanwhile, Emily was putting in her last earring when a knock at her door made her jump slightly. "Come in," she called.

James entered, looking every bit the dashing gentleman in his tuxedo. He stopped, mesmerised, as he took in Emily's appearance.

"Oh, Emily, you look wonderful," he breathed, awe and admiration mingling in his voice.

Emily wore an ivory ball gown that seemed spun from dreams. Layers of luxurious silk and delicate tulle formed a bodice that hugged her curves, shimmering subtly in the light. The sweetheart neckline was edged with intricate lace, complementing the diamond necklace and earrings she'd chosen earlier. The skirt cascaded around her in soft, billowing waves, the tulle catching the glow of the room and lending her an ethereal quality, while the silk beneath added a soft satin sheen. Every detail radiated elegance and timeless romance. Minimal makeup enhanced her natural beauty, letting her bright eyes and warm smile shine.

James offered his arm, and she took it with a gentle smile. "Why, thank you, kind sir," she said softly.

As they began their descent, the soft swish of her gown echoing off the polished floors, Marc and Mary reached the bottom of the staircase. They paused, drawn to the approaching couple.

"Oh, Marc, look at her! She looks incredible!" Mary whispered, awe lacing her voice.

Marc's eyes followed Emily, and for a long moment, he simply couldn't breathe. The sight of her, radiant and flawless, stole the air from the room. She was more than beautiful—she was mesmerising, every movement a blend of grace and strength. His chest tightened, a mix of admiration, longing, and the sharp pang of frustration at the unspoken tension between them.

Mary noticed Marc's gaze lingering, and her expression softened. "She's stunning, isn't she?"

Marc's jaw tightened, his eyes never leaving Emily as she descended the staircase with James. "Yes… beyond words," he admitted, though his tone carried a quiet edge of something unspoken.

As they moved gracefully down the stairs, Emily laughed up at James, who gazed at her with pride that softened even his sharpest features. She carried herself with effortless elegance, her tall, statuesque frame commanding the attention of everyone in the room. Her golden-brown hair was swept into an intricate chignon, loose tendrils curling to frame her face delicately. A diamond necklace and matching earrings adorned her slender neck, each stone catching the chandelier light and scattering it in tiny, dazzling flashes that enhanced her radiant aura.

Her ivory ball gown seemed alive, flowing like liquid moonlight. The bodice hugged her curves perfectly, the layers of silk and tulle in the skirt cascading in a soft, ethereal wave with each step. Its understated elegance drew every eye to her, allowing the diamonds and the gentle glow of her skin to shine. She was breathtaking, a vision of grace and poise.

As they reached the bottom of the stairs, Mary whispered with admiration, "Emily, you were right—it was worth the wait. You look incredible."

Emily blushed, tucking a curl behind her ear. "Thank you, Mary. You look beautiful too; that green suits you perfectly."

Marc finally found his voice, stepping closer, his gaze unwavering. "You look lovely, Emily," he said, though his understatement could not mask the intensity behind his words. She smiled politely, nodding in acknowledgment, though a flicker of disappointment crossed her eyes at the simplicity of his compliment.

James, beaming with pride, turned toward Marc. "I think we have the two most beautiful women at the ball, don't you, Marc?"

"Definitely," Marc replied, his voice clipped, the warmth missing from his words as his eyes stayed fixed on Emily.

# Chapter Eighteen

In the ballroom, James and Emily glided through the crowd, her gown shimmering beneath the soft glow of crystal chandeliers. They paused to exchange pleasantries and laugh at shared anecdotes, Emily's melodic laughter weaving seamlessly with the music. Every movement she made was poised, enchanting, yet Marc could see the subtle restraint in her smiles, the way she kept her emotions carefully tucked beneath her composed exterior.

From the edge of the dance floor, Marc watched quietly, his expression unreadable, though the tension in his shoulders betrayed him. Emily noticed him only briefly, feeling the weight of his gaze as she danced with James and shared two graceful dances with her father. Several men approached, offering polite bows and invitations to dance, but James intercepted each with a light-hearted charm. "I've made my fiancée promise to keep me as her main focus tonight," he laughed, deflecting their advances with ease.

Later, while Emily and James were speaking with Mary, James sighed softly. "I need to talk to John for a minute." He turned to Emily, brushing his lips gently across her forehead. "Stay here with Mary," he said, a quiet reassurance in his voice before walking away.

Mary's gaze lingered on Emily fondly. "You're so lucky to have James. He's going to be a wonderful husband."

Emily's lips curved in a soft, contented smile. "Yes… I think so too."

Mary's expression shifted, a wistful note creeping in. "I just wish Marc would find a nice girl."

Emily tilted her head, curiosity piqued. "Oh? Why's that?"

Mary sighed, the wistfulness deepening. "I'd love to have a sister, someone close. But I know it won't happen. Marc has always said he'll never let his heart overrule his head. He's content to have brief flings and move on."

A chill ran through Emily, the words settling like ice against her chest. She glanced at Marc across the room, his eyes still fixed on her every movement, and a complex knot of emotions tightened inside her. Desire. Frustration. Worry. And the painful awareness that the man who stirred her soul so deeply was a man who had built walls too high to scale.

For a fleeting moment, she wondered if those walls might someday crumble—and what it would cost both of them if they did.

Mary was chatting about something trivial, but Emily's mind had long drifted elsewhere, pulled relentlessly toward Marc. She tried to focus, tried to smile and nod, but her thoughts refused to settle.

Then, a chill ran down her spine. A man was staring at her—intense, unblinking—and an instinctive unease settled deep in her chest. She had already noticed two others strategically positioned across the ballroom, quiet, silent observers rather than guests. They hadn't mingled or danced, but their eyes followed her relentlessly, their gazes cold and calculating. Every time she shifted her attention, it seemed they shifted too, tracking her movements with unnerving precision.

Emily's stomach twisted, a rising sense of panic pricking at her. Her feet shifted nervously, and she forced her eyes back to Mary, leaning closer as if proximity could anchor her.

"I've noticed those three men haven't danced with anyone," she whispered, voice low, "and they keep staring at me. It's… it's starting to freak me out."

Mary chuckled softly, trying to reassure her. "Oh, don't worry about them, Emily. They're the bodyguards Marc hired to watch over you."

Emily froze. "What?" Her voice cracked with a mix of shock and outrage.

Mary frowned. "I thought you knew."

"No! I didn't," Emily snapped, heat rising in her chest. "Excuse me, Mary—I need to speak with your brother."

Without waiting for a reply, she pushed through the crowd, weaving past swirling gowns and laughing couples until she reached Marc, who was talking with Irene and Ray. She caught his attention with a sharp tug on his arm, and he immediately excused himself, following her as she stormed outside.

They moved quickly toward the quiet of her mother's garden, eventually stopping behind a tall, flowering hedge. The soft strains of the ballroom music drifted through the night air, a delicate contrast to the storm brewing between them.

Emily turned on him, fists clenched, eyes blazing. "How dare you hire bodyguards!" she spat, her voice rising with every word. "Strangers watching me? Following me? Spying on my every move?"

Marc drew a deep, steadying breath, instantly understanding the source of her fury. "Emily, dammit," he said, his tone firm but controlled. "It was for your own good. I couldn't risk leaving your safety to chance tonight. You have to understand—"

"My safety is not your responsibility!" she cut him off, her chest heaving with frustration. "You're not my fiancé, Marc. You have no right to do this! None!"

The tension of the night—and Marc's barely contained frustration—finally snapped. His jaw tightened, and for a fleeting moment his eyes darkened with something raw, a volatile mix of anger and need. Instead of answering her, he stepped forward, seized her by the waist, and pulled her into his arms, capturing her mouth in a fierce, possessive kiss.

Emily froze, startled by the suddenness of it—but the intensity of his touch unravelled her almost instantly. Her resistance melted; she wrapped her arms around his neck and drew him closer. Marc's grip softened, his roaming hands sliding to her back, moulding her body to his. When his palms cupped her bottom and pressed her firmly against the hard evidence of his arousal, a soft gasp escaped her.

Her fingers tangled in his hair as she kissed him back with equal urgency. Their breathing grew ragged, filling the silent garden as everything beyond the two of them slipped away.

Emily whimpered when Marc's hand moved to her breast, his thumb brushing her hardened nipple through the fabric of her dress. The sensation shot straight through her, making her arch into him, a soft moan trapped against his lips.

"I want you, Em," Marc murmured against her mouth, his voice rough, desperate. "I can't stand being near you and not touching you."

As he lifted her skirts, sliding his hand beneath them, his fingers found the damp heat between her thighs. Emily shuddered at the first brush of his touch, her head falling back as a soft cry broke from her.

"Marc!" she sobbed, clutching his shoulders as his hand slipped inside her silk underwear, his fingers exploring her wet folds with devastating certainty.

His touch was firm yet achingly gentle, coaxing her higher and higher until her body trembled with need. When he found her most sensitive spot, he circled it with slow, deliberate precision, each movement building pressure, feeding the fire he'd sparked. His mouth didn't leave hers—he swallowed every gasp, every cry, every broken sound she made.

Emily's world spun as pleasure washed over her in wave after wave. She clung to Marc as her body shattered under his touch, the intensity stealing her breath, her strength, everything but him. Her legs threatened to buckle, but he held her, solid and unyielding, keeping her anchored.

When the tremors finally faded, Marc lifted his head and gently lowered her skirt. He steadied her, his hands lingering possessively at her waist before he stepped back.

"I may not be your fiancé," Marc said, voice calm but burning with certainty, "but I'm the one you truly want. Be honest with yourself, Emily. The way you respond to me, the way you lose yourself in my arms—" He paused, eyes locked on hers. "It proves I'm right. And deep down… you know it."

Without waiting for a response, Marc turned and walked away, leaving Emily breathless and shaken, her heart pounding with emotions she wasn't prepared to face.

He was right. She did want him. But the desire only tangled her thoughts further, leaving her mind in a storm of confusion and guilt. *How could she feel this way when James—James, who had loved her so faithfully—was waiting for her?* She pressed a hand to her chest, steadying the rapid beat of her heart, and drew in a deep breath, forcing herself to regain composure. Slowly, deliberately, she smoothed the folds of her gown and made her way back to the ball.

She stayed against the wall, trying to appear serene, when Mary found her. The night was winding down, and the guests who had travelled for the ball were beginning to drift toward the wharf, ready to return to the mainland.

Mary chattered cheerfully about the men she had danced with, teasing and laughing, and asked if Emily had enjoyed herself. Emily smiled faintly, giving the polite assurance she knew Mary expected. But the smile didn't reach her eyes. Beneath it, the storm of longing, guilt, and frustration raged on.

As the evening drew to a close, exhaustion pressed down on her like a heavy cloak. She bid James and Marc goodnight, forcing herself into the motions of civility, and then followed Mary upstairs, their footsteps echoing softly in the quiet corridors. Mary sighed dreamily beside her.

"You're so lucky. James is wonderful. I hope I find someone like him one day," Mary murmured.

A sharp pang of guilt jabbed at Emily's chest. Mary was right—she was lucky. Lucky to have James, with his unwavering love and gentle devotion. And yet, the truth she couldn't speak gnawed at her: she had betrayed him, even if only in heart and impulse. She felt like a liar, a cheat, undeserving of the man who had given her everything.

"You'll find someone special," Emily replied softly, forcing a smile, masking the turmoil beneath. She added lightly, with a laugh that felt hollow, "You deserve nothing less."

But the words rang false to her own ears. As they continued up the stairs, her thoughts shifted inexorably to Marc. A sharp ache gripped her chest, catching her breath. The realisation hit with painful clarity: Marc would never consider marrying her. He wanted her, yes—but only on his terms, only for fleeting moments. His actions, though intoxicating, had made that impossibly clear. She had been blind. Foolish. Consumed by hope, by desire, by the dangerous thrill of being wanted.

Later, as she undressed and prepared for bed, the weight of the day pressed heavily upon her. The silk of her nightgown slipped over her skin, but it offered no comfort against the turmoil inside. Her mind replayed Marc's touch, his gaze, the heat of his words—every moment she had allowed herself to forget reason. *What was she supposed to do now? How could she reconcile the pull of desire with the loyalty she owed to James?*

Sleep seemed impossibly distant, the night stretching long and lonely. She needed time to think, to sort through the tangled web of her heart—but she could not do it with either James or Marc near. For the first time in days, Emily felt the true weight of the choices she had made pressing down on her, and she wondered if she would ever find clarity—or peace.

# Chapter Nineteen

The last day of the anniversary house party passed in an almost surreal calm, the kind that felt fragile, as though any sudden movement might shatter it. Emily spent most of it by her father's side, wandering the sprawling estate. Their conversation flowed easily, touching on childhood memories, her mother's laughter, and John's musings on retirement. On the surface, it was comforting, even idyllic—but beneath it, guilt gnawed at Emily relentlessly.

Her mind kept wandering, drawn in fragments to James's quiet, protective attentiveness, and to Marc's brooding, magnetic presence lingering at the edges of her thoughts. Her father never mentioned her distraction, but she could feel his awareness of it. She hated herself for allowing him to feel sidelined, for letting her desires and confusion intrude on this time with him.

Still, John was patient as always. He listened to her stories, even the incomplete, meandering ones, never demanding more, though the wistful glint in his eyes betrayed how much it meant to him.

The warm hum of cicadas echoed through the air as they strolled along the familiar jungle paths, their steps creating a rhythmic crunch against the earth. Shafts of golden sunlight pierced the thick canopy, illuminating patches of moss and vibrant greenery in scattered bursts. Emily trailed her hand along the rough bark of a tree, letting her fingers brush over the soft moss.

"You know, Dad," she murmured, her voice quiet as though afraid of disturbing the stillness, "sometimes I forget how beautiful this place is. It's like our own little paradise."

John smiled, his deep voice tinged with nostalgia. "Paradise, yes. Your mother loved this place. She always said it was where the world stood still, where everything felt right."

Emily's chest tightened at the mention of her mother. The familiar ache of loss settled over her. "I've been thinking…maybe I'll stay a few extra days after everyone leaves this afternoon. It's been so hectic. I could use some quiet."

John slowed, his expression darkening slightly with concern. "Do you think that's wise? With everything that's been happening lately?"

"The only people left will be the staff," Emily replied, brushing a strand of hair from her face. "You've known them for years. They're practically family. What's there to worry about?"

John stopped, frowning, his brow furrowing. "Emily, I trust them, I do. But after the snake, and that flowerpot almost hitting you… I can't shake the feeling that we need to be careful."

Emily exhaled, crossing her arms in mild frustration. "Dad, I'll be fine. You're worrying too much."

"I'm your father," John said firmly. "It's my job to worry. Let's talk to James first. He should weigh in."

Her irritation flared. "Do we really need to consult James? I can make my own decisions, Dad."

John's gaze softened, his voice quieter now. "You're right, you can. But James loves you. He's been worried sick about you all week. This isn't just about you—it's about him too."

Emily bit back a retort, frowning but nodding reluctantly. The last thing she wanted was an argument with her father.

As they continued along the shaded path, the tension gradually eased. Lighter conversation returned—memories of her mother teaching her to climb trees, John's thoughts on downsizing his company, the wedding plans that still felt like a dream.

The estate was bathed in the golden haze of late afternoon, the air rich with the scent of damp earth and blooming flowers. For a while, everything felt normal, almost peaceful.

Then, without warning, the fragile calm shattered.

A faint whoosh split the air, barely audible over the jungle's hum. Before Emily could react, a sharp, searing pain tore through her upper arm. She gasped, stumbling backward as an arrow embedded itself with a resounding thunk into the tree trunk behind her.

"Emily!" John's voice rang out, sharp with panic, as he lunged forward to steady her. His arms caught her before she collapsed entirely, eyes darting to the dark stain spreading across her blouse.

"It's…an arrow," Emily choked out, her voice trembling. She pressed her hand to the wound, trying to stem the bleeding.

John's face hardened, fear masked by steel. "We need to get you back to the house. Now."

Blood trickled down her arm, leaving a dark trail along the jungle path as John half-carried her, navigating the twisting route with desperate haste. Emily's vision blurred, the world tilting, but she clung to her father's steady presence, drawing strength from his firm grip.

They burst into the clearing, breaking through the trees into the garden and toward the terrace. The sound of laughter floated across the air—James, Marc, and Mary at the table, voices light and carefree.

James spotted them first, his face freezing in terror. "Emily!" he shouted, leaping from his chair.

Marc followed close behind, jaw tight, eyes narrowing as he took in the sight of Emily's bloodied sleeve. "What the hell happened?" His voice was low, dangerous, every syllable sharp with barely contained anger.

"She was shot with an arrow," John said sharply, easing Emily into a chair. "It came out of nowhere."

Mary gasped and rushed inside for the first aid kit.

James dropped to his knees beside Emily, hands hovering over her trembling form. "Are you okay? Is it bad? God, you're bleeding—"

"I'm fine," Emily said shakily, her pale face betraying the pain. "I don't think it hit anything vital."

Mary returned with scissors, cutting carefully around the wound. "We need to clean it before it gets infected," she said briskly, her voice steady, a calm anchor amidst the chaos.

Marc stood apart, fists clenched, muttering under his breath. "This is the third time. This is insane."

James's jaw tightened, his fear transforming into anger. "We need to find out who's doing this. Now."

Marc didn't wait. "I'm going to check the perimeter," he said, voice cold, resolute.

"Be careful," John warned, but Marc was already moving toward the jungle, every muscle coiled and alert.

James stayed close to Emily, hands trembling as he helped Mary clean and bandage the wound. His voice softened, cracking slightly. "I won't let anything happen to you. I swear it."

Emily looked up at him, eyes wide and glistening. "I know," she whispered, though fear still gnawed at her. Whoever had done this had come terrifyingly close this time.

Once the wound was secured, they gathered on the terrace. Most guests had retreated to their rooms or cabins, preparing for the launch back to the mainland in about an hour.

"I'm staying here for a couple more days," Emily said, breaking the tense silence.

James and Marc exchanged a wary glance. "Do you think that's wise?" James asked carefully.

Marc's lips thinned, but he remained silent.

"I am staying," Emily said firmly, though her voice wavered slightly under their watchful stares.

"The bodyguards will stay, then," James said, leaving no room for argument.

"No!" Emily shot back, arms crossing instinctively—then winced as a sharp pain flared in her arm.

"Sweetheart," John said gently, his voice steady and concerned, "you need to be reasonable. We're all worried about you."

Mary added, calm but pragmatic, "What if just one bodyguard stays? That shouldn't be too restrictive."

All eyes turned to Emily. She exhaled, shoulders slumping, the fight draining from her. "Fine…only one," she muttered reluctantly.

With that settled, they all made their way to the wharf.

Emily stood beside her father, watching the last of the guests board the launch. The house would soon be empty, leaving her alone with her thoughts—and with the faint hope that solitude might offer the clarity she so desperately craved.

Marc, James, Mary, and her father lingered as the boat prepared to depart, each farewell feeling heavier than the last.

Emily hugged Mary tightly, drawing comfort from her warmth despite the emotional exhaustion that clung to her. "Send me your number so we can stay in touch," she said softly.

"I will," Mary promised, eyes glistening with unshed tears. Though their time together had been brief, Mary had become a comforting presence, and Emily felt an ache as she let her go.

Her father was next. He pulled her into a long, grounding embrace, his strength anchoring her in the moment. "Take care of yourself, darling," he murmured. "Rest, clear your mind. You deserve it."

Emily nodded, throat tight. "I will."

She watched him walk away, her chest heavy. He had always wanted the best for her, even when she struggled to understand what that truly was.

Then came James. He brushed his lips to hers, a gentle, restrained kiss. "Let me know when you're back," he said softly. "We'll have dinner—just the two of us."

"I will," she whispered, voice trembling. His steady presence had been a balm, yet a part of her recoiled with guilt. She loved him—truly—but her heart was tangled, pulled toward directions she wasn't ready to face.

Finally, there was Marc.

He lingered as the others stepped back, his presence commanding, drawing the air taut around them. Without a word, he wrapped her in a familiar embrace, arms strong, steady, and protective. He pressed a soft, almost apologetic kiss to the top of her head before releasing her.

Their eyes met, and for a fleeting, heart-wrenching moment, Emily glimpsed something raw in his gaze—pain, regret, and a depth of emotion she couldn't name.

He leaned close, lips brushing her ear as he murmured, "I'm sorry."

Emily's breath hitched, her heart twisting painfully. She didn't know if his apology was for the tension of the past days, the unspoken longing between them, or something deeper still. Quietly, she thought to herself, so am I.

Marc stepped back, his retreat deliberate, as if leaving were a struggle in itself. When he finally boarded the launch, Emily remained frozen on the dock, her hand pressed lightly to her chest, trying to tame the storm of emotions whirling inside her.

As the boat pulled away, she watched until it vanished over the horizon. Her heart was heavy, her thoughts a tangled mess of guilt, longing, and confusion. And yet, amid it all, a small part of her clung to hope—the solitude awaiting her over the next few days might finally give her the clarity she so desperately needed.


Emily stayed on the island for another week, seeking solace in solitude. She filled her days swimming in the turquoise waters, tending the lush gardens, and reclining on the terrace with a book in hand. Yet, no matter how serene her surroundings, her mind refused to be still. The quiet only left room for thoughts that gnawed at her—guilt, longing, and confusion, each one heavier than the last.

She missed Marc, and the admission cut deeper than she cared to acknowledge. She knew it was wrong. He had made it abundantly clear: he wanted passion, not permanence. He sought fleeting indulgence, not commitment. And yet, she craved whatever fragments of him were offered, even at the cost of her own heart.

The memory of their kisses haunted her—not for the act itself, but for the intensity, the thrill, the fire that had ignited between them. It was a stark contrast to James, whose love was steady, unwavering, and utterly safe. James was everything she should desire: devoted, patient, kind. And yet, Marc had awakened a part of her she hadn't known existed, a side that hungered for danger, for intensity, for a connection that scared and exhilarated her in equal measure.

The guilt twisted in her chest, sharp and relentless. Mary's words echoed mockingly in her mind: Marc will never marry. He'll never let his heart override his head. He's content to bed them for a time and then move on. She had been foolish—blinded by desire, allowing herself to fall for a man who would never offer her the permanence she needed.

Her heart ached with shame. She was a cheat, undeserving of James's trust and love. If she truly loved him, she would have drawn the line with Marc before it had ever escalated. Yet here she was, caught between longing and loyalty, passion and responsibility, each choice tearing at her from different directions.

By the end of the week, Emily knew she could no longer hide from the truth. She had to face James, to confess, to end the pretence that had bound them together. The thought filled her with dread, but she knew it was the only way forward—the only path that might offer a chance at redemption, even if it meant breaking the heart she cherished most.

# Chapter Twenty

The next day, Emily told James she would be returning. His bright, expectant smile made her chest tighten with guilt, but she steeled herself—she would face him with honesty, no matter how difficult. With the bodyguard dismissed, convinced he was no longer needed, she made her way to her fiancé's office, deliberately timing her visit to avoid Karen, who was out to lunch.

Standing before James's door, Emily took a steadying breath and knocked softly.

"Enter," came his familiar voice.

She stepped inside. James looked up from his desk, a warm smile lighting his face. "Welcome back," he said.

Emily returned the smile, though hers was hesitant. "Can we talk?"

James set down his pen, his expression shifting to seriousness. "Of course. Have a seat."

They both sat, and he leaned forward slightly, brow furrowed. "Actually, Emily... I need to talk to you too."

Surprised, Emily opened her mouth, but they spoke at the same time.

"I can't marry you," they said in unison.

Silence fell, the words hanging heavy in the air.

"What?" they echoed, startled, then broke into a shared, nervous laugh.

James gestured for her to speak first. "You start."

Emily swallowed hard, folding her hands in her lap. "I've been thinking a lot, James. And... I've realised that while I care for you deeply, my feelings aren't what they should be for marriage."

James's face remained calm, his eyes searching hers.

"I love you," she continued, her voice trembling, "but not in the way you deserve. It's more like the love of a brother. You deserve someone who can give you their whole heart—and I can't."

He exhaled slowly, nodding as if finally giving voice to a truth he'd carried for too long. "Emily... I've been feeling the same way. I do care for you—deeply—but it isn't the kind of love that can sustain a marriage. And I think, somewhere inside, we both knew that." His voice softened. "We're both at that stage where we wanted the next chapter—a family, a partner—and we held onto the idea that we could give that to each other. Maybe that's why neither of us ever pushed the issue of intimacy."

A blend of relief and sadness washed over her, loosening the tension she had carried for weeks. For the first time, she felt like she could breathe.

Quietly, she slipped off her engagement ring and placed it in his hand. "I'm so sorry, James. I hope… I hope you don't hate me."

James curled his fingers around the ring, his expression steady and kind. "Hate you? Never." His voice was warm, sincere. "If anything, I'm grateful we're being honest— with ourselves and with each other. And I really hope we can still be friends."

Emily placed her hand over his. "We will. I won't let this change that."

He stood and pulled her into a warm embrace. "You're one of a kind, Emily. I'm lucky to have you in my life."

As they pulled apart, he hesitated. "There's something else," he said cautiously.

Emily tilted her head, curious. "What is it?"

He paused, then admitted, "I've developed feelings for Mary. And… she feels the same. We've been talking, and we'd like to see where it leads."

Emily blinked in surprise, then a genuine smile spread across her face. "That's wonderful, James. Truly."

"You're okay with it?" he asked, visibly relieved.

"Of course," she said softly. "You both deserve happiness."

At that moment, the door opened, and Mary stepped in. She froze, eyes wide, as she took in Emily and James together. "Oh… I'm sorry!" she stammered.

Emily turned to her with a gentle, reassuring smile. "No, wait."

Mary hesitated, uncertainty flickering across her face.

Emily crossed the room and wrapped her in a heartfelt embrace. "James told me. I'm so happy for you both."

Relief washed over Mary, and she hugged her back tightly. "Thank you, Emily. I was so afraid of hurting you."

"You haven't," Emily said sincerely, pulling back slightly to meet her eyes. "We'll always be friends."

Mary smiled, and James joined them, his expression soft and full of gratitude.

Emily turned to him with a playful glint in her eye. "I'd better go tell my father. Wish me luck."

James's brow furrowed slightly. "I can come with you."

"No," she said firmly, yet kindly. "This is something I need to do on my own."

She gave him one last warm smile. "Be happy, James."

"You too, Emily," he said softly, watching her walk out, a quiet pride and affection in his gaze.

As Emily stepped out of the office, a lightness lifted her chest. Even with the difficult conversation ahead, for the first time in what felt like forever, she felt certain she was on the right path.

Heading toward her father's office, Emily felt a flicker of relief—Jeremy's desk was empty. He must be at lunch. She was grateful for the privacy; this wasn't a conversation she wanted overheard. Taking a steadying breath, she knocked lightly.

"Come in," her father's deep, familiar voice called.

Emily pushed the door open, offering a warm, nervous smile. John looked up from the papers scattered across his desk. The usual sternness in his gaze softened as he met her eyes.

"Hello, sweetheart. Welcome back," he said, leaning back in his chair. "What brings you here?"

"Do I need a reason to visit my wonderful father?" Emily teased, crossing the room to kiss him on the cheek. She settled into the chair across from him, willing her nerves to settle.

John chuckled, a twinkle in his eyes. "Flattery will get you everywhere, my dear."

Emily let out a soft laugh, but it quickly faded. Her smile dimmed as she clasped her hands tightly in her lap, the weight of what she was about to say pressing down on her.

"Dad," she began softly, her voice trembling. "There's something I need to tell you."

Concern creased his brow as he leaned forward. "What is it, sweetheart? You know you can tell me anything."

Emily inhaled deeply, summoning courage. "James and I… we've decided to end our engagement. I returned his ring."

The words hung heavy in the quiet office. Emily's heart raced as she watched her father's expression shift—surprise, confusion, and finally, a tender concern.

"You're calling off your engagement?" he asked carefully. "But… I thought you two were happy."

Emily nodded, her hands tightening. "We were, in a way. But it's not the kind of happiness that builds a marriage. I love him, Dad—but not in the way a wife should love her husband. It's… more like the love of a brother."

John's face softened, and he reached across the desk to take her hand. "Emily, all I want is for you to be happy. If this feels right to you, then I support you completely. I'm proud of you for being honest with yourself—and with James."

Her throat tightened, and she blinked rapidly to keep tears at bay. "Thank you, Dad. That means so much."

Before she could say more, the door opened quietly, and James stepped inside. His calm, steady presence filled the room, and he offered Emily a small, reassuring smile before turning to her father.

"Sorry to interrupt," James said, walking toward them. "I thought it best to be here while Emily talks to you."

John's gaze shifted between them, a flicker of understanding dawning. "James," he said warmly, "this was a mutual decision?"

James nodded, standing beside Emily. "Yes, sir. We had a heartfelt conversation and realised that while we care for each other deeply, it's not the kind of love that should lead to marriage."

Emily's eyes softened as she glanced at him. "We're better as friends, Dad. And we don't want to lose that."

John leaned back, exhaling slowly. Relief softened his features. "Well, as long as you're both at peace with this, that's all that matters. I'm proud of you both for handling it with such maturity."

Emily's chest swelled as she squeezed James's hand in silent thanks. Her father's understanding felt like the final piece of closure she needed.

James met her gaze, then John's. "Thank you for your support, sir. It means a lot to both of us."

John rose, extending a hand to James. "You'll always be family, James."

James accepted it with a grateful smile. "That means a lot, sir." He excused himself, leaving Emily and her father alone.

John studied her for a long moment, pride and love shining in his eyes. "You've grown into an incredible young woman, Emily. I know this wasn't easy, but you handled it with grace."

Emily smiled through her tears. "Thank you, Dad. That means the world to me."

They spent a few minutes talking about lighter matters, the conversation easing the heaviness of the moment. When Emily finally left the office, her heart felt lighter.

With her father's support, James's friendship, and her own clarity, she finally felt certain she had made the right choice—and that she was ready to move forward.


Over the past week, Marc had noticed a subtle shift in Mary's routine. Each evening, as he worked through the endless boxes from his move, she would dress carefully, slip on her jacket, and step out into the night. At first, he dismissed it—Brisbane was still new to her, and he assumed she was simply exploring the city, discovering its hidden corners, or meeting new people. But as the nights piled up—seven in a row—and her returns grew later and later, a gnawing unease settled in. There was something about her behaviour, a restless energy that didn't fit, that made his chest tighten and his mind race.

That evening, as Mary slid into her coat and reached for the door, Marc realised he could no longer ignore it. He set down his laptop, rising from the couch, and spoke, his tone casual but edged with an undercurrent of tension, a thin veil over the coil of curiosity—and something darker—that had been building all week.

"You've been going out a lot lately," he said, glancing up at her. "What's going on?"

Mary paused, her hand on the doorknob, and turned to him with a practiced, casual smile. "I'm going out with James again," she said lightly—but the moment the words left her lips, her expression froze. She hadn't meant to speak his name aloud; they had agreed Marc didn't need to know yet.

Marc's reaction was instant, sharp, and cold. "James?" he repeated, his voice tightening. "What the hell? Is he cheating on Emily?"

"No! No, it's not like that," Mary said quickly, stepping back, her cheeks flushing crimson.

Marc's eyes narrowed, his tone hardening. "Then you'd better tell me exactly what it is like."

Mary hesitated, glancing down before meeting his intense gaze. "Emily..." she began, but the word caught in her throat.

Marc leaned forward, the tension in his chest coiling like a spring ready to snap. "Emily what?" he pressed, his voice low and urgent. "Is she back?" Two long weeks had passed since he last saw her, and the memory of her absence gnawed at him—especially the memory of how she had trembled in his arms, completely undone by him.

Mary exhaled slowly. "She returned about a week ago."

Marc's pulse quickened. "Have you… have you seen her?" he asked, struggling to keep his voice steady, though his heart pounded against his ribs.

Mary tilted her head, a faint look of puzzlement on her face. "Yes, I saw her at the start of the week."

"How is she?" His voice steadied now, but inside, it was anything but calm.

"Oh, surprisingly well," Mary said with a small, almost casual smile. It was the wrong kind of smile—one that stoked his anger without warning.

Marc's expression darkened. A cold, rising wave of frustration and possessiveness swept over him. "Does she know you're going out with… with her fiancé?" His jaw clenched, his fists tightening involuntarily.

Mary blinked, composed but cautious. "James isn't her fiancé."

Marc froze. The words hit like a physical blow. His legs felt unsteady, and he sank onto the couch, trying to absorb the revelation. "What…?" he whispered faintly, voice trembling despite his effort to mask it.

Mary's gaze softened, concern flashing in her eyes. "Marc… are you okay? You look pale."

He ignored her, the image of Emily returning her ring, ending things with James, flooding his mind in vivid, torturous clarity. "What do you mean, he's not her fiancé?" he asked again, quieter this time, almost to himself.

"She returned the ring at the start of the week," Mary explained, her voice steady despite a faint blush. "They ended things. Emily gave James and me her blessing. Please don't be upset. James and I… we've developed feelings for each other. After Emily ended things, he told her about us. She hugged us both, smiled, and said she was happy for us. I mean… I really care for Emily. I'm grateful to have met her."

Marc barely heard the rest. His mind was elsewhere, fixated on Emily. The vivid memory of her hand slipping the ring from her finger, her eyes glistening with unshed tears, and the weight of her decision to sever the future she'd built with James—it all pressed down on him. His chest ached with a thousand unspoken questions.

"Marc?" Mary's voice drew him back, a tether to the present. "Are you listening?"

He blinked, forcing himself upright. Without responding, he grabbed his phone and keys from the table, leaning down to press a quick, almost distracted kiss to Mary's cheek. "Yeah… I'm fine. Enjoy your date," he muttered, though the words carried none of the warmth they usually did.

Before Mary could respond, Marc strode out of the apartment, leaving her standing in the doorway, her brow furrowed in confusion, watching him go.

As the elevator descended, Marc's thoughts twisted and collided like storm clouds. *Emily was unattached.* The words echoed in his mind, but instead of bringing relief, they only tightened the hollow knot in his chest. *A surge of longing mingled with uncertainty—did this change anything between them? Was there still a chance, or had too much time passed?*

He didn't have the answers. He only knew he couldn't sit still. Fingers trembling slightly, he pulled out his phone and called the security team he used, his voice low, controlled, yet edged with urgency. "Emily Sinclair's address. The one from her safety checks. I need it. Now."

The response came almost immediately, precise, and efficient. Marc's jaw clenched as he tapped the address into his GPS, his pulse hammering in tandem with the rapid beat of his thoughts. Without hesitation, he slid into his car, the engine roaring to life as streetlights streaked past, blurring into gold and silver ribbons in the night.

Questions raced through his mind—*what would he say when he saw her? Would she even want to see him?* Could he risk the possibility of rejection after all that had passed?

But doubt was fleeting. One thought anchored him: Emily had returned James's ring. And somehow, that single fact had upended everything he thought he knew. Everything he wanted.

He gripped the steering wheel tighter. Whatever happened next, he couldn't let this moment slip away.

# Chapter Twenty-One

Emily stepped out of the shower, steam curling around her like a soft veil, and reached for the fluffy white bathrobe hanging on the hook nearby. She wrapped it snugly around her damp body, the warmth a comforting contrast to the cool air brushing her skin and picked up a towel to gently squeeze the water from her hair. The quiet of the evening settled over her, a fragile serenity she rarely allowed herself to enjoy.

She padded barefoot across the hardwood floor, the faint hum of the city outside barely audible through the thick windows. Her apartment, dimly lit and serene, felt like a sanctuary tonight. The gentle rhythm of raindrops tapping against the glass mirrored the slow cadence of her thoughts, soothing yet stirring a restless ache deep in her chest.

After tying the robe securely at her waist, she wandered toward the kitchen. The cool tiles underfoot sent a shiver up her spine as she opened the fridge, scanning its contents for a light snack. The quiet was almost meditative until a sudden, sharp knock at the door shattered the stillness.

Emily froze, her heart skipping a beat. *Who could possibly be here at this hour?* Her pulse raced as a swirl of questions and apprehension flooded her mind. Slowly, hesitantly, she moved to the door, her fingers trembling as they slid the lock open. She cracked it just a fraction, peering into the dimly lit hallway—and her breath caught.

Marc stood there, rain-slicked, and formidable, his broad shoulders rising and falling as though he had run for miles. The water glistened on his jacket and clung to the dark strands of hair falling across his forehead. His gaze, intense and unflinching, locked onto hers, and Emily's chest stuttered with a mixture of longing and disbelief.

"Marc?" she whispered, her voice trembling. Seeing him like this, soaked and earnest, made her pulse surge, yet confusion tangled with the sudden heat of her desire. "Why are you here?"

His eyes softened, though a flicker of urgency remained. "I needed to see you," he said simply, the raw edge in his voice sending shivers down her spine.

Emily's fingers gripped the edge of the door. Her thoughts collided with her emotions in a chaotic storm: hope, fear, longing, and caution all warring for dominance. "How did you even... find me?" she asked, her tone sharper than she intended.

Marc stepped closer, resting a hand lightly against the doorframe. "It doesn't matter," he murmured, his voice steady but vulnerable. "Please, Em... can I come in?"

Her instinct screamed to shut the door, to protect herself from the sudden surge of emotions he ignited. But another part of her—the part that had missed him far more than she would admit—hesitated. Before she could decide, he nudged the door open a little further. She didn't stop him.

"I came to see you," he repeated, softer now, almost a plea. The vulnerability in his voice made her chest ache with a longing she couldn't name.

"Why?" she breathed, her words barely audible. Her mind raced with questions, yet her body betrayed her, drawn to the warmth radiating from him.

Marc stepped inside, closing the door with a soft click that felt final and intimate all at once. He turned to face her, his hands resting gently on her shoulders. The touch was light, almost tentative, as if he feared she might recoil.

"I've missed you," he said, his voice thick with emotion. His hands tightened ever so slightly, drawing her closer, anchoring her in his presence. "More than I can put into words."

Emily wanted to resist, to demand answers, to hold her fragile composure. But the ache in his voice shattered her defences. Instinctively, she leaned into him, allowing his strong, steady arms to envelop her. She surrendered to the warmth and the familiarity, letting herself melt against him.

"I missed you too," she murmured, her voice muffled against his chest, almost involuntary.

For a long moment, they simply stood there, wrapped around each other, the outside world fading into insignificance. The steady beat of Marc's heart beneath her ear was a grounding rhythm against the tempest swirling in her own chest.

Then, as if pulled by an invisible force, Marc slowly stepped back, his gaze locking with hers. Time stretched, suspended between them, heavy with unspoken truths and desires. Every subtle movement—the tilt of his head, the way his lips parted slightly—sent tremors of anticipation through her.

And then, with deliberate slowness, he leaned closer, the space between them collapsing, each heartbeat bringing them nearer, until the warmth of his presence pressed against her entirely.

Their lips met, and an electric fire ignited between them, fierce and consuming. A low, rough groan escaped Marc as he drew her closer, pressing her body against his with a hunger that bordered on desperate. Every brush of his lips against hers was deliberate, teasing, coaxing, and yet there was an urgency that stole her breath, leaving her trembling beneath his touch.

Emily's body responded instinctively, every nerve alight, a heated ache unfurling deep within her. Soft curves pressed against hard, unyielding muscle, every inch of her pulled into his magnetism. The kiss spiralled, feverish and urgent, a storm of passion neither could deny, and beneath it all, a raw, primal desire burned—an intensity that made her heart pound and her skin ache for more.

Marc's hands glided over her with reverent insistence, memorising the contours of her body, lingering over the places that made her shiver. When his fingers brushed the belt of her bathrobe, he paused, seeking permission in her gaze. Emily's lips curved in a slow, knowing smile, trust shining from every look.

With a gentle tug, he loosened the belt, letting the robe slip from her shoulders and pool around her feet. She stood before him, bathed in the silver glow of the moonlight streaming through the window, every line of her illuminated in a soft, intimate radiance.

Marc stepped back just slightly, his eyes raking over her form with awe and restrained hunger. His chest rose and fell unevenly, the tension coiling tight in his arms, his restraint hanging by a delicate thread.

"You take my breath away," he murmured, his voice hoarse with longing. "You're incredible... absolutely beautiful."

For the first time in her life, Emily didn't feel self-conscious. Every doubt, every insecurity melted away, leaving only the undeniable pull of need coiling through her, the desperate ache to feel him closer, to let the world fall away until it was just the two of them, lost in the madness of desire.

Marc's gaze softened as he reached for her again, his hands sliding along her sides with a tenderness that contradicted the heat in his eyes. "I can't... stay away from you," he whispered, voice rough and intimate, a confession as raw as the ache between them.

Emily's pulse thrummed in response, her own whisper barely audible. "Then don't."

The words, so simple yet so potent, sent a shiver racing through them both. In that instant, the world beyond the apartment ceased to exist. There was only the ache, the warmth, and the magnetic pull drawing them together, relentless, and undeniable.

Without another word, Marc lifted her effortlessly into his arms. The feel of her pressed against him—the soft weight, the heat of her skin—made his chest tighten. Every step to the bedroom was deliberate, measured, yet charged with an urgency neither could ignore. He laid her down gently, reverently, as if she were the most fragile treasure in existence.

Even as he stripped away his clothes with a purposeful swiftness, his eyes never left hers. There was a fire in them, tempered by tenderness, a balance of desire and reverence that made Emily's heart pound.

Hovering above her, Marc's fingers traced the curve of her cheek, featherlight, sending sparks crawling across her skin. His gaze held hers, dark and smouldering, a storm barely contained. "Do you even know what you do to me?" His voice was low, rough around the edges, a growl tempered by an almost painful restraint.

Emily's lips parted in a breathless whisper, the warmth of anticipation curling through her. "Show me," she said, her voice soft but firm, an invitation, and a challenge all at once.

Marc's lips curved into a slow, predatory smile. He lowered his mouth to hers, letting the kiss build gradually, a delicious tension that promised more, each brush of his lips igniting her senses further. Every movement, every touch, was measured yet charged with longing, the quiet intimacy between them intensifying the heat that roared beneath the surface.

A strangled cry tore from her throat as he cupped her breast, his palm hot against her sensitised skin. He groaned low in his chest, flicking his thumb over her hardened peak—once, then again when she arched into him with a helpless whimper. Their mouths fused, the kiss deep and drugging, tongues tangling, breath mingling, until nothing existed beyond the blistering intensity of their connection.

His hands roamed over her body—learning her, mapping her. When he found the silken curve of her thigh, he stroked her with deliberate slowness, igniting a fresh rush of heat between her legs.

Then he tore his lips from hers, dragging them down her body in a scorching trail. His mouth closed over one taut nipple, his tongue flicking, teasing, before he sucked deeply, pulling a broken moan from her lips.

Her fingers tangled in his hair, her breath coming in ragged bursts as he kissed his way lower—down the smooth plane of her stomach—his lips and tongue worshipping every inch.

He pushed her thighs apart and reached between them. She gasped when his fingertip slid over her slick, satin heat—stroking, circling, coaxing more from her. Kneeling between her legs on the bed, he lowered his head.

And then he tasted her.

Pleasure detonated inside her. It was so intense her hips shuddered beneath him. He held her steady, swirling his tongue through her wetness, drinking every sound she made.

Then he was devouring her—tongue stroking, circling, teasing the tight bud of her pleasure until she writhed beneath him, sobbing his name. When he slid a long, masculine finger inside her, she nearly came undone. She was tight—so tight—her muscles gripping him. He withdrew slowly, then thrust in again, setting a torturous rhythm that dragged her higher, and higher, until she was teetering on the edge.

"Oh… Marc, please." Her voice was fractured, pleading.

He groaned against her, the vibration sending another jolt ripping through her. "You taste incredible," he murmured, breath warm against her fevered skin.

Tremors slammed through her. Her back arched off the bed as she held her breath, eyes squeezed shut, lips parted in a silent gasp. His tongue stroked her with its full width—rough, relentless—then softened, twirling her with the delicate flick of its tip.

Her entire body tightened—arching once more—

—and she exploded with a scream of ecstasy.

Another strangled cry tore from her as wave after wave crashed over her. He held her through it, his mouth lingering, drawing out every last shudder until she collapsed beneath him, trembling and utterly wrecked.

Slowly, reverently, Marc kissed his way back up her body, tracing every dip, every curve, worshipping her with every touch. He hovered over her again, his body settling between her parted thighs, the heavy weight of his arousal pressing intimately against her softness.

Their eyes met.

No words were needed.

He wanted her.

She needed him.

And neither of them would deny it any longer.

Marc bent and claimed her lips in a deep, searing kiss. She could taste herself on him—a heady reminder of the pleasure he'd just given her. His hardness nudged at her entrance, poised at a threshold they could never uncross.

She was ready—hot, wet, aching for him.


She moaned, the sound low and desperate, as he guided his thick, throbbing shaft against her slick heat, circling the swollen tip over her entrance in slow, maddening strokes. Her body trembled beneath him, hips lifting, seeking more.

When he could no longer fight the pull of her, he aligned himself and pushed forward—deep, so achingly deep—into her tight, hot sheath. The sensation slammed into him, a rush of pleasure so fierce, so consuming, it punched the breath from his lungs.

"Oh—!" A sharp pain sliced through Emily, catching her off guard. Her body tensed, nails digging into his shoulders as a small gasp escaped her.

Marc froze instantly, every muscle locking. He lifted his head, searching her face, shock flickering there—followed by something deeper. Concern. Awe. Reverence.

His voice came rough. "You're a virgin?"

Emily held his gaze, defiant, steady. She reached up, cupped his face, and pulled him into a slow, sensual kiss.

As their mouths parted, she whispered, "I was a virgin. I'm not anymore."

Then she tilted her hips, just enough to pull a long, low groan from deep inside him.

His restraint shattered.

Bracing his hands against the mattress, he thrust into her again—deeper—another groan breaking from his chest. Pleasure crashed through him hard enough to make him struggle for breath.

Emily's discomfort dissolved, replaced by something fierce and consuming. The pleasure built—swift, relentless—until it swallowed her whole. The sounds leaving her lips were wild and raw, unrecognisable. She clung to him, her fingers digging into the muscles of his back, her body rising to meet each thrust, matching him, answering him, their passion burning hotter, hungrier.

He drove into her again… and again… skimming the razor-thin edge of control. Her sudden cry tore through the air as she clenched around him, her fingernails digging into his shoulders. He froze—every muscle coiled—eyes squeezed shut as he fought the brutal, exquisite urge to let go too soon.

With a strained breath, he forced himself to slow, thrusting deep… deliberate… making her feel every thick, pulsing inch as he filled her completely. Her breaths turned into soft, frantic little pants, her body arching toward him as he moved, lifting her higher… and higher.

Then it hit her again.

A shudder rolled through her—then a tidal wave—and she screamed his name, raw and breathless.

"Marc…"

He felt it too. The urgency. The fierce, seductive pull of her body gripping him—dragging him deeper—unravelling every shred of restraint he had left.

Their mouths crashed together, hungry, desperate, devouring each other as their bodies moved in perfect, frantic rhythm.

Pleasure tore through her, white-hot, consuming. Her body clenched around him in sharp, pulsing waves, pulling him with her, holding him captive in her release.

Marc groaned against her throat, the sound rough and helpless, his hands clamping around her hips as he thrust hard—burying himself to the hilt—as her tight, molten heat milked him mercilessly.

With a deep, guttural growl, he broke—his body seizing as he spilled into her, his climax crashing over him so violently it stole the breath from his lungs and left him trembling in her arms.

They lay tangled together, bodies slick with sweat, chests rising and falling in uneven breaths.

Then Marc kissed her again—soft, tender, achingly sweet. Such a contrast to the raw passion moments before that Emily's heart clenched painfully. Tears stung her eyes, but before they could spill, Marc bent and kissed them away.

A little while later, he rolled onto his side and gathered her close, cradling her in the firm curve of his arm. He pressed a lingering kiss to her forehead, his touch gentle, reverent.

Exhausted, Emily drifted into a deep, blissful sleep.

But Marc remained awake, staring at the ceiling as a heavy realisation settled over him.

She had been a virgin.

Something he had never imagined.

He had assumed James had been intimate with her—*why wouldn't he have been?* But now he knew the truth. James had never touched her.

*No one had.*

The revelation sent something sharp and primal through him—possessive, protective, fierce. She had given herself to him. Trusted him with something precious.

A slow smile curved his lips as he pulled her even closer, brushing one last kiss against the top of her head.

Only then did he finally let sleep take him.

# Chapter Twenty-Two

Emily stirred as the first golden rays of morning filtered through the curtains, casting a warm glow over the room. A delicious heat surrounded her—solid, strong, unmistakably Marc. His arms were wrapped around her, his body pressed intimately against hers, his breath slow and steady against the back of her neck.

She shifted slightly, nestling deeper into his embrace, and a low, contented groan rumbled in his chest.

As she began to turn toward him, his arm tightened, stilling her.

"Don't move," he murmured against her ear, voice thick with sleep and desire. "Just feel."

A shiver ran through her as his lips brushed the sensitive curve of her neck, placing slow, lingering kisses there. His hands slid up her body, cupping her breasts, his fingers teasing the already firm peaks. Emily gasped softly, her body arching instinctively into his touch.

Marc's mouth curved in a knowing smile against her shoulder as his thumbs grazed her nipples, sending ripples of pleasure straight to her core.

She squirmed, breath hitching, her body tuned entirely to his. Pressing her round, perfect backside against the hard length behind her, she felt him inhale sharply. His hand slipped lower, fingers trailing down her stomach with maddening slowness.

When he found her slick, heated centre, Emily let out a strangled moan.

Marc hummed in approval, nibbling lightly at her ear. "So wet for me," he murmured, his voice a velvet caress.

She trembled as his fingers began their slow, deliberate torment—stroking, circling, applying exquisite pressure. Every touch lit her up, molten heat unfurling through her veins.

"Marc…" she gasped, sobbing on a breath. "Please."

His lips brushed her neck, warm and teasing. "Tell me what you need, sweetheart."

"You," she whispered, voice raw and trembling. "I need you."

Marc's fingers continued their lazy, devastating exploration, teasing her until she pushed her hips back, silently begging for more.

"Please, Marc. I need you," she whimpered, desperation cracking her voice.

"Do you want me inside you?" he murmured darkly into her ear.

"Yes… I need to feel you inside me," she breathed.

That was all he needed.

He lifted her thigh and positioned his thick, rigid length at her entrance. With a slow, smooth thrust, he filled her completely—stretching her, claiming her—letting her feel every inch. A deep groan rumbled from his chest as he buried himself in her heat.

"Em…" he moaned, emotion thickening his voice.

They moved together in a slow, intoxicating rhythm, perfectly in sync. His thrusts were deep and deliberate, each one sending a new shockwave spiralling through her.

Emily gripped his arm, her body tightening around him as pleasure coiled inside her—tight, urgent, impossible to contain. A wave of pure ecstasy slammed into her, ripping through her in relentless pulses. She cried out his name as her body clenched around him, dragging him with her.

Marc groaned, his rhythm breaking, thrusts turning sharp with need. He pounded into her welcoming heat until control snapped. He shattered, release pouring into her in hot, shuddering pulses, a deep groan tearing from his chest.

They collapsed together, tangled in sheets and limbs, bodies still humming with aftershocks of pleasure.

Marc pressed a soft, lingering kiss to her shoulder, his lips warm and tender.

Emily sighed, contentment blooming in her chest as she nestled closer. With his arms wrapped securely around her, safe and sated in his embrace, she slipped into a deep, peaceful sleep.

Marc waited until her breathing evened out, the gentle rise and fall of her chest telling him she was finally lost in a deep, untroubled sleep. Reluctantly, he eased himself from her warmth, careful not to disturb her. He dressed quickly, each movement precise, his mind unwilling to linger on the thought of leaving her side.

Before stepping away, he lingered, standing over her for a moment. The soft glow of the bedside lamp painted her features in a tender light, highlighting the curve of her cheek, the delicate arch of her lips, the peaceful expression that made his chest ache with a mixture of longing and protectiveness.

Leaning down, he brushed a gentle kiss across her temple, feather-light, as if committing the memory of her to his soul. Emily stirred beneath his touch, a soft murmur escaping her lips, but she didn't wake. Her body shifted slightly, settling deeper into the comfort of sleep, and Marc allowed himself the briefest smile.

For a heartbeat, he just watched her, the quiet intimacy of the moment settling around him like a fragile, sacred cocoon. Then, with a final, almost reverent glance, he stepped back, hesitated, and softly closed the door behind him, leaving her in the quiet sanctuary of her dreams.

Sunlight filled the room when Emily woke. Warm. Golden. Deceptively soft. She reached out instinctively, her arm stretching across the mattress—

Empty.

Her fingers touched nothing but cool sheets.

A hollow pang shot through her. *Of course he was gone. What else had she expected?* Marc Winters didn't stay. He didn't wake up next to the woman he'd spent the night with. He didn't offer explanations.

He simply took what he wanted—

And left.

Her chest tightened, the disappointment sharp enough to make her swallow hard. She didn't blame him—not really. She'd made her choice as much as he had. Still, the ache lingered.

Rising from bed, she froze at the sight of the faint stain of blood on the sheets. Heat rushed to her cheeks. Oh God. She snatched the sheets off quickly, tossing them in a bundle before heading for the shower.

By the time she emerged, dressed in a loose sundress and with damp hair brushing her shoulders, she'd convinced herself to breathe. To move on with her morning. To eat something.

She padded into the kitchen, opening cupboards, trying to distract herself from the heaviness twisting inside her—

Until a loud, hard knock jolted through the apartment.

Her heart leapt into her throat.

Marc.

Maybe he had come back.

Hope surged so fast it stole her breath. She hurried to the door and pulled it open—

Her world slammed to a stop.

Jeremy stood there, rigid and pale, his expression carved with something cold and unnervingly intense.

"Jeremy?" Emily managed, her voice unsteady. "What are you doing here? Is my father okay?"

His eyes locked onto hers with disturbing clarity. "We need to talk," he said, too calm. Too steady.

A warning curled through her stomach. "Jeremy—"

He shoved the door hard, forcing it open. The sudden impact sent her stumbling backward. Before she could recover, he stepped inside and kicked the door shut, the lock sliding home with an ominous click.

A chill rippled through her.

"Jeremy," she whispered, fear creeping up her spine, "what are you doing?"

He lunged, grabbing her shoulders in a bruising grip. His face twisted, desperation and fury tearing through his features. "You shouldn't have led me on, Emily," he spat. "You should love me. Not them. Not Fraser or Winters."

Emily's pulse hammered. "Jeremy, stop. Let go of me!"

"You don't understand," he hissed, shaking her. "They don't love you like I do. They never did. You were always meant for me. You belong to me."

Panic flared. She twisted, clawing at his hands, trying to break free. "Jeremy, I'm not with anyone! I'm not with them!"

"You're lying!" he roared.

He shoved her backward. She fell onto the couch; her breath knocked from her lungs. Jeremy loomed over her, hands pinning her down.

Emily fought—kicking, pushing, screaming—her heart slamming against her ribs. "Get off me! Jeremy, stop!"

He leaned closer, face contorted with furious obsession. "Winters and Fraser poisoned you against me. They took you away."

"No!" Emily cried, her voice ragged. "You're scaring me! Stop!"

Her strength was slipping, her body trembling beneath his weight. Summoning the last of her power, she let out a piercing scream—

Jeremy's arm snapped forward, striking her across the face.

White-hot pain bloomed, a burst of light behind her eyes. She cried out, the sound sharp with panic and agony.

"Stop!" she sobbed, her vision blurring. "Please—stop!"

But his rage only grew. Fury twisted his features into something unrecognisable.

Her sundress bunched under his grip, fabric tearing with a harsh rip as he yanked at it. She shrieked, terror surging through her like fire.

"You're mine," he snarled. "You always were. I'm done waiting."

Her body shook. She thrashed, desperate, voice cracked and pleading—

"Help! Someone—!"

Footsteps thundered in the hallway. Heavy. Fast. Closing in.

Before the sound had fully registered, the door exploded open with a violent crash— splintering wood, metal screaming, force shaking the walls—

And someone charged into the room.

# Chapter Twenty-Three

Marc walked down the hallway, a small bag of pastries in hand, steam still curling from the warm paper. He felt lighter than he had in years, his thoughts drifting back to the peaceful rise and fall of Emily's breathing, the softness in her smile as she slept. For the first time in a long time, he felt… hopeful.

But beneath that rare sense of peace, something unsettled churned in his chest—an inexplicable tug of unease he couldn't quite name.

As he neared her apartment, a sound sliced through the quiet corridor.

A scream.

Not just any scream—Emily's scream.

Marc froze mid-step, the world narrowing to a single point. For a fraction of a second his lungs refused to work, and then—

Adrenaline detonated inside him.

He sprinted, the bag of pastries dropping forgotten to the floor as he tore through the hallway. He reached her door and twisted the handle.

Locked.

No time.

Marc slammed his shoulder into the door, the impact jarring bone. The frame splintered but held. With a growl torn from somewhere primal, he hit it again—harder. Wood cracked, hinges shrieked, and on the third blow the door burst inward, crashing against the wall.

And then his blood turned to ice.

Emily was pinned to the couch, her body twisted beneath Jeremy's weight. Her sundress was torn open, the delicate lace of her bra exposed, her face streaked with tears—terror etched into every line of her expression. Jeremy's hands clawed at her; his mouth twisted with rage and obsession.

Marc didn't think.

He didn't breathe.

He launched.

He ripped Jeremy off her with a ferocity he didn't know he was capable of, throwing him across the room. Jeremy hit the floor hard, scrambling upright in a daze—but Marc was already on him.

His fist connected with Jeremy's jaw—one brutal crack.

Another punch, this one heavier, fuelled by righteous fury and the image of Emily's terrified eyes burned into his mind.

Jeremy swung back, landing a wild hit to Marc's ribs, but Marc barely registered the impact. He drove forward like a storm, grabbing Jeremy by the collar and slamming him against the wall before bringing his fist down again and again.

The room filled with the violent symphony of fists hitting flesh, Jeremy's choked cries, the brutal thud of bodies colliding. The coffee table shattered as Marc hurled him onto it, glass exploding beneath Jeremy's weight.

Jeremy lay groaning, barely conscious.

Marc didn't spare him another glance.

His entire world narrowed to Emily.

She was curled into herself on the couch, trembling violently, her breath coming in sharp, broken gasps. Tears streamed down her cheeks, her hands clutching the torn edges of her dress as if trying to hide from the world.

"Emily," Marc breathed, crossing the room in two strides.

He knelt beside her and pulled her into his arms, holding her against him as though he could shield her from everything—past, present, future. She collapsed against his chest, gripping his shirt with shaking fingers.

"I was so scared," she whispered, voice fractured. "He just—he just forced his way in."

Marc cradled the back of her head, pressing a fierce kiss into her hair. His voice trembled with rage he could barely contain. "I'm here. You're safe now. I promise you, Em… he'll never touch you again. I shouldn't have left you. I only went to get us some breakfast."

Emily pulled back slightly, looking up at him with watery eyes. "I thought…" She hesitated, her voice faltering.

Marc searched her face, realisation dawning, his heart twisted painfully. His expression softened. "You thought I left for good, didn't you?"

She nodded silently, her throat tight.

Marc's voice dropped to a quiet, earnest murmur. "I would never disappear on you. Not after last night. Not ever."

Her lips parted on a shaky breath as she nodded, the fear in her gaze slowly giving way to something fragile… but hopeful.

Marc wrapped an arm around her again, pulling her against him as he glanced at Jeremy's limp form on the floor.

"Once the police deal with him," he murmured into her hair, "you and I are going to talk. Really talk."

Emily nodded again, her fingers curling weakly into his shirt, clinging to him with the last of her strength.

This time, she didn't have to say the words.

He was already holding her close.

Marc pulled out his phone with a hand that still trembled from adrenaline and dialled the police. His voice was clipped, urgent, controlled only by force of will as he relayed the situation. When he hung up, he sank onto the couch beside Emily and pulled her gently into his arms.

She didn't resist. Her head rested against his chest, her shaky breaths warming the fabric of his shirt. Every time she inhaled unevenly, a pulse of anger shot through him—not at her, but at the man who had dared to lay a hand on her.

He held her tighter, steadying his own breathing so she could mirror it, grounding her in the rhythm of his heartbeat.

Sirens echoed faintly from the street below, growing closer, louder. Emily flinched at the sound, and Marc stroked a soothing hand down her back. "They're coming," he murmured. "You're safe, Em. I've got you."

Moments later, a rapid succession of footsteps approached the apartment. Uniformed officers flooded inside, doing quick sweeps, assessing the scene with practiced efficiency. Marc stayed right beside Emily as chaos erupted around them.

Jeremy still lay sprawled across the shattered coffee table, unconscious, his swollen face an ugly mix of blood and bruises. Two officers knelt beside him, checking for signs of awareness and securing him while paramedics wheeled in a stretcher. Even as they lifted him, an officer snapped cuffs around one wrist—protocol for violent offenders.

Emily clutched Marc's hand at the sight, her nails digging into his skin.

A female officer approached gently, her tone soft. "Emily, we'll need your statement."

Marc didn't leave her side. He stayed standing behind her as she sat on a chair, his hand resting protectively on her shoulder while she recounted the events—sometimes stumbling, sometimes pausing, sometimes swallowing back tears.

The longer she spoke, the tighter Marc's jaw became, yet he forced himself to stay silent. This moment belonged to her.

When Jeremy was finally taken out on the stretcher, a seasoned detective stepped forward—a calm, steady presence amid the wreckage.

"We've got Jeremy Saunders in custody," he said. "He'll be transported to the hospital for evaluation, then booked on multiple charges, including assault and attempted sexual assault."

Emily's breath hitched at the words, terror flickering across her face. Marc's hold on her shoulder tightened protectively.

The detective continued, his voice gentle. "We'll need detailed statements from both of you. Once processed, he'll be held in custody. A restraining order will be put in place to ensure he can't approach you again. Right now, your focus should be on your safety and well-being."

A tear slid down Emily's cheek, and Marc pulled her into his arms.

"You're safe now," he murmured quietly, his lips brushing the top of her head. "I'm right here. I'm not going anywhere, Emily. Not now, not ever."

For the first time since the attack began, she let herself believe him.

Once the last officers finished their assessment and explained the next steps, the apartment fell into a stunned quiet. The space, once her sanctuary, now felt fractured—broken glass, overturned cushions, a torn dress, and a violation of trust that lingered like a cold shadow.

Emily dressed slowly in her room, her hands trembling. Marc waited outside the door, patient, silent, but alert—ready to shield her from anything.

When she emerged, pale and shaken, he gently guided her to the car. She moved like someone walking through smoke, disoriented and fragile. Marc opened the passenger door for her, his touch soft, careful.

The drive to the police station was silent. Emily stared out the window, her fingers twisting nervously in her lap. Marc's hands gripped the steering wheel with white-knuckled tension, fury simmering beneath his calm exterior.

At the station, they were escorted into a quiet interview room. Officers offered water, tissues, reassurance—Emily barely noticed. She gave her statement, voice trembling, eyes bright with unshed tears. Marc gave his own next, precise, and controlled, though anyone watching him closely could see the storm behind his eyes.

Then came the part he hated most—watching as female officers gently photographed Emily's injuries.

Bruises along her arms.

Dark marks on her legs.

The swollen welt blooming across her cheek.

The small, sharp cut where Jeremy's ring had grazed her skin.

Marc's fists clenched so tightly he felt his nails break skin. But he forced himself to stay calm, to stay present, to stay what she needed.

When it was finally over, Emily sagged into her chair, drained.

She turned to him, her voice barely a whisper. "I… I can't go back there. The door's broken, and even if it weren't… I wouldn't feel safe."

Marc didn't hesitate. "Wherever you want to go, I'll take you."

She lowered her gaze, gathering her courage. "My father's estate. He needs to know. And… I'd feel safer there."

Marc nodded immediately. "Then that's where we'll go."

He rose and offered her his hand. She took it, her fingers cold and trembling. He enfolded them gently in his own warmth.

And as they walked out of the station together, Marc's grip tightened, anchoring her—silent, steady, and unmistakably hers.


The drive to John's estate was quiet, the hum of the engine the only sound between them. The tension in the car was thick but oddly comforting, a silent solidarity that both anchored and reminded them of the chaos they had just survived. Emily leaned her head against the window, the city lights blurring past as her thoughts spiralled—fear, relief, and uncertainty all jostling for dominance. She shivered slightly, the memory of Jeremy's aggression still vivid in her mind.

Marc stole glances at her, noting the slight tremor in her fingers, the way her jaw was set as if bracing against some invisible weight. He wanted to speak, to say something—anything—to soothe her, but words felt insufficient. All he could do was stay near, and he prayed that was enough.

The towering gates of the estate appeared in the distance, their black iron bars a symbol of safety and sanctuary. Emily exhaled, a small sigh of relief escaping her lips for the first time in hours. Marc reached over, his fingers brushing hers in a grounding squeeze.

"We'll get through this," he murmured, voice low but resolute, carrying a weight of promise.

Emily nodded silently, her gaze fixed on the estate ahead. She didn't know exactly what 'getting through this' would entail, but for the first time since the attack, she felt a flicker of hope. Marc's presence beside her was a tether to that hope, and for now, that was enough.

As they pulled into the driveway, her eyes immediately caught James's car parked near the front entrance. Her chest tightened—a reminder that the world outside her fragile bubble of safety had not paused. James was often here for meetings with her father, but in this moment, the familiar sight brought a jolt of tension she wasn't prepared for.

They entered the grand home, the familiar scent of polished wood and fresh flowers greeting them. The house had always been a haven, but now it felt oddly foreign, a quiet witness to the trauma she carried with her. Even the silence seemed charged, heavy with anticipation, as if the walls themselves had absorbed the echoes of the morning's events.

Emily approached the study, her hand trembling slightly as she knocked softly. The sound of her knuckles against the door felt deafening in the hush. "Come in," John's voice called, calm but tinged with curiosity.

As she stepped inside, both James and her father's eyes immediately found her. James's attention snapped from the papers before him to her trembling form, concern overtaking every other thought. Behind him, John's gaze mirrored the same mixture of worry and confusion. Both men's eyes locked onto her as if trying to shield her from the weight of the world.

"What the bloody hell happened to you?" Their voices merged in unison, thick with disbelief and fear.

Before she could answer, James closed the distance and enveloped her in a protective embrace. "Who hurt you?" His voice broke slightly as he stroked her back, hands trembling, betraying the depth of his worry.

John stepped closer, his own hand resting firmly on her shoulder. The solidity of his touch was a tangible reminder of unwavering protection. Marc stayed slightly behind, a silent sentinel, his expression dark but calm—a quiet testament to the support he offered, fierce and unyielding.

Emily finally let go of her restraint. The emotions she had bottled up since the attack surged forward, a torrent of tears and trembling that wracked her body. She recounted the ordeal—Jeremy's intrusion, the violence, the fear—her voice quivering, the words spilling out like a dam breaking. Relief mingled with lingering terror, and the full weight of the trauma she had endured threatened to overwhelm her.

Her father's jaw tightened as fury overtook him, his arms pulling her close as if his embrace alone could shield her from harm. "Thank God you're safe," he muttered, brushing a hand through her hair, his voice a mixture of comfort and barely restrained rage.

Emily, still shaking, glanced at Marc. "Can we… can we stay here? Just for a while?" Her voice was a whisper, fragile but earnest. "I don't want to be alone."

John didn't hesitate. "Of course, you can stay. You're safe here, Emily. No question." His certainty was absolute; a promise she clung to like a lifeline.

But then Emily's gaze flicked to James, who had shifted slightly, his attention moving to Marc. There was a low, simmering intensity in his eyes, a silent warning coiled beneath the surface. "You and I need to talk," he muttered, voice dropping into a growl, every syllable threaded with controlled anger.

Marc didn't flinch. He met James's gaze evenly, understanding the silent challenge but refusing to back down. He gave a subtle nod, acknowledgment without surrender.

Sensing the tension escalating, John spoke quickly, his voice firm but gentle. "Emily, why don't you take a bath? It'll help with the bruises and calm your nerves." He placed a reassuring hand on her back, guiding her toward the stairs. "I'll make sure the staff prepares your room. Get some rest, sweetheart. You need it."

# Chapter Twenty-Four

As Emily and her father exited the room, the door clicked softly shut behind them, leaving Marc and James alone. The air between them crackled with unspoken fury, and James wasted no time letting it spill over.

"What the hell do you think you're playing at?" James thundered, his voice bouncing off the walls like a physical blow. His eyes burned with a mixture of fear and rage, every muscle in his body coiled for confrontation.

Marc opened his mouth, intending to respond, but James was already advancing, his stride purposeful, his fists clenched at his sides.

"You can't treat Emily like your other women," James spat, venom dripping from every word. "She's not some passing fling. She's decent. She's good. Damn it, Marc! She's innocent! You can't just—"

Marc cut him off, his own voice low, cold, and unwavering. "I know that. And it's none of your damn business. I'm with her now. Deal with it."

James let out a harsh, bitter laugh, the sound hollow with frustration. "Deal with it?" he echoed, taking another step closer, eyes flashing. "You really think it's that simple? How long until you get bored, Marc? How long before you toss her aside like every other woman who's fallen for your charm? Because you will. And when you do, she'll be destroyed. She's not like the others—you'll break her."

Marc's jaw tightened, fists curling at his sides, but his gaze didn't waver. The words stabbed at him, threatening to unravel the control he'd maintained, yet he refused to flinch. His voice was steel, low, and unwavering.

"I won't toss her aside," he said firmly.

James scoffed, a sharp, incredulous sound. "Bullshit. You don't do relationships. You don't believe in them. You've said it yourself. So, tell me—how long before you prove me right?"

Marc's chest tightened. He opened his mouth, ready to fight back with words, with that familiar armour of charm and arrogance—but what came out instead was quieter, raw, and unvarnished, even shocking to himself.

"I love her."

Silence slammed into the room like a physical force.

James froze mid-step, his fury momentarily eclipsed by disbelief. His mouth opened slightly, then closed, as if testing the reality of the words. His brow furrowed, eyes searching Marc's face for a hint of jest—but found only absolute truth.

Marc stood rigid, feeling the gravity of the admission settle over him. He hadn't planned to say it—not aloud, not now—but there it was, unavoidable and liberating. His voice, when he spoke again, carried the weight of certainty.

"I love her, James. I'm not going anywhere."

James's expression faltered, a flicker of doubt and conflict passing across his features. The anger remained, simmering beneath the surface, but it was tempered now by something else—something that mirrored his own love and fear for Emily.

Marc exhaled slowly, letting the truth solidify in the space between them. "I love her," he repeated, softer this time, quieter but no less fierce. "And I'm here. For good. If she'll have me."

Before James could respond, the door opened. John stepped inside, his presence commanding yet calm, a stabilising force amidst the storm. His eyes flicked between the two men, assessing the lingering tension with a measured gaze.

"Marc, Emily's asking for you," John said, his voice steady but threaded with authority. "She's in the second room on the left at the top of the stairs."

Marc's shoulders relaxed slightly, relief washing over him. He needed to see her, to speak the words he'd finally admitted, to reassure her and stake his claim on the love he no longer denied.

"Thank you, John," Marc said, his tone sincere. "I'll go to her now. We need to talk."

As he moved toward the door, the weight of the confrontation lingered in the room, a silent challenge left between him and James. Marc didn't flinch; he had no doubts. His heart was set.

He paused at the base of the stairs, drawing a deep, steadying breath. Thoughts of Emily flooded his mind—her laughter, her tears, the fierce warmth in her eyes. I love her. The words pulsed like a drumbeat in his chest, liberating, consuming, undeniable. Nothing—no past, no fear, no obstacle—would stand in the way of the life he wanted with her.

With that resolve anchoring him, Marc began his ascent, each step a promise: to protect her, to cherish her, to never let her go.

He moved swiftly up the stairs, his urgency clear, heart hammering in his chest. Emily needed to know—needed to feel—how deeply he cared, how utterly present he was for her. The thought of her alone, vulnerable, even for a moment, made his pulse spike.

At the door of her room, he paused, taking a steadying breath. The soft sound of running water drifted through the slightly ajar bathroom door, a soothing rhythm that calmed him just long enough to steady his nerves. "Emily?" he called softly.

"I'm in here," she replied, her voice warm and inviting, laced with that trust that always disarmed him.

Marc eased the door open and froze for a heartbeat, his breath catching at the sight before him. Emily was reclined in a bubble-filled bath, her figure partially submerged, the water curling around her in soft, frothy swirls. She looked serene, but there was a vulnerability in the curve of her shoulders, the gentle tilt of her head, that made his chest tighten.

Her gaze met his, and she offered a gentle smile, a simple, wordless invitation. "Join me?"

Marc's lips curved in a soft, affectionate smile. "Are you sure?"

"Yes. Please." Her hand reached toward him, open, trusting, and he felt a warmth bloom through his chest.

Without hesitation, Marc shed his clothes, stepping into the warm bath behind her. He settled close, wrapping his arms around her as she leaned back against his chest. A soft sigh escaped her lips, and he felt the tension drain from her body, mingling with the relief that echoed through him.

"Mmm… that's better," she murmured, her head tilting back slightly, exposing the graceful curve of her neck. Marc brushed a strand of damp hair away and pressed a careful, reverent kiss to the soft skin, savouring the intimacy of the moment.

"Emily," he murmured, his voice thick with emotion.

"Mmm?" she replied, her eyes half-closed, hazy with contentment.

"I love you," he whispered, the words raw and unguarded, as though speaking them aloud might make them tangible, inseparable from the beating of his heart.

For a heartbeat, she stiffened in his arms. Panic flared in him—*had he misjudged the timing? Had he pushed too far?* But then her gaze lifted, searching, and his fears melted away. There was no doubt, no hesitation in her eyes.

She slowly turned to face him, her hands brushing along his arms, grounding him as she whispered, trembling but certain, "I love you too."

Relief and joy surged through him, mingling with a fierce protectiveness and a quiet awe. He lowered his lips to hers in a kiss that was tender, reverent, and lingering, as though he could convey every ounce of his devotion through that single, careful contact.

Pulling back slightly, he rested his forehead against hers, voice soft but unwavering. "I don't want to hurt you. Ever."

Emily tilted her face into his hands, letting him cradle her, letting herself absorb the safety and the love radiating from him. "I know," she whispered. "And I trust you."

Marc's heart swelled. In that moment, surrounded by the warmth of the bath, the rising steam, and the quiet intimacy of their embrace, the world outside ceased to exist. There was only Emily, and the love he had longed for, returned, fierce and undeniable.

She gazed up at him, vulnerable yet certain, her trust unmistakable in the way she moved—shifting to straddle his hips, water rippling softly around them. His arousal pressed firmly against her, and a quiet gasp slipped from her lips.

"I know you never would," she murmured, her voice thick with certainty.

Her mouth found his again, this time urgent and hungry. Her hands roamed across his chest, tracing the hard lines of muscle, feeling the power beneath his skin. Marc cupped her breasts, his thumbs brushing over her taut, aching nipples. He stroked the tender blush-pink peaks with slow, deliberate fingertips. Her lips parted on a silent gasp as pleasure raced through her.

Then he drew her down to him, capturing one aching nipple in his warm, wet mouth.

She moaned aloud as a spark of heat shot through her, tension coiling low and tight in her belly. He moved to her other breast, cupping its weight in his large hand, squeezing gently as he suckled her deeply. Her moan deepened as he stroked his hands over her body.

He lifted his head to claim her lips again, kissing her with raw hunger as his hands slid down her bare shoulders, tangling in the wet silk of her hair.

"Marc… please," she breathed against his mouth, her plea searing through him.

She wrapped her fingers around his long, thick arousal. Taking a steadying breath, she aligned their bodies, watching his face closely as she lowered herself onto him—slowly, deliberately—drawing him deep inside her.

His head fell back with a choked gasp.

She began to ride him—slow at first, finding her rhythm—then faster as need overtook her, water sloshing around them. Her lips parted, her expression fervent, almost glowing with pleasure.

"Marc," she gasped.

His mouth found her neck, placing open-mouthed kisses along her damp skin. "I love hearing you say my name," he murmured, voice thick with desire. "I used to fantasise about you saying it like this."

She rode him harder, faster, gripping his shoulders as the intensity built. Marc looked up at her beautiful face, her eyes squeezed shut in a pleasure so fierce it made his breath catch.

He caught one taut nipple in his mouth, tongue flicking, sucking, drawing another helpless moan from her. He moved to the other, his hands tightening on her hips, guiding her movements as the pleasure coiled tighter between them.

"Marc… please," she whimpered, breathless, desperate.

Marc's hand slipped between them, his fingers finding the sensitive bundle of nerves that sent shockwaves through her.

Emily shattered with a cry, her body trembling around him. The sight of her—head thrown back, mouth parted in pure ecstasy—undid him.

A guttural groan tore from his chest as he followed her over the edge, his release crashing through him. "Emily," he gasped, voice raw with emotion.

For a long moment they remained entwined, wrapped around each other as their breaths slowly steadied. His hands traced lazy circles along her back, her cheek warm against his shoulder.

"I don't think I'll ever get enough of you," Marc murmured, his voice rough and unguarded. "You drive me crazy."

Emily smiled against his skin, pressing a soft kiss to his neck. "Good," she whispered, her breath warm and teasing.

Marc chuckled, arms tightening around her. "We should get out," he said, though he made no effort to move.

Emily sighed, melting against him. "Mmm. Soon," she replied lazily, savouring the quiet, sated comfort of his embrace.

A little while later, Marc stepped out of the bath and dried himself off before carefully lifting Emily from the water. Her skin—soft, warm, glistening with droplets—seemed to glow under his hands as he stood her up and gently dried her, his touch delicate yet assured as it moved over every curve.

Emily whispered, amusement threading through her voice, "I could get used to this."

Marc's answer was a low, sensual murmur against her ear, his lips brushing the delicate shell. "I hope so. Because I intend to take care of you forever."

He lifted her easily into his arms and carried her toward the bedroom. Her slight weight pressed against him, her breath warm against his neck—a comfort he knew he would never take for granted. He laid her down on the bed, the cool sheets a striking contrast to the heat of her skin. Sliding in beside her, he gathered her close, her head tucked beneath his chin as she melted into him. The softness of her body, the steady rise and fall of her breath, settled something deep inside him—something he hadn't even realised was restless.

After a quiet moment, Marc spoke, his voice low and resonant with meaning. "That night on the island when you were nearly killed... I wanted you so badly." He paused, fingers idly tracing the curve of her shoulder. "But I couldn't make love to you. Not after you told me that kissing me made you feel ashamed. I couldn't risk you waking up the next day feeling guilty about being with me."

Emily's chest tightened. Memories she'd long tried to bury stirred—fear, confusion, anger, all tangled together. "I'm sorry," she whispered, the remorse thickening her voice.

Marc shook his head gently, brushing a stray lock of hair from her cheek. "No, sweetheart. You don't owe me an apology." His gaze softened. "I didn't want to be another man who touched your body and left you emptier. I wanted you—your heart, your soul. All of you."

Emily lifted her face, her eyes luminous as they met his. "You have it," she said, her voice barely above a breath, but steady with certainty.

Marc's heart tightened with a slow, almost aching warmth. He tilted her chin and brushed his lips against hers—soft at first, then deepening into something tender, consuming, full of promise. Soon, they were lost in each other again, bodies entwined beneath the sheets, the world beyond the room forgotten.

They stayed tangled in one another far longer than they intended, the afternoon drifting into evening as they lingered in the intimacy of every whispered word, every touch, every shared breath. Eventually, they dressed—slowly, with gentle smiles and lingering caresses—before making their way downstairs to the dining room.

The sight of her father, James, and Mary sitting at the table brought a quiet sense of grounding, a reminder that even after chaos, life found its way back to normalcy. Emily and Marc shared a soft smile, their bond deepened, strengthened, unshakeable.

Mary, who had arrived a little earlier, broke the silence, her voice soft with concern. "I can't believe what you went through, Emily, James just told me. I'm so glad Marc was there for you." She looked at Marc with a mixture of gratitude and surprise. She had never imagined Marc, with his complicated past, would fall in love, but seeing him now with Emily made it clear he had changed. "I'm glad Marc has finally fell in love, and with someone as wonderful as you."

"Thank you, Mary," Emily said, her voice warm as she reached for Marc's hand. "I know I'm lucky."

Marc lifted her hand to his lips, kissing it gently, his voice full of emotion. "You don't know how lucky I feel."

James, who had been watching the scene unfold with a mixture of amusement and disbelief, broke in with a smirk. "You know, Marc," he said, his tone teasing but affectionate, "when I told you about Emily and said you'd love her, I didn't mean it quite like this."

The group erupted in laughter, the tension of the past weeks dissipating in the warmth of their shared moment. Marc, remembering how this woman he'd met on New Year's Eve had been James' fiancée, spoke up. "Maybe not, but I'm glad I found her. I've got you to thank for that. I lost her on New Year's Eve, but you helped me find her again."

James looked taken aback for a moment, then smiled with a chuckle. "New Year's Eve? But it was March when you two first met."

Marc and Emily exchanged a look, then burst into laughter. Between shared smiles and intertwined hands, they explained everything—the New Year's Eve encounter, the kiss that neither of them forgot, the spark that started it all.

James, still processing the revelation, grinned. "So, I never had a chance," he said, reaching for Mary's hand. "But it all worked out in the end."

Everyone laughed again, the room filled with a sense of relief and joy. They had all been through so much, but now, in this moment, they were safe, together, and ready to face whatever came next.

# Epilogue

After the terrifying incident, Emily made the life-changing decision to leave her apartment. The space that had once felt like a safe haven now held too many haunting memories, and the thought of being alone there became unbearable. Instead, she and Marc moved into her father's sprawling estate, which quickly became their sanctuary. The estate, with its vast grounds, numerous wings, and absolute privacy, offered them both the perfect balance of solitude and luxury. Though they relished the peace of their new home, they still occasionally used the apartment for quiet nights alone, taking comfort in the familiarity it offered.

Meanwhile, James and Mary's relationship had flourished in the months since. Their love was undeniable, and the couple had recently gotten engaged, to the delight of everyone around them. Marc and Emily were thrilled for them, often spending time together as they celebrated the couple's joy and supported them through the exciting wedding plans. James and Mary were building a life full of happiness and shared moments, and Emily and Marc couldn't have been more pleased for them.

John, Emily's father, was overjoyed to have his daughter and her partner living under his roof. His pride and happiness were visible in everything he did, but his playful hints about wanting grandchildren had become a running joke. Marc and Emily laughed off his remarks, teasing him about his eagerness for the next generation. Although Emily wasn't opposed to the idea, they both agreed that such decisions would come when the time was right. For now, they were focused on their love and the life they were building together.

As for Jeremy, justice had finally been served. He was convicted on all charges, sentenced to years in prison. However, just months after his incarceration, he met a tragic end when he was killed by another inmate in a violent altercation. Despite the horrors he had caused in her life, Emily felt a strange sense of closure. Marc, though concerned for her well-being, respected her decision to attend his funeral. He feared that Emily's compassionate heart might lead her to seek forgiveness, but he admired her empathy. It was one of the reasons he had fallen in love with her—her capacity to care even in the most difficult of circumstances.

With New Year's Eve on the horizon, Emily's father had invited her to attend a prestigious party in Sydney, the same event she had gone to the previous year for one of his key clients. Though she had initially agreed, her excitement was tempered by Marc's inability to accompany her due to a critical business meeting. Despite the disappointment, Emily found solace in knowing that she had Marc's unwavering support, even if he couldn't be by her side physically. She would return to him, to the warmth and love of their shared life, no matter what the night had in store.

As Emily stepped out of the penthouse suite, she paused for a moment in front of the elevator mirror, admiring her reflection. She had chosen to wear the same elegant blue dress from last year, the one that had felt perfect on that unforgettable night she had met Marc. The shimmering fabric clung to her figure, the daring slit revealing just enough of her leg with every step she took. The royal blue made her feel radiant, and the memory of that first encounter filled her with warmth. She smiled, touched by the memory, but also eager for what the evening would bring.

The party was in full swing when Emily arrived at the grand ballroom. The soft hum of conversation, the clinking of glasses, and the sparkle of the chandeliers cast a magical atmosphere over the crowd. Emily moved through the room with ease, her beauty and poise drawing admiring glances, but despite the festive surroundings, her heart was heavy. Without Marc by her side, everything felt a little less bright, a little less complete.

Her beauty did not go unnoticed. Her hair cascaded in soft waves around her shoulders, and the sapphire necklace she wore sparkled brilliantly, catching the light as she moved. Though she exuded confidence and elegance, a small part of her felt empty, her thoughts constantly drifting back to Marc and the warmth he brought to every moment they shared.

As she made her way to the bar, hoping to steady herself with a drink before mingling, she was surprised to find the area crowded. But then, out of the corner of her eye, she spotted someone who immediately captured her attention. Leaning casually against the counter, his back to her, was Marc. His broad shoulders filled out his sharp suit effortlessly, and the moment their eyes met, her heart fluttered.

Marc turned toward her, a warm, unmistakable smile spreading across his face. He had a way of looking at her as if she were the only person in the room. His gaze held nothing but affection, and that smile—it was as charming and confident as ever.

"I was hoping you'd wear that dress," he said, his voice rich with warmth as he spoke her name. Emily felt a rush of joy, disbelief mixing with excitement as she hurried toward him.

"I thought you couldn't make it?" she asked, her voice a mixture of surprise and happiness.

Marc chuckled softly, his eyes never leaving hers. "I wouldn't have missed this for the world," he replied. "New Year's Eve is our special night."

The words hung between them, thick with meaning. They stood there for a moment, the world around them fading as they shared a private moment amidst the crowd. Marc reached out, his fingers brushing lightly against hers, and Emily felt an electric spark shoot through her.

The night unfolded like something from a dream. They spent the evening laughing, dancing, and stealing intimate moments away from the crowd, their connection growing with every shared glance and whispered word. As midnight approached, the energy between them shifted. The anticipation was palpable. This night, it seemed, was different—more profound.

As the final seconds of the year ticked away, Marc gently took Emily's hand, his fingers trembling slightly as he led her away from the revelry. They made their way to a quiet corner of the terrace, where the city skyline stretched out before them, lit up with the vibrant energy of the night. But in that moment, the only thing Marc saw was Emily.

He stopped and turned to face her, his heart racing. The moonlight illuminated her face, casting a soft glow that made her look even more beautiful. Marc's voice was a whisper, but the weight of his words was undeniable.

"Emily," he began, his eyes full of vulnerability, "you've been the light in my life. Every day with you is a gift. I can't imagine my future without you in it. I don't want to."

Before Emily could respond, Marc dropped to one knee, his heart pounding in his chest. He pulled out a small velvet box, the city lights around them seeming to dim as he opened it, revealing a breathtaking sapphire ring. The deep blue of the sapphire gleamed in the moonlight, surrounded by a halo of brilliant diamonds, each one shimmering like stardust.

"Will you marry me?" he whispered, his voice thick with emotion.

Tears welled up in Emily's eyes, her heart swelling with love and joy. Her hand flew to her mouth in shock as she struggled to find words. Finally, she smiled through her tears, her voice full of certainty.

"Yes," she whispered. "Yes, I will."

As the clock struck midnight, fireworks exploded in the sky, but in that moment, time seemed to stand still. Marc slid the ring onto Emily's finger, his hands trembling with emotion. He lifted her chin gently, leaning in to kiss her—a kiss that was tender and full of promises yet to be made.

When they finally pulled away, Marc's grin was wicked, his eyes sparkling with affection. "Maybe we could start working on those grandchildren your father keeps asking for?" he teased, his voice low and affectionate.

Emily laughed, her heart soaring. "Yes, please," she whispered, knowing that whatever the future held, it would be a beautiful journey, full of love, laughter, and endless possibilities.

As they stood there, wrapped in each other's arms, with the fireworks above and the city lights below, they knew their love had only just begun. And together, they would write the next chapter of their story, a life full of love, adventure, and all the dreams they had yet to fulfil.

# The End

# The Billionaire's Secret Baby

## Alison Reid

A complete standalone romance

Previously published individually

# Chapter One

The flashbulbs popped like tiny explosions, strobing the night in bursts of blinding white. Billionaire Adrian Werrington stood stiffly beneath the ornate archway of the Langford Imperial, one of Manhattan's most opulent hotels, his expression unreadable, his posture carved from control. At thirty-six years old, he was tall and broad-shouldered, with the kind of athletic build that hinted at discipline rather than vanity.

His tailored black tuxedo fit like it had been stitched to his frame, crisp and understated, just like the man inside it. Midnight-dark hair, swept neatly back, gave sharp contrast to eyes the colour of cold steel—a piercing blue that rarely betrayed what he was thinking.

He exuded intelligence, precision, and quiet power—exactly what the world expected of him. Exactly what he no longer had the energy to uphold.

His jaw was set, his hand resting lightly at the small of his wife's back. It was a gesture for the cameras, nothing more. He hated touching her now. Hated even being close to her. But he'd made his bed—trapped himself in this elegant, soulless prison—and now he had no choice but to lie in it, smiling.

Cleo leaned into him, radiant in a floor-length crimson gown that shimmered under the lights. Her perfectly coiffed blonde hair curled just so over one shoulder, her red lips curved in a smile designed to seduce cameras and silence critics. She looked like a dream.

But she felt like ice.

"Smile, darling," she purred under her breath, never breaking her pose.

Adrian complied, his expression polished and controlled — the look he'd mastered over years of boardrooms and press conferences. To the watching world, he was every inch the powerful billionaire husband. Devoted. Unshakable. Lucky.

Inside, he was suffocating.

He'd built empires with ruthless precision. Outmanoeuvred rivals, read markets like maps. People called him one of the sharpest minds in finance. And yet, he hadn't seen her coming.

Cleo had fooled him—completely. Not just with her beauty or those carefully timed tears, but with the one thing he'd always wanted: the promise of a family. A real family.

Even now, he sometimes woke up in the quiet hours of the morning, staring at the ceiling, wondering how he'd let it happen. He'd always prided himself on being sharp, unshakable. He'd built an empire by seeing through people, through pretences. But with Cleo, he'd been blind.

She told him she was pregnant. He proposed. Married her within weeks. Then, just after the wedding, she said she lost the baby.

He was devastated. Gutted. He'd already imagined holding his child, teaching them how to ride a bike, building a life around something more than boardrooms and bank balances. But Cleo? She moved on like it had been a passing inconvenience. When he gently suggested they try again, she shook her head with a tight smile and said, "I couldn't go through that again… not yet."

That was over a year ago.

She still refused. Always with an excuse, a deflection, a sudden migraine, or a charity event that required her attention. Now, he saw the truth. She never intended to give him a child. Never intended to build anything real with him.

Now he was trapped beside a woman who looked like perfection but had no soul to speak of.

And he only had himself to blame.

They moved forward, Cleo waving delicately to photographers, her laughter light and false as they entered the ballroom. The annual Bennett Foundation Gala glittered with chandeliers and opulence. Champagne flowed, conversations buzzed, and the city's elite swirled in designer labels and practiced charm.

Adrian drifted through it all like a man underwater.

"Adrian, my boy!" A hearty slap to his shoulder yanked him from his thoughts. Gregory Langford, an old family acquaintance, beamed up at him. "And Cleo, you stunner. You two are just—" he gestured vaguely, "—perfection. The golden couple."

Cleo leaned in with a sultry laugh and touched Gregory's arm. "You're too kind."

Adrian offered a tight smile, murmured something polite, and moved away as soon as he could. The ballroom felt airless, every conversation rehearsed, every glance loaded with expectation. He hated these events. He hated this world.

But most of all, he hated pretending.

He found his escape in a quiet corner by the terrace doors, his gaze drifting past the glass. Outside, beneath the soft glow of fairy lights, a couple stood with their toddler. The little boy, barely walking, toddled clumsily between his parents' legs, giggling as he clutched a balloon.

Adrian's chest tightened.

The child's laughter rang out, pure and unrestrained, and for a brief moment, the weight of the gala disappeared. He imagined what it would feel like — to hold a child of his own, to read them a bedtime story, to tuck him in at night. To be a father. It was all he ever wanted.

He clenched his fist around his champagne glass, the delicate stem straining beneath the pressure.

Cleo was still withholding what he wanted most. A child. A future. Something real. He was sick of waiting, sick of the deflections and the carefully delivered excuses.

They hadn't touched each other in over a month—longer if he was honest with himself. Their marriage was a cold performance, polished for the world, empty behind the scenes.

He didn't love her. He didn't even like her.

What he wanted was simple: a family. A woman to love. A life that wasn't just luxury and headlines but warmth, laughter, something true.

And Cleo… Cleo was not that woman.

"You're sulking," her voice sliced through his thoughts, silk laced with steel. She appeared beside him in a whisper of perfume and satin, not even glancing toward the terrace or the small family beyond the glass. "You're ruining the illusion. At least pretend to enjoy yourself."

He looked at her, studied the flawless features the world adored. So beautiful. So hollow.

"I'm sick of the illusion and tired of pretending," he said flatly.

Her smile didn't waver, but her eyes narrowed, sharp as glass. "You think you're the only one with regrets? Trust me, darling. This isn't exactly my dream, either. I thought you loved me when you proposed."

"And I thought I'd be a father." His voice was low, bitter. "But you refuse to even try."

Her smile cracked, the steel behind it hardening. "This isn't the time or place," she hissed through her teeth. "So put on your smile and act like you love me. For the cameras. For the board. For everyone who's betting on this marriage."

She slipped her arm through his, her grip firm, controlling — a private warning in a public moment. Together, they turned toward the dance floor, a vision of effortless elegance, the picture of bliss.

And Adrian Werrington — billionaire, husband, prisoner — forced another smile and walked back into the lie.

The ride home was silent.

Their driver weaved through the Manhattan streets while Cleo scrolled aimlessly on her phone, her expression smooth and unreadable. Adrian stared out the tinted window, his reflection superimposed over the city lights—sharp suit, polished appearance, vacant eyes.

When they stepped into the penthouse, the silence followed them, thick and suffocating. Cleo kicked off her heels and let her silk shawl slide from her shoulders onto the marble floor. She turned to him with an easy, practiced smile.

"I thought tonight went rather well," she said, gliding toward the bar to pour herself a drink. "People were watching us all evening. You looked divine."

Adrian didn't respond. He walked to the far end of the living room, unbuttoning his cuffs, stripping off the layers of performance like armour he no longer wanted to wear.

"I think we should separate," he said quietly.

The crystal clinked against the decanter as Cleo's hand faltered. She turned slowly, her expression blank with surprise. "I'm sorry, what?"

"I said we should separate." His voice was calm now—measured, detached. "This isn't working, Cleo. It never really did. We got married because you were pregnant... and then you weren't."

A silence bloomed between them, wide and heavy.

Then—tears. Immediate. Perfect. Her lower lip trembled, eyes glistening as though on cue. "Adrian... you don't mean that. You've just been under pressure lately. The board, the press—it's gotten to you."

She crossed the room, silk whispering around her legs, and reached up to touch him, her hands smooth and practiced as they slid over his chest. "Let's not do this tonight. Come to bed with me. We can talk in the morning."

He stepped back, the rejection clear in every line of his body. "I'm not interested."

The softness in her gaze flickered, then vanished. Her mouth tightened, and the tears dried up just as quickly as they'd come. "You'd really throw away everything? After all we've built?"

"All we've built," he repeated, voice low. "You mean the performance. The PR. The illusion of a happy marriage. We haven't built anything real."

"You're being dramatic."

"I've been sleeping in the guest room for over a month, Cleo," he said, unmoving. "And you haven't seemed to mind."

She stared at him, caught off guard—not by the words, but by the finality in them. Her mask cracked, just slightly, revealing the cold calculation behind the tears.

Without another word, Adrian turned and walked away, his footsteps echoing down the marble hallway. The soft click of the guest room door might as well have been a slammed one.

He loosened his tie, sat on the edge of the bed, and let the silence fold around him.

Not peace—he didn't know what peace felt like anymore.

But this… this was quiet. And that was a start.

Adrian stared at the ceiling of the guest room, the morning light bleeding in through the sheer curtains like a slow confession.

He hadn't slept.

Not deeply, anyway. His body had shut down at some point out of sheer exhaustion, but his mind hadn't stopped. Not when the conversation replayed itself again and again in different tones, different variations—her voice weeping, then mocking, then nothing at all.

He sat up slowly, elbows resting on his knees. The tie he'd tossed on the floor last night lay coiled like a noose near the bedpost.

*Separation.*

He'd said the word aloud. For the first time.

And for the first time in months, something inside him had settled. Not peace, not yet—but a kind of clarity. The fog was lifting. His path was sharp, inevitable.

He showered, dressed, and fastened his cufflinks with mechanical precision—like armour. Like a man preparing for war, not another day at the office.

When he stepped into the kitchen, Cleo was already there.

White robe. Espresso in hand. Scrolling through her phone like the night before had been a casual conversation about table linens. Her face was as flawless as ever—no puffy eyes, no mascara smudges. Just pristine detachment, elegant and empty.

Once, he'd mistaken that cool control for confidence. Now, it just looked like glass. Cold. Reflective. Breakable.

He didn't speak.

Neither did she.

They were past the shouting stage. Past the negotiations, the rehearsed apologies, the hollow makeups.

This was silence now. Mutual withdrawal. The last stretch of a dying performance.

And for Adrian, that silence confirmed it.

Separation wasn't just necessary.

It was survival.


By the time Adrian stepped into his private elevator, he already had his game face on— the one the world knew. The one he'd learned to wear at ten years old when his father told him men with emotions didn't last in finance.

The ride to the top floor of Werrington Wealth was smooth, but the storm inside him brewed with a silent, bitter precision. As the doors opened, he was met with the familiar scent of wood polish and lilies, the echo of productivity humming like a hive around him.

He nodded at his assistant, barked out a clipped "Good morning," and strode into his office.

But the moment he closed the door, he exhaled.

That's when he saw it—her handwriting.

Heidi Gibson, his CFO, had left a folder neatly centred on his desk, exactly where she knew he'd find it. He recognised the way she looped her H's. Precise. Elegant. No-nonsense. Like her.

He exhaled and raked a hand through his hair before sinking into his chair. The report was exactly what he needed—numbers, projections, data points. The cold, predictable world of finance. A world he could control.

But halfway down the first page, his eyes drifted to the clipped note.


***Updated with the revised index factors. Let me know if you want to review in person. —***
***H.G.***

Professional. Efficient.

Still… something about her lingered. In his thoughts. In the air.

She'd only been here three months. And in those three months, he had started to notice things. Small, inconsequential things—at first. The way she bit her lower lip when she was deep in thought. How she pushed her sleeves up when the numbers got serious. Her expressive face, the curve of her neck when she tilted her head in challenge.

She was beautiful, but not like Cleo. Cleo's beauty was curated—airbrushed perfection, sculpted and styled. Heidi's was something else entirely. Natural. Unforced. Quietly magnetic.

And beyond the surface, she was brilliant. The most impressive CFO he'd ever worked with. Sharp. Strategic. Grounded.

He shouldn't notice. He knew that.

He was still married—even if the marriage was unravelling thread by thread.

But the truth was harder to ignore with every passing day.

He was noticing everything about her.

And that… was becoming a problem.

# Chapter Two

The executive floor of Werrington Wealth smelled like money.

Not the kind count in bills or digital portfolios, but the kind woven into polished glass, Italian leather, and the subtle perfume of fresh-cut lilies—always white, always delivered on Mondays. It was the scent of power, precision, and curated perfection.

Heidi Gibson stepped off the private elevator and adjusted the folder under her arm. Her heels clicked against the marble floor with a confident, measured rhythm. She looked every inch the part: tall and svelte in a tailored navy sheath dress that skimmed her figure like it had been made for her. Her long, golden-brown hair fell in loose, glossy waves down her back, framing a face that stopped conversations.

Her skin was flawless, the kind that caught light and held it. Almond-shaped green eyes scanned the hallway with quiet calculation, framed by perfectly arched brows that gave her an air of sharp intelligence. Her lips—full, soft—were the kind men remembered without meaning to—were painted in a muted rose that matched the understated elegance of the rest of her.

Professional. Impeccable. Unshakable.

But beneath the smooth surface, her mind was already racing through index projections, acquisition strategy, and—against her better judgment—the man waiting at the end of the corridor.

Adrian Werrington.

The name alone sent a flicker of tension through her spine. Heidi tightened her grip on the folder and kept walking toward his office, her heels quieter now against the marble. It was early—early enough to slip in, drop the report on his desk, and be gone before he arrived. That's how she managed it lately. Distance. Control. Because proximity to Adrian did something to her. Something no man ever had.

Three months. That's how long she'd been at Werrington Wealth. Long enough to learn the rhythms of the place—the politics, the power plays, the relentless pressure. But also, long enough to see beneath the gloss. This empire didn't run on ambition or brilliance alone. It ran on precision. And fear.

And then, there was him.

Adrian Werrington.

He was the axis around which the whole machine turned. Everything the press painted him to be—charismatic, visionary, impossibly composed. The kind of man who made silence feel like a strategy and a glance feel like a verdict. But behind the perfectly tailored suits and razor-sharp intellect… there was something else.

Something quieter. Sadder.

He was handsome—devastatingly so—with that effortless confidence that turned heads in any room. Smart in a way that didn't just command respect but demanded it. And unfortunately, married.

Still, Heidi had seen glimpses of the man behind the mask. Fleeting cracks in the otherwise impenetrable facade. Moments he probably didn't realise anyone had seen.

The subtle tension in his jaw when Cleo's name was mentioned.

The way his gaze would drift during strategy meetings, unfocused, as though the skyline outside offered a better reality than the one he was stuck in.

Like he wasn't just thinking—he was trying to escape.

It made her wonder.

What was he running from?

Or worse… who?

And then there was her.

Mrs. Cleo Werrington—equal parts designer gown and dagger smile. Heidi had met her once, briefly, in the executive lounge. One handshake. One glance. That was all it took. Cleo had looked her over like she was an outfit she didn't care for. Like Heidi's mere presence was something to be tolerated, not acknowledged.

That had been enough.

Heidi shook the thought off, forcing her focus back to the now as she returned to her office. The quiet click of the door closing behind her was oddly grounding. She slid into her chair with her usual poise, powered up her screen, and pulled up the latest report.

There was work to do.

The revised forecast after the Asia-Pacific setback needed finalising before ten, and she refused to let a pair of cold blue eyes—or a certain inconvenient marriage—distract her from what she did best.

Because Heidi Gibson had earned her place here.

And she wasn't about to let anyone—even him—knock her off balance.

Heidi stood at the head of the conference table at ten thirty sharp, tablet in hand, her posture poised and effortless. The navy dress she wore skimmed her figure with clean lines and no embellishment—precisely her style. Understated. Unapologetically refined. She didn't need dramatic flair or a raised voice to command attention.

She was attention.

Adrian sat at the far end of the table, arms crossed, one brow slightly raised as he watched her. She was mid-presentation, guiding the executive team through the revised forecast in response to the Asia-Pacific downturn. Her voice was even, clipped, every word deliberate. No wasted language. No nervous energy. Just clarity and calm control.

She was right—on all of it. He knew it. They all did.

But Adrian wasn't just listening to her words. He was watching her. The way she moved, the way she held the room without trying. That sharp mind packaged in elegance. Green eyes cool, focused. Long golden-brown hair worn down, catching the light as she turned slightly toward the projection screen. God, she was beautiful.

Too beautiful.

And it was becoming harder to pretend he didn't notice.

When she paused to breathe, one of the VPs jumped in with a condescending chuckle. "Those numbers are a little ambitious, don't you think? Maybe let's temper the optimism."

Heidi didn't flinch. "If I tempered the numbers every time a man in a $5,000 suit got nervous, we'd be bankrupt by now."

A beat of silence. Then, a low ripple of amusement around the table. Adrian's mouth twitched before he could stop it.

She glanced at him—just briefly. And something passed between them. Recognition. Unspoken.


After the meeting, the others filed out, leaving her to gather her things. Adrian remained in his seat, pretending to check his phone, but really… he was watching her again. The grace in her movement. The precision. She intrigued him more than he wanted to admit.

She was halfway to the door when she paused, turned, and hesitated.

"Did you get a chance to look at the updated revised index factors?" Heidi asked, her voice low and even, carefully professional. "I left it on your desk this morning."

Adrian looked up from his screen, caught off guard—not by the question, but by the softness in her tone. It wasn't casual, exactly. But it wasn't distant either.

"I did," he said. "Thank you. It was sharp work."

She gave a small nod, the corner of her mouth twitching in something close to a smile. "Well… the Q4 projections are aggressively boring and wait for no man."

That intrigued him. The faintest curve of amusement broke across his face—a rare, unguarded smile. The first real one in days.

"Or woman," he replied quietly.

Heidi smiled back, subtle but warm. She turned, heels clicking against the polished floor as she headed for the door. Adrian watched her go, something unspoken flickering in his eyes.

The door closed softly behind her.

And the silence that followed didn't feel quite so empty anymore.


Heidi stepped into her office and let the door click shut behind her, the soft snick sounding louder than it should in the quiet. She leaned back against the cool wood; eyes closed for a beat and exhaled slowly. Her pulse was doing that thing again—racing beneath her skin like it had every right to betray her over a single look. A simple thank-you. A smile.

God help her.

She crossed the room with quick, precise steps and dropped her tablet onto the desk with more force than necessary. Then stood there for a moment, staring at it like it might scold her. Her hand came up to pinch the bridge of her nose, a grounding gesture.

Get it together, Gibson.

He was married. He was the CEO. Your boss. Completely untouchable, and entirely the wrong kind of dangerous.

And yet… that look. That moment in the boardroom when their eyes had locked and the air had thinned around her, quieting everything else like the world had taken a breath and held it. It was fleeting. Barely a heartbeat long. But it landed like gravity. Like inevitability.

She dropped into her chair and swivelled toward the floor-to-ceiling windows, Manhattan's skyline glittering like a jewel box below. Busy. Dazzling. Ruthlessly alive. Unlike her thoughts, which refused to stay in the neat mental compartments she worked so hard to build.

She hadn't planned to speak to him at all after the meeting. She usually didn't. Better that way. Simpler. But when she'd seen him still sitting there after the room had cleared—shoulders drawn, jaw tight, the weight of something unspoken hanging around him like smoke—she'd felt it. That tug. That soft pull of empathy… of interest. Of him.

He looked like a man unravelling slowly, thread by deliberate thread.

And still, he'd been courteous. Attentive. Grateful. Not because he had to be—but because he chose to be.

It would be so much easier if he were arrogant. If he looked through her like glass or treated her like decoration or dismissed her ideas with a smirk and a half-listen. But he didn't. He listened. He read. He thanked her.

And that—that—was the problem.

She turned back to her desk, pulling the Q4 forecast toward her, eyes scanning the numbers without really seeing them. Instead, they caught on the empty stretch of desk where his last report still sat—marked by a single handwritten note in the margin. Just a line of thanks. No flourish. No signature. Just…

*Thanks. A.*

He didn't have to write it. He never had before.

She bit her bottom lip, a slow exhale feathering past her mouth.

Why did he write it?

And why, no matter how hard she tried, couldn't she stop thinking about him?

It was after ten when Adrian found himself standing outside her office door.

He had no real reason to be there—no pressing issue, no urgent file to deliver. Nothing that couldn't wait until morning. And yet, here he was, standing like an intruder, heart pacing for reasons he didn't fully understand. No, that wasn't true. He understood perfectly. He knew she was still working. He always did.

The executive floor was silent now, cloaked in the hushed stillness that came after hours. The soft hum of recessed lighting and the occasional creak of settling beams filled the space. He glanced over his shoulder, confirming the hallway was empty, though he already knew it was. Everyone else had gone home.

Everyone but her.

His knuckles brushed the polished wood as he knocked—softly, almost hesitantly. He knew it was a risk. Unprofessional. Ill-advised. But he couldn't help himself.

Not tonight.

"Come in," came her voice—low, composed, but unmistakably hers.

He opened the door slowly.

And there she was.

Heidi sat at her desk, posture still straight despite the hour. Her hair was swept back now, no longer cascading in those soft, loose waves. The glow of the desk lamp framed her face, casting delicate shadows under her cheekbones. She wore no makeup—just a faint smudge beneath her eye that hinted at how long she'd been here.

Even stripped of polish, she was striking. Maybe even more so.

"Adrian." Her voice held a flicker of surprise, her gaze drifting briefly to the papers in his hand before settling on his face. "Is everything all right?"

He hesitated, pulse kicking up again. He could've fabricated a reason—a file, a question, something. But the truth refused to stay buried tonight.

"I…" He exhaled, then met her eyes. "I noticed your light was still on. I wanted to make sure you were okay."

A pause.

She looked at him, expression unreadable. "I'm fine, thanks. Just wrapping up some Q4 details."

He nodded once, stepping inside—but left the door open behind him, like that crack of space between them somehow made it safer. Less… intimate.

"Well, don't work too late," he said, his voice softer than he meant it to be.

For a brief second, something in her gaze shifted. A flicker of warmth. Then—just as quickly—it vanished, replaced by the cool professionalism she wore like armour.

"I won't," she said. "I'm nearly done."

He lingered a moment longer than necessary, eyes tracing the curve of her shoulder, the slight crease between her brows. She looked tired. But more than that—she looked lonely. And that unsettled him in ways he wasn't prepared to unpack.

"Okay," he said quietly. "Have a good night, Heidi. I'll see you in the morning."

She nodded, her expression unreadable once more. "Good night, Adrian."

He turned and stepped back into the hallway.

The door clicked softly shut behind him.

And the silence that followed somehow felt louder than anything else.


Heidi shut down her computer without finishing the last slide.

Her fingers moved mechanically, muscle memory guiding her through motions her mind had long since abandoned. Her focus was elsewhere—stuck in the quiet space he'd left behind.

She grabbed her coat, shrugged it on, and flicked off the desk lamp. The office dimmed into shadow, the only light now spilling from the city outside—Manhattan glittering like it always did, beautiful and indifferent.

She didn't say goodbye to anyone. There was no one left to hear it.

By the time she stepped into the elevator, her reflection in the mirrored doors looked composed, unreadable. Just as it should be. Just as it always was.

She climbed into the waiting Uber without checking the plates. She didn't need to. This late, the streets were quiet, and the car smelled faintly of coffee and some too-sweet cologne that clung to the upholstery.

Heidi sank into the leather seat, clutching her bag to her chest like it might anchor her. Her gaze drifted to the window, watching the blur of lights and shadows slide past.

But her mind wasn't on the city.

It was still on him.

Adrian Werrington.

The way he'd said her name tonight—softly, like it meant something. Like she meant something.

The knock on her door hadn't startled her. She'd known it was him. Somehow, she always knew. Maybe it was the rhythm of his steps. Maybe it was something else—some kind of emotional radar she wished she could shut off.

She could still feel the echo of him in the room. The faint imprint of his presence. The weight of the silence he left behind.

He shouldn't have come.

And she shouldn't have cared.

But she did. More than she wanted to admit. More than was smart. More than was safe.

Her fingers tightened around her bag as the car rolled to a red light, taillights ahead flaring crimson in the glass. She caught her own reflection in the window—tired eyes, soft mouth, the shadow of conflict ghosting across her face.

She was slipping. Letting him get too close. Letting herself get too close.

And for what?

A look? A smile? A late-night visit that didn't mean anything—or worse, meant too much?

He was married.

That should've been the end of it. The boundary, the wall, the hard stop.

But tonight, had felt like a beginning. And beginnings, she knew, were far more dangerous.

The light changed. The car moved on.

So did she—at least, on the surface. Back to the apartment that wasn't quite home, back to her high-rise solitude and spreadsheets and smart decisions. Back to pretending this wasn't happening.

But in the quiet, beneath it all, the ache remained.

And for the first time in a long time…

Heidi didn't want to be alone.

# Chapter Three

The penthouse was quiet when Adrian stepped through the door.

Too quiet.

Not that he expected anything else. Cleo's car wasn't in the garage, and her coat hadn't been on the hook. She was likely at some overpriced restaurant downtown, sipping champagne with her equally plastic circle of friends, gossiping in hushed tones about people they pretended to admire and quietly despised.

Good. He didn't want her here tonight.

He didn't want to pretend.

Adrian shrugged off his coat, tossed it onto the back of the leather armchair, and loosened his tie with one hand as he made his way toward the study. The overhead lights cast a soft, golden glow over the dark walnut shelves, rows of books and framed degrees staring back at him like silent witnesses.

He hadn't been in here in weeks.

It still smelled faintly of the Cuban cigars his father used to smoke—an indulgence Adrian never took up himself. He crossed to the desk, pulled open the bottom drawer, and began sifting through old files. Alan, his lawyer and friend, had asked him earlier that day to gather a few things: bank statements, prenuptial agreements, their marriage license. The paperwork that marked the beginning of something he now intended to end.

Separation.

He'd said the word out loud for the first time last night.

And it had felt right. Clean. Like air after a storm.

There was no fight left between them—just the echo of what used to be. And lies. So many lies.

Adrian flipped through folders, scanning dates and headers, sorting out what he needed. His jaw ticked when he came across their wedding certificate. White vellum, gold embossed lettering. A lie wrapped in elegance.

He was about to close the drawer when something caught his eye—an envelope tucked between two estate documents. He frowned and pulled it out, the flap already opened, the paper inside folded twice.

*Letterhead. Mount Clair Medical Group.*

Curiosity—or maybe something darker—made his fingers still.

He unfolded the paper.

And the world stopped.

*Patient: Cleo Lester.*

*Procedure: Bilateral Tubal Ligation.*

*Date of Procedure: October 11th*

Adrian stared at the words.

His pulse spiked, a heavy thud in his chest.

He read it again. Slower this time.

Tubal ligation. A sterilisation procedure.

*Dated eighteen months ago.*

His mind seized.

But Cleo had claimed she was pregnant twelve months ago.

The math didn't just speak—it screamed.

She'd looked him in the eye. Tearful. Convincing.

Told him they'd lost the baby.

That she'd miscarried.

And he had believed her.

He'd mourned. Blamed himself. Worked less. Tried harder.

Tried to be better for a child that had never existed.

Adrian's breath snagged—sharp, cold, catching like glass in his throat.

The page crackled as his hand curled around it.

She hadn't lost a baby.

She had never even been pregnant.

The truth landed like a gut-punch—visceral, final.

She'd lied.

Manipulated him.

Used a phantom pregnancy to corner him, guilt him, control him.

He married her for the child.

There had never been a child.

Who does that?

Rage rose like a slow boil. At first a buzz in his ears. Then louder, hotter, all-consuming.

He stood frozen, staring at the page like it might set fire to the room.

And then everything began to click into place—

Her sudden urgency to marry.

The emotional games.

The illusion of family just long enough to trap him in a vow he never would've made otherwise.

He should've trusted his instincts. He had—once. But he'd buried them beneath duty. Image. Guilt.

No more.

Adrian crossed the room and flung the report onto the desk like it was poison.

His reflection caught in the window—jaw clenched, shoulders squared, eyes hard.

He wasn't sad.

Not anymore.

He was done.

And tomorrow, Cleo would find out just how done.


Adrian arrived at Werrington Wealth before seven. The city was still shaking off its sleep, but he was wide awake—sharpened by fury and clarity.

His driver had barely put the car in park before Adrian was out and striding toward the building, keyed in by security, his mind already racing through the next steps. Today, the charade ended.

The corridor lights on the executive floor were dimmed, still in night-mode, casting everything in a cool, steel-hued glow. The silence was welcome. Familiar. But it did little to quiet the storm inside him.

He turned the corner—just steps from his office—when he saw her.

Heidi.

She was walking toward him, a to-go coffee in one hand, the other casually tucked into the pocket of her tailored trousers. Hair pulled into a low twist. No makeup except for a muted swipe of colour on her lips. Calm, focused, always pulled together.

Their eyes met.

He tried to smooth his expression, but she caught something. She always did.

"Morning," she said, offering a small smile. "You're in early."

"So are you," he replied, voice lower than usual.

She tilted her head slightly, studying him. "Big day?"

He paused, unsure how much his face had betrayed him.

"Something like that," he murmured.

Her eyes searched his. "You okay?"

There it was—gentle, unassuming concern. Not prying. Not performative.

Real.

Adrian swallowed the knot in his throat and gave her a faint smile. "I will be."

She nodded, slow and knowing. "Let me know if you need anything."

And then, because she knew better than to push, she stepped past him, heels quiet against the marble.

But not before he turned slightly, watching her retreat down the corridor.

Steady. Graceful. Grounding.

Adrian inhaled deeply and turned toward his office, slipping inside before the rest of the building came to life.

He closed the door behind him, loosened his tie, and reached for his phone.

It rang twice before a familiar voice picked up.

"Alan Bishop."

"It's me," Adrian said.

Alan didn't miss a beat. "You ready?"

Adrian stared at the city beyond his office window, the sun just beginning to rise behind the skyline.

"Yes," he said. "Let's move forward with the separation."

"Understood. I'll start the paperwork. Fast, clean, no mess—just like we discussed."

"There's more," Adrian added, his voice tightening. "I found something last night. A medical report. Cleo had a tubal ligation. Eighteen months ago."

Silence on the other end.

"She told me she was pregnant a year ago. Said she miscarried. But this report proves she couldn't have been pregnant at all."

Alan let out a slow breath. "Jesus."

"She lied," Adrian said flatly. "Used a fake pregnancy to get me to marry her. I just didn't know how far it went."

"Well, now you do," Alan said. "And with that on top of everything else? This won't just be quick. It'll be bloodless. You've got an ironclad prenup, and with fraud on her part? She walks away with nothing. Not even sympathy."

Adrian leaned back in his chair; eyes fixed on a single point in the skyline.

"Good," he said quietly.

"Want me to deliver the papers myself?" Alan asked.

"Yes. Thanks. I can't… I can't stand to look at her."

"I don't blame you," Alan said. "Truth be told, I never liked her."

Adrian gave a humourless huff. "I don't think I ever did either. Not really."

There was a beat of silence, and then Alan's voice returned, more measured. "All right. She'll have everything by this afternoon. We'll keep it clinical, clean, and fast."

"Perfect."

Adrian ended the call and set the phone down, letting the quiet stretch.

The city was waking up—its buzz faint through the triple-paned glass—but in here, it was still. Still enough for the weight of it all to settle.

It was done.

Or at least—the beginning of the end.

And for the first time in a long time… he felt the tightness in his chest begin to ease. A sliver of space where guilt had once lived. Where performance had taken up residence.

Then, unbidden, his mind drifted.

To Heidi.

The way she'd looked at him in the corridor. The calm in her voice. The genuine concern. The kind he hadn't known in years.

He wondered if she could see it on him—the unravelling of a life he never wanted, and the faint outline of something better just beginning to emerge.

He wasn't sure what came next.

But he was sure of this: *he wanted her in it.*


Adrian sat at the small conference table in his office, jacket off, sleeves rolled neatly to his forearms. Across from him, Heidi sat with her tablet, posture as precise as ever, though the edges of her expression had softened.

They were knee-deep in the Q4 projections, cross-checking variables, debating strategies. But the atmosphere was different today—lighter somehow.

Adrian felt it.

Relief had been a quiet companion all morning. The kind that didn't shout but whispered: you did the right thing.

He'd made the call. The papers were on their way. And every breath since had felt a little easier.

Heidi glanced up from a note and arched a brow. "You really think the board won't flinch at that much deviation from last quarter?"

"They'll flinch," Adrian said with a dry smile. "But they'll get over it once the returns hit."

Heidi laughed softly, shaking her head. "Arrogant and right. Dangerous combination."

Adrian leaned back slightly, mirroring her smile. "You say that like it's a bad thing."

Just then, the office door flew open with a crack.

Cleo.

Her heels struck the floor like gunshots. Designer coat slung carelessly over one arm; sunglasses still perched on her head like a crown. Her lips were twisted into a venomous smile as her eyes landed on Heidi.

"So," she said, voice like acid. "This is the tart you're leaving me for?"

Heidi's smile vanished in an instant, her body going still. She didn't speak—but her eyes lifted to Adrian's, guarded and unreadable.

Adrian stood sharply. "Enough, Cleo. Get out. I'm having a meeting with my CFO."

Cleo laughed, bitter and theatrical. "Oh, CFO, is that what we're calling it now?"

"I will not do this with you here," Adrian said, voice firm, low. "Leave. Now."

"I will not," Cleo snapped, stepping further into the room like she owned it. Her gaze stayed glued to Heidi, dripping with disdain. "I don't want a divorce. I'll fight you. I'll drag it out for years if I have to."

Adrian's eyes locked onto hers, his voice steady—dangerously calm. "I don't think that's wise, Cleo. Because if you push this… I'll make sure everyone knows you faked a pregnancy to trap me into marrying you."

Cleo's mouth dropped open in theatrical offense. "I didn't fake it."

"Really?" Adrian said, his voice deceptively calm as he lifted an eyebrow. "How exactly does someone get pregnant six months after a tubal ligation?"

Heidi's head snapped up, her eyes wide. She looked between them, startled. Adrian wasn't joking.

The silence hung thick for a moment.

Heidi began to rise from her seat, her spine straightening, chin tilting slightly in quiet resolve. Her professionalism wrapped around her like armour. "I'll give you both a moment," she said evenly.

"No," Adrian said, turning toward her. His hand came to rest on her shoulder—firm but gentle, deliberate. "Stay."

His voice wasn't loud. But it carried weight.

Heidi froze, eyes lifting to his. And for a breathless moment, something passed between them. Not just understanding—but solidarity. Trust.

Cleo blinked, thrown by the gesture. For the first time, she faltered.

"I… I didn't… I never did that," she stammered, her usual poise fraying at the edges.

"I have the medical report. You did it eighteen months ago. And you claimed to be pregnant twelve months ago." He let the silence stretch, each word sinking in like a stone. "So no, Cleo. You were never pregnant. You never lost a baby. You just lied. And let me grieve something that didn't exist."

She faltered, the colour draining from her face.

"You want me to walk away with nothing?" she whispered.

"You deserve nothing," Adrian said, ice in his voice, "after all the lies you've told. But you might still get something—if you don't make this ugly."

Cleo's expression shifted like a flicked switch. She moved closer, slowly, her voice dipping into a sultry register. She placed her hands on his chest like a plea wrapped in seduction. "Adrian… we can work this out. You're just upset."

He peeled her hands off him with a grimace of disgust. "Get out, Cleo. We are done."

Her composure crumbled. "I don't care what you say. I will fight this."

Adrian exhaled, steadying himself. Then he shifted tone—pragmatic, cool. "You're not entitled to anything. But if you walk away quietly, I'll offer you a settlement. Nothing extravagant. Just enough to move on with some dignity."

That made her pause. Her chin lifted a fraction, eyes narrowing with suspicion. "You're bluffing," she said slowly. "You wouldn't actually tell people."

"I would," Adrian replied, voice like steel. "And I will. Try me."

Her expression twisted. "All you ever cared about was that damn baby."

"I cared because you knew how much I wanted to be a father," he said, jaw tightening. "And you used that knowledge to trap me."

Cleo said nothing. But the fire in her eyes wavered, the certainty beginning to crumble.

Then, with a sharp pivot, she turned on her heel and stormed out—

the door snapping shut behind her like the crack of a gavel.

Adrian stood motionless for a long moment, his jaw tight, his hands curled into fists at his sides. The room still crackled with the remnants of Cleo's venom.

He finally turned, his gaze finding Heidi. She hadn't said a word—hadn't moved—but her eyes were wide, her expression unreadable.

"I'm sorry," Adrian said quietly. "She had no right to speak to you like that."

Heidi shook her head once, slowly. "I'm fine. Are you okay?"

His lips lifted in a wry, tired half-smile. "I will be."

Heidi didn't press. But the way she looked at him—steady, searching—made it clear she wasn't just asking to be polite.

Adrian sat down again, the weight of the confrontation settling in his bones. Across the table, Heidi still hadn't touched her tablet. The air between them felt different now.

Charged.

Quiet, but not empty.

"Do you want to leave this for another time?" she asked gently, nodding toward the Q4 projections.

Adrian exhaled slowly, rubbing a hand across the back of his neck. "You must think I'm an idiot."

Her brow lifted, surprised. "Why would I think that?"

"Because I fell for her lies."

Heidi's voice was steady, kind—but firm. "An idiot is the last word I'd use to describe you. You believed someone you trusted. That doesn't make you foolish, Adrian. It makes you human. And her…" She hesitated just briefly. "It makes her a manipulator."

Adrian's mouth curved—not quite a smile, but something close. Tired. Grateful. "You're a good person, Heidi."

She gave him a soft look—one that didn't try to fix, explain, or excuse.

She just saw him.

"You are too," she said quietly. "Even if you don't feel like it right now."

Adrian held her gaze for a moment longer, something unspoken lingering in the space between them. Then, as if by silent agreement, they both turned back to the projections.

They carried on with the meeting as though nothing had happened. Numbers, graphs, forecasts—business as usual. But the silence between words felt fuller now. Weighted. Changed.


Later, when Heidi returned to her office, she closed the door quietly behind her and leaned against it for a long moment.

The calm exterior she'd worn all afternoon remained intact—but just barely. Inside, her thoughts spun, replaying everything. The confrontation. Cleo's sharp, accusing tone. Adrian's voice, cool and devastating: *'How exactly does someone get pregnant six months after a tubal ligation?'*

But more than any of that, it was the way he'd looked at her. Right before he asked her to stay.

The weight of his hand on her shoulder—firm, steady, deliberate.

He *trusted* her.

That was what stuck.

She crossed the room and sank into her chair, but her fingers hovered above the keyboard, motionless.

Heidi didn't let herself hope for things she couldn't name. Not usually. Not safely.

But today... something had shifted. A line had blurred. A door, maybe, cracked open.

And part of her—quiet, cautious—wasn't ready to pretend it hadn't.

She just didn't know what scared her more—that it was real... or that she might already want more.

# Chapter Four



*Two weeks later…*

The ballroom at the Fairmont gleamed with soft gold light and the clink of champagne flutes. Crystal chandeliers sparkled overhead as the city's elite gathered to honour Roger Felton, one of Werrington Wealth's longest-standing board members, retiring after a decade of service.

Heidi moved through the crowd with graceful ease, her emerald gown sweeping elegantly behind her. It was a floor-length silk creation—simple but devastating. The bodice hugged her frame with quiet confidence, and the back dipped just low enough to be daring without losing sophistication. Her honey brown hair was pinned into a low chignon, soft tendrils brushing her jaw. No necklace. Just a pair of delicate diamond earrings and that signature calm that drew attention without demanding it.

She either didn't notice the heads that turned—or chose not to.

But Adrian noticed.

He saw her the moment she stepped into the room, as if the air shifted around her. His breath caught—just for a moment—and the rest of the room blurred.

God, she looked incredible.

She hadn't spoken much to him these past two weeks. There had been moments— quiet exchanges in meetings, brushes of tension laced with something warmer—but she always pulled back just before anything could deepen. And he understood. Or at least, he tried to.

But tonight… it was impossible not to feel it.

Especially now when she looked like that.

Adrian moved toward her, brushing past executives and board members, not stopping until he was at her side. "Heidi."

She turned, her expression warm, though still edged with the restraint she wore like armour these days. "Adrian."

"You look…" His voice dipped, caught somewhere between admiration and something deeper. "Stunning."

A small, guarded smile touched her lips. "Thank you. You clean up pretty well yourself."

He gave a low chuckle. "I do my best."

There was a pause, charged and quiet, before she asked, almost tentatively, "How are you?"

He met her eyes, and in them she saw the weight he'd been carrying. "Better," he said, voice rougher than before. "It'll be over soon. Thank God."

"I'm glad." Her voice was soft, sincere. "You deserve to move on."

He opened his mouth to respond—but didn't get the chance.

"Well, isn't this cozy?"

Cleo.

She stood beside them in a glittering silver sheath that sparkled like tinsel—tight, loud, and screaming for attention. Her smile was more a snarl, her gaze glued to Heidi with thinly veiled disdain.

Adrian's jaw tensed. "Why are you here?"

Cleo gave a breezy shrug. "Oh, relax. Roger and I go way back. Besides"—her eyes flicked toward Heidi with feigned innocence— "I couldn't miss the chance to meet the woman who's been monopolising your attention lately."

Heidi's expression didn't falter, but something subtle shifted—like a door quietly closing behind her eyes. She turned, her tone polite but cool. "If you'll excuse me—"

"No." Adrian stepped forward, his voice gentle but urgent. His hand brushed her arm, a quiet plea in the gesture. "You don't have to go."

But she was already moving, her heels soft against the marble floor, her presence slipping away like breath on glass.

Adrian turned to Cleo, his voice dropping to a steel-edged whisper. "If you make a scene tonight, the deal is off."

Cleo arched a brow. "I didn't make a scene."

"You're circling one." He took a step closer, the calm in his voice more dangerous than any raised tone. "The NDA is part of the settlement. Five million is more than generous. But if you so much as raise your voice in front of my team—or drag any of them into this—you walk away with nothing."

Cleo's smile curled, cold and possessive. "You're not fooling anyone, Adrian. It's obvious. You're obsessed with her."

"That's enough."

Her eyes glittered. "So quick to defend your precious CFO. What's so special about her, anyway? She's nothing."

He didn't rise to the bait. Didn't even look at her. He just turned and walked away, leaving her in a haze of envy, rage—and the faint trace of her own expensive perfume, now soured with bitterness.


Later that evening, Heidi stood at the marble sink in the ladies' room, pressing a cool, damp cloth to the back of her neck. The heat of the ballroom—its glittering lights, murmured conversations, and ever-watchful eyes—had finally caught up with her. She'd spent most of the night navigating careful distances: from Cleo, from Adrian, and most of all, from herself.

She didn't hear the door until it clicked shut behind her.

"You're not fooling anyone," came the voice, low and cutting. "You're after Adrian."

Heidi turned slowly, the cloth still in her hand.

Cleo leaned against the door, arms crossed, a smug tilt to her mouth. Her reflection in the mirror was sharp-edged, brittle with jealousy.

"Am I?" Heidi said, her voice calm. "Even if I were—and I'm not—that's none of your business."

Cleo stepped forward, her stilettos striking the tile with deliberate rhythm. "He's not interested. He doesn't get involved with employees. That's all you'll ever be."

Heidi met her gaze, steady and unflinching. "If you're trying to shake me, it's not working."

"You should be shaken," Cleo snapped, her mask slipping. "He'll use you. Chew you up and spit you out like everyone else."

Heidi tilted her head, her tone quiet but sharp. "If he's really not interested…, why are you so desperate to convince me?"

Cleo's eyes flashed. Her silence was answer enough.

Heidi didn't linger. She stepped past her, poised and composed, and reached for the door. "Maybe you should just walk away with your dignity. Before you lose that too."

She didn't look back as she left, but the sound of the silence she left behind felt louder than anything Cleo could've said. In the mirror, Cleo's reflection fractured, the anger and desperation cracking through the gloss.

Back in the ballroom, Heidi paused just inside the door.

Something had shifted.

For weeks, she'd buried her feelings, built walls with logic and professionalism. But tonight, had stripped everything bare—Cleo's bitterness, Adrian's unwavering loyalty, and the truth pulsing steadily in her chest.

She scanned the crowd, found him across the room.

And this time, she didn't hesitate.

She walked to him.


Adrian felt her before he saw her. A subtle shift in the air, the faintest trace of jasmine and something warmer—like the ghost of her skin against his.

He turned, and there she was.

"Hello," he said, his voice low, laced with something that sounded dangerously close to longing.

Heidi met his gaze, calm and unreadable, but something flickered beneath her polished exterior—resolve, maybe. Or surrender.

"Hi," she breathed, her voice soft but certain. It brushed against him like silk, quiet but impossible to ignore.

They stood in silence for a moment too long. Around them, the music of the ballroom dulled into nothing, as if the world itself was holding its breath.

"You look…" His eyes swept over her, reverent, disbelieving. "Beautiful doesn't even come close."

Her lips lifted in a wry smile. "You already said that."

"I know." His gaze lingered. "And I'll probably say it again."

She laughed then—quiet, breathless—and for the first time in weeks, it wasn't laced with caution.

"I need to dance," she murmured, a teasing lift to her brow. "Do you know anyone who might be interested?"

Adrian stepped in, closing the last of the space between them. He extended his hand, palm open, steady.

"It would be my greatest pleasure."

Heidi slid her hand into his, her fingers cool against his palm, but her touch sent a rush of heat up his arm. Adrian led her to the dance floor, weaving through the crowd as if no one else existed.

The music had slowed, the kind of elegant waltz people barely paid attention to anymore. But Adrian did. He placed a hand gently at the small of her back, drawing her close, and her other hand settled against his chest—steady, warm, real.

They began to move, gliding effortlessly into step, their bodies slipping into a rhythm that felt instinctive. Natural. Intimate. Heidi tried not to think about how right it felt— how effortlessly her hand fit in his, how his touch at the small of her back steadied her more than she cared to admit.

For a moment, they said nothing. The silence between them wasn't awkward—it was thick with unspoken things, weighted and electric.

"You've been avoiding me tonight," Adrian said at last, his voice low, just for her.

"I've been trying," she admitted, her eyes fixed somewhere just past his shoulder. "So Cleo has nothing to throw back in your face."

His lips lifted in a quiet, knowing curve. "That's thoughtful. But unnecessary."

Heidi looked up then, meeting his eyes. "She complicates everything, Adrian. And we work together. She already thinks we're involved."

"She can think whatever she wants," he said, voice calm, resolute. "I stopped caring about her version of the truth a long time ago."

Heidi hesitated. "I hope you find some peace when it's finally over."

Adrian's grip tightened slightly at her waist, steady but unintrusive. "Let's hope so."

They didn't speak again, not as the music carried them through the next turn, not as the distance between them subtly closed. They simply moved together, caught in a quiet understanding, the world narrowing to the space between their bodies.

And it left both of them a little breathless.


They spent the rest of the night circling each other in the safest way they knew how— talking. About work, travel, books they'd half-read, and food they'd rather be eating. Sometimes they mingled with others, shared light laughter, toasted to the retiring board member with practiced smiles. But no matter who they spoke to, their eyes kept finding each other.

It was late when Heidi finally glanced at her phone. She turned to him with a soft smile. "I should go."

"I'll take you home," Adrian offered instantly.

She shook her head. "No, I'll get an Uber. It's fine."

"Please," he said, his voice dipping into that rare mix of firm and gentle. "I insist."

She hesitated, then nodded once. "Alright."

They rode in silence most of the way—comfortable, reflective silence. The city passed by in a soft blur of lights as the limousine carried them to her apartment building.

When it came to a stop, Heidi reached for the door, but Adrian was quicker. "I'll walk you up."

"That's not necessary."

"I know," he said, already stepping out, "but I want to."

She sighed, half-smiling, and let him follow her inside.

At her door, she turned to him, grateful but composed. "Thank you. For the ride. For tonight."

"You're welcome." He meant it.

She reached for her keys—then froze as his hand closed over hers.

It was instinct more than decision. A current that had been humming between them all evening suddenly surged to life. Her breath hitched, heart stuttering in her chest as his eyes met hers—dark, searching, unspoken words flickering in their depths.

And then he kissed her.

There was nothing tentative about it. No pause. No hesitation. Just heat and hunger, crashing into them like a wave they could no longer outrun. Weeks—months—of restraint dissolved in an instant. His hand slid to the side of her face, thumb brushing her cheek as his mouth claimed hers, fierce and unrelenting. It tasted like everything they hadn't said. Everything they'd buried.

She responded before her mind could catch up, her fingers curling into the lapel of his jacket, pulling him closer. The kiss deepened, urgent and consuming, his body pinning hers gently against the door. She felt herself falling, the world narrowing to the pressure of his lips, the thundering in her chest, the way he held her like he'd never let go.

But then—she pulled back.

Breathless. Shaken.

Her eyes flew open, wide, and startled, her chest rising and falling with the effort to steady herself. "That wasn't a good idea," she whispered, her voice low and trembling with something she wasn't ready to name—something dangerously close to need. Or hope.

He didn't speak. He just looked at her, like the moment had cost him something. Like he'd do it again anyway.

And that—more than the kiss—was what made her heart ache.

Adrian stepped back slightly, chest rising and falling, his hands falling to his sides. "Yes," he said quietly. "Sorry."

Neither moved for a moment. Just two people standing on opposite sides of a line they'd both just crossed.

Then she turned, unlocked the door, and slipped inside—closing it with a soft click that felt louder than it should've.

And Adrian stood there, staring at the door like it might open again.

But it didn't.


After slipping out of her gown and into a soft nightgown, Heidi stood in front of the bathroom mirror, toothbrush in hand, completely still. Her reflection stared back at her—wide-eyed, flushed, unsettled.

Her lips still tingled.

That kiss.

She couldn't stop replaying it—the way his hand cupped her cheek so gently, reverently. The way his mouth found hers with a hunger he hadn't tried to hide. The way she had responded, without thought or hesitation, like it was inevitable.

And the way she'd pulled back—not because she wanted to, but because she had to.

It hadn't been just a kiss.

That was the problem.

With a sigh, she set the toothbrush down and ran her fingers through her hair, trying to shake the memory loose. But it clung to her like heat in her skin, refusing to fade.

This couldn't happen again. She couldn't let it happen again.

And yet…

As she padded into her darkened bedroom, her heart still racing, she knew sleep wouldn't come easily.

Not when a kiss that should've been a mistake had felt so heartbreakingly right.


Adrian didn't go home right away.

He told his driver to take the long way back—didn't care where, as long as the city lights blurred past the windows and the silence inside the car stayed undisturbed.

He sat with one elbow resting on the door, his fingers pressed to his lips like they might still hold the shape of her kiss.

He shouldn't have kissed her.

He knew that. He knew it.

But when she'd looked up at him at her door—eyes soft, voice grateful, walls lowered just enough to let the real Heidi show through—he'd been powerless. It hadn't felt like a choice. It had felt inevitable.

And the way she kissed him back…

God.

He replayed it in flashes—the way her fingers curled into his jacket, the small gasp she gave when he deepened the kiss, the way she'd leaned into him like she didn't want it to stop. Like maybe she felt it too.

But then she pulled away.

*'That wasn't a good idea.'*

She was right. Of course she was.

This—whatever this was—was a bad idea wrapped in worse timing. He wasn't free yet. Not entirely. And she deserved more than half-measures and complications.

But none of that made it easier to ignore how she felt in his arms.

Back at his penthouse, he poured himself a drink he didn't really want and stood at the window, looking out over the city like it might offer him answers. The skyline glittered in the dark, cold, and perfect.

Heidi wasn't like this city.

She wasn't all sharp edges and steel.

She was warmth. She was steadiness. She was the voice in his head when everything else was noise. And he couldn't stop thinking about the way she looked at him before he kissed her—as if some part of her had been waiting for it too.

He took a sip of scotch; let it burn its way down.

He couldn't afford to want her.

But he already did.

And the worst part?

He didn't regret the kiss.

Not even a little.

# Chapter Five

The following week unfolded in quiet, practiced denial.

At Werrington Wealth's headquarters, the office hummed with its usual rhythm—clicking keyboards, murmured conversations, the occasional ring of a desk phone. But beneath the routine, something had shifted.

Heidi felt it the moment she walked in Monday morning.

Adrian was already in his office, the door half-closed, shades drawn just enough to suggest he didn't want to be disturbed. And maybe he didn't. But she felt his presence anyway, like a current humming low beneath the floor.

Their first meeting was at nine.

She entered the conference room early, professional and composed, flipping through her notes with steady hands that didn't reflect the knot in her stomach. When Adrian walked in a few minutes later, their eyes met for a fraction too long.

"Good morning," he said, his voice as even as ever.

"Morning," she returned, just as calmly.

They didn't mention the kiss.

They didn't mention the silence after it, the way she'd turned the key and closed the door without a goodbye. They didn't mention how close they'd come to stepping over a line that couldn't be uncrossed.

Instead, they talked earnings projections. Strategy decks. Investor meetings. Every word was precise. Efficient.

Professional.

But it didn't stop the way her pulse quickened when he stood behind her at the whiteboard, just a little too close. It didn't stop the flicker in his eyes when she brushed past him to plug in her laptop. Every shared glance was loaded with unsaid things. Every silence too loud.

By Wednesday, it was driving her mad.

She caught him watching her during a board prep call—his expression unreadable, jaw tight. And when she looked up, he didn't look away. Just held her gaze for a second too long before shifting back to his screen.

That night, she dreamed of the kiss.

Thursday, they passed in the hallway outside the elevators. She nodded politely. So did he. Their arms brushed as they moved past each other, and it was like touching a live wire.

Friday, they worked late.

The office was quiet, the halls dimmed, the staff long gone. Heidi was gathering her things when she heard his voice behind her.

"Heidi."

She turned, carefully blank. "Yes?"

His eyes searched hers—tired, unreadable, heavy with something he wouldn't name. "Have a good weekend."

"You too," she said, after a beat.

And that was it.

He didn't step closer. She didn't stop him when he turned away.

But her hand lingered on the strap of her bag, her breath shallow, her lips pressing together like they still remembered the feel of his.

They were pretending.

But the space between them was already filled with everything they weren't saying.

And it was only a matter of time before it spilled over.


The next week passed in a blur of restraint.

Adrian kept his distance—not because he wanted to, but because it was the only way to stay sane. The kiss had undone him in a way nothing else had in years. He'd replayed it more times than he cared to admit—the feel of her lips against his, the soft hitch of her breath, the way she leaned into him like she'd been holding that need just as long.

And then she'd pulled away.

She was right, of course. It wasn't a good idea. Not with the divorce still looming, the lines between them still blurred by circumstance.

So, he let the silence stretch taut between them. Let professionalism mask the pull that threatened to swallow him whole. He watched her move through the office with that same quiet fire, that elegance he'd come to crave—and said nothing.

But inside, he was unravelling by the inch.

It had been two weeks since he'd kissed her, and all he could think about was doing it again.

By Friday, the divorce was finalised.

Cleo had signed the papers in a glass-walled conference room, her expression icy and triumphant as she slid them across the table. Five million in cash, plus the penthouse. She behaved as if she'd won some great prize.

Adrian didn't react.

He was a billionaire—her settlement was a drop in the ocean of what he was worth. He was lucky Alan had insisted on a watertight prenup from the start. Still, Cleo had taken the one thing he couldn't imagine wanting anymore.

The penthouse.

Once, it had been a dream—clean lines, breathtaking views, the kind of home you built a future in. But not anymore. Every inch of it reeked of her: cold silences, arguments that never ended, perfume that used to intoxicate and now made his stomach turn. It was a monument to everything their marriage had failed to be.

Let her have it.

He'd already packed what mattered. The rest could rot with the memories.

That evening, he stayed late—not because there was work to do, but because the idea of walking into an empty hotel suite felt unbearable. The skyline outside his office burned in streaks of crimson and gold, the city slipping into twilight. He stood by the window, a glass of scotch in hand, the silence a rare kind of comfort.

His suit jacket lay forgotten on the couch, his tie loose, top buttons undone. Sleeves rolled to his elbows. He barely recognised the man reflected in the window—tired, yes, but strangely lighter. Like something heavy had finally fallen away.

He was just draining the last sip of his drink when the door clicked open behind him.

He turned, instinctively alert.

Heidi stood in the doorway, file in hand, surprise flickering across her features. "Oh— I didn't think anyone was still in."

Adrian's gaze softened, something unspoken settling between them. "Neither did I."

She hesitated. "I just came to drop off the quarterly projections."

"Thanks," he said, voice low and even.

She stepped farther in, her heels quiet against the floor, movements careful. She set the report on his desk, her fingers brushing the edge like she needed the grounding.

He didn't move.

But his eyes never left her.

She looked up. For a second, they just…stood there. No titles. No barriers. Just Adrian and Heidi, suspended in something electric and unspoken.

"Have a good weekend," she said softly.

She turned to leave, but before she could take a step—

"Heidi."

She stopped. Looked back.

"Yes?"

He crossed the room slowly, deliberately, setting his empty glass on the desk beside her report.

And then he kissed her.

There was no thought, no hesitation—just need. Raw and burning. The taste of her had haunted him for weeks, and now that she was here, close enough to touch, he couldn't help himself.

His hand slid to the side of her face, his fingers threading into her hair, and he kissed her like a man starved. Like he'd been drowning for two weeks, and she was the air he'd been gasping for.

And then—God, then she kissed him back.

Her hands were on his chest in an instant, not pushing him away but pulling him closer. Her mouth parted beneath his, soft and urgent, and he groaned low in his throat as she responded—hungrily, almost desperately. Her fingers curled into the open collar of his shirt, tugging him toward her, and all the tension they'd been holding in snapped like a rubber band stretched too far.

It was chaos after that. Controlled only by instinct.

He lifted her onto the edge of his desk without breaking the kiss, knocking a pen holder to the floor as she clutched at his shoulders, pulling him into the cradle of her hips. She gasped when his hands gripped her thighs, dragging her closer, and the sound of it— breathless, wanton—nearly undid him.

Heidi's fingers dove into his hair, and her head tilted to deepen the kiss. It wasn't tentative anymore. It was all heat and friction, weeks of suppressed desire boiling over in a rush that made Adrian feel like he'd been lit from within.

His hands slid up beneath the hem of her blouse, fingertips grazing bare skin, and she shivered beneath his touch. Her legs wrapped around his waist without thinking, anchoring him to her, grounding them both in a moment that had been building from the first time she'd ever looked at him like she saw the man behind the mask.

There was no office. No consequences. No Cleo. No past.

Just the two of them—wanting, taking, tasting.

Adrian kissed her like he didn't care what came next—like everything after this would be secondary to having her now. And Heidi gave into it, clung to him like she'd been holding back too long and finally—*finally*—had permission to let go.

Her blouse came off first, his hands making quick work of the buttons as he bared her inch by inch, his mouth trailing heat along the curve of her neck, the line of her collarbone. She arched beneath him, breath catching as his hands explored her skin— slow, reverent, like he was memorising her by touch.

He lifted his head, eyes dark, jaw tight with restraint. "Tell me to stop," he said, voice hoarse.

She didn't hesitate. "Don't."

That one word shattered the last of his control.

His mouth found hers again, deeper this time, devouring. He wanted to taste every sound she made, every breathless gasp and soft moan. She tugged at his shirt, pulling it free from his slacks, fingers sliding over the hard planes of his chest, nails scraping lightly as she pushed it off his shoulders.

He groaned when her hands mapped over his bare skin, her touch both tentative and bold, like she couldn't decide whether to savour or consume. Her mouth found the line of his throat, his jaw, then lower, kissing a path down his chest, and it made him dizzy, the way she worshipped him with every kiss.

Adrian's hands gripped her hips, sliding her to the edge of the desk again, and he sank to his knees, looking up at her like a man kneeling before his salvation. She blinked down at him, lips parted, chest heaving, completely wrecked—and more beautiful than he'd ever seen her.

"Adrian," she breathed.

"I need to taste you."

And then he did.

She gasped as his mouth found her—slow at first, teasing, like he wanted to drive her mad before giving her what she needed. Her fingers wound into his hair, her thighs trembling around his shoulders as he worked her with his tongue and lips and relentless pressure until she shattered, crying out his name like a prayer.

He didn't stop until she pulled him up to her again, desperate for more, for all of him.

They barely made it through the next few minutes. His slacks undone, her skirt hiked up, their bodies pressing, grinding, seeking. When he finally entered her, it was with a groan that seemed to shake him to his bones.

She gasped, clinging to him, her nails digging into his back, and he kissed her to swallow the sound.

They moved together like they'd been made for this—every thrust deep and slow, every roll of their hips a quiet devastation. Her forehead rested against his, breath mingling, their eyes locked in something more than lust. It was personal. It was intimate. It was everything he hadn't let himself feel.

When she came again, it was with a soft cry against his neck, her whole body trembling as she fell apart in his arms. The feel of her unravelling around him—the way she clung to him, like she didn't want to let go—sent him over the edge seconds later. He buried his face in her shoulder and came with a low, broken groan, spilling into her as the last thread of restraint snapped.

He didn't move for a long time.

Neither did she.

Their breath mingled in the quiet hum of the office, both of them wrapped in a silence too intimate to name. His forehead rested against hers, one hand cradling her jaw like it was something precious, the other pressed gently to the curve of her back. Her skin was warm against his, soft and real in a way that made everything else feel distant.

He didn't want to pull away.

Didn't want the moment to end.

But reality always came knocking.

Eventually, he drew back just enough to look into her eyes, searching for something. Permission. Clarity. A reason not to want more.

What he found instead was vulnerability. Hers. His. Tangled together in the space between them.

He brushed his thumb across her cheek, then dropped his gaze to her lips—kissed them once, gently. Almost apologetic.

Then: "Come with me."

She blinked. "What?"

"To my hotel," he said, voice rough and low. "I've been staying at the Four Seasons. Just for the night. No pretending, no walking away before we've figured out what this is. Just… come with me."

Heidi's breath caught. She looked down, then away, and for a moment, he thought she might say no.

But she didn't move from his arms.

Didn't try to put distance between them.

Instead, her hands curled around the fabric of his shirt, holding on. And after a beat, she looked back at him with something like resolve in her eyes.

"We've already crossed the line," she said quietly. "Might as well see what's on the other side."

Adrian exhaled, not relief—something deeper.

He nodded once, kissed her again, and whispered against her lips, "Let's go."


The elevator ride is quiet, charged. Heidi leans against the back wall, arms loosely folded, her eyes on the numbers ticking upward. Adrian standing beside her, close but not touching, hands in his pockets like he's keeping them there on purpose. The silence isn't awkward—it's expectant. Like neither of them dares speak in case they break the spell.

The hotel suite was quiet when they stepped inside, the soft sound of the door clicking shut behind them loud in the stillness.

Adrian set his keycard on the credenza without turning on the lights. The city shimmered beyond the floor-to-ceiling windows, a breathtaking skyline that couldn't compete with the woman standing beside him.

Heidi hovered just inside the door, her fingers lightly skimming the edge of her coat, her expression unreadable. She wasn't unsure—he could tell that much. She was just… absorbing. The night. The choice. Him.

He turned to her slowly, his voice a soft echo in the dark.

"You okay?"

She nodded, a faint smile tugging at her lips. "Are you?"

"I will be," he said. "If you stay."

That was all it took.

She stepped toward him, unfastening her coat as she moved. He watched it fall to the chair behind her, then crossed the space between them with careful restraint, his hands sliding to her waist. They stood like that for a moment—close but not yet kissing, their breath mingling, the anticipation building again.

And then she reached for the top button of his shirt.

That was the beginning of the unravelling.

He kissed her again, slower this time, savouring it. Their mouths moved in perfect sync—less frantic than before, but no less intense. Her hands slid over his chest as she pushed his shirt from his shoulders, fingertips grazing bare skin like she needed to relearn him.

Adrian groaned softly as her touch stirred something low and hot inside him. "God, I've wanted this," he whispered against her mouth.

"Me too," she said, and the quiet honesty of it undid him.

He lifted her gently—effortless, reverent—and carried her to the bedroom, laying her down on the crisp sheets like she was something precious. She watched him the whole time, eyes dark and searching, as if waiting to see if he'd change his mind.

But there was no room for doubt.

Not anymore.

He kissed her again, deeper now, and her arms came around his shoulders, anchoring him as their bodies pressed together. Clothes came off piece by piece—slow, deliberate—until there was nothing between them but skin and heat and that trembling, unspoken thing neither of them had dared name until now.

Adrian slid a hand over her ribs, across her stomach, reverent in his touch. "Tell me what you want."

Heidi's breath caught. "You."

That single word was a balm and a flame.

When he entered her again, it was slower this time—achingly so. Like he needed to feel every inch of her, memorise every gasp and sigh. She met him with equal intensity, her fingers threading into his hair, her legs wrapping around him to pull him deeper.

They moved like they were rediscovering the world in each other. No rush. No shame. Just two people finally allowed to feel everything they'd been suppressing.

He kissed her through every soft moan, every whispered plea, until her voice broke on his name, and she came apart beneath him, clutching him like she never wanted to let go.

He followed a moment later, burying his face in her neck, the world narrowing to the sound of her breath, the feel of her body around him, the knowing that nothing would ever be the same again.

After, they lay tangled in the sheets, bodies still flush, breath slowly returning to normal. Heidi's hand rested over his heart, her head on his shoulder. Adrian didn't speak—just pressed a kiss to her hair and pulled her closer.

The night turned into the next day, then the night, then Sunday morning.

They made love on the living room floor, in the shower, in the bath, in the bed—again and again. They couldn't get enough of each other. It wasn't just the physical, though that burned hot and insatiable. It was the way Adrian looked at her now, without walls. The way Heidi touched him, without hesitation. They moved together like they were trying to memorise one another, like this—this rare stillness, this aching closeness—was something borrowed and beautiful and not to be wasted.

They ordered room service and didn't leave the suite. They ate with bare feet curled under them on the couch, shared bites from the same plate, laughed softly over spilled champagne and ridiculous late-night movie choices.

They didn't talk about work.

They didn't talk about what came next.

They stayed in the moment, wrapped in a fragile kind of joy that neither of them had known how much they needed until it was right there between them. Adrian held her like he never wanted to let her go. And Heidi, for once, didn't try to think her way out of the way she felt.

# Chapter Six

Heidi left on Sunday in the late afternoon, her hair still damp from their last shower, her lips swollen from too many kisses that felt like promises neither of them were ready to make. She kissed him goodbye at the door, soft and lingering, then slipped out with a quiet see you tomorrow and a look that said she didn't want to go.

And that was when reality set in.

The moment the door clicked shut, the silence in the suite turned heavy. Adrian sat on the edge of the bed, a glass of untouched whiskey in his hand, staring at nothing while the soft echo of her laughter still lingered in the room. He hadn't wanted to think about what waited outside that room. But the outside world didn't wait for permission.

By evening, the news had broken.

*WERRINGTON DIVORCE SHOCKER: GOLDEN COUPLE SPLIT AFTER ONE YEAR OF MARRIAGE.*

The headlines were everywhere—financial news blogs, society columns, business gossip sites. Cleo's publicist had been busy, spinning the narrative with practiced precision. Their one-year marriage, painted in glossy photographs and charity gala appearances, had officially come to an end.

But that wasn't the part that made Adrian's jaw tighten.

It was what came next.

*INSIDE SOURCES CLAIM THE CAUSE OF THE SPLIT WASN'T MONEY— BUT ANOTHER WOMAN. WERRINGTON WEALTH'S NEW CFO, HEIDI GIBSON.*

Adrian stared at the screen, the words blaring back at him with sharp, cold finality.

There it was.

The speculation. The judgment. *The scandal.*

People had always loved the illusion of his perfect marriage. Now they'd devour the mess of its ending.

But this? Dragging Heidi into it?

It made his blood boil.

They didn't know the truth—that he and Cleo had been over long before Heidi ever came into his orbit. That Heidi wasn't the reason the marriage failed—she was the reason he'd finally walked away from something that had been killing him in slow, quiet ways.

Still, it didn't matter what was true.

Not in the court of public opinion.

Not in an industry where perception could be everything.

Adrian set down his glass, jaw clenched, already thinking about how to protect her—how to get ahead of the story, how to keep this from becoming something that would hurt her career or reputation. She didn't deserve to be caught in the fallout of his broken past.

She deserved better than that.

Better than him.

And for the first time since Friday night, the glow of the weekend dimmed beneath the shadow of what came next.


Heidi had no idea what was waiting for her Monday morning.

She'd gotten home early Sunday night, her body deliciously sore, her skin still carrying the memory of Adrian's touch. The suite had felt like another world—one where time didn't exist, and reality had been put on mute. She'd stepped out of it reluctantly, like surfacing from a dream she wasn't ready to wake from.

At home, she'd just stripped out of her clothes, slipped between the sheets, and fell into the deepest, most content sleep she'd had in years.

But by 8:47 a.m. Monday morning, the spell had shattered.

The first sign was the whispering.

It started as she walked through the sleek glass doors of Werrington Wealth's headquarters—polite greetings that came with too-wide smiles and quick glances that flicked away the second she met them. Her heels clicked against the tile, the sound oddly sharp in the sudden quiet that followed her through the reception area.

Then came the silence in the elevator. The way the junior analysts from finance stopped talking mid-sentence when she stepped in. She smiled anyway, kept her posture straight, her gaze forward. But her stomach twisted.

She reached her floor and walked out into more of the same: conversations halting, eyes trailing her, hushed murmurs just under the surface.

She didn't know what had happened—yet. But she felt it in her bones.

Then she saw it.

On her desk, left by some well-meaning assistant, was a neatly printed article from The Wall Street Ledger. She picked it up with steady hands.

## *CFO OR FEMME FATALE? WERRINGTON DIVORCE SPARKS SCANDAL.*

Her breath caught.

Beneath the bold headline was a subheading that made her stomach turn:

*SOURCES SAY BILLIONAIRE ADRAIN WERRINGTON'S NEW CFO WAS MORE THAN JUST A COLLEAGUE—INSIDERS ALLEGE SHE'S THE REASON HIS MARRIAGE ENDED.*

Heidi stood frozen, the article trembling between her fingers.

There were blurry photos embedded in the piece—her and Adrian dancing at the retirement party two weeks ago.

She lowered the paper slowly, the office around her tilting sideways for just a second. Her pulse pounded in her ears.

She knew the truth.

She knew she had nothing to do with the demise of his marriage. That nothing had happened until the divorce was finalised. That their weekend together had been private, sacred even. Something only they knew about.

But now…

Her career. Her reputation. Everything she'd worked so hard to build—suddenly in the crosshairs of a story she hadn't signed up for.

She felt the ground shift beneath her, a slow sinking dread pressing against the fragile bubble she hadn't realised she'd been living in.


It was early Monday morning when Adrian found her in the solarium of the penthouse, she now called hers. Sunlight streamed through the floor-to-ceiling windows, glinting off the marble floors and catching in the sleek wave of her perfectly styled hair. She was lounging on a cream-colored chaise, barefoot, in silk loungewear, a mimosa in hand and a smug little smile dancing on her lips.

She didn't even look surprised to see him.

"Adrian," Cleo purred, setting her glass down with exaggerated grace. "To what do I owe the pleasure?"

He didn't bother with pleasantries. He stepped into the room like a man on a mission, his jaw tight, his eyes cold. He hadn't seen her since the final signatures were inked— since she took the penthouse, the cheque, and left his life with a self-satisfied smirk. But this—this was war.

"You planted the story," he said flatly. "About me and Heidi."

Cleo blinked once. Slowly. "What story?"

"Don't play dumb." His voice was steel. "The article in the Ledger. The so-called 'inside source.' The implication that Heidi caused our divorce."

She tilted her head, feigning innocence. "Are you implying I would leak something to the press?"

He didn't flinch. "I'm saying you already did."

Cleo gave a soft laugh, all feigned offense and manufactured grace. "You're giving me far too much credit. I have better things to do than feed gossip to tabloids."

"You always did enjoy controlling the narrative," he said, stepping closer. "But let me make something clear—if you're trying to ruin Heidi's reputation out of spite, I will bury whatever's left of yours."

Cleo's smile faltered—just for a second. Then she rolled her eyes. "God, Adrian. You're so dramatic."

He didn't move. "I want the name of whoever leaked it."

"I didn't leak anything." She stood now, arms folded, face hardening. "Do you really think I need to lift a finger for this to blow up? You were photographed together."

"The timing—the wording—it's designed to make her look like she seduced me out of my marriage, which is complete bull,"

"Well," she said sweetly, "you did look pretty seduced dancing with her."

He advanced a step, voice low. "We were over long before she came into the picture. And you know it."

Cleo's eyes flashed. "Of course I know it, Adrian. But you think the rest of the world cares? You think the board, the press, your investors care about your timeline?"

He stared at her, seeing her for exactly who she was—every inch the woman who had once known how to get under his skin and now took pleasure in trying to claw at the person he cared about.

"I didn't do it," she said finally, cool and clipped. "Not this time. But don't expect me to clean up your mess either. You want to play house with your CFO? Fine. Just don't cry when it gets complicated."

Adrian's voice dropped to a warning growl. "If you come after her again—directly or indirectly—I swear to God, Cleo, I'll come after you with everything I've got."

Cleo gave a slow, practiced shrug. "You always did like your little threats."

"They're not threats," he said, turning to go. "They're promises."

And then he was gone, leaving behind nothing but the fading echo of his footsteps and the first flicker of real fear in Cleo's perfectly lined eyes.


Not long after leaving Cleo, Adrian stood by the tall windows of his office, the city sprawled out beneath him like a kingdom he no longer wanted to rule. The phone was pressed to his ear, his jaw tight, shoulders tense. The scandal had already started its slow, brutal burn through the news cycle—every headline screaming about betrayal, power plays, and boardroom affairs. He knew how these things worked. He'd helped shape a few narratives himself over the years. But this time, the person at the centre of it wasn't him. It was Heidi.

And that was unacceptable. She was innocent.

Alan's voice came through the line, calm but clipped. "It's going to be bad, Adrian. They're going to turn her into a villain."

"I know," Adrian said, watching the headlines scroll across the screen in his office:

"I spoke with PR," Alan continued. "We can issue a statement, deny everything, shift the blame back to the press… but it won't kill the story. Not without blood."

Adrian closed his eyes, his hand tightening around the phone. "What are you saying?"

"I'm saying the only way to protect her reputation is to give the press something bigger. Something truer. If they knew the marriage was a lie—if they knew Cleo faked a pregnancy to trap you—it would change the narrative. Completely."

Adrian didn't speak.

Alan sighed. "Look, I know you probably don't want that to come out. But it's the only way."

There was a long pause.

Adrian's eyes drifted toward the desk across the room—the one where he'd finally lost control, where he'd tasted everything he'd been denying with Heidi for months. The memory burned hot beneath his skin, but it wasn't lust that gripped him now—it was purpose.

Alan's voice broke the silence, gentler now. "Is your CFO's reputation worth all this, Adrian?"

Adrian didn't blink. "Yes."

Alan let that settle. A beat of silence passed between them.

"Then you have two options," he said finally. "Talk to Cleo. Convince her to release a statement—say the marriage was already over, that Heidi had nothing to do with it. Or we go public ourselves. The medical reports are ready."

Adrian nodded once, jaw set. "I'll speak to her. But if she doesn't say it by midnight, we release everything."

Alan's voice was cold steel. "We give them the truth. And let them choke on it."


An hour later Adrian stepped inside the penthouse for the second time that day. The concierge had let him up without announcement—Cleo still had privileges, but he still had keys. That balance of power was about to shift permanently.

Cleo was lounging in the sunken living room, scrolling through her phone with feigned nonchalance. The moment she saw him; her mouth curved into a smile that didn't reach her eyes.

"Back so soon?" she said, setting the phone down. "I take it not everyone's swooning over your CFO."

Adrian didn't respond immediately. He crossed the room with the slow, deliberate calm of a man who had already decided how this would end.

"I'm not here to debate the fallout," he said coolly. "I'm here to give you a choice."

Cleo arched a brow. "A choice?"

He stopped in front of her, eyes cold, jaw tight. "Tomorrow, I'm releasing a full account of what ended our marriage. The truth. Including the faked pregnancy."

Her expression flickered—but only for a second. "You wouldn't."

"I will," he said. "Unless you speak to the press tonight. You tell them what you and I both know—that our marriage was over months before Heidi Gibson entered the picture. That it was appearances, not affection, holding us together."

Cleo stood, arms folding across her chest. "And if I don't?"

"Then I go public with everything. The doctors' reports. The falsified bloodwork. The NDA you tried to get me to sign to keep me quiet. All of it."

"You'd humiliate me?" she hissed, voice sharp with disbelief. "Destroy me?"

"No," Adrian said, his voice low and even. "You did that the moment you tried to destroy someone who had nothing to do with your lies."

Cleo's facade cracked, just slightly. "You always did like playing the hero."

"This isn't about playing anything." He stepped closer, towering over her now. "It's about ending this. You said you wanted to be free—well, here it is. But I won't let you rewrite history just to make yourself feel better. Heidi isn't your scapegoat."

"And if I tell the truth," she said bitterly, "what do I get?"

"You get to keep what dignity you have left," he said. "You get to walk away with the narrative you crafted—glossy, graceful, on your terms. Or you get dragged through every headline in the country as the woman who tried to fake a child to trap a billionaire."

Silence stretched between them. Cleo's jaw clenched. Her hands trembled slightly, barely perceptible.

"You have until midnight," Adrian said finally. "After that, the truth goes out with or without your voice in it."

He turned and walked to the door.

"And Cleo?" he said over his shoulder.

She didn't respond.

He looked back, his gaze sharp. "Next time you try to come for someone I care about; be sure you can survive the blowback."

Then he left, the door shutting behind him with the finality of a chapter ending.

# Chapter Seven

By Monday afternoon, when Adrian finally knocked on her office door, the weight of the moment tightened across his shoulders like a noose.

"Come in," Heidi called, her voice flat, tired.

She looked up as he entered. Not angry—just worn down, like life had taken too many pieces from her. There was a hollowness in her eyes, a quiet kind of ache, like someone who'd been bracing for impact far too long.

"Adrian."

"I came to let you know what's going to happen," he said.

She leaned back in her chair, arms folding loosely. "I already know. The press has their narrative. I'm the woman who destroyed your marriage."

He flinched, the word hitting sharper than it should've. "Cleo's making a statement tonight."

That got her attention. Her brow lifted. "What kind of statement?"

"She's going to tell the truth—that the marriage was over long before you ever walked into this office."

Heidi blinked, stunned. "She agreed to that?"

"I gave her a choice," he said. "Tell the press, or I do. And if I do, I tell them everything. The real truth."

The colour drained from her face. She rose slowly from her chair.

"No," she breathed. "Adrian, you can't do that."

"I can," he said. "And I will."

"You'd expose all of it? That she faked a pregnancy? That the entire marriage was built on a lie?"

His jaw tensed. "If that's what it takes to clear your name."

She stared at him; disbelief etched across her face. "You're giving up your privacy, your control, your dignity—for me? Why would you do that?"

"Because you're innocent," he said simply. "And you don't deserve to be crucified for something you didn't do."

She turned away, her voice quiet but trembling. "Adrian, this will follow you for the rest of your life."

"Then let it," he said quietly. "I've spent a year protecting a lie. I won't let her control the narrative anymore."

She turned back to him, tears shining in her eyes. "You're blowing up your own life, Adrian."

He stepped closer, the distance between them crackling with everything unsaid. His voice was rough with regret. "I already blew it up the day I married Cleo. That was my choice. My damage. None of this is on you."

Her gaze dropped, her shoulders drawing in. "You know what happened this weekend… it can't happen again."

Adrian didn't respond right away. He just looked at her, as if memorising her face, the lines of heartbreak and strength written into it.

Finally, he nodded. "I know."


Adrian read the press statement from Cleo Werrington for the third time, the words scrolling across the screen like a carefully rehearsed monologue.


*Adrian and I have shared years of our lives together, but unfortunately, not all stories end the way we hope. The truth is our marriage was effectively over long before Heidi Gibson ever stepped foot inside Werrington Wealth. She had nothing to do with the end of our marriage. Adrian and I were simply not well-suited. We tried—truly we did—but that chapter of our lives closed a long time ago. I wish him the best as we both move forward separately.*


A clean break. Sanitised, even. But it was something.

His phone buzzed in his hand. Alan.

"This should calm the waters," Alan said without preamble. "You've got three sympathetic headlines already. 'Cleo Werrington Sets Record Straight.' That kind of thing."

Adrian leaned against the edge of his desk, staring out at the city skyline, washed in the soft glow of night. "Let's hope so."

There was a pause on the other end of the line before Alan asked, more softly now, "So Adrian, tell me—what is Heidi to you anyway? Are you… interested in her?"

Adrian exhaled, the breath leaving him slowly, thick with the weight of everything unsaid. His fingers curled tighter around the phone, knuckles pale.

"If she wasn't my CFO," he said quietly, his voice stripped of pretence, "yes. I would be."

Alan was silent for a beat. Then, gently, "But she is."

Adrian closed his eyes. "Which means it can't happen."

A pause.

*Not yet.*


The press storm that had once felt like a tidal wave receded almost overnight. Cleo Werrington's carefully crafted statement had done what even the most expensive publicist couldn't—diffuse the drama. The narrative shifted from scandal to sympathy, and for the first time in weeks, Heidi could walk through the halls of Werrington Wealth without sensing eyes burning into her back.

To her relief, the whispers stopped. The sidelong glances faded. But the ache inside her didn't.

The real problem wasn't the press—it was Adrian.

Being near him was becoming unbearable.

It wasn't the tension of a secret anymore; it was the longing. The craving. Every time she walked past his office, her steps faltered. Every time he spoke in a meeting, her body reacted like a live wire had been touched. She saw him in every reflective surface, every late-night email, every breathless pause before she opened a door, hoping—dreading— that he'd be there.

Heidi had thought that crossing that line with him—that night in the office, and everything that followed in the suite—might have satisfied the hunger, given her clarity.

It had done the opposite.

Now she couldn't forget how his hands felt on her skin. How his mouth had found hers like it had been waiting all his life to do it. How he'd looked at her afterward, not like a man full of regret, but like a man utterly undone.

There had been near misses. Moments where she almost let herself give in.

Once, she'd stayed late and he'd come into her office with two cups of coffee, the silence between them deafening as she reached for the mug and their fingers brushed. She pulled her hand back like it had touched a live wire. He hadn't said a word—but the look in his eyes had made her breath catch.

Another time, during a board prep meeting, their knees had accidentally touched under the table. It was a flash of contact—half a second—but her entire body had felt it. So had his. She saw it in the way he swallowed hard, in the way his pen paused mid-note.

They were unravelling slowly.

Carefully.

Inevitably.

And still, she avoided him. Not out of anger. Not even out of fear.

Out of self-preservation.

Because if she let herself fall again, there would be no coming back.

And she didn't know if her heart could survive loving him completely, only to have to pretend again by morning.


The silence in his new penthouse wasn't peaceful—it was punishing. Every room felt colder now. Even the whisky in his glass tasted dull.

He stared out over the city skyline, lights blinking like distant promises he no longer believed in. He'd spent the last two weeks holding himself back with the kind of discipline he used to pride himself on. Now, it felt like a slow form of torment.

Cleo's press release had done its job—he hadn't received a single call from the board in days. The tabloids had backed off, the whispers at the office had all but stopped, and Heidi's reputation had been restored.

But his peace hadn't returned.

If anything, the quiet only made him more aware of what he couldn't have.

Heidi Gibson was everywhere.

In the rustle of paper across the boardroom table. In the smell of coffee outside his door. In the echo of her heels down the corridor. She didn't avoid him—not completely— but she kept her distance. Always professional. Always composed.

But he could see it in her eyes. That flicker of restraint. That hesitation. That same pull that was undoing him more and more every damn day.

They'd been circling each other like fire and oxygen. One spark away from burning down everything they'd built.

He hated that he couldn't touch her. Hated even more that he wanted to. The memory of her—bare beneath him, breathless and soft, her body arching into his—haunted him in moments he was supposed to be focused. The way she'd looked up at him in the hotel suite, like she felt it too, like she knew this was more than a mistake.

And then she'd disappeared behind professionalism again. Like it had never happened. Like he hadn't held her all night.

He'd told Alan the truth.

If she weren't his CFO, he wouldn't hesitate. He'd be with her. Fully, unapologetically.

But she was his CFO. And she had everything to lose.

He couldn't ask her to risk that.

*Could he?*

Adrian turned from the window, running a hand down his face. He hadn't gotten to the top of Werrington Wealth by making impulsive decisions. But nothing about how he felt about Heidi made sense. It made him question every choice he'd made before her.

He picked up his phone. No new messages.

He wanted to text her. To tell her he couldn't stop thinking about her. That he missed her voice, her laugh, the way her eyes softened when she looked at him like she was trying not to fall.

But he didn't.

Instead, he opened her last email, reread her clinical report about quarterly forecasts, and stared at her name on the screen like it could answer the questions screaming in his chest.

How long can I keep pretending this doesn't matter?

And worse—how long can she?


Thursday afternoon.

It had been nearly four weeks since she'd felt Adrian's hands on her skin, his mouth against hers, his body tangled with hers in a moment she still relived in the quiet hours of the night.

And it was slowly driving her out of her mind.

Heidi sat in the glass-walled conference room, surrounded by Werrington Wealth's top executives. The fluorescent lights overhead buzzed faintly, and she blinked hard, trying to focus on the spreadsheet projected on the screen.

But the numbers swam.

She'd barely slept all week. Food had lost its appeal, replaced by a queasy discomfort that lingered from morning until late afternoon. She'd chalked it up to stress. After all, she was the woman the press had whispered about, the woman Cleo Werrington had defended in a surprise press release.

That kind of pressure clung like a second skin.

But this was something else.

Her body felt foreign. Heavy. Off-balance. And right now, the heat in the room was unbearable. She shifted in her seat, blinking away the grey creeping into her vision.

"…we'll need to reevaluate the forecast if we want the board's approval," someone said. She couldn't even tell who. It was all a blur.

She reached for her water, her hand trembling as she brought it to her lips.

Then the room tilted.

The sounds became distant, warped.

"Heidi?" someone said.

And then everything went black.


Adrian was on his feet before her body hit the floor.

"Heidi!"

Panic tore through him like fire. The conference table scraped back as he lunged forward, dropping to his knees beside her. Her skin was pale, her forehead clammy, her lips parted as her chest rose and fell in shallow breaths.

"Call the paramedics!" someone shouted, but Adrian was already pulling off his suit jacket, slipping it beneath her head.

"Heidi, stay with me," he whispered, brushing the hair from her face, the back of his fingers pressing lightly to her cheek.

He didn't care that half the executive team was watching.

He didn't care that protocol would call this inappropriate.

All he saw was her.

The woman who haunted his thoughts. The woman he couldn't stop wanting. The woman he was sure he was falling in love with.

And she was unconscious in his arms.

Her lashes fluttered slightly, a soft sound leaving her throat.

"Adrian…?" she murmured, barely audible.

"I'm here," he said immediately. "You fainted. Help is on the way. Just stay with me, alright?"

She blinked up at him, dazed, and confused, her gaze anchoring to his. Something passed between them then, fragile, and unspoken. Fear, vulnerability… and something deeper.

Adrian gritted his jaw, holding her close without caring who saw. All the restraint, all the waiting—it didn't matter now.

Not if something was wrong.

He couldn't lose her.

Not now.

Not ever.


The boardroom had never been so quiet.

The sleek glass walls, once a symbol of power and precision, now loomed like transparent sentinels—witnesses to a moment no one quite knew how to interpret. The executive team had been ushered out quickly, their murmurs of concern fading behind the hush of closing doors, while paramedics moved in with efficient calm.

Heidi lay conscious now, her body angled carefully on a folded jacket—Adrian's, though no one had said it aloud. A thin sheen of perspiration clung to her forehead, her lashes damp, her breath steadying in uneven waves. The colour was slowly returning to her cheeks, but her stillness held a fragility that made even the seasoned paramedics tread gently.

One of them, a young woman with a calm voice and a clipboard in hand, adjusted the cuff on Heidi's arm. Beside her, her partner uncapped a water bottle and passed it to Heidi.

"You're stabilising," the paramedic said with a professional kind of kindness. "Your blood pressure's coming up. You're dehydrated—that's likely what caused the fainting."

"I'm fine," Heidi whispered, her voice raw with fatigue. "Just need a minute."

"You need more than a minute," the woman replied, not unkindly. "You need proper rest, hydration, and a checkup with your GP as soon as possible. No arguments."

Heidi didn't give any. She nodded once, almost imperceptibly, her fingers tightening slightly around the bottle.

Outside, Adrian paced.

His tie was half-loosened, his phone forgotten in his hand. Unread messages pulsed on the screen, demanding attention he couldn't spare. Every few seconds, he glanced toward the glass door, willing it to open, willing someone to give him news that didn't make his gut twist into knots.

He hadn't breathed properly since he'd seen her fall.

The image was etched into him now—Heidi crumpling in that designer dress, her body collapsing in a silence so loud it had drowned everything else. For a moment, just one agonising beat, she hadn't moved. And he'd felt something split in him.

The door finally creaked open.

One of the paramedics stepped out, clipboard under her arm, her gaze scanning until it landed on him. She closed the door softly behind her, preserving what little privacy remained.

Adrian was beside her in an instant. "Is she alright?"

"She's stable," the paramedic said. "But she's exhausted and severely dehydrated. Her vitals are normalising now, but she needs to take this seriously. We're not transporting her—she insisted she's okay—but she must see her doctor. Soon."

Adrian's jaw clenched, but he nodded. "I'll make sure of it."

The woman paused, then softened her tone. "She needs real rest. No work. No stress. No long nights in boardrooms. And someone to keep an eye on her."

He didn't answer—just nodded again, tighter this time.

With a quiet nod, she moved past him, her partner trailing behind.

The hallway fell silent again.

Adrian stared at the closed door, the same glass he'd stood behind countless times—only now, it felt like a barrier he didn't know how to cross.

He wanted to go to her.

To sit beside her.

To make her drink that damn water, to carry her out if she so much as hesitated.

To say everything he hadn't said.

To admit what he'd only just begun to understand—that she mattered more than he'd let himself believe.

But that door wasn't just glass.

Not anymore.

Not since the hotel.

Not since she'd started pulling away, brick by brick, with that same quiet grace that was now keeping him out.

He raked a hand down his face, trying to calm the drumbeat of his heart.

When the door opened again, Heidi stood there.

Pale, but upright. A bottle of water gripped in one hand. The other braced against the doorframe, as if she wasn't quite convinced, she could hold herself up without it.

Their eyes locked.

Time suspended, just long enough for the breath in his lungs to catch.

"Are you okay?" he asked, stepping forward instinctively—then stopping himself.

"Yes." Her voice was soft. "Just need to go home. Rest."

"I'll call you a car—"

"I've already ordered one." She glanced away, then back. "Thank you… for before."

He nodded, the words sticking in his throat. "Anytime."

She turned slightly, ready to walk away.

"Heidi."

She stopped.

He stepped forward, just enough for his voice to lower. "Please see your doctor. Don't make me come looking if you don't."

Something flickered in her expression—elusive and unreadable. Not anger. Not indifference. Just something she wasn't ready to let him see.

"I will," she said quietly. "I promise."

Then she was gone.

He watched her retreat down the hallway, her heels clicking softly on the marble, the sound too fragile, too final.

Her posture was composed, but he saw it—the tremor in her hand as she checked her phone. The subtle wobble in her steps. The way she blinked hard, too many times.

And something inside him twisted.

Something dangerous.

Something permanent.

Something he didn't know how to name—

Only that it wouldn't go away.

# Chapter Eight

The sterile smell of antiseptic clung to the air, sharp and clinical, as Heidi sat on the edge of the examination table. The paper beneath her crinkled with every nervous shift. A blood pressure cuff lay discarded on the counter, and her blouse was still slightly wrinkled from the rushed exam. She stared at the closed door, her fingers woven tightly together in her lap.

She hadn't expected to be here today.

She hadn't expected any of this.

After the episode in the boardroom, she'd promised she'd see her doctor. But promises were easy to make when you were light-headed and surrounded by concerned professionals. Now, alone in a quiet exam room, the reality of it all sat heavy on her shoulders.

The door clicked open.

Dr. Lively, a woman in her mid-forties with warm eyes and a no-nonsense energy, stepped in, holding a slim tablet. She glanced at Heidi, then at the vitals on her screen.

"Well," she said gently, "you weren't kidding when you said the last few weeks have been stressful."

Heidi gave a tired smile. "Understatement of the year."

Dr. Lively approached, tapping her screen before setting the tablet on the counter.

"Heidi," she said, her tone shifting ever so slightly, "your labs are back."

Heidi straightened unconsciously. Something about the doctor's voice—measured, steady—tightened the air.

"Your blood sugar was low. You're dehydrated, and your iron levels are slightly below where they should be," the doctor continued. "Nothing alarming—just signs your body's been running on fumes."

"Yeah," Heidi murmured. "That sounds about right."

"And…" Dr. Lively paused. A small, meaningful breath. "Your HCG levels are elevated."

Heidi blinked, confused. "I'm sorry—my what?"

Dr. Lively's smile was soft. "Congratulations, Heidi. You're pregnant."

The room stilled.

Heidi stared, unmoving, her brain slow to register the words. They didn't sound real. Not in this room. Not after the week she'd had. Not after barely keeping it together for the last two months.

"Pregnant," she echoed faintly.

Dr. Lively nodded. "About four weeks based on the hormone levels. We'll do an ultrasound soon to confirm gestation and make sure everything is progressing normally."

Heidi shook her head slowly, more in disbelief than denial. Her hand moved unconsciously to her abdomen.

"But I—" Her voice faltered. "I didn't… I wasn't planning…"

"You wouldn't be the first woman to be surprised," the doctor said gently. "But now that we know, the most important thing is taking care of you. You need more rest, more fluids, and absolutely no skipping meals. Your body's already working overtime."

A breath caught in Heidi's chest. A thousand thoughts collided in her mind—Adrian, the boardroom, the hotel, the silent space she'd built between them like armour. The future, sudden and fragile, had arrived without knocking.

Dr. Lively tilted her head, watching her. "Do you want a moment?"

"No," Heidi said quietly. "I'm okay. Just… processing."

"That's normal." The doctor handed her a small printout with follow-up instructions. "Schedule a prenatal appointment this week. And call me if you feel faint again—don't wait."

Heidi nodded, still not quite trusting her voice. The doctor smiled once more, then stepped out, giving her the room.

And suddenly, it was just her.

Her and the quiet hum of the fluorescent light overhead. Her and the paper-covered table. Her and the invisible shift in her world.

*Pregnant.*

The word echoed in her mind, not sharp, but soft. Trembling. It didn't feel real yet. But it was there now. Anchored. Permanent.

She exhaled slowly, her hand still resting protectively over her abdomen, her heart thudding louder than it had in days.

A baby. *His baby.*

The thought bloomed quietly inside her, unexpected but strangely warm. She hadn't planned this—God, not even close—but something deep and instinctive stirred at the realisation. A smile touched the corners of her lips, soft and tentative. She was… happy. In the middle of the chaos, the fear, the uncertainty—she was happy.

But then came his name.

Adrian.

Her smile faded, replaced by a knot of worry that curled in her stomach. How was he going to react? Could she even tell him?

He'd just clawed his way free from a cold, calculated marriage—one built on a lie about a child that never existed. And now, weeks later, she was carrying his.

No. She couldn't tell him. Not yet.

She wouldn't be the woman who trapped him, who reignited his worst fears. And more than that, she wouldn't accept a ring given out of guilt or obligation. She wouldn't marry a man who didn't love her—not even Adrian Werrington.

Especially not Adrian Werrington.

Her throat tightened as she pressed her fingers lightly against her belly, her eyes stinging. God, what was she going to do?

It wasn't just her anymore.

And somehow, that made everything feel both impossibly fragile—and fiercely, undeniably real.


It was Saturday afternoon, and Heidi still hadn't made up her mind about how to deal with her pregnancy. The weight of the decision pressed down on her, making every thought feel heavier than the last. She hadn't expected to feel so lost, so uncertain, but here she was, pacing her apartment in the quiet hours of the afternoon, grappling with the truth inside her.

She knew she couldn't keep the secret forever. She intended to tell Adrian before the baby was born, but not yet. It was too soon. He had just gotten out of a loveless marriage; one built on lies. How could she burden him with more? How could she add this to his already overwhelming life?

The fear of his reaction twisted in her chest. Would he see her as just another complication? Another mess? She didn't want to be that for him—not after everything.

A knock on the door broke her train of thought, and she froze.

She hadn't expected company—not today. Not now.

Her pulse quickened as she walked toward the door, instinctively smoothing her hand over her stomach, as if the simple gesture could calm the storm inside her. She hesitated, breathing deep, before finally pulling the door open.

"Adrian."

His name slipped from her lips in a whisper, edged with surprise and something softer— something that warmed the chill that had settled in her chest over the past few days.

He stood there, tall and commanding, his dark eyes locking with hers, a storm of emotion swirling behind them. His hair was slightly tousled, like he'd run his hands through it more than once on the drive over. And instead of his usual sharp suit and silk tie, he wore jeans and a charcoal-gray T-shirt that hugged his frame in a way that made it hard for her to breathe.

There was something different about him today—less armour, more rawness. Something in his expression looked… unguarded. Real.

For a long, suspended moment, neither of them said anything. The air between them was thick with everything they hadn't said, everything they couldn't.

"I came to see if you're okay," he said at last, his voice low and steady, but threaded with something she couldn't quite name—concern, guilt, maybe more.

Heidi swallowed hard. She'd told herself to keep her distance. That space was necessary. But now, standing here, with him on her doorstep, the ache of wanting him near swelled too strong to ignore.

"I feel much better," she said quietly, stepping aside to let him in.

He hesitated for just a beat, then crossed the threshold, his presence filling the space like he belonged there.

"You look much better," he said, his eyes scanning her face, as though memorising the return of colour to her cheeks.

Her apartment wasn't large, but it was warm and inviting—tasteful, functional, feminine. The living room flowed into the kitchen in a soft open-plan layout. A cream sofa sat in front of a modest bookshelf and a low coffee table scattered with design magazines and half-read novels. The kitchen was neat, with brushed steel appliances and pale wood cabinets that gleamed in the afternoon light filtering through sheer white curtains.

"Coffee?" she offered.

"Yes, please," he said, his voice quieter now.

He moved to the kitchen bench and perched on one of the stools, watching her as she moved around the kitchen with graceful ease—measuring out the coffee, filling the kettle, her every motion fluid despite the turmoil swirling inside her.

And he watched her like he didn't want to miss a single second. Like her every breath, every glance, every quiet motion around the kitchen meant more than he could admit out loud.

They made small talk over coffee—light, easy, careful. She told him she'd caught up on sleep, he told her the board meeting had been rescheduled. Neither of them mentioned the deeper things—the collapse, the fear in his eyes, the way her body had trembled afterward. They weren't ready. Not yet.

But something simmered beneath the surface, a quiet urgency neither of them could name.

When the mugs were empty and the silence stretched a little too long, Adrian rose from his seat.

"I'm glad you're feeling better," he said softly, his eyes lingering on hers.

She walked him to the door, her bare feet whispering across the floor. When she reached for the handle, her hand paused—hovered there, trembling slightly.

He didn't move to leave. Neither of them did.

Their eyes met, and time seemed to pause, the silence thick with everything they hadn't said but somehow understood.

"Heidi," he whispered, her name falling from his lips like a prayer.

She turned to him slowly, her heart pounding so hard she thought he might hear it in the quiet. Her breath caught in her throat, lodged somewhere between hope and hesitation, between everything she wanted and everything she was afraid of.

Then he whispered her name again—so soft, so reverent it nearly broke her—and before she could think, before she could talk herself out of it, he kissed her.

There was no caution in it. No room left for restraint. His hands cupped her face like she was something fragile, something cherished, and the feel of his lips on hers was both new and achingly familiar. Her fingers curled into the front of his shirt, holding him close, grounding herself in the solidity of him.

Time unravelled. The world beyond her small apartment dissolved, leaving only the two of them suspended in the quiet hum of something inevitable.

He kissed her again and again, as if trying to memorise the shape of her mouth, the sound of her sighs. When he pulled back for breath, his forehead rested against hers, and in that shared silence, everything between them shifted.

He guided her backward gently, his hands never leaving her skin, past the sofa, into the softened golden light pouring in through the windows. Each step brought them closer to something unspoken, something that had always existed beneath the surface.

Every kiss deepened the ache between them; every touch erased a piece of the distance they'd fought so hard to maintain. His fingers slid over the curve of her waist, under the hem of her shirt, reverent and slow, as though rediscovering her all over again.

When he laid her down, it wasn't just desire—it was devotion. The kind that hummed in the air, in every brush of lips, every whispered breath.

They made love like it meant something—because it did.

There was no rush. Only the soft rhythm of bodies moving in sync, of hands holding on like they never wanted to let go. It was tender and intense, a slow-burning confession neither of them had found the words for.

I missed you.

I need you.

I never stopped.

She moaned his name, quiet and broken, and he buried his face against her neck, breathing her in like she was air.

Afterward, the world returned in hushed tones and warm skin. Heidi lay draped against him, her cheek pressed to his chest, the steady thrum of his heartbeat beneath her ear. His arms held her like he'd been waiting a lifetime to do so, his fingers tracing gentle, absentminded circles down the length of her back.

She didn't know how to tell him yet. The words hovered on the edge of her lips, caught somewhere between longing and fear, tangled up with the secret blooming quietly inside her.

She wanted him—God, she wanted him. Every slow breath, every brush of his fingers against her skin, every heartbeat synced with his—it all tethered her to something deeper than she was ready to name. The truth of what he meant to her pulsed in every silent moment between them. But the deeper that truth sank in, the heavier the weight of what she hadn't said became.

This can't keep happening.

Not like this.

She couldn't keep falling into him when she was carrying something so monumental—something that would change both their lives forever. She couldn't keep losing herself in the feel of his touch while hiding the truth that lived quietly inside her, growing stronger by the day.

He had just broken free from a woman who lied to keep him. And now she carried the kind of truth that could bind him, too—whether he wanted it or not.

And then there was her own fear. Her career. The life she'd built with so much control and intention now felt like it stood on the edge of something uncertain, unpredictable. Could she really balance it all? The woman she'd fought to become, and the mother she was about to be.

Her fingers curled against his chest, and she closed her eyes.

This shouldn't be happening.

But God… she didn't want it to stop.

They ate takeout cross-legged on the floor, laughing over spilled soy sauce and arguing light-heartedly about which movie to stream. It felt easy—dangerously easy. The kind of comfort that made her forget the world outside her apartment, the decisions waiting just beyond the walls.

By the time the credits rolled, they were curled up together on the couch, her head on his shoulder, his hand resting on her thigh like it belonged there. No tension. No distance. Just warmth.

Later, in the quiet hush of her bedroom, they came together again.

It wasn't rushed. It was softer this time, slower—like they had all the time in the world. Like they'd finally surrendered to something that had been waiting for them all along. His mouth brushed hers with reverence, his hands moving over her body like he was relearning every inch. And she let him. Let herself forget everything except the way it felt to be his—to be wanted, seen, known.

She knew it should stop.

Knew it was dangerous, living in this suspended world where reality hadn't quite caught up.

But God… she wanted him.

She wanted the way he touched her like she was the only thing that mattered. The way he looked at her after, like he was seeing something sacred.

She wanted him so much, even if she didn't know how this ended.

It was Sunday afternoon by the time Adrian knew he had to leave. The sun filtered through the pale curtains, casting soft golden light across the room, and for a while, he'd let himself pretend this was normal. That he belonged here, tangled in sheets that smelled like her, sipping coffee from her favourite chipped mug, watching her move around her apartment like she wasn't already part of him.

But time didn't pause for them. And eventually, the weight of reality settled in his chest.

He pulled on his shirt slowly, eyes on her as she sat on the edge of the bed, her legs curled beneath her, her hair still mussed from sleep and something else he couldn't stop remembering.

He didn't want to go. But more than that, he didn't want to leave this… undefined.

He turned to her, voice quieter than he intended. "What now?"

He hadn't meant to sound so uncertain. Adrian Werrington was never uncertain. But with her—Heidi—it was different. She made him want things he'd long stopped believing he could have. Real things. Scary things.

She looked up at him, and for a moment, he thought she might answer with certainty, might give him something solid to hold onto.

But her gaze wavered, and her voice was barely above a whisper.

"I don't know."

And somehow, that truth—so simple, so raw—hurt more than anything else ever could.

Adrian's jaw tensed. He stepped closer, the calm unravelling from his voice.

"I want to see you again, Heidi."

She looked up at him, heart hammering in her chest. "We can't, Adrian. We work together."

That did it.

His expression darkened—not with cruelty, but frustration. He ran a hand through his hair, pacing a short line across her living room.

"I don't give a damn who knows," he bit out. "Let them talk. Let them speculate. I want to be with you. Isn't that enough?"

Her lips parted, but she couldn't speak right away. She stood, wrapping her arms around herself.

"It's not about gossip, Adrian. You're the CEO. You'll survive a scandal. I won't." Her voice trembled, even as she tried to hold it steady. "This world doesn't forgive women the way it forgives men. Especially women like me who've worked twice as hard to be taken seriously."

He stared at her, the fire still in his eyes—but behind it, something softer flickered. Understanding. Pain.

"So, what then?" he said quietly. "We just pretend this didn't happen. That it doesn't mean anything?"

She blinked fast, her throat tightening. "It means everything."

And that was the worst part.

She was already breaking her own heart.

Adrian looked at her like he was on the edge of something—like words were fighting to break free from his throat—but none of them made it past his lips. Just a long, quiet breath. A faint, reluctant nod.

Then he turned.

He moved to the door without another word.

And she didn't stop him.

He stepped out, the distance between them growing with each quiet footfall. He left without a backward glance, without a single word to fill the aching silence he left in his wake.

She stood frozen, staring at the door, her arms wrapped tightly around herself as if that could hold in everything threatening to break loose.

It wasn't until she heard the door click shut behind him—soft, final—that her composure cracked. The silence that followed was unbearable.

Tears welled up and spilled over before she could stop them.

She had chosen her silence. Her boundaries. Her career.

But in the stillness of that empty apartment, it didn't feel like strength.

It felt like losing him.

# Chapter Nine

Heidi had refined avoidance to an art.

Emails instead of face-to-face conversations. Calls rerouted through her assistant. In meetings, she sat at the far end of the table, voice clipped, expression neutral, posture pristine. All business. No room for anything else.

Adrian noticed every deflection. And every one of them made him want to put his fist through a wall.

It had been eight weeks since the weekend at her apartment. Eight weeks since her skin had burned beneath his hands, since she'd said his name like it mattered—like he mattered. Since he'd finally crossed the line, he'd been toeing for what felt like a lifetime.

And now? She wouldn't even look at him.

He stood in the doorway of the glass-walled conference room, jaw tight, watching her slip her laptop into her briefcase with clinical efficiency. The rest of the team had already filtered out, still murmuring about quarterly projections and the Berlin expansion.

She knew he was there. She just didn't care.

He waited. Then, quietly, "Heidi. Can we talk?"

Her hands didn't pause. "We just did. The audit team's numbers are solid. We're prepped for the presentation."

"You know that's not what I meant."

A soft sigh escaped her lips. Then—finally—she looked up. Her eyes were tired. Guarded. Not cold but calculated. Like she was balancing too many things at once and couldn't afford to let one slip.

"Adrian." She said his name like a period. "It was a mistake. We were a mistake. We were emotional. It shouldn't have happened."

He stared at her. The words doused him like ice water.

"A mistake?" he repeated. "Is that what you're calling it?"

Her lips twitched into something that might've been a smile if it hadn't been so hollow. "I don't think either of us need that kind of complication."

"Heidi, for God's sake. You think I just sleep with my CFOs when I'm having a rough week?"

She flinched—barely—but he saw it.

"I think we were both vulnerable," she said, quieter now. "And I think it can't happen again."

Something twisted in his chest. Confusion. Frustration. A sharp edge of something too raw to name.

"You're acting like none of it meant anything."

She met his gaze, steady and quiet. And for one brief, devastating second, he saw it— the truth. The ache she was trying to bury. The fear coiled just beneath her perfect composure.

"It can't mean anything," she said softly. "You're my boss. There's already talk. There's always talk. And I'm not going to be the woman who slept her way into a headline."

Adrian stepped closer, careful. "You're not collateral to me."

Her eyes flickered. Softened. But only for a heartbeat.

"Even if I believed that… it doesn't change anything. We don't get to have this."

Every move he made felt like skating on cracking ice—one misstep, and she'd vanish completely. And that scared him more than he wanted to admit.

She'd always been composed, controlled. Brilliant. And now she was using that same brilliance to shut him out—methodically, professionally, perfectly.

"Heidi," he said, voice low. "Talk to me. Really talk to me. I know something's going on."

"I'm fine."

Too fast. Too smooth.

He didn't buy it. Not for a second. But he also couldn't force her to tell him. And that—the powerlessness—nearly unmade him.

He was Adrian Werrington. He dictated boardrooms. He rewrote contracts with a look. He made kings out of corporations.

But with her?

He was helpless.

She slid her bag over her shoulder and met his eyes one final time.

"Please," she said, quietly. "Let's not make this harder than it already is."

And then she walked away—heels sharp against the polished floor, head high, shoulders straight. Like she hadn't just ripped something vital out of him.

Adrian stood there, fists clenched, heart a wreck of questions he couldn't answer.

He didn't know what she was hiding.

But whatever it was, it was slowly, silently destroying them both.


The waiting room smelled like lemon disinfectant and cheap perfume. Soft instrumental music played from a speaker overhead, too serene to match the storm churning in Heidi's chest.

She sat alone, ankles crossed, fingers curled around the edge of her bag. Twelve weeks. That's what they'd told her when she'd scheduled today's appointment. Twelve weeks, one day, and a few hours, depending on the scan.

Twelve weeks of pretending everything was fine.

The nurse called her name gently, as if afraid to disturb her. Heidi stood and followed her through a short hallway into the exam room, answering questions with clipped politeness. Blood pressure, weight, a few murmured reassurances.

"Your doctor will be right in," the nurse said, and left her with a paper gown, a folded sheet, and too much silence.

Heidi changed quickly, cold creeping across her skin as she perched on the edge of the exam table. She pressed her palms to her thighs, steadying herself. She hadn't wanted to come. But she had to. If not for herself, then for the tiny, flickering heartbeat inside her.

A knock. The door creaked open, and Dr. Velasquez entered, smiling warmly.

"Well, you look tired—but you also look like you're hanging in there," she said, setting down the tablet. "Let's take a peek at this little one, shall we?"

Heidi nodded. Her throat was too tight for words.

Moments later, the gel was cool on her skin. The wand moved across her abdomen, and then—there it was.

The sound filled the room.

A soft, rhythmic flutter. Fast. Steady. Alive.

A heartbeat.

Heidi blinked hard. She wasn't going to cry. Not here. Not in front of anyone.

Dr. Velasquez angled the screen so she could see the faint outline. "Twelve weeks, measuring right on track. Strong heartbeat. Everything looks good, Heidi."

She managed a small smile. "That's… good."

"You haven't brought anyone with you," the doctor said gently, not quite asking, but close.

"No," Heidi said quickly. "It's just me."

There was a pause. Then Dr. Velasquez nodded, professional as ever. "Well, you're doing great. I'll give you a few minutes to clean up, then we can go over the bloodwork and next steps."

When she was alone again, Heidi stared at the monitor a moment longer. She wasn't just pregnant.

She was going to be someone's mother.


Later that night, her mother's voice came through the phone that evening, soft and measured, like it always was when she knew Heidi was holding back.

"Tell me what's going on, sweetheart. You sound… far away."

Heidi sat on the floor of her apartment, knees tucked to her chest, the ultrasound photo resting on the coffee table like a secret. Like a confession.

"I had an appointment today," she said quietly. "Twelve weeks. Healthy heartbeat."

A breath on the other end of the line. "Oh, honey…"

"I haven't told him." Her voice cracked. "I can't."

"Is he married?"

"No. Divorced." A pause. "But it's complicated."

Her mother didn't respond right away. "Do you love him?"

Heidi closed her eyes. "Yes. But I can't tell him about the baby."

"Why not?"

"Because he is my boss. Because he was trapped by his ex-wife over a pregnancy. Because I've worked my whole life to be taken seriously, and this—this would make me look like a cliché. The pregnant employee. The scandal."

"You're not a scandal," her mother said firmly. "You're a human being. And that baby growing inside you? That's not a mistake, Heidi."

"I'm scared, Mum." Her voice dropped to a whisper. "I don't know how to do this. I don't know what he'll say. I don't even know if he wants this."

Her mother's voice softened even more. "You don't have to have all the answers tonight. But you do have to stop trying to carry this alone."

A tear slid down Heidi's cheek. She didn't wipe it away.

"I don't know how to tell him," she said. "And I'm not ready to hear him say something I can't unhear."

Silence stretched between them.

Finally, her mother spoke, gentle and sure. "Then wait. Wait until you're ready. But don't wait forever. Some truths only get heavier the longer you hold them."

Heidi looked down at the grainy black-and-white photo on the table. A tiny, perfect secret. A heartbeat she couldn't ignore.

Maybe not today. Maybe not tomorrow.

But soon.

Because this child deserved a father who knew they existed.

And maybe—just maybe—she deserved to be loved, even in the messy middle of it all.


Adrian stood by the window in his office, arms crossed, watching the city move like a living organism—bright, fast, and relentless.

He couldn't concentrate.

Emails piled up. His calendar blinked with meetings. But none of it touched him. His thoughts kept circling back to her.

To Heidi.

Twelve weeks. That's how long it had been since the weekend that changed everything. Since he'd kissed her, touched her, tasted her for the first time. Since she'd let herself fall into him like she'd needed it just as badly.

And then she'd pulled away.

At first, he'd told himself it was temporary. A cooling-off period. A return to boundaries and professionalism. They'd made a mistake, she'd said. They needed space.

But space had turned into silence.

She was barely in the same room with him anymore unless protocol demanded it. Her emails were terse. Her voice in meetings was cool, detached, stripped of every trace of intimacy. She smiled for everyone else—but not for him.

And it was starting to feel personal.

He didn't want to be the asshole boss who couldn't take no for an answer. He wasn't that man. But he also wasn't blind. He knew Heidi. Knew how she carried herself, how she hid things behind that impeccable composure.

And something was off.

Worse than off.

She was hiding something.

He saw it in the way she touched her stomach when she thought no one was looking—a small, absent gesture that made his pulse slow. He saw it in how pale she'd been lately, how exhausted. And there was that day last week when she disappeared midday, no explanation, and returned looking like she'd been crying in her car.

Adrian turned from the window and paced to his desk, jaw tight.

She wasn't just avoiding him. She was protecting herself.

From him.

He hated it.

He wanted to believe this was about work boundaries, about fear of office gossip or fallout. But deep down, something colder had started to gnaw at the edges of his thoughts.

What if it was something else entirely?

What if she was sick?

What if she was hurt?

What if—

His phone buzzed. A text from Alan:


***Lunch later? Or are you brooding over your CFO again?***


Adrian didn't reply.

Instead, he sank into his chair and opened the company calendar, scrolling through Heidi's week. She had a few meetings blocked out, some time off she hadn't explained, and an innocuous two-hour window labelled "appointment."

Adrian exhaled slowly.

That was the third one this month.

He stared at the screen for a long time.

Then he leaned back, rubbing a hand over his mouth, his chest tight with something unfamiliar.

It wasn't just professional distance. It wasn't regret. And it sure as hell wasn't indifference.

She was carrying something she wouldn't share. And whether she liked it or not, he felt it too.


Heidi stood in front of the mirror in the executive lounge, adjusting the soft cream blouse she'd chosen carefully that morning. The fabric draped over her belly just enough to hide the gentle swell, but she could see it—feel it—growing more obvious every day.

Fourteen weeks.

She smoothed the hem and took a steadying breath. Today was the day.

She had rehearsed it a dozen different ways. Calm. Clear. No expectations. Just the truth.

*'I'm pregnant. It's yours. I don't want anything from you, Adrian—I swear. I would never keep your child from you.'*

She would say it with dignity. With strength. Because whatever came after, her child deserved honesty. And so did he.

It was becoming torture not being able to talk to him. To touch him. To pretend like their weekend together hadn't unravelled her. Her body still ached for him at night, even when her mind warned her to keep her distance.

But the silence was killing her. And she was tired of being afraid.

She turned away from the mirror, one hand automatically coming to rest on her stomach. It had become a habit—protective, subconscious, instinctual.

The hallway was quiet as she stepped out, her heels clicking softly on the polished floor. Adrian's office was at the end, the door still closed. She'd timed it perfectly. He had a small break before his next meeting. She just had to reach it. Just had to get the words out.

But halfway there, the door opened.

And Cleo stepped out.

Heidi stopped in her tracks, heart dropping like a stone.

Cleo Werrington looked like a woman who didn't lose—sleek red dress, stilettos, diamonds at her throat like a warning. Her lips were curved into that faintly amused smile she always wore, like she'd just remembered something wicked and was saving it for later.

And then she saw Heidi.

Her gaze swept down, pausing—lingering—on the way Heidi's hand protectively cupped her abdomen.

Heidi dropped it immediately, but it was too late.

Cleo's smile sharpened.

"Well," she said, her voice silk-wrapped venom. "I see someone's been busy."

Heidi forced herself to keep her chin high, her tone neutral. "Cleo."

But Cleo only stepped closer, eyes glittering with amusement. "So, this is the angle now? You're going to trap him with a baby? Very retro. I didn't think you had it in you."

The words hit like a slap. Sharp. Mean. And not entirely unexpected.

"I'm not trapping anyone," Heidi said quietly, her throat tight. "I don't know what you're talking about."

Cleo laughed—a soft, mocking sound that made Heidi's stomach turn. "Oh, sweetheart. Do you honestly think you can hide it for much longer? You think a baby is your golden ticket? That he's going to what—fall madly in love with you? Marry you? Be the doting father? He's not going to fall for that one, again."

Heidi didn't respond. She didn't trust her voice.

Cleo leaned in, her perfume cloying and expensive. "You're not the first woman to think a child will give you leverage. Hell, I even tried. But here's the problem with betting on Adrian—he only plays games he can win."

The moment stretched, cruel and cold.

Then Cleo stepped back, tossing her hair over her shoulder.

"Best of luck," she said breezily. "You'll need it."

And with that, she sauntered down the hall, heels tapping out a triumphant rhythm as if she hadn't just gutted Heidi in a single conversation.

Heidi stood frozen.

Her hand found her stomach again. Protective. Shaken.

She had been so close. So close to telling him.

But now her heart felt too bruised. Her confidence cracked in half.

Because Cleo's words had hit a nerve she hadn't even known was exposed.

What if Adrian did think that?

What if everyone did?

Heidi turned away from Adrian's office and walked back the way she came, her steps quick and sharp, but the weight in her chest felt like it was pulling her down with each movement. Her head was down, her throat burning from the sharp sting of Cleo's words. They rattled in her mind, over and over again, and the ache was unbearable. She couldn't even stomach the idea of seeing Adrian now, knowing that the moment she'd been dreading had arrived, and she hadn't been able to face him.

Today wasn't the day after all.

Instead of going to Adrian's office, Heidi found herself heading to the HR department. She hadn't planned it. She hadn't thought about what she was going to say—she only knew she needed to leave. Right now.

She pushed the door open and stepped into the quiet office, where Laura, the HR assistant, looked up from her computer. She gave Heidi a polite smile, but it quickly faded as she saw the tension in Heidi's face.

"Is everything okay?" Laura asked, her voice gentle.

"I need to leave," Heidi said, her voice tight, strangled with emotion. "I have a family emergency. I need to go today. I'm so sorry, but it can't be helped."

Laura blinked, clearly surprised. "Of course, Heidi. Do you need any help with your leave of absence paperwork?"

"No," Heidi replied quickly, shaking her head. "I don't have time. I'll figure it out later. Just... just let them know I'm gone, please."

Laura's concern was evident, but she didn't press. She just nodded, pulling up a form to note Heidi's leave. "Take care of yourself," she said softly, handing Heidi the paperwork without further comment.

Heidi barely registered it as she grabbed the papers and turned away, her mind already elsewhere.

She hurried back to her office; her stomach twisted in a knot. The weight of everything she was about to leave behind—the responsibilities, the commitments, the impossible situation she'd put herself in—pressed on her with the force of a thousand pounds.

She didn't even give herself time to think about it. She packed her things quickly—papers, personal items, her laptop—anything she might need. There was no room to second-guess. No room to feel sorry for herself. She just had to get out.

Once everything was packed, Heidi walked down the hallway, avoiding eye contact with anyone. She didn't even bother saying goodbye to her colleagues, the people she had worked alongside for months. It felt like another life; one she wasn't a part of anymore. The door to the elevator closed behind her with a finality she could taste in the back of her throat.

She didn't look back as she left the building.

It wasn't until she arrived at her apartment that she finally allowed herself to take a deep breath. She had to leave. It wasn't just for the sake of the baby; it was for her own sanity. She'd never been good at running, but right now, it was the only option. She had to go somewhere she could think, somewhere away from Adrian and the mess they'd created.

She threw a few clothes into a suitcase, grabbed a few essentials, and shoved everything into an uber, which took her to the bus station.

The bus ride to Princeton was long. She could hardly sit still, constantly shifting in her seat, trying to ignore the gnawing ache in her stomach. She leaned against the window, watching the world pass by in a blur.

There were moments when she caught herself imagining what might have been if she'd been braver. If she had told Adrian the truth sooner. But she couldn't. Not yet. She wasn't ready.

The bus rumbled through the streets of New Jersey before stopping at the Princeton station, and Heidi stepped off, feeling like a stranger in her own life.

She looked around, inhaling the cool air of Princeton. The town was quieter than she remembered, more peaceful. And for a moment, she thought maybe she'd found a tiny piece of peace for herself.

Her mother's house was just a short walk away. She spoken to her mother two weeks ago. She didn't let her know she was coming, but she knew she'd be there for her. She always was.

Heidi's mind was clouded with the storm of emotions—guilt, fear, confusion, and longing. She needed to get away from everything for just a little while. To breathe without the constant pressure of her decision looming over her.

But even as she walked toward her mother's front door, she knew the truth was coming. She couldn't run forever.

And she couldn't keep Adrian in the dark forever, either.

She didn't know how long she'd stay. She only knew she had to leave before the truth crushed her completely.

# Chapter Ten

The skyline was beginning to blur.

Adrian sat behind his desk, his tie loosened, the amber light of his office dimmed to match the early evening haze outside. Another board meeting behind him. Another quarterly forecast that meant nothing without her insight. He'd asked for the latest numbers three times. Laura had reminded him they were already on his screen.

Still, he waited for Heidi to walk through the door with her notes, her wit, her cutting honesty.

But the silence stretched.

He rubbed the bridge of his nose, the dull ache behind his eyes pulsing harder with each passing second. Unable to sit still, he rose from his chair and walked down the hall to Heidi's office. The door was open.

Laura stepped out, a folder clutched tightly to her chest, her expression unreadable—but something about it made his chest tighten.

"Heidi's not here," she said quietly. "I was just coming to let you know. She had to leave—said it was a family emergency."

Adrian's eyes narrowed. "What emergency? When?"

"About two hours ago," Laura said, her voice a little strained now. "She packed up her office this afternoon. Cleared everything out."

He stared at her, stunned. "That's not possible. She wouldn't just leave. Not without speaking to me."

Laura gave a slow, reluctant nod. "I thought the same. But she's gone. No goodbyes. No explanation. Just... walked out."

A cold flush crept over his skin.

"She looked upset," Laura added gently. "But Adrian—she looked wrecked. Like she hadn't slept in days."

He turned toward the nearest window, the city skyline shimmering beneath the setting sun, distant and indifferent. His hands curled into fists.

"She wouldn't just leave," he muttered, more to himself than to her. "Not like this."

Laura hesitated. "I think she's been hurting for a while. Whatever pushed her over the edge... it wasn't small."

He didn't answer. Couldn't.

His silence was a fortress—one Laura didn't try to breach.

After a moment, she turned and quietly returned to her office, leaving him standing alone outside Heidi's empty doorway.

Then his phone buzzed.

It was Heidi.


*Adrian,*

*I'm sorry. I need space, and I need time. Please don't look for me. This has nothing to do with the company. It's me. I just—I'm not okay.*

*Thank you for everything.*

*Heidi*


He read it twice. Three times. The words began to blur, and this time it wasn't the skyline.

Not okay.

She wasn't okay.

And she was gone.

He stood motionless for a long moment before reaching for his phone and dialling her number. Straight to voicemail.

Then again.

And again.

When the third call failed, he threw the phone onto the desk and stared at her door she used to walk through ten times a day.

He wasn't going to let this end in silence.

Not this time.

The small cottage sat quietly at the edge of a sleepy street, its porch light glowing like a beacon in the late dusk. Heidi stood on the front steps, her hands trembling around the strap of her overnight bag, heart pounding against her ribs.

It had been a long bus ride and a short walk—and her body ached from exhaustion. But the real weight pressing on her was emotional. Bone-deep. Suffocating.

The door opened before she could knock.

Her mother's face appeared in the doorway, lined with worry. "Oh, sweetheart."

Heidi collapsed into her mother's arms without a word, the sob catching in her throat. Her mother pulled her inside, shutting the door quietly behind them as if afraid noise might break her further.

They sat on the worn floral sofa in the living room, warm lamplight casting soft shadows on the walls. Heidi held a cup of tea she wasn't drinking, the steam curling against her cheek as her mother sat beside her, one hand resting on her knee.

"I think I ruined everything," Heidi said quietly. Her voice was hoarse, like it had fought its way out from under weeks of silence.

Her mother said nothing, only gave her hand a gentle squeeze.

"I didn't mean to fall in love with him," she continued. "It just… happened. I thought I could keep things professional, that I could pretend I didn't feel what I felt. But I failed at all of it."

Her mother's brows furrowed slightly. "Is this about the man you've been working for? The CEO?"

Heidi nodded, swallowing the lump in her throat. "Adrian Werrington. He's—he's everything I didn't know I needed. Smart, infuriating, loyal to a fault. And I—I broke it. I broke us."

She set the tea down on the coffee table with shaking hands.

"His wife, Cleo, lied to him. Faked a pregnancy to trap him. He was emotionally checked out of that marriage long before I ever—before we…" She shook her head. "But when I got pregnant, I couldn't tell him. I couldn't risk him thinking I was like her. That I had manipulated him."

Her mother's sat quietly, waiting, listening.

"After the divorce Cleo tried to cause trouble for me, but Adrian calmed it all down. I was going to tell Adrian today about the baby, but she was there and got in my head. I couldn't breathe in that building anymore, couldn't think. So, I left."

She let the silence hang between them, her mother processing the storm she'd just unleashed.

"I love him," Heidi whispered. "I love him in that terrifying, irreversible way. But I'm so scared. Scared of being the mistake in his life. Scared of what happens if I stay, and worse—what happens if I don't."

Her mother exhaled slowly, tucking a strand of Heidi's hair behind her ear. "You've always carried the weight of the world like it's your job, Heidi. But maybe it's okay to let someone else carry you, just this once."

Heidi looked down, her voice barely audible. "If he calls… if he somehow finds out I'm here—please, don't tell him."

Her mother didn't respond immediately. Then she gave a slow, careful nod. "If that's what you need, I won't say a word."

"Thank you," Heidi whispered, tears slipping silently down her cheeks.

Her mother pulled her close again, holding her tightly as the night deepened around them. And for the first time in weeks, Heidi let herself fall apart in the safety of someone else's arms.


Alan stood in the middle of Adrian's office, arms crossed, his expression a sharp mix of irritation and concern.

"Tell me what the hell is going on with you," he demanded.

Adrian didn't look up right away. He sat behind his desk, motionless, sleeves rolled to his elbows, tie undone, every inch the portrait of a man quietly unravelling.

"Heidi left," he said finally, voice low and ragged. "I can't find her."

Alan's brow furrowed. "Your CFO, Heidi?"

"Yes."

"Well, hire another one," Alan said flatly, like it was just another box to tick off his crisis management list.

Adrian's head snapped up, eyes dark with something volatile. "It's not that simple."

Alan's arms dropped. "Why? You're acting like the world ended. You've got a company to run, a board breathing down your neck, a reputation—"

"Because I damn well love her."

The words landed like a gunshot.

Alan blinked. "You... what?"

Adrian pushed up from his chair, pacing now, the admission cracking something wide open inside him.

"I love her," Adrian said again, his voice more intense this time. "I've been in love with her for months. I just didn't realise it until she was already gone. She left without a word—no goodbye, no note, nothing. Well... a short text telling me she wasn't okay. And I can't fix it. I can't fix us because I don't know where she is."

Alan's tone softened. "Fix what, exactly?"

Adrian scrubbed a hand over his face, his jaw tight. "We slept together."

"You what?" Alan's eyebrows shot up.

"After the divorce, we slept together. I've never felt like this for any woman. When we were together, it was... extraordinary."

Alan leaned back, processing the revelation. "I knew something was going on, but not this. Why do you think she left?"

"Cleo. The divorce. The scandal. I let it all spiral. I didn't protect Heidi when it counted. I let Cleo twist the narrative, let the media chew her up. I dragged Heidi into my mess, and she nearly lost everything because of it." Adrian stopped pacing, his breath unsteady. "She trusted me, Alan. And I failed her."

Alan was silent for a long moment. "And you're just now telling me this?"

Adrian let out a bitter breath. "I didn't plan on falling for her. Hell, I fought it. But she's the only thing in my life that's felt real in years." His voice cracked, low and gutted. "I've built empires. Fought battles most men wouldn't come back from. But I don't know how to survive this. Not without her."

The room went still.

Then Alan exhaled, his voice no longer sharp but weighted with something like understanding. "So, what are you going to do?"

Adrian turned toward the window, the city glittering like it might swallow him whole.

"I have to find her," he said quietly.

"How?"

"I don't know. I even called her mother. She doesn't know where she is either." A pause. "It's been two months."

The cursor blinked on the screen like a heartbeat—steady, relentless, reminding her that once she hit 'send', there would be no going back.

Heidi sat at her mother's kitchen table, her hands trembling faintly as she re-read the message for what must've been the hundredth time. It didn't get easier. If anything, each word cut deeper the longer she stared at them.

*Adrian,*

*I have to tell you something that may come as a shock. I'm pregnant. He's yours. Yes, it's a boy.*

She swallowed hard. The truth had been a stone in her throat for weeks now, growing heavier with every heartbeat, every flutter from the tiny life inside her. She had imagined so many ways to tell him—over dinner, maybe, or on a quiet morning in bed when their world still felt simple. But life hadn't waited. And neither had Cleo.

*I know I should have told you straight away, but you had only got out of an unwanted relationship. I didn't want to burden you with another. The day I left, I was going to tell you, but Cleo came out of your office, and she guessed. She got in my head. Told me that you would think I was trying to trap you. But I'm not.*

Heidi blinked against the heat behind her eyes. Cleo's voice still echoed in her mind— icy, sharp, cruelly composed. *'You think a baby is your golden ticket? That he's going to what—fall madly in love with you? Marry you? Be the doting father? He's not going to fall for that one, again.'*

The words had dug deep, unearthing every insecurity Heidi had tried to bury.

*I don't want anything from you, Adrian. I will never stop you from seeing your son.*

She reached for her tea—cold now—trying to steady herself with the familiar hum of her mother moving about the house in the background. She didn't know what Adrian would feel when he read this. Shock. Anger. Betrayal. Maybe all of it. But at least he would know.

*I'm 22 weeks along, only eighteen more to go.*

It was surreal. Twenty-two weeks of growing a life in silence. Twenty-two weeks of pretending she wasn't counting kicks, wasn't dreaming in flashes of dark hair and storm-grey eyes. Their son. Hers and Adrian's.

*I'm at my mother's home in New Jersey. Please don't be angry with her. I made her promise not to tell you I was here. I am truly sorry.*

She hesitated then; fingers poised over the keyboard. This part hurt the most—not because it was untrue, but because it was. She hadn't just hidden to protect herself. She'd done it to protect him, too. From the scandal. From the chaos. From her.

*I didn't mean for any of this to happen. I didn't mean to fall in love with you.*

A tear slid down her cheek. She didn't bother to brush it away.

*But please don't worry about that. I will get over it eventually. I don't want you to feel obligated to say or do anything. Please give me that courtesy.*

She stared at the word courtesy for a long moment. It felt too formal for a man whose mouth had traced every inch of her skin, who knew how she took her coffee and the stories behind every scar. But she had to protect herself, even now. Even with him.

*If you are interested, I'm getting a scan done the day after tomorrow. If you would like to come, you are welcome. But please—you don't have to.*

*Please don't hate me.*

*Love always,*

*Heidi*

She exhaled. It wasn't perfect, but it was honest. And she didn't have the strength for perfect anymore.

Her finger hovered over the send button.

For a heartbeat, she imagined him reading it—brows drawn, jaw tight, that unreadable mask he wore when emotion clawed too close to the surface.

Then she clicked 'send'.

The screen blinked.

It was done.

She closed the laptop and pressed a hand to her belly, whispering into the quiet.

"He knows now, little one."

Outside, the wind stirred the late-spring leaves, and somewhere—miles away—a man would soon read words that would change everything.


Adrian hadn't slept.

The city was painted in muted grey; the skyline blurred behind morning fog as he stood at the floor-to-ceiling window in his penthouse. Coffee untouched. Tie abandoned. His phone sat on the counter behind him, taunting him with its silence. Two months. Sixty-two days. Fifteen messages he never sent.

Then it buzzed.

He turned slowly, not expecting much—some board update, a reminder, maybe Alan again demanding he get his act together. But then he saw the name.

Heidi.

His chest tightened.

He crossed the room in three strides, thumb trembling slightly as he opened the email. It wasn't long. It didn't need to be.


*Adrian,*

***I have to tell you something that may come as a shock…***

He read it once. Then again.

And again.

By the third time, he was sitting on the edge of the sofa, elbows on his knees, the email glowing from his phone like a torch in the dark.

*I'm pregnant. He's yours. Yes, it's a boy.*

He closed his eyes. A boy. His son. The truth bloomed in his chest and hollowed it out all at once. He felt like the wind had been knocked out of him.

She'd been going to tell him that day. That same awful day.

But Cleo had beaten her to it.

His jaw clenched, rage and regret flashing through him like a spark meeting gasoline. Of course, Cleo had guessed. Of course she'd twisted the moment into something poisonous.

*She got in my head. Told me that you would think I was trying to trap you…*

"She was trying to protect me," he murmured aloud. The realisation hit hard. Heidi had been protecting him—his name, his freedom, his future. Even when he hadn't protected her.

*I don't want anything from you…*

God, she really believed that. That he might think of her as just another trap. Another lie. A heartless gold digger, like Cleo.

He scrolled down to the end, heart pounding as he reached the part that hurt most:

*I didn't mean to fall in love with you. But please don't worry about that. I will get over it eventually.*

His hands tightened around the phone.

*She loved him.*

And she'd left, believing he didn't love her back.


*I'm 22 weeks along… getting a scan the day after tomorrow… you're welcome to come… but please—you don't have to.*


He stood abruptly. Like hell he wasn't going.


*Please don't hate me.*


How could he hate her, how could she think that. He loved her, more than he had ever loved anyone. And now she was carrying his baby… *his son.*

He didn't know what he'd say. Didn't know how to undo the damage he'd done. But one thing was certain—he wouldn't let her face that ultrasound alone. Not again. Not ever.

He grabbed his keys and coat, already dialling.

"Ben," he said when his driver picked up. "I need you at the building in five. We're going to New Jersey."

He hung up and looked down at the message one last time.


*Love always,*

*Heidi.*


His thumb hovered, then tapped 'Reply'.


*Heidi,*

*Thank you for telling me. I'm on my way.*

# Chapter Eleven

Heidi's hands trembled slightly as she read Adrian's message for the third time.

***Thank you for telling me. I'm on my way.***

Short. Measured. Controlled.

No exclamation marks. No questions. No hint of emotion. Just pure Adrian Werrington—contained, precise… unreadable.

Was he angry? Shocked? Relieved? She couldn't tell. And she hated that it still mattered—how his words, his tone, his stillness could unravel her so completely. But the fact that he was coming—that he hadn't ignored the message, hadn't sent his assistant or responded with a hollow 'we'll talk later'—it had to mean something.

*Didn't it?*

Heidi slipped her phone into her jacket pocket, exhaling as she smoothed a trembling hand over the gentle curve of her stomach. Then she stepped into the sitting room, where her mother was gently setting down a steaming mug of chamomile tea beside the knitting basket.

"Mum, I'm just going for a walk," she said quietly.

Her mother looked up, warmth and concern mingling behind tired eyes. "Alright, sweetheart. Just don't go too far. It's still a bit chilly out."

"I won't," Heidi murmured with a tight smile. She wrapped her scarf around her neck, looping it twice before stepping outside.

The morning light was pale and crisp—the kind of spring brightness that didn't quite bring warmth but promised it was coming. She took a deep breath, the cold air stinging her lungs in the best way, sharpening the edges of her spinning thoughts.

This was her ritual. Every morning since she'd returned to New Jersey: Walk first. Think later.

She moved past the corner bakery where the scent of fresh bread spilled into the street, past the tiny park with its rusting slide and crooked benches, past the library steps where she used to read in the summers. Her boots crunched over gravel and sidewalk grit, and with each step, the familiar rhythm of home steadied her.

But nothing could steady the flutter in her chest.

Not today.

Adrian was coming.

She paused near the little churchyard fence, brushing her fingers over the iron railing, then let her hand drift to her stomach.

"He's coming to see you, baby," she whispered, her voice soft, breaking the silence like a secret. "Can you believe it?"

The weight of it—the impossible truth of it—settled over her with equal parts joy and fear.

A tentative smile tugged at her lips. It wasn't peace. Not yet. But it was something like hope. Small, quiet, persistent.


Adrian had just turned the corner when he saw her.

He hadn't even told the driver to stop yet. The car idled at a red light just outside the quiet, tree-lined neighbourhood where Heidi had grown up. And then—through the window—he saw her.

Her hair was loose, catching the morning light like threads of gold. Her hands were tucked into the pockets of her coat; her face framed in a softness he hadn't seen in months. There was something achingly delicate about her. And yet—she glowed.

Adrian leaned forward in his seat, his voice tight. "That's her. Pull over."

Ben eased the car to the curb.

Adrian's breath caught.

She looked... luminous. Fragile. Unbelievably real. And when her hand moved instinctively to the swell of her stomach—his child—something inside him fractured and reformed all at once.

She hadn't noticed the car.

He stepped out slowly, as if one sudden move might break the spell. His pulse thundered in his ears.

"Heidi."

She turned, startled. Their eyes met—and time stilled.

For a heartbeat, they just looked at each other. All the distance. All the longing. All the things unsaid. It was there, in the silence between them.

Then Heidi moved—no hesitation, no fear—just emotion. She launched herself into his arms, burying her face against his chest as the sobs came freely now, raw, and unrestrained.

Adrian wrapped his arms around her like he never wanted to let go.

Not again.

*Never again.*

"I'm sorry." Her voice was muffled against his chest, thick with emotion. "I should have told you."

Adrian held her tighter, one hand cradling the back of her head as if anchoring her to him. His voice was low, rough with feeling. "Heidi, I'm sorry."

He pulled back just enough to look into her eyes, his own filled with something raw and unguarded.

"For not making you feel like you *could* tell me. For not showing you that I would never—not for a second—think you were anything like Cleo."

Her breath hitched, tears still clinging to her lashes.

"You're nothing like her," he said softly. "You're everything she wasn't. Honest. Brave. Good."

He cupped her face gently, his thumb brushing away a tear. "And I should've made sure you knew that. From the start."


Adrian gently guided her toward the car, his hand warm and steady on the small of her back. He opened the door for her, helping her inside with a care that made her throat tighten. Once she was settled, he slid in beside her, close enough that their arms brushed.

"Ben, the Graduate Hilton," he instructed the driver, his voice calm but firm.

"I need to let my mother know where I am," Heidi said softly. "She'll worry."

"Call her," Adrian replied, turning to face her. "Because we need to talk."

She nodded and pulled out her phone. Her fingers trembled slightly as she dialled.

"Mum? It's me. I'm with Adrian... Yes, I'm okay. I just needed to talk to him, that's all. I'll call you later, I promise." A pause. Then a soft smile. "I know. I love you too."

When she hung up, she tucked the phone away and leaned back, exhaling slowly.

Her mother was relieved. And, surprisingly, happy.

Neither of them spoke for the rest of the ride, but the silence between them wasn't heavy anymore. It was filled with things waiting to be said, emotions that had been buried too long.


When they reached the hotel, Ben pulled up to a private entrance. Adrian stepped out first, offering his hand once again as Heidi emerged. He didn't let go. Not as they walked through the polished lobby. Not in the elevator. Not even as he opened the door to his suite.

The moment it closed behind them, they were alone. Finally.

Heidi went into Adrian's arms the moment the door shut, as if she'd been holding her breath for weeks and only now could exhale. He kissed her—slow, deep, aching with all the things he hadn't said, all the time they'd lost.

They clung to each other, foreheads pressed together, their breaths mingling. They both knew there were words waiting to be spoken, truths to untangle—but not yet. Not now.

Right now, they needed this.

They needed each other.

Without breaking their gaze, Adrian lifted her effortlessly, cradling her close as he carried her to the bed. He paused in front of it, setting her down gently so she stood before him. There was reverence in his touch, in the way his fingers slid over the buttons of her coat and helped it slip from her shoulders.

She reached for him too, tugging at his jacket, his shirt, her hands hungry and sure. With every layer shed, they came closer—not just in body, but in something deeper. In the quiet, breathless place where fear had once lived, there was only yearning now.

When Heidi was bare before him, Adrian just looked at her. His eyes roamed slowly over her body, lingering on the soft curve of her breasts, the new fullness in her hips, the gentle roundness of her belly. His hands followed, smoothing over the slight swell with a tenderness that made her eyes sting.

"You're more beautiful than I remember," he whispered, voice rough with awe. "Even more now."

He dropped to his knees before her, his hands on her waist, his forehead resting gently against the place where their child grew.

And for a moment, neither of them moved—just breathed. Just held on.

Because this, right here, was everything.

He kissed her swollen belly—softly, reverently—his lips lingering as if in silent conversation with the life growing inside her. Then he stood, eyes locked with hers and gently guided her back until she lay against the cool sheets, her hair fanned out like a golden halo on the pillows.

Adrian hovered over her for a moment, just looking—tracing the changes time and love and pregnancy had left on her body. She was softer now, fuller, her curves more pronounced. He ran his fingers slowly along the delicate new lines of her, from the swell of her breasts to the curve of her waist and the gentle round of her stomach. Every inch of her told a story he hadn't been there to witness, but one he ached to honour now.

"You're different," he murmured, brushing a thumb across her ribcage, his voice low and awed. "But not in the way you think. You're more… you."

Heidi blinked up at him, breath trembling. "You don't—"

"I do," he cut in softly, kissing her again. "Every inch. Every change. It's you, Heidi. And I've never wanted anyone more."

He moved with care—more deliberate, more attentive than ever before. There was no rush, no frenzy, just the slow burn of rediscovery. He kissed her collarbone, her shoulders, her wrists. Touched her like she might break, even though he knew she was stronger than anyone he'd ever met.

When he finally entered her, they both gasped—him from the overwhelming sensation of being inside the woman he hadn't stopped dreaming about, her from the relief of being made whole again.

They moved together slowly, their bodies finding a rhythm as familiar as it was new. She clung to him, fingers digging into his back, their breaths falling into sync, their murmured names the only sound in the room. Her body had changed, yes—but it welcomed him still, maybe even more so now. And he held her like she was everything—because she was.

Every movement, every kiss, was a vow.

And when they finally collapsed together, skin to skin, breath to breath, Adrian held her tightly, one hand resting protectively over her belly, as if he could shield them both from the world.

He whispered into her hair, "I love you, Heidi. I always will."

She stiffened.

Adrian felt it instantly, the way her body tensed beneath his. Slowly, she turned in his arms, her eyes finding his with something wary and uncertain swimming in their depths.

"Please don't, Adrian."

His brow furrowed. "Don't what?"

"Don't say that... not because of this." Her hand moved to rest on her stomach, protective, hesitant. "I know you'll love this baby. We both will. But you don't have to tell me you love me because of it."

He stared at her, stunned. "Is that what you think?" he asked, voice low, controlled. "That I only said I loved you because you're pregnant?"

She looked away, blinking quickly. "You married Cleo because you thought she was."

He inhaled sharply, then sat up a little, the hurt clear in his expression but softened by understanding. "I did," he admitted. "And it was the worst mistake of my life. But not once—*not once*—did I ever tell Cleo I loved her. Because I didn't. Because I couldn't."

He reached out, cupping her cheek, gently urging her to meet his eyes again.

"Because you're the only woman I have ever loved, Heidi. Before the pregnancy. Before we made love for the first time. Before everything."

Her eyes filled, lips parting slightly as though to argue—but nothing came out. The look on his face silenced every doubt that had been gnawing at her for months.

"I didn't come for the baby," he continued, his voice thick. "I came for *you*. And I'm staying... for both of you."

She leaned into his touch, letting his words settle deep—past the fear, past the doubts—into the part of her that had always waited for him, even before she understood she was waiting.

"Say it again," she whispered.

"I love you," he said, his voice raw, steady. His forehead rested against hers, their breaths mingling. "I love you so much it terrifies me."

A tremulous smile broke through the emotion on her face. "I love you too. I have from the day I met you. I didn't know it at the time, but... there was always this pull toward you I had to resist."

"I felt it too," he murmured. "Every day. You walked into my life and everything started shifting. I just didn't realise you were the change I needed."

"I wanted to tell you about the baby," she admitted softly, fingers brushing over the curve of her stomach, "but I didn't want to complicate your life—not right after you got out of that… unwanted relationship."

Adrian let out a breath, brushing a thumb over her cheek. "I won't lie, Heidi. I'm upset I wasn't there from the beginning. That I missed the first kicks, the scans, the cravings… all of it. But I do understand why you didn't tell me." He paused, his voice thick with feeling. "I'm just glad I know now. That I'm here now."

Her eyes shimmered with tears, not from sorrow, but from the overwhelming sense of relief and love. "I was always going to tell you," she said, her voice barely above a whisper. "Because I know how much you want to be a father."

He lowered his head and kissed her—softly, reverently.

"And I want to be one with you, Heidi. Only you."

She smiled—the brightest, most radiant smile he'd ever seen—and flung her arms around his neck, laughter bubbling up like sunlight. "I'm so happy," she said, her voice catching on joy.

He wrapped his arms around her tightly, holding her as though he'd never let her go. "So am I," he murmured into her hair, then gently pulled back to look into her eyes. "You're not going to tell me you're worried about a scandal again, are you?"

She met his gaze with unwavering certainty. "No," she said simply. "As long as I know you love me, I don't care what anyone thinks."

Adrian let out a long breath—the kind that only came after months of holding everything in. "Thank God," he said, half-laughing, half-reeling. "I don't think I could go through that again."

"Neither could I," she whispered, pressing a kiss to his lips. "But we don't have to. Not anymore."

He kissed her back, slowly and deeply, the future finally unfolding between them— clear, unshaken, and theirs.


Soon after, they got dressed, lingering in the warmth of each other's presence before the reality of the day pulled them forward. There was a softness to their movements now—a kind of reverence in the way Adrian helped her zip up her dress, the way Heidi smoothed his collar, her hand brushing over his chest like she needed to feel his heartbeat one more time before stepping out into the world.

When they arrived at her mother's house, the front door opened before they could knock. Judy stood there, arms crossed, eyes sharp with concern that melted into cautious relief the moment she saw Heidi safe, standing beside Adrian, her hand tucked into his.

"I'm so sorry I couldn't tell you where Heidi was," Judy said to Adrian after he introduced himself properly, his voice low and respectful.

"I understand," Adrian replied, his tone sincere. "You were protecting your daughter. I'd have done the same."

Judy studied him for a moment, as if trying to measure the weight of his intentions. Then she nodded, and something unspoken passed between them—an acknowledgment of love's complexity, and of second chances hard won.

Heidi stepped forward and hugged her mother tightly, whispering, "I'm okay now, Mum. We're okay."

Judy held her for a moment longer, then pulled back just enough to glance down at her daughter's belly. Her voice wavered, soft with emotion. "And soon I will be a grandmother?"

Heidi nodded, her eyes glistening. "Yes."

Judy's gaze shifted back to Adrian. "Then I suppose we all have some catching up to do."

Adrian reached for Heidi's hand again, intertwining their fingers. "I'd like that very much."

# Chapter Twelve

The hum of the ultrasound machine was soft, rhythmic, almost soothing. But Heidi could feel the anxious energy humming beneath Adrian's composed exterior. He sat beside her in the small, dimly lit exam room, one hand gently holding hers while the other rested stiffly on his thigh, his knuckles taut.

His navy blazer was slung over the back of the chair; the sleeves of his shirt rolled halfway up his forearms. There was something almost boyish about him like this—slightly undone, out of his element. Vulnerable.

"This might feel a little cold," the sonographer said kindly as she spread the gel across Heidi's belly. "Just relax and look at the screen."

Adrian's grip tightened around her fingers instinctively; his eyes locked on the monitor like he was afraid to blink.

Heidi turned to watch him instead.

His expression shifted the moment the image came into focus. First confusion—then awe. Then something deeper. Something unspoken.

"There's your baby," the sonographer said softly, moving the wand slowly. "Nice and active today. Heartbeat looks strong."

Adrian leaned forward slightly. His jaw clenched, and he exhaled through his nose like he was trying to keep himself in check. Heidi felt the pressure of his thumb sweep across her knuckles, almost absently, like he needed the grounding of her touch.

"He's beautiful," Heidi whispered.

He turned to her then, his voice rough with emotion. "He is."

Adrian looked back at the screen. The tiny curve of a nose. A fluttering heartbeat. A hand that seemed to wave before curling into a fist.

Heidi blinked against the sudden sting in her eyes.

The sonographer smiled gently and turned the screen a little more toward them. "Would you like to hear the heartbeat?"

Adrian nodded once, too overcome to speak.

The sound burst into the room like a galloping drum—fast, strong, impossibly alive.

Adrian's eyes closed.

Heidi had never seen him like this. Not even when he held her in the dark after their first night together. Not even in the stillness of his hotel suite when he traced her name against her skin like a prayer.

This was different.

This was surrender.

"He's okay?" he asked finally, his voice strained with something she couldn't quite name.

"He's perfect," the sonographer said. "Everything looks exactly as it should."

Heidi watched him breathe again. Really breathe. The tension in his shoulders eased, his thumb still tracing soothing patterns across her skin.

"Would you like to take some pictures home?" the tech asked.

Heidi nodded, but it was Adrian who spoke. "All of them. Please."

When it was over, and the images were printed and tucked into an envelope, they stepped out into the corridor, walking slower than usual, like they were both reluctant to leave the sacred stillness of that room.

Adrian held the envelope in one hand, staring down at it like it was treasure.

"I didn't know," he said quietly. "I mean—I knew he was real. Of course I did. But seeing him…"

He trailed off, shaking his head slightly.

"It changes everything, doesn't it?" Heidi said, her voice soft.

Adrian stopped walking. Turned to face her. His eyes searched hers.

"It does," he said. "You do."

He reached up, brushing a stray curl behind her ear, letting his fingertips linger along her jaw.

"I don't want to miss anything else, Heidi."

She swallowed hard, her heart full.

"You don't have to," she whispered.

He stepped closer, his forehead pressing to hers, the envelope crinkling slightly in his hand between them. "You make me want to be brave," he said. "For him. For you. For the life we didn't plan—but that I want more than anything."

Her breath caught. The warmth of him, the weight of those words—it was everything.

"I'm scared," she admitted.

"I am too," he said. "But I'm here."

And for the first time in months, Heidi believed it.

He wasn't just there.

He was *with* her.


After the ultrasound, they walked hand in hand out to the waiting car. The afternoon sun was soft behind the clouds, casting a silvery sheen over the city as the driver held the door open.

Adrian helped her in, his hand lingering at the small of her back before sliding in beside her. As soon as the door shut and the car pulled away from the curb, he spoke.

"Penthouse, thanks, Ben," he said smoothly to the driver.

Heidi's eyes flicked toward him. Something about the word tightened her chest. Penthouse.

She turned slightly in her seat, her voice calm, but guarded. "I thought Cleo got the penthouse."

"She did," Adrian replied without looking at her. Then he added, as if it were obvious, "I bought a new one."

"Oh." It came out smaller than she meant it to. She looked out the window, watching the city blur past.

The idea of him moving on, of buying a new place, a fresh space untouched by the ghost of Cleo or the broken pieces of their marriage—it comforted her.

They pulled up in front of a discreet, luxury apartment building on Fifth Avenue, a sleek awning stretching over the entrance. A doorman greeted Adrian by name and tipped his hat politely to Heidi.

Ben drove off as Adrian guided her inside, his hand resting lightly on her lower back. The lobby was all marble and clean lines, modern and warm, hushed, and private. They stepped into a private elevator, Adrian swiping a sleek black keycard.

Heidi glanced at him as the elevator began to rise. Her heart was beating faster now. She couldn't tell if it was excitement or nerves.

When the doors opened directly into the penthouse, she stepped out and gasped.

"Wow," she breathed. "It's… gorgeous."

And it was. Soft, ambient lighting cast a golden glow over a wide-open living space with glass walls overlooking Central Park. The furnishings were modern, but lived in. Clean lines softened by texture—leather, velvet, brushed wood. A fireplace flickered in the corner. Beyond the kitchen, a long hallway disappeared into what she assumed were the bedrooms.

She turned to say something—maybe to tell him the view felt like a dream or that she could already see herself waking up here with him—when the soft buzz of the intercom interrupted the moment.

Adrian moved to the panel near the wall and pressed a button. "Yes?"

A voice crackled through the speaker. Adrian listened, then replied, "Send him up. Thanks."

Heidi tilted her head, brows lifted. "Who's that?"

He turned toward her, casually adjusting the cuff of his sleeve. "My lawyer. And my friend."

"Alan, right?" she asked, her voice thoughtful. "I met him once… I think it was my first week working for you. He came by the office with those ridiculous Halloween cupcakes."

Adrian's smile tugged wider. "That's him. And they were not ridiculous. They were amazing."

Before Heidi could say more, the elevator dinged, the smooth doors gliding open.

Alan stepped out, not immediately seeing her. He was in his usual tailored suit, holding a thick folder under one arm and tapping away at his phone. The second he looked up and spotted Adrian, his expression shifted to one of exasperated relief.

"Where the hell have you been?" he said, not bothering with a greeting. "You've missed two calls, the board's losing its mind about the revised Singapore deal, and your PR team is—"

Then he saw Heidi.

"Oh—sorry." Alan stopped mid-sentence, blinking as he took her in. "Didn't realise you had company."

Heidi offered a polite smile, one hand resting lightly over her bump in a protective, instinctive gesture.

Adrian chuckled and stepped forward, his tone rich with warmth and pride. "Alan, have you met Heidi?" He looked over his shoulder at her with something tender in his eyes. "The mother of my son."

Alan's eyes widened just slightly. For all his legal training and professional composure, he wasn't quite prepared for that.

"I—uh—wow." He extended a hand, recovering quickly. "Heidi. Of course. I've heard… well, a lot lately. It's good to finally meet you properly."

Heidi shook his hand, her expression soft but a little cautious. "Nice to see you again."

Alan glanced at Adrian, then back to Heidi, his expression warm but assessing—curious in the way old friends always are when faced with something new and meaningful. "Congratulations, both of you. And—if I may—you're glowing. Pregnancy really suits you."

Adrian shot him a mock-warning look, one brow arched. "Careful. Compliment her too much and I'll have to throw you out. I'm very protective these days."

Alan laughed, holding up both hands in surrender. "Message received. No poetic flattery, just factual admiration."

Then his tone shifted, softer, more sincere as he looked at Adrian again. "But seriously, man… I'm happy for you. You look different. Lighter. Better than the last time I saw you."

"That was probably my fault," Heidi said quietly, a small smile tugging at her lips.

Alan chuckled, eyes twinkling with amusement. "I like her, Adrian. She's honest."

Adrian glanced at Heidi, his voice low but full of affection. "That's one of the many reasons I love her."

Heidi excused herself with a warm, polite smile, murmuring something about pregnancy requiring more bathroom breaks, then gracefully disappeared down the hallway. Her voice was light, almost teasing, but the way she moved—elegant even beneath the subtle weight of motherhood—left an imprint on the room.

Adrian's eyes followed her until she was out of sight. There was a softness in his gaze, something quiet and reverent, as though just watching her steadied something inside him.

Alan waited a beat, then crossed his arms with a knowing smile. "So… that's the woman who brought Adrian Werrington to his knees?"

Adrian snorted, crossing to the bar with an easy stride. He poured two glasses of scotch, the amber liquid catching the light. "I was already on my knees," he said, handing a glass to Alan. "She just didn't walk past. She saw me there… and helped me up."

Alan raised a brow, taking a slow sip. "You're serious about her."

Adrian didn't blink. "More than I've ever been about anything. She's the one."

The room fell into a thoughtful quiet. Alan watched him closely, then nodded, slower this time. "I can tell. You look different, man. Not just lighter—though you do—but grounded. Like you're actually here for once, not three steps ahead or buried in the past." He paused. "Hell, even happy. When's the last time I saw that?"

Adrian leaned against the bar, one hand in his pocket, the other cradling his drink. "Maybe… never."

Alan's smile dimmed into something more serious. "I was worried after Cleo. Then when Heidi left, I thought…" He shook his head. "You didn't look like a man who was surviving. You looked like a man who'd already given up."

"I know." Adrian's voice dropped, more gravel than silk now. "I almost had."

Alan tilted his head. "So, what happened?"

"She left because she was pregnant… and she thought I'd think she was like Cleo. That she was trapping me." He stared down into his glass. "But Heidi? She was trying to protect me. Even if it meant breaking her own heart."

Alan let out a low whistle, shaking his head. "She's *nothing* like Cleo."

"She's everything Cleo wasn't," Adrian said quietly.

There was another pause, the silence heavy but not uncomfortable. Alan studied his friend, then offered a nod. "She's good for you."

Adrian's lips curved into a rare, honest smile—quiet, almost reverent. "She's everything I didn't know I needed."

Alan chuckled. "Careful, you're starting to sound like a Hallmark movie."

Adrian raised his glass in a small toast. "She's the only woman I've ever loved. And I'm going to marry her."

Alan lifted his brows. "Congrats, mate."

"I haven't asked yet," Adrian admitted, "but I will."

They clinked glasses with a soft chime, the moment quietly monumental.

"And the baby?" Alan asked, voice gentler now.

Adrian's entire expression shifted—lit from within. "A boy. Twenty-two weeks today. I saw his heartbeat. His hands. His spine. I didn't think I'd ever have this. A real family." He looked toward the hallway where Heidi had disappeared. "But I want it. With her. All of it."

Alan gave a rare, genuine smile, emotion flickering behind his eyes. "Then don't screw it up."

Adrian let out a quiet laugh. "That's the plan."


The three of them decided to go out for dinner, choosing a quiet French bistro nestled on a tree-lined side street—one of those hidden gems only true locals knew about. Inside, the air was warm with the scent of butter and herbs, the soft flicker of candlelight dancing over linen-covered tables. Crystal glasses chimed gently against fine porcelain, and murmured conversations filled the air like a gentle melody. It was intimate, elegant, and effortlessly romantic.

They settled into a curved leather booth near the back. Conversation flowed easily, laughter bubbling up over shared stories and old memories. Alan had a quick wit and an infectious charm, and to Adrian's quiet satisfaction, Heidi met him beat for beat—smart, warm, and effortlessly disarming.

By the time dessert arrived, Alan was recounting a disastrous sailing trip Adrian had once insisted on, complete with stormy seas, seasick investors, and a broken mast.

Heidi was laughing, genuinely, her hand resting on her baby bump. "Please tell me there are photos."

"Oh, there are photos," Alan said gleefully, wagging his fork. "I'll send them to you. Adrian looked like a drowned hedge fund rat."

Adrian groaned dramatically, leaning back with a shake of his head. "This was a mistake. Bringing the two of you together? Absolute betrayal."

Alan smirked. "You'll survive. Barely."

Adrian turned to Heidi, eyes warm, voice low with mock indignation. "Should I be jealous?"

She looked at him over the rim of her water glass, lips curling into a soft, knowing smile. "You're the only man I ever want."

Something in the way she said it silenced him. No teasing, no coyness—just truth. A quiet vow woven into the flicker of candlelight.

Adrian reached across the table, brushing his fingers lightly over hers.

Alan, watching them, gave a little shake of his head and raised his glass. "To love that sneaks up on you and refuses to let go."

Heidi laughed softly. "And to friends who embarrass you with stories over crème brûlée."

They toasted, glasses clinking gently above the flickering flame.

And for the first time in a long time, Adrian Werrington felt like a man who had everything.


The city glittered below them, lights scattered like stars caught in glass. Back in the penthouse, the air felt still, sacred, like it was holding its breath just for them.

Adrian poured them both a glass of water—no wine, not when she was carrying his son—and brought hers over in the same way he always brought her something now: with care, with reverence, with fingers that lingered as they passed the glass.

Heidi slipped off her heels and curled her legs beneath her on the cream-coloured velvet sofa, her hand resting gently over her bump. Adrian sank down beside her, undoing the top button of his shirt, the tension of the evening rolling off his shoulders.

"You were wonderful tonight," he said softly, watching her.

She tilted her head, amused. "I had a good time. Alan's a riot."

Adrian chuckled, setting his glass down and leaning toward her, elbows on his knees, gaze steady. "Alan's half in love with you already."

Heidi raised a brow, lips curling into a sly smile. "Well, he's going to be disappointed then." She reached out, fingers brushing the inside of his wrist. "You're the only man for me."

The words were light, but they landed like truth always does—quiet, deep, irrevocable.

Adrian stared at her, his expression unreadable for a beat. Then he stood, abruptly but not coldly, and walked into the bedroom without a word.

Heidi blinked, heart skipping. "Adrian?"

"Come here," he called, voice low, but steady.

She followed, padding barefoot across the warm floor. When she stepped into the room, the lights were dimmed, the city shimmering through the glass behind him. He was standing beside the bed, something small in his palm.

For a moment, she just looked at him—his rolled sleeves, his open collar, the way his heart looked like it was beating right at the edge of his skin.

He stepped forward. "I didn't want to do this tonight. I was going to wait. Make it special. Dress up. Champagne. Music." He gave a breathless laugh. "But nothing feels more right than this. Just you. Just *us*."

She stared at him, heart thudding, mouth slightly parted.

"I've loved you since before I was ready to admit it."

Her eyes blurred, lips trembling. "Adrian…"

He took her hand, pressing something cool and delicate into her palm.

"I don't care where we live, or how this looks, or what anyone says. I only care about one thing."

He dropped to one knee.

"Heidi Gibson, will you marry me?"

The ring in her hand caught the light—a simple, stunning oval diamond, delicate and timeless, set in a band of gold that felt like forever.

Her breath caught. "Yes," she whispered, the word falling from her lips like a promise.

Adrian stood slowly, cupping her face in both hands, pressing his forehead to hers as he exhaled shakily.

"Yes?" he repeated.

She nodded, smiling through tears. "Yes. God, yes."

Their kiss wasn't rushed. It wasn't frantic. It was slow, deep, sure—the kind of kiss that rewrote everything that came before it.

Adrian eased her down onto the bed with gentle, reverent hands, laying kisses over her cheek, her jaw, the soft curve of her throat.

"I love you," he murmured, again and again. "I love you."

She ran her fingers through his hair, pulling him closer. "I'm yours."

When he finally slid the ring onto her finger, it gleamed like a secret between them.

And in the hush of that night, with the city outside and their future ahead, they made love slowly—like two people who had finally stopped running, finally stopped hiding.

And who had found, in each other, everything they'd ever needed.

# Chapter Thirteen

Heidi returned to Werrington Wealth the following Monday, stepping back into her role as CFO with quiet determination. It was as if no time had passed—her name was back on the reports, her calendar filled within hours, and her sharp instincts picked up right where they'd left off.

Adrian had made her promise—twice, and with narrowed eyes—not to push herself too hard. She'd nodded sweetly, kissed him on the cheek… and promptly ignored him. Meetings stacked up. Reports were analysed. Contracts negotiated with her signature poise and precision. It felt good to be needed again, to have her mind fully engaged, even if her ankles were swollen by noon and her back protested every long stretch at her desk.

The news had broken earlier that week, splashed across finance blogs and society columns alike:

**_BILLIONAIRE ADRIAN WERRINGTON ENGAGED — RELATIONSHIP WITH CFO HEIDI GIBSON CONFIRMED._**

One headline, however, made her pause—just long enough to feel a flicker of unease:

**_IS NEW FIANCÉE TO BILLIONAIRE ADRIAN WERRINGTON PREGNANT?_**

Adrian had caught the furrow in her brow when she first saw it. He'd simply reached for her hand and said, "Let them speculate. We know the truth. That's all that matters." And in that moment, it really was.

There were a few more headlines floating around—brief commentary, a grainy photo of them walking hand in hand outside his penthouse. But the frenzy faded quickly. Perhaps it was the calm professionalism they maintained at work. Perhaps it was the way they looked at each other—undeniably real, undeniably in love.

Whatever the reason, the press lost interest. But they didn't.

They were building a life. They were expecting a child. And every whispered conversation behind boardroom doors or sidelong glance in the lobby was just background noise.

Heidi was exactly where she wanted to be—by Adrian's side, doing what she loved, carrying a life they'd created together. The world could watch, speculate, or move on.

She didn't care.

Because for the first time in a long time, she had everything that mattered.

On Friday, as the late afternoon sun spilled warm, golden light across her office, Adrian walked in with Alan at his side.

Alan leaned in and kissed Heidi's cheek, grinning broadly. "Adrian, I've got to say—I really like your choice of second wife better than your first."

Adrian gave him a look, equal parts amused and exasperated. "You seem to be making a habit of kissing my fiancée a little too often."

Alan shrugged, unbothered. "She's very kissable."

Heidi arched a brow, her lips curling into a wry smile as she zipped up her laptop case. "Flattery from the board is always appreciated."

Adrian moved to lean against her desk, the quiet fatigue of a long week visible in the slope of his shoulders. "We've got to sort out the Singapore contracts. I'll be in meetings for hours—I probably won't be home until late."

She nodded, still packing. "No problem. I'll see you when you get in."

He pulled her into his arms, pressing a warm kiss to her lips, lingering just a second too long for Alan's comfort. "Make sure you eat something," Adrian murmured.

"I will." She laughed. "You worry too much."

Alan chuckled, crossing his arms. "About you? He definitely does."

Adrian didn't deny it. He just held her a little tighter before releasing her. "Ben will take you home."

Heidi touched his cheek, a quiet moment passing between them. "Okay. Don't work too late."

"I will try to be home as soon as I can."

As Adrian and Alan disappeared down the corridor, Heidi glanced down at her bump—growing a little more each day—and smiled. The world outside the glass walls of

Werrington Wealth might still be chaotic, but in this moment, in her heart, everything felt exactly as it should be.

About thirty minutes later, Adrian and Alan were deep into contract negotiations in the executive lounge of the Werrington suite.

"I still don't like Clause 7.4," Alan said, adjusting his glasses. "It gives too much discretion to the local partners on performance metrics. We need a tighter definition or a safeguard."

Adrian nodded. "Agreed. Let's propose a rewording—tie it to quarterly returns and fixed KPIs. I don't want surprises six months down the line."

They were just diving into the next section when Adrian's phone lit up. With a quick glance, he tapped the speaker button, his eyes back on the document in front of him.

"Ben? Everything okay?" Adrian asked casually.

What followed froze the air in the room.

A wall of noise burst through the speaker—sirens screaming, car horns blaring, and men shouting over each other. The sharp whine of metal being torn open cut through it all like a knife.

"She's unconscious!" someone yelled.

Then another voice—urgent, panicked. "We need to get her out of there, now!"

A third man shouted, voice tight with horror, "God—she's pregnant!"

Adrian shot upright, his spine ramrod straight. "What the hell's going on, Ben?" His voice was sharp, commanding, laced with rising panic.

Alan's head snapped up too, his expression instantly grim.

There was a burst of static, then Ben's voice finally broke through, choked, and rushed, trying to make himself heard over the chaos. "Mr. Werrington—it's Miss Gibson."

Adrian went cold, his blood turning to ice.

Ben didn't wait for a response. "A truck—its brakes failed—came flying down Fifth and slammed into the car at the 42nd intersection. It hit hard, passenger side. She was pinned. We couldn't get to her. Emergency crews had to cut through the door."

"Is she—?" Adrian couldn't finish the sentence.

"She's unconscious," Ben said, breath ragged. "Breathing. Barely. They're loading her into the ambulance now—New York-Presbyterian."

Adrian was already moving, grabbing his jacket with trembling hands, eyes blazing. "I'm on my way."

Alan stood too, pale and shaken. The contract was forgotten. There was only one priority now.

And Adrian's heart had just been loaded into the back of an ambulance.


Adrian burst through the sliding glass doors of New York-Presbyterian, Alan right behind him. The antiseptic smell hit him first—then the chaos. Nurses, patients, gurneys, overhead announcements blaring codes he didn't understand. None of it mattered.

"Where is she?" Adrian demanded, voice raw, eyes wild as he scanned the crowded ER.

Ben was standing near the triage desk, still in his driver's uniform, his face ashen, hands clenched at his sides. The moment he saw Adrian, he stepped forward, but he didn't speak—he couldn't. Guilt and devastation were written all over him.

"She's here," he choked out finally. "They rushed her in—no one's told me anything else."

Adrian didn't wait. He stormed up to the triage nurse, slamming his hand on the counter. "Heidi Gibson. She was just brought in—car accident, pregnant. I need to know if she's—"

The nurse looked up, her face calm but firm, practiced in dealing with people in panic. "Sir, she's being evaluated now. A trauma team is working on her. As soon as a doctor can speak with you, they will."

"I don't want a doctor—I want to see her!" Adrian snapped. His voice cracked under the strain. "She's pregnant. She was unconscious. You have no idea how long she—she could be—" He turned away, his hands raking through his hair as he paced in a tight, desperate circle. "God, I should've taken her home—I should've—"

"Adrian," Alan said gently, stepping between him and the nurse. "Breathe. You're no good to her like this. We're here now. Let them work."

But Adrian couldn't breathe. His chest felt like it was collapsing in on itself, each inhale jagged, as if laced with shards of glass. An image of Heidi in a mangled car—bleeding, trapped, alone—replayed behind his eyes in an endless, torturous loop.

He couldn't stop seeing her hand in his that morning—warm, trusting—and before he left her this afternoon her fingers brushing his cheek in a soft, lingering goodbye.

*'I'll try to be home as soon as I can'*, he'd told her.

That was it.

Not *I love you.*

Not *You're my world.*

Just that. A promise wrapped in routine, spoken without knowing it might be the last thing he'd ever say to her.

And now, with her life hanging in the balance, it was all he could hear—over and over—like a haunting echo he couldn't silence.

He sank into one of the waiting room chairs like his legs had given out. Alan sat beside him, a steady presence, while Ben stood off to the side, shoulders slumped, still staring at nothing.

The minutes crawled by in slow, torturous silence, broken only by the occasional voice over the hospital intercom or the squeak of hurried footsteps on polished tile.

Ben sat across from Adrian, his face pale, eyes haunted. "I'm so sorry, sir," he said quietly, his voice thick with guilt. "I should've—"

Adrian shook his head, cutting him off. "No," he said, voice hoarse. "Don't. It's not your fault, Ben. You were not driving the truck." But the words felt hollow. Nothing could undo what had happened.

Alan sat beside him, a steady presence amid the storm. "She's strong, Adrian," he said, his hand briefly gripping Adrian's shoulder. "So is the baby. You have to believe that."

But Adrian couldn't speak. He just stared ahead, jaw clenched, one leg bouncing restlessly. The thought of losing her—*of losing* them—sliced through him like a blade.

He had only just gotten her back. They had just started imagining a future.

And now… now he was terrified it might all be taken from him.

And still—no word.


Almost an hour had passed. Sixty unbearable minutes where every second dragged like a lifetime. Adrian had paced a trench into the hospital floor, his hands shaking, his eyes bloodshot with fear. Alan had tried to get him to sit, to drink water, to breathe—but it was useless. Adrian was locked in a silent, desperate war with every terrifying possibility playing on repeat in his mind.

Then—*finally*—the doors to the trauma wing swung open.

A doctor stepped out, still in scrubs stained with blood—Heidi's blood.

"Heidi Gibson," she said.

Adrian was there in an instant. "I'm her fiancé—Adrian Werrington. Tell me. Please."

"Heidi is stable for now. She's still unconscious, but her brain scans show no swelling or bleeding at this point. That's good news."

Adrian exhaled shakily, but she didn't stop there.

"She does, however, have a partial placental abruption. That means the placenta is starting to separate from the uterine wall. It's small, but real. She's losing some blood internally, and the baby's oxygen supply is being compromised."

Alan's hand went to Adrian's shoulder. "Oh God."

Adrian tried to stay grounded, but the room tilted a little. "What does that mean for them?"

The doctor's voice was even, but her words landed with weight. "We're monitoring both closely. The baby's heart rate is fluctuating, but not in the danger zone yet. Our hope is to delay delivery—even just a few more days. At 23 weeks, every day makes a difference."

Adrian looked up, sharply. "And if you can't delay?"

"If either Heidi's condition declines, or the baby's heart rate drops further, we'll have to perform an emergency C-section."

Alan whispered, "Can he survive at 23 weeks?"

She paused. "It's possible. The NICU team is ready. But it would be an uphill battle. At 23 weeks, the baby is extremely premature. There's a significant risk of brain haemorrhages, underdeveloped lungs, vision, and hearing loss… and a high mortality rate."

Adrian's throat closed. "And Heidi? If you wait… what are the risks?"

"Worsening abruption could lead to severe haemorrhage, organ failure, even death. She can't tell us how she feels. She can't speak up if something changes. That makes things unpredictable."

Adrian stared at her, jaw clenched. "So, what you're saying is… I might have to choose."

The doctor looked at him gently, her voice quieter now. "We hope it won't come to that. But yes, if things worsen quickly, we may ask for a decision. Right now, we're trying to give them both a chance."

A heavy silence fell.

Finally, Alan asked the question neither of them wanted to say out loud.

"If it comes down to one… who has the better chance?"

She hesitated. "Medically? Heidi. But we'll do everything in our power to save them both. That's our promise."

Adrian nodded, slowly. "Then you do everything. You fight for both of them. Every second, every breath."

"We will," the doctor said softly. "I'll update you if anything changes."

Heidi was fighting for her life.

And so was their son.

Adrian's hands curled into fists. He looked like he might collapse. Alan gripped his shoulder, steadying him. Ben stood behind them both, looking gutted.

"I need to see her," Adrian said, breathless. "Please. I need to be with her."

The doctor gave a slow nod. "We're transferring her to ICU now. One of you can come in shortly."

Adrian's heart was thundering, but all he could hear was the sound of her voice in his memory, soft and laughing that morning.

He didn't care what rules he had to break.

He wasn't leaving her side.


A nurse led Adrian down a long, sterile hallway that felt like it stretched for miles. Each step felt heavier than the last, his breath shallow, chest tight. The white walls blurred around him, and the soft hum of hospital machinery sounded like a roar in his ears. He barely registered the people he passed—doctors, nurses, patients. None of them mattered. Only her.

The ICU doors opened with a quiet hiss, and the nurse turned to him gently. "She's stable for now. You can stay for a few minutes. Just… be prepared. There's swelling from the head trauma, and she's hooked up to multiple monitors."

Adrian nodded, though he didn't really hear her. His heart was pounding too loud.

Then he stepped inside.

There she was.

Heidi looked so small in that bed—too still, too pale. Tubes and wires snaked out from under the blankets, a heart monitor beeping steadily, too slow for his liking. Her face was bruised, a cut near her temple covered in a butterfly stitch. Her long lashes rested against skin that looked almost translucent. Machines surrounded her, but none of them could tell him what he needed to know: if she'd wake up… if she'd survive.

Adrian's breath caught. His legs nearly gave out.

He sank into the chair beside her bed, trembling, and reached for her hand. It was warm, but limp in his grasp. He clutched it tightly and pressed it to his lips.

"I'm here, sweetheart," he whispered, his voice hoarse. "I'm right here."

A sob rose in his throat, but he forced it down.

"I should've been with you. I should've—" He broke off, shaking his head as his eyes filled. "You were just going home. That's all. And now—God, Heidi, please… just wake up. Just give me one sign you can hear me."

He pressed his forehead to the back of her hand and closed his eyes.

"You can't leave me. Not like this. I haven't even told you—" His voice cracked. "I haven't told you how you changed my life."

The machines kept beeping. The only reply was silence.

Adrian sat there, heart breaking with every passing second, holding onto her like she was the only thing keeping him breathing—because she was.


The nurse returned, her expression gentle but firm. "Mr. Werrington, I'm sorry… I have to ask you to leave."

Adrian didn't even blink. "No."

She sighed. "I understand that this is hard, but—"

"No," he said again, sharper this time. "I'm not leaving her."

A moment of hesitation passed, then she quietly slipped out. A few minutes later, the door opened again—this time with the attending physician in tow, a man in his fifties with kind, tired eyes, and a clipboard in hand.

"Mr. Werrington," the doctor said, "I've been told you're unwilling to leave. I need you to understand—we're monitoring her and the baby around the clock, and we need access to do our work."

Adrian stood, his expression ragged, barely holding it together. "Do what you need to do. I won't get in the way. But I'm not leaving her side."

The doctor studied him for a moment, then looked at the machines, at Heidi's still form, at the way Adrian held her hand like it was the only thing keeping him alive.

Finally, the doctor nodded. "Then stay. Just... stay out of the way. And talk to her. It can help more than you know."

Adrian exhaled a breath that shook. "Thank you."

The doctor gave a quiet nod and stepped out with the nurse. When the door closed behind them, Adrian pulled the chair close to the bed again, sat down heavily, and took Heidi's hand in both of his.

The monitors hummed with quiet life—Heidi's heartbeat slow but steady, the baby's a delicate echo beside it, holding on.

He brought her hand to his lips, kissed it gently, then leaned forward and whispered, his voice hoarse, barely more than breath.

"You're not leaving me. Do you hear me? I just found you."

# Chapter Fourteen

Adrian wasted no time after Heidi was stabilised. Within hours, he had Ben coordinate the logistics to bring Judy Gibson, Heidi's mother, from Princeton to New York. There was no question of cost or convenience—only proximity.

He secured a suite for her in the hotel adjacent to the hospital, the closest accommodation available, so she could visit Heidi as often as she wanted. Judy came every day, her presence quiet but grounding, often holding her daughter's hand in silence or speaking softly to her, as if trying to coax her back with maternal will alone.

Adrian gave them space when she arrived, slipping away to shower, shave, and change into something clean before returning to his post beside Heidi's hospital bed. But he never stayed away for long. He couldn't. The minutes stretched too painfully when he wasn't near her.

Days blurred into nights, the sterile rhythm of the ICU his new reality. Nurses came and went. Monitors beeped in a mechanical lullaby. Meals went uneaten. Time became something meaningless—measured only in her shallow breaths and the slow drip of IV fluids.

Adrian stayed. He read aloud to her from the novel she'd left in her office, his voice low and steady even when his heart felt like it was fracturing one breath at a time. He played the soft classical playlists she loved, the ones she listened to when working late into the night. He spoke to her belly, resting his hand gently over the bump that had grown slightly fuller in the days since the accident.

He promised the world to their unborn son—beaches and bedtime stories, piano lessons, and messy pancakes on Sunday mornings. He begged for time, just enough time to right every wrong, to love Heidi the way she deserved, to be the man she believed he could be.

He couldn't bear the thought of losing either of them.

Sometimes he laid his head on her stomach, whispering nonsense stories, imagining what the baby would look like, imagining tiny kicks in response. Sometimes he simply cried, quietly, in the darkened room when the world had gone still, and no one could see.

And still—no change.

No flutter of fingers. No flicker of lashes. Just the persistent beep of the heart monitor and the rhythmic hiss of machines keeping her alive.

On the seventh day, Alan showed up unannounced.

Adrian was sitting in the armchair by Heidi's bed, eyes hollow, hair dishevelled, stubble darkening his jaw. He looked up, startled, as Alan stepped into the room with a paper bag of food in one hand and worry creasing his usually impenetrable features.

"I figured you wouldn't be eating," Alan said gruffly, setting the bag down on the table. "So, I brought real food. None of that vending machine crap."

Adrian didn't answer right away. His gaze drifted back to Heidi.

Alan crossed his arms and studied his friend in silence. "Jesus, Adrian. You look like hell."

"I feel worse," he muttered.

"I'm not here to lecture you," Alan said, softer now. "But you need to sleep. Eat. Breathe. She wouldn't want you destroying yourself while she's fighting for her life."

Adrian's throat bobbed. "I can't leave her."

"I'm not saying leave. I'm saying… let people help you. Let me help you."

Adrian stood slowly, walking to the window. He stared out at the hospital courtyard, bare trees shifting in the wind like brittle bones.

"She left to protect me because she loved me," he said quietly. "She was pregnant and scared, and I didn't see it. I didn't fight hard enough for her when it mattered. And now…"

Alan waited.

"And now I sit here and watch machines breathe for her. I talk to a belly and pretend it's enough." His voice cracked. "But it's not. It never will be. I can't lose her, Alan. I can't breathe without her."

Alan placed a steady hand on Adrian's shoulder. "Then don't let this be the end of the story. You want her to come back to you? Be here when she does. In one piece."

Adrian didn't move, but he nodded once.

Alan left him with the food and the silence, knowing anything more would be too much. He would check in again. That's what brothers did, even the ones you chose.

Still—no change.

Until day thirteen.

The alarm screamed at 3:42 a.m.

Adrian jolted awake in the chair beside Heidi's bed, his heart slamming against his ribs as red lights pulsed and monitors shrieked. The shrill, mechanical symphony of crisis fractured the stillness of the ICU, and for a disoriented moment, he couldn't breathe.

"What's happening?" he rasped, already on his feet, stumbling forward as nurses swarmed the room like a wave of white coats and clipped urgency.

One nurse checked Heidi's oxygen saturation—dropping rapidly. Another was already on the phone at the wall unit, rattling off vitals in quick succession. The lead nurse, Janelle—the one who never flinched—was already dragging the intubation cart toward the bed.

"Her oxygen's crashing," she said. "Lung function's deteriorating fast."

A second alarm joined the first, shriller and more insistent.

Adrian turned to the foetal monitor—its screen glowing ominously. The baby's heart rate was slowing.

"Decels confirmed," one of the neonatal nurses said urgently. "We've got foetal bradycardia. Heart rate's dipping into the red."

Adrian felt his chest tighten like a vice. "No," he said, voice cracking. "No, no, no…"

The room filled with more bodies—doctors, nurses, someone from respiratory, NICU staff. Dr. Rowan, the trauma attending, swept in still fastening his lab coat, his tone clipped and razor-sharp.

"She's in acute respiratory failure," he said. "We need to intubate immediately."

Another voice: "The baby's not tolerating the stress. We're seeing late decels. Could be related to the placental abruption."

Placental abruption.

The words hit Adrian like a punch to the chest. He remembered the term from that terrifying night of the accident—partial separation of the placenta. It had stabilised, they'd said. But now…

"She's haemorrhaging," another nurse called. "Small but steady—origin's the placenta."

"She's twenty-five weeks," Adrian said hoarsely, eyes darting from Heidi to the monitor. "The baby's… too small."

"The baby has a fighting chance," said the NICU nurse. "We've delivered younger. But every minute counts."

A new presence stepped in—Dr. Kinari, the high-risk OB. She glanced at the monitor, the blood pressure readout, the oxygen levels, then looked directly at Adrian.

"We need your consent," she said, calm but firm. "If we stabilise Heidi first, we may lose the baby. If we deliver now, surgery could kill Heidi—her body is failing, and the placental abruption complicates everything."

Adrian's knees threatened to buckle.

"We don't have time to do both," she continued gently. "You're her medical proxy. You have to tell us—if it comes down to it, who do we save?"

The words were a blade across his soul.

He looked down at Heidi—his brilliant, beautiful, maddening Heidi—her face pale and still, her body tangled in IV lines and sensors, a quiet battlefield.

She looked fragile. Too fragile for this.

But beneath the thin blanket, her rounded belly rose and fell, impossibly steady, impossibly brave. The child inside—the one he wanted more than anything—still fought, even now. Their child.

Adrian felt like he was being ripped in two.

All his life, he had imagined fatherhood like a fairytale—Sunday mornings in pyjamas, a baby asleep on his chest, teaching tiny fingers to play piano keys, laughter echoing through a sunlit kitchen. But none of it mattered without her.

He couldn't lose *her*.

He couldn't be without *her*.

His voice trembled as he said, "Heidi…"

Dr. Rowan stepped closer. "We'll do everything we can. But we need a decision."

Adrian stared down at her, heart breaking. He thought of all the moments they hadn't had yet—her smile in the morning light, her voice teasing him over dinner, the sound of her laughter wrapped around the walls of a shared home.

She had changed him. Made him softer. Stronger. Whole.

She was his beginning. And his end.

He took a shaking breath and forced the words past the ache in his throat. "Save her," he whispered.

A heartbeat of silence.

Then motion erupted—orders flying, scrubs brushing past him as they wheeled her out of the room. One team headed for ventilation. Another readied an emergency surgical suite in case her vitals deteriorated further.

Adrian stood frozen in the echo of fading footsteps and beeping machines.

He pressed a trembling hand to the bed, the spot where she'd lain moments before, and whispered, "You come back to me. Do you hear me? You come back."

The door swung closed.

And he was alone with the silence that remained.


The double doors to the surgical theatre slammed open with a clang that echoed like thunder.

Adrian stood just beyond them, scrubbed out, dressed in sterile blues, but barred from going any farther. The glass window between him and the operating room felt like a wall a thousand miles thick. On the other side, a controlled chaos unfolded—voices clipped, movements precise, urgency painted across every face.

Heidi lay motionless on the table beneath a halo of sterile light. Drapes covered her body except for the swell of her belly and her pale, delicate face, framed in a nest of tangled hair and oxygen tubing. Machines beeped. A ventilator hissed. Monitors blinked like stuttering stars.

"BP's still dropping. Seventy-two over forty-one."

"She's bleeding into the uterus—abruption site is worsening."

"Start the transfusion. Type O-negative. Hang another unit."

Adrian's hands curled into fists at his sides.

"She's strong," Judy whispered beside him. She stood like a sentinel, a mother carved from steel and fear, watching her daughter be torn open by fate. "She's stronger than this."

Inside the OR, Dr. Kinari's voice rang above the controlled storm.

"We're going for a classical caesarean. Vertical incision—faster access. Let's move!"

Scissors snapped. Metal clinked against metal. Adrian couldn't breathe.

He didn't understand how the world hadn't stopped spinning.

Didn't understand how the stars hadn't gone dark when they said he might lose them both.

Then—sharp and clear—

"I've got the baby!"

A breath held.

A silence so thick it felt like drowning.

"Cord's wrapped twice around the neck—get me suction—"

The NICU team swarmed in.

The seconds stretched out like an eternity.

And then—

A sound.

Thin. Raspy. Struggling.

But there.

A cry.

*A cry.*

Adrian's knees buckled and he gripped the edge of the observation rail as the tiniest, angriest scream he had ever heard shattered the tension in the room like glass under pressure.

"He's breathing," someone confirmed. "Spontaneous respiration. Apgar six."

"Get him to the isolette. NICU team, go!"

They moved like lightning, transferring the tiny infant—so small he could've fit in Adrian's two palms—into a sterile pod. Tubes. Sensors. Oxygen. But alive. *Alive.*

His son.

But joy hadn't yet touched Adrian's chest—because Heidi still wasn't moving.

"BP's unstable," Dr. Rowan said. "Clamp that bleeder—she's losing volume faster than we can replace."

"She's throwing PVCs," called the anaesthesiologist. "We're nearing cardiac threshold."

"She's in DIC," someone muttered. "Coagulation cascade's failing."

Adrian's vision tunnelled.

"No," he said aloud, his voice low, raw. "No, no, no…"

Inside the OR, Dr. Kinari leaned over the surgical field, her voice fierce. "We're not losing her. Not today."

Her hands moved like a symphony—commanding, relentless.

"Graft it. Pack the uterus. More plasma. Another epi push. Now."

Minutes bled into more minutes. Adrian couldn't tell how many. He couldn't tell if he was standing, floating, or dreaming. Just that the woman he loved was dying—*or surviving*—beneath his helpless gaze.

Then—

The monitors slowed.

Settled.

Beep. Beep. Beep.

"Pressure's stabilising," someone said. "Bleeding's controlled. We've got her back."

Adrian sagged against the wall.

"She's in sinus rhythm," the anaesthesiologist confirmed.

"She's going to need ICU," Dr. Rowan said, "but she's made it through surgery."

Dr. Kinarip exhaled slowly, her gloves streaked with blood, sweat glistening at her temples. "Let's close her up. Carefully."

Adrian pressed both hands to his face and shook with a sob that finally, finally escaped.

She was alive.

They both were.

His son had cried into the world, and Heidi—*his Heidi*—had fought through the impossible.

They had survived.

And in that sterile, too-bright hallway, as a nurse came to lead him toward the NICU and whispered, "Would you like to meet your son?"—he found himself weeping like a man reborn.

# Chapter Fifteen

The NICU was hushed, blanketed in soft light and the rhythmic hum of life-saving machines. It smelled faintly of antiseptic and something warmer—something almost sacred.

Adrian stepped through the glass doors as if entering hallowed ground.

A nurse greeted him with a gentle smile. "Mr. Werrington?" she asked softly, as if louder words might rupture the delicate miracle inside.

He nodded, his throat too tight to speak.

"Your son is stable," she said. "He's breathing with assistance, but he's strong. A fighter. You can see him now."

She led him down a row of isolettes—each one a world of hope and fragility—until she stopped beside one near the window.

"There he is."

Adrian looked.

And the world… stopped.

Inside the temperature-controlled incubator, nestled in blankets no bigger than a doll's blanket, was the smallest human being he had ever seen. His skin was nearly translucent; his head covered in the finest dusting of dark hair. Wires and tubes threaded around him like ivy, monitoring every breath, every beat, every flicker of movement.

But he was alive.

His tiny chest rose and fell.

His mouth opened in a faint, silent mewl.

Adrian moved closer, slowly, reverently.

"He was 1 pound 13 ounces," the nurse said, checking a screen. "But he's doing well for a twenty-five weeker. Strong reflexes, responsive to sound."

Adrian barely heard her. He was kneeling now, both hands pressed against the clear plastic wall of the isolette, staring at this impossibly small, impossibly fierce boy.

His son.

"Can I… touch him?" he whispered.

The nurse smiled. "Yes. Through the port. Just your fingertip, gently."

He reached in through the side panel and extended his index finger.

And the baby, as if drawn by instinct, curled his tiny hand—no bigger than a grape—around it.

Adrian choked on a breath.

Tears welled and spilled freely.

"You're here," he whispered, voice cracking. "You made it."

His thumb gently stroked the baby's arm. "You scared the hell out of me, you know that?" He swallowed. "But you held on. Just like your mum."

His eyes drifted closed for a moment, overwhelmed.

"I haven't picked a name yet," he murmured. "Your mum and I… we didn't get that far."

He opened his eyes again, locking onto that impossibly small hand clutching his finger with surprising strength.

"You will have to wait for your name until your mum wakes up."

Adrian smiled through tears.

His son shifted slightly, a faint twitch in his legs.

Adrian pressed his forehead to the glass.

"Your mum's still fighting," he whispered. "But she's coming back. I know she is. And when she wakes up, I'm going to tell her everything. About this moment. About you."

He stayed like that for a long time—speaking softly, gently, to the child who had changed everything. To the son he had almost lost.

To the life he would now do anything to protect.

And as the sun rose outside the hospital windows, painting the city in streaks of pink and gold, Adrian Werrington made a silent promise to the sleeping miracle in the incubator:

*He will always protect him.*

And soon, neither of them would ever have to face this world without Heidi again.

The walk back to Heidi's room felt heavier than it had that morning. Maybe it was the weight of everything he now carried—love, fear, gratitude... *awe.* Or maybe it was simply that part of him didn't want to let go of the moment he'd just had with his son. Their son.

*Our son.*

Adrian stepped into the room quietly, careful not to disrupt the delicate stillness. The machines were still there, dutiful, and tireless. Heidi remained unmoving, pale against the sea of white linens, her breathing assisted by tubes that hissed in gentle rhythm.

But something had changed.

There was colour in her cheeks—faint, but there. Her pulse read stronger. Her body, still so frail, no longer looked like it was slipping.

She was fighting.

Adrian sank back into the chair at her bedside, taking her hand gently between both of his. "Hi, sweetheart," he whispered, his voice low, reverent.

He rubbed slow circles over her knuckles, his thumb lingering on the soft curve where her engagement ring should be. It rested in his pocket now, waiting—just like he was. It would return to her finger, and this time, a wedding band would sit beside it. As soon as she was better.

"There's someone you need to meet," he said softly.

He took a breath, emotion catching in his throat.

"He's... perfect, Heidi. He's so small. So impossibly small. But he's here. He's breathing. Fighting."

Adrian reached into his pocket and pulled out his phone, already open to the photo the NICU nurse had taken. He held it out, just in case—just in case her eyes fluttered open and she could see it.

"He's got your mouth," he continued, smiling through a tear. "And your quiet strength. I swear, he wrapped his hand around my finger and wouldn't let go."

He set the phone on the bedside table, screen up, the picture still glowing softly. He kissed her hand, resting his forehead against it afterward.

"I thought I lost both of you," he whispered. "And I—I couldn't choose. But they made me. They made me say the words. And I chose you, Heidi. Because if I'd lost you..."

His voice cracked. He sat up again, looking at her face.

"I knew you wouldn't leave him," he said. "Even if I had to choose… you'd never let go. You'd find your way back to him."

He reached out and gently brushed a lock of hair from her temple.

"I need you to come back now, sweetheart," he said quietly. "He's here. He's waiting for you. We both are."

The machines beeped steadily. The air held its breath.

Adrian didn't move.

He kept her hand cradled in his, and he began to hum softly—Clair de Lune, the first piece he'd heard her listening to in her office one night when she worked late. The memory swelled inside him like a prayer.

And somewhere, beneath the layers of sedation and stillness, a single finger twitched against his palm.

It was small.

It could've been nothing.

But Adrian sat bolt upright, staring at her hand, breath frozen in his chest.

Then—another twitch.

And this time, she made a sound. A faint, broken exhale. A whisper of breath caught in her throat.

Adrian leaned close, tears spilling freely now.

"Heidi, I'm here. Our son is here. We're waiting. Come back to us."

He kissed her temple, holding her hand as if it were the most fragile treasure he'd ever been given.


Everything was heavy.

Her limbs, her lungs, her thoughts.

Like floating underwater in a dream where you try to scream, but the sound never comes. Where light filters dimly through the surface but never quite reaches you. Where your name echoes faintly, over, and over, but you can't answer.

*Adrian.*

She knew that voice. Even through the thick, muffled fog that clung to her mind like wet wool, she knew it. Deep and low, like warmth on a cold night. He was speaking—

no, pleading—and every word brushed against her like a touch she couldn't feel but somehow still knew.

*'Hi, sweetheart…'*

That word tugged at her—sweetheart—a name only he used. A name that felt like arms around her waist, forehead kisses in elevator shadows, promises whispered into tangled sheets.

She wanted to answer. God, she wanted to open her eyes and say his name and feel his hand in hers. But her body wasn't listening. Her body had been through war, and her mind was caught somewhere between here and not-here.

*'There's someone you need to meet…'*

Her baby.

Her heart tried to leap, but it was more like a flutter, a tremble deep inside her ribs. He was talking about the baby. Our baby.

*'…so small. So impossibly small. He's breathing. Fighting.'*

Fighting…

Tears pooled behind her closed lids, even as her face remained still. She wanted to scream—to reach for him, to hold her son. She wanted to know if he was okay, if Adrian was okay, if this was real or some cruel delusion crafted by her brain.

He kept talking, his voice growing tighter, breaking apart in places where emotion spilled out too fast to catch. She caught only fragments.

*'…they made me…'*

*'…chose you…'*

*'…couldn't lose you…'*

*'…he's waiting…'*

A soft melody filled the air, brushing against the fog in her head like a breeze trying to stir dead leaves. Clair de Lune. He was humming it. She could almost feel the music vibrating through the air, vibrating through him. It was beautiful, like it always was—wistful and full of longing.

She followed it. Let it pull her through the weight, through the fear, through the place where pain had once screamed but now only pulsed gently, distantly.

And then—

A warmth. Her hand. His lips on her skin.

"You're the strongest woman I've ever known," he said, his voice a vow. "And I'm never letting you go again. Not for anything. Not for anyone."

He pressed a kiss to her forehead—gentle, reverent—as monitors beeped steadily in the background, bearing witness to the quiet, impossible miracle unfolding between them.

And for the first time in weeks, the darkness lifted.

Because she had come back.

And so had hope.

# Chapter Sixteen

Heidi's recovery unfolded like spring after a brutal winter—slow, tentative, but unstoppable. Each day brought her a little closer back to herself, and to the life she had nearly lost.

The morning after she first opened her eyes, Adrian was still holding her hand when she woke again, his head bowed beside her. He lifted his gaze the moment her fingers flexed.

"You stayed," she whispered.

"I told you I'm never leaving."

Strength returned to her in small, stubborn increments. They weaned her off the ventilator. Then came sips of water. Broth. Yogurt. She graduated to a soft diet by the third day and demanded real coffee by the fifth. Adrian tried to deny her. She glared at him until he relented.

"I've had a tube down my throat, a near-death experience, and thirty-seven stitches," she rasped. "I think I've earned caffeine."

Her mother visited daily, carrying homemade soup and gentle scoldings. Judy rarely cried, but the way she looked at Heidi—like she couldn't believe she was real and whole—was enough to undo them both. She smoothed Heidi's hair, adjusted her blankets, and kissed her forehead like she was five years old again.

On the sixth day, Alan arrived with a bag of chocolate truffles and zero decorum. "You look like hell," he said cheerfully. "But less like hell than a week ago."

Heidi chuckled—then winced. "Don't make me laugh. It hurts."

"Then I'm doing my job right." He gave her a wink. "Honestly, I just came to make sure Adrian was still showering."

"Barely," she muttered.

Alan dropped into the visitor's chair. "You scared the hell out of us, Gibson."

"Yeah," she said softly. "I scared myself, too."

He stayed for an hour, trading jokes, and half-serious advice about raising sons and surviving corporate warfare. Before he left, he pressed her hand with surprising gentleness. "You're tough as hell, you know that?"

"Don't let that get around," she said with a tired smile.

On the seventh day, Ben came.

He hovered awkwardly at the door, clutching a small arrangement of white daisies and baby's breath—sweet and unassuming, like he didn't want to overstep.

"I wasn't sure if I should come," he said. "After everything…"

"Don't be silly," Heidi interrupted, reaching for his hand. "You helped save my life."

"I stalled. I froze. I—I didn't know what to do—"

"You called Adrian. That's what mattered." Her voice was quiet but clear. "None of this was your fault."

Ben's eyes glossed. He nodded, swallowing hard. "The baby's doing well. Everyone's calling him the NICU rockstar."

Heidi blinked at that. "I haven't seen him yet," she said. "They said soon. That I need more strength. But I feel like I've been waiting my whole life."

Ben gave her a soft smile. "He's going to know how loved he is."

That evening, Adrian walked in with a wheelchair.

"Ready?" he asked, eyes shining.

She blinked. "Is it time?"

He nodded. "He's ready for you."

Wrapped in a soft robe, her IV line taped down and a nurse at her side, Heidi let Adrian wheel her through the hospital corridors. Every hallway felt like a pilgrimage. Every turn a breath held. When they finally reached the NICU doors, she thought her heart might give out from anticipation alone.

Then—there he was.

Tiny. Swaddled.

Sleeping in a softly lit isolette.

A tangle of wires and monitors surrounded him, but none of it could distract from the miracle of his chest rising and falling. The nurse opened the isolette and gently lifted the baby, placing him against Heidi's chest as she settled into the kangaroo care chair.

She gasped.

He was so small. Not even five pounds. But real. Warm. Alive.

Her arms trembled as they closed around him, the warmth of his skin against hers stealing her breath. Tears slipped silently down her cheeks.

"Hi, little one," she whispered, pressing a kiss to his downy head. "I'm your mum."

Adrian knelt beside her, his hand resting over hers, over the impossibly small body they now shared.

"Heidi," he murmured, voice choked. "You did it."

She looked at him through tears. "We did."

The machines kept beeping. Nurses kept moving. But in that chair, holding her son, Heidi felt the world slow to a quiet, perfect stillness.

Everything she had fought for was in her arms.

And for the first time since the accident, she let herself believe—

They were going to be okay.


Naming a child should've been the easiest thing in the world. But for two people who had battled through trauma, love, and loss to get here, it became something sacred.

They sat beside their son's isolette, the soft hum of the NICU machines rising and falling like a lullaby. His progress over the last week had stunned even the doctors. He'd gone from struggling with oxygen levels to breathing with minimal support, from barely tolerating touch to curling his impossibly tiny fingers around theirs.

"He's got a will of steel," Adrian murmured one morning, his gaze fixed on the baby's face. "Like you."

Heidi smiled, her fingers tracing slow circles on her son's blanket. "No," she whispered. "That's you. He held on because you did."

Adrian turned to her, quiet for a long moment. "We should give him a name that means something. Strength. Legacy. Something he can grow into."

Heidi nodded, eyes soft with emotion. "What about William?"

Adrian blinked. "That was my grandfather's name."

"I know. You told me once. Said he taught you how to ride a horse and how to never flinch in front of the press."

A smile curved his lips. "William it is."

She touched the baby's cheek. "And Henry. For your father."

Adrian inhaled, visibly moved. "William Henry Werrington," he said slowly. "Strong. Noble. Like he was born to carry the name."

Heidi nodded, eyes misty. "It's perfect."

Adrian bent and kissed her temple. "He's going to be just fine. I know it now."

Alan arrived later that day, tossing a bag of gourmet pretzels on the bed like it was contraband.

"Missed me?" he grinned.

Heidi smirked. "You only come bearing snacks. Never flowers."

"I figured you'd rather eat than smell things."

Adrian stepped in from the adjoining NICU room, coffee in hand, and Alan gave him a long look. "You look like someone let you sleep for more than three hours."

"I didn't," Adrian said flatly, handing Heidi her coffee before dropping into the corner chair. "But William's doing better."

Alan raised an eyebrow. "You finally gave the kid a name?"

Adrian nodded. "William Henry. After my grandfather and father."

Alan gave a low whistle. "Well damn. He's destined for great things now."

Heidi smiled. "He's already exceeded expectations. He's strong. Brave. Just like his father."

Adrian shook his head, but a flicker of pride lit his expression. He brushed a gentle hand over Heidi's knee.

"You need to go back to work," she said suddenly.

He blinked. "What?"

"You haven't been to the office in weeks."

"I'm not leaving you. Or him."

"I'm not asking for forever," she said gently. "Just a few hours a day. You need the distraction. And your team probably thinks you died."

Alan chimed in. "We actually had a bet going on how long it would take before you completely cracked and tried to install a mobile command centre in the NICU."

"I did consider it," Adrian muttered.

"Adrian," Heidi said, voice soft but steady. "You've been my anchor. But you also need space to breathe. To be you again. The company needs you."

Alan leaned forward. "And I need my partner back. Just for a few meetings. Maybe a merger or two."

Adrian sighed, rubbing the back of his neck. "You're both ganging up on me."

Heidi smiled. "Because we love you."

That silenced him. After a beat, he kissed her hand and stood. "Fine. Half a day tomorrow. But I expect fifteen text updates. Minimum."

"Sixteen," she teased.

He shook his head, smiling as he left the room.

Alan waited until the door clicked shut. Then he let out a breath and slumped into the chair beside her. "He scared the hell out of me, you know."

Heidi looked at him, surprised.

"I've known Adrian Werrington for over twenty years. I've seen him close billion-dollar deals without blinking. But when you got hurt… he broke. And I didn't know if he'd come back from that."

Heidi reached for his hand. "I'm sorry I scared you."

He gripped her hand tightly. "Just do me a favour, okay?"

"Anything," she said softly.

"Don't ever get hurt again. Seriously. My heart can't take it."

A laugh escaped her, breathy and light, even as her ribs gave a protesting throb. "Deal. But only because it's you."

They sat in an easy silence after that, their fingers still laced. The soft rhythm of the monitors pulsed around them like a gentle heartbeat—life moving forward, quietly, insistently.

The door creaked open. Adrian stepped back into the room, coffee in one hand, his brow lifting slightly when he caught sight of their intertwined fingers.

"Should I be worried?" he asked, feigning suspicion.

Alan didn't miss a beat. "I'd steal her in a heartbeat, mate—but she won't have me."

Adrian smirked, walking toward them. "Good. Because I'd have to kill you."

Heidi rolled her eyes. "You two are ridiculous."

Adrian leaned down, pressing a kiss to her forehead, his voice low. "Only about you."

And for the first time in what felt like forever, Heidi let herself feel the peace of being loved—fiercely, completely, and without fear.

Adrian returned to work slowly, reluctant at first, his heart tethered to the sterile corridors of the hospital and the fragile, miraculous life fighting behind the glass. For the first week, he only managed half-days, his thoughts always drifting back to the NICU and the quiet room where Heidi continued to heal. But eventually, the rhythm of business pulled him back in, and full days resumed.

Still, he never really left them.

Every hour, almost without fail, a text would arrive on Heidi's phone.

*Did William lift his fist again like he's ready to throw a punch?*

*Tell him his father said bedtime is not negotiable.*

*How's my girl? You sleeping enough? You smiling yet?*

Heidi would smile; her heart warmed every time and answer them all. Short replies at first—still tired, still sore—but filled with the kind of affection she had once tried so hard to hide. Now, it came easily. Naturally. Like breathing.

One night, when the nurses had dimmed the lights and the quiet hum of monitors was the only sound, Adrian arrived with two coffees and a softness in his eyes. He kissed her temple, whispered something about William outgrowing his preemie onesie already, and sat beside her on the edge of the bed.

Then he reached into his coat pocket and slowly opened his hand, revealing the engagement ring she hadn't seen since the day of the accident. It sat in his palm like a promise unbroken, a symbol of everything they'd nearly lost—and everything they'd fought to keep.

"I've been carrying this every day," he said, his voice quiet, thick with emotion. "Hoping you haven't changed your mind."

Tears welled in her eyes—not from doubt, but from the weight of all they'd endured. She couldn't speak at first, just nodded as her fingers trembled. He took her hand gently and slid the ring back where it belonged, the gesture reverent, sealing something sacred between them.

Then, barely above a whisper, she said, "Never."

He exhaled—slow, shaky, like he'd been holding his breath since the day he almost lost her.

Every day, William grew stronger. His breaths no longer needed help. He still looked impossibly small, but his cries had become louder, his limbs more insistent, his tiny fingers wrapping around theirs like he meant to hold on forever. The doctors marvelled at him—at his fight, his tenacity. Heidi called him her little warrior, and Adrian never corrected her. He agreed with every word.

Heidi's recovery kept pace. Slow, steady, almost stubborn in its determination. The colour returned to her cheeks, the fire to her spirit. The pain faded, leaving behind only the love.

Eventually, Judy packed her things to return home. But not before she pulled Adrian aside near the elevators and looked him dead in the eye.

"I didn't know what to think of you, the first time I met you," she said. "But I do now."

He smiled.

"Thank you," she said, her voice thick with emotion. "For loving my daughter like you do. For showing up when it matters most."

He nodded, unable to speak for a moment. Then, "She saved me too, Judy. In more ways than you'll ever know."

They hugged quietly, and Judy gave him one last look before turning toward the exit. "You bring my grandson to see me when he's ready. And don't wait too long, Werrington."

"We won't," he promised.

And then—after weeks of monitors and midnight vigils, of whispered lullabies through the glass and waiting for miracles—the day came.

Discharge papers signed. Car seat tested. Nurses crying quiet tears. Heidi's hand in Adrian's as they walked out the hospital doors, their son nestled against her chest.

William Henry Werrington, tiny but fierce, was finally going home.

# Chapter Seventeen

The penthouse felt different.

Heidi stepped across the threshold, clutching William gently to her chest in his soft carrier, and took a breath. The familiar scent of home—clean linen, lemon wood polish, and a hint of Adrian's cologne—wrapped around her like a memory.

Adrian hovered behind her, one hand on the small of her back, the other lugging the overstuffed diaper bag like it was a briefcase made of explosives. He'd already tripped twice getting it out of the car, muttered a curse under his breath, and declared that baby gear was "designed to test a man's patience and balance."

Now, he was trying to look confident. He was failing adorably.

"Okay," he said, clearing his throat. "I have a surprise for you."

Heidi turned, brows raised. "Another one? You've already brought me home. That's enough."

"Not quite," he said, his eyes twinkling. "Come with me."

He led her slowly down the hallway, his hand brushing hers. When they stopped outside one of the spare bedrooms, Heidi's heart beat a little faster.

Adrian paused. "Ready?"

He opened the door.

Heidi stepped inside—and froze.

The room had been transformed.

Soft cream walls were accented with delicate sage green panels, warm and soothing. A white crib sat beneath the window, dressed in the softest linen sheets and a knitted blanket. A glider chair waited in the corner beside a small bookshelf already half-full, its shelves lined with storybooks and plush animals. On the far wall, elegant wooden letters spelled out WILLIAM, with a small crown carved above the 'W'.

She blinked, overwhelmed. "Adrian…"

"I had help," he rushed to say. "Judy supervised the paint. Alan picked the armchair, which is shocking, honestly. And I may have had a meltdown over mobile colours."

She laughed softly, the sound catching in her throat. "It's perfect."

He stepped beside her, fidgeting with the straps of the carrier as if afraid to disturb William. "I wasn't sure if I should wait for you. But I wanted it to feel like he belonged here. Like we all did."

Heidi turned toward him, her eyes misty again. "We do."

Adrian exhaled. "Good. Because I have no idea how this diaper pail works, and I think I may have installed the changing table backwards."

"You tried to assemble furniture alone?"

"I'm a CEO, not a carpenter."

Heidi leaned against the crib, watching him fumble with a baby wipe dispenser like it was a puzzle box. "You're trying too hard. It's adorable."

"I am not adorable," he grumbled, poking the lid. "I'm rugged and capable and incredibly intimidating."

"You're wearing a burp cloth on your shoulder."

He paused. Looked. Groaned. "Damn it."

She giggled, stepping forward. "Come here, Mr. Intimidating."

He met her halfway, his arms wrapping gently around her as she nestled into his chest, William safely curled between them. The quiet hum of the penthouse settled around them—soft, safe, and still.

"I never imagined this," Heidi whispered. "Not after everything. Not like this."

He kissed her hair, his voice low. "Neither did I. But now I can't imagine anything else."

They stood there a long time, in the room built from love and second chances, their son breathing steadily between them.

Home, at last.


Finally, after what felt like an eternity of cautious intimacy and sleepless nights, Heidi was given the all-clear.

The doctor's words were clinical, almost offhand: "You've healed beautifully. You can resume all activities as you feel comfortable."

But to Heidi, they were anything but clinical. They were permission. Permission to be close again. To bridge the space that had existed—not out of lack of love, but out of necessity—between her body and Adrian's.

Because she missed him.

Desperately.

It wasn't just the physical ache, though that was there, humming quietly beneath her skin. It was the absence of what they were—what they'd always been—in those most intimate moments. The stolen kisses in the hallway were sweet, and his arms around her in bed were comforting, but it wasn't enough. Not anymore. She needed to feel him again. Needed to remember what it meant to love him with her whole body, not just her heart.

She didn't tell him the doctor had cleared her. Not right away. She wanted to show him.

That night, after William was asleep and the dishes were done and the world had gone quiet, Heidi slipped into their bedroom while Adrian was in the shower. She changed into the softest silk chemise she could find—nothing extravagant, just simple and ivory and hers. She didn't even bother with makeup. Her body, though softer and still a little foreign to her, carried the quiet pride of survival. Of motherhood. Of transformation.

When Adrian walked into the room, towelling off his hair, he stopped in his tracks.

His eyes swept over her, slow and stunned, as though he were trying to reconcile this vision with the woman he'd been holding at night for months.

"You're beautiful," he murmured, voice hoarse, towel forgotten in his hand.

Heidi stepped toward him, heart pounding. "The doctor said I'm healed."

He stared at her for a moment—long enough that she thought maybe she'd made a mistake. But then he crossed the room in three strides and pulled her into his arms like he'd been holding his breath for weeks.

The kiss started gently. Reverently.

But it didn't stay that way.

It deepened with a hunger neither of them had realised they'd been suppressing. It was messy, tender, and raw, and by the time they reached the bed, both were trembling— more from emotion than desire.

He was careful with her. Almost too careful.

"You don't have to be delicate," she whispered against his mouth. "I'm not breakable anymore."

He paused, forehead pressed to hers, eyes shining in the low light.

"It's not that," he said quietly. "I just... I've never wanted something to be right so badly."

She pulled him closer. "It already is."

And when they finally came together, it wasn't about heat or urgency. It was slow and reverent, filled with whispered apologies neither of them needed to make and promises neither of them spoke aloud. His hands trembled as they touched her, rediscovering the curves he already knew by heart. She wept, just a little, when he kissed the faint line of her scar, as if it were holy.

And when he moved inside her, they both stilled—overcome by the immensity of it. Of them.

It wasn't the first time.

But it felt like it was.

Like everything before had been a prologue, and this—this quiet, tear-soaked, soul-baring union—was the real beginning.

Afterward, they lay tangled together, her head on his chest, his hand resting protectively over her waist. Neither of them spoke for a long time.

Until finally, Adrian's voice broke the silence.

"I didn't know I could love you more," he whispered, lips brushing her temple. "But I do."

And Heidi, wrapped in the warmth of his arms, of their life, whispered back the only thing she could.

"I know. Me too."

William was three months old, a chubby-cheeked, bright-eyed bundle of joy with a laugh that could melt the iciest of moods. That afternoon, the sun poured through the living room windows in golden shafts, catching in the fine strands of his wispy hair as Adrian lay sprawled on the rug beside him. He was on his stomach, making exaggerated faces while holding up a soft cloth book that made crinkling sounds William found utterly fascinating.

Heidi stood in the doorway, sipping tea and watching them, her heart so full it felt impossible to contain. This—this life, this man, this child—none of it had been planned. But it had become everything.

Adrian looked up mid-goofy grin and caught her watching. His expression softened, eyes lingering on her like he still couldn't believe she was real.

Then, casually—so casually it caught her off guard—he asked, "How much longer are you going to make me wait to marry you?"

Heidi blinked, lowering her mug. "Excuse me?"

He smirked. "You heard me."

She burst into laughter, cheeks flushing. "I'll marry you right now if you like."

He raised a brow, as if testing her. "You would."

"Yes," she said simply, walking over to sit beside him. "Absolutely."

Adrian sat up straighter, propping William in his lap, who immediately began trying to chew on his father's knuckle. "Don't you want a huge white church wedding with all the trimmings? Fancy dress, dramatic aisle moment, string quartet, swans?"

"Swans?" she teased, lifting William from his lap and planting a kiss on his soft head. "Now that would be dramatic."

"You know what I mean," Adrian said, suddenly serious. "People expect it. Especially from me."

Heidi tilted her head, eyes thoughtful. "Adrian… if this past year hasn't taught me anything else, it's that I honestly don't care what people expect."

She looked down at William, then back up at the man who had once been just her boss, then her lover, and now—her everything.

"I care about us. And about this little guy. I care about real things. The people who show up for you when you're falling apart. The ones who sit next to your hospital bed and don't ask for anything in return. The ones who stay, even when they have every reason to run. That's what matters to me."

Adrian's jaw tensed, and he reached over to tuck a strand of hair behind her ear.

"You are going to be the most beautiful bride," he said quietly, voice rough with emotion.

Heidi smiled, eyes damp with unshed tears. "So… city hall tomorrow?"

"God, I love you," he muttered, pulling her close with one arm as William squealed happily in her lap.

"And I love you," she whispered, resting her forehead against his. "I'd marry you in a bathrobe, in the rain, on a Tuesday if it meant you were mine."

Adrian kissed her—soft and slow, right there on the rug with their son gurgling between them.

"Maybe not tomorrow but soon, just be ready," he said, grinning against her lips. "But I draw the line at bathrobes."

# Chapter Eighteen

Heidi had no idea.

Saturday morning began like any other, with William babbling at an ungodly hour and Adrian bringing her coffee in bed while she nursed their son. He kissed her temple and murmured something about her mum wanting to spend time with her—just a girl's day out, he said, to spoil her a little. She didn't question it. She'd been in sweats and messy buns for three straight months, and her mother had been itching to "glam her up" for weeks.

So, she went. Her nails were done in a soft blush tone. Her hair was curled into long, loose waves. Makeup was applied with gentle precision by a woman who said, "You're going to glow even more in a few hours." Heidi had laughed, thinking it was just mum talk.

All the while, her mother doted on William, bouncing him on her lap and humming lullabies as Heidi sat in a salon chair, amused by how serious everyone was treating her like a VIP. Still, no alarms went off in her head. It was just a nice day, a thoughtful treat after months of diapers and hospital visits and sleep deprivation.

When they finally pulled up in front of the building that afternoon, her mum squeezed her hand and whispered, "Just wait," with a twinkle in her eye.

Heidi stepped into the penthouse and froze.

The lights were dimmed, replaced by a soft, golden glow of hundreds of flickering candles. Flowers—white peonies and cream roses—lined the living room, the entry table, the windowsills. Scattered petals blanketed the floor like confetti from some divine celebration. There was music playing softly in the background, the soft strains of a string quartet version of "Can't Help Falling in Love."

And everywhere she looked, she saw familiar faces: her mother, Alan, Ben, their closest friends, and colleagues—all smiling, holding champagne flutes, watching her with open affection.

"What's happening?" she whispered.

Then she saw him.

Adrian stood at the far end of the living room, in a perfectly tailored black suit, crisp white shirt, no tie. His hair was neatly styled, but the warmth in his eyes was pure Adrian—calm, steady, filled with the kind of love that reached straight into her soul. William was cradled in a soft white onesie in Alan's arms nearby, cooing as if he understood the magic in the air.

Adrian walked toward her slowly, one hand in his pocket, the other reaching for hers.

"You said you'd marry me any day," he said with a quiet smile.

She blinked, stunned. "Yes... I did."

"Well," he said, lifting her hand to his lips, "today's the day."

He pressed a kiss to her fingers, then gestured gently toward the hallway. "Your dress is on our bed."

Heidi swallowed hard, her throat thick with emotion. "You planned all this?"

"I've been planning it for weeks," he admitted softly. "I wanted it to be perfect. No stress, no expectations. Just us, the people we love... and a promise."

She stared at him, dazed. "Adrian..."

He cupped her face, his thumb grazing her cheek. "Go get dressed, sweetheart. I've waited long enough."

Her heart thundered as she turned, tears already forming. She walked to their bedroom and gasped when she saw the dress laid out on the bed.

It was elegant and understated—just like her. A simple ivory silk gown with delicate lace at the shoulders and a row of tiny satin buttons down the back. Next to it sat a small velvet box holding pearl earrings, and a hand-written note in Adrian's unmistakable script.


*I'll love you in every version of forever. Come find me at the altar.*


She pressed the card to her chest and let the tears fall for just a moment—tears of joy, of disbelief, of every impossible thing that had led to this moment.

Then she slipped into the dress, took a deep breath, and walked back into the glowing warmth of the home they'd built together—ready to become his wife.

Heidi stepped into the living room transformed into a dreamscape, her bare feet silent against the soft carpet strewn with petals. The music changed as she appeared— something slow and romantic, carried by strings and quiet piano. Every head turned toward her, but her eyes only found Adrian.

He stood beneath a soft floral arch, framed by the panoramic windows where the afternoon sun spilled golden light across the floor. His breath visibly caught when he saw her. And then he smiled—this stunned, reverent smile that made her knees weak. Alan nudged him gently and whispered something, probably reminding him to breathe.

Her mother kissed her cheek and took William from her arms with a teary smile, stepping back into the small crowd of loved ones as Heidi made her way to him.

When she reached Adrian, he took both her hands in his, fingers firm and warm, grounding her in the moment. Their officiant—a friend of Adrian's family—stood nearby, but even he seemed to fade into the background.

"You're breathtaking," Adrian whispered.

Heidi laughed softly, her eyes already shimmering. "You clean up pretty well yourself."

There was laughter from their guests, a gentle wave of warmth and support that wrapped around them like a second set of vows.

They hadn't written traditional ones. They didn't need them. They were beyond rehearsed speeches and borrowed words. When it came time, the officiant simply nodded to Adrian.

He turned to her fully, still holding her hands.

"I think I started loving you the moment you challenged me in the boardroom," he said, voice low, thick. "And every day since has been a lesson in how love changes a man. You've changed me, Heidi. You've taught me how to show up, how to be soft, how to stay. You made me a father—" his voice faltered briefly— "and now you're going to be my wife. And I promise you, I'll never take a single second of that for granted."

Her breath hitched. She squeezed his hands tightly.

When it was her turn, she smiled through her tears.

"I never thought I'd end up here," she said. "Not like this. Not with you. But I have never been more sure of anything than I am of you. Of us. You are my safety, my home, my fiercest love. And every time I look at our son, I see you—the good, the strong, the gentle in you. You have given me everything I didn't even know I needed. And I swear, I'll love you with every breath I have left."

Adrian drew in a slow breath, and she watched as tears filled his eyes—his control finally breaking.

The officiant asked for the rings, and Alan stepped forward with a proud grin, handing over the simple white gold bands nestled in a velvet box.

Adrian slid hers on first, his hands trembling slightly. Then she returned the gesture, whispering a kiss to his knuckles when it was done.

"I now pronounce you husband and wife," the officiant said gently. "You may kiss—"

Adrian didn't wait for the rest.

He pulled Heidi into him, kissed her with reverence and hunger, with every unspoken promise poured between parted lips. Their friends and family erupted in soft cheers and teary applause.

And then, the best surprise of all.

From the back, her mother stepped forward, carrying William—now dressed in the tiniest white tuxedo onesie, complete with a navy bowtie.

The crowd cooed and laughed as Adrian reached for him, lifting him up between them.

"Look, buddy," he whispered. "Mummy's my wife now."

Heidi reached out to stroke William's cheek, and he babbled something unintelligible, waving one tiny hand like he was giving his blessing.

Adrian kissed his son's head, then Heidi's, and held them both close as the candles flickered around them and sunlight bathed their new beginning.

It wasn't just a wedding. It was a homecoming—for all three of them.


The penthouse was quiet now, the last of the guests having said their goodbyes hours ago. The soft hum of the city was muted behind the floor-to-ceiling windows, casting a golden glow across the polished floors. William was spending the night with Judy, giving them their first night alone in what felt like forever.

Heidi stood barefoot by the window in her wedding dress, holding a glass of champagne she hadn't touched. Her hair was coming loose in soft waves, and the candlelight shimmered over the delicate fabric of her gown. Adrian leaned in the doorway, still in his black suit, his bowtie now undone and hanging around his collar.

He watched her for a moment. Just watched. As if committing the image to memory.

She turned slowly and smiled at him. "It still feels surreal."

"You're my wife," he said softly, as if trying the words on for size. "You have no idea how good that sounds."

"I think I do," she murmured, setting the glass aside.

He crossed the room in three slow steps, stopping just in front of her, his fingers brushing along the edge of her jaw. "Tired?"

"A little," she said, tilting her face into his touch. "But not enough to sleep. Not yet."

Adrian exhaled a quiet breath and pressed his forehead to hers. "I want to remember this. This version of us. Right here. Right now."

"You mean the married version?" she teased.

He gave a low chuckle. "The peaceful version. The calm before the storm of toddlerhood."

She laughed too, and that sound was everything. Light, happy, home.

He bent down and kissed her gently, reverently, then deeper—slow and exploratory, like they had all the time in the world. She melted into him, her hands sliding around his waist, fingers curling into his shirt. When he pulled back, their foreheads still touching, his voice was rough with emotion.

"I love you," he whispered.

She nodded, tears prickling at the corners of her eyes. "I know. I love you too."

They moved in tandem to the bedroom, shedding layers not in a rush but with quiet intention. Her dress pooled to the floor, and his jacket joined it, followed by buttons and kisses and soft touches that built like a promise. When he laid her back against the sheets, he didn't speak—he didn't need to. His hands, his lips, the way he looked at her… it said everything.

He made love to her slowly, reverently, as if rediscovering her—each curve, each sigh, each whisper of her name. And she gave herself over to him completely, wrapping herself around him, grounding him in the knowledge that this—this—was theirs. No more stolen moments. No more holding back. Just love. Just them.

Afterward, they lay tangled in each other, his hand resting gently over her stomach, her head on his chest, their legs intertwined beneath the sheets.

"Mrs. Werrington," he said with a lazy, satisfied smile.

"Mmm," she replied, tracing a slow circle over his chest. "I like the sound of that."

"You sure I didn't ambush you today?"

"Adrian…" She tilted her head to look up at him. "It was perfect. You made it perfect."

He kissed her forehead. "Good. Because I plan on doing this forever."

She smiled, her heart full.

"Forever sounds just right."

The golden city lights wrapping the room in a gentle glow, they drifted to sleep in each other's arms—husband and wife, soulmates, home.

# Epilogue

The late afternoon sun bathed the backyard in golden light, laughter ringing through the air as children darted between balloon arches and picnic blankets. Colourful streamers fluttered in the breeze, and the remains of a thoroughly demolished piñata lay scattered across the grass.

Adrian slid his arms around Heidi's waist from behind, his chin resting lightly on her shoulder. The scent of vanilla cake and fresh grass lingered in the air, mingling with the shrieks and giggles from the trampoline.

He tightened his hold and kissed the side of her neck. "Can you believe William is five?"

"No," Heidi said softly, her eyes following their son as he chased a group of friends, his superhero cape flying behind him. "And I can't believe Jessica is almost three."

Adrian exhaled against her skin, his breath warm with love and memory. The fear of those dark months still lingered, tucked away in the quiet corners of his mind where the what-ifs liked to hide.

When Heidi had first brought up the idea of having another baby, Adrian had shaken his head, his voice low and firm. He couldn't. Not again. He couldn't bear the thought of losing her—not after everything they'd been through. The thought alone had hollowed him out.

But Heidi, with her quiet strength and unwavering heart, had slowly chipped away at his fear. She didn't beg. She just believed—in their love, in the life they were building, in the possibility of something more.

And when the test turned positive, it had nearly undone him. Joy and dread had collided in his chest—a silent storm of hope and terror.

The doctors had been cautious. "High-risk," they'd said. "Every step must be monitored closely."

Adrian watched her—closely. He relearned the language of her body. Every small victory—no swelling, no fainting, a steady heartbeat—felt like a miracle. He hovered, he worried, he measured time by the rhythm of her breathing, by how she moved, how much she worked. He loved her with a kind of reverent terror.

And now, as sunlight spilled across their yard and their daughter's laughter rang out, he pressed another kiss to Heidi's neck and held her tighter—grateful for the life they had dared to choose.

Jessica had arrived with a fierce cry and a full head of dark hair—perfectly healthy. Perfectly theirs.

"I thank God every day that you convinced me," he murmured, voice thick with emotion. "I didn't know how much I needed her until she was here."

Heidi smiled and threaded her fingers through his, where they rested over her stomach. "I'm just glad you trusted me… trusted us."

The patio doors opened behind them, and Mary, their 55-year-old nanny with a heart of gold and the patience of a saint, stepped outside holding a tray of juice boxes. "Anyone need a top-up?" she called cheerfully.

A small herd of children raced toward her like she was the queen of snacks.

"Mummy!" Jessica's tiny voice broke through the chatter. She ran up, curls bouncing, her fists full of candy. "Look how many lollies I got from the piñata!"

Heidi bent down to admire the loot, her smile full of maternal pride. "That's amazing, sweetheart."

Adrian grinned, ruffling his daughter's hair. "Good job, honey. You're a piñata pro."

Jessica beamed and scampered off again, barefoot, and fearless, to join the others at the cake table. William now wore a party hat and was roaring like a dinosaur.

Heidi leaned into Adrian's chest, her voice soft but certain. "You were right, you know."

"About what?"

"The backyard. The house. All of this."

He pressed a kiss to her temple, his eyes sweeping over the scene—friends mingling, children playing, love stitched into every corner.

"We built something good," he said.

"No," Heidi corrected, turning to face him. "We built something great."

Their lips met in a kiss—soft, sure, and full of everything they had fought through to find one another.

Around them, life moved—wild and beautiful, ordinary, and extraordinary.

And in the centre of it all stood the two of them. A family. A love story that had survived the unthinkable.

As they pulled apart from the kiss, the words slipped from both their lips at the same time, soft and certain—

"I love you."

Spoken in perfect unison, like one heart echoing through two souls.

That day, beneath the sunlight and the sound of their children's laughter, Heidi knew with unwavering clarity:

They had everything they'd ever need.

And they were finally, truly home.

# The End

# The Wrong Sister

## Alison Reid

A complete standalone romance

Previously published individually

# Chapter One

Elena Dutton sat across from Cole Blackwell in the glass-and-steel aerie of his Manhattan office, framed by floor-to-ceiling windows and a skyline that glittered with power. The city stretched endlessly behind her—steel, glass, ambition—and she wore it like a second skin. New York suited her. It always had. As though everything it represented—capital, control, inevitability—already belonged to her.

She crossed one elegant leg over the other, the movement precise and unhurried, practised to the point of instinct. Nothing about Elena Dutton was accidental. Not the immaculate fall of her cream suit, not the understated diamonds at her throat, not the calm, appraising gaze she fixed on him as though he were the one being assessed.

On the table between them lay a slim leather folder—Dutton Group embossed discreetly on the cover. Inside were documents that had already shifted the ground beneath one of the oldest private companies in the country.

"This arrangement makes sense," Elena said evenly. "You're not a man who would marry for love."

Cole studied her over the rim of his coffee cup. Most women hesitated before saying something like that—softened it, dressed it up, followed it with a smile meant to reassure. Elena delivered it as a statement of fact. Clean. Unvarnished. Efficient.

She held his gaze without blinking.

"Blackwell Capital already holds two proxy seats," she continued smoothly, as if reciting figures everyone in the room already understood. "Your people are embedded in the advisory committee. The preliminary agreements are signed. The succession contingencies are drafted."

She gestured lightly toward the folder.

"This"—her lips curved, cool and assured— "is simply the final piece."

There it was.

No coyness. No illusion that this meeting was about romance. This was about formalising what was already in motion. About optics. About permanence.

Cole set his cup down slowly, the porcelain clicking softly against the glass surface of his desk. "You're very direct."

"I prefer efficient," she replied without apology. "Sentiment complicates things. Neither of us benefits from complication."

He leaned back in his chair, fingers steepled, watching her carefully.

"And you're confident you can deliver controlling interest."

"I'm my father's heir," Elena said without hesitation. "Publicly. Legally. And in every way that matters." She paused just long enough to let the statement settle. "When William Dutton steps down, the board will need continuity. Stability. Someone the markets trust."

"And you believe that person is you."

"I know it is," she corrected coolly.

Cole's gaze sharpened—not at her confidence, but at the ease with which she wore it. She didn't posture. She didn't oversell. She believed it. Entirely.

"What about your sister?" he asked casually. "Will Lauren retain any position once succession is finalised?"

Elena didn't blink. She gave a faint, dismissive shrug, as though the question barely deserved oxygen.

"No. I'll retain controlling interest. Lauren isn't suited to leadership at that level." Her tone was neutral, almost bored. "She's irrelevant to the structure."

The words landed between them with quiet finality.

Cole absorbed it without comment.

Elena Dutton was beautiful—undeniably so. Tall and willowy, her bearing spoke of generations of privilege and careful grooming. Old money. Impeccable education. A woman raised for boardrooms, charity galas, and influence exercised behind polished smiles rather than force.

She understood leverage instinctively. Timing. Optics. She knew when to speak and when to let silence do the work. And she never once questioned her place at the top.

That certainty—absolute, unexamined—was precisely what made her convincing.

And precisely what made this deal viable.

"My father's health is declining," she continued after a moment, her voice steady despite the weight of the admission. "When he's gone, the board will fracture unless there's a clear line of succession. You provide that. Strength. Certainty. A name investors trust."

"And you," Cole said evenly, "gain mine."

She inclined her head. "Status. Security. Consolidation. I'm under no illusions, Cole. This would be a partnership—not a fairy tale."

Good, he thought. Fairy tales were expensive. Partnerships were profitable.

He glanced briefly at the city below—traffic pulsing like arteries carrying capital and momentum—then returned his attention to her.

"There would be expectations," he said.

"Of course," Elena replied smoothly. "Public appearances. A united front. Strategic alignment."

"I would expect an heir."

"I have no objection," she said without pause. "Once that obligation is met, we can live separate lives."

He studied her for a long moment. "And emotionally?"

"I don't require love," Elena said calmly. "I require respect. And discretion."

Cole nodded once.

At the time, it had seemed… sufficient.

The arrangement settled something inside him. Not relief exactly—more a sense of order restored. Variables contained. Outcomes projected.

"I have the Dubai trip," he said. "Soon."

"I know." Elena's eyes sharpened with interest. "Your investors value stability. An engaged man reads differently than a single one."

A faint smile tugged at the corner of his mouth. She really was exceptionally well informed.

"Then we should use that trip to see how well we fit," he said. "Publicly, at least."

"That would be sensible," she agreed. "And efficient."

He nodded once. "My legal team will draft a marriage contract. A comprehensive one. Prenuptial terms, asset protections, succession clauses."

"Of course," Elena said smoothly. "I'd expect nothing less. My lawyers will want to review it, but I don't foresee any complications. We're aligned."

That sealed it.

Cole rose, extending his hand across the desk. "Then I think we understand each other."

Elena stood as well, placing her hand in his. Her grip was firm, her gaze unwavering, her expression already calibrated for whatever public narrative they would soon present.

"We do," she said. "This will work very well—for both of us."

"I agree."

"I'll organise a dinner with my father in the next couple of days," she added. "We can begin laying the groundwork."

As she released his hand and turned toward the door, Cole felt the familiar satisfaction of a deal neatly struck.

No risk. No uncertainty. No unnecessary emotion.

Just power aligning with power—clean, controlled, and entirely devoid of sentiment.

Exactly the way he preferred it.


After Elena left, the office felt unusually quiet.

Cole rose from behind his desk and moved to the floor-to-ceiling windows, his hands settling loosely in his pockets as he looked out over the relentless pulse of New York City. Traffic surged far below like a living organism—horns, lights, ambition colliding at every intersection. This city understood him. It rewarded certainty. It punished hesitation. And it never pretended sentiment mattered more than power.

His reflection stared back at him in the glass.

Thirty-five. At the height of his power.

Tall. Broad-shouldered. Dark hair cut with military precision. A clean-shaven jaw set in habitual control. Piercing blue eyes that missed very little and revealed even less. His body bore the mark of discipline rather than indulgence—hours in the gym carved deliberately into an already punishing schedule, strength built and maintained with the same ruthless focus he applied to business.

There was nothing soft about him. Nothing accidental.

Every line, every muscle, every restraint had been earned.

Cole Blackwell had everything men spent lifetimes chasing—wealth, influence, authority. And he had achieved it without illusion, without sentiment, without ever allowing emotion to weaken his grip.

Exactly as he intended.

Elena Dutton was the same.

Practical. Composed. Intelligent in the ways that mattered. She understood the nature of the agreement without romantic delusion clouding her judgement. No fantasies. No expectations of devotion. No demand for more than what had been explicitly negotiated.

A marriage contract. A prenup. Clearly defined assets. Succession contingencies. Public unity. Private autonomy.

Clean terms.

That alone placed her above most women he encountered.

Love, on the other hand, had never interested him.

Love was a liability.

He had seen what it cost—empires softened, decisions compromised, men undone by things they could neither control nor contain.

Cole preferred certainty. Contracts. Outcomes that could be enforced.

Love offered none of that.

Desire was different.

Desire was simple. Predictable. Easily satisfied.

Cole dated beautiful women all the time—models, socialites, actresses drawn to proximity to power. They wanted access. He wanted release. No one pretended otherwise. He took what he wanted, enjoyed it, and walked away before expectations could form.

Clean. Efficient. Contained.

Exactly how he preferred it.

Marriage, for him, had never been about intimacy. It was a strategic instrument—something to be leveraged, not felt. Elena understood that. She didn't want his heart. She wanted his name. His position. His future.

And in return, she offered him exactly what he wanted.

As Cole continued to watch the city surge and glitter below, he felt nothing but satisfaction. The path ahead was clear. Controlled. Profitable.

No emotion.

No risk.

*Just power—aligning precisely where it belonged.*


Twenty-six-year-old Lauren Dutton sat in the quiet library of her family's estate; her laptop balanced on her knees as spreadsheets and financial reports glowed softly across the screen. The room smelled faintly of old books and polished wood; a tangible reminder of legacy and history pressed into every surface.

Her platinum-blonde hair—usually worn in loose waves cascading to her waist—was pulled into a severe bun, a deliberate choice that signalled focus over vanity. Emerald eyes, normally hidden behind her glasses, moved steadily across figures and projections with practiced precision, catching discrepancies most people would never notice.

She didn't care whether anyone noticed her beauty. It was irrelevant—often inconvenient. Lauren had learned early that attention lingered where it didn't belong, that it distracted from competence and diluted authority. So, she avoided it by design, dressing plainly and purposefully, unwilling to let her appearance interfere with the things she intended to command, calculate, and control.

What mattered was being taken seriously.

Not admired. Not desired.

Respected.

Unlike her sister.

Elena chased attention as though it were currency, mistaking admiration for influence and appearance for power. For Lauren, beauty was incidental. Intellect, discipline, and quiet authority endured—and she had no intention of letting anything obscure that.

Tall, willowy, and deliberately understated, Lauren had long since grown accustomed to fading into the background—especially beside Elena. Her sister was a study in polish and presentation: hair always perfectly styled, makeup applied with practiced precision, every outfit curated to flatter and command attention. Elena's beauty was undeniable, but it was also constructed—maintained with effort, intention, and hours spent perfecting an image designed to be admired.

Lauren's was different. Quieter. Unmanufactured. She didn't need cosmetics to soften her features or carefully chosen clothes to make a statement. She had never learned the rituals of mirrors and makeup tables because she'd never needed to. But she had never thought of that as something to be proud of, either. It simply… was.

Elena walked into rooms and people turned. Doors opened. Conversations bent toward her. She knew how to shine—how to be seen.

Lauren never tried to compete.

Not because she couldn't—but because she didn't want to.

She loved her sister. Truly. They shared a childhood, a family, a history that mattered. But they were built differently, driven by different priorities. Elena valued admiration, status, and the reassurance that came with being wanted. Lauren valued competence, substance, and the quiet satisfaction of being trusted. Neither was wrong. They simply stood on opposite sides of the same coin.

Influence earned quietly lasted longer than power demanded loudly.

Gregory Wade—her closest friend and confidant since childhood—had reminded her of that very fact just that morning, in his usual dramatic fashion. He'd flopped onto the arm of her chair, studied her critically, then declared, "People are blind, Lauren. Absolutely blind. You're the more beautiful daughter."

She'd rolled her eyes, already reaching for her coffee, but he wasn't finished.

"But you hide it," he'd added, thumping her shoulder affectionately. "And you're smart enough not to care. Everyone thinks Elena is the star of the show. They're wrong."

Lauren had smiled faintly at that—not in agreement, but in affection. Gregory always saw her clearly.

And he wasn't wrong about the rest, either.

While Elena charmed her way through charity galas and boardroom dinners, Lauren was the one who could read a balance sheet at a glance, anticipate risk before it surfaced, and dismantle a weak argument without raising her voice.

She didn't perform intelligence.

She applied it.

The library door opened without a knock.

Lauren looked up instantly.

Her father, William Dutton, stood in the doorway, his presence still commanding despite the illness that had begun to hollow him out. He had lost weight—there was no disguising that—but his posture remained upright, his shoulders squared by decades of leadership. His steps were slower than they once had been, measured now, but his eyes—emerald like hers—were as sharp and assessing as ever.

They found her immediately.

And lingered there longer than they ever did on Elena.

"I need your thoughts," he said simply.

The words carried weight. They always did.

Lauren closed her laptop and set it aside without hesitation. "Of course, Father. What's on your mind?"

He crossed the room and gestured toward the chair opposite her desk. "Succession."

The word settled heavily between them, thick with implication.

Lauren's chest tightened. "Father—"

"You know my health is failing, Lauren," he said calmly, as though discussing a quarterly forecast instead of his mortality.

She stood abruptly, emotion flaring despite her usual restraint. "Don't say that," she said softly, her voice betraying her. "You're not—"

William reached for her hand, his grip warm, steady. "It's all right, sweetheart," he said gently. "I have to think about these things now. Ignoring them won't change the outcome."

She swallowed hard, nodding even as dread pressed into her ribs. She loved her father more than anyone in the world. The thought of losing him felt unbearable—like standing at the edge of a future she wasn't ready to face.

"I know," she whispered. "I just… I hate it."

He gave her hand a reassuring squeeze before releasing it and sitting. "The board will fracture when I'm gone," he continued, his tone shifting back into the deliberate cadence of a man who had built an empire. "You know the men we're dealing with—investors, trustees, legacy partners. They respect names. Influence. Power."

His mouth tightened slightly. "They do not respect sentiment."

Lauren exhaled slowly. "So, you want Elena positioned as—"

"No," William said, cutting in quietly but firmly.

She stilled.

"I want you."

The words landed with quiet force.

"You are already running this company in everything but name," he continued. "You manage operations. You stabilise risk. You anticipate market shifts before my advisors even realise there's a problem. The board comes to me, but the solutions come from you."

Lauren's throat tightened. "Father—"

"I intend to transfer fifty-one percent of the company into your control," he said evenly. "A controlling interest. Enough to prevent any internal power struggles. Enough to ensure continuity."

She stared at him, stunned. "Elena will be furious."

William's expression softened, but his resolve did not waver. "Elena is charismatic. She is visible. But she does not understand this company. And she does not want to. She wants the title, not the responsibility."

Lauren shook her head slowly. "She's your eldest—"

"And you are my successor," he said simply. "This company needs leadership, not performance. It needs someone who understands that power is not taken— it is carried."

Silence stretched between them.

"I know this puts a burden on you," he added quietly. "And I would not ask it of you if I didn't believe—completely—that you are the only one capable of protecting what we've built."

Lauren closed her eyes briefly, steadying herself. When she opened them again, her voice was calm, resolute.

"If you trust me," she said, "then I won't let you down."

William smiled then—proud, unmistakable. "I never doubt you," he said. "Not for a moment."

In the hush of the library, surrounded by legacy and truth, Lauren understood something with crystalline clarity.

This wasn't about inheritance.

It was about responsibility.

She hesitated, then asked softly, "She's not going to be happy. Are you going to tell her?"

"I will—but not yet," William said without hesitation. "And I'd like you to keep this between us for now. I'll explain it when the time is right. She'll understand. You're the logical choice. You know what you're doing."

Lauren masked her reaction behind a composed expression, but inside, warmth spread—familiar and grounding. The quiet reassurance of being seen. Truly seen.

She loved her father fiercely—not only for the man he was, but for the respect he gave her when the world so often overlooked her. That respect had been her compass her entire life.

"Thank you for trusting me," she said simply.

His lips curved into the faintest smile. He didn't need to say more. The look he gave her carried everything—confidence, faith, certainty.

She had been preparing for this her whole life.

Elena might charm the board and captivate investors with elegance and polish, but Lauren would run the company. Quietly. Efficiently. And without spectacle.

And no one—not even Elena—would realise that the true power behind the Dutton empire belonged to the daughter they had always underestimated.

William rose slowly and rested a hand on her shoulder. "Thank you, sweetheart."

Lauren stood and wrapped her arms around him.

She loved her father, yes—but more than that, she cherished his trust.

And no one would ever take that from her.

# Chapter Two

Lauren sank back into the leather chair in the library and released a long, deliberate sigh. Late afternoon sunlight streamed through the tall windows, catching in the air and turning drifting dust motes into flecks of gold. The room was quiet, steeped in the familiar comfort of old books and polished wood— usually a refuge. Today, it felt like a holding cell.

Across from her, Gregory perched on the edge of the chaise, one arm draped casually along the back, studying her with open amusement.

"You look like you've just been sentenced," he said, smoothing the lapel of his impeccably tailored jacket.

"I might as well have been," Lauren replied, snapping her laptop shut. The soft click echoed through the room with finality. "There's a family dinner tonight. Cole Blackwell is coming. Elena invited him."

Gregory's eyebrows shot up. "*The* Cole Blackwell?" A grin spread across his face. "The billionaire who's photographed with a different woman every week. The one society pages treat like a rotating cover model?"

"Yes," Lauren said flatly. "That one."

She hesitated, then added, "And I have a feeling Elena thinks they're heading toward an engagement."

Gregory sat up straighter. "Engaged?" He let out a low whistle. "Well. She would think that. He's basically the prize of the century in her world."

"Exactly," Lauren said, her tone dry. "Untouchably wealthy. Powerful. Beautiful in that aggressively curated way. The kind of man magazines describe as 'elusive' when what they really mean is emotionally unavailable."

Gregory snorted. "And famously allergic to commitment."

Lauren nodded. "Which makes it even more absurd. I can't recall them ever going on a proper date. No dinners. No holidays. No anything that resembles an actual relationship." She rose and crossed to the window, folding her arms as she looked out across the grounds. "But Elena doesn't need substance. She needs optics."

Gregory leaned back, folding his arms. "So, less romance, more… acquisition."

Lauren glanced over her shoulder. "If you asked her, she'd call it destiny. If you asked me, I'd call it branding."

"And he?" Gregory asked. "What's in it for him?"

Lauren shrugged lightly. "Attention. Admiration. A beautiful woman on his arm who doesn't ask for more than he's willing to give." Her voice remained calm, but there was certainty beneath it. "He's seen with a new woman every week, Gregory. Models. Actresses. Heiresses. Elena probably thinks being the one who keeps him would be the ultimate win."

Gregory's grin widened. "And you?"

"I think a marriage built on appearances and convenience is a slow-motion disaster," Lauren replied evenly. "And I don't have the time—or the patience—to pretend otherwise."

He tilted his head. "You realise you might be asked to be maid of honour."

She rolled her eyes, though the corners of her mouth betrayed a flicker of amusement. "Unlikely. Elena and I operate on entirely different planes." She paused, then added with cool honesty, "But if she believes marrying Cole Blackwell will make her happy… I suppose she's welcome to find out for herself."

Gregory raised his coffee cup in mock salute. "To Cole Blackwell—serial bachelor—and Elena Dutton, convinced she's the exception."

Lauren smirked faintly, then returned to her desk, reopening her laptop. Numbers and projections bloomed back onto the screen—reliable, rational, uncomplicated.

Let Cole Blackwell and Elena perform their little spectacle tonight.

Lauren had no intention of being drawn into it.

She had far more important things to do.


Lauren descended the grand staircase of the Dutton estate with unhurried precision, each step measured, deliberate. Her posture was flawless; her expression composed to the point of cool detachment. She wore a navy-blue dress that did nothing to flatter her tall, willowy frame—by design. Her platinum-blonde hair was twisted into a severe bun, glasses settled firmly on her nose like a barrier rather than an accessory.

She looked exactly as she intended to: competent, unadorned, unimpressed.

Across the sitting room, Elena was everything Lauren was not trying to be.

Her sister glowed in a champagne-coloured gown that clung gracefully to every curve, her dark hair styled in soft, glossy waves. She laughed easily, leaning into Cole Blackwell with effortless intimacy, her hand resting on his arm as if it belonged there.

Cole stood beside her, tall and immaculately dressed, his presence confident without being showy. He surveyed the room with the ease of a man accustomed to power and admiration, his blue eyes sharp, calculating. He and Elena were already engaged in conversation with their father, perfectly positioned—visually, socially.

Lauren crossed to the sideboard and poured herself a drink, watching the tableau with open disinterest. When Cole's gaze flicked toward her, it was brief and dismissive—taking in the plain dress, the glasses, the severe bun. A faint smirk curved his mouth before he turned back to Elena.

Predictable.

Dinner was announced, and they took their places at the table. Lauren sat opposite Cole, diagonally removed—close enough to engage, far enough to remain detached.

Midway through the first course, Elena lifted her glass. The soft chime cut cleanly through the conversation.

"I thought we should let everyone know," she said brightly, "that Cole and I are considering getting engaged."

William Dutton blinked, genuine surprise slipping through his polished restraint. "That's… unexpected," he said carefully.

Lauren lifted her glass slowly, eyes never leaving her sister. "Considering," she echoed, tasting the word. Then her gaze slid to Cole. "Is that the same as wanting to marry each other, or is it more of a… preliminary discussion?"

Cole turned toward her fully now, irritation flashing across his features before he masked it. "I wasn't aware marriage required romantic theatrics to be legitimate."

"Ah," Lauren said thoughtfully. "So, love isn't required."

Elena's smile tightened—just slightly.

Cole's lips curved with cool confidence. "Love is optional. Compatibility is essential."

Lauren tilted her head. "That's an interesting way of saying mutual tolerance."

Cole leaned back, fingers lacing together. "Some of us prefer realism over fantasy."

"And some of us," Lauren replied evenly, "find it extraordinary that people willingly bind their lives together for optics." She took a sip of her wine. "It sounds… exhausting."

William cleared his throat. Elena laughed too quickly and slid her hand possessively over Cole's arm.

"Lauren," she said lightly, "you always turn everything into a debate."

Lauren smiled—polite, detached. "Only when the logic is flawed."

Cole's eyes narrowed, irritation sharpening before something else crept in—interest.

"For someone who disdains marriage," he said coolly, "you seem unusually invested in how others approach it."

"I'm not invested," Lauren replied without hesitation. "I'm entertained." She paused, just long enough for the word to land. "And who said I disdain marriage?"

That gave him pause.

"I hope one day I find a man who loves and respects me as deeply as I love and respect him," she continued calmly. "Then—and only then—would I consider marriage."

Cole studied her more closely now, his earlier dismissal gone. "You're certain you'll find that kind of love and respect?"

"Yes," Lauren said evenly. "And if I don't, I would rather be alone than tied to a man who feels less than I do."

That earned her a long, measuring look. This time, Cole didn't smirk. He watched her—really watched her—as if reassessing a variable he'd discounted too quickly.

Elena lifted her glass, her smile polished and bright. "Let's not ruin dinner," she said smoothly, reclaiming the moment with practiced ease.

"I'm not attacking anyone," Lauren said calmly, her gaze never leaving Cole. "I'm simply stating my beliefs."

Elena's smile tightened. "Not everyone thinks like you, Lauren."

Lauren finally broke eye contact with Cole and turned to her sister. "You're right, Elena." She raised her glass, her tone sweet, impeccable. "I wish you and Mr Blackwell all the happiness in the world."

Outwardly, the tension eased. Conversation resumed. Plates were cleared. Wine was poured.

But something had shifted.

Lauren spoke only when necessary, her observations concise and precise. Cole found himself listening more closely than he intended—irritated by her certainty, unsettled by her refusal to impress him.

She didn't flirt.

She didn't soften.

She didn't yield.

And when their gazes met across the table—hers cool and unimpressed, his sharpened with reluctant curiosity—it was unmistakable.

They didn't like each other.

And for the first time in a very long while, Cole Blackwell found that... intriguing.

Later, after Cole and Elena disappeared and the house settled into quiet, Lauren found her father alone in his study. She paused at the threshold until he looked up.

"Father," she said gently, "Cole Blackwell is... impressive."

"He is," William replied. A small, knowing smile tugged at his mouth. "But you didn't like him."

"Marrying for appearances is ridiculous," Lauren said evenly. "And I believe Elena is making a mistake."

William sighed, the weight of disappointment visible in the slight slump of his shoulders. "I had hoped my daughters would marry for love." His gaze softened, turning distant, as though memory had reached out and claimed him. "Your mother and I did. It mattered."

The words stirred something deep in Lauren's chest.

Her mother—Joan Dutton—had been gone three years now, but the imprint she'd left was indelible. Joan had once told Lauren, with quiet amusement and unapologetic certainty, that she'd met William Dutton and married him within a month. Everyone had said it was reckless. Too fast. A mistake born of infatuation rather than sense.

They had been wrong.

Her parents had never stopped loving one another—not through the pressures of the company, not through public scrutiny, not through time itself. Their marriage hadn't been strategic or convenient. It had been chosen. Every day. Joan had believed, fiercely and without compromise, that love was not a weakness but a foundation.

Lauren carried that belief like a compass.

"Marrying for power rarely ends well," she said quietly, the truth of it shaped by both observation and inheritance.

"I know," William murmured, almost to himself. Then he looked at her again, his gaze steady now, searching. "I was glad to hear you won't be so inclined, Lauren."

She shook her head once, firmly. "Never. I want more than that."

A faint, relieved smile touched his lips. "Good. I would like to believe that at least one of my daughters will have a happy marriage."

"So would I," Lauren replied softly. "I hope one day I'll meet a man I can truly love."

William's expression warmed. "That's all I've ever wanted for you and Elena," he said simply. "But she's on her own path."

Lauren nodded, understanding the unspoken complexity of that truth.

As the moment settled, warmth spread through her chest—not pride, but something steadier and deeper. Reassurance. She had her father's respect, earned quietly over years of consistency and clarity. And beneath that respect lay something even more meaningful: the legacy of a love that had been real, enduring, and uncompromised.

It was the kind of love she refused to settle for anything less than.

Even now.

Especially now.


Elena lingered at the door, one manicured hand resting lightly on Cole's sleeve as the butler withdrew and the house settled into its customary, curated quiet. The kind of silence money bought—thick with tradition, expectation, and unspoken rules.

She smiled up at him, confident, polished, already inhabiting a future she believed was inevitable.

Cole barely noticed.

His attention was still caught on the dinner table. On a pair of emerald eyes behind sensible glasses. On a voice that had dismantled him without raising its volume once.

Lauren Dutton.

She hadn't challenged him for effect. She hadn't tried to score points or dominate the room. She had simply asked a questions—and waited. Letting his own words expose themselves.

No flirtation.

No nerves.

No performance.

Just certainty.

It unsettled him.

Most people—women especially—either deferred to him or leaned into charm, angling for advantage, attention, or leverage. Lauren had done neither. She hadn't smiled to soften her words. Hadn't sought his approval. Hadn't appeared remotely impressed.

If anything, she'd looked faintly… bored.

As though she'd assessed him, found his worldview limited, and moved on.

He disliked that more than he cared to admit.

She didn't resemble her sister in any obvious way. No curated glamour. No strategic neckline. The dress she wore was understated to the point of severity, designed to conceal rather than entice. Her hair was pulled back in a style that did it no favours, glasses plain and functional. There was no visible effort to compete with Elena's polish.

She could be overlooked—easily.

And yet she hadn't been.

Because beneath the restraint was something sharp. Real intelligence. Not decorative. Not performative. The kind that listened more than it spoke, that measured before responding, that asked questions which unsettled rather than entertained.

He had noticed her hair—an unusually striking shade, rare and luminous when the light caught it. A pity she wore it like that. And she wore no makeup at all, yet her skin was flawless, her lips naturally pink, full without artifice. Unadorned. Unapologetic.

That, too, irritated him.

Elena squeezed his arm gently, pulling him back into the present. "I'm sorry about Lauren," she said lightly. "She can be… intense."

Cole summoned a polite smile. "Opinionated."

Elena laughed softly. "She always thinks she knows better than everyone else."

He didn't respond.

Because he wasn't convinced she didn't.

What lingered with him most wasn't Lauren's challenge—it was William Dutton's reaction to her. The way her father had listened. Not indulgently. Not patiently.

Seriously.

As though her words carried consequence. As though her opinions shaped outcomes.

That hadn't escaped him.

Lauren Dutton was supposed to be the quiet one. The plain sister. The afterthought. The spare.

Instead, she felt like a variable he hadn't accounted for.

And Cole Blackwell despised miscalculations.

Elena shifted closer, already speaking about future dinners, charity appearances, the optics of being seen together more often. He nodded at the appropriate moments, said the expected things, played his role with practiced precision.

Yet an unwelcome truth pressed in.

He and Elena hadn't even been on a proper date.

No stolen glances.

No shared laughter.

No heat.

They hadn't even kissed.

Their understanding was clean. Efficient. Entirely devoid of chemistry.

And unbidden—unwanted—his thoughts betrayed him.

What would it be like to kiss Lauren?

Not for appearances. Not as strategy.

But to see if that composure fractured.

To feel whether that quiet certainty softened—or sharpened—beneath his mouth.

To discover whether she would pull away… or meet him with the same steady intensity she brought to everything else.

The thought landed heavy. Dangerous.

Cole stiffened, irritated—most of all with himself.

Lauren Dutton hadn't wanted anything from him.

And for the first time in a very long while, that didn't just make a woman interesting—

It made her dangerous.

# Chapter Three

Lauren had chosen the small bistro just off the park for lunch—quiet, discreet, far enough from the Dutton offices to think without interruption. She sat opposite Gregory at a corner table, her salad untouched, fingers wrapped loosely around a glass of sparkling water. The tension in her shoulders hadn't yet eased.

She had come straight from her father's office.

William only went in on his good days now—days when pain was manageable and his mind sharp enough to spar with markets and projections. Today had been one of those days. A gift. Fragile, fleeting, precious.

Gregory studied her over the rim of his iced coffee. "You have that look," he said lightly. "The something-important-just-happened-and-you're-not-ready-to-talk-about-it look."

Lauren exhaled, leaning back in her chair, letting the tension ease slightly. "Father is at the office today."

Gregory's expression softened. "That's… good."

"It was," she agreed. "He was clear. Focused. Annoyingly perceptive, as always." She paused, then added, "We talked about Dubai."

That caught his interest immediately. "Ah. Dubai *Dubai.* Not just flashy towers and overpriced brunches, then."

"No," Lauren said dryly. "The investment consortium."

She set her glass down and folded her hands neatly on the table, slipping effortlessly into analysis. "It's a closed consortium—sovereign-backed capital mixed with private equity. Old Gulf money, institutional investors, and a handful of global players who prefer to move quietly. Energy infrastructure, logistics corridors, data hubs—they're positioning Dubai as the connective artery between East and West."

Gregory whistled softly. "Subtle."

"Dangerously so," Lauren replied. "They don't court attention. They court leverage. Whoever partners with them early gets access to markets most Western firms can't touch without years of groundwork."

"And your father wants in," Gregory said.

"He does—if the terms are right," Lauren corrected. "He wanted to go himself, take me with him. Investors rarely deal with single men, but they would have made an exception for him as a widower."

Her voice remained calm, but something tightened briefly behind her eyes. Gregory noticed. He always did.

"But he can't," he asked softly.

"No." She shook her head once. "The travel alone would be too much—the climate, the schedule, the strain. He knows it. I know it. But Elena has told him she will be attending. With Cole—as his fiancée."

Gregory arched a brow. "Of course she is."

Lauren's lips curved faintly, but there was no humour in it. "Father said—" She paused, hearing the words echo in her mind, measured but hopeful— *'Hopefully your sister will get the information that we need while she is there. I think the Dutton Group should be involved if possible.'*

She repeated them aloud, word for word.

Gregory tilted his head. "That's… optimistic."

Lauren let out a soft, breathless laugh. "That's exactly my concern. Elena will enjoy the optics—the galas, the introductions. Cole will enjoy the access." She lifted her gaze, sharp and unwavering. "But this consortium doesn't reward charm. It rewards preparation."

"And Elena isn't exactly known for her due diligence," Gregory observed.

"She isn't," Lauren agreed calmly. "Which means whatever information she brings back will be filtered—through Cole, through ambition, through whatever version of events best suits them."

Gregory's mouth curved into a wicked smile. "Has Elena even noticed you're practically running the company now?"

"Of course not," Lauren replied without hesitation.

Gregory leaned forward, lowering his voice. "So… what are you going to do?"

Lauren's fingers tightened briefly around her glass before she deliberately relaxed them. "What I always do. Prepare for the possibility that she comes back with half the picture—or worse, a narrative designed to steer the company into a position that benefits Blackwell Capital more than it does us."

Gregory smiled slowly. "Meaning you'll already have the other half."

She met his gaze, cool and assured. "I already do. I've been tracking the consortium's movements for months—shell entities, advisory overlaps, silent partners. If the Dutton Group is going to be involved, it will be on our terms."

Gregory lifted his glass in a mock toast. "To the underestimated daughter."

Lauren finally picked up her fork, her appetite returning at last. "To getting the information we actually need," she said quietly. Her gaze drifted briefly out the window, calculating, measuring. "I would prefer to be going myself, but unfortunately, that won't be the case. The only silver lining… is that I won't have to spend a week in Cole Blackwell's presence—or my sister's, for that matter."

A faint, wry smile tugged at her lips, but it didn't reach her eyes. There was no humour in her assessment, only clarity. She knew exactly what challenges lay ahead—and exactly how to prepare for them.


Just as Gregory reached for the bill and signalled to the waiter, Lauren's phone rang.

She glanced at the screen and answered immediately. "Hello."

"Lauren, it's your father." William's voice was tight, controlled in the way it only ever was when he was holding something together by sheer force of will. "Your sister has been in a car accident. I'm on my way to the hospital now."

Lauren's spine straightened. She wasn't close to Elena—had never been—but the words landed heavily all the same. Whatever their differences, she would never wish harm on her sister.

"I'll meet you there," she said without hesitation.

She ended the call and looked up to find Gregory watching her, concern already etched into his expression. "Everything okay?"

"Elena's been in a car accident," Lauren said evenly. "She's in hospital."

"Oh no." Gregory was on his feet immediately. "Come on—I'll drive you."

Lauren nodded, a quiet wave of relief settling through her. She was perfectly capable of handling things on her own—she always had been—but having Gregory beside her made the weight easier to carry. His support was steady, unquestioned. Welcome.

They reached the hospital quickly, the atmosphere shifting the moment they stepped inside—sterile air, hushed voices, the low hum of urgency beneath it all. William was already there, standing as soon as he saw them.

"Lauren." He crossed the waiting area in two long strides and pressed a kiss to her cheek, his hand lingering briefly at her shoulder. Then he turned to Gregory, offering a warm, grateful handshake. "Thank you for bringing her."

"Of course," Gregory said simply.

Lauren took in her father's drawn expression, the tension he hadn't quite managed to hide. Whatever differences existed between the sisters, this was still his child lying behind those hospital doors.

And that mattered.


A short while later, a nurse approached and asked them to follow her down the corridor. The three of them were led into a small consultation room—neutral walls, a round table, a box of tissues placed deliberately at its centre. It was the kind of room designed for conversations that were never easy.

Moments later, the doctor entered.

He was in his early forties, calm and composed, his white coat immaculate, a tablet tucked under one arm. His expression was professional but not detached—measured, careful, the look of a man accustomed to delivering difficult information with clarity rather than drama.

"Mr. Dutton," he said, inclining his head politely. "Ms. Dutton."

Lauren straightened slightly, her hands folding together in her lap, her focus sharpening. Gregory remained beside her, close but unobtrusive.

"Your daughter was involved in a high-speed collision," the doctor continued. "The impact caused multiple injuries, but I want to reassure you first—she is stable, conscious, and out of immediate danger."

William released a breath he'd been holding, his shoulders lowering a fraction.

"She has a fractured right femur," the doctor explained, glancing briefly at his tablet. "It was a clean break, but significant enough to require surgical intervention. We've already taken her to theatre to stabilise the bone with internal fixation. The surgery was successful."

Lauren nodded once, absorbing the information. "And neurologically?" she asked.

"A mild concussion," he replied, meeting her gaze with quiet respect. "She was briefly disoriented at the scene but is now alert and responsive. We'll monitor her closely over the next twenty-four to forty-eight hours to ensure there's no swelling or delayed complications."

"What about other injuries?" Lauren asked.

"A fractured clavicle on the left side," he said. "It will heal without surgery but will require immobilisation. She also sustained several deep lacerations to her arms and shoulder from broken glass. Those have been cleaned and sutured. There's significant bruising, but no internal bleeding."

William's jaw tightened. "How long will she be here?"

"At least a fortnight," the doctor replied. "Possibly longer, depending on pain management and how she responds to physiotherapy."

Lauren glanced briefly at her father, already aware of the implications—both personal and professional.

"You can see her shortly," the doctor added. "She's asking for you."

William nodded, emotion flickering briefly across his face. "Thank you, Doctor."

As the man left the room, Lauren reached out and rested a steady hand over her father's. "She's going to be alright," she said quietly—not as reassurance, but as fact.


Soon after, a nurse led them down the softly lit corridor to Elena's room. The steady beep of monitors grew louder as they approached, the air carrying the familiar, sharp scent of antiseptic. William's pace quickened despite his effort to appear calm.

Elena lay propped up against white pillows, her skin pale but her eyes open and alert. One leg was encased in a cast and elevated, her left arm secured in a sling, dark bruising already blooming along her collarbone and shoulder. A thin line of stitches traced her forearm, stark against her skin.

William moved to her side immediately, lowering himself carefully into the chair beside the bed. He took her hand gently, as though afraid even that might hurt her.

"How are you feeling, love?" he asked softly.

Elena managed a small, tired smile. "Sore," she said honestly, her voice faint but steady. "But alive."

Her gaze shifted then, taking in all of them—her father, Lauren, Gregory—lingering for a moment longer than expected, emotion flickering beneath her composed exterior. "Thank you for coming."

Lauren stepped to the other side of the bed, Gregory's arm settling instinctively around her shoulders, a quiet anchor she hadn't realised she needed. She placed her hand lightly on the mattress, close enough for Elena to see without touching any injured skin.

"Of course we would be here, Elena," Lauren said calmly. "You're not facing this alone."

For a brief moment, the usual distance between the sisters faded, replaced by something gentler—shared history, shared blood, and the fragile relief that comes when disaster stops just short of tragedy.

Lauren stayed a little longer, speaking quietly with her father while Elena rested, her eyes drifting closed between sentences. When the room settled into a comfortable hush, Lauren straightened and glanced at her watch.

"I should get back to work," she said calmly. "I'll see you at home, Father."

William nodded, squeezing Elena's hand once more before looking up at Lauren. "Drive safely."

Lauren turned to her sister, her expression composed but sincere. "I'll be back tomorrow," she said. "Get better soon." She placed her hand gently on Elena's uninjured shoulder—brief, careful, reassuring.

Elena looked up at her and offered a tired smile. "Thanks for coming, Lauren. Gregory."

Gregory inclined his head. "Anytime."

They stepped into the corridor together, the soft click of the door closing behind them. Gregory's arm remained draped loosely around Lauren's shoulders as they walked, an instinctive gesture neither of them questioned.

Halfway down the hall, they slowed.

Cole Blackwell stood near the nurses' station, having just arrived—immaculately dressed, expression composed. He stopped short when he saw them. His gaze went first to Lauren, sharp and assessing, then dropped to Gregory's arm around her shoulders.

Something unreadable crossed his face.

Lauren noticed—but didn't react. She kept her gaze forward, posture unaltered, as though nothing at all had changed. Gregory, sensing the shift, didn't move his arm.

Cole's jaw tightened almost imperceptibly as they passed him, the faintest pause betraying his irritation.

For reasons he couldn't immediately name, the sight bothered him far more than it should have.

A nurse directed Cole down the corridor and pointed him toward Elena's room. He adjusted his jacket automatically, composure snapping back into place as he approached the door, then pushed it open.

Elena lay propped up against white pillows, her colour still pale, one leg immobilised in a cast, her arm secured in a sling. The machines beside her bed hummed softly, a quiet reminder of how close things had come. William sat in the chair beside her, leaning forward, one hand clasped around hers, his expression etched with concern.

Elena's eyes lit the moment she saw Cole.

"Cole," she said, a faint smile curving her lips despite the pain. "You came."

"Of course I did," he replied, crossing the room in long, purposeful strides. He stopped at the foot of the bed, his gaze taking in the injuries before returning to her face. "How are you feeling?"

She let out a weak huff of laughter. "Like I've been hit by a car."

William gave a small, strained smile at that, squeezing her hand gently. Cole inclined his head toward him in greeting, but his attention remained fixed on Elena, his expression carefully attentive—concern worn like a perfectly tailored suit.

Inside, however, his thoughts were anything but calm.

The Dubai trip loomed large in his mind—four days away, meticulously planned, strategically vital. They were not convinced that he was settling down into matrimony. That was the only way he had secured his place with the consortium on the understanding that he would attend with his fiancée. Appearances mattered to those investors. Stability. Continuity. A united front.

He took in Elena's cast, the sling, the careful way she shifted against the pillows, and the reality settled with sharp clarity.

She wouldn't be able to travel.

Which meant he wouldn't either.

The inconvenience hit first—cold, immediate, unwelcome. Meetings postponed. Momentum stalled. Access delayed. He had already positioned himself, already moved pieces into place, and now one variable had collapsed the entire sequence.

It irritated him far more than he allowed to show.

He kept his expression composed, concern carefully calibrated, but beneath it his mind recalculated, stripping the situation down to cause and effect. The investors hadn't invited him because of his track record alone. They had invited him because he had promised them something they valued: the optics of permanence, of alliance, of a man anchored rather than untethered.

Without Elena at his side, the invitation would evaporate.

And Cole Blackwell despised having his plans disrupted—especially by circumstances he couldn't control.

# Chapter Four

The quiet stretched between them like a taut wire, each second heavy with unspoken thoughts, until Elena's soft voice finally cut through it. "I'm sorry, Cole. I won't be able to make the Dubai trip."

He didn't flinch, didn't even shift his gaze from her in the hospital bed. "Yes. I'm aware of that," he said, his tone measured and clipped. There was no anger, no frustration—at least none he allowed to surface. Yet beneath that calm exterior, a storm of irritation coiled tighter with every passing second, simmering just beneath the surface.

Elena hesitated, her fingers twisting the edge of the hospital blanket. "What… what will you do?" she asked, uncertainty threading her words.

Cole finally turned, his dark eyes sharp, calculating, and unyielding. "I'll adjust," he said smoothly. "Plans are meant to be executed, Elena." He took a small step back, letting the weight of his words hang heavy between them. "The investors won't be happy if I show up without a partner," he added, the faint edge of determination sharpening his tone. "I will find someone else to accompany me."

Elena's chest tightened. A flicker of irritation—and something more, a pang of jealousy—sparked behind her calm mask. "I hope… this doesn't change our plans for the future?" she asked, her voice low, almost challenging.

Cole's gaze settled on her, unwavering and commanding. "No. No, you are the perfect wife for me," he said firmly. "This"—he gestured toward her bandaged injuries, a reminder of her vulnerability— "doesn't change that. But I will need a partner to present as my fiancée. These investors are adamant… single men simply aren't acceptable."

Elena's lips pressed together, a spark of resentment mingling with a deeper longing. She wanted to argue, to insist he couldn't take another woman—but even as the words formed in her mind, the truth settled painfully: this alliance with Cole was business, not love.

Her father, William, sat quietly nearby, observing. He listened as Elena and Cole discussed their impending engagement and marriage with the precision and detachment of a corporate merger. It unsettled him—a man who had always believed, as he did, that two people should marry only for love. Yet he had long ago accepted that both his daughters were grown enough to make their own choices.

A thought flickered through his mind. He had wanted to meet the investor consortium in Dubai himself, but his current health made that impossible. Another idea surfaced, tentative but practical. He chose his words carefully. "Why don't you take Lauren in her place?"

Cole blinked, momentarily forgetting William was even there, and glanced at him with a raised brow. Elena's eyes widened, a mixture of disbelief and alarm as she turned to her father. "Lauren…?"

William nodded, the idea gaining traction in his mind. "Yes."

Cole's expression remained sceptical, his dark gaze sharpening. "I'm not sure that's an option," he said cautiously.

Elena paused, her mind racing as the pieces fell neatly into place. Lauren. Safe. Predictable. Unremarkable. No one like her could ever challenge Elena's position or siphon off the influence and status that came with Cole's name. Relief surged through her, quickly followed by a sharp sting of envy—not for Cole himself, but for the power and opportunities he represented.

A small, deliberate smile curved her lips. "Actually, Cole," she said, her tone carefully measured, every word brimming with calculation, "Lauren might be the perfect choice."

William observed the subtle cunning in Elena's expression. He knew his daughter had always underestimated her sister—dismissed Lauren as plain, timid, or lacking ambition—yet the quiet strength and measured composure Lauren displayed were exactly what this situation required.

Cole considered the situation carefully, analysing every possibility. Plenty of women he knew would leap at the chance to accompany him—but most would misread it as more than business. They would cling, distract, and fail to hold an intelligent conversation unless it revolved around fashion, gossip, or trivialities. Lauren, however, was different. Intelligent, self-contained, unassuming—she would not demand his attention or disrupt the delicate balance he needed. She was plain, unobtrusive, perfectly suited for the role.

He studied them both and finally asked, his tone calm, precise, and measured, "Would she agree to it?"

Elena's smile deepened, sharp yet subtle, her calculation clear. "If Father asked her, she would."

"She would have to pose as my fiancée," Cole added, turning his gaze to William. "Would she agree to that?"

William allowed a small, knowing smile to tug at his lips. He understood Lauren well—she had wanted to meet this consortium almost as much as he did. "Yes," he said, confidence in his voice. "I think I could persuade her."


"You can't be serious, Father… with Cole Blackwell?" Lauren's eyes widened in exasperation as she stared at him, the incredulity in her voice barely contained.

William's expression remained calm, deliberate, but firm. "It's the perfect solution, Lauren. I know how much you wanted to go on the Dubai trip, and this is your chance."

Lauren bit her lip, feeling the pull of reason against her unease. The opportunity was rare, the chance to meet the investors firsthand invaluable—but the thought of being tied, even as a façade, to Cole Blackwell made her stomach twist. "And… what about Elena?" she asked cautiously, brow furrowed. "How does she feel about me… posing as her fiancé's fiancée?"

William's gaze softened slightly, though there was no hesitation in his answer. "Elena already agreed."

Lauren's head snapped up. "She did?"

"Yes," he said, a faint smile tugging at his lips. "And besides, it's not like they're in love. You should have heard them discuss their engagement—it was more like a corporate merger than a romance."

Lauren suppressed a laugh. "I can just imagine."

Her father's smile deepened, though his eyes were sharp with expectation. "Exactly. This isn't about romance—it's about opportunity."

Lauren exhaled slowly, ambition and unease twisting together in her chest. Posing as someone else's fiancée wasn't exactly appealing—but the chance this represented was too valuable to ignore. This was a rare opening, a stepping stone she couldn't simply walk away from. Already, her mind began ticking through the possibilities: how she could manoeuvre, how she could maintain control, and how to ensure this situation worked entirely in her favour.

"Alright, Father. I'll go," she said finally, her voice steady, though her mind raced with calculation. "It's… a good opportunity."

"Thank you, Lauren," he said, pulling her into a brief, firm hug that carried both pride and expectation.

Lauren straightened immediately as she stepped back, her resolve hardening. "I'll go see Elena first, then Cole. I'll make sure they understand the plan."

Inside, she felt the thrill of control, the subtle power of knowing she was stepping into a situation most would shy away from. Every glance, every word, every interaction could be carefully managed to her advantage. This was her chance—and she would take it, on her terms, with precision, poise, and a quiet satisfaction that no one, not even Cole or Elena, could touch.

Lauren made her way to the hospital room first, pausing at the door to take a breath before stepping inside. "How are you feeling today?" she asked, keeping her tone light, almost casual.

"Terrible," Elena complained, flopping back against the pillows. She had never been a good patient, always dramatic whenever she was unwell—not like Lauren, who simply got on with things.

Lauren offered a small, sympathetic smile. "So… Father talked to me about Dubai?"

Elena's eyes flickered with curiosity, then sharpened with understanding. "And?"

Lauren nodded. "Yes. I just came to let you know I've agreed to go."

A slow, approving smile spread across Elena's face, though it was tinged with relief—and a subtle edge. "Oh, good. I was worried he'd take one of his… bimbos. At least you won't turn his head."

Lauren felt the insult prickle, wrapped neatly in praise, but she didn't flinch. She let the comment hang in the air; her mind already focused on the opportunities ahead. Let Elena stew in her theatrics—this was business, and Lauren knew exactly how to play her part.

She lingered a little longer, listening to Elena's litany of complaints about the bed, the nurses, and the lack of proper pain relief. Each exaggerated sigh and dramatic gesture was another reminder of how different she was from her sister. By the time Lauren stepped out of the room, she thought she might need a dose of pain relief herself—if only to recover from enduring her sister's dramatics.

Next stop was Cole Blackwell's office. Lauren had never been there before, and she didn't have an appointment. The sleek glass building and the quiet hum of the elevator made her pulse quicken—not with fear, but anticipation. She wasn't sure what to expect, though she reminded herself firmly: this was business, not personal. Every word, every gesture, every glance would be calculated. She had a role to play, and she intended to play it flawlessly.

As she straightened her shoulders and adjusted the strap of her bag, she let a small, private thrill ripple through her. This was her chance—to navigate a world most would hesitate to enter, to wield influence quietly, and to emerge unshaken. One careful step at a time, and she would ensure that when she walked into Cole Blackwell's office, she walked in on her terms.


Cole was reviewing a report his CFO had just emailed when the intercom buzzed.

"Yes?" he said.

"There's a Lauren Dutton here to see you, Mr. Blackwell."

He raised an eyebrow. Unexpected. "Send her in."

Lauren entered, composed as always. Her hair was pulled back into a severe bun, glasses perched perfectly on her nose. No makeup—but Cole noted silently she didn't need any; her skin was flawless. The shapeless dress she wore was unflattering—he thought she would look far sharper in a tailored suit—but she carried herself with a quiet confidence that drew his attention anyway.

"Miss Dutton. What do I owe this pleasure?" Cole asked, leaning back in his chair, eyes sharp and unreadable.

"I've come to discuss Dubai," she said, her tone controlled. "My father has asked me to accompany you on this trip."

"Ah, yes. You do realise you will need to pose as my fiancée," he said, the corner of his mouth lifting slightly, testing her reaction.

A flicker of discomfort—and irritation—crossed her face, but only for a moment. She met his gaze evenly. "Yes. I do."

"Will that be a problem?"

"I don't think so," she replied, calm, precise. "As long as we have separate rooms, I'll be fine."

Cole studied her a beat longer, taking in the way she measured her words, the calculated steadiness in her posture. She wasn't like the others—she wouldn't fawn or stumble. That made her useful. Dangerous, in a way.

Lauren, meanwhile, was already calculating her own approach, noting how little Cole revealed and how much control she could quietly maintain. She would play her part perfectly—business first, appearances second. Every word, every movement, every pause would be deliberate. She had no intention of giving him—or anyone else—the slightest advantage.

"Well, I am grateful to you for agreeing to this," Cole said, tone even, almost cold. "It was unfortunate your sister had the accident."

"Yes. I'm sure that was a terrible inconvenience to your plans," Lauren replied, smooth, edged with veiled disdain.

Cole's eyes flicked briefly to her, noting the subtle bite in her words, but he chose to ignore it. Bigger matters required his focus. "Well, if you are posing as my fiancée, you will need this."

He opened his desk drawer with deliberate precision and pulled out a small, elegant box. Flipping it open, he revealed a massive baguette-cut diamond solitaire.

Lauren's eyes widened, her carefully composed face betraying the faintest flicker of surprise. "Surely you don't expect me to wear my sister's engagement ring," she said, lifting an eyebrow. The challenge in her tone was unmistakable.

Cole regarded her coolly, expression unreadable. "Not your sister's… yet," he said evenly. "It will be expected—for appearances."

He extended the ring toward her. "Try it on. It may need to be resized."

Lauren took it in her hands, turning it over. The diamond gleamed brilliantly under the office lights—a symbol of wealth, influence, and the authority this arrangement would confer. She felt the weight of the opportunity it represented, and despite herself, a small part of her mind acknowledged it. Still, she maintained her composure. She would wear the ring if it served her purpose, but she would not flaunt it.

Sliding it onto her ring finger, she noted with satisfaction that it fit perfectly.

Cole's dark gaze lingered on her hands. They were surprisingly delicate, elegant in a way he hadn't anticipated. For a brief, unbidden moment, he imagined those hands brushing across his chest, soft against bare skin. He immediately shook off the thought, forcing his attention back to business. "Well," he said, masking his discomposure, "it looks like it fits perfectly."

Lauren slid the ring off and instinctively reached to hand it back. She had never imagined wearing an engagement ring when she wasn't in love. Marriage had always been about love—and only love. This arrangement, orchestrated between her sister and Cole, made her blood run cold.

"Maybe you should hang onto it until we get there," she suggested, voice calm, measured—but with a subtle edge of control.

"Nonsense," Cole replied, sliding it back toward her. "You'll need to get used to wearing it."

Lauren slipped the ring on again, expression flawless, though inside, a storm of calculation—and a flicker of something unbidden—stirred. She would play the part perfectly, for now, because it served her.

"Very well," she said. "When do we leave?"

"The day after tomorrow," he answered smoothly. "We'll travel on my private jet. I'll let you know when a limousine will pick you up from your father's estate."

Lauren inclined her head, already thinking ahead. "Good. We'll need to go over a few things on the flight. I'll need to understand your routines, preferences… and you mine."

"Agreed," he said, dark eyes fixed on hers. "We need to come across as a united front."

"Agreed." She turned toward the door, her stride confident and unhurried, every movement measured. Just before crossing the threshold, she paused. She glanced back at him then, her gaze lingering deliberately—mischievous, knowing, entirely unafraid.

"I'll see you in a couple of days," she said lightly. "Have a lovely day, Mr. Blackwell."

"Cole."

The single word cut through the space between them—quiet, firm, unmistakably intentional.

She stopped mid-step.

Slowly, she turned back, one brow lifting in faint surprise. "Excuse me?"

"You need to call me Cole," he said, low, deliberate, a flicker of attention and expectation behind his eyes.

"Oh... yes, of course... Cole," she said, testing the name carefully on her tongue.

The subtle shift sent a shiver through him he hadn't anticipated. Lauren offered one last, faint, knowing smile, then turned and left—back straight, unwavering, refusing to look back—but the echo of her presence lingered.

Cole leaned back in his chair, staring at the empty space. The click of the closing door still echoed in his mind. For the first time, he felt a flicker of unease.

He had expected this arrangement to be straightforward—business, appearances, nothing more. Lauren was supposed to be safe. Predictable. Undistracting. Yet the way she carried herself, so measured, so quietly commanding, unsettled him in ways he hadn't anticipated.

He shook his head slightly, forcing his thoughts away from the memory of her precise movements, her voice, the way she'd said his name. The professional boundaries he had set felt fragile.

*Was this a mistake?* He told himself it was all business. Yet the thought of her close, poised to represent him flawlessly, and the way she had quietly claimed control of the situation... it gnawed at him.

Cole's jaw tightened. Women like her were rare—not manipulators, not charmers—but simply existing with quiet authority made them far more dangerous than any of the others. Maybe this wasn't going to be as easy as he thought.

# Chapter Five

Lauren made her way to Gregory's law office, the familiar city streets a comforting backdrop to her thoughts. The bustle outside contrasted sharply with the controlled purpose she carried inside her. She reminded herself: this was business, not socialising.

Gregory looked up from his desk as she entered, and his face lit up with genuine enthusiasm.

"Lauren! What a surprise! What brings you here?" he asked, rising from his chair, a mix of curiosity and delight in his eyes.

Lauren smiled, a hint of mischief in her expression, and held up her hand—her fingers adorned with the engagement ring.

Gregory's jaw dropped, a mixture of shock, delight, and mock annoyance flashing across his face. "You… you're engaged?!"

She shook her head, laughing softly. "No. Not engaged—at least, not in the usual sense. This is Cole Blackwell's ring."

Gregory froze, staring at her as if she'd just announced something impossible. "What?!"

Lauren leaned against his desk casually, letting him absorb the news fully before continuing. "My father arranged it. I'll be accompanying him to Dubai… posing as his fiancée. It's strictly for appearances."

Gregory ran a hand through his hair, half exasperated, half fascinated. "Lauren… only you could get yourself tangled up in something like this."

She grinned, the corner of her mouth tilting knowingly. "Exactly. Only me."

She explained the situation in detail, her tone calm and measured, every word chosen carefully to convey control and purpose. Gregory listened intently, nodding and smiling at the appropriate moments, eyes wide with disbelief at how effortlessly she had been pulled into such a high-stakes arrangement.

"Well," he said finally, leaning back in his chair, "this is the opportunity you've been hoping for, isn't it?"

"Yes," she admitted, "but I'm not exactly a fan of being in Blackwell's company—especially when he plans to marry my sister. Still… beggars can't be choosers."

Gregory raised an eyebrow. "When do you leave?"

"The day after tomorrow," Lauren replied, her voice steady, though her mind was already racing through the calculations—timelines, appearances, contingencies. "And I'll be away for at least eight days."

Gregory whistled softly, shaking his head with a mix of admiration and disbelief. "Only you, Lauren. Only you could turn a business trip into… well, whatever this is."

Lauren chuckled, letting herself enjoy a brief moment of satisfaction. "What can I say."

"He's going to be in for a bit of a shock when he sees you in all your glory," Gregory reasoned, shaking his head.

"I honestly don't care what he thinks," Lauren replied lightly. Then her mouth curved into a mischievous smile as she glanced down at her plain, straight dress. "But I won't deny—it might be a little fun seeing his face when I show up in something other than my… work clothes." She allowed herself a subtle, fleeting thrill at the thought of having that small measure of control over the situation.

Gregory grinned. "I wish I could be a fly on the wall. Maybe you could record it for me."

Lauren laughed, genuine and unguarded. "Maybe."

He studied her for a moment, expression softening. "He's not going to know what hit him. You're far more beautiful than Elena could ever be. You shine from the inside, Lauren—and the outside package?" He gestured toward her with a grin. "Absolutely exceptional."

Then he laughed and sighed theatrically. "If only I wasn't gay."

Lauren's smile softened. "I would have snapped you up years ago, Gregory. You're my soulmate."

Their shared laughter lingered, easy and familiar, grounding her in a way nothing else quite could. She allowed herself a moment of warmth before the calculation returned. She was stepping into a role fraught with power, influence, and subtle politics—and she would play it perfectly.

Lauren rose from the chair. "I better go. I actually need to do some shopping. It's been ages since I've had to dress up. I usually leave that to my sister."

"I wish I could come and help, but alas, work calls," he said with mock regret. He came around the desk, giving her a quick hug and a peck on the cheek. "I love you, Lauren. Take care of yourself… and whatever you do, don't fall in love with Cole Blackwell."

Lauren burst out laughing. "Are you kidding me? He treats a marriage proposal like a hostile takeover. There's no chance of that ever happening."

"He wouldn't deserve you anyway," Gregory said cheekily, grinning from ear to ear.

Lauren shook her head, still smiling. "You're impossible."

"And you love me for it," he shot back with a wink, making her laugh again as she headed toward the door, every step measured and purposeful, ready to take on Dubai on her terms.


Lauren was packed and ready when the limousine arrived. Her father waited for her at the door with a hug and a kiss on the cheek.

"Call me if you need anything, Father," she said softly, her tone tinged with genuine concern. "I actually don't like leaving you."

Her father, clearly having one of his bad days, managed a small, reassuring smile. "Nonsense, Lauren. You're going to be exactly where you need to be," he said, though his eyes betrayed the worry he tried to mask. "Besides, I have Mr. and Mrs. Mansel to look after me." His long-time butler and housekeeper were loyal, steadfast, and utterly dependable.

Lauren allowed the driver to load her two suitcases into the car, sliding into the opulent back seat as the door closed behind her. She studied the interior with a flicker of amusement. Cole Blackwell likes to travel in style, she thought, letting herself appreciate the understated luxury.

The drive to the airport was quiet, a chance for Lauren to review in her mind the role she was about to play. At the private jet customs area, the driver brought out both suitcases. Cole was already waiting, his dark eyes assessing her with that usual intensity.

He raised an eyebrow. "Is that all you're bringing?" His tone carried a hint of incredulity—he was used to women traveling with six, sometimes eight suitcases, even for a weekend. Then he remembered: Lauren Dutton was practical, not obsessed with fashion. He adjusted his expectations accordingly.

"I have everything I need," she replied evenly, her voice calm, confident, betraying none of the slight thrill she felt under his scrutiny.

Cole's gaze lingered, and for the first time, he saw her in something other than the shapeless, sack-like dresses she usually wore. Her hair was still swept back in its usual bun, glasses perched perfectly on her nose, but her outfit was strikingly different—skin-tight jeans that accentuated her figure, paired with a simple, fitted top. When she bent to pick up a bag, he caught an unexpected glimpse of the curve of her backside, and a subtle, involuntary tightening ran through him.

He straightened, forcing himself to mask the reaction. Lauren, unaware of the effect she had, stood with the poise, and control she always carried. Yet Cole couldn't deny the subtle shift—the way she moved, confident and precise, drawing attention without effort. *This is going to be more complicated than I thought*, he admitted silently.

The jet gleamed on the tarmac, sleek and imposing, its presence unmistakably Cole Blackwell—power, precision, and unapologetic wealth. Lauren followed him up the steps, acutely aware of the way his hand hovered near her back, close enough to guide her but never quite touching. It was deliberate, she realised. Everything about him was.

Inside, the cabin was quiet luxury—cream leather seats, polished wood, soft ambient lighting. It felt more like a private lounge than an aircraft. Lauren paused only a moment, taking it in, before moving toward one of the seats.

"Your seat's here," Cole said, gesturing to the one beside his. Not across. Beside.

Of course.

Lauren inclined her head and sat, crossing her legs with effortless grace. The movement drew his attention again—damnably so—and he forced his focus elsewhere as the door closed and the engines began their low, steady hum.

A flight attendant offered champagne. Cole accepted. Lauren shook her head. "Sparkling water, please."

Another point of difference, Cole noted. Most women would have taken the champagne without hesitation.

As the jet began its ascent, silence settled between them—not awkward, but watchful. Calculated.

"We should go over a few things," Cole said finally, breaking it. "Public behaviour. Expectations."

"Agreed," Lauren replied. "We'll need a consistent story. How we met, how long we've been together, what you like people to believe about us."

His mouth curved slightly. "You're very methodical."

"I don't leave things to chance," she said, meeting his gaze steadily. "Especially not when appearances matter."

He studied her then—not just her face, but the way she held herself, composed and quietly formidable. She wasn't nervous. She wasn't dazzled. And that unsettled him more than he cared to admit.

"In public," he said, "we'll be affectionate. Nothing excessive, but enough to be believable."

Lauren nodded once. "I can manage that."

"And in private?"

Her brow lifted just slightly. "In private, we maintain boundaries."

For a moment, something unreadable flickered in his eyes. Then he gave a short nod. "That works."

She glanced down at the ring still resting on her finger, the diamond catching the cabin light. It felt heavier up here—more symbolic. More dangerous.

"I'll wear it when necessary," she added calmly. "But I won't play the part more than required."

Cole leaned back in his seat, watching her from beneath lowered lashes. "You don't do anything you don't want to, do you?"

"No," she said simply. "Neither do you."

A beat passed. Then, unexpectedly, he laughed—quiet, low, almost surprised. "You're right."

Lauren turned her gaze toward the window as the clouds drifted past, her reflection faintly visible in the glass. She felt it now—the shift. The line they were walking, thin and treacherous.

Beside her, Cole remained still, but his thoughts were anything but. This was supposed to be straightforward. Controlled. Yet with every measured word, every subtle glance, Lauren Dutton was dismantling his expectations piece by piece.

And as the jet carried them toward Dubai, one thing became uncomfortably clear to him—

Lauren wasn't just stepping into his world.

She was about to challenge it.

The hum of the engines settled into a steady rhythm as the jet levelled out, the cabin lights dimmed to a soft glow. Lauren adjusted in her seat, glancing toward Cole as he loosened his cufflinks with methodical precision.

"We should lock down the finer points," she said evenly. "Before someone asks a question neither of us is prepared for."

Cole turned slightly toward her. "Agreed. Where do you think we met?"

She considered it. "Not at a gala. That would invite too many follow-up questions."

"Good point."

"A charity board meeting," she suggested. "Something discreet. You were funding a project my father was advising on."

His mouth curved faintly. "Plausible. And flattering."

"And we've been together long enough that an engagement isn't rushed," she added. "But not so long that people expect a wedding date immediately."

"How long?" he asked.

"Eight months," she said after a beat. "Long enough for stability. Short enough for mystery."

Cole studied her, impressed despite himself. "You're good at this."

"I've had practice," she replied lightly. "Watching my sister."

A silence followed—not uncomfortable, but thoughtful.

"And in public?" he asked. "How do we behave?"

Lauren folded her hands neatly in her lap. "Comfortable. Familiar. Touches that look unconscious rather than performative. You reach for my hand without thinking. I lean in when you speak. Nothing excessive."

His gaze dropped briefly to her hands before lifting again. "And in private, we remain as we are now."

"Exactly," she said calmly.

Something unreadable flickered in his eyes, gone as quickly as it appeared. "Understood."

A flight attendant passed quietly through the cabin. Lauren shifted, uncrossing her legs. "I'm going to use the bathroom before we land."

She rose smoothly, steadying herself against the seat as the jet hit a pocket of rough air. The turbulence came without warning—sharp, sudden.

The floor seemed to drop out from under her.

"Lauren—"

She didn't have time to grab anything before she lost her footing. Momentum carried her sideways—and straight into him.

Her body landed in his lap, her hands braced instinctively against his chest, her breath knocking from her lungs as the jet jolted again.

For half a second, neither of them moved.

Then Cole felt it.

The instant, involuntary reaction of his body—hard, undeniable, utterly unwelcome.

Shock ripped through him.

Lauren froze too, acutely aware of the way his arms had come up around her without thought, anchoring her there, the solid heat of him beneath her far more noticeable than it had any right to be.

"I—" she began, flushing, trying to pull back.

"Stay still," he said tightly, more command than request, as another shudder ran through the aircraft.

His voice was controlled, but his jaw was clenched hard enough to ache. He was painfully aware of her—her weight, her warmth, the faint scent of her shampoo—aware in a way he absolutely should not have been.

The turbulence eased.

Lauren shifted immediately, mortified, scrambling back to her feet. "I'm so sorry—"

"It's fine," he said quickly, too quickly, forcing his hands back to his sides as though they'd never touched her at all. "Turbulence."

She nodded, not quite meeting his eyes, and moved down the aisle, her composure returning with every step.

Cole leaned back in his seat the moment she was gone, closing his eyes briefly.

*What the hell was that?*

That reaction had been instinctive. Physical. Completely outside his control.

He exhaled slowly, forcing calm back into his body, his mind already snapping into discipline mode. This was dangerous. Not because of her clumsiness—but because of how easily she'd undone him without trying.

When Lauren returned a few minutes later, composed once more, neither of them mentioned what had happened.

But the air between them had changed.

And both of them knew it.

# Chapter Six

The descent into Dubai was smooth, the city revealing itself beneath the jet in a glittering sprawl of glass, steel, and ambition. From her window seat, Lauren took it in with a strategist's eye—wealth concentrated into spectacle, power made visible. It was exactly the kind of place deals were sealed behind closed doors and appearances were everything.

Beside her, Cole had returned to his composed silence, but it felt different now. Tighter. More deliberate. He reviewed documents on his tablet, jaw set, posture immaculate, yet Lauren sensed the vigilance beneath the calm. He was guarding something—himself, perhaps.

When the jet touched down, the cabin hummed softly as the engines powered down. A flight attendant moved quietly through the aisle, preparing for disembarkation. Lauren reached for her handbag, smoothing her expression into professional neutrality.

"Remember," Cole said as they stood, his voice low, controlled, pitched for her ears alone. "Once we step outside, we're on."

She met his gaze steadily. "Of course."

The heat hit them the moment the cabin door opened—thick, dry, unapologetic. Lauren instinctively straightened, adjusting her posture as the stairs descended. Cameras weren't present—this wasn't a public arrival—but staff were watching. Always watching.

Cole placed a hand at the small of her back.

It was light. Brief. Correct.

And yet, Lauren felt it immediately—the deliberate choice of contact, the silent acknowledgement of their roles. She didn't flinch. Instead, she leaned in just slightly, enough to make it natural, believable. His hand remained for a second longer than necessary before he withdrew it.

He noticed. So did she.

At the base of the stairs, a small delegation waited—hotel staff, security, a local liaison. Cole's demeanour shifted seamlessly into command mode. Confident. Charismatic. Untouchable.

The drive into the city passed in a blur of luxury vehicles and mirrored towers. Inside the limousine, silence settled again, thick but not uncomfortable. Lauren watched the city roll by, her reflection faint in the tinted glass.

"We'll be staying at the Al Qasr," Cole said eventually. "One suite. Separate bedrooms."

Lauren turned her head slightly, meeting his gaze. "As agreed."

A pause followed—brief, deliberate, charged.

"There will be a welcome dinner tonight," he added. "Key investors. Informal, but appearances matter."

"I'll be ready," she said calmly.

He glanced at her then—not at her clothes, not at the ring, but at her face. Composed. Unreadable. Unmoved by the city's excess or his presence.


At the hotel, staff swept in efficiently, luggage disappearing, keys produced. The entrance opened into a vast marble lobby, all soaring arches and gilded accents, sunlight streaming through towering glass panels that caught and fractured it into gold. The space hummed with low voices and discreet movement—guests, executives, hotel staff, security. Not loud. Just attentive.

Lauren registered it instantly.

Eyes.

Not overt, not intrusive—but assessing. Curious. The kind that catalogued status and relevance within seconds.

Cole felt it too.

Without a word, without even glancing at her, he reached for her hand.

The contact was instinctive—decisive. His fingers closed around hers with practiced ease, warm and sure, the gesture so natural it startled her. Lauren's breath caught for half a second, her gaze flicking to their joined hands.

She didn't pull away.

Instead, she adjusted—turning slightly toward him, letting her shoulder brush his arm, letting the moment settle into something believable. Necessary. Around them, a few heads turned. A hotel concierge smiled knowingly. Somewhere behind them, a phone lifted briefly, then lowered.

Cole's thumb shifted once against her knuckles—an unconscious movement that betrayed more awareness than the role required.

He felt her respond—not tightening, not resisting—just… allowing.

They walked forward together.

"This way, Mr Blackwell," the concierge said smoothly. "Welcome back."

Back. As if this were already established. As if she belonged here.

"This is my fiancée, Lauren Dutton," Cole said, his tone effortless, practiced, carrying just far enough.

The word landed differently now—anchored by the weight of his hand around hers, by the quiet certainty of the performance.

Lauren smiled, poised and warm, her free hand extending gracefully. "Thank you. It's lovely to be here."

Cole glanced down at her then—briefly, sharply—not at her smile, but at the ease with which she wore the moment. How seamlessly she fit beside him. Too seamlessly.

Only once they reached the private lift did he release her.

The doors slid shut with a soft, muted click, sealing them into sudden quiet.

The absence of his touch was immediate.

Lauren flexed her fingers once, subtly, as if grounding herself. Cole stared straight ahead, jaw set, expression unreadable.

"For tonight," he said after a beat, voice controlled, eyes fixed on the rising floor numbers, "we arrive together."

Lauren inclined her head. "Naturally."

The lift ascended in silence.

Neither mentioned the flight.

Neither acknowledged the hand-hold.

Neither commented on how easily the lie had taken shape.

But as the doors opened onto their floor, Cole was acutely aware of one undeniable truth—

This arrangement had crossed its first invisible boundary.

And he wasn't entirely sure which of them had done it.

The suite at the Al Qasr was everything Lauren had expected—and more.

Cole keyed them inside, and the doors opened to a space that felt less like a hotel suite and more like a private residence designed for royalty. High ceilings soared overhead, crowned with intricate detailing, while soft, recessed lighting cast a warm glow across polished marble floors. Floor-to-ceiling windows framed a sweeping view of the Arabian Gulf, the water catching the late afternoon sun like scattered gold.

The living area was expansive yet intimate—plush cream sofas, dark carved wood, silk cushions embroidered with gold thread. The air carried a faint, soothing scent of jasmine and sandalwood. Quiet luxury. Impeccable control. Very Cole Blackwell.

Lauren took it in without comment, though inwardly she appreciated the restraint. Nothing ostentatious. Everything deliberate.

"There are two bedrooms," Cole said, setting his jacket aside with habitual precision. He gestured down the corridor. "Both with ensuites. You can take whichever you prefer."

She glanced briefly in either direction, then back at him. "I don't mind."

The words landed heavier than she intended. Cole stilled for a fraction of a second. He was used to preferences, demands, strategic choices dressed as indifference. This—this genuine lack of concern—caught him off guard.

"Very well," he said after a beat. "The one on the right gets the morning light."

"Then I'll take that one," she replied easily.

Another pause. Subtle. Noted.

"I'll give you some time to rest," he said, glancing at his watch. "Dinner with the consortium is this evening. Be ready in two hours."

Lauren nodded. "I will." No negotiation. No fuss.

She picked up her bag and walked toward the bedroom, her heels quiet against the marble. At the door, she paused only long enough to say, "See you shortly," before closing it behind her.

The room was a sanctuary. Soft creams and muted golds, a king-sized bed dressed in crisp white linen, sheer curtains drifting in the air-conditioned breeze. Beyond the sleeping area, the bathroom unfolded like a private spa—deep soaking tub, stone surfaces, candles already lit, plush towels folded with meticulous care.

Lauren exhaled, tension slipping from her shoulders for the first time since leaving home. She stripped off her clothes without ceremony, leaving them neatly folded on a chair, then sank into the steaming bath. The water wrapped around her, easing muscles she hadn't realised were tight.

For a few blessed moments, there was no Cole Blackwell. No Dubai. No carefully constructed façade. Just warmth. Silence. And the steady rhythm of her own breathing as she closed her eyes, gathering strength for the role she was about to play.


Cole watched the bedroom door close behind her, the soft click echoing faintly through the suite. He remained where he was for a moment longer than necessary, hands resting loosely at his sides, his mind anything but still.

Lauren Dutton was… impressive. Not in the usual way women tried to be. There had been no performance, no calculated charm, no attempt to ingratiate herself into his space. She had stepped into the suite with quiet appreciation, chosen a room without drama, and accepted his schedule without question. No demands. No negotiation. No subtle power plays disguised as preference.

That alone set her apart.

Most women he travelled with—dated, engaged, paraded beside—treated luxury like a stage. They needed to be seen appreciating it, reacting to it, claiming it. Lauren had simply entered as if she belonged there, neither intimidated nor impressed.

That unsettled him more than he cared to admit.

He moved toward the window, loosening his tie, his reflection faint in the glass as the sun dipped lower over the Gulf. He had built his life on control, precision, and appearances—and she fit the first two far better than he'd anticipated.

The third, however… his jaw tightened slightly.

Lauren's mind was sharp. Her composure flawless. Her understanding of the role—better than Elena's ever had been, if he was honest. But tonight mattered.

First impressions with the consortium were everything. Their expectations were rigid, traditional, unforgiving.

And Lauren's wardrobe…

He exhaled through his nose, already anticipating the problem. She dressed for function, not effect. Those shapeless dresses she favoured—perfect in a boardroom, disastrous at a formal dinner in Dubai where image was currency. He had dated models, socialites, women who instinctively knew how to dress for power, to command a room before they ever spoke.

If Lauren walked in wearing one of her sack-like dresses, hair scraped back, minimal makeup—selling the engagement would become… complicated. Not impossible, but harder than it needed to be.

And that annoyed him. Everything else about her made the lie feel dangerously believable.

Cole straightened, resolve snapping back into place. If necessary, he would handle it. He always did. This was business, after all—and appearances could be managed.

Still, as he glanced once more toward the closed bedroom door, an unfamiliar thought surfaced, uninvited and unwelcome.

He wasn't worried she'd embarrass him.

He was worried she might surprise him.

And in his world, surprises were the most dangerous of all.


Lauren took her time.

For once, there was no schedule dictating her movements, no expectation pressing down on her shoulders. The suite was hushed, cocooned in luxury, and the muted sounds of the city far below barely registered as she let herself unwind. She began with a long, steaming bath, letting the water curl around her like a warm embrace. The tension from the flight, the airport, the scrutiny— all of it melted away as her muscles loosened and her thoughts quieted. This moment—private, indulgent, entirely hers—was a rare luxury she allowed herself.

Afterward, she washed her hair thoroughly, letting the familiar ritual ground her. When she finished blow-drying it, she paused, fingers hovering over the brush. Then she made a deliberate choice.

She left it down.

Lauren almost never let her hair fall freely. It was impractical, distracting, and invited attention she generally didn't want. Gregory adored it—he often said it was criminal she hid it away. Her father loved it too, always smiling softly whenever she let it spill down her back. But tonight required something different.

Her platinum-blonde hair cascaded in a silky waterfall down to her waist, glossy and impossibly soft. Every subtle movement caught the light, framing her face with effortless elegance, softening her usual severity, and lending her an aura that drew attention without effort or artifice. It was mesmerising, even to herself.

She removed her glasses and replaced them with contacts. Glasses had been her shield for years—a quiet barrier that allowed her to navigate her work with precision. Contacts left her eyes exposed, the vivid green startling against her pale skin, almost luminous in the suite's soft lighting. It was a small risk—but a deliberate one.

Her gaze shifted to the wardrobe. She didn't need flashy. She didn't need attention-grabbing. This was about balance—respectful, composed, undeniably elegant.

Fingers brushed past brighter, louder options. She dismissed anything too bold, too brash, too designed to pull eyes toward her. Finally, she selected a black dress, its hem falling just past her knees. She remembered reading long ago that modesty mattered here—certain lines shouldn't be crossed. The dress was form-fitting without shouting, skimming her curves with understated confidence.

Her body, lean and sculpted from dawn runs and disciplined Pilates, carried the dress with quiet poise. It was strapless at first glance, but small, elegant sleeves framed her shoulders, leaving her collarbones bare. Clean. Refined. Graceful.

Lauren studied herself in the mirror, turning slightly, lifting her chin, assessing every detail with critical, practiced eyes.

Jewellery crossed her mind—but this time she didn't dismiss it entirely. Instead, she chose a pair of simple drop diamond earrings, delicate and understated, catching the light softly as she fastened them. A subtle echo of the brilliance on her hand. Nothing flashy. Nothing competing. Just enough to complement the ring.

Her gaze drifted to the diamond on her finger. It would still be the star tonight—brilliant, commanding—but accompanied by quiet company that enhanced rather than overshadowed it. She lifted her hand slightly, the facets catching the light, deciding that this would be the statement. Let that be what people noticed first. Let everything else serve as the backdrop.

Makeup was next—minimal, deliberate. Soft foundation, a touch of contour to enhance her natural bone structure, a subtle hint of colour on her lips, and her eyes defined just enough to coax out the vivid green that could be arresting if noticed. It was her face, but sharpened, elevated, perfected without betraying the effort.

Satisfied, she stepped back and surveyed the ensemble as a whole. Everything balanced—hair, dress, jewellery, makeup, posture. She was ready. She wasn't nervous. She was prepared.

Sliding into her stilettos, she felt the small boost of confidence they gave, not height, but poise. One last steadying breath, a mental review of the rules, the story, the role she had rehearsed a thousand times in her head. This was her moment to command the room, to move with authority, to appear effortless.

She opened the bedroom door and paused in the threshold, absorbing the living area where Cole waited. Calm. Composed. Unaware that she was about to dismantle every assumption he had made about her.

Lauren moved forward, letting her gaze drift casually over the suite—the furniture, the art, the view—but every step measured, every motion deliberate. She hadn't needed to announce herself. Her presence alone was enough.

And as her reflection caught in the glass of the living area, she allowed herself a small, almost imperceptible smile. Tonight, she was not just stepping into Cole Blackwell's world—she was about to make him notice that she belonged there on her own terms.


Cole was in the living room, the dark blue of his tailored suit emphasising the breadth of his shoulders, a crisp white shirt beneath, and a perfectly knotted tie. He looked every inch the impeccably composed billionaire, as always. He was just taking the last swallow of a fine, amber Scotch he had poured for himself, letting the warmth settle in, when he heard the soft click of Lauren's door opening.

He turned slowly, expecting the usual practical Lauren: hair tied back, glasses perched neatly on her nose, perhaps a simple, utilitarian dress. But the moment his eyes landed on her, the Scotch threatened to freeze in his throat.

Lauren emerged, hair cascading down her back in a shimmering platinum wave that fell all the way to her waist, every strand catching the light, glossy and impossibly soft. The black dress she wore hugged her form perfectly—subtle, elegant, striking without exaggeration. The strapless neckline framed her collarbones just enough to be noticeable, the faint sleeves softening the edges of her shoulders. Her green eyes glimmered under the soft lighting, the expertly applied makeup highlighting them without masking her natural beauty. Simple drop diamond earrings mirrored the sparkle of the engagement ring on her hand, understated yet impossible to ignore.

Cole's breath caught. She was breathtaking. Not fragile or delicate, not posed, or artificial like the women he often encountered in his world of models and socialites. This was commanding, quiet, poised—effortlessly magnetic. Every step she took radiated control, confidence, elegance. And Cole, who prided himself on ironclad composure, felt every ounce of control slipping away.

He straightened, shoulders back, but it was useless. She had him entirely off-balance, and for the first time in years, he questioned whether he could maintain the façade he had mastered so meticulously.

She stopped a few feet away, gaze steady and unwavering, locking with his in a way that felt deliberate yet effortless. Cole, man of precision and control, felt the faint, unwelcome stir of vulnerability—an unfamiliar flutter he had no intention of admitting. He had underestimated her entirely.

"Do I pass muster?" she asked, quiet, teasing, challenging.

"Yes," he said instantly, a touch too quickly, as if the word could anchor him. *Damn it. Get it together.*

"Yes," he repeated, trying to steady his voice. "You look…" His words faltered. There were no words that could encapsulate the presence in front of him.

"Passable," she finished for him, the small, knowing smile tugging at her lips both infuriating and captivating him.

Without waiting for his response, she began to glide toward the suite door, measured, self-assured, leaving him momentarily frozen, scrambling to reclaim the composure he had so easily commanded in every other situation.

He stepped forward, unable to resist, eyes drawn to the cascade of platinum hair tumbling down her back. Every instinct screamed to reach out, to run his fingers through it, to feel the silky strands under his hands. He had been with women who demanded attention, women who curated every movement, every glance—but none had ever held him like this. None had rendered him unmoored with nothing more than a step into a room.

Cole swallowed hard, forcing his gaze away, yet the image burned into his mind: Lauren, radiant, poised, untouchable, yet magnetic in a way that made his calculated restraint falter. Every line of her posture, every subtle movement was a quiet command, and he found himself responding instinctively.

This wasn't supposed to happen. She wasn't supposed to affect him. She was the placeholder, the safe, predictable option. Yet she had shattered that expectation effortlessly.

# Chapter Seven

Lauren and Cole left the suite together, moving with the quiet, assured confidence that had marked every step since their arrival. Her heels clicked softly against the polished marble floor, each measured step a subtle rhythm of poise and self-possession. Cole led the way toward the elevators, his posture impeccable, the dark blue of his tailored suit sculpting the broad strength of his shoulders. Lauren followed just slightly behind, allowing him to set the pace, though he could feel the weight of her presence like a magnetic pull at the edge of his awareness—a silent, compelling challenge to his carefully calibrated control.

The elevator ride was a study in muted tension, the soft hum of machinery underscoring the hush between them. The mirrored walls reflected their careful symmetry, and Lauren stole a brief glance at her reflection—not to admire herself, but to reassure that her platinum hair lay flawlessly over her shoulders and that the black dress hugged her form with understated elegance. Cole, meanwhile, found his gaze straying involuntarily to her profile, a tight coil of awareness twisting through his chest, unacknowledged, yet impossible to ignore.

When the elevator doors opened onto the dining level, the rich aroma of exotic spices and refined cuisine greeted them like a warm current. The lighting was low and intimate, designed to flatter—polished wood tables gleamed beneath soft amber light, crystal glassware fracturing it into a thousand muted sparkles. The men of the investor consortium were already gathered, forming small clusters alongside their partners, exchanging polite laughter and murmured conversation, the subtle cadence of diplomacy filling the room.

Their attention shifted almost immediately.

Not abruptly—this was not a room given to obvious stares—but with the quiet recalibration of interest. Conversations softened. Heads turned. Lauren felt it as much as she saw it, the subtle awareness of being assessed, catalogued.

Cole felt it too.

Without conscious thought, his hand came to rest at her waist.

The contact was firm, unmistakable. Possessive enough to signal intimacy, measured enough to remain appropriate. Lauren's breath caught, her instinctive reaction sharp and immediate—but she didn't step away. Instead, she adjusted her stance, leaning into him just slightly, aligning herself with his body as if it were the most natural thing in the world.

Cole's fingers flexed once, settling more securely.

"Well," he murmured near her ear, voice pitched low, meant only for her, "we've made an impression."

Her lips curved faintly. "Apparently."

They moved forward together, his hand remaining at her waist as they approached the table. It felt… easy. Too easy. Lauren was acutely aware of the heat of his palm through the thin fabric of her dress, of the subtle pressure that guided her without directing her. The awareness irritated her—how quickly her body adjusted, how naturally she accepted the contact.

"Ladies and gentlemen," Cole said smoothly when introductions were called for, his voice calm, assured. "May I introduce my fiancée, Lauren Dutton."

The word landed with weight.

Lauren offered her hand, her smile warm but controlled. "It's a pleasure to meet you."

She felt Cole lean closer, just enough to reinforce the image. His thumb brushed lightly against her side—an unconscious movement, she realised, not for the audience but for himself. The gesture lingered a fraction longer than necessary before his hand eased away, only to return when they were guided toward their seats.

As she settled to his left, Cole angled his chair slightly toward her, his presence a steady anchor. Conversation flowed easily, wine was poured, plates were arranged. To Lauren's left sat an Arab prince—polite, charming, unmistakably intrigued. His attention was flattering, intelligent, edged with admiration that went beyond courtesy.

Lauren handled it with practiced grace.

She spoke thoughtfully, laughed softly at the right moments, engaged with insight rather than flirtation. Yet Cole tracked every exchange, every glance the prince allowed himself to linger too long. His jaw tightened almost imperceptibly.

When Lauren made a dry, unexpectedly witty observation about international markets, the prince laughed outright—genuine, delighted. Before Lauren could temper her response, laughter escaped her as well. Real laughter. Unguarded.

The sound startled them both.

Lauren felt the warmth bloom instantly, unbidden, spreading through her chest. She hated it—hated how easy it felt, how alive the moment was. She straightened subtly, schooling her expression, but the damage was done.

Cole watched her laugh—and felt something sharp and unwelcome twist in his chest.

It wasn't admiration. Not entirely.

It was possession.

He leaned closer, his arm sliding behind her chair, fingers resting lightly at her shoulder. "Careful," he murmured, lips near her temple. "You're outshining us all."

She glanced at him, amused despite herself. "Is that a complaint?"

"An observation," he replied, but his tone was edged, restrained.

The prince leaned closer, clearly engaged. Cole didn't hesitate this time. His hand lifted, fingers brushing back a loose strand of Lauren's hair, tucking it behind her ear with practiced intimacy. The gesture was soft, familiar—and lingered.

Too long.

Lauren's breath stilled. The warmth intensified, traitorous and unwelcome. She could feel the light graze of his knuckle against her skin, the awareness sparking between them. For a moment, the room faded—the voices, the movement, the weight of expectation.

Then Cole withdrew, his expression carefully neutral.

He hated the reaction that followed. The satisfaction. The quiet, visceral certainty that the message had been received.

The prince noticed. The smallest falter crossed his features before he masked it with polite composure. Cole caught it instantly—and felt no guilt.

Lauren shifted slightly closer to Cole, a deliberate choice, subtle but unmistakable. Her shoulder brushed his arm. She told herself it was for appearances. Told herself the warmth flooding her veins was nothing more than adrenaline.

She didn't believe it.

Cole did not miss the movement. His hand returned to her shoulder, firmer now, anchoring her at his side. The line between performance and instinct blurred, dangerously thin.

As conversation resumed, Cole realised—with a flicker of unease—that he was no longer entirely acting.

And Lauren, smiling politely as she lifted her glass, knew with quiet certainty that she resented how right his presence felt beside her.

After dinner, the guests were ushered into a spacious, softly lit room for drinks and dancing. The air hummed with muted laughter, clinking glasses, and the faint strains of a live string quartet. Lauren was about to lower herself onto a plush settee when the prince stepped forward, his movement smooth and deliberate. He extended his hand, his dark eyes locking briefly with hers. "Would you care to dance with me?"

Cole, engaged in a deep conversation with another gentleman, didn't notice. Lauren hesitated for only a heartbeat, a faint, polite smile forming at the corners of her lips. She wanted to dance. She placed her hand in the prince's, letting him lead her gently toward the polished dance floor.

Once there, he pulled her into his arms a bit too closely at first, the proximity testing boundaries with the familiarity of practiced charm. Lauren, ever aware, shifted subtly—an almost imperceptible adjustment that created just enough space to assert her own presence without breaking the rhythm. The movement was graceful, controlled, and perfectly measured, yet it did not escape the prince's notice; for the briefest moment, his confident poise faltered.

Lauren's posture remained impeccable, every movement conveying that she was no passive participant. Her head tilted slightly, her gaze clear and assured, and the faint lift of her chin communicated both elegance and quiet authority. Even in this delicate dance, she controlled the narrative.

The prince, leaning in slightly to match the tempo of the music, insisted she call him Ahmed. "You have remarkable insight on global markets for someone your age, Miss Dutton. Do you advise your father directly on investments?"

"Please, call me Lauren," she replied with a calm, courteous smile, her posture flawless. "I do, occasionally. My father values diverse perspectives, and I've been fortunate to accompany him on a few international negotiations. It's taught me that understanding context is just as important as the numbers themselves."

"Indeed. Context is everything. And you seem very confident navigating it," Ahmed said, his gaze lingering on her attentively, assessing her as much as he listened.

"Confidence comes from preparation. One cannot afford hesitation when decisions have far-reaching consequences," Lauren replied evenly, inclining her head with quiet assurance, holding his gaze without wavering.

"And yet you manage to remain… graceful while doing so," Ahmed added, a faint, appreciative smile tugging at his lips.

Lauren let out a soft, controlled chuckle. "Grace is as much about timing and restraint as it is about style. The same principles apply whether in a ballroom or a boardroom." Her words were light, yet deliberate, every syllable measured.

Ahmed leaned in slightly, intrigued. "You have a rare combination of intellect and poise, Lauren. It's… refreshing."

Lauren acknowledged the compliment with composed courtesy, her expression steady. "Thank you. I find it important to separate admiration from distraction, especially in professional or formal settings."

"Wise. Most people forget that." Ahmed shifted subtly closer, his presence deliberate but measured, testing boundaries while maintaining a formal air.

"How long have you been with Mr. Blackwell?" he asked, his tone curious but respectful.

"Eight months," Lauren replied evenly. "We only recently became engaged."

"Ah," he said softly, a shadow of regret in his expression. "Yes, that is a pity."

Lauren laughed lightly, the sound melodic yet controlled, letting it remain elegant and unruffled. But Ahmed's gaze remained serious, thoughtful, the corners of his eyes narrowing ever so slightly as though weighing the implications behind his words.


From across the room, Cole caught fragments of the dance as if through fractured glass—the subtle incline of Lauren's head toward Ahmed, the elegant shift of her posture as she responded to his lead, the faint smile that curved her lips when he murmured something meant only for her. None of it was inappropriate. None of it breached decorum.

And yet every measured movement sent a low, controlled surge of possessiveness through Cole's veins.

It was instinctive. Immediate. Unwelcome.

His jaw tightened fractionally, shoulders locking into rigid alignment as every ounce of his meticulously honed restraint snapped into place. He had positioned himself where he could see them clearly—too clearly—and now he could not look away. Ahmed's hand rested lightly at Lauren's waist, guiding her with practiced ease, his head bent close enough to suggest intimacy without demanding it.

Cole's fingers curled slowly around the stem of his glass.

*She was his.*

The thought came sharp and absolute, cutting through logic and reason alike. It irritated him—this reflexive certainty, this primal sense of claim that had nothing to do with contracts or appearances. He had agreed to play a role, nothing more. Yet as Lauren laughed softly at something Ahmed said, her green eyes bright beneath the warm glow of the chandeliers, she seemed… luminous. Untouchable. Entirely unaware of the quiet storm she had stirred in him.

That, more than anything, unsettled him.

Cole excused himself from the conversation he'd been holding, movements deliberate, unhurried, though his muscles were coiled tight beneath the tailored fabric of his jacket. He waited until the music softened and the dance drew to a close. As Ahmed guided Lauren toward the edge of the floor, Cole moved— intercepting them with effortless authority.

His hand slid over Lauren's fingers, closing around hers with decisive certainty.

"Come, sweetheart," he murmured, voice low, firm, pitched for her ears alone. "I need to feel you in my arms again."

The words were intimate. Too intimate.

Lauren blinked, momentarily caught off guard by the possessive edge in his tone, by the subtle pressure of his grip. But she recovered instantly. Her composure never faltered. She didn't flinch or hesitate—only inclined her head slightly, accepting the transition as if it were inevitable.

Ahmed stilled, his polite smile tightening almost imperceptibly as he registered the shift. He gave a small bow, all grace and restraint. "Thank you for the dance, Lauren. I hope we have the chance to speak again while you are here."

"I would like that," Lauren replied evenly, her tone courteous, measured—yet there was an unspoken finality there that made the boundaries unmistakable.

Cole felt it immediately.

His grip tightened just enough to be felt—a quiet reminder, a private signal meant for her alone. Heat radiated from his palm, a promise and a warning entwined. Before she could step fully away, he drew her into his arms, close and unyielding, claiming the space she occupied with unmistakable intent.

Lauren made a subtle movement, a reflexive attempt to create distance—but his voice stopped her.

"Don't," Cole said quietly.

The single word carried weight. Authority. Something darker beneath.

She lifted her gaze to his, unflinching, searching his face with calm precision.

"You are my fiancée," he continued, his tone controlled, measured, as if he were reminding himself as much as her. "And it would only be natural that you are close."

"Of course," she replied evenly, though her pulse betrayed her, skittering beneath his hand where it rested at the small of her back.

He stepped closer, aligning their bodies with deliberate intent. There was no mistaking the contact now—the warmth, the solid press of him, the awareness crackling between them like static. Lauren inhaled slowly, refusing to let it show how deeply she felt it. Cole, despite every disciplined instinct screaming caution, could not deny the visceral response her proximity provoked.

The room seemed to recede.

Music softened into a distant hum, conversation dissolving into background noise as they began to move together. His hand settled firmly at her waist, guiding her with unspoken command. Her other hand rested lightly against his chest, fingers splayed over his jacket, close enough to feel the steady thrum of his heartbeat beneath.

"Put your head on my shoulder," Cole said softly, his mouth near her ear. The request was deliberate. Intimate. Dangerous.

Lauren hesitated, a faint, almost playful curve touching her lips. "Isn't that a bit... forward?"

"No," he countered quietly, certainty threaded through every syllable. "We've only recently become engaged. This is expected. Isn't it the honeymoon phase?"

Her eyes flickered up to his, testing, questioning—aware of the excuse, of the truth beneath it. Slowly, gracefully, she complied. Her head settled against his shoulder, her body fitting into his with an ease that stole his breath.

The effect was immediate.

Her warmth seeped into him, her soft exhale brushing his throat, her scent—subtle, unmistakably hers—flooding his senses. Cole's chest tightened painfully. He had invited this. And already, he knew it had been a mistake.

Irresistible. Unwise. Entirely beyond his control.

His hand shifted at her waist, fingers flexing unconsciously as if anchoring himself. Lauren tilted her face slightly, her cheek brushing the line of his jaw, close enough that he could feel the whisper of her breath against his skin. The movement was accidental—or perhaps not. For a suspended heartbeat, they stilled.

Too close.

Cole's gaze dropped to her mouth.

The world narrowed to the faintest distance between them, to the undeniable pull urging him to close it. His lips hovered near hers, breath mingling, the temptation sharp and immediate. One inch closer—and restraint would shatter.

Lauren felt it too. She went utterly still, aware of the dangerous proximity, of the moment balanced on a knife's edge. Her fingers curled slightly against his chest, then relaxed—as if reminding them both where the line lay.

The music shifted.

Reality rushed back in.

Cole drew a controlled breath and pulled away just enough to break the spell, his expression carefully neutral, though his pulse betrayed him. When the dance finally ended, a quiet, hard-earned relief washed through him.

For one reckless moment, he had feared he might act on impulse.

Something irreversible.

Like kissing her senseless in the middle of the dance floor—and not caring who saw.

# Chapter Eight

When they stepped away from the dance floor, Cole decided, almost instinctively, to take Lauren's hand in his. Not possessively—not in the way the world would read it—but to ensure she did not drift too far from him amid the crowd. She attempted to withdraw her hand, a faint, polite resistance in her fingers, but he tightened his grip just enough to make his intent clear. This was where he wanted it to remain.

"I said stay close," he murmured, low and controlled.

Lauren's green eyes met his, calm, slightly amused. "I don't plan on wandering off," she replied, her tone light yet carrying that quiet certainty he had begun to notice.

Before he could respond, two elderly investors approached, their polite smiles and courteous nods signalling formality, yet curiosity shimmered in their eyes.

"Ah, Mr. Blackwell," the taller one said, "and your fiancée. What a pleasure. I've heard much about the family enterprise. Miss Dutton, your insights tonight were… enlightening."

Lauren inclined her head slightly, serene yet confident. "I'm glad to hear that," she replied evenly. Then, with careful precision, she added, "It's always fascinating to hear perspectives from different generations. Sometimes the best opportunities are found in the margins between experience and fresh insight."

Cole froze almost imperceptibly. Opportunities… perspectives… The words lodged in his mind like a spark. Elena's assumption—that Lauren was irrelevant, inexperienced—suddenly seemed naïve, almost reckless.

Once the investors moved on, Cole's brows knitted, curiosity and suspicion sharpening his gaze. "Lauren…" His voice was low, controlled, yet edged with the need for clarity. "Were you… repeating something they said? Or are you…?" He let the question hang.

Lauren's lips curved into a faint, knowing smile. "Or am I what?" she prompted lightly, unflustered, unguarded.

Cole's eyes narrowed. "Am I to understand that you actually know…?"

"I am quite capable of holding my own," she said evenly, measured, firm. "I earned a business degree—with honours. I've been involved in my father's company for years, participating in strategy sessions, financial planning, and negotiations. I'm not repeating hearsay—I have a voice, and I've earned the right to use it."

Cole's jaw tightened as the truth settled with uncomfortable clarity: he might have negotiated the wrong deal entirely—with the wrong sister.

Elena had seemed the logical choice. Refined. Beautiful. Groomed for public life. She had sat across from him in his office and spoken his language fluently—contracts, optics, leverage. Their arrangement had been precise, almost elegant in its efficiency. A marriage structured around a comprehensive prenup. Clearly delineated assets. Succession contingencies spelled out in advance. Proxy board seats for the Dutton Group once the Dutton transition occurred. Public unity, private autonomy. An heir produced on an agreed timeline, after which they would live largely separate lives.

No emotion. No expectation of fidelity beyond discretion. No confusion.

At the time, it had seemed… sufficient.

*But Lauren?*

Lauren had substance. Poise. An intellect sharp enough to challenge his own without ever needing to announce itself. She wasn't trained for appearances—she commanded rooms without effort. And standing here, watching her navigate investors with quiet authority, he felt something shift beneath the foundations of every assumption he'd made.

He exhaled slowly, frustration mixing with an unfamiliar respect. Lauren wasn't a placeholder. She wasn't irrelevant. She was formidable—and he had underestimated her completely.

For the first time since negotiating with Elena, Cole questioned whether the engagement he had so meticulously planned was the right move at all. Everything with Elena had been measured and contractual: her ambition, her belief that she would inherit the Dutton Group, the optics of stability an engagement would project to his investors. The prenup had already been outlined. The public narrative curated. Even the expectations of succession and governance discussed in unemotional terms.

He had wanted a foothold in the Dutton Group. That had been the beginning and the end of it.

But watching Lauren now—listening to the subtle precision of her insights, the way investors leaned in when she spoke—he felt the ground shift. She was more than capable. More than aware. Not a ceremonial wife or a boardroom ornament. She could run the company. And unlike Elena, she believed in something he had always dismissed as a weakness.

Love.

Elena had been content with appearances, power, and convenience. She had agreed to a contract disguised as a marriage, complete with legal safeguards to ensure neither party ever truly owed the other more than what was written on paper. Cole had convinced himself he was the same—that logic and strategy could govern his personal life just as ruthlessly as his empire.

But standing here, with Lauren beside him, the line between calculation and desire blurred.

He hadn't planned for this. He had planned an alliance. An image. A legally fortified union designed to satisfy markets, boards, and succession lawyers. Not this unsettling awareness that the variables might be wrong—that he had negotiated the perfect deal with the wrong person.

He replayed the evening in his mind: Lauren handling investors with calm authority; the way she anticipated risks before they were voiced; the depth of her understanding when strategy shifted unexpectedly. Elena's dismissal of her sister as irrelevant echoed sharply now—not just incorrect, but dangerously so.

William Dutton was no fool. *Why would a man like that overlook someone like Lauren?*

Cole ran a hand over his jaw, frustration threading with something far more destabilising. His life had been built on control—on predictability, precision, and leverage. Yet Lauren defied all of it. She challenged him. Unsettled him. Forced him to reconsider plans he had believed unshakeable.

And then there was the attraction.

He hadn't anticipated its intensity—or its persistence. It had begun in his office, watching her slide the engagement ring onto her finger, imagining it pressed against his skin, the warmth of her hand against his chest. On the jet, when she had fallen into his lap, the reaction had been visceral, instinctive, bypassing logic entirely. And now, seeing her here—poised, radiant, fully aware yet untouched by the attention around her—he knew the desire wasn't fading.

It was intensifying.

But desire was one thing. Marriage was another.

Lauren wouldn't settle for contracts and contingencies. She would want love. And love was something he had never planned to offer—never believed in, never accounted for.

Then the thought struck him with brutal force: if Lauren truly was William Dutton's heir—as he now increasingly suspected—every carefully laid step he had taken to secure influence within the Dutton Group was suddenly unstable. The control he prized so highly felt precarious, slipping through his fingers.

"Earth to Cole," Lauren said lightly, a small smile playing at her lips.

He exhaled, dragging his focus back to the present, and turned toward her. "Sorry," he murmured, his voice low and carefully composed.

"I think we should call it a night," she said, calm and decisive.

Cole nodded, even as his thoughts continued to churn.

"Yes," he agreed, a faint smile ghosting his features. "I think we've made quite the impression."

For the first time in years, the future he had so meticulously engineered no longer looked certain.

And that both unsettled him—and intrigued him more than he cared to admit.

They moved through the remaining guests with polished ease, exchanging courteous smiles, handshakes, and murmured farewells. When they reached the prince, he took Lauren's hand and pressed a bold kiss to her knuckles, entirely unfazed by the fact that Cole still held her other hand. Lauren's expression remained perfectly composed, but Cole felt the familiar tightening in his chest all the same.


Once they arrived at their suite, Lauren kicked off her heels and sank onto the sofa, finally allowing herself a moment to breathe and relax.

"Drink?" Cole asked, his voice low, casual, yet carrying a subtle edge of concern.

"Yes, please. Brandy," she replied, settling back into the cushions.

He poured a measure and handed it to her. "The prince is taken with you," he remarked, teasing lightly.

Lauren lifted the glass, a faint smile tugging at her lips. "Yes, he doesn't seem put off by the fact that I'm engaged," she laughed softly.

"Does that happen often?" Cole asked, curiosity threading his tone.

"What?" she tilted her head, amusement in her green eyes.

"Men fawning over you," he clarified, raising an eyebrow.

Lauren took a slow sip of brandy, letting the warmth spread through her. "When they see past the façade I maintain," she said, calm, measured, almost teasing. Even in her ease, there was authority in her words—a quiet reminder that she was no ordinary woman.

Cole leaned back against the sofa, captivated. "Why do you maintain the façade?" he asked genuinely, though a part of him already feared the answer.

Her expression softened, thoughtful. "Men don't take you seriously when you're a woman," she said quietly, firm yet reflective. Then, with the faintest shrug, she added, "And when you add blonde hair into the mix… it's a whole other level of assumptions."

Cole's chest tightened. Her composure wasn't a trick—it was deliberate, precise strategy. Every word, every movement, confirmed what he had been sensing all evening: she was capable, aware, and utterly unshakable.

He found himself leaning closer, almost unconsciously, drawn to the combination of intellect, poise, and subtle warmth radiating from her. His usual ironclad control felt suddenly porous, challenged by her effortless command of presence.

"Do you… enjoy being underestimated?" he asked softly, half curiosity, half admission of the intrigue she stirred in him.

Lauren's lips curved into a small, knowing smile. "It has its advantages," she replied. "You can observe, calculate, and act while others are distracted by assumptions. Sometimes, it's quite useful."

Cole's hand itched to brush a stray lock of platinum hair from her face, to claim just a fraction of the space her calm authority occupied. But he forced it down, keeping his composure. Instead, he let his gaze linger, tracing the curve of her jaw, the steady rhythm of her breathing, the quiet confidence radiating from her. Desire and respect warred within him, leaving him painfully aware that this—Lauren—was nothing like he had expected.

"Well, for what it's worth," he said finally, voice low, deliberate, "I don't think you should ever hide that hair of yours."

Lauren tilted her head, a faint smile tugging at her lips. "You sound just like Gregory," she said lightly. "He loves running his fingers through it and telling me I'm mad for hiding it."

Cole's brow furrowed, his jaw tightening almost imperceptibly. "Gregory?" His tone was clipped, the edge betraying an unexpected spark of possessiveness—and irritation he hadn't anticipated.

Lauren's green eyes met his, steady, unfazed. "Yes. A friend of mine. Actually… my best friend," she said lightly, teasing yet composed.

"Not your boyfriend?" Cole asked cautiously, hoping he hadn't revealed too much of his curiosity—or concern.

She laughed softly, a sound that made him grit his teeth slightly. "No, not my boyfriend," she replied, playful. "My last boyfriend was… about six months ago. And I might add, Gregory hated him from the start."

Cole's jaw worked subtly as he absorbed the information. Hated him. Not jealousy exactly—but a tight coil of awareness, sharpening his instincts about ownership, protection, and boundaries.

Lauren leaned back slightly on the sofa, her posture relaxed but entirely intentional. "He has a way of reading people," she added casually. "He sees past the surface, and he's never shy about telling me what he thinks. Sometimes I wish I could see the world through his eyes."

Cole's gaze dropped to her hands, fingers brushing the rim of her brandy glass, and he couldn't help the quick, possessive thought: *I want to be the one whose opinion matters that much.*

"And you?" Lauren asked lightly, arching a brow, teasing yet sharp, reading the undercurrent in his gaze. "Girlfriends? Before Elena, of course."

Cole's lips twitched—a half-smile, half-restraint—but his eyes remained steady. "I don't do girlfriends," he said softly, deliberate, the words carrying confidence and quiet warning.

Lauren's green eyes sparkled with amusement and curiosity. "Of course. Well, soon you'll be married to my sister. I wish you luck with that," she said, playful yet incisive.

"You and your sister don't get along?" Cole asked, leaning a fraction closer, his interest sharpening, an edge beneath the casualness of his tone.

"It's not that we don't get along," Lauren replied smoothly. Her posture remained elegant, her voice calm and measured. "We're just… very different. Elena prefers to live off my father's wealth. I prefer to contribute to it—to earn my place, to understand the business from the inside."

Cole's jaw tightened almost imperceptibly as her words settled. So, Elena isn't the only one with ambition. This sister—this one—is something else entirely. Intelligent. Capable. And potentially far more dangerous than anyone realises.

"She doesn't have much to do with the company?" he asked, carefully neutral.

Lauren laughed softly. "No. She wouldn't know a spreadsheet from a balance sheet."

Cole went very still. If that was true, the logic of succession made no sense at all. Elena's confidence, her certainty—it suddenly felt less earned than assumed.

"The thing that bugs me most about Elena," Lauren continued, then added with a small shrug, "or any woman who does this, is that she's content relying on a man for everything she wants. Not that she has to—she's wealthy in her own right. As am I."

"You don't rely on your father's money," Cole said, not a question.

"God, no." Lauren shook her head. "I have too much self-respect." Then she flushed slightly, realising how it sounded. "I shouldn't have said that."

Cole merely shrugged. "You were being honest. There's nothing wrong with that."

She studied him for a moment, then set her glass down on the coffee table and rose gracefully to her feet. "Well, I think it's time for bed. I will say this, Cole… you're not as arrogant as I first thought."

He lifted a brow, saying nothing, his gaze following her every movement.

"But Elena," she added, tilting her head slightly, a faint, knowing smile touching her lips, "and your approach to marriage…" She shook her head once. "Is not the way I would approach it."

His curiosity flared. "And how would you approach it?" he asked quickly, leaning forward, genuine interest threading his voice.

Lauren paused, green eyes locking with his—steady, unflinching. "Honestly? I'd base it on respect. Partnership. Honesty." A beat. "And love. Not appearances. Not strategy. Not convenience. Not money. A marriage should be a union of equals—not a transaction. Not a chess move."

Something shifted in Cole's expression—admiration, certainly, but something sharper, more dangerous glinting beneath the surface. *And here I thought I knew all the rules.*

"I can't understand how any man could respect a woman who simply leans back and expects everything handed to her, when she's perfectly capable of earning it herself," she said, her tone measured, edged with quiet fire. "And wouldn't the man in question prefer to be wanted for himself, not for what he could give?"

Cole considered her words, thoughtful, but remained silent.

Lauren's lips curved into a small, composed smile, her eyes glinting with quiet satisfaction. "Goodnight, Cole."

"Goodnight, Lauren," he murmured, his voice dropping to a lower, almost intimate timbre, as if the night—and this moment—belonged solely to them.

He watched her go, her figure retreating down the hallway until the door closed softly behind her. The subtle click of the latch resonated like a final punctuation, and Cole finally let out the breath he'd been holding, a slow exhale that carried away some of the tautness coiled in his chest.

*Four more nights.* Four more nights of being in her orbit, breathing the same air, watching her move through the world with that infuriating grace, intelligence, and unshakable poise. Four nights of knowing he was supposed to maintain control, to stick to the plan he had so meticulously crafted, and four nights of realising, with an unsettling thrill, that control was slipping through his fingers.

He leaned back against the wall, pressing a hand to his forehead, as if he could physically shove the thought away. *How am I going to survive this?* And he didn't just mean resisting the desire that roared in his chest whenever she was near. No—it was far more than that. It was her mind, her confidence, her principles, her laugh; the way she navigated every room, every conversation, with quiet authority. Each glance, each word, left him acutely aware of how much of himself he was already giving away, even before he had consciously allowed it.

Cole closed his eyes for a moment, letting the darkness behind his eyelids provide a small, fragile barrier. He had planned, calculated, maneuvered—and yet, Lauren Dutton had arrived like a storm, unravelling everything he thought he knew about strategy, desire, and, most dangerously, himself.

Four more nights. He ran the number through his mind again, and a tight, almost feral edge tugged at the corner of his composure. *Four nights. Survive it?* No, he realised sharply. He didn't want to survive. He wanted to understand, to anticipate, to somehow wrest control… but the truth was terrifying and undeniable: for once, the rules were no longer his to command.

And somewhere deep, beneath the irritation, the pride, and the possessiveness, a dangerous spark of exhilaration burned.


When Lauren closed the door to her bedroom, her thoughts lingered on what she had just said. She meant it—Cole wasn't as arrogant as she had first assumed—but beneath the calm certainty of her words, a different, more troubling awareness was stirring. She felt a pull toward him, a magnetic tug she knew she needed to resist.

He was her sister's fiancé. That was a line she could never cross, no matter how compelling the attraction, no matter how the warmth of his presence unsettled her.

Her mind drifted back to the jet, to the moment she had landed in his lap, the brief, reckless fantasy that had flashed through her mind—wanting, just for an instant, to kiss him, to test if his desire mirrored her own. But that was unthinkable, utterly out of bounds. Desire alone would not justify action, and she had no intention of betraying the trust of her sister—or herself.

Still, the thought lingered, sharp and insistent, a quiet reminder that some lines, no matter how clear, could feel impossibly difficult to uphold.

# Chapter Nine

Cole was already at the table when Lauren emerged from her bedroom.

Morning light streamed through the floor-to-ceiling windows, casting the suite in soft gold, and for a moment he forgot the report open beside his coffee. She wore a tailored charcoal pantsuit that skimmed her figure perfectly—clean lines, sharp shoulders—professional yet undeniably feminine. Her platinum hair was pulled into a high ponytail, sleek and purposeful, exposing the graceful line of her neck.

She looked… dangerous.

Sexy, in a way that had nothing to do with intention and everything to do with confidence.

Cole forced his gaze back to his tablet, though his attention had already betrayed him. He cleared his throat, reached for his coffee, anything to anchor himself.

"Did you sleep well?" he asked, deliberately neutral.

"I did, thank you," Lauren replied easily, moving toward the coffee machine. "And you?"

"Yes," he said automatically.

A lie.

He'd slept in fragments—half-dreams, half-thoughts—too aware of the quiet room beside his, of the memory of her warmth on the dance floor, of her breath against his throat. He'd spent hours staring at the ceiling, replaying conversations, glances, moments he should not be cataloguing with such care.

She poured herself coffee and turned toward him, and he looked up again despite himself.

"I'll be leaving shortly," he said, slipping back into familiar territory—business, schedules, control. "I have a closed-door roundtable this morning. Global strategy. Energy markets, infrastructure and logistics, currency risk." He paused, glancing at his watch. "It'll run most of the morning. I'll see you at lunch."

Lauren nodded, expression composed. "Of course."

But something flickered behind her eyes—calculation, anticipation.

Only then did it fully register.

He had no idea.

Her father had moved quickly, decisively, the moment Lauren had agreed to accompany Cole on the trip. Her presence here hadn't been symbolic or social—it was strategic. The Dutton Group would have a voice at that table, and William Dutton had chosen her to carry it.

Lauren wrapped her fingers around her mug, hiding her smile.

She could correct him now. Clarify. Watch surprise—or irritation—flash across his face.

But she didn't.

Some things were better revealed in context.

"Have a productive meeting," she said lightly.

Cole stood, gathering his jacket and phone. "I always do."

As he passed her, close enough to catch the faint scent of her perfume, he hesitated—just a fraction too long—then continued on toward the door.

Lauren watched him leave, thoughtful.

He would see her soon enough.

Not as his fiancée.

But as his equal.

And when he did, she was very curious to see whether Cole Blackwell would admire the move… or resent it.


The boardroom was designed to intimidate.

Floor-to-ceiling windows overlooked the desert coastline, the glass tinted just enough to remind everyone inside that privacy was absolute. A long oval table dominated the space, polished dark wood, discreet microphones embedded at every seat. This was not a room for posturing. It was where decisions were made quietly—and fortunes shifted accordingly.

Cole took his seat with the practiced ease of a man who belonged here. Legal counsel and analysts lined the perimeter, silent, observant. Across the table sat the core investors: sovereign fund directors, infrastructure magnates, old money with newer appetites. At the head, the consortium chair cleared his throat.

"Let's begin. Energy markets first."

Charts flickered to life on the screen—supply constraints, geopolitical choke points, renewable transitions delayed by logistics bottlenecks. The discussion was sharp, efficient. Men spoke in measured tones, trading figures, and forecasts like currency.

Cole contributed when appropriate, controlled, and precise. He was midway through a point about risk mitigation in emerging markets when he felt it—a subtle shift in the room.

Lauren had entered quietly.

Not late. Deliberate.

She didn't take a seat beside him, as he had assumed she would. Instead, she moved to the opposite side of the table, to a place already marked with a discreet leather folder embossed with the Dutton Group insignia.

Cole's attention snapped to it.

That wasn't decorative.

The consortium chair glanced up, nodded once. "Ms Dutton. Glad you could join us."

Ms.

Not fiancée. Not guest.

Lauren inclined her head politely and took her seat, posture composed, expression serene. She opened the folder with practiced ease, scanning the briefing as if she'd already memorised it.

Cole felt a faint tightening in his chest.

So, this wasn't courtesy attendance.

This was representation.

The discussion moved on—logistics corridors, port congestion, infrastructure vulnerabilities tied to currency instability. A senior investor spoke confidently about hedging exposure through layered contracts and regional diversification.

Lauren listened. Didn't interrupt. Didn't rush.

Then, when the room settled into a brief pause, she spoke.

"May I ask a clarifying question?"

Her voice was calm, unassuming—but it carried.

The chair nodded. "Of course, Ms Dutton."

Lauren lifted her gaze, green eyes steady. "If we're assuming currency volatility as a secondary risk, aren't we underestimating its role as a primary amplifier? Particularly in regions where infrastructure financing is dollar-denominated but revenue streams are local."

A few heads tilted.

She continued, unhurried. "Even diversified logistics networks become fragile if currency devaluation erodes operational margins faster than contracts can be restructured. The exposure isn't geographic—it's temporal. The lag between shock and response."

Silence followed.

Not dismissal. Not discomfort.

Consideration.

One of the older investors leaned forward slightly. "You're suggesting time risk outweighs location risk."

"I'm suggesting they're inseparable," Lauren replied evenly. "And that mitigation strategies should prioritise adaptive mechanisms over static hedging."

The chair nodded slowly. "Interesting."

Another investor spoke, this time addressing her directly. "What would you propose instead?"

Lauren didn't hesitate. "Convertible infrastructure financing tied to performance benchmarks, indexed to currency movement. It preserves liquidity without forcing premature divestment."

There it was.

A quiet reframing.

The discussion pivoted—subtly, unmistakably. Questions followed, not challenges. Clarifications, not corrections. The room began orbiting her point, reshaping assumptions around it.

Cole watched it happen, his expression carefully neutral.

But inside, something shifted.

They weren't indulging her.

They were listening.

Responding.

Building on her analysis.

A man two seats down referenced Lauren's framework when making his next point. Another nodded in agreement, scribbling notes.

Cole felt a strange, unwelcome combination of admiration and unease.

This wasn't Elena's world of optics and positioning. This was substance. Command. Precision.

And Lauren was entirely at home in it.


As the session drew to a close, the chair summarised the discussion, pausing deliberately. "We'll revisit currency exposure using Ms Dutton's recommendations as a baseline."

Cole's gaze flicked to Lauren.

She didn't look at him. Didn't seek acknowledgment. She simply closed her folder, composed as ever, as though she hadn't just redirected the room.

In that moment, Cole Blackwell understood something with unsettling clarity.

He hadn't brought her here as his fiancée.

She hadn't come to stand beside him.

She had come to sit at the table.

And the room—this room—had accepted her without question.


He finally caught up with Lauren in their suite just as she stepped out of her bedroom, a slim tablet tucked beneath her arm, her jacket already draped over it as if she were still half in the world she'd just left.

"Why didn't you tell me?" Cole demanded.

The words came sharper than he intended, frustration cracking through his usually measured tone.

Lauren stopped.

Not startled. Not defensive.

She turned slowly to face him, her green eyes steady, assessing—far too composed for a woman who'd just blindsided him in a closed-door strategy session.

"Tell you what?" she asked calmly.

"That you were attending the roundtable," he said, stepping closer. "That you were representing the Dutton Group. I walked into that room thinking you were there as—" He cut himself off, jaw tightening. "As my fiancée."

"And instead?" she prompted, arching a brow.

"And instead," he said tightly, "you were one of the most influential voices at the table."

A beat passed.

Then Lauren's lips curved—not smug, not apologetic. Certain.

"You told me you'd see me at lunch," she said evenly. "You didn't ask where I'd be before then."

"That's not the point."

"No," she agreed softly. "It isn't."

She shifted the tablet to one hip, her posture relaxed, unguarded—and somehow more commanding for it. "You assumed," she continued, "that I was here to smile politely and support you. That was never the arrangement."

Cole's gaze sharpened. "It was my arrangement."

"And this," she said gently, meeting his eyes without flinching, "was my father's."

The words landed cleanly. Decisively.

"You knew I wouldn't like being blindsided," he said.

"I knew you wouldn't," she replied. "But I also knew you'd respect what I did once you saw it."

His silence confirmed it.

Lauren took a step closer now, lowering her voice—not to placate him, but to make sure he understood. "I don't operate in shadows, Cole. I don't trade on deception. I just don't announce myself unless it's necessary."

"And you didn't think this was necessary?"

"I thought my work would speak for itself."

It had.

Cole exhaled slowly, frustration warring with something far more unsettling—admiration. "You changed the direction of that discussion."

"Yes," she said simply. "Because the risk models were flawed."

A pause.

"You let them listen to you," he said.

"I didn't let them do anything," she corrected. "They chose to."

The distinction hit harder than anything else.

She glanced toward the sitting area, then back at him. "If you're angry because I surprised you, I understand that," she said. "But if you're angry because I proved I belong in that room…" She let the thought hang.

Cole held her gaze, the tension thick, charged, undeniable.

"That," he said quietly, "isn't why I'm angry."

Lauren studied him for a long moment, then nodded once, as if she'd already known.

"Good," she said. "Then we're clear."

And as she walked past him toward the sitting room, Cole realised with a jolt of clarity that the problem wasn't that Lauren had disrupted his plans.

It wasn't just that she had surprised him.

What unsettled him most was not the surprise—it was that she was rapidly becoming impossible to plan around at all.

"Your problem, Cole," Lauren said calmly, moving past him to sit on the sofa, utterly unhurried, "is that you're a bit of a control freak. You like to plan everything."

He bristled—but he didn't interrupt.

"There are moments in life," she continued, folding one leg beneath her, composed and certain, "that simply can't be planned."

She met his gaze then—not challenging him, not apologising either. Just stating fact.

"My father and I were meant to be part of this consortium," she explained. "But his health wasn't strong enough for him to attend."

Cole's expression shifted, subtly.

"Then Elena had her accident," Lauren went on, her voice steady, measured. "And my father saw an opening. A solution. So, he took it."

She gave the smallest shrug. "Which is why I'm here."

Silence stretched between them.

Cole realised—with a mix of irritation and reluctant admiration—that she hadn't stepped into this role by chance. She had been chosen. Trusted. Positioned.

And that unsettled him far more than the surprise ever had.

"So, William played me?" Cole said at last, his voice low, controlled, though something brittle edged the words.

Lauren didn't flinch. She rose slowly, meeting his gaze head-on. "No," she said evenly. "He outmanoeuvred you."

His jaw tightened.

"There's a difference," she continued, unruffled. "Playing someone implies deceit. My father was transparent. He assessed the circumstances, weighed the risks, and acted in the best interests of his company."

"And I was collateral?" Cole asked, steel flashing in his eyes.

"No," Lauren replied without hesitation. "You were a variable. One he knew could adapt."

That landed harder than any accusation.

She stepped closer—not invading his space, but near enough that he felt the shift in the air between them. "You needed a fiancée. My father needed me here."

Her gaze held his. "We didn't plan for you and Elena to get engaged. We didn't plan her accident. None of this was scripted—but we adapted."

"Elena and I are not engaged," Cole said sharply, defensively.

"She believes it's only a formality before you are," Lauren replied quietly. "And if the accident hadn't happened, she'd be standing here with you instead of me."

Cole exhaled slowly, tension coiling in his shoulders. He hated that she was right.

He hated even more that he respected it.

"You're not angry," he observed.

"I have no right to be," Lauren said simply. "This was business. And you understand business better than most."

She headed toward the door, glancing over her shoulder. "So… are you coming to lunch, or do we need to continue this little negotiation first?"

"You're very impressive, you know that," Cole said, his tone low, almost reluctant.

Lauren's lips curved into a bright, disarming smile, the kind that made his chest tighten. "That's the nicest thing you've ever said to me," she replied softly. "Thank you."

# Chapter Ten

That evening, the prince was hosting a cocktail party accompanied by an exhibition of his personal art. Lauren emerged from her bedroom, she was breathtaking. She wore a floor-length, one-shoulder silk gown in a deep ruby red that clung to her in all the right places, the fabric catching the light with every subtle movement. Her hair was softly curled, swept over one shoulder to cascade down her bare skin, and long ruby drop earrings nearly brushed against her collarbone. Her makeup was flawless, a touch more dramatic than the night before, highlighting her green eyes and full lips.

Cole met her in the living room, impeccably dressed in a black tuxedo. The sharp lines of the suit mirrored his precise posture, but his gaze softened entirely as it landed on her.

"You look… stunning," he said, his voice low, deliberate, betraying more emotion than he intended.

Lauren offered a small, composed smile, but there was a glint of something teasing in her eyes. "Thank you," she replied, her voice calm, controlled—but the effect she had on him was anything but.


They arrived at the cocktail party together, the grand hall buzzing with soft conversation, the clink of glasses, and the muted notes of a string quartet weaving through the space. The prince's collection of personal art adorned the walls—bold abstracts, intimate portraits, landscapes that seemed to breathe under the ambient lighting. Guests in elegant evening wear circulated in clusters, exchanging polite laughter and subtle glances.

Cole kept a steady hand lightly at the small of Lauren's back, guiding her through the crowd with controlled ease. His dark eyes scanned the room, noting every subtle reaction: a raised eyebrow, a fleeting glance, the whispered curiosity as people took in Lauren's striking gown and her confident poise.

Before he could relax, an old acquaintance intercepted him, blocking his path with a broad smile and an enthusiastic handshake. "Cole! It's been ages! You simply must catch me up on—"

Lauren murmured beside him, calm, poised, "I'll continue looking at the artwork." Her voice was smooth, almost teasing, and she allowed a faint, polite smile to brush her lips.

Cole inclined his head briefly in response, a subtle acknowledgment, then turned his attention to the gentleman, the practiced ease of his manner slipping seamlessly into conversation. He allowed himself a fraction of a second to notice Lauren slip away, gliding toward the far side of the room with her head held high, her gown flowing like liquid silk with every step.

As soon as Lauren turned a corner to examine a striking abstract painting, out of sight from Cole, the prince appeared. Smooth, deliberate, and purposeful, he moved through the room with an ease that made the other guests' part like water around a stone. His dark eyes immediately found Lauren, tracking her movements with the quiet precision of someone accustomed to being noticed.

"Lauren," he said, low and warm, the faintest undertone of interest threading his words. "I was hoping I'd find you."

Lauren turned slightly, offering a polite smile—composed, alert, radiating quiet confidence. "Your collection is remarkable," she said evenly, her tone neutral, her posture poised, every gesture carefully measured.

The prince closed the distance, moving just a fraction too close, his presence charged with subtle intent. "Your insight this morning—on the intersection of global markets and infrastructure—was impressive. I'd very much like to hear more," he said, his gaze lingering, testing boundaries with an easy, deliberate charm.

Lauren replied with measured grace, "Thank you. It's always fascinating to see how strategy and perception intersect—whether in business or in art."

His smile deepened, intrigued, leaning just enough closer to suggest intimacy without overstepping. "Perhaps a private discussion over a drink?" His tone carried a carefully calculated pressure.

Lauren felt the pull—there was no denying he was handsome, charismatic, and the kind of man who would draw attention. She allowed a careful smile to play at her lips, aware of the risk. As far as everyone was concerned, she was Cole's fiancée, and this line could not be crossed.

Before she could respond, Cole's presence snapped into her periphery. In one effortless step, he was at her side, his dark gaze fixed on the prince. "I'm afraid I'll have to disappoint you, Ahmed," he said, his voice low, controlled, carrying a quiet edge of warning. "My Lauren doesn't have private discussions with the opposite sex."

The prince's eyes flicked to Cole, a polite—but unyielding—smile on his lips. "Of course," he said smoothly, though the glint of intrigue in his gaze never wavered.

Lauren's heartbeat surged, a mix of relief, amusement, and a simmering heat that made her aware of every brush of air between them. Cole had arrived just in time, drawing a line she could not—and would not—cross.

The prince excused himself with a courteous nod, and Lauren let out a quiet, relieved breath. "Thank you," she whispered, her voice soft.

Cole did something even he hadn't expected. He bent his head, close enough that his lips brushed hers in a fleeting, deliberate kiss—gentle, claiming, and charged with all the tension that had been building between them. Lauren's breath hitched, and for a heartbeat, the world narrowed to just the two of them, the art, and the unspoken pull that neither could deny.

Lauren's body stiffened for a heartbeat, every nerve alight, caught between shock, desire, and the iron line she had drawn for herself. Her mind screamed at her to pull back, to remember that her sister was Cole's fiancée, not her, but every instinct—the warmth of his mouth, the quiet strength behind his touch— threatened to undo her resolve.

She didn't move, didn't resist, but the faint intake of her breath betrayed her. Her fingers flexed around Cole's strong forearm, grounding herself as the world seemed to contract around the two of them.

Cole lingered just long enough for the tension to hum between them, letting the kiss linger at the edge of more without ever fully crossing the line. When he finally drew back, his gaze captured hers, dark and unreadable, holding an unspoken promise and warning all at once.

Lauren's pulse raced, her lips tingling from the brief contact, and she realised, with a mix of exhilaration and dread, that surviving the rest of this trip in his orbit was going to be far more complicated than she had ever imagined.

"What was that for?" she asked, her voice low and breathless, more a challenge than a question.

Cole didn't answer. *What could he say?* The truth—*I couldn't help myself*— wasn't something he could admit. His gaze flicked toward the prince, still lingering nearby, and a sharp, hot spike of possessiveness shot through him. The thought of anyone—even a man as polished and composed as Ahmed—leaning too close to Lauren, speaking too intimately, ignited something he hadn't expected: *jealousy.*

He flexed his fingers subtly around hers, an unspoken claim, and for a long moment, said nothing at all, letting the quiet heat between them speak louder than words ever could.

Later, when the evening finally ended and they returned to the suite, Lauren offered a simple "goodnight" and retreated to her room. Inside, she sank onto the bed, her pulse still racing, mind tangled in turmoil. That kiss—it was only a kiss; she tried to tell herself—but she couldn't shake the memory of his lips against hers.

No. This couldn't happen. He was engaged to her sister. A line existed, clear and unbreakable. And yet... by God, she wanted to kiss him back. She wanted to pull him close, to feel the strength of his arms around her, to let herself lose herself in the intensity of it—like a lover would.


As Lauren disappeared into her room, Cole watched her go, every movement burned into his mind. He should not have kissed her.

He could still feel the memory—the soft press of her lips, the faint warmth and subtle pressure, the delicate give and take that had sent a jolt through him. It was a sensation he had no right to crave, and yet it had rooted itself deep in his memory. The more he thought about it, the more he wanted it again—wanted her again.

This was why he shouldn't have done it. He was meant to keep his hands, his lips, his attention in check. She was his soon-to-be sister in-law, a line he could never, ever cross. And yet now, he knew. He knew what her lips felt like, and that knowledge burned through him, gnawing at his control like fire.

He ran a hand over his jaw, forcing himself to breathe, to steady the storm raging inside him. Logic demanded restraint. Reason insisted on control. But desire... desire was relentless.

He had only spent two days in her orbit, and already his usual discipline, his meticulous restraint, seemed to have evaporated. And they still had three more nights together. Three more nights in close proximity, where every glance, every subtle movement, threatened to unravel him further.

With hard, reluctant clarity, he admitted the truth: the kiss had changed everything. He didn't just want to hold her again—he wanted to kiss her, to taste her, to feel that impossible closeness once more. And the terrifying part? He wasn't sure he could resist it.

The next morning, neither of them mentioned the kiss.

They shared breakfast in quiet harmony—polite, measured, almost careful—each of them keenly aware of what went unspoken. By mid-morning, the atmosphere shifted from personal restraint to professional focus.

The group was seated around a long, polished conference table, laptops open, data decks projected onto the screen. In the corner stood a detailed scale model of the proposed renewable energy plant—a vast sprawl of solar arrays and wind turbines, engineered with meticulous precision.

"Projected ROI over five years is expected to reach twelve percent," the lead analyst said, advancing the slide. "This includes operational efficiencies, anticipated government subsidies, and projected energy output."

Lauren lifted her hand slightly, not interrupting, simply claiming space. When she spoke, her voice was calm, clear, and assured.

"I appreciate the analysis," she began, "but I'm curious whether the model fully accounts for currency fluctuation risk and potential permitting delays. Either could significantly affect net returns—particularly in years three and four."

A murmur rippled around the table.

Cole felt his jaw tighten as he watched her—composed, precise, entirely in her element. The analyst blinked, momentarily thrown.

Lauren continued, unfazed. "The assumed operational efficiency also appears optimistic. A five-percent underperformance would reduce ROI closer to nine-point-five percent. Factoring in realistic variance and mitigation strategies may alter both investor expectations and overall project feasibility."

Silence followed—brief, weighted.

Then one of the older investors leaned back in his chair, fingers steepled, studying her with open interest. "You sound like someone who's been in the room before," he said, a note of genuine respect in his voice.

Lauren met his gaze steadily, offering a small, professional smile. "I've had the privilege of observing—and contributing to—several of my father's projects. You learn a great deal when you're given a seat at the table instead of standing on the periphery."

Cole's gaze lingered on her.

He had known she was intelligent. Capable. But watching the room respond to her—seeing seasoned investors recalibrate in real time—made the truth impossible to deny.

Lauren wasn't an accessory.

She wasn't a convenient stand-in or a polished illusion designed to appease investors.

She was William Dutton's heir.

The truth settled with quiet, undeniable force, reshaping everything Cole thought he understood. There was no world—corporate, strategic, or ethical—in which William would ever pass her over in favour of Elena. Not permanently. Not without consequence. Elena had presence, ambition, charm. But Lauren had substance. Vision. Authority earned, not demanded.

The board would see it. The market would sense it. And the company—already delicately balanced—would fracture under the wrong leadership.

With Lauren, it wouldn't merely endure.

It would thrive.

The implications landed hard and fast, unfolding with ruthless clarity. Lauren wasn't simply the safer choice—she was the only viable one. Which meant the engagement he had orchestrated with Elena, once tidy and advantageous, was now untenable. A liability masquerading as strategy. In business terms, it was flawed. In reality, it was indefensible.

And in truth—his truth—it was already obsolete.

The realisation carried with it a sharper edge, one that cut deeper than corporate calculus. Cole felt an unfamiliar urgency tighten in his chest, a rare disruption to the order he prized so carefully. This wasn't impatience. It wasn't irritation.

It was necessity.

The arrangement with Elena could not be allowed to continue—not for appearances, not for convenience, not for a single day longer than required. Every hour it remained intact only compounded the damage.

He would end it when he returned to New York.

Decisively. Cleanly.

Because some mistakes could be managed.

Others, if left uncorrected, became catastrophes.

And Cole Blackwell did not tolerate either.


After lunch, there was a narrow pocket of free time before the evening's charity ball—an unscheduled pause that should have been welcome. Cole used it as an excuse.

"I have work to take care of," he told Lauren evenly, already standing, already withdrawing. The words were true enough to pass scrutiny, though not in the way she might assume.

She accepted it without comment, offering a brief nod before turning back to her tablet, composed and self-contained as ever. The ease with which she let him go unsettled him more than if she had questioned it.

Cole retreated to his bedroom and closed the door behind him with deliberate care, shutting out the low hum of the suite, the distant murmur of staff, the presence of her. Silence settled instantly, thick, and unforgiving.

He crossed the room and perched on the edge of the bed, elbows resting on his knees, fingers interlaced loosely as he stared at the polished floor. For several seconds, he did nothing at all.

The weight of his attraction to Lauren pressed in on him—persistent, unrelenting, impossible to dismiss.

It wasn't the sharp, uncomplicated pull he was used to. This was slower. More invasive. It threaded itself into his thoughts, disrupted his focus, lingered long after she'd left the room. He found himself replaying moments he hadn't given permission to matter—the warmth of her laughter at dinner, the way she fit against him on the dance floor, the steady calm in her gaze when he looked at her too closely.

Control had always been his refuge. His advantage. He excelled at compartmentalisation—at keeping desire contained, emotions secondary to strategy. Lauren made a mockery of that discipline without trying.

Cole dragged a hand through his hair and exhaled slowly. This was a distraction. An inconvenience. One he should be able to manage.

And yet.

He had wanted her close today. Had needed it, even. The possessiveness that had surged through him then still unsettled him now—not because it existed, but because it had felt instinctive. Unquestioned. He hadn't calculated it. He hadn't decided it.

It had simply been there.

Cole straightened, rolling his shoulders as if physically shrugging off the thought, and reached for his laptop. Emails populated the screen—figures, projections, negotiations that required precision and clarity. Normally, this would ground him. Anchor him.

Instead, his mind kept drifting.

Lauren, standing beside him.

Lauren, meeting his gaze without flinching.

Lauren, warm and steady in his arms, unaware of how close he'd come to losing control entirely.

His jaw tightened.

This could not continue unchecked. Whatever this pull was—this quiet erosion of his carefully constructed distance—it needed boundaries. He needed distance. Time. Perspective.

And yet even as he told himself that, another truth pressed in, unwelcome and insistent.

Distance hadn't dulled the awareness so far.

It had sharpened it.

Cole closed the laptop without sending a single reply and leaned back, staring up at the ceiling. The evening loomed ahead—the charity ball, the public performance, the role they would step back into with effortless polish.

He knew he would be composed again by then. Controlled. Untouchable.

But for now, alone in the quiet of the room, he allowed himself one unguarded thought before burying it where it couldn't interfere.

Lauren Dutton was becoming a liability.

And he was no longer certain he wanted to mitigate the risk.

# Chapter Eleven

Lauren was perfectly content to let Cole retreat into his work. She welcomed the distance—for now. She'd been itching to call Gregory all morning, the need for a familiar voice humming beneath her skin, but first… a long, indulgent, warm bath.

She sank into the tub with a sigh, the water curling around her like an embrace, soothing tight muscles and washing away the lingering tension of the morning. Steam rose in lazy tendrils, fogging the mirrors and blurring the sharp edges of reality. She'd lit candles—soft golden light flickering against the tiled walls— and for a little while, the world beyond the suite simply didn't exist. No Cole. No Elena. No expectations. Just quiet, warmth, and the gentle rhythm of her own breathing.

When the water finally cooled, she emerged reluctantly, drying herself off slowly, savouring the plush warmth of the towel as it clung to her skin. She slipped into a silk robe, the fabric whispering over her body, and retrieved her phone from the vanity. Gregory's name glowed on the screen.

Her thumb hovered for a moment. She smiled to herself—then tapped.

"Hello, gorgeous," Gregory's cheerful voice came through almost instantly, warm and teasing, like he'd been waiting.

"Hi, Gregory. How are you? Sorry, I know it's early there."

"Not that early," he replied with a faint chuckle. "Just gone eight. You know me—I'm an early riser. So… how's it going with Cole?"

Lauren felt an unexpected flutter in her chest and shrugged, even though he couldn't see her. "Oh, he's… not as arrogant as I thought he'd be." She paused, choosing her words carefully. "He's actually pleasant to be around."

"Pleasant," Gregory repeated. "That sounds loaded."

She laughed softly, but the sound lacked conviction. Her mind betrayed her— last night's kiss, the way Cole's gaze lingered too long, the constant, simmering tension she couldn't seem to escape. "Even… interesting, in a lot of ways."

Gregory's voice sharpened, the teasing edge fading. "Wait. Is something happening there that I should know about?"

Lauren's breath caught. She forced a light laugh. "No! No, of course not."

"Lauren…" Just her name, drawn out, layered with knowing. He'd always been like this—able to hear what she didn't say, to catch the hesitation beneath her words.

She exhaled slowly, curling a strand of still-damp hair around her finger, grounding herself. "He's… Cole is…" She faltered, then tried again. "He's nothing like I expected."

There was a brief pause on the other end of the line.

"Lauren," Gregory said gently, "your tone says something is going on. I can hear it. You're not telling me everything."

Her fingers tightened around the phone. The pull of honesty tugged at her, the comfort of confiding in someone who truly knew her. But admitting anything about Cole—about the way he unsettled her, the way her heart reacted to him—felt dangerous.

"Gregory," she said softly, almost a whisper, "I don't know what it is. Not yet. I just… needed to talk to someone I trust."

"Okay," he said, affection threading through his voice. "Spill."

She smiled despite herself. "He's almost engaged to my sister."

"The operative word there being almost," Gregory replied. "You like him. I mean—like him?"

She couldn't lie to Gregory. And she didn't want to. "Yes. I do. But it can't go anywhere. He's almost engaged, and he thinks love is a myth."

"Love?" Gregory said incredulously. "You think you love him?"

"No—no," she said quickly, honestly. "Not that. But I am… attracted to him."

Gregory laughed, clearly caught off guard. "Wow. I did not see that coming."

"Neither did I," Lauren admitted, her voice softer now. "I don't know what to do. There's this pull toward him I can't explain. It's stronger than I expected, and I can't seem to ignore it."

His tone shifted again, caution creeping in. "Lauren… has anything physical happened?"

She hesitated, biting her lower lip. "No… well—oh. He did kiss me."

"He kissed you?" Gregory echoed, disbelief and concern mingling.

"Yes, but I don't think it was… personal." She frowned, trying to make sense of it. "The prince has been pursuing me, and I think Cole did it to assert his claim. To stake his ground."

"A prince?" Gregory asked, clearly intrigued. "You're just going to drop that in casually? Tell me more."

"Ahmed," she said carefully. "He's… nice. Intelligent. Handsome. Confident. And he's made it very clear he doesn't care that I'm supposedly engaged to Cole. He's pursuing me openly."

Gregory whistled softly. "So, you've got a royal suitor and a billionaire marking territory at the same time. That's… impressive. And complicated."

Lauren laughed quietly, some of the tension easing. "Complicated doesn't even begin to cover it. But it's not about Ahmed. He's charming, and yes, there's an attraction—but it's Cole. I didn't expect to feel this way about him. Not like this."

Gregory was silent for a moment. Then, "Lauren… you know your heart better than anyone. You need to be honest with yourself about what you want, even if it scares you. But also—be careful. He's Cole Blackwell. That man doesn't do anything halfway. And once he wants something…" He paused. "He doesn't let go easily. And he wants your sister."

A soft sigh slipped from her lips. "I know. That's the problem. I can't betray Elena."

"Then don't plan," Gregory said gently. "Just be aware. Watch what he does. How he treats you. But don't let him—or anyone—push you into something you're not ready for."

Lauren swallowed, the weight of his words settling alongside the undeniable pull in her chest. "Gregory… I think he's already pushed me farther than I thought I could go."

There was a pause. Then his voice dropped, teasing but sincere. "Lauren Dutton, you've always been clever. Just don't get lost in someone else's orbit without knowing where it leads."

She chuckled, warmth flooding her cheeks. "Thanks, Gregory. I just needed someone to talk to. Someone who wouldn't judge me for… feeling things I shouldn't."

"You'll figure it out," he said warmly. "You always do. Just don't let anyone— even a prince—make decisions your heart isn't ready to handle."

She smiled, relief and yearning weaving together. "I'll try. And Gregory?"

"Yes?"

"I should have recorded his reaction when he actually saw me," she said, a soft giggle escaping.

He laughed. "Ah ha. I knew it would floor him."

She nodded, smiling to herself. "He couldn't speak for a little while. It was… quite satisfying."

"I can only imagine," Gregory said. "Serves him right."

Her smile softened, emotion threading her voice. "Thank you—for being the one person I can always trust to tell me the truth. I love you."

"Always, Lauren," he replied, steady and sincere. "And I love you too."


When Lauren emerged from her bedroom, the soft glow of the suite's lamps cast a warm halo around her. She was dressed in a royal blue strapless satin gown, the fabric hugging her curves perfectly, a daring slit revealing just enough of her long, toned leg to make it impossible for anyone to look away. Her hair was swept into an elegant updo, a few loose tendrils framing her face, and the subtle shimmer of sapphire earrings caught the light with every movement.

Cole stood in the living area, already impeccably dressed in a dark charcoal tuxedo. His eyes, dark and intense, tracked her every movement as if memorising the moment. There was a raw, almost palpable tension in the air; he wanted nothing more than to sweep her into his arms, to press her against him, to take that gown off slowly and deliberately—an indulgence he knew he could not allow himself, no matter how badly he wanted to.

"You look ravishing," he murmured, his voice low, husky with an emotion he couldn't quite hide.

Lauren felt a faint blush rise to her cheeks, hearing the sincerity behind his words. "Thank you," she replied, her voice smooth but tinged with warmth. "You look very handsome yourself."

Cole's gaze lingered, drinking her in, before nodding toward the door. "The charity ball is at the Armani Hotel in the Burj Khalifa. The terrace overlooks the city—it's spectacular at night. Shall we?"

Lauren allowed herself a small, teasing smile, slipping her hand into his. "Lead the way, Mr. Blackwell."

As they stepped into the chauffeured limousine waiting to whisk them through the heart of Dubai, the city lights stretched endlessly before them, a glittering tapestry below. The hum of the engine, the scent of her perfume, the press of his hand against hers—it all combined to make her pulse quicken. She knew tonight would be long, filled with glances, conversations, and the subtle undercurrent between them that neither could fully ignore.

Cole, meanwhile, couldn't take his eyes off her, even as the car wound its way toward the hotel. The thought of the night ahead—the elegant ballroom, the glittering guests, and the inevitable proximity to her—made his chest tighten with both anticipation and restraint.

The Burj Khalifa loomed above, its pinnacle vanishing into the velvet night sky, a beacon of power and prestige. Inside the Armani Hotel, the lobby shimmered with crystal chandeliers, polished marble floors reflecting the ambient golden glow. Every detail whispered elegance—modern, sleek, and intoxicating. This wasn't just a charity event; it was a stage for influence, for whispers in gilded corners, and for... dangerous temptation.

Lauren leaned slightly closer to Cole as they stepped into the awaiting cityscape of lights outside the floor-to-ceiling windows. The flutter in her chest was equal parts excitement and caution. This night wasn't merely about appearances—it was a collision of desire and duty, a test neither of them were sure they could navigate unscathed.

The ballroom unfolded before them like a jewel. Crystal candelabras cast a soft radiance across the polished floors, catching the glimmer of champagne flutes and sequined gowns. Soft classical music floated through the air; a string quartet tucked into a corner. Guests in tailored tuxedos and flowing gowns moved gracefully, some laughing lightly, others engaged in intense conversation. The air was a mixture of perfume, polished leather, and anticipation.

A passing waiter offered a tray of champagne, and Cole deftly lifted two glasses, handing one to Lauren with a glance that lingered just long enough to send warmth rushing through her. She murmured her thanks, and they began to circulate, weaving between groups of influential guests.

They exchanged pleasantries, shared polite laughter, and admired the eclectic contemporary artwork displayed for the evening. The music swelled, and couples drifted onto the dance floor. Cole stayed close, his presence a quiet, magnetic force, his hand brushing the small of her back whenever they moved.

Every subtle touch, every deliberate lean toward her felt calculated—and impossible to ignore. His dark eyes held hers longer than necessary, and Lauren felt the familiar flutter of butterflies she hadn't experienced in years, if ever.

He smiled—small, knowing, and almost dangerous in its subtlety. While meant to maintain the illusion of their engagement, each smile, each gentle contact stirred something reckless in her chest. Her mind warned her of boundaries, of reason, of off-limits men—but her body didn't listen. Every turn, every sway, every brush of his hand tested her resolve.

And in the glamour of Dubai, under the warm glow of chandeliers and the low hum of conversation, she realised this night would etch itself into both of them in ways neither could forget.

Cole extended his hand, his gaze intense, leaving no room for hesitation. "May I have this dance?" His voice was low, smooth, carrying the quiet weight of a promise he wasn't ready to speak aloud.

Lauren hesitated just a heartbeat before placing her hand in his. "Yes," she said softly, a faint smile tugging at her lips despite the tug-of-war inside her.

The music shifted, and they moved to the centre of the dance floor. The crowd blurred; the world contracted until it was just them. Cole's hand pressed to the small of her back, drawing her closer than etiquette allowed. She rested her head lightly against his shoulder, breathing in the warmth of him. He held her a fraction tighter than necessary, anchoring himself to her presence, to the reality of her.

He didn't know what to call the pull that drew him to her—part desire, part possessiveness—but he knew he had to resist it. He shouldn't let it go too far. And yet, with every turn of the dance, every brush of her fingers against his hand, he felt his control slipping.

When the dance ended, Lauren stepped back reluctantly. Cole's hand lingered at the small of her back a moment longer than needed, the warmth of her skin, the softness beneath his touch, intoxicating.

Just then, Ahmed appeared, moving through the crowd with confident precision. His smile was polished, his gaze steady. "May I have this dance?"

Lauren's heart jumped, and she glanced up at Cole, silently hoping he might refuse, might claim her again. But he said nothing, his jaw tight, expression unreadable. The silence was deliberate, and the sting of it pricked her chest. He was letting her go.

With a faint, polite smile, Lauren placed her hand in Ahmed's. "I would love to."

Ahmed drew her onto the dance floor, guiding her with measured elegance. His presence was commanding yet courteous, close enough to make her pulse quicken without letting decorum slip entirely. She moved with grace, matching his steps, aware of the coil of tension in her chest—the memory of Cole pressing her close still burning.

As the music drew to a close, Ahmed didn't return her to Cole, who was deep in conversation with a prominent investor. Instead, he inclined his head toward the terrace. "Come," he said softly, "I want to show you the view."

Lauren followed, the cool night air brushing against her bare shoulders, carrying the faint scent of jasmine from the hotel gardens below. The terrace opened onto a sweeping panorama of Dubai—an endless sea of glittering lights reflected in the creek, the Burj Khalifa rising like a silver spire into the night sky, the city pulsing with life even at this late hour.

Ahmed guided her to the balustrade, his hand brushing hers in a fleeting, deliberate touch that sent a small shiver through her. She leaned slightly against the railing, letting her eyes drink in the spectacle. "It's breathtaking," she murmured. "I don't think I've ever seen anything like this."

Ahmed's voice was calm, smooth, carrying a quiet authority that drew her attention even more than the cityscape. "See that?" he said, pointing toward the lights of the old creek district. "The architecture there blends the traditional with the modern. You can almost feel the history in the stones."

He turned slightly, sweeping his hand to indicate the glittering marina below. "And there—the yachts, the water reflecting the towers—it's one of my favourite views in the city. It's peaceful, in a way, despite all the energy around it."

Lauren's gaze followed his gestures, and she felt the gentle pull of his presence behind her. Without thinking, she leaned a fraction back, and then she felt it— the warmth, the proximity. Ahmed had moved closer, his chest nearly brushing her back, his presence magnetic and grounding.

He reached forward and rested his hands lightly on her shoulders. The contact was firm but careful, protective rather than possessive, his fingers brushing against the soft curve of her neck. Lauren's breath caught, a subtle heat blooming in her chest. The cool night air did nothing to diminish the warmth radiating from his touch.

"I want you to see it fully," he murmured, his voice low, intimate, threading against her ear. "The way the city glimmers, the way it feels alive."

She tilted her head, allowing her gaze to sweep over the skyline once more. Lights twinkled across the creek, reflected in gentle ripples on the water, while the iconic silhouette of the Burj Khalifa loomed above them, brilliant and untouchable. Everything shimmered—the city, the night, the air between them.

Ahmed's hands remained on her shoulders, steady and warm, grounding her even as a swirl of conflicting emotions ran through her. She could feel his measured strength behind her, the calm confidence in his posture, the subtle weight of intention in his touch. It was intimate, electric, and completely controlled—a gesture that made her heart race and her mind reel all at once.

"Beautiful, isn't it?" he said, his tone softening. "The city, the night... it's easy to get lost in it."

Lauren swallowed, acutely aware of the pull of his presence, the magnetic connection that seemed to hum in the air around them. "It's... incredible," she whispered, her voice soft and breathless. "Thank you for showing me."

Ahmed's fingers flexed slightly where they rested on her shoulders. He lifted one hand and gently tilted her chin up and back until their eyes met in the reflection of the city lights beyond the glass. For a suspended moment, the world seemed to still—as if the city below and the stars above had quietly drawn back, leaving only the two of them on the terrace, the air charged, the night alive with possibility.

Behind her, Lauren could feel his controlled strength, the subtle tension in his stance, the unmistakable warmth of a man acutely aware of her—yet restraining himself, just enough, to respect the fragile boundaries of the moment.

"It's almost as beautiful as you," he murmured.

# Chapter Twelve

Cole, having excused himself from the conversation with the investor, scanned the room for Lauren. She hadn't mentioned stepping away, and a sudden, cold knot of apprehension tightened in his chest. He had originally thought giving her a little space—letting her move freely, letting Ahmed have his moment—would be the prudent, sensible thing to do. A way to keep his own emotions in check.

But now, standing on the edge of the crowded ballroom, every instinct screaming, he realised how wrong that idea had been. Where would a man like Ahmed take a woman he was clearly interested in? The answer was obvious: somewhere private. The terrace.

Cole's steps were deliberate, silent, every sense sharpened. The chatter and clinking glasses of the party faded into the background as he moved. And then he saw them: Lauren, framed by the soft glow of the terrace lights, her hair lifted by the night breeze, eyes fixed on the city below. Behind her, Ahmed leaned in just slightly, his hands resting lightly but deliberately on her shoulders. The gesture was casual, confident, intimate—and it drove a spike of heat through Cole's chest.

Their faces were mere inches apart, and for a heartbeat, the world seemed to pause. Cole's chest tightened. A surge of jealousy and anger—sharp, raw, overwhelming—left him momentarily breathless. He had never felt this for anyone—not for a woman, not like this.

Every instinct roared at him: to cross the terrace in a single stride, to pull Lauren into his arms, to stake a claim that was as much about protection as it was desire. His mind fought it, telling him to remain composed, to let her make her own choices—but his body, his heart, his entire being refused to listen.

Cole's dark eyes narrowed, watching Ahmed's practiced charm and Lauren's soft, attentive response. The sight ignited a possessive fire he couldn't deny, a primal need that made his jaw tighten. He had thought distance would help, thought restraint would be the right choice—but seeing them like this, feeling the tension radiating from every inch of her posture toward another man, made it clear: he didn't want space. He wanted her. *Only her.*

A low, controlled breath left Cole's lips, though inside, a storm raged. Every calculated thought about appearances, decorum, even the engagement to Elena—they all fell away under the weight of raw, undeniable desire.

And with that, he made a decision. Not rash, not reckless, but deliberate. He would reclaim her attention, her presence, and leave no doubt where she belonged.

Cole stepped onto the terrace, his dark gaze locking on Lauren. "Sweetheart," he said, voice low and warm, threading affection through the edge of steel, "this is where you got to."

His eyes flicked to Ahmed's hands resting on Lauren's shoulders, calm and confident just moments before. Cole raised a single, slow eyebrow—a silent, razor-sharp warning: *hands off.*

Ahmed's smile was polite, his composure intact, though the faint tightening around his eyes betrayed reluctance. Slowly, carefully, he withdrew his hands, raising them in a subtle, gentlemanly gesture. "I was just showing the view to your charming fiancée," he said, his tone courteous, measured, yet underscored with a hint of hesitation.

Lauren felt the tension coil like electricity between the men—controlled, polite, but undeniable. She could see the restraint in Ahmed, the barely concealed edge in Cole, the quiet war simmering in the space between them.

Cole stepped closer to her, close enough that the heat from his body brushed hers. His hand rested lightly at her side—not on her shoulders, not yet claiming fully, but enough to make the point. "Thank you for keeping her company," he said evenly, voice smooth, dangerous, "but I'm here now."

Ahmed nodded, lips pressed into a polite line and gave a small bow of acknowledgment. "Of course. I will leave you."

He stepped back, leaving them alone, but the faint stiffness in his posture spoke volumes—he had been forced to retreat, reluctantly, unwillingly. The terrace, the view, the night air—they were now Cole's domain, and Lauren felt it, the magnetic pull of him surrounding her, anchoring her to a space that was suddenly and completely theirs.

Cole's eyes softened as he turned to her, but the smouldering intensity never left them. "Are you alright?" he asked quietly, though the sharpness in his tone carried the underlying message: *no other man should claim even a moment of her attention.*

Lauren swallowed, her pulse still racing, caught between relief and a thrill she couldn't quite name. "I—I'm fine," she whispered. "It's... beautiful out here."

"It certainly is," Cole murmured, his gaze locked on her, and it was clear he wasn't speaking about the view. His hand brushed hers lightly, a deliberate, teasing contact that sent a jolt of heat through her, making her knees weaken ever so slightly.

The night seemed to pause around them.

Beyond the terrace railing, the city sprawled endlessly below—a vast, glittering mosaic of light and movement, glass towers rising like sentinels against the velvet dark. Cars traced thin ribbons of gold through the streets far beneath them, the distant pulse of life continuing as if untouched by what had just passed between them.

But for this moment, none of it mattered.

All that existed was the charged space between them—and the unspoken claim Cole had made without words, without hesitation.

Lauren's breath caught as she lifted her gaze to his.

His eyes were dark, intent, stripped of their usual cool detachment, holding her with an unwavering focus that made the air feel heavier, denser. There was no calculation in his expression now. No strategy. Just certainty. Possession restrained by discipline rather than doubt.

The pull of him was undeniable.

It settled low in her chest, spreading outward in a slow, intoxicating wave that loosened her careful control. Every rational thought wavered beneath it—the sensible objections, the reminders of boundaries and consequences—until all that remained was the acute awareness of being exactly where she was meant to be.

And with exactly who she was meant to be with.

The thought startled her with its clarity.

She inhaled slowly, grounding herself in the cool night air, but even that did little to dull the warmth humming beneath her skin. Cole hadn't moved closer. He didn't need to. His presence alone felt enclosing, deliberate, as if he had drawn an invisible line around them both.

They remained there in silence for several long minutes, standing side by side, facing the view yet acutely aware of each other. The city lights flickered below, distant, and impersonal, while above them the sky stretched wide and endless.

Lauren let the quiet settle, let the moment breathe, knowing instinctively that rushing it would break something fragile and rare.

Eventually, she turned toward him.

"Would you mind," she asked softly, her voice calm despite the undercurrent of feeling she made no attempt to name, "if we left?"

Cole looked at her then—really looked at her.

Her face was serene, composed, but her eyes held a depth that hadn't been there before, something open and resolute all at once. Not retreat. Not hesitation. A choice.

Understanding flickered across his features, followed by something quieter. He nodded once.

"Of course," he said simply.

The single words carried no disappointment. No pressure. Only agreement.

And as they turned away from the railing together, leaving the city and its glittering distractions behind, both were acutely aware of the same undeniable truth—

Nothing had been resolved.

But nothing, after this, would ever be the same.


The limousine ride back to the hotel passed in silence.

Not an awkward silence—no need for conversation filled with pleasantries or deflection—but something heavier, charged, settling into the plush leather interior with them. The city slipped past the tinted windows in streaks of light and shadow, distant and unreal, while inside the car the air felt dense, expectant.

Lauren sat beside Cole, her posture composed, hands folded neatly in her lap. She stared ahead, focusing on nothing and everything all at once, acutely aware of the small, undeniable distance between them. Inches. Mere inches.

It felt deliberate. Necessary.

She fought the instinct to shift closer, to let her shoulder brush his arm, to close the space that seemed to hum with possibility. The urge startled her with its persistence. This wasn't infatuation. This wasn't recklessness. It was quieter than that—and far more dangerous.

She shouldn't feel this.

He was almost engaged to her sister.

The reminder rose like a shield, rigid and familiar. Elena. The arrangement. The inevitability that had once seemed fixed and unquestioned. Lauren clenched her fingers together, grounding herself, refusing to indulge the warmth that lingered from the terrace, from the way he had looked at her as if the rest of the world had fallen away.

She turned her gaze briefly toward the window, forcing distance not just in space, but in thought.

Beside her, Cole was equally still.

He sat with his back against the seat, one arm resting along the side of the limo, gaze forward, expression carefully neutral. Anyone watching would have seen composure. Control. A man entirely at ease.

The reality was far less contained.

The attraction between them pressed at him relentlessly, no longer sharp and fleeting, but steady—insistent in a way that demanded acknowledgment. It had stopped being a momentary lapse, something he could dismiss by sheer force of will. It followed him now. Sat beside him. Breathed in the same quiet space.

It was becoming a distraction.

One he was finding harder—and more dangerous—to ignore.

Cole exhaled slowly, jaw tightening as his thoughts veered where he didn't want them to go. Lauren's calm presence unsettled him precisely because it felt so natural. Because he didn't have to imagine what it would be like to reach for her—he already knew. He'd felt the warmth of her, the quiet certainty with which she met his gaze, the way she neither yielded nor retreated.

Then there was the other concern. The one he could no longer compartmentalise.

Elena.

The pending engagement loomed now not as a solution, but as an obstacle— one he had already, irrevocably, decided would not move forward. The realisation had come with surprising clarity, cutting through strategy and ambition alike.

Ending it would cost him.

The foothold he had intended to secure within the Dutton Group would vanish with it. Years of careful positioning, of calculated advantage, undone by a decision he hadn't anticipated making so soon—or so decisively.

And yet, as he sat there beside Lauren, the cost no longer felt negotiable.

Because he knew, without doubt, what William Dutton already understood.

Lauren was the heir.

Not Elena. Never Elena.

Lauren had the insight, the discipline, the quiet authority that could not be manufactured or inherited by title alone. With her, the Dutton legacy would strengthen. Expand. Endure.

The truth settled heavily in his chest, unmistakable and final.

Cole glanced sideways, just once.

Lauren hadn't moved. Her expression was serene, composed, her gaze still fixed outward—but something in the line of her shoulders suggested restraint rather than ease. As if she, too, were holding herself in place by sheer force of will.

The thought tightened something in him.

The limousine rolled to a smooth stop beneath the hotel's portico, the soft brake bringing them back into the present. Neither spoke immediately. Neither moved.

They exited the car with the same controlled distance they had maintained inside it, slipping once more into public composure.

But both carried the same quiet certainty with them as they stepped into the light—

This was no longer just an arrangement.

And pretending otherwise was becoming impossible.

As soon as they stepped into the suite, the silence deepened.


The lights came on automatically, casting a soft glow over the elegant space, but neither commented on it. The night still clung to them—too close, too unresolved. Lauren paused just inside the entryway, her composure immaculate, her movements precise, as though nothing about the evening had unsettled her.

"Goodnight, Cole," she said evenly.

The words were polite. Final. Deliberately ordinary.

Cole turned toward her, surprised by how quickly she had retreated behind formality. For a moment, he considered saying something—anything—that might slow her departure. But he didn't. He simply inclined his head.

"Goodnight, Lauren."

She offered a brief nod, already stepping away, heels quiet against the marble as she crossed the living area toward her bedroom. Cole remained where he was, watching her retreat with a stillness that belied the tension tightening in his chest.

She didn't look back.

At her door, Lauren paused just long enough to rest her hand against the handle, her shoulders lifting slightly with a controlled breath. Then she opened it, slipped inside, and closed it behind her with careful restraint, the soft click echoing far louder than it should have.

Only then did she allow herself to lean back against the door.

*Two more nights.*

The thought came unbidden, sharp, and insistent.

Only two more nights before this would end. Before they would board a plane and return to New York. Before distance, reality, and obligation stepped back into place.

Two more nights to maintain control. To remember who she was meant to be. To remind herself that this—whatever it was—could not be allowed to become anything more.

Lauren closed her eyes briefly, pressing her palm flat against the cool wood.

Two more nights, she told herself again, as if repetition might make it easier.


In the living area, Cole stood exactly where she had left him.

The suite felt suddenly larger. Emptier.

He stared at the closed door to her room, acutely aware of the quiet now separating them. The evening replayed itself with ruthless clarity—the terrace, the unspoken understanding, the way she had asked to leave without explanation. He exhaled slowly, jaw tightening.

Two more nights.

The same thought surfaced, unwelcome and heavy.

It should have been a relief.

Instead, it felt like a countdown.

# Chapter Thirteen

The next two days unfolded in a relentless blur of meetings and presentations.

From early morning briefings to late afternoon strategy sessions, the schedule allowed little room for reflection—and Cole suspected that was exactly why Lauren had welcomed it. She was composed, precise, relentlessly professional. In boardrooms and conference halls, she was once again William Dutton's daughter, not his fake-almost-fiancée, not the woman who had unsettled Cole's equilibrium with a single look held too long.

They worked seamlessly together. Efficient. Polished. Untouchable.

Which only made the distance between them more noticeable.

On the first evening, as preparations were made for dinner, Lauren stopped him near the suite's entrance, her expression serene but guarded.

"I'm going to sit this one out," she said calmly. "I've developed a headache."

Cole studied her for a moment longer than necessary. Her posture was straight, her voice steady, her gaze unwavering. Too controlled. Too deliberate.

*A lie.*

He recognised it instantly—not with irritation, but with understanding. Whatever she was avoiding, it mirrored his own instinct to retreat, to put space between them before something irreversible occurred.

"Of course," he replied evenly. "I'll let them know you're unwell."

Her lips curved faintly, appreciative but distant. "Thank you."

As he left the suite alone, Cole told himself it was for the best. Distance, even temporary, was a form of discipline. A necessary correction. The pull between them had grown too pronounced, too charged to ignore.

And yet the absence followed him.

The dinner was held in one of the hotel's private dining rooms, all low lighting and refined elegance. Conversation flowed easily as plates were served and wine poured, but Cole was acutely aware of the empty seat beside him. He kept his focus on the discussion at hand, responding with practiced ease, though part of his attention remained fixed on what was missing.

It didn't go unnoticed.

Halfway through the meal, Ahmed leaned slightly toward him, his tone polite but edged with genuine concern. "Your fiancée—is she okay?"

Cole's fingers stilled around his glass.

"She wasn't feeling well earlier," he replied smoothly. "Nothing serious."

"I see." Ahmed nodded, but his gaze lingered. "She seemed… quite fatigued yesterday. I hope she's resting."

The concern was real. Unaffected. And it put Cole immediately on edge.

He forced a measured smile. "Lauren doesn't often slow down. She'll be fine."

Ahmed inclined his head, but the exchange left a faint tension in its wake. Cole felt it settle low and sharp, unwelcome, and insistent. It wasn't suspicion that unsettled him—it was the reminder that Lauren's absence had created space. Space for attention. For interest.

For others.

As the evening wore on, Cole found his focus slipping more often than he liked. Each time conversation lulled, his thoughts returned unbidden to the suite—to Lauren alone, deliberately withdrawn, choosing restraint over proximity.

And for the first time since arriving in Dubai, Cole felt something dangerously close to regret.

Not for attending the dinner alone.

But for allowing distance to feel like relief—when it was already beginning to feel like loss.


On the last night, Lauren knew she couldn't claim a headache.

Avoidance had served its purpose, but absence would only draw more attention now. Tonight mattered—socially, politically, strategically—and she would not give anyone cause to speculate. Least of all Ahmed.

She dressed with deliberate care.

The black silk gown skimmed her body like liquid shadow, elegant in its simplicity, the cut designed to suggest rather than reveal. It moved when she moved, catching the light in subtle waves that made her appear both untouchable and impossibly present. Against the dark fabric, her hair was striking—platinum-blonde locks falling loose down her back, reaching her waist in a gleaming cascade that felt almost defiant in its beauty.

She regarded her reflection briefly, expression calm, resolute.

Tonight, she would be impeccable.

When she stepped into the living area, Cole looked up—and forgot, for a fraction of a second, how to breathe.

He had been fastening his cufflinks, posture relaxed, mind focused on the evening ahead. The sight of her arrested him completely. His gaze swept over her without apology, dark and intent, taking in the fall of her hair, the elegant line of her shoulders, the quiet confidence she wore as effortlessly as the dress itself.

He couldn't take his eyes off her.

Lauren paused, meeting his gaze with composed awareness. She neither preened nor retreated—simply allowed the moment to pass, as if his reaction were inevitable and therefore unremarkable.

"You look… stunning," he said at last, the word emerging more controlled than he felt.

"Thank you," she replied evenly, smoothing an imaginary crease at her hip. "Shall we?"

The drive to the venue passed with restrained conversation, the city lights once again blurring past the windows. Cole was acutely aware of her beside him— the soft sheen of silk, the faint scent of her perfume, the way she sat perfectly still, as though conserving energy for the performance ahead.

When they arrived, the atmosphere shifted immediately.

The venue was alive with conversation and music, the hum of influence and expectation woven through the air. As Cole and Lauren entered, attention turned as it always did—but this time, it lingered.

Ahmed spotted them almost instantly.

He broke away from his group with unmistakable purpose, crossing the room in long, confident strides. His gaze was fixed on Lauren, appreciation open and unapologetic, his smile warm as he approached.

"Lauren," he greeted, bowing slightly as he reached them. "You look radiant tonight."

Before Cole could respond, Ahmed extended his hand toward her, his focus narrowing as if Cole were no more than a formality at her side.

Lauren accepted the greeting with practiced grace, her smile polite, controlled. "Thank you. It's good to see you again."

Cole's jaw clenched.

He felt it—an immediate, visceral tightening low in his chest, sharp and unwelcome. Ahmed's ease, his confidence, the clear intention in the way he positioned himself closer to Lauren than necessary—all of it scraped against Cole's restraint.

His hand came to rest at Lauren's lower back, firm and unmistakable.

Possessive.

The message was subtle, but it was not ambiguous.

Ahmed's eyes flicked briefly to the contact before returning to Lauren's face, his smile tightening just a fraction. "I hope you're feeling better this evening," he said. "I was concerned when you were unable to join us."

"I'm perfectly well," Lauren replied calmly, aware of the tension now threading the space between the two men. "Thank you for asking."

Cole leaned in slightly, his voice low, meant for Ahmed as much as her. "Lauren insisted on being here tonight."

The words were neutral. The implication was not.

As they stood there, Lauren poised between them, Cole became acutely aware of how thin his control had grown. This was no longer irritation or professional rivalry.

It was the unmistakable recognition that he did not like anyone else looking at her as though she were an option.

And he was no longer certain how much longer he could pretend otherwise.


After dinner, the music swelled through the room, rich and rhythmic, drawing guests toward the dance floor in a slow, inevitable tide. Lauren felt it before she saw it—the shift in energy, the subtle loosening of formality as conversation gave way to movement.

Ahmed turned to her with an easy smile. "May I?"

It was polite. Expected. Perfectly timed.

Lauren hesitated only a fraction of a second before nodding. "Of course."

She felt Cole's hand at her back tense immediately.

Too late.

Ahmed guided her onto the floor with practiced confidence, his palm settling at her waist, his other hand enclosing hers. The music was smooth, unhurried— designed for closeness without impropriety. Lauren moved easily, letting training and instinct take over, her expression serene, her posture flawless.

From the edge of the floor, Cole watched.

Every controlled step, every subtle turn, every moment of proximity scraped against his restraint. Ahmed leaned in slightly as he spoke, his mouth close to Lauren's ear, his attention wholly fixed on her. Lauren responded with polite focus, her body language neutral—but the intimacy of the dance did its work regardless.

Cole's jaw locked.

This was not strategy.

This was not business.

This was another man's hand at her waist.

The thought was sharp, possessive, undeniable.

He didn't wait for the song to end.

Cole crossed the floor with decisive purpose, cutting through the dancers without apology. Ahmed registered him a second too late.

"Lauren," Cole said, voice calm, controlled, and utterly immovable.

She looked up, startled by the authority in his tone.

"May I?" he added—though it was not a question.

Ahmed's hand lingered for a heartbeat longer than necessary. "We were just—
"

Cole stepped closer, his presence eclipsing the space between them. His hand replaced Ahmed's at Lauren's waist, firm and certain, his fingers splaying as if they had always belonged there.

"I know," Cole said coolly. "That will be all."

The air around them tightened.

Ahmed straightened, his expression composed but cool. "If Lauren wishes—"

"She does," Cole replied without looking away from her.

Lauren felt the claim land—public, unmistakable. Heat flared low in her chest, equal parts shock, and awareness. She should have objected. Should have corrected him.

She didn't.

Ahmed inclined his head stiffly and stepped back, disappearing into the crowd.

The music continued, but everything else fell away.

Cole drew Lauren closer, aligning their bodies with deliberate precision. Her breath caught as the full weight of his presence settled around her—solid, commanding, impossibly familiar. His hand tightened at her waist, grounding her, claiming her.

"You didn't have to do that," she murmured, her voice steady despite the tremor beneath it.

"Yes," he replied quietly. "I did."

They moved together, slow and controlled, their steps seamless. Lauren's hand rested against his shoulder, fingers curling into the fabric of his jacket as if by instinct. Cole lowered his head slightly, his mouth close to her ear.

"I don't like being tested," he said softly. "And I don't share."

Her pulse spiked. "You're almost engaged to my sister."

His hold tightened fractionally. "Not for much longer."

The words hit her like a blow—soft, devastating, impossible to ignore.

She tilted her head back, meeting his gaze. His eyes were dark, intent, stripped of all calculation. For a suspended moment, they stopped moving altogether, bodies close, breath mingling.

Too close.

Cole's gaze dropped to her mouth.

The distance between them narrowed to nothing but intention. Lauren felt the pull—sharp, undeniable—as his hand slid slightly higher at her back, drawing her in. Her lips parted involuntarily, her breath brushing his.

One more second—

Lauren turned her face just enough to break the spell, her forehead resting briefly against his shoulder instead.

Cole exhaled slowly, a controlled breath dragged from deep in his chest.

They continued to dance, but the shift was irreversible.

Around them, the room buzzed on—unaware, indifferent—but the line had been crossed. Not physically.

Emotionally.

And as the music faded, Cole knew with absolute clarity that he was done pretending this was temporary.

Lauren didn't know what to make of Cole's declaration.

*Not for much longer.*

The words replayed themselves in her mind with unsettling persistence, echoing beneath the composed surface she presented to the world. He had said them quietly, decisively—without hesitation or explanation—leaving no room for interpretation and yet offering no clarity at all.

She should have dismissed them.

Should have told herself they were nothing more than impulse, a territorial reflex born of proximity and pride.

But she couldn't.

Because something had shifted. Not just in him—but in her.

Lauren had always been precise about her emotions. Careful. She did not indulge in fantasy or romantic projection. Attraction, she understood. Chemistry. Desire. Those were reactions—biological, fleeting, manageable.

This was different.

What she felt for Cole had moved beyond physical awareness, beyond the heat and tension that flared when he touched her or looked at her too closely. It had crept in quietly, insidiously—through shared silences, mutual respect, the way he listened when she spoke, the way he saw her.

She trusted him.

The realisation startled her more than anything else.

She trusted his judgment. His competence. His steadiness. She trusted the space he gave her, the way he never diminished her intelligence or softened his expectations for her comfort. Somewhere along the way, admiration had deepened into something far more dangerous.

*She was falling in love with him.*

The truth settled heavily in her chest, both undeniable and terrifying in its clarity.

And that was precisely the problem.

Cole Blackwell did not believe in love.

He had made that clear from the beginning—not with bitterness or drama, but with calm, unwavering certainty. Love, to him, was an illusion. A liability. Something that distracted, weakened, distorted judgment. He believed in control. In structure. In outcomes he could predict and manage.

*What place did love have in that world?*

Lauren exhaled slowly, steadying herself as the weight of it pressed in. She could already see the fault lines forming—her growing vulnerability set against his impenetrable logic, her hope quietly taking root where his scepticism ruled.

If she allowed herself to fall fully, there would be no halfway. No retreat without cost.

And if Cole truly did not believe in love, then whatever passed between them— however intense, however real it felt in the moment—might never become the thing she needed it to be.

That knowledge did not stop her feelings.

It only sharpened them.

Lauren straightened, lifting her chin slightly as if bracing herself against what lay ahead. She would not beg for something he could not give. Would not mistake possession for devotion, or desire for commitment.

But neither could she pretend this was nothing.

What had taken root between them was no fleeting attraction she could dismiss with logic or discipline. It had grown in the spaces between words, in shared glances held too long, in the way he challenged her without condescension and protected her without smothering. It was steady, deliberate—unnervingly real.

Because for the first time in a very long while, her heart had chosen.

Quietly.

Decisively.

Without consulting her reason or asking permission from her caution.

The realisation left her breathless, not with excitement, but with the gravity of it. Love, when it came uninvited, carried consequences. It demanded honesty, reciprocity—things she could not assume from a man who had made his disbelief so clear.

And she had no idea whether Cole Blackwell would ever choose her in return.

Not fully. Not in the way that mattered.

Until he did—until his actions aligned unmistakably with his words—she would not surrender to the pull between them. Would not mistake desire for devotion or allow herself to be swept into his arms by a moment that might never become a future.

Restraint, she knew, was not weakness.

It was self-respect.

So, she would hold the line, no matter how fiercely the urge pressed in—to lean into his strength, to seek refuge in his certainty, to believe that wanting her would be enough.

Until he chose her—openly, irrevocably—she would remain where she was.

Steady.

Watching.

Waiting.

# Chapter Fourteen

By the end of the evening, the atmosphere had softened into polite exhaustion—the hum of success, contracts discussed and impressions made, the quiet satisfaction of a night that had unfolded precisely as intended.

Guests began to take their leave in small clusters. Handshakes turned into cheek kisses, warm but restrained, the customary gestures of diplomacy and courtesy. Lauren received them with composed grace, offering smiles and soft words, her posture elegant, her presence impeccable.

One by one, the delegates leaned in to kiss her cheek.

Brief. Respectful. Correct.

Cole was several steps away, engaged in farewells of his own, his attention momentarily pulled elsewhere as he exchanged final words with investors and advisors. Lauren sensed his absence even before she registered Ahmed's return.

He approached her quietly.

"Lauren."

She turned to face him, offering a polite smile. "Your Highness."

Ahmed's expression softened, the formal reserve of the evening easing into something more personal. He placed his hands lightly on her shoulders, the gesture gentle, deliberate—intimate without being overt.

"It was a pleasure to meet you," he said warmly.

Before she could respond, he bent toward her.

His kiss brushed her cheek—but not as the others had. It lingered a fraction longer, landed closer to her mouth than courtesy dictated. Close enough that she felt his breath, close enough that the boundary blurred.

Lauren stilled.

She did not step back. She did not lean in.

She held herself perfectly neutral—composed, unyielding, uninviting— allowing the moment to pass without giving it weight.

"Thank you," she replied evenly as he straightened. "The pleasure was mine."

But the air had shifted.

Across the room, Cole turned just in time to see it—the placement of Ahmed's hands, the angle of his head, the unmistakable intimacy of the gesture. Something dark and immediate flashed through his eyes, his expression tightening as he registered the proximity.

*Too close.*

The word struck with clarity and force.

By the time Cole reached them, Ahmed was already stepping back, his expression unreadable, his farewell impeccable.

"Until we meet again," Ahmed said smoothly.

Lauren inclined her head in acknowledgment.

Cole arrived at her side, his presence immediate and unmistakable, his hand settling at the small of her back with a possessive certainty that brooked no challenge.

"Yes," Cole said coolly, eyes fixed on Ahmed. "Until then."

The words were polite.

The meaning was not.


The suite door closed behind them with a muted click, sealing out the noise of the evening and trapping the tension inside.

Lauren moved first, slipping off her heels and placing them neatly beside the console table. Her movements were calm, deliberate—too calm, calculated almost, as if daring him to react. She walked toward the floor-to-ceiling window, the city lights glittering below, casting her silhouette against the glass.

Cole remained where he was, jacket still on, pulse hammering in his chest. The jealousy he had held at bay all evening surged now, hot, and unforgiving. He could still see it—the angle of Ahmed's head, the placement of his hands, the way that kiss had lingered just a heartbeat too long. Too close. Intimate in a way that crossed a line he hadn't expected to be crossed.

"Why did you let him do that?" Cole asked sharply, the words slicing through the quiet.

Lauren turned slowly, her back still to him. "Do what?"

"Kiss you like that," he said, voice clipped, the control in it stretched thin by the burn of possessiveness. "Touch you like he had the right."

Her brows lifted slightly, just enough to signal mild surprise—or defiance. "It was a customary farewell."

"That was not customary," Cole snapped. "And you know it."

Silence stretched between them, taut and brittle, each word unspoken carrying a weight neither dared to release.

Lauren folded her arms, her expression cooling. "You're reading far too much into it."

"No," he said, taking a deliberate step closer. "I'm reading exactly enough."

She met his gaze steadily, her tone measured. "I didn't encourage him."

"I didn't say you did," he countered, jaw tight.

"But you're implying it," she pressed, voice sharper now. "You're standing here interrogating me as though I owe you an explanation."

His chest tightened. "You're supposed to be my fiancée."

The word landed hard, echoing off the walls.

"But I'm not, am I?" she said quietly, almost a whisper. "My sister is."

That stopped him, the words slicing through the certainty he thought he had.

For a moment, the only sound was the hum of the city beyond the glass, distant and indifferent.

"I told you that engagement isn't happening," Cole shot back, sharp, frustrated.

"You told me nothing," she said, voice trembling slightly with controlled anger. "You made a vague declaration in the middle of a dance floor and expected me to… what? Trust it?"

His hands clenched at his sides. "I don't like other men touching you."

"That," she said sharply, "is not my problem."

"It is when you let it happen," he countered, voice low, dangerous.

Her eyes flashed, fire and frustration igniting. "I did not let anything happen. I behaved with dignity and restraint—something you might consider trying."

The words struck him like a physical blow.

Cole turned away abruptly, dragging a hand through his hair. "You have no idea what it was like watching him look at you like that."

"And you have no idea what it's like being looked at like an object you can claim," she replied, voice steady, precise. "I am not a bargaining chip between powerful men."

He faced her again, dark eyes ablaze. "That's not how I see you."

"Then stop treating me like something that can be taken from you when we aren't even together. It's all a charade, Cole. None of it's real."

The space between them vibrated with everything unsaid—desire, fear, longing, restraint.

He stepped closer despite himself, stopping just short of touching her. "This is not nothing," he said quietly, voice low, controlled, yet taut with barely suppressed emotion.

"I know," she replied, barely above a whisper, shoulders squared, but her pulse betraying the truth.

"Then don't pretend you don't feel it too."

She swallowed, heart hammering, but didn't look away. "Feeling something does not give you ownership."

His chest rose and fell sharply. "You think I want this?"

"I think," she said softly, "you want everything on your terms."

The accusation landed with a dull thud. He opened his mouth to respond, to argue, but she had already made her decision.

"I'm going to bed. Goodnight, Cole." She gave him one last look, sharp and measured. "This will all be over tomorrow. Then you and Elena can start making plans for the future."

He just stood there, watching her retreat, every inch of her body, the sway of her hips, the quiet authority in her step. The door clicked softly shut, leaving him alone.

The suite suddenly felt too large, too empty. The echo of her words rang louder than any raised voice, reverberating off the walls, bouncing off his thoughts, amplifying the heat of jealousy still burning in his chest.

But beneath it was something far more dangerous, far more insistent:

Regret.

By the time the bedroom door closed behind Lauren, the tears had already started, sliding silently down her cheeks. She pressed her palms to her face, as if she could smother the ache in her chest, the wild, unrelenting pull of emotions she couldn't name—or control.

She felt like a fool. Falling for a man who didn't believe in love was one thing, but falling for a man who would be marrying her sister? That thought twisted in her gut like a knife.

Every rational part of her screamed to stop, to step back, to protect herself, but her heart refused to listen. It throbbed with the memory of his touch, the intensity in his gaze, the magnetic way he made her feel seen, desired, alive.

And yet, the reality of Cole's world, of their tangled lives, pressed in around her. Desire and longing warred with reason, leaving her trembling in the quiet suite, unsure whether to laugh at her own foolishness—or cry.

She sank onto the edge of the bed, burying her face in her hands, the tears sliding unchecked now, hot, and helpless. Love—or something dangerously close to it—had claimed her, even as the impossible, the reckless, the forbidden stretched out before her like a challenge she wasn't sure she could survive.

The next morning, after very little sleep, Lauren decided to shower and pack before emerging from the bedroom. She moved slowly, shaking off the haze of restless thoughts and the weight of the previous night. By the time she stepped out, she wore skin-tight jeans and a fitted white T-shirt, her hair still damp and slightly tousled from the shower, her presence casual yet effortlessly captivating.

Cole sat at the small writing desk near the window, a large envelope open before him, papers spread out in careful order. He didn't look up immediately, absorbed in the contents, but the faint crease between his brows betrayed a mind still racing.

"Morning," Lauren said softly, breaking the silence, her voice carrying just enough warmth to make him glance up.

"Morning," he replied, eyes flicking to her briefly before returning to the papers, though the tension in his jaw suggested he hadn't expected her to appear so soon. He held up the envelope, tilting it slightly toward her. "The consortium has made their decision on who they will be partnering with. They want Blackwell Capital and the Dutton Group, as well as the prince." His jaw clenched imperceptibly.

Lauren stepped closer, curiosity piqued despite herself, her gaze scanning the neatly typed letter and the logo of the consortium at the top. "My father will be happy," she said, voice soft, cautious.

Cole didn't respond immediately, watching her reaction carefully. His dark eyes lingered on her as if weighing something far heavier than a piece of paper. Finally, he said, low and measured, "He should be. You've done an exceptional job this week."

"Thank you," she murmured, a hint of a smile brushing her lips. She turned toward the door, then paused. "What time do we leave?"

Cole looked up at her, meeting her gaze briefly before checking his watch. "The jet will be ready to depart within the hour."

She nodded slowly, taking in his words, letting the reality settle around her.

The flight passed quietly. Lauren had fallen asleep not long after take-off, her head resting gently on Cole's shoulder. He wanted, desperately, to wrap his arm around her, to hold her close, to tell her that the pull he felt for her—the longing, the desire, the ache—wasn't an illusion. It was *real*.

But he couldn't. Not yet. Not until he told Elena that their plans to marry were over. Not only because it was painfully obvious she was not the heir William Dutton had intended, but because he could not imagine standing at the altar with her, knowing every beat of his heart, every moment of his life, would ache for Lauren.

He watched her sleep, chest rising and falling, warmth radiating through the thin fabric of her T-shirt, and the ache in his chest deepened. He didn't want to let her go. He couldn't.

And yet, for now, he had to wait.

The charade was finally over.

At JFK, the bustle of the airport—the rolling luggage, the distant announcements, the hurried footsteps—felt like a distant hum compared to the storm swirling between them. They no longer had to pretend to be engaged. The masks, the polite smiles, the carefully choreographed gestures of ownership and obligation—all of it could fall away.

Lauren adjusted the strap of her bag over her shoulder, her heels clicking softly on the polished floor. She moved toward her town car, a small smile tugging at her lips, a mixture of relief and lingering tension coiling in her chest.

Cole fell into step beside her, his presence like a shadow she couldn't escape, dark and magnetic. He didn't speak immediately, just let his gaze linger on her, tracing the curve of her jaw, the soft fall of her hair, the way her body moved with casual grace.

When they reached her car, the driver standing politely at attention as he loaded her suitcases into the trunk, Lauren hesitated. The night air felt suddenly charged, thick with things unsaid. She glanced back at Cole, her hand resting lightly on the open car door.

"Thank you… for everything," she said softly, her voice warm, threaded with the strain and uncertainty of the past days.

For a split second, he simply looked at her—really looked at her—as if committing the sight of her to memory. Then his hand shot out before she could move, fingers closing around her elbow. Not rough. Not gentle either. Possessive. Certain.

"Don't go just yet," he said, his voice low, edged with something dangerous, something barely restrained.

Her breath caught.

Before she could form a response, he pulled her toward him. The movement was decisive, unyielding—and then his mouth was on hers.

The kiss was immediate. Devastating.

It wasn't careful or tentative. It wasn't the polite brush of lips they'd shared before. This was hunger unleashed—days of restraint, of stolen glances and unfinished moments, colliding all at once. His lips claimed hers with raw urgency, heat flaring between them as if a match had finally been struck.

Lauren gasped into the kiss, the sound swallowed by his mouth, and instinct took over. Her hands slid up his chest and around his neck, fingers threading into his hair as she pressed closer, fitting herself against him as though she had always known exactly where she belonged. The world narrowed to the feel of him—the solid strength of his body, the heat of his skin, the way his kiss demanded rather than asked.

Cole groaned softly, the sound vibrating against her lips. One hand settled firmly at the small of her back, anchoring her to him, while the other came up to cradle her face, his thumb brushing her cheek with a tenderness that stood in stark contrast to the ferocity of his kiss. It was as if he couldn't decide whether to devour her or worship her—so he did both.

The kiss deepened, slowed just enough to become devastating. His mouth moved against hers with deliberate intent, learning her, savouring her, as though he had waited far too long for this and had no intention of wasting a second. Lauren melted into him, every thought dissolving, every doubt burned away by the certainty of his touch.

They broke apart only when the world insisted—when breath became unavoidable when reality pressed back in. Her breathing came in short, uneven bursts, her hands still gripping his jacket. Cole's chest rose and fell just as hard, his forehead dropping to rest against hers as if he needed the contact to stay upright.

Their eyes locked.

The spark between them was undeniable now—no longer contained, no longer denied. It crackled in the space between them, electric and alive.

Cole's lips brushed hers again, slower this time, softer. Almost reverent. As if sealing something.

"You're mine," he murmured, low and intense, the words not a claim so much as a truth spoken aloud.

The shiver that ran through her had nothing to do with the cold.

Before Lauren could respond, he stepped back, his dark gaze never leaving hers, and walked toward his waiting limousine with a purposeful stride, every movement measured, controlled—but still exuding the fire of desire that hadn't dimmed for even a moment.

Lauren hesitated for just a heartbeat, torn between the pull of him and the need to go. She slid into the town car as the door opened, the driver already waiting, hands poised on the wheel, the engine quietly purring to life.

As the car began to pull away, she glanced up through the window—and there he was. Cole stood at the door of his limousine, tall, immovable, every inch the image of dark, magnetic control. His eyes were fixed on her, burning with an intensity that made her stomach tighten, her chest ache, and her pulse spike all at once.

For a fleeting moment, the bustling airport, the noise of the world, even the separation itself—all of it faded. There was only Cole, and there was only her, and the undeniable truth of what they wanted, what they felt, lingering like electricity between them.

And then the car rounded the corner, carrying her away—but the image of him, watching, waiting, claiming, remained etched in her mind. Lauren exhaled shakily and lowered her gaze, trying to steady the storm inside her chest. That was when she saw it.

The ring.

Her breath caught as she stared down at her left hand, the diamond glinting softly in the muted light of the car's interior. Elegant. Imposing. Never meant for her. It sat there like a quiet accusation, heavy with intention and consequence.

She turned her hand slowly, the stone catching the light with every movement, and her throat tightened. In the rush of departure, the ache of goodbye, the heat of that final kiss—she had forgotten to give it back to him.

A hollow laugh escaped her, brittle and soft. Of course she had.

The ring was meant for her sister. A future she didn't belong in. A promise that wasn't hers to keep. And yet it rested against her skin as though it had always been there, as though it had chosen her anyway.

Lauren curled her fingers into her palm, closing her hand around it, her chest aching with the weight of everything unspoken. Tomorrow, she told herself. She would return it tomorrow.

But as the city blurred past the window and Cole's words echoed in her mind— *You're mine*—she couldn't ignore the unsettling truth settling deep in her bones.

Nothing about this felt temporary.

And nothing about that ring felt easy to let go of.

# Chapter Fifteen

The car rolled through the familiar streets, past iron gates and sweeping trees, until the Dutton estate came into view—grand, imposing, steeped in legacy. Lauren felt the weight of what awaited her inside: her father, her sister, the unspoken consequences of choices made, and the tangled emotions that had followed her across continents.

But as the driver stepped out and opened her door, she paused, taking a slow, steadying breath. For a moment, the stress of the past week faded, replaced by a quiet, grounding thought: she had done it. She had represented the Dutton Group with poise, intelligence, and determination. She should be proud of what she had accomplished.

She stepped onto the stone path and was met at the front door by the butler, who inclined his head respectfully.

"Welcome home, Miss," he said warmly, his voice carrying that quiet steadiness that had been a constant in her life.

Lauren returned his smile. "Thank you, Mansel." Then, almost immediately, she asked, "Is my father in his study?"

"Yes, Miss," he replied, leading her down the familiar corridor toward the study, the walls lined with portraits and memories of generations past.

The study door opened, and William Dutton rose from behind his desk the moment he saw her. His face lit up, a mixture of pride and relief shining in his eyes.

"Welcome home, sweetheart," he said, pulling her into a brief, affectionate embrace. "I'm so proud of you—you got our name at the top table."

"Thanks, Dad," Lauren replied softly, a smile tugging at her lips. Then her gaze drifted past him, scanning the room as a question surfaced. "Is Elena home yet?"

"No," he answered with a small shrug. "The doctors want her to stay in for a few more nights."

Lauren let out a slow, relieved smile. At least, she thought, she wouldn't have to endure Elena's constant chatter—or her inevitable judgment—just yet. The quiet sense of relief mingled with pride, and for the first time in hours, she allowed herself a moment to breathe.

She stood there, feeling both grounded and restless, aware that while one chapter of obligations had ended, the one that truly mattered—Cole—was still very much unresolved.

Cole watched Lauren's car disappear into the distance, her figure swallowed by the hum of the city and the blur of passing traffic. A tight ache gripped his chest, deep and unfamiliar, a sharp twist of longing he had never known before.

It wasn't just the departure—it was her. The way she had moved, the sway of her hair in the wind, the curve of her shoulders, the quiet confidence in her stride. She belonged to the world, and yet, in that fleeting moment, she had belonged only to him.

And then his mind drifted back to that kiss. The kiss they had shared—just moments ago was already seared into him like fire. He had kissed her softly before, a brush of lips that had been sweet, tender… but that had been nothing compared to this. That kiss had been electric, a jolt of heat that had left him raw, trembling, desperate.

It wasn't just desire. It was a claim, a confession, and a warning all at once. He had tasted her, felt her, and in that instant, every ounce of restraint he had fought to maintain shattered.

Cole ran a hand over his face, jaw tight, heart hammering. He wanted to go after her, to pull her back, to tell her that what they had shared wasn't just a fleeting moment. That kiss had said what words could not—and he would not allow it to be the last.

The ache in his chest deepened, a gnawing hunger that clawed at him relentlessly, making him want—more than anything—to rewrite the rules, to seize the next step, to claim what had always been maddeningly, impossibly just out of reach.

And yet, he stayed rooted, hands gripping the edge of the limousine seat, watching the road blur beneath the city lights. The hum of traffic, the distant shouts of the night, even the soft purr of the engine—all of it faded into the background. Some things, some people, could not be chased. Not yet.

Not until the obstacles were gone. Not until the path was clear.

And the largest obstacle of all sat squarely in his path: *Elena.*

Cole exhaled slowly, jaw tight, dark eyes narrowing as he ran through the conversation he had to have, the words that would strip away pretence and obligation. He couldn't afford hesitation, couldn't afford compromise—not when the prize, the woman who had captured him utterly, was at the other end of it all.

He had to tell Elena the truth. Not gently. Not politely. Not carefully.

He had to make sure she understood that their plans, their engagement, everything, were over. Completely.

Only then could he go after Lauren without reservation, without restraint, without the gnawing guilt that had already begun to eat at him.

And even as the thought of seeing her, touching her, holding her close ignited a fire in his chest, he knew: first, he had to clear the path. First, he had to face Elena.

And then… then Lauren would be his.


Cole didn't wait.

By the time his limousine reached the city, the decision had settled into something hard and immovable inside him. This wasn't a conversation he could postpone, soften, or dress up in half-truths. The longer he delayed, the more dishonest it became—not just to Lauren, but to himself.


The private hospital suite was quiet when he arrived, washed in muted afternoon light and carrying the faint scent of antiseptic and flowers. Elena was propped against crisp white pillows, her hair perfectly styled despite the circumstances, a tablet resting on her lap as she scrolled absently.

She looked up, surprise flickering briefly across her face before smoothing into a pleased smile.

"Cole. I didn't expect you so soon."

He didn't return the smile.

He closed the door behind him carefully, deliberately, as if sealing the room against interruption. He remained standing, hands in his pockets, posture rigid.

"We need to talk," he said.

Something in his tone made her straighten. "What's on your mind?" she asked lightly, though her eyes sharpened. "Is everything all right?"

"No," he replied simply. "It isn't."

Silence stretched between them.

She tilted her head. "I assumed the trip went well. The consortium—"

"This isn't about the consortium," he cut in, calm but unyielding. "It's about us."

Elena set the tablet aside. "Did something happen in Dubai?"

"I did a lot of thinking," he said. "About our arrangement. About us."

The word hung in the air, brittle.

She frowned. "Like what?"

"There is no 'us,' Elena," Cole said quietly. "Not anymore."

The colour drained from her face, then rushed back in a sharp flush.

"What are you talking about? We're engaged."

"No," he replied, his gaze steady, unwavering. "We were planning to be. That's not the same thing. And it's not happening."

Her laugh was short, incredulous. "You can't be serious."

"I am."

"You don't just end something like this on a whim," she snapped. "Our plans— your board—the Dutton Group—"

"I don't care," he said evenly. "Not about that."

She stared at him as though he'd spoken a foreign language. "Since when?"

"Since I realised it's not important enough to justify marrying the wrong person for the wrong reasons."

The words landed like a blow.

Elena's eyes narrowed. "Is this about my sister?"

Cole didn't answer immediately. He didn't need to.

Her breath hitched. "Did she say something? She's always been jealous of me. Did she convince you—"

"Lauren didn't say a thing," he cut in firmly. "And let's be honest—you never wanted me. You wanted the position. The future. The security."

"That was never a secret," she shot back, though her voice wavered.

"I know," he said. "But it's not enough for me anymore."

She looked away, jaw tightening. "So, what—you're throwing everything away because of… what?"

"That doesn't concern you," he replied quietly. "I've simply decided I don't want to marry you."

She looked back at him then—really looked—and whatever she saw in his expression made her go still.

"This was never going to work," he continued. "You deserve someone who wants you without hesitation. Without doubt. And I am not that man."

Tears welled in her eyes, though her chin lifted stubbornly.

"I know this is because of Lauren. She's said something—"

"She said nothing," Cole said flatly.

Elena looked away, blinking rapidly. "You're ruthless," she whispered.

"You knew that when we negotiated this arrangement," he replied. "But I won't marry you when my heart is already elsewhere."

"Heart," she scoffed softly. "You don't have one. You said you didn't believe in love."

"I was wrong," he said simply. "It turns out I do."

She stared at him in stunned silence.

Cole moved toward the door, then paused. "I'm sorry, Elena. But this ends now."

When he left the room, he didn't look back.

And for the first time in longer than he could remember, Cole Blackwell felt something dangerously close to relief.

Now there was nothing standing between him and the woman who had undone him.

Nothing—except whether Lauren would still let him come close.

Lauren missed Cole.

The realisation had settled into her chest sometime in the early hours of the morning, heavy and undeniable. They had been back for barely a day, yet the absence of him felt disproportionate, like something essential had been removed without warning. The house was familiar, comforting—but it felt quieter without the weight of his presence, without the awareness of him somewhere nearby.

She had dreamt of him.

Not just fleeting images, but vivid moments that lingered long after she woke—his mouth on hers, that kiss replaying with merciless clarity. In her dream, it hadn't ended at the airport. It had deepened, slowed, turned into something unguarded. She had imagined what it would feel like to rest against his chest, to fit there as though it had always been meant for her. To be held by him, claimed by him, not as part of a charade but because he wanted her—only her.

The thought made her chest ache.

She rolled onto her side, staring at the soft morning light filtering through her curtains, her hand curling instinctively against the pillow as though it might become him if she wished hard enough. She wondered what it would be like to give in completely, to let herself be possessed by the intensity she knew lived just beneath his control. To stop resisting the pull that had wrapped itself around her so tightly she could hardly breathe without thinking of him.

It was ridiculous, she told herself. Reckless. Dangerous.

And yet, the memory of his voice, his gaze, the way he had kissed her—not carefully, not politely, but as though he had reached a breaking point—refused to fade.

Lauren closed her eyes again, her heart beating just a little too fast, knowing with a quiet certainty that whatever this was between them, distance hadn't weakened it.

If anything, it had only made the longing sharper.

She lifted her hand, her gaze catching on the ring still circling her finger.

She hadn't taken it off.

The diamond glinted softly in the morning light, elegant and unmistakable. She could buy a thousand rings without a second thought—any cut, any stone, any setting she pleased. But this one… this one meant something. It carried weight. Memory. Possibility.

And to her surprise, she didn't want to remove it.

Her thumb brushed over the smooth band, a faint smile tugging at her lips, equal parts wistful and unsettled. The ring wasn't hers. It had never been meant to be. And yet, it sat there as though it belonged, as though it had found the hand it had been waiting for all along.

Lauren exhaled softly and pushed the covers back, rising from the bed. She carried the thought with her into the bathroom, letting the shower steam up around her, warm water cascading over her shoulders and washing away the remnants of restless sleep. She stood beneath it longer than necessary, lost in thought, the image of Cole and the feel of that ring refusing to loosen their hold.

When she stepped out of the bathroom, she reached automatically for her usual armour—the shapeless dresses, the soft layers meant to blur rather than reveal, the glasses she wore like a shield, her hair pulled back into something neat and forgettable.

Then she stopped.

She thought of the way Cole had looked at her. Not politely. Not casually. But as though he had seen her—every line, every curve, every quiet strength she usually hid. As though she had stepped out from behind the disguise and he had been waiting for her all along.

Slowly, deliberately, she chose something different.

She dressed as if she wanted to be seen. Not just by him—but by the world. The fabric skimmed her body instead of concealing it, flattering without trying too hard. She left her hair loose, letting it cascade down her back in soft waves, unrestrained, unapologetic.

She paused in front of the mirror.

She looked good.

Confident. Alive. Like a woman no longer content to fade into the background of her own life. Her gaze drifted to her hand—and there it was, still catching the light. The ring. She didn't question it. Not yet.

Lauren gathered her things, slipping her phone into her bag just as a familiar name flashed across the screen—a reminder of plans already made.

Gregory.

Brunch would be safe. Easy. Familiar. A chance to talk, to breathe, to anchor herself in something that made sense.

As she headed out, sunlight spilling down the hallway and warming her skin, Lauren told herself it was just a ring.

But deep down, she knew better.

# Chapter Sixteen

The café was already humming when Lauren arrived—sunlight spilling through wide windows, the clink of cutlery and low conversation wrapping the space in an easy, familiar warmth. Gregory was seated at their usual table near the window, jacket draped over the back of his chair, espresso untouched as he scrolled absently on his phone.

He looked up the moment he saw her—and stilled.

"Well," he said slowly, standing to kiss her cheek, his eyes sweeping over her with unmistakable approval. "Someone looks… different."

Lauren smiled, a little self-conscious, as she slid into her seat. "Different good or different alarming?"

"Very different good," he replied, sitting back down. "So. Tell me everything. How was the trip?"

She wrapped her hands around her coffee cup, grateful for the warmth. "Productive. Exhausting. Successful." She hesitated, then added, "The consortium accepted the Dutton Group."

Gregory's eyebrows shot up. "Lauren—that's huge."

"It is," she said, a flicker of pride breaking through. "Blackwell Capital is in as well. And…" she paused, lips curving faintly, "so is Prince Ahmed."

Gregory laughed softly. "Of course he is. I assume he was charming and infuriating in equal measure."

"Utterly," she agreed, relaxing a fraction. "But it worked. All three parties. My father was thrilled."

"As he should be," Gregory said warmly. Then his gaze drifted—subtle, perceptive—down to her left hand resting against the cup.

The ring caught the light.

He didn't say anything at first. Just watched her for a beat too long.

Lauren noticed. Of course she did. She shifted slightly, angling her hand away. "Oh—this," she said quickly, lifting it anyway with a light laugh. "Temporary. I just… didn't want to misplace it."

Gregory's mouth twitched. "You didn't want to misplace it," he repeated mildly.

"Yes," she said, a little too fast. "I forgot to give it back. That's all."

"Uh-huh."

She frowned. "What?"

He leaned back in his chair, folding his arms, studying her with that unnerving calm she'd known for years. "You're talking about it like it's yours."

"It's not," she insisted. "It belongs to Elena. I just—had a lot going on."

"And yet," he said gently, "you're still wearing it. You didn't forget it existed. You forgot to give it back."

Lauren opened her mouth to respond—then closed it again.

Gregory tilted his head. "Tell me about Cole."

Her pulse spiked. "What about him?"

"The way you're saying his name," Gregory said quietly. "The way you're not saying his name."

"That's ridiculous."

"Lauren," he said softly, not unkindly. "You're in love with him."

The words hit her like a physical blow.

Her breath caught. "No," she said immediately. "I'm not."

"You didn't even think about it," he noted. "You just denied it."

"I barely know him," she argued. "And he doesn't even believe in love."

Gregory smiled sadly. "That's not a rebuttal."

She shook her head, colour rising to her cheeks. "I'm attracted to him. That's all. It was intense. Temporary. Complicated."

"And the ring?" he asked gently.

She glanced down at it, her throat tightening. "It doesn't mean anything."

Gregory reached across the table and covered her hand with his. "It means something to you. And that's enough."

Lauren swallowed, her eyes stinging despite herself. "It can't go anywhere," she whispered. "It shouldn't."

Gregory squeezed her fingers once. "Love rarely asks permission," he said softly. "And it never waits for the timing to be convenient."

She looked away, blinking rapidly, the truth pressing in from all sides.

"I'm not in love," she said again, quieter this time—less certain, as though saying it softly might make it true.

Gregory didn't argue.

He simply smiled at her with knowing affection and said gently, "Then you're already in trouble."

Almost on cue, her phone lit up on the table between them.

Cole.

The name glowed far brighter than it should have, as if the universe itself were conspiring against her. Gregory's gaze flicked to the screen, then back to her face, his smile turning rueful.

"Well," he murmured, "speak of the devil."

Lauren's breath hitched. For a moment she simply stared at the phone as it vibrated insistently, her pulse echoing its rhythm. Then she turned it face down, the motion deliberate, final.

She didn't reach for it.

Gregory lifted a brow. "You're not answering."

"No," she said, too quickly. She folded her hands together, as if to keep herself from changing her mind.

"Lauren," he said softly, "you can't avoid him forever."

"I know," she replied, her voice barely above a whisper. "I just… need time."

"To do what?"

She hesitated, then admitted, her voice dropping to something raw and unguarded, "To figure out how to deal with him when he's married to my sister."

The words sat heavy between them.

Gregory studied her for a long moment, his expression softening with something like concern. "And what if he doesn't give you time?"

Her throat tightened. She glanced at the phone again, still face down on the table, as though she could feel his presence through the glass and metal. Cole Blackwell was not a man accustomed to waiting. He pursued. He decided. He took.

"Then," she said quietly, forcing the words past the knot in her chest, "I suppose I'll have to be brave enough to face him… and Elena."

The admission left her breathless.

The phone finally fell silent, the vibration ceasing abruptly—but the absence of sound felt louder than the ringing ever had. As if something unresolved, something inevitable, had merely paused rather than disappeared.

Lauren wrapped her fingers around her coffee cup, grounding herself in its warmth, even as she knew—deep down—that time was already slipping through her fingers.

It had been three days and countless unanswered phone calls.

Cole slapped his phone down on the leather seat beside him, jaw tight, irritation simmering just beneath the surface. Lauren was avoiding him. That much was obvious. What he couldn't understand—what gnawed at him relentlessly—was why.

His limousine moved smoothly through the city traffic, en route to yet another meeting he no longer cared about, when something outside the window caught his attention.

Gregory.

Cole's gaze sharpened instantly. He remembered him clearly—the hospital corridor, the easy familiarity, Gregory's arm draped around Lauren's shoulders in a way that had struck far too close to possession for comfort.

"Stop the car," Cole snapped.

The driver barely had time to react before the limousine eased to the curb. Cole was already out the door, the city noise rushing in around him.

"Gregory?" he called.

Gregory was walking away from the courthouse, briefcase in hand, his stride purposeful. He slowed, then stopped, turning toward the voice. Recognition dawned, and his eyebrows rose in mild surprise as his eyes landed on Cole Blackwell.

"Well," Gregory said coolly, a faint smile touching his lips, "this is unexpected."

Cole strode up to him, extending his hand, the motion deliberate, controlled. "Hello, Gregory. I'm Col—"

"I know who you are… Mr. Blackwell," Gregory interrupted smoothly, his grip firm as he shook Cole's hand. The brief moment of contact carried a quiet strength, a subtle warning that he wasn't someone to be underestimated.

Cole's jaw tightened, though his eyes remained steady. "Please… call me Cole."

Gregory's faint smile deepened, his eyes glinting with amusement. "And what can I do for you, Cole?"

Cole held his gaze, the hum of the city fading around them. "I was hoping I could talk to you about Lauren."

"That depends on what," Gregory said cautiously, his tone calm but measured.

"Have you seen her?" Cole asked, his voice tightening. "I've been trying to call, and she won't answer."

Gregory's eyebrows lifted. "She still isn't answering?"

Cole's curiosity sharpened, a flicker of frustration crossing his face. "No. She's… avoiding me, it seems."

Gregory hesitated for a moment, then said carefully, "I was with her when you called the first time."

Cole's chest tightened, a pulse of something sharp and raw hitting him. "So… she is avoiding me."

Gregory studied him for a beat, then nodded slowly. "Yes. At least for now."

Cole let out a low breath, trying to steady himself, the hum of the city seeping back in as the weight of his frustration settled hard. He hated it—hated being kept at a distance from her, hated the ache in his chest that seemed to grow every time he thought about her.

"But why?" he asked, voice tight.

Gregory's eyes softened, perceptive as always. "I think Lauren thinks it's better if she doesn't get too close… to the man her sister is going to marry."

Cole ran a hand through his hair, jaw tight. "I'm not. That's what I've been trying to let her know."

"You're not?" Gregory asked, raising an eyebrow.

"No," Cole said firmly. "I talked to Elena the day we got back. It's over."

"Oh, I see," Gregory said, a smirk tugging at his lips. "And what do you need to speak to Lauren for, then?"

Cole hesitated; the words knotted in his throat for a moment. But he should be able to trust Gregory—if Lauren did, then perhaps he could too. He took a slow breath, voice low but steady.

"I think… I'm in love with her," he admitted.

Gregory's smirk softened into something warmer, knowing. "Well," he said, leaning back slightly, "that explains a lot."

Cole didn't smile. He only stared ahead, the confession feeling heavier in the open air than it had in the quiet of his mind—but also, somehow, a little lighter.

"I need to see her," Cole said after a pause, his jaw tight, his voice almost urgent. "Can you talk to her?"

Gregory studied him for a long moment, the corner of his mouth twitching in amusement. Then he leaned forward slightly, voice calm but edged with mischief.

"I have a better idea."


Lauren stood before the mirror, the soft morning light filtering through the curtains casting a gentle glow across her face. Her reflection was flawless—her hair, her dress, every detail meticulously in place—but her eyes told a different story. They were stormy, restless, brimming with a quiet turmoil that no makeup could disguise.

The gown she wore was a floor-length, fire-engine red masterpiece that hugged her figure in all the right places before flaring gently at the hem. The bodice was structured, cinching her waist with subtle boning and a sweetheart neckline that accentuated her collarbones and the delicate slope of her shoulders. The fabric shimmered faintly as it caught the light, flowing in soft, elegant folds that whispered as she moved.

Her platinum blonde hair was swept to one side, the rest tumbling over her shoulder in soft, glossy waves. A diamond-encrusted comb held it back just enough to reveal her face, catching the light with every tilt of her head. The ensemble was striking—powerful, feminine, impossible to ignore—but even standing there, perfectly styled, she felt the weight of absence pressing on her chest.

It had been a week. Seven days since they had returned from Dubai. Cole had stopped calling after the third day, each unanswered phone call a silent echo in her mind. By the fourth day, it was clear—he had given up.

Lauren tried to steel herself, to summon some sense of relief, but the truth was undeniable. It hurt. Her chest ached, her thoughts were consumed by him, and the emptiness left in his absence felt raw, permanent.

No, she told herself, staring into her own eyes in the mirror. No more hiding. Be honest with yourself, Lauren. You're devastated.

And for the first time, she allowed herself to really feel it.

She let out a slow, shuddering sigh. Maybe it was for the best—he was marrying her sister, after all. The thought stabbed at her with guilt. She hadn't gone to see Elena since returning, not wanting to confront the awkwardness. She knew she shouldn't feel jealous—but she did. The unspoken tension that would inevitably settle between them felt unbearable to imagine.

Her father's words echoed softly in her mind: *She'll be back home soon.*

Soon, yes—but for now, she kept her distance, alone with her thoughts, with the echo of a kiss lingering in her memory, and the weight of a longing she could neither escape nor tame.

The doorbell rang, cutting through the quiet of the house. That would be Gregory. She had agreed to be his date for a charity dinner dance. She often accompanied him to dinners and cocktail parties, so when he asked, she hadn't hesitated.

She took a slow breath, smoothed the front of her dress, and made her way to the door, bracing herself to step into the world... even if a piece of her heart still belonged somewhere else.

Descending the stairs, she found Gregory at the front entrance, deep in conversation with her father.

William spotted her first. "Oh, there she is! Lauren, you look gorgeous."

"Thank you, Dad." She leaned up and kissed him lightly on the cheek, smiling despite the flutter in her chest.

Gregory whistled softly, his eyes lighting up as he took in her appearance. "Wow… you look stunning, Lauren. I'm going to be the envy of the entire party."

Lauren felt a faint blush rise to her cheeks, the compliment both flattering and grounding. She let herself smile, grateful for the normalcy, even if her thoughts kept drifting back to someone she shouldn't be thinking about.

Cole stood in the bathroom, steam curling around him like a soft haze, his skin still damp from the shower. The scent of soap lingered in the air, mingling with the faint cologne he had chosen for the evening. He reached for his tuxedo, fingers brushing over the crisp fabric, but paused for a moment, letting the weight of the week press down on him.

A whole week. Seven long days since he had last seen her. Seven days of unanswered calls, of pacing, of imagining her in someone else's arms—even if it was just a fleeting thought. He ached to see her.

Gregory hadn't been able to secure him a ticket to the dinner portion of the charity ball, but he had organised for Cole to at least be there for the dancing. And more importantly, he had promised that Lauren would be there.

*Finally.* He would see her again.

The thought sent a shiver down his spine, a mix of anticipation and something more—something raw, unrelenting, and impossible to ignore. He straightened, running a hand through his damp hair, the memory of her smile, the curve of her lips, the way she carried herself, all flashing unbidden in his mind.

Tonight, he would see her. And he would not let a single moment slip away.

They were halfway through dinner when Lauren suddenly felt it—a prickling at the back of her neck, the subtle weight of someone's gaze fixed on her. She shifted slightly in her seat, glancing around, trying to ignore it, but the feeling refused to dissipate.

Gregory noticed her sudden stillness. "What's wrong, Lauren?" he asked, concern knitting his brow.

She looked at him, a flicker of unease in her eyes. "I… I feel someone is watching me."

Gregory's hand brushed lightly against hers under the table, steadying. He glanced at his watch, calculating. Not yet. It couldn't be Cole—not yet.

Before he could say more, Lauren's lips curved into a controlled, almost imperceptible smile, and she nodded toward a table two across. "What is he doing here?" she whispered.

Gregory followed her gaze, his eyes narrowing in mild amusement. There, seated with his usual air of composed confidence, was Ahmed. His eyes were fixed on her, unwavering, intense, yet polite.

Lauren turned back to Gregory, the smile now carefully painted across her lips, hiding the flutter of emotions beneath. "Prince Ahmed is here," she said softly, a hint of exasperation lacing her tone.

Gregory leaned back slightly, a knowing look in his eyes. "Well," he said dryly, "that explains the feeling of being watched."

Lauren let out a quiet sigh, adjusting her posture, forcing herself to focus on the conversation at the table, but the weight of his gaze remained, electric and impossible to ignore.

# Chapter Seventeen

As soon as dinner was over, Ahmed navigated through the small crowd and found Lauren standing with Gregory, engaged in light conversation.

"Lauren, how lovely to see you again," he said, his voice smooth, eyes holding a spark of something unspoken.

She turned, her smile radiant, practiced yet genuine. "Prince Ahmed! What a pleasure to see you here. What brings you to New York?"

"Partly business," he said, the words carrying a clear, playful innuendo that left little doubt his presence had more than one purpose. His gaze lingered on her just a heartbeat too long.

Lauren glanced at Gregory. "Gregory Wade—this is Prince Ahmed."

Gregory stepped forward, hand extended with polite confidence. "Pleased to meet you."

Ahmed took his hand, shaking it smoothly, then turned his attention back to Lauren. "And where is your fiancé?"

Lauren's fingers brushed the engagement ring still adorning her left hand, a secret comfort she hadn't yet removed. She smiled, letting the glint of the diamond add weight to her words. "Unfortunately, he couldn't make it tonight."

Ahmed's eyes held a flicker of amusement, as though he both understood and was happy at her answer, but he didn't press. Instead, he allowed a small, charming smile to tug at his lips, leaving the air between them charged and deliberate.

As soon as the music started he turned to Lauren. "Can I have this dance?"

"Of course." She took his extended hand Gregory smiled at her as Ahmed led her to the dance floor.

He didn't give her time to protest.

As the music swelled, his hand slid confidently to the small of Lauren's back and he drew her into his arms, close enough that she could feel the steady strength of him, the heat through the fine fabric of his jacket. The dance floor seemed to recede as they moved together, his steps smooth and assured, guiding her effortlessly through the rhythm.

He danced beautifully—controlled, elegant, every movement precise. One hand held hers lightly, the other anchored her at her waist, his thumb brushing there now and then in a way that felt intentional. Lauren followed his lead, her body responding despite herself, the glide and turn of the dance drawing her closer with each measure. Around them, couples swayed and spun, but Ahmed's focus never left her. His gaze stayed fixed on her face, dark and intent, as though she were the only woman in the room.

When the music slowed, he drew her closer still, their bodies aligned, her breath catching as his hand pressed more firmly at her back. It was intoxicating—dangerous in its ease, in the way it made her forget, just for a moment, everything she was supposed to remember.

The final notes faded, applause rippling around them, but Ahmed didn't immediately release her. Instead, he leaned in, his voice low near her ear. "Come. Let me show you the view."

Before she could answer, he guided her from the dance floor, his hand remaining at her waist as he led her through the tall glass doors and onto the terrace. The cool night air brushed against her bare arms, the city lights stretching endlessly below them, brilliant and alive.

He steered her gently backward until she felt the solid marble column at her back. One arm lifted, bracing his hand beside her head, caging her in without quite touching. With the other, he reached out and tipped her chin upward, forcing her to meet his gaze.

The world seemed to narrow to the space between them—the quiet hum of the city below, the soft rush of her own breath, the unspoken tension hanging thick in the air. Ahmed was close, close enough that she could feel the warmth radiating from him, the promise in his touch, the deliberate intimacy of the moment pressing in from all sides. It would have been easy to give in, to let the seduction of the night and his practiced charm carry her forward.

But it wasn't him she saw.

Even as Ahmed's gaze held hers, even as his hand steadied her chin and his presence caged her in, her thoughts betrayed her. She imagined different eyes looking down at her—darker, more intense. A different strength surrounding her. A different voice murmuring her name.

Cole.

The realisation struck hard and sudden, tightening her chest. This moment, charged and dangerous as it was, felt hollow because the man standing before her was not the one she wanted. Not the one whose absence had carved itself into her heart over the past week.

And standing there, balanced on the edge of temptation, Lauren understood with painful clarity just how deep she had fallen—because no matter how intoxicating the moment was, she was wishing, with everything in her, that it was Cole in front of her instead.


Cole scanned the ballroom, his gaze cutting through the crowd with purpose until it landed on Gregory. He straightened and made his way over, every step driven by anticipation and nerves coiled tight beneath his calm exterior.

"Ah, there you are," Gregory greeted him the moment he approached. There was something in his tone—too measured, too careful. "We have a problem."

Cole's brow furrowed. His eyes flicked instinctively around the room again. "She didn't come," he said, the disappointment unmistakable in his voice.

Gregory shook his head once. "Worse."

Cole stilled. "Worse?"

"Prince Ahmed is here."

For a split second, everything went quiet. Then Cole felt it—the sharp, immediate surge of heat in his chest, possessive and furious, flooding his veins.

"Ahmed is here," he repeated, the words flat, dangerous.

His jaw tightened, his hands curling slowly at his sides as his gaze swept the room anew, no longer searching just for Lauren—but for the man who had dared to put his hands on her before.

"Where?" Cole demanded, already scanning the exits, his body coiled tight with urgency.

Gregory lowered his voice. "He danced with her, then they disappeared. I've been looking, but I can't find them."

"Damn it." Cole dragged a hand through his hair, his mind already racing ahead. Where would Ahmed take a woman when he wanted privacy when he wanted her attention undivided?

The answer came instantly.

"The terrace," he said, more to himself than to Gregory. His jaw set, resolve hardening into something unbreakable. "I think I know where they are."

He turned back to Gregory, eyes fierce but grateful. "Thank you. I'll never forget this." He held out his hand.

Gregory didn't hesitate. He took it, his grip firm, his expression serious. "Just look after her. Lauren's special."

"I know," Cole said quietly. "And I will."

Then he was already moving, cutting through the ballroom with purpose, every step carrying him closer to the woman who had claimed him completely—whether she knew it yet or not—as he headed straight for the terrace.

He saw them before they saw him.

They stood at the far end, partially shielded by a marble column, the city lights spilling around them like a private stage. Cole slowed, stopping just short of stepping into their line of sight, allowing himself one brief, dangerous moment to take it all in. Lauren stood tall and composed, her emerald gaze steady as it met Ahmed's. There was no hesitation in her posture, no uncertainty—only quiet confidence, the kind that didn't need to announce itself. It struck Cole then, hard, and sharp, that this was exactly where he was meant to be.

This was the line.

His jaw tightened. His hands curled slowly into fists at his sides, every muscle coiling with restrained force. Possessiveness surged through him, fierce and unrelenting. This was not a man he could dismiss. And Lauren… Lauren was his. The certainty of it thundered through his veins, making his pulse hammer in his temples.

"Lauren," Ahmed murmured, his voice low and intimate, carrying easily across the short distance. "You must know I find you extremely attractive. I haven't been able to get you out of my mind." His gaze lingered, unashamed, tracing the elegant lines of her silk-clad figure. "Your mind is sharp—formidable even—and your beauty…" A slow smile curved his lips. "Magnificent."

Heat flared beneath Cole's collarbone, sharp and unwelcome.

Ahmed reached for her hand, lifting it deliberately, as though nothing in the world could rush him. He pressed his lips to her palm—an intimate, possessive gesture that sent a flash of white-hot anger through Cole's chest. "Why don't you tell your fiancé you've had second thoughts," Ahmed continued softly, "and allow me to take you away from all of this? I would make you very happy."

Cole didn't move.

Every instinct screamed at him to intervene, to cross the space and end it—but he forced himself to wait. To watch. To trust her.

Lauren smiled then—not coy, not flustered, but calm. Assured.

"Ahmed," she said gently, her tone warm but unmistakably firm, "you flatter me. Truly." She withdrew her hand with quiet grace, reclaiming her space. "But I'm in love with my fiancé." Her eyes held his, steady and unwavering. "I would never betray him. I am a woman of honour."

She rested her hand lightly on Ahmed's arm—not an invitation, but a courteous boundary. "Please understand. I appreciate your offer, but I can't accept it."

Cole's chest tightened painfully.

*I'm in love with my fiancé.*

He wanted—needed—that to be true.

Ahmed studied her for a moment, then smiled, a touch of resignation softening his expression. "Ah… alas," he said lightly. His gaze flicked past her shoulder, finally noticing Cole standing there, before returning to her. "You are a very rare woman. I hope Cole Blackwell knows exactly how fortunate he is."

Cole stepped forward.

"I do, Ahmed," he said, his voice low, controlled, and utterly certain as he came to Lauren's side. His presence was immediate, solid, his gaze locking onto hers with an intensity that stole her breath. "Believe me. I do."

Lauren stilled, startled by the sound of his voice, by the force of him beside her. Her breath caught as their eyes met—questions, emotion, and something dangerously close to hope flickering between them.

Ahmed stepped back, reading the moment with practiced ease. A knowing smile curved his mouth. "I'm glad to hear it." He inclined his head toward Lauren in a respectful bow, then turned and disappeared back into the glow and music of the ballroom, leaving the terrace—and the night—charged with everything that had almost been said.

And everything that was about to be.

Silence settled between them.

Lauren and Cole remained where they were, the night humming softly around them, the city lights a distant blur. Neither of them looked away. Cole moved closer, close enough that she could feel the heat of him, the tension coiled tight beneath his control, like a wire pulled to breaking point.

"You're here," she whispered, the words barely sound, more breath than voice.

Before his mind could catch up—before logic or restraint could intervene—his arm slid around her waist, firm and unmistakably possessive. His other hand threaded into her hair, and the softness of it stole his breath. Softer than he'd imagined. Softer than he had any right to know.

He lowered his head and kissed her.

Not a careful kiss. Not a polite one.

It was hungry and urgent, the kiss of a man who had denied himself too long and had finally surrendered. Lauren's breath caught, her body going utterly still for one suspended heartbeat—shock, heat, longing colliding all at once.

Then instinct took over.

Her arms slid up around his neck, fingers curling into the fabric of his jacket as she pulled him closer and kissed him back. Not softly. Not cautiously. Her mouth moved against his with fierce intent, matching his hunger stroke for stroke, her lips parting as she leaned into him, surrendering to the heat that had been building between them since the moment they met.

The kiss deepened, unrestrained now, filled with want and days—weeks—of things left unsaid.

Cole groaned softly against her mouth, the sound vibrating through her, his hold tightening at her waist as if he feared she might disappear if he loosened his grip. Time blurred. The music from inside, the city, the world beyond them faded until there was only the press of his body, the intoxicating pull of his kiss, and the dangerous truth pounding through her veins.

This didn't feel like a mistake.

It felt inevitable.

He pressed closer, the solid heat of him leaving no space for doubt or denial, and Lauren gasped at the unmistakable awareness of how deeply she affected him. The realisation sent a shiver racing through her, straight to places she had been trying very hard not to acknowledge.

Her hands slid into his hair, fingers threading through the thick strands, nails grazing his scalp. His reaction was instant—a low, rough sound torn from his chest, dark and unguarded.

He broke the kiss just long enough to steal her breath before his mouth traced along her jaw, unhurried, reverent. His lips lingered at her throat, learning her, revelling in the way her body responded without permission.

A soft moan slipped free before she could stop it.

God, this felt good.

Too good.

She didn't want to stop. And judging by the way Cole's breath had gone uneven, the way his grip tightened as if she were something essential, neither did he.

"God," he murmured thickly against her lips, "I want you so bad it hurts."

That was what shattered the spell.

Not because she didn't want him—she did, with an intensity that frightened her—but because reality crashed back in, cold and unyielding.

Elena.

Lauren brought her hands up to his shoulders, firm this time, pushing him back. He released her instantly, as though the contact had burned him, staring at her with a look of pure confusion—almost loss.

"What?" he asked, breathless.

"Cole, stop," she said, her voice shaking despite her effort to steady it. "This can't happen."

"Why?" The word came out raw, stripped bare.

"Elena," Lauren said softly but clearly. "You're almost engaged to her."

"No," he replied at once. "I'm not."

She stilled. "What?"

"I ended it," he said, searching her face, needing her to believe him. "The day we got back from Dubai. I told her it was over."

Lauren blinked, genuinely stunned, the world tilting just slightly beneath her feet.

"You… ended it?"

"Yes," he said, the truth laid bare between them at last.

Her heart lurched, the sound of it suddenly loud in her ears. "What—why?" she asked, her voice barely above a whisper, as if speaking any louder might fracture the moment.

Cole exhaled slowly, dragging a hand through his hair. The controlled, unshakeable man she knew was clearly fighting to keep himself steady. When his gaze locked onto hers, it was unflinching—painfully honest.

"Because I realised I couldn't go through with it," he said quietly. And that much was entirely true. What he didn't say—what he couldn't yet put into words—was that the engagement had never truly been about Elena. It had been about strategy. About legacy. About William Dutton's heir.

Only now did the truth stand stark and undeniable before him.

The heir he had calculated for… wasn't Elena.

It was Lauren.

"And because pretending stopped being possible when I realised I'm in love with you," he added, his voice low, deliberate. The words carried a weight that made her stomach twist and her chest ache all at once.

"You love me?" she whispered, disbelief and wonder threading through her tone. "You don't believe in love."

"I didn't," he said simply. He stepped closer, lifting her chin gently until she had no choice but to meet his eyes. They were dark, intense, stripped bare of every defence. "Not until I met you."

Her breath caught.

"I love you, Lauren Dutton."

The world seemed to still.

"I…" Her voice wavered, emotion rushing in too fast, too overwhelming. Then she exhaled, surrendering to the truth she had been denying for far too long. "I love you too."

The admission left her lips softly, reverently, as though it were something fragile.

Then reality nudged its way back in, quiet but persistent. "Is she… okay?" she asked gently. The concern was genuine. She knew Elena hadn't loved Cole, not in the way love demanded—but there were other wounds. Pride. Humiliation. The sting of being left behind.

Cole's expression softened, though the intensity never fully left his eyes. "She was angry," he said honestly. "Hurt. But she understands." He paused, then added with quiet certainty, "And she knows I won't change my mind."

He held her gaze, unwavering, and in that look Lauren saw it—the same resolve that had unsettled her from the start, the same certainty that made him dangerous and irresistible all at once.

She drew in a slow breath, her emotions tightening into a dizzying knot—relief, fear, longing, hope—all tangled together. Nothing in her life had prepared her for this moment. For this clarity. For the way everything suddenly felt terrifyingly real.

And still, she leaned closer.

Cole's hand brushed hers, light but deliberate, and the contact sent a shiver racing through her. His thumb lingered, as if memorising the feel of her.

"Lauren," he murmured, his voice rough, intimate, vibrating with restrained emotion, "this changes everything."

She didn't pull away.

"I know," she whispered.

And for the first time, standing there beneath the open sky with the city humming around them, Lauren allowed herself to believe that maybe—just maybe—everything was finally falling into place.

# Chapter Eighteen

Cole rested his forehead against hers, their breaths mingling, his voice low and urgent. "Can we get out of here?"

She smiled, a real one this time—soft, luminous. "And go where?"

"My penthouse."

Her answer wasn't spoken at first. Instead, she slid her hands up his chest, feeling the steady thrum of his heartbeat beneath the crisp fabric of his tuxedo. Her fingers curled into the lapels of his jacket, pulling him down into a kiss that burned with intent. When she broke it, her lips brushed his as she murmured, "Get me out of here."

He didn't waste a second.

Moments later they were moving through the ballroom together, the world blurring at the edges. As they reached the exit, Lauren paused just long enough to say, "I need to let Gregory know."

"He already does," Cole replied smoothly.

She stopped and looked at him. "He was in on this?"

Cole's mouth curved into a rare, genuine smile. "I like Gregory."

She laughed softly, the sound light and relieved, and then they were stepping into his waiting limousine, the door closing behind them with a quiet finality— shutting out the night, the doubts, and everything that had once kept them apart.

She leaned back against the seat, resting her head briefly on his shoulder, savouring the warmth, the closeness, the electric tension humming between them. The limousine glided through the streets of New York, each stoplight and turn stretching the delicious anticipation—a slow, teasing prelude to the night that awaited them.

Minutes later, they arrived at a towering glass building in the heart of Manhattan. Its sleek façade gleamed beneath the night sky, a monument to wealth, power, and the life Cole commanded. A doorman greeted them with a polite nod as the limousine slid to a stop, but Cole barely acknowledged him, his focus fixed entirely on Lauren.

As they stepped into the private elevator, the doors slid closed, enclosing them in soft, warm light. Cole's gaze swept over her slowly, unhurried, unmistakably appraising, and she felt herself melt beneath its intensity.

"Every time I see you, Lauren… I need you in my arms," he confessed, his voice low, edged with a roughness that sent a shiver through her.

Lauren smiled, her heart racing. "Good," she teased softly, pressing herself closer as the elevator began its silent ascent.

The doors opened to reveal his expansive penthouse, the city skyline stretching endlessly beyond floor-to-ceiling windows. The apartment was sleek, modern, and unmistakably luxurious—plush furnishings, muted lighting, carefully chosen art—but none of it could compete with the woman standing beside him. Cole's gaze lingered on her, dark and heated, as he closed the distance between them.

"Welcome to my home," he murmured, his hands sliding to her waist, pulling her flush against him. She tilted her head back, her lips brushing his as they sank into a deep, lingering kiss. The city buzzed far below, oblivious to the storm of desire igniting in Cole's penthouse.

Lauren's fingers tangled in his hair, tugging him closer. Cole's hands roamed her body with a confidence that made her pulse race, and yet the spacious intimacy of the penthouse—private, undeniably theirs—made every touch feel amplified, heightened, impossible to ignore.

He lifted her effortlessly, carrying her to the oversized sofa and setting her down with careful, possessive reverence. "You look absolutely exquisite tonight," he said, his lips finding hers again in a kiss that was both urgent and deliberate.

Lauren responded without hesitation, pressing herself against him, tasting, feeling, savouring every second. The penthouse, the city, the world beyond the glass walls—all of it disappeared. There was only them, their need, and the intoxicating, unrelenting pull neither could deny.

Cole's hands traced her back, sliding down to her hips, drawing her impossibly close, as though he needed to imprint every inch of her into memory. Her breath caught in ragged gasps, mingling with his, and the room seemed to shrink until there was nothing but the two of them, caught in the storm of heat, desire, and unspoken emotion.

When they finally broke apart for air, their foreheads remained pressed together, breaths tangled, hearts racing. Cole's voice was low, roughened by emotion, threaded with something both dangerous and unexpectedly tender.

"Lauren… you have no idea what you do to me."

Her chest rose and fell rapidly, exhilaration and fear twisting together in her stomach until she could no longer tell them apart. She lifted her gaze to his, eyes dark and searching. "I think I do," she whispered. And she knew—on some instinctive, undeniable level—that they both did.

Without another word, Cole bent and scooped her into his arms. Lauren let out a soft gasp, her arms looping instinctively around his neck, as if she belonged there. He kissed her as he carried her, unhurried yet purposeful, into his bedroom, as though this moment was inevitable rather than reckless.

He set her gently on her feet beside the bed, his hands lingering at her waist, reluctant to let her go. Then, with deliberate care, he reached up and removed the comb from her hair. It spilled free, cascading down her back in long, platinum waves.

He slid his fingers through it, massaging her scalp slowly, reverently, as if committing the feel of her to memory. "Your hair is beautiful," he murmured, his thumb brushing her temple. "Just like the rest of you."

Then his mouth claimed hers again—deeper this time, hungrier—as though the last of his restraint had finally fractured. Lauren kissed him back without hesitation, her hands pushing his jacket from his shoulders. It slid to the floor, forgotten, as if nothing else in the world mattered.

His hands returned to her hair, fisting gently as he kissed her, anchoring her to him. Lauren's fingers worked quickly at his bow tie, tugging it free and tossing it aside with the jacket. Her hands moved to the buttons of his shirt, undoing them one by one, the smooth warmth of his skin beneath her touch sending a thrill through her as she pulled the fabric loose from the waistband of his trousers.

Cole groaned softly against her mouth, the sound vibrating straight through her, as if her touch alone was undoing him. And in that moment—standing beside the bed, tangled together, caught between impulse and intention—neither of them could pretend this was anything less than inevitable.

Her hands roamed his chest, exploring the solid warmth beneath his shirt, memorising the steady beat of his heart as if it were something she might need to recall later. Cole's breath hitched at her touch, and his hands slid around her waist, fingers warm, sure, reverent.

He found the zipper at the back of her dress and paused for the briefest moment—as if giving her the chance to stop him, to change her mind. She didn't. Instead, she leaned closer, her forehead brushing his, her silent consent unmistakable.

Slowly, deliberately, he drew the zipper down.

The soft whisper of fabric filled the room as the tension in the dress released, the silk loosening beneath his hands. The gown slipped from her and pooled at her waist, revealing her bare skin, luminous in the low light. She wore no bra—she didn't need one—and the sight of her stole what little breath he had left.

Cole stilled, his hands tightening slightly at her hips, his gaze moving over her with open awe, not possession but appreciation. Something raw crossed his face, something unguarded.

"My God…" he murmured, voice thick, reverent. "You're stunning."

Heat flushed her skin, not from embarrassment, but from the way he looked at her—as if she were extraordinary, as if this moment mattered. She reached for him then, needing the reassurance of his touch, the weight of his attention, as the space between them dissolved once more.

And whatever lay ahead—uncertainty, consequences, questions neither of them had answers to—faded beneath the simple, undeniable truth pulsing between them: this was real, and neither of them wanted to turn away.

Cole's hands moved over her with a tenderness that made her breath catch, his touch confident yet reverent as his mouth claimed hers again. The kiss deepened, slow and unhurried, stealing the last of her caution. A soft gasp escaped her as sensation rippled through her, every nerve alive beneath his hands.

She answered him instinctively, fingers fumbling at first before finding their purpose, undoing the front of his trousers with a quiet urgency that matched the way his breath faltered against her lips. They barely broke the kiss, foreheads brushing, mouths still seeking, as fabric gave way and barriers fell.

His hands slid to her waist, guiding the fallen silk lower, the gown slipping past her hips to pool at her feet. It felt impossibly intimate—this shared rhythm of touch and breath, this wordless agreement that neither of them wanted to slow down.

They were still kissing, still clinging to each other, caught in the heady space between restraint and surrender—where thought dissolved, and all that remained was heat, connection, and the knowledge that whatever they were stepping into together would change them both.

Both naked now, Cole lifted her with surprising gentleness and laid her carefully on the bed, as though she were something precious, something to be cherished rather than claimed. The sheets were cool beneath her skin, a stark contrast to the heat pulsing between them.

For a moment, he simply looked at her.

His gaze traced her slowly, reverently, as if committing every detail to memory. His hand followed, gliding down the length of her body with a tenderness that made her throat tighten, his touch filled with awe rather than urgency.

"You are so beautiful," he said quietly, the words raw and unguarded, stripped of his usual control.

Lauren reached for him, her fingers curling around his wrist, grounding him, pulling him closer. He lowered himself beside her, gathering her into his arms, her body fitting against his as though it had always known where it belonged.

He kissed her then—not rushed, not demanding—but deep and consuming, a kiss that spoke of choice rather than impulse, of wanting rather than taking. She melted into him, her hands sliding into his hair, her breath hitching as the world narrowed to the warmth of his mouth and the steady beat of his heart against hers.

She pushed him gently but decisively onto his back, straddling him with slow, electrifying confidence. Her hair spilled forward in a soft, silken curtain, framing her face and cascading over her breasts as she looked down at him—unapologetic, luminous, utterly sure of herself. In that moment, she looked like a siren, all quiet danger and irresistible allure.

Her hands slid over his chest, unhurried, exploratory, learning the warmth and strength beneath her palms. She felt the way his muscles tightened instinctively at her touch, the way his breath deepened, control slipping in measured degrees. A low groan escaped him, rough and unguarded, his head tipping back against the pillows as if surrendering to her lead.

Lauren leaned down, her lips brushing his throat, lingering there just long enough to make him restless. She traced a slow path along his collarbone, her mouth following, teasing rather than claiming, letting anticipation do its work. Each kiss was deliberate, each pause calculated, until his hands flexed at his sides, fighting the urge to pull her closer.

"Lauren…" Cole rasped, her name heavy with need, stripped of all restraint.

She smiled—soft, knowing, just a little wicked—and lifted her head, meeting his gaze. The look in her eyes stole what little breath he had left. This wasn't haste or hunger alone. This was choice. This was want.

His erection stood hard, thick, waiting for her. Heat flooded her, her pulse stuttering as she wrapped her hand around him, stroking once—slow, deliberate, devastating. His breath hissed out, his entire body tensing beneath her touch.

She lowered her head slowly, her lips parting as she leaned in. Her breath ghosted over him—hot, trembling—and then her tongue brushed gently over the swollen head of him, a soft, tentative flick meant to taste him. Cole's hands balled into fists at his sides, fighting for control.

"God…" he groaned again, raw, pleading.

She took him into her mouth—slow, deliberate, inch by inch—her lips stretching around him with careful precision. Her hands wrapped around the rest of him, stroking in perfect rhythm with the motion of her mouth, a synchronised dance of tease and release.

His hips jerked involuntarily, breath shattering in ragged gasps as she drew him deeper, inch by inch, teasing him with a torturous, deliberate pace. She pulled back just enough to tease, to torture, then engulfed him again, each motion wringing another strangled, guttural sound from him.

Cole's fingers threaded into her silken hair, tugging lightly, steadying himself as the pleasure surged, building unbearably high. His chest rose and fell in uneven bursts, his hips rocking forward, chasing the exquisite torment she gave him.

"You… you feel incredible," he groaned, voice rough, low, desperate.

She looked up at him through the strands of her hair, lips slick and glistening, eyes shining with heat and mischief. Her tongue traced the underside of him, moving in a slow, torturous rhythm that left him gasping, trembling.

Every movement, every subtle shift of her mouth and hands, unravelled his restraint further. The control he had clung to—the careful, deliberate calm he had maintained—crumbled with each moan he couldn't hold back.

He hit the back of her throat, a deep groan tearing from him. She pulled back just enough to breathe, only to drag him back in, sinking deeper, lips and tongue coaxing, teasing, commanding all at once.

"God… Lauren," he gasped, his hands tightening in her hair, the need, the want, the sheer desperation rolling off him in waves.

She hummed around him, a soft, low vibration that made his toes curl, every nerve alight. Her fingers tightened their rhythm, stroking, matching the pace she set with her mouth, a perfect harmony of control and abandon.

Cole's head dropped back against the pillow, his breath ragged, a tremor running through him as he fought against the mounting pleasure threatening to consume him. Each inch, each pull, each deliberate pause sent shivers of ecstasy through him, twisting tighter in his chest until the only thing that existed was the delicious torment of Lauren—her, completely, unapologetically, driving him past the edge.

"Enough," he growled, his voice rough and barely controlled.

Before she could react, he caught her wrists and pulled her upright in one fierce, instinctive motion. Their bodies collided, heat and urgency crashing together, and his mouth claimed hers in a kiss that was anything but restrained—deep, hungry, and unmistakably certain. There was no hesitation now, no space for doubt or second thoughts. Only want.

The world narrowed to the press of him against her, the rough slide of his hands along her arms as if he needed to reassure himself, she was real, that this moment wasn't some illusion he might wake from. Her breath hitched as she clutched at his shoulders, the force of the kiss stealing the ground from beneath her.

In a swift, fluid movement, he turned them, guiding her back onto the bed. She landed against the cool sheets, the contrast sending a shiver through her just as his weight followed, solid and sure. His hands roamed her body with reverent urgency, learning every curve, every reaction, as though memorising her.

He lifted his head just enough to look at her, his expression dark with desire and something deeper—something dangerously close to awe. And in that charged stillness, before anything else could happen, Lauren knew with absolute certainty: there was no going back from this.

A soft, involuntary moan slipped from her lips, as he cupped her breast, his palm hot against her sensitised skin. He groaned low in his chest, flicking his thumb over her hardened peak—once, then again when she arched into him with a helpless whimper. Their mouths fused, the kiss deep and drugging, tongues tangling, breath mingling, until nothing existed beyond the blistering intensity of their connection.

His hands roamed over her body—learning her, mapping her. When he found the silken curve of her thigh, he stroked her with deliberate slowness, igniting a fresh rush of heat between her legs.

Then he tore his lips from hers, dragging them down her body in a scorching trail. His mouth closed over one taut nipple, his tongue flicking, teasing, before he sucked deeply, pulling a broken moan from her lips.

Her fingers tangled in his hair, her breath coming in ragged bursts as he kissed his way lower—down the smooth plane of her stomach—his lips and tongue worshipping every inch.

He pushed her thighs apart and reached between them. She gasped when his fingertip slid over her slick, satin heat—stroking, circling, coaxing more from her. Kneeling between her legs on the bed, he lowered his head.

And then he tasted her.

Pleasure detonated inside her. It was so intense her hips shuddered beneath him. He held her steady, swirling his tongue through her wetness, drinking every sound she made.

Then he was devouring her—tongue stroking, circling, teasing the tight bud of her pleasure until she writhed beneath him, sobbing his name. When he slid a long, masculine finger inside her, she nearly came undone. She was tight—so tight—her muscles gripping him. He withdrew slowly, then thrust in again, setting a torturous rhythm that dragged her higher, and higher, until she was teetering on the edge.

"Cole, please." Her voice was fractured, pleading.

He groaned against her, the vibration sending another jolt ripping through her. "You taste incredible," he murmured, breath warm against her fevered skin.

Tremors slammed through her. Her back arched off the bed as she held her breath, eyes squeezed shut, lips parted in a silent gasp. His tongue stroked her— rough, relentless—then softened, twirling her with the delicate flick of its tip.

Her entire body tightened—arching once more—then she exploded with a scream of ecstasy. A strangled cry tore from her as wave after wave crashed over her. He held her through it, his mouth lingering, drawing out every last shudder until she collapsed beneath him, trembling and utterly wrecked.

# Chapter Nineteen

Cole flipped her onto her stomach with a sure, commanding touch that sent a tremor straight through her. The shift of his hands—firm on her hips, guiding her knees beneath her—made her feel weightless, wanted, completely claimed. She felt the heat of him behind her before he even touched her, his presence a dark, overwhelming force that made her breath catch.

Her body reacted before her mind could form a thought. She pushed back against him, deliberately rubbing her aching, swollen centre against the hard, head of him glide over her slick folds. Slow. Teasing. Excruciating. Each circle, each stroke over her entrance made her entire body tighten with anticipation. Her breath hitched, her thighs quivered, her fingers fisting in the sheets as he dragged pleasure out of her one aching inch at a time.

"Cole…" The word slipped out as a broken moan. She wasn't sure if she was begging or warning him—or herself.

Her hips tilted back instinctively, searching, inviting, needing. She was so wet, so ready, that even the slightest brush of him had her trembling.

And then he finally gave in.

He pressed forward, sinking into her with a deep, deliberate thrust that stole her breath—half shock, half relief. The stretch of him filled her completely, a slow, consuming slide that seemed to erase every other thought. Her arms trembled, forehead pressing to the sheets, as a long, low moan tore from her throat.

"God, Lauren… you're so tight," he groaned, voice rough with need.

Every nerve in her body burned with sensation. She felt him—every inch, every pulse, every shiver of restraint as he moved within her. Her walls clenched involuntarily, pulling him deeper, drawing a sharp, ragged breath from him behind her.

"Hard… fast," she gasped, voice breaking on the words as she pushed back, needing more. "Please."

His hands tightened on her hips, fingers digging in possessively.

Then he gave her exactly what she wanted.

He drove into her—fast, fierce, unrelenting. The sound of their bodies meeting filled the room, each slap of skin sending sparks racing through her nerves. Her moans grew louder, raw, and uncontrollable. Her fingers clawed at the bedspread, her body moving instinctively with his, chasing every thrust as if she could vanish without it.

"Lauren…" he groaned behind her, voice dark, rough, and ragged. "You feel so perfect."

Perfect. The word struck her harder than the pleasure tearing through her. Perfect—for him, with him. Her body trembled at the thought alone.

Tension coiled inside her, tight and white-hot, winding higher with every thrust, every gasp, every relentless movement of his body. Her hips moved on their own, matching him stroke for stroke, need for need. She felt him everywhere—inside her, against her skin, in every frantic sound escaping her lips.

Then it hit.

The orgasm tore through her violently, her scream muffled against the sheets as her body convulsed around him. She clamped down instinctively, feeling his rhythm stutter, hearing him groan—a guttural, helpless sound—as he drove into her again, deeper.

"Cole…"

Her name slipped from her lips like a plea, a confession she hadn't meant to voice. It carried need, trust, and a surrender so complete it stole his breath.

The sound of her—of her surrender—hit him hard.

Cole went utterly still, jaw tightening as he fought the instinct to collapse into the pull between them, to lose himself entirely. His eyes closed for a brief, tortured second as he drew in a ragged breath, forcing control back into his body. Not yet.

With deliberate care, he slipped out of her molten heat, guiding her onto her back once more, every movement careful despite the urgent fire thrumming through him.

"Look at me," he murmured, low, roughened by feeling rather than command. "I need to see you when I come."

Her eyes met his—wide, luminous, shining with everything she couldn't speak—and in that instant, the air between them crackled, heavy with unspoken desire.

He drove into her, deep and deliberate, each stroke slow and purposeful, every inch of him igniting a trail of fire through her. Her breaths fractured into frantic, soft pants, her body arching, seeking, pulling him closer with every movement.

Again and again, he thrust, skimming the thin edge of control, building tension that coiled tight and relentless. She cried out beneath him, every nerve alight, her hands digging into his skin—sharp, claiming, desperate.

Then she shattered again—harder this time—her cry slicing straight to him. Her body clenched around him, urgent and greedy, dragging him deeper into the same exquisite abyss.

"Lauren—" His voice broke into a rough groan, raw and primal, as the world fractured inside him. His hands gripped her hips, holding her tight as he buried himself fully inside her. Her tight, honey-slick warmth pulled him past the point of restraint.

A guttural, instinctive growl tore from his chest as he spilled into her, shuddering, every breath caught in the force of it. He stayed pressed deep against her, heart hammering in sync with hers, the intensity almost unbearable. Nothing—no touch, no kiss, no longing—had ever undone him the way she did.

When the tremors finally ebbed, Cole lowered his forehead to hers and kissed her again—slow, reverent, as if marking the fragile, profound truth of what they'd shared. Lauren met him with the same quiet intensity, her lips open, her hands threading into his hair, their kiss unhurried yet brimming with the wonder of each other.

He rolled onto his side and drew her with him, settling her against his chest as though it was the most natural place in the world for her to be. One arm curved securely around her, holding her close, while his other hand drifted up, fingers threading through the long, silky fall of her hair. He stroked it absently, tenderly, grounding himself in the feel of her warmth, her weight, her presence.

Lauren rested her cheek against his skin, listening to the steady beat of his heart beneath her ear, her breathing gradually matching his. The room was hushed, the city beyond the windows distant and unreal, as if time itself had paused to give them this moment.

Wrapped together, neither spoke. Words felt unnecessary. Whatever this was—unexpected, dangerous, undeniably real—it lingered between them, soft and powerful, as he held her and wondered how something so unplanned could already feel so inevitable.

The next morning, long before the sun had edged the horizon with light, they found each other again. The world outside the room was still wrapped in shadows, the hush of early morning granting them a space that belonged only to them.

Cole slid into her from behind, the warmth of her body welcoming him like it had been waiting all night. A low groan escaped him, deep and guttural. "I don't think I'll ever get enough of you," he murmured against her neck, his voice rough with need.

Lauren arched back into him, shivering at the contact. "Yes… more," she breathed, her fingers clutching the sheets, curling into the sensation of him filling her.

"You want more, baby?" His lips ghosted over the shell of her ear as his hand drifted along her hip, teasing, steady, claiming.

"Yes," she gasped, body trembling in response.

He slipped almost all the way out, drawing back just enough to tease, and then drove in hard, the motion strong, deliberate, reverberating through them both. "Jesus… you feel like heaven," he groaned, pressing close, every movement a blend of fire and control.

Her head fell forward against the pillow, a soft, raw moan escaping her lips. The room was filled with the rhythm of them, the low sounds of pleasure mingling with the quiet of the early dawn. She felt him behind her, hard and insistent, and the intensity of his need mirrored her own, echoing every shiver, every gasp.

He rolled his hips, coaxing, teasing, and she trembled around him, gripping the sheets until her knuckles whitened. "Yes… just like that," she whispered, voice ragged with breath and desire.

Cole's chest pressed against her back, his hands steady at her hips, anchoring her to him as he moved with slow, delicious precision. Each thrust was measured, controlled, yet filled with the urgent desire that had been simmering between since the day they met.

"God, Lauren…" His voice dropped, low and intimate, vibrating through her. "I could lose myself in you forever."

She shivered at the confession, a wave of heat and longing washing over her. "Don't… don't stop," she begged, barely more than a whisper, her body arching instinctively toward him.

And he didn't stop. He drove into her with a slow, powerful rhythm, the intimacy of the moment—the closeness, the surrender—binding them in a way that went far beyond the physical. The outside world didn't exist. There was no past, no future, no engagement, or obligations. There was only this—only the two of them, entwined, hearts and bodies echoing the same need, the same desire, the same ache for each other.

Cole's movements became faster, sharper, but never uncontrolled, each thrust hitting a rhythm that had them teetering on the edge together. Lauren's back arched against him, every nerve alive, every breath a tremor of need. Her hands gripped the sheets, nails digging in, as her body clenched around him, pulling him deeper.

"I… I'm close," she gasped, her voice ragged, low moans breaking through the quiet of the room.

Cole's lips found the curve of her shoulder, biting lightly, nipping, marking, as he whispered, "Then come for me, baby. Let go for me."

Her fingers tangled in the sheets, her body quivering with the mounting intensity. The heat, the pressure, the raw, consuming need between them built higher and higher, coiling tighter with every pulse of his hips.

"God… Cole," she breathed, voice shaking. Her legs tightened, pressing him closer, and the first wave hit her, tearing through her like fire and electricity all at once. She cried out softly, her body trembling as she came, every fibre of her responding, every nerve alight.

Cole groaned, deep and guttural, a sound that shook through her, and he held her close, feeling the contraction of her body around him. The sensation, the closeness, the surrender—it pushed him over the edge. With a shuddering thrust, he followed, the world narrowing to the warmth of her, the beat of her heart, the soft gasps and moans that wrapped around him like fire.

They clung to each other through the aftermath, his hands tracing her sides, rubbing soothing circles along her back, as her head falling back against his chest. Their breaths mingled, ragged, uneven, the intimacy of the release leaving them raw and aching in the best possible way.

"You… you feel incredible," Cole murmured, voice low and husky, lips brushing the top of her head. "I… I will never get enough of you."

Lauren let out a soft laugh, half a sigh, half a moan, pressing herself closer. "Neither will I," she whispered back, warmth and exhaustion threading through her words. "That… was amazing."

And for that quiet, suspended moment, the world outside ceased to exist. The city, the engagement, even the complications—they all melted away. There was only Cole, only Lauren, and the raw, unshakable bond that had finally, fully, claimed them both.

They drifted back into sleep tangled together, the night lingering just a little longer than it should have.


When it was finally time to rise, Cole moved first—sudden, decisive, full of restless energy. Before she could ask what he was doing, he had scooped her up effortlessly, her surprised laugh filling the room as she wrapped her arms around his neck.

"Cole?" she asked, amused, still half-asleep.

"We need a shower," he said simply, eyes bright, mouth already curved in that dangerous smile she was beginning to recognise.

And as he carried her toward the bathroom, Lauren had the distinct sense that whatever this was between them—it wasn't slowing down. Not even close.

Steam filled the bathroom, curling around them like a private cocoon. Cole washed himself quickly, efficiently—impatient in a way that made Lauren smile. When he turned his attention to her, everything slowed.

His hands moved over her with reverence, unhurried, as if he were memorising her all over again. Warm water traced the lines of her shoulders, her back, her hips, while his touch followed, deliberate and tender. Lauren leaned into him, her eyes drifting closed, every nerve ending humming beneath his palms.

"Cole…" she breathed, already unsteady.

He rested his forehead against hers, water cascading over them, his breath uneven, his voice rough with everything he was holding back. "I know," he murmured, the words barely audible beneath the spray.

The restraint shattered anyway.

In one fluid motion, he lifted her, and her breath caught as her legs instinctively wrapped around him, anchoring herself to the only solid thing left in the world. Heat flared between them—swift, consuming—and the space around them seemed to dissolve, leaving only the closeness of their bodies, the echo of water, and the soft, urgent sounds neither of them tried to silence.

Her hands clutched at his shoulders, fingers digging in as his mouth found hers. The kiss was deep and claiming, as though he were trying to pour everything he felt into that single connection. Time blurred. Thought vanished. There was only this—need, recognition, inevitability.

He pressed into her, then pulled back, then thrust again, each movement deliberate, full of raw hunger. His lips captured hers again, fierce, and unrelenting, and against her mouth he said the words that shattered everything.

"Marry me."

Her eyes flew open. "What did you say?"

He didn't pull away. Didn't hesitate. His forehead pressed to hers, his voice low, certain, utterly unguarded.

"I said marry me."

"Cole—"

"I mean it," he said, his voice rough with feeling. "I love you, Lauren. I want you. I want a life with you."

"But—"

"No buts." His groan was reverent, almost a plea. "I love you. Marry me."

The world tilted. Her heart thundered in her chest, every doubt drowned by the truth in his eyes, by the way he held her as if letting go was no longer an option.

"I love you too," she breathed, the words torn from somewhere deep and unprotected.

"Then marry me."

Her head fell back, a shiver racing through her as emotion overwhelmed her. "Yes," she said, the word trembling but sure. "Yes."

Then it became a storm—fast, urgent, desperate—like they couldn't get enough of each other. Her back pressed against the cool tiles while he drove into her, over and over, every thrust sending sparks through her nerves, until finally, shattering together, they cried each other's names like a prayer, hearts pounding and bodies spent in the echo of their need.

After they were dried, Cole dressed quickly in trousers and a crisp white shirt, the ease of his movements belying the intensity of what had just passed between them. He picked up the phone and called down to the concierge, speaking in a low, efficient tone as he arranged for clothes to be brought up for Lauren—details handled, as always, without fuss.

"You didn't have to do that," she said softly, settling onto the sofa in the penthouse living room, still wrapped in his plush bathrobe. The fabric smelled faintly of him—clean, warm, familiar already.

He crossed the room and bent in front of her, brushing a stray strand of damp hair from her face, his fingers lingering at her cheek. His dark gaze held hers, teasing but unmistakably tender.

"I would be perfectly content for you to stay in my bathrobe," he murmured, a faint smirk tugging at his mouth, "but people might give you funny looks when we go and see your father."

Lauren laughed, the sound light and genuine, the tension she'd been carrying for days finally loosening in her chest. For the first time in longer than she could remember, she felt entirely at ease—safe, seen, and undeniably his.

She tilted her head, studying him. "Why are we going to see my father?"

His expression shifted, the teasing fading as something deeper took its place—steady, deliberate, unshakeable. He straightened slightly but didn't move away, his hands resting on her knees as if anchoring them both to the moment.

"Because," he said quietly, "I just asked you to marry me." His thumb brushed over her skin, slow and certain. "And I intend to do this properly, Lauren."

Her breath caught, the words settling into her like a promise.

"You're worth it," he added, voice low and sincere. No grand declarations. No flourish. Just truth.

The simplicity of it undid her. Emotion swelled in her chest before she could stop it, and a single tear slipped free, tracing a warm path down her cheek.

Cole noticed instantly. His thumb came up, brushing it away with a tenderness that stole what little breath she had left. "Hey," he murmured, his forehead resting briefly against hers. "That's a happy tear, I hope."

She laughed softly, a little unsteady, and nodded. "It is. I just… I never expected this. Any of it."

He pressed a kiss to her temple, his arm tightening around her, holding her close. "Neither did I," he admitted. "But I've never been more certain of anything in my life."

# Chapter Twenty

It was late afternoon as the limousine rolled through the familiar streets, past iron gates and sweeping trees, until the Dutton estate came into view—grand, imposing, steeped in legacy. Lauren felt the weight of what awaited them inside: her father, her sister, the consequences of choices made.

But as Cole stepped out of the car and offered her his hand, she realised something important.

She wasn't facing any of it alone.

Hand in hand, they walked toward the house—toward truth, toward confrontation, toward the future—secure in the knowledge that whatever came next, they would meet it together.


They were met at the front door by the butler, who inclined his head respectfully.

"Good evening, Miss," he said warmly.

Lauren smiled. "Evening, Mansel." Then, almost immediately, "Is my father in his study?"

"Yes, Miss. And I'm pleased to say he's having a good day today."

Relief softened her expression. She glanced at Cole, then took his hand and led him down the familiar corridor toward the study.

The door opened, and William Dutton rose from behind his desk at once. His face lit up when he saw her.

"Hello, sweetheart," he said, pulling her into a brief, affectionate embrace. Then he turned to Cole, extending his hand. "Blackwell. What do I owe the pleasure?"

Cole shook his hand firmly, meeting his gaze with calm respect. "Sir, I was hoping we might have a private word."

William's brows lifted slightly, curiosity sparking, but he nodded without hesitation. "Of course."

Lauren felt the moment stretch. She squeezed Cole's hand gently, a silent show of support. "I'll leave you two to talk," she said softly.

She stepped out, closing the door behind her.

The room fell quiet.

Cole turned back to William, straightening instinctively, every sense sharp, focused, exposed. This—this—was more intimidating than any boardroom standoff or hostile negotiation he had ever faced. There were no strategies here. No leverage. Just truth.

"Sir," he began, his voice steady despite the thrum in his chest, "I'd like to ask for your daughter's hand in marriage."

For the first time since Cole had met him, William looked genuinely surprised. His brows lifted slightly, his gaze sharpening before a slow, knowing smile curved at the corner of his mouth.

"Which daughter?" William asked dryly, though his eyes missed nothing.

Cole didn't hesitate. Not even a heartbeat.

"Lauren," he said simply.

The room went quiet.

William studied him in silence, the weight of years—of fatherhood, judgment, and fierce love—settling into the pause. Cole didn't look away. He didn't flinch. He stood there and let himself be measured.

At last, William leaned back, folding his hands together. "Do you love Lauren?"

"Yes." The word came instantly, unguarded. "More than I thought was possible."

Something shifted in William's expression—approval, relief, perhaps even satisfaction.

"Well," William said after a moment, a glint of both warmth and steel in his eyes, "I was hoping you'd say that." He gestured to the chair opposite him. "Now sit down, Blackwell. If you want my blessing, we're going to have a proper conversation first."

Cole exhaled slowly and did exactly as he was told.

William wasted no time. "Three weeks ago, you and Elena were talking about getting engaged."

Cole had expected it. He nodded once. "That was a mistake." He didn't soften it, didn't hedge. "To be honest, sir, I never thought I would fall in love."

William's gaze sharpened, not unkindly. "And yet you expect me to believe you are—in a matter of weeks?"

"Yes," Cole said without flinching. "Because what I feel for Lauren isn't convenient. It isn't strategic. It isn't something I chose. It happened whether I wanted it to or not."

"You've only known her a very short time," William said quietly.

"I know," Cole replied. "And that terrified me at first. But everything about this—about her—feels right. When I'm with Lauren, I don't calculate. I don't plan three steps ahead. I don't wonder what the outcome will be." His jaw tightened. "I just know I don't want a future that doesn't include her."

William studied him for a long moment, his expression unreadable, the silence stretching just long enough to feel intentional.

"And Lauren," he asked at last, his voice steady, "does she feel the same?"

Cole didn't hesitate. Not even for a heartbeat.

"Yes," he said simply.

William nodded once. "I will need to speak to her before I give you an answer."

"I understand," Cole replied. He leaned forward slightly, urgency threading through his control. "But I want you to know this—I promise to make her happy. I would do anything for her. And I will spend the rest of my life proving that I deserve her."

William held his gaze, weighing the words, the conviction behind them.

The silence that followed wasn't heavy. It was deliberate.

And for the first time, Cole felt as though he wasn't just asking for something priceless—

he was beginning to earn it.


Lauren waited in the living room, pacing once, then forcing herself to stop. She stood by the window, hands clasped together, watching the late afternoon light spill across the lawn—but not really seeing it. Every second stretched, taut with anticipation, until it felt like an age had passed.

Finally, the study door opened.

Her father stepped out first.

Lauren straightened instantly. William crossed the room and stopped in front of her, his hands settling gently on her arms, grounding, familiar, steady. He looked at her closely, the way he always had when something truly mattered.

"Is this what you want?" he asked quietly.

She didn't hesitate. Not even for a heartbeat.

"Yes, Father." Her voice was firm, sure. Then softer, truer still: "I love him."

Something shifted in William's expression—relief, pride, certainty. He nodded once.

"That's all I needed to hear," he said simply.

He kissed her cheek, lingering just long enough to convey everything words didn't need to. "Congratulations, sweetheart."

Lauren's breath left her in a rush. She turned—and there was Cole.

He stood just inside the doorway, watching her with an intensity that made her chest ache. No calculation. No restraint. Just open, unmistakable emotion.

She crossed the room to him, and the moment she reached him, his hands came up to cradle her face, his thumb brushing her cheek as if to reassure himself she was really there.

"Well?" she whispered.

His smile was slow, profound, and filled with something unshakable. "He gave me his blessing."

Her eyes filled instantly. She laughed and cried at the same time, pressing her forehead to his.

"I told him I love you," she murmured.

His voice was thick when he answered. "I know. And I told him I intend to spend the rest of my life proving I deserve you."

She slid her arms around his waist, as he pulled her close, holding her there in the quiet of her childhood home—no negotiations, no strategies, no power plays.

Just love.

And forever, finally beginning.

That night, they kept things simple—dinner at the estate with her father. Elena was still in the hospital and wouldn't be home until the following day, which gave Lauren a temporary sense of relief. She wasn't ready for that conversation yet. Not the explanations. Not the fallout. Tonight, she just wanted peace.

The three of them sat together at the long dining table, the atmosphere warm and unhurried. William was in good spirits, asking thoughtful questions, watching Cole with quiet approval. Cole, for his part, was respectful and attentive, never overstepping, never posturing—just present. Lauren noticed it all, the way he listened, the way he met her father's gaze without challenge or insecurity. It made her chest ache with affection.

When dinner ended and Cole prepared to leave, she walked him to the front hall. The house was quiet, the soft glow of the sconces casting gentle shadows along the walls.

Before she could say anything, he pulled her into his arms and kissed her—slow, tender, and deeply certain. The kind of kiss that promised tomorrow without demanding it.

When he rested his forehead against hers, Lauren smiled up at him.

"Can we have dinner tomorrow night?" she asked softly. "I really want you to get to know Gregory properly."

His smile widened, easy and genuine. "I'd love to."

Relief and happiness washed through her. She kissed him once more, lingering this time, before letting him go.

As she watched him leave, Lauren knew the hardest conversations still lay ahead.

Lauren arrived at the restaurant first, the soft evening light of New York filtering through the large windows, casting a warm glow across the elegant interior. She chose a quiet table in the corner, the flicker of candlelight reflecting off her sapphire-blue dress. Her fingers nervously traced the rim of her glass, anticipation and excitement twining in her chest. Cole had been delayed— thirty minutes, he had said—but that gave her a few moments to settle before her oldest friend arrived.

When Gregory appeared, his broad smile and easy stride immediately brightened the space. He closed the distance between them in two quick steps and enveloped her in a warm, familiar hug. "I can't believe my Lauren is actually engaged," he said, his voice full of amusement and awe. "And you look radiant."

Lauren laughed softly, leaning into the embrace for a moment longer than necessary. "I'm in love," she admitted, her eyes glimmering.

Gregory pulled back just enough to look at her, his gaze sharp but affectionate. "I can see that," he said, a knowing smile tugging at the corner of his lips. He gestured to the seat across from her. "You've never looked happier."

She smiled, a little shyly, but full of warmth. "It's… different. Everything feels different with him."

Gregory's expression softened. "I've never seen you this… alive," he said, sliding into the chair opposite her. "It's good to see, Lauren. Really good."

For a moment, the noise of the restaurant faded. It was just the two of them, the easy familiarity of years of friendship giving way to the thrill of new love. Lauren felt her chest lift with the truth she had tried to contain: she had never been more certain of anything in her life.

Then, as if on cue, Cole finally arrived, slipping through the restaurant doors with that effortless presence that always made her heart skip. Lauren's pulse quickened, and Gregory's eyes twinkled knowingly as he watched her face light up. Cole strode to the table, his dark eyes immediately finding Lauren's, a small, teasing smile tugging at his lips.

Gregory stood, extending his hand. "It's good to see you again, Gregory," Cole said smoothly.

"Likewise," Gregory replied with a grin, "I'm looking forward to seeing if you are good enough for my Lauren."

Cole chuckled, a deep, easy sound that resonated through the corner of the restaurant. "I'll try not to disappoint."

That was all it took. The ice broke instantly. Conversation flowed naturally between the two men, each volley of dialogue sparking laughter and camaraderie. Gregory's easy humour and teasing remarks drew genuine chuckles from Cole, who responded with sharp, witty comebacks that had Lauren beaming across the table. They debated light-heartedly over recent business ventures, exchanged travel anecdotes, and even playfully argued over the merits of steak versus seafood. Every so often, Cole's gaze flicked to Lauren, softening with a tenderness that made her chest swell.

When Cole excused himself to the restroom, Gregory leaned slightly closer, his voice low. "I like him," he murmured, an approving glint in his eye.

Lauren smiled, warmth flooding through her. "I'm glad. I wanted you to get along."

"I think I understand why you fell for him," Gregory added, a conspiratorial grin spreading across his face. "He's... solid. Loyal. Smart. And he clearly makes you happy."

Lauren's eyes glistened, the corners crinkling with joy. "He does," she whispered.

When Cole returned, Gregory quipped with a mischievous grin, "I hope this means Lauren will be letting her hair down more often... literally."

Cole laughed, the rich sound drawing a few curious glances. "I certainly hope so. It's a travesty to hide it."

Gregory turned to Lauren, his expression softening. "I like this guy, Lauren. I think he's a keeper."

Cole reached across the table, brushing his fingers against hers. "I'm glad you think so," he murmured, his voice low and sincere. Lauren felt a shiver of warmth at the touch, at the reassurance in his tone. For the first time in a long while, she allowed herself to breathe fully, feeling certain that the people she loved—and who loved her—were all in alignment.

And for that moment, everything else—the obligations, the pressures, the uncertain future—faded. It was just them, laughter and warmth and a quiet certainty that this was right.


After dinner, Cole and Lauren waved goodbye to Gregory as he slid into his Uber. Lauren watched until the car disappeared into the city lights, a soft smile lingering on her lips. Then she turned to Cole, who had already opened the door to his waiting limousine. The sleek black interior reflected the glow of streetlights as they settled into the plush leather seats.

Cole leaned back slightly, his gaze sliding over her with open curiosity—and unmistakable amusement. "So," he drawled, voice easy, unpressured, as if the decision itself belonged entirely to her. "Where to?"

Lauren didn't answer with words. Her fingers brushed his as she leaned in, capturing his mouth in a bold, lingering kiss that left no room for doubt. When she pulled back, just enough to breathe, her voice was low and husky with intent. "Your place," she murmured. "If I don't get you naked soon, I may actually go mad."

Cole's laugh was deep and warm, vibrating through the cabin. He reached up, tucking a loose strand of hair behind her ear, his fingers lingering at her jaw, his thumb brushing her skin with lazy promise. "Mad, hmm?" he said softly, dark eyes glittering. "That's a risk I'm willing to take." His mouth curved. "But fair warning—I plan to drive you absolutely insane first.."

A shiver traced its way down her spine at the promise. Lauren leaned back against the seat, resting her head on his shoulder, breathing him in, letting the anticipation coil tight and delicious between them.

The moment they stepped into his penthouse, restraint vanished.

Lauren's fingers slid into his hair, tugging him closer as if instinct alone guided her, as if she'd been waiting for this exact second. Cole's hands came to her with assured familiarity, every touch deliberate, unhurried, devastating— mapping her, claiming her, reminding her how inevitable this had always been. The space around them—open, private, unmistakably theirs—seemed to magnify everything. The heat. The tension. The certainty thrumming between them.

With effortless strength, Cole lifted her, carrying her down the hall to the bedroom as though there were nowhere else she could possibly belong. He set her down gently, reverently, like something precious—and already his. For a heartbeat, he rested his forehead against hers, breathing her in, grounding himself, before his lips found hers again. The kiss was urgent but restrained, loaded with everything he'd held back.

"I've wanted you like this all night," he confessed, the raw honesty in his voice leaving no room for doubt.

Lauren didn't hesitate. She pressed into him, met his kiss with equal hunger, equal certainty, her hands sliding over him as though she were finally home. The penthouse dissolved. The city beyond the glass fell away.

There was only them—this moment, this pull, and the intoxicating truth neither of them had the strength, nor the desire, to fight any longer.

# Chapter Twenty-One

The next morning, Cole had an early meeting. The sky beyond the windows was just beginning to lighten, the city still wrapped in a rare hush. He dressed quietly, careful not to wake her, but Lauren stirred anyway, blinking sleepily as he turned back toward the bed.

He leaned down and kissed her—slowly, reverently—lingering as though he were committing the moment to memory. There was no urgency in it, no hunger, only warmth and something deeper, steadier. Something that settled in his chest and refused to let go.

"The limousine will take you home," he said softly, brushing his thumb along her cheek. His touch was gentle, unhurried, as though he had nowhere else he needed to be.

She smiled, reaching for his hand. "You'll call?"

"I will," he promised without hesitation, pressing one last kiss to her forehead before forcing himself to straighten and step away.

"I love you," Lauren whispered.

"I love you too."


Those words stayed with Lauren all the way to the Dutton estate—warm, grounding—until the moment she stepped inside.

The house was quiet, sunlight filtering through tall windows.

Then she saw Elena.

She was seated on the sofa, her injured leg elevated on a cushioned ottoman, encased in a rigid brace. Pale. Still. But her eyes—sharp, glittering, alive with something dangerous—tracked Lauren the instant she entered.

"Well," Elena said coolly. "You finally decided to come home."

Lauren's stomach tightened. "Elena… I didn't know you were back. How are you feeling?"

Elena let out a short, humourless laugh. "Physically? Trapped in this brace. Emotionally?" Her gaze hardened. "Betrayed by my own sister."

Lauren stopped a few steps away, her heart pounding. "Elena, I'm sorry. I never meant for this to happen. I didn't plan to fall in love with him."

Elena studied her carefully now, as if dissecting her. Then she smiled—slow, sharp, and cruel.

"And he told you he loves you too, didn't he?"

Lauren hesitated, then nodded. "Yes."

That smile widened. "God, Lauren." Elena shook her head in mock pity. "For someone who prides herself on being intelligent, you're heartbreakingly naïve."

"He does love me," Lauren said, though the words felt suddenly fragile in her mouth.

"No," Elena snapped, her composure cracking just enough to feel real. "He doesn't. He can't. Cole Blackwell doesn't believe in love. He never has. He told me that himself."

Lauren swallowed.

Elena leaned back against the sofa, wincing slightly as she adjusted her leg, then continued—measured now, deliberate. "While I was stuck in a hospital bed, Father came to see me yesterday. We talked. About your engagement. About the company. About succession."

Lauren frowned. "What does that have to do with Cole and I?"

Elena's eyes locked onto hers. "Oh, everything."

She let the word hang, then continued, her voice low and lethal.

"Do you know why Cole and I were going to get married? It wasn't romance. It wasn't affection." Her lips curved in a thin, knowing smile. "It was strategy. Access. Power."

Lauren felt the first real fracture inside her chest.

"He wanted a foothold in the Dutton Group," Elena said calmly. "And I believed I was my father's heir. The controlling interest. The majority vote." She leaned back slightly, watching Lauren's face. "We made it very efficient. Blackwell Capital already holds two proxy seats. His people are embedded in the advisory committee. Preliminary agreements were signed. Succession contingencies were drafted."

Each term landed like a blow—clinical, undeniable.

"This wasn't hypothetical," Elena continued. "It was happening. The framework was in place. All that was left was the marriage contract and the prenup to formalise it."

Lauren's breath came shallow now, her pulse pounding in her ears.

Elena tilted her head, studying her. "And then Father made it clear. Succession wasn't going to me." A pause. Deliberate. "It was going to you."

"So..." Lauren whispered.

"So," Elena said softly, relentlessly. "While you were dazzling investors and charming rooms full of men twice your age, Cole worked it out. You were the real heir. The one Father respects. The one the board listens to." Her gaze sharpened. "The one who would hold the majority."

Lauren swayed slightly, gripping the back of the chair.

"And you," Elena went on, her tone almost conversational, "believe marriage is about love. Not leverage. Not contracts. Not power." A faint smile. "So, Cole adjusted his strategy."

Each word felt surgical.

"He couldn't get what he wanted through me anymore," Elena said. "So, he ended it. And suddenly—miraculously—he fell in love with you."

The room seemed to tilt.

"You think it's coincidence?" Elena pressed. "That the moment he realises you are the successor, he starts looking at you differently? Touching you? Kissing you? Saying all the right things at exactly the right time?"

Lauren's hands curled into fists at her sides, nails biting into her palms as her mind betrayed her. Moments replayed with brutal clarity—the timing she hadn't questioned, the urgency she'd mistaken for passion, the certainty she'd taken on faith.

Too perfect.

Too seamless.

Elena watched the realisation flicker across her sister's face and smiled, slow and satisfied.

"He gave you exactly what you wanted," she said softly, almost kindly. "Love. Promises. A future." Her eyes glittered. "And you walked straight into it."

The words echoed, heavy and suffocating.

Silence pressed down on Lauren's chest, making it hard to breathe. Her throat burned. She wanted—desperately—to argue. To defend him. To say Elena was wrong.

But doubt had already slipped inside her. Cold. Sharp. Lodged deep.

"I trust him," Lauren whispered. The words sounded thin, fragile—more a plea than a declaration. More for herself than for Elena.

Elena's expression didn't soften.

"That's your mistake," she said quietly. "He doesn't want you, Lauren. He wants the company. And once he has it?" She shrugged lightly. "He'll forget about you. Men like him always do."

Something inside Lauren broke—not loudly, not dramatically—but cleanly. Like glass under pressure. Like something that would never fit together the same way again.

Elena leaned forward then, her voice calm, poisonous.

"If you don't believe me," she said, "ask him yourself. Ask him why we were getting engaged. Ask him if he already knew you'd be the heir when he started falling in love with you."

Lauren didn't move.

"Go on," Elena pressed. "If you don't believe your own sister—find out for yourself."

Her gaze dropped pointedly to Lauren's hand.

"That ring," Elena said flatly.

Lauren's breath caught.

"That ring was bought for me," Elena continued. "He hasn't even had the decency to buy you one of your own—like a man in love would. Instead, he lets you wear a ring meant for another woman." Her mouth curved in a thin, merciless smile. "That's not love, Lauren. That's convenience."

Lauren stared at the ring as if seeing it for the first time. What had once felt symbolic now felt wrong—heavy, borrowed, false.

She believed her.

And that belief hurt more than anything Elena could have said.

Because doubt, once planted, had taken root.

And it was already destroying her.


Lauren didn't say another word to Elena. She couldn't—not without shattering completely. She turned and walked out of the room on unsteady legs, each step heavier than the last, her chest tight as if the house itself were pressing in on her.

Upstairs, she closed the door to her bedroom and leaned back against it, eyes squeezed shut. Her heart was racing, her thoughts a tangled, relentless storm. The ring on her finger felt unbearably heavy now. Wrong. She slid it off and set it carefully on the dresser, as though touching it any longer might break her altogether.

There was only one person she could talk to. One person who knew her well enough to hear what she couldn't yet say.

Her hands trembled as she picked up her phone and tapped Gregory's name.

He answered on the second ring.

"Lauren?" His voice shifted instantly—gentle, alert. "What's wrong?"

That was all it took.

"I think I've made a terrible mistake," she said, her voice breaking on the last word.

"Hey—hey," Gregory said softly. "Slow down. I'm here. Talk to me."

She sank onto the edge of the bed, staring at the floor as if it might anchor her. "Elena's home," she said. "She… she told me things. About Cole. About why he was going to marry her."

There was a pause, then, carefully, "Okay. What did she say?"

Lauren swallowed hard. "She said the engagement was never about her. That it was about the Dutton Group. About access. Influence." Her breath hitched. "She said Cole only changed course when he realised I was the heir. That he knew I believed in love—and used that."

Gregory didn't interrupt. He let her speak. He always did.

"And the ring," Lauren continued, her voice hollow now. "Gregory… the ring I'm wearing? He bought it for Elena. Not me. He never even gave me one of my own."

Silence stretched on the line—heavy, careful.

"She told me to ask him," Lauren whispered. "To ask him if he knew I'd inherit the company. To ask him why they were getting engaged in the first place." Her voice cracked. "And the worst part is… I believe her. I don't want to—but I do."

"Lauren," Gregory said gently, "that doesn't mean she's right. It means she knew exactly where to strike."

"I know," she said miserably. "But doubt is there now. And I can't unfeel it. Everything feels… tainted."

Gregory exhaled slowly. "Okay. Listen to me. You are not foolish. You didn't imagine what you felt. And you don't give your heart easily—you never have."

"I gave it to him," she whispered. "And now I don't know if it was real. Or if I was just… convenient."

"Hey," Gregory said firmly, warmth edged with steel now. "You don't get to reduce yourself like that. Not after everything you are."

Tears slid silently down her cheeks. "What if I was wrong about him? What if I let myself believe because I wanted it so badly?"

"Then you do what you've always done," Gregory said softly. "You ask the hard questions. You demand the truth. And you protect your heart until you have it."

She nodded, even though he couldn't see her.

"I'm so scared," she admitted. "Because if Elena's right… I don't think I'll survive it."

Gregory's voice gentled again. "You will. Because you're stronger than you think. And whatever happens, you're not alone. I'm right here."

Lauren closed her eyes, gripping the phone like a lifeline.

"Thank you," she whispered. "I don't know what I'd do without you."

"You don't have to," Gregory replied quietly. "Not now. Not ever."

And for the first time since she'd walked through the front door, Lauren let herself cry—softly, brokenly—held together only by the steady sound of Gregory's voice on the other end of the line.

Lauren knew she couldn't sit with the doubt any longer. It would rot her from the inside if she did. She had to hear it from him—had to look him in the eye and ask the questions that were tearing her apart.

She showered, letting the hot water run until it nearly scalded, hoping it might wash away the ache in her chest. It didn't. When she dressed, she chose simple lines, armour more than clothing, and slid on oversized sunglasses to hide eyes still red and blotchy from crying. She barely recognised the woman staring back at her in the mirror—composed on the surface, fractured underneath.

An hour later, she stepped into the sleek glass tower that housed Cole Blackwell's offices.

Upstairs, Cole was seated at his desk, reviewing reports, absently humming under his breath. He hadn't stopped smiling all morning. Everything felt aligned—his business, his future, his heart. Lauren had rearranged his world in the best possible way, and he wasn't fighting it.

The intercom buzzed.

"Mr Blackwell, there's a Lauren Dutton here to see you."

His smile widened instantly. "Send her in."

He stood as the door opened, already moving toward her, anticipation warm and easy in his chest. But the moment she stepped inside, something shifted.

She didn't smile.

Her posture was rigid; her face guarded behind dark lenses. She didn't remove her sunglasses. And when he reached for her—arms opening automatically— she flinched. It was a small, instinctive movement, but sharp enough to land like a blow.

Cole stopped short, confusion flashing across his face.

"Lauren?" he said quietly. "What's wrong?"

She took a breath, steadying herself, then slowly slid the sunglasses off and met his eyes. The vulnerability there—raw, wounded, barely contained—hit him harder than any accusation ever could.

"We need to talk," she said, her voice controlled, but only just.

His brow furrowed. "Of course." He gestured toward the seating area. "Sit down. Tell me what's going on."

She didn't sit.

She remained standing, hands clenched at her sides, as if sitting might cause her to fall apart completely.

"I want you to tell me the truth," she said.

The air in the room tightened, thick with tension.

Cole's expression shifted—alert now, cautious. "Okay…"

"Why were you going to marry Elena?"

He went very still. She noticed immediately.

"Because she offered a foothold in the Dutton Group," he said at last, his voice steady, unembellished. "When she inherited the company."

The words cut deeper than she expected.

He opened his mouth to continue, but she lifted her hand, stopping him.

"Did you know?" she asked, eyes locked on his. "Before Dubai. Did you know my father intended me to succeed him?"

"No."

Her breath hitched. "Did you work it out while we were there?"

"Yes, but—"

She raised her hand again, firmer this time.

"Which day?" she asked quietly. "The second, or the third?"

He swallowed.

"Third," Cole said finally. Not defensive. Not evasive. Just honest. "I suspected it on the second day. By the third… I was certain."

Silence stretched between them—thick, dangerous, unforgiving.

Her chest tightened painfully.

Lauren felt the last fragile thread inside her snap.

"So, Elena was right," she said quietly. "It started as business."

"Yes," he admitted, his voice low. "But that's not what it became. Not with you."

Her laugh was hollow, broken. "You see the problem, don't you?" she asked. "How am I supposed to separate what's real from what isn't?"

Cole crossed the room slowly, deliberately, stopping a careful distance away. He didn't touch her.

"Because what I feel for you has nothing to do with the Dutton Group."

"How can you say that?" she demanded, emotion finally spilling free. "You fell in love with me at exactly the moment it suited your business interests."

"That's not fair," he said softly.

"Isn't it?" she shot back. "You told me you didn't believe in love. You don't do girlfriends. And suddenly you're proposing—using a ring you bought for my sister."

That one landed.

He winced. "Lauren—"

"Stop," she said, holding up a hand. "I need you to understand something." Her voice shook now. "I didn't fall in love with you because of what you could give me. I can buy my own jewellery—but you let me wear a ring meant for another woman."

"I can fix that."

She shook her head. "Why didn't you think to do it before? Was it because all of this was just convenience?"

"No."

She ignored him. "I fell in love with you because I thought you chose me. *Me.*"

He looked stricken. "I did choose you."

"But did you choose me," she asked, her voice breaking, "or did you choose the company that comes with me?"

The question hung between them, heavy and merciless.

Cole looked at her—really looked at her—and for the first time since she'd walked in, the easy confidence he wore cracked.

"I chose you," he said, fierce and raw.

Tears welled in her eyes, unbidden. "I don't know if I can believe that yet."

She opened her purse, her hands trembling, and pulled out the ring. Crossing the room, she placed it carefully on his desk, the soft clink unbearably loud in the silence.

"Lauren, don't—"

"I need time," she said quietly. "I need space to figure out if what we had was real… or if I just wanted it to be."

She hesitated, then turned toward the door, her heart aching with every step away from him.

Just before she left, she paused.

"I loved you with my whole heart," she said softly.

He answered without hesitation. "I still love you."

She didn't look back.

# Chapter Twenty-Two

Cole didn't move.

The door closed with a soft, final click, and the sound echoed far louder in his head than it should have. For a long moment, he simply stood there, staring at the place where Lauren had been, as if she might reappear if he waited long enough.

She didn't.

The office felt wrong without her—too large, too polished, too empty. The air itself seemed thinner, harder to breathe.

His gaze dropped to the desk.

The ring lay there, a small, gleaming circle of accusation. He stared at it, his chest tightening until it bordered on pain. God, he should have told her. All of it. The moment he'd realised the truth in Dubai. The moment the deal with Elena became irrelevant. The moment his priorities had shifted so violently it had frightened him.

But he hadn't.

He had waited. Managed. Controlled. Assumed there would be time.

Time had been his greatest miscalculation.

Cole dragged a hand through his hair and exhaled sharply, the sound rough, unfamiliar. He had built his life on timing—on precision, on knowing exactly when to act and when to hold back. And yet when it had mattered most, when honesty should have come before strategy, he had failed her.

Elena had beaten him to it.

The thought burned.

Elena, with her half-truths sharpened into weapons, her perfectly placed omissions. She hadn't lied—not outright—but she hadn't needed to. The truth, delivered without context, without the emotion behind it, had been enough to destroy everything.

And Cole had handed her that opportunity.

He turned abruptly and slammed his fist into the wall, the impact sending a dull ache up his arm. He barely registered it. Physical pain was easier. Familiar. This—this hollow, sickening regret—was not.

He should have told Lauren. Should have sat her down, looked her in the eye, and said: *This started as business, but you changed everything. I chose you before you even knew there was a choice.*

Instead, he had let her believe the past was settled. Let her wear a ring that had been meant for another woman. Let silence do the damage.

"Idiot," he muttered to the empty room.

For the first time in his adult life, Cole Blackwell felt something dangerously close to panic.

He replayed her face when she'd asked the question—the exact moment hope fractured into doubt. The way her shoulders had squared, defences rising with painful dignity. She hadn't screamed. She hadn't begged. She had simply withdrawn, taking her heart with her.

That hurt more than anger ever could.

He crossed to the desk and picked up the ring, curling his fingers around it until the diamond bit into his palm. It meant nothing now. Powerless. Useless. A symbol of everything he had once wanted—and everything he had been wrong about.

He had always believed love was a liability.

Now he understood the truth with brutal clarity.

Love was the risk he should have taken sooner.

And if he lost her because he had waited—because he had tried to manage the truth instead of trusting it—he would deserve every second of the emptiness settling into his chest.

Cole straightened slowly, resolve hardening beneath the regret.

This wasn't over.

He had made a mistake—but he would not let it be the final one.

Not when the only woman he had ever loved was walking away believing he had never truly chosen her.

He would fix this.

Even if it cost him everything else.

The Dutton family chapel was quiet in the way only sacred spaces ever were—thick with stillness, heavy with history. Pale afternoon light filtered through the stained-glass windows, casting fractured colours across the stone floor and the simple wooden pews.

Gregory paused just inside the doorway.

Lauren sat at the front, alone.

She hadn't heard him enter—or perhaps she had and simply didn't care. Her shoulders were bowed, her hands clasped so tightly in her lap that her knuckles had gone white. Her hair, usually immaculate, hung loose and unkempt around her face. She looked smaller somehow, drawn inward, as though grief had physically hollowed her out.

The sight of her struck him like a blow to the chest.

She looked like she was wasting away.

Her dress hung looser than it should have, the lines of her body sharper, her posture rigid with exhaustion. Her father had told him she'd spent the last two days down here, and now he believed it. Dark shadows bruised the skin beneath her eyes, her complexion pale in the soft wash of candlelight. Whatever strength she normally radiated—calm, capable, unshakeable—had been stripped bare, leaving only devastation behind.

"Lauren," Gregory said softly.

She flinched at the sound of his voice, then slowly turned. Her eyes were red-rimmed, glassy, rimmed with fatigue and something far worse than tears. Heartbreak.

"Oh," she whispered, as if surprised to see him. "Hi."

Gregory crossed the aisle in long, measured steps and sat beside her on the pew. Up close, it was even worse. Her hands trembled faintly. There was a fragility to her now that terrified him.

"How long have you been here?" he asked gently.

She shrugged, a small, helpless motion. "I don't know. It's quiet here."

That alone told him everything.

"You haven't been eating," he said carefully.

Her lips curved in a faint, humourless smile. "Food feels… unnecessary."

Gregory swallowed hard. "Sleep?"

She shook her head. "Every time I close my eyes, I see his face. Or I hear his voice. Or I hear my sister's."

The words cracked on the last syllable.

Gregory's jaw tightened. He resisted the urge to pull her into his arms—not because he didn't want to, but because she looked like she might shatter if he touched her too suddenly.

"I'm worried about you," he said quietly.

She finally looked at him then—really looked at him. Her composure fractured, just for a moment.

"I don't know how to fix this," she whispered. "I don't know how to trust what was real and what wasn't. I don't know how to stop loving him, and I don't know how to survive loving him either."

Tears slipped free, silent, and devastating, tracing slow paths down her cheeks.

Gregory reached out then, unable to stop himself, and covered her clasped hands with his own. They were cold.

"You don't have to fix anything right now," he said firmly, anchoring his voice for her when she clearly couldn't. "You just have to breathe. Eat. Sleep. Let the people who love you hold the weight for a while."

She shook her head weakly. "I trusted him," she said. "I trusted myself." Her breath hitched. "And I was wrong."

"No," Gregory said at once. "You weren't wrong to love. You weren't wrong to believe in him. That part—that part was brave."

She let out a broken sound that was halfway between a laugh and a sob, then folded forward, pressing her forehead against her clasped hands.

Gregory stood and pulled her gently into his chest, this time not hesitating. She went willingly, collapsing against him as though she'd been holding herself upright by sheer force of will alone.

He wrapped his arms around her, holding her as she finally cried—quiet, wrecked sobs shaking her thin frame.

"I feel like I'm disappearing," she whispered against his shoulder.

"You're not," Gregory said fiercely, tightening his hold. "I've got you. I'm not going anywhere. And neither is the woman you are. This pain doesn't get to erase you."

She clung to him, breathing unevenly, tears soaking into his shirt as the chapel held them in its silence.

Gregory stared ahead, jaw set.

Cole Blackwell had done this—whether he'd meant to or not.

And Gregory knew, with absolute certainty, that something was going to have to change.


Three days.

That was how long it had been since Cole had last seen Lauren walk out of his office without looking back.

It felt like a lifetime.

His penthouse was unbearably quiet. His bed cold and untouched. His phone a constant weight in his hand—every vibration a disappointment, every silence a reminder. He had sent flowers the first day. White lilies. Her favourite. No response. Text messages followed—measured at first, then raw, honest, stripped of pride.


*Please talk to me.*

*I know I hurt you, but I love you.*

*I'm not giving up on us.*


Nothing.

No reply. No acknowledgement. Not even a rejection.

Cole sat behind his desk now, staring at a financial report he hadn't absorbed a single word of. He hadn't slept properly. Hadn't shaved. The sharp edge he usually carried—the confidence, the control—had dulled, worn thin by absence.

The intercom buzzed.

"Mr Blackwell, Gregory Wade is here to see you."

Cole looked up sharply. His pulse kicked. "Send him in."

The door opened moments later, and Gregory stepped inside. He took one look at Cole and stopped short.

"Well," Gregory said slowly, shutting the door behind him. "You look like hell."

Cole huffed a humourless breath. "Nice to see you too."

Gregory didn't sit. He crossed the room, arms folded, eyes sharp and assessing—the same intensity Lauren used when she was cutting through nonsense.

"She hasn't spoken to me," Cole said quietly. "Nothing."

"She's spent the last three days in the family chapel," Gregory replied. "I don't think she even knows you've sent flowers or texted."

Cole's chest tightened at the thought. She was suffering because of him.

"She's barely eaten. Barely slept," Gregory continued, his voice low, almost pained. "I'm genuinely worried about her."

Silence settled between them—dense, heavy, but not hostile.

Gregory exhaled slowly, lifting his gaze to meet Cole's squarely. "All right," he said, voice firm, just enough to make Cole take notice. "I'm going to ask you something, and I want the truth. No corporate spin. No strategy. No carefully chosen words."

Cole straightened, bracing himself instinctively. "Okay."

"Do you love my best friend?"

The question landed clean, unyielding. There was nowhere to hide.

"Yes," Cole said immediately, without hesitation, without qualifiers. "I love her."

Gregory watched him carefully, searching his face, his posture, the tension in his jaw. Cole didn't look away. Didn't soften it. Didn't try to justify it.

After a long moment, Gregory nodded once.

"Good," he said. "Because if I thought for even a second you didn't, I wouldn't be standing here."

Cole swallowed. "I know I hurt her."

"You did," Gregory agreed. "Badly."

"I never lied to her about my feelings."

"No," Gregory said quietly. "But you didn't tell her everything when it mattered."

Cole closed his eyes briefly. "I know."

Gregory moved closer, resting a hand on the back of the chair opposite the desk but still didn't sit. "Lauren doesn't doubt your intelligence or your ambition. She doubts whether she was chosen—or simply convenient."

"That's not what she was to me," Cole said, his voice roughening. "She was never that."

"Then you'd better prove it," Gregory replied. "Because right now, all she can hear is Elena's voice in her head."

Cole's jaw tightened. "Elena twisted everything."

"Of course she did," Gregory said. "That woman had always caused problems for Lauren. But doubt doesn't need truth to grow. It just needs silence."

Cole looked up sharply. "So, what do I do?"

Gregory studied him for a moment, then finally pulled out the chair, and sat.

"You stop chasing her with flowers and words," he said calmly. "She's heard the words. Now she needs certainty."

"How?" Cole demanded. "She won't even see me."

Gregory leaned forward. "You show her—without asking for anything back—that she comes first. Before the Dutton Group. Before strategy. Before leverage."

Cole frowned. "What does that look like?"

"It looks like risk," Gregory said simply. "Real risk. The kind you can't spin."

Cole leaned back, the weight of it settling in. "I'd walk away from the company deal."

Gregory's brows lifted slightly. "Would you?"

"Yes," Cole said without pause. "If that's what it takes."

Gregory nodded again, more firmly this time. "Then you start there."

Cole met his gaze. "You believe me."

"I do," Gregory said. "And I don't do that lightly."

He stood, smoothing his jacket. "Lauren loves deeply. But once she feels like someone's love came with conditions…" He shook his head. "That cuts her to the bone."

Cole's voice was low. "I never meant to hurt her."

"I know," Gregory said. "But intent doesn't erase impact."

He turned toward the door, then paused.

"One more thing."

Cole looked up.

"If you want her back," Gregory said quietly, "you don't convince her you love her. You show her she doesn't have to compete with anything for you ever again."

The door closed softly behind him.

Cole sat there for a long moment, staring at nothing.

Then he reached for his phone—not to text her, not to plead—but to make a decision.

Because for the first time in his life, winning wasn't about strategy.

It was about choosing her.

# Chapter Twenty-Three

Cole didn't hesitate.

The moment Gregory's words settled, something inside him aligned with brutal clarity. This wasn't a negotiation. This wasn't strategy. This was the only move that mattered.

He picked up the phone.

"Cancel the call with Zurich," he said when his assistant answered. "And clear my schedule. I need the board—now."

Within the hour, Cole stood at the head of the long glass table, the skyline stretching behind him like a reminder of everything he'd built. His executives watched him carefully, sensing the shift before he spoke.

"I'm withdrawing Blackwell Capital from any present or future negotiations involving the Dutton Group," he said evenly.

Silence slammed into the room.

One of the board members blinked. "Cole—this partnership puts us in an unparalleled position—"

"I know exactly what it does," Cole cut in. "Which is why I'm ending it."

Another voice cut in, sharper. "This was months in the making."

"And it's done," Cole replied. "Effective immediately. No proxy seats. No preliminary agreements. No succession contingencies. Nothing."

They stared at him as if he'd lost his mind.

He hadn't.

"This isn't a pause," he continued, tone calm, unshakeable. "It's a full withdrawal. Put it in writing. Issue the releases. I don't want ambiguity. I don't want leverage lingering in the margins."

A beat of stunned silence passed.

"May we ask why?" someone finally ventured.

Cole's jaw set—not with anger, but with absolute conviction. "Because I refuse to build my future on something that cost me the woman I love."

No one argued. No one could.

Cole didn't wait for permission. He turned and walked out, decision final, power cleanly severed.


Next stop: the ring.

The thought hit him hard as he moved down the corridor. He'd been an idiot—an unforgivable one—to let the woman he loved wear a ring meant for her sister. Worse, he hadn't even chosen it himself. He'd delegated it. Handed the task to a personal shopper like it was a line item on a list. Efficient. Impersonal. Empty.

That ring meant nothing.

The one he wanted Lauren to wear—if she ever would—had to come from him. From his hands. From his heart.

It couldn't be safe. Or convenient. Or expected.

It had to be unique. Bold. Intelligently designed. Elegant without being delicate. Strong without being loud. A piece that didn't apologise for taking up space.

Just like her.

Cole slowed, resolve settling deep and steady in his chest.

If he was going to ask her to trust him again—if he was going to ask her to choose him—then this time, every choice would be his.

No shortcuts.

No strategies.

No substitutions.

Only the truth.


Lauren's footsteps echoed softly against the polished floors of the Dutton estate as she entered the house from the chapel. Her heart still felt heavy, weighed down by the doubts and revelations of the past. She barely noticed the quiet elegance of the foyer until a familiar voice called softly from the study.

"Lauren," her father said.

She turned to see William Dutton standing there, arms open. He pulled her into a firm, reassuring hug—the kind that made her feel both small and entirely safe at once. "Come, sit with me," he said, guiding her to one of the deep leather chairs by his desk.

Lauren sank into the seat as he took the one opposite her. His eyes searched hers, steady and unwavering. "I know you're struggling," he began gently. "Struggling to believe that Cole loves you… for you—and not for the company."

She swallowed hard, the question still raw in her mind.

"I want you to hear this from me," he continued. "When he came to me to ask for your hand… I was completely convinced. And I still am. Cole Blackwell loves you, Lauren."

He let that sink in before continuing quietly. "He showed me in every way a man could—the way he carried himself, the way he looked at you, the way he talked about you."

"When Elena and he were thinking about getting engaged, I never even had that conversation with him—because he didn't care about Elena. She was a means to an end."

"But when you returned from Dubai and asked to speak with me privately, it was a big deal for him. He told me he never thought he'd be having this conversation with the father of a woman he loved. But he loved you enough to want to do it right."

"He didn't hesitate. He didn't try to finesse it. He wanted it right… because he loves you. He was nervous, yes, but he understood how important it was. That alone should tell you everything you need to know."

Lauren blinked, the lump in her throat making it hard to speak.

"And if that isn't enough," her father added, reaching for a folder on his desk, "then you need to know this." He slid it across to her. "Blackwell Capital has just sent a press release to their shareholders. They are stepping away from any interest in the Dutton Group—permanently. No proxy seats. No preliminary agreements. No succession contingencies. They've withdrawn entirely."

Her hands trembled as she took the papers, reading the bold declaration. The words burned through the fog of doubt clouding her heart. She looked up at her father, awe and relief mingling in her gaze.

"Lauren," he said softly, leaning back, his expression calm but resolute, "trust me. He chose you. Not the company. Not convenience. You."

For the first time in days, Lauren allowed herself to believe it. The relief was overwhelming but then she started to think, will he forgive me for doubting him.

She looked up at her father, her green eyes wide and uncertain, vulnerability finally surfacing. "Is… is he going to forgive me?" she asked quietly, her voice trembling with a mix of fear and hope. "For doubting him?"

William Dutton's expression softened, and he leaned forward slightly, placing a reassuring hand over hers. "Lauren," he said, steady and patient, "if he didn't love you—truly, completely—you wouldn't even be asking that question. The fact that it matters to you tells me everything you need to know about him. He's not perfect. He's not without pride. But he loves you, and love—real love—survives doubt, if both sides are willing to fight for it."

Lauren swallowed, her throat tight, trying to absorb the certainty in her father's voice. She wanted to believe him, wanted to let it anchor her, but a part of her still trembled.

"Remember," he continued gently, "he asked for your hand because he wanted you. Not the company, not appearances, not convenience. You. And the fact that he risked that—because of how he feels about you—means he already knows the real stakes. And he's willing to take them."

Lauren let out a slow, shaky breath, the weight of fear and guilt battling against the flicker of hope blossoming inside her. "I just… I don't want to lose him," she whispered.

"You won't," her father said firmly, his eyes locking with hers. "Not if you're honest, and not if you let him know you trust him the way he's trusted you. He'll forgive you, Lauren. Because love like this… it doesn't disappear overnight. It fights. And so should you."

Lauren lingered in the study a moment longer, letting her father's words settle in her chest like a lifeline. Her doubts still flickered at the edges of her mind, but for the first time in days, hope had a foothold. She took a deep, steadying breath and looked up at William.

"Thank you, Dad," she said softly, her voice trembling with gratitude. "For believing in me… and in him, even when I couldn't."

He smiled, a quiet, knowing expression. "You're stronger than you think, Lauren. Now go. Fix this. Before doubt has another chance to take hold."

Her heart pounded as she left the study, closing the door gently behind her. Upstairs, she moved quickly through the halls, almost running, urgency lifting her in a way she hadn't felt in days. She reached her room and closed the door, locking the quiet behind her. The decision was made. She was going to see Cole. She was going to tell him she loves him—and beg him to take her back.

First, she needed to feel like herself again. She stripped off her day clothes and stepped into a hot shower, letting the water wash away the heaviness clinging to her like a second skin. She lingered beneath it, imagining him waiting, imagining the warmth of his presence and the intensity of his gaze.

When she stepped out, she wrapped herself in a towel, her mind racing with a thousand things she wanted to say—and a thousand she feared she might stumble over. She dressed carefully, choosing an outfit that was effortless yet elegant: something that made her feel confident, that reminded her that she was worth loving not for what she could offer, but for who she was. Her hair fell in soft waves over her shoulders, her lips were subtly tinted, her eyes brightened to catch his attention.

Once ready, she grabbed her phone and ordered a town car, her fingers trembling with anticipation. Each passing minute stretched unbearably as she waited for it to arrive. She checked herself one last time in the mirror, taking a deep breath and whispering to her reflection, "I can do this. I have to do this."

The car pulled up outside the building, sleek and black, waiting like a silent accomplice. She slid inside, pressing a palm against the cool leather seat as the city blurred past the windows. Her stomach twisted with nerves, but beneath it was an unshakable determination.

The penthouse came into view—a shimmering tower of glass and steel against the late afternoon sky. Lauren's pulse quickened as she stepped out of the car, smoothing her dress and bracing herself for what awaited inside.

The concierge greeted her politely. "How can I help you?"

"I'm here to see Cole Blackwell. Lauren Dutton," she said.

"Ah, Miss Dutton," he replied, a knowing glance. "Mr. Blackwell instructed that if you arrived, to send you straight up."

"Thank you," she said, her voice steady despite the fluttering in her chest.

The concierge led her to the private elevator, swiped his card, and pressed the penthouse button. The doors slid closed, and her heart jumped with a mixture of hope and fear.

She took a steadying breath, lifted her chin, and tried to summon all the confidence and love she could muster. She had come this far. Now it was time to face him—and hope he would open his arms to her again.

Cole stood on his balcony, gazing out at the bustling city below, every thought consumed by her. He missed her—more than he had allowed himself to admit. Then the elevator dinged. His chest tightened. He had instructed the concierge to send only one person straight up. Could it be her?

The elevator doors slid open with a quiet whoosh, revealing the sleek marble floor of Cole's penthouse. Lauren stepped out, heels clicking softly against the polished surface. She froze for a heartbeat, taking in the expansive space—the floor-to-ceiling windows, the muted lighting, the city sprawling endlessly beyond. It was all Cole: precise, controlled, untouchable.

Then she saw him.

Cole turned at the sharp echo of her heels, and for a suspended moment, neither of them moved. The expansive penthouse seemed to shrink, the city beyond the windows melting into a distant, muted hum. Every thought, every doubt, every ache of longing crystallised in his gaze as it locked onto hers.

"Lauren," he breathed, his voice low, rough, threaded with a vulnerability he rarely allowed anyone to see.

She swallowed hard, her pulse hammering in her ears. Step by tentative step, she closed the distance between them, hands trembling slightly. "Cole… I—forgive me," she whispered, her voice trembling with the weight of everything left unsaid.

He moved then, like a force of inevitability, closing the gap in an instant. Arms encircling her, pulling her close, grounding her. "There's nothing to forgive," he murmured against her hair, his chest warm against hers. His voice softened, edged with an honesty that made her heart stutter. "Do you… forgive me?"

She couldn't wait. She cupped his face in her hands, feeling the tension there, the longing, the restrained passion he tried so hard to contain. Her lips found his, trembling at first, then firm, demanding, seeking.

Cole didn't hesitate. His hands threaded into her hair, holding her as if she were the only thing in the world that truly mattered. The kiss deepened, fierce and unrelenting, as if the days of pain, doubt, and distance had been condensed into this single, electric moment. Every hesitation, every misstep, every misunderstanding melted away beneath the intensity of their reunion.

When they finally broke apart—just enough to breathe—their foreheads rested together, hearts hammering in sync. His eyes, dark and intense, searched hers as if memorising every flicker of emotion.

"I've missed you," he whispered, his voice hoarse.

"I've missed you so much," she breathed back, her hands still pressed against him, anchoring herself in the undeniable truth: they had found each other again, and nothing would make her let go this time. "I'm sorry."

"There is nothing for you to apologise for," he said gently. "There was nothing wrong with you being afraid," he said quietly. "Loving someone is scary."

He brushed a soft kiss over the tip of her nose. "And I love you more than anything, Lauren. I need you to believe that."

"I do," she whispered. "And I love you too."

Something in his expression softened—relief, devotion, something dangerously close to reverence.

Then he kissed her again—slowly at first, savouring the reunion, the relief, the certainty. But the restraint didn't last. It shattered, replaced by a consuming need that neither of them tried to stop. Their lips moved together with desperate precision, every touch, every brush of skin igniting the passion they had fought so hard to contain.

Cole's hands roamed her back, pulling her flush against him, while hers traced the hard planes of his chest, memorising, claiming. The kiss deepened—urgent, electric, overwhelming—a release of weeks of tension, longing, and suppressed emotion.

When they finally broke apart, both of them gasping for air, their foreheads rested together once more, breaths mingling, hearts racing in unison.

Cole took her hand and guided her gently to the sofa. "Wait here," he murmured.

She nodded, her pulse still racing.

He disappeared into the bedroom and returned moments later, something small cradled in his palm. Without hesitation, he dropped to one knee.

Lauren's breath caught. Tears spilled freely now.

He opened his hand, revealing a stunning square-cut emerald, flanked by large diamonds on either side—bold, striking, unmistakable.

"Marry me, Lauren," he said, his voice steady but thick with emotion. "Not because of business. Not because of legacy. Not because of anything that comes with you. But because I love you. All of you. Only you."

She couldn't speak. She only nodded, tears streaming down her cheeks.

Cole slid the ring onto her finger, his hands steady, reverent.

"I chose this for you," he said softly. "Because the colour reminded me of your eyes. And because it's unique and bold—just like you."

Lauren looked down at her hand, then back at him, her heart so full it felt like it might break open.

"Yes," she whispered, voice shaking with joy. "Always yes."

# Epilogue

Lauren walked the marble-lined halls of Dutton-Blackwell, the soft click of her heels echoing through a space that had once felt intimidating—and now felt like home. Sunlight streamed through towering glass walls, casting reflections over the company's crest etched into polished stone: two legacies, now one.

She smiled to herself as she made her way towards her husband's office.

Five years.

It hardly felt real sometimes.

Today was their anniversary, and despite the years that had passed, her heart still fluttered when she thought of Cole—of the man who had once believed love was a liability and now built his life around it.

Her thoughts drifted, unbidden, back to their wedding day.

Cole had insisted on a celebration worthy of history. She'd argued gently—told him she would have been perfectly content with family, a few close friends, and the quiet reverence of the Dutton family chapel. But he had shaken his head, cupping her face with absolute certainty.

"I want the world to see you," he'd said. "To know that you chose me—and that I chose you."

And so, it had been the wedding of the century.

She would never forget the moment the doors opened and she stepped into the aisle on her father's arm. The hush that fell over the crowd. The way Cole's breath caught as if the world itself had stilled. The devotion written so plainly across his face it stole hers away.

Not pride.

Not possession.

Love.

Pure and unguarded.

And in the front row, Elena had been smiling—truly smiling. Not the polished, social smile she had perfected over the years, but something softer. Real. Lauren remembered the way her sister's eyes had shone, the squeeze of her hand just before the ceremony began.

Not long before the wedding, Elena had come to her quietly, almost nervously, and confessed she was in love. Really in love. With Troy. A man who hadn't impressed her with wealth or status, but with laughter, steadiness, and the simple way he saw her.

Lauren had been genuinely happy for her.

And Elena, in a moment of rare honesty, had laughed and admitted the truth they had both always known—that a marriage between her and Cole would have been a disaster. What Cole and Lauren shared was something entirely different. Something neither of them could have manufactured, no matter how carefully they tried.


Her father had lived two more years after that day. Long enough to see both his daughters settled, fulfilled, and thriving. Long enough to hold his grandson—William Henry Blackwell—born exactly twelve months after the wedding, a perfect, solemn little miracle with his father's eyes and the unmistakable Dutton determination already etched into his gaze.

The light of their lives.

Lauren swallowed softly at the memory, gratitude and love wrapping around her heart as surely as it always had.

She and Cole had spoken to her father often during those final months—about the future, about the company, about legacy. It had been William himself who had smiled and said, "Merging the two would make me very proud."

And so, they had.

One year after his passing, Blackwell Capital and The Dutton Group became Dutton-Blackwell. The transition, though monumental, had been far smoother than either of them had expected. Perhaps because it had never been about power.

It had always been about partnership.

Lauren slowed as she reached Cole's office. Andrew, Cole's longtime assistant, looked up from his desk with a knowing grin.

"Morning."

"Good morning," she replied warmly. "Is he available?"

Andrew chuckled. "For you? He always is."

She smiled in thanks and knocked lightly on the door.

"Come in," Cole's voice called.

The moment she stepped inside, his head lifted. His expression softened instantly, that familiar, devastating smile spreading across his face. He rose without hesitation and came around the desk, already reaching for her.

"There's my mother-to-be," he said, sliding a hand over her gently swollen belly, reverent as ever, as if the simple act still amazed him. His palm lingered there, warm, and protective. "How's the little one today?"

Lauren laughed softly, covering his hand with hers. "Gymnastics, I think. Either that or plotting world domination."

Cole grinned, the familiar spark lighting his eyes as he leaned in to press a tender kiss to her temple. "Must run in the family."

She relaxed fully against him, breathing him in—the scent of him, the solid reassurance of his arms. Five years later, and he could still undo her with a touch. With a look. With the quiet certainty of belonging she felt every time he held her like this.

"Happy anniversary," she whispered, her voice thick with emotion. "You should have woken me."

He chuckled softly. "Every day with you is an anniversary," he said, brushing his thumb along her arm. "And besides, I didn't want to disturb you. You looked so peaceful." His mouth curved, unmistakably cheeky. "And I knew you didn't get much sleep last night."

She slapped his chest lightly, laughter spilling free. "I'm not complaining," she said, then tipped her head back to smile up at him. "Are you?"

He pulled back just enough to meet her eyes, his expression full of devotion and mischief in equal measure. "Not on your life."

Her heart swelled, full to the point of aching—of love, of history, of the future growing beneath her ribs. This life. This man. This family they had built together.

"Oh," she added casually, though her eyes sparkled, "Gregory is taking William for the night."

Cole's brows lifted, slow understanding dawning.

"So," she continued, sliding her arms around his neck, "I thought I might spoil my husband."

His smile turned downright dangerous as he drew her closer, one arm firm around her waist, the other still resting protectively over her belly. "Best anniversary gift I could ask for," he murmured. Then his voice lowered, warm and certain. "But I think it's my turn to spoil you."

He bent his head and kissed her—slow, unhurried, the kind of kiss built from years of knowing exactly how to touch her. When he finally pulled back, his forehead rested against hers, his eyes closed for a brief moment as something old and distant surfaced in his mind.

There had been a time when he'd believed love was a liability. A weakness. A risk no rational man should take. He'd built his life on control, strategy, certainty—on never needing anyone.

God, how wrong he'd been.

The last five years had been the best of his life. Better than any deal he'd closed. Better than any victory he'd ever claimed. Their son—four years old now, curious, and fearless, already too smart for his own good—was the centre of his world. And their daughter would arrive in only a few short months, already rewriting his heart in ways he hadn't known were possible.

He opened his eyes and smiled at the woman who had given him all of it.

"Do you know how lucky I feel?" he asked softly, brushing his nose against hers, the gesture intimate and instinctive. "Every single day."

She smiled back, just as tender. "As lucky as me."

Then her expression shifted, turning serious in that way that always had his full attention. "You have made me the happiest wife I could ever have hoped for," she said quietly. "I never doubt your love. You cherish me every day, in all the small ways that matter most." Her voice wavered just slightly. "And I want you to know how grateful I am for that. I love you, Cole. I always will."

Something tightened in his chest. His smile wobbled, his eyes turning suspiciously glassy, emotion he never bothered to hide from her anymore.

"I love you more," he said, voice thick but steady. "Forever."

He pulled her into him, holding her as if this—*this*—was the axis his entire world turned on.

And for both of them, standing there wrapped in love, laughter, and everything
they had fought for, built, and chosen—there was no greater success than that.

# The End

# Before You Go…

If you fell for these characters and want more love stories filled with emotion, passion, and second chances, my newsletter is where I share them first.

**You'll receive:**

- 💜 Early access to new releases

- 💜 Exclusive reader-only content and extras

**Join my reader list here:** https://alisonreidauthor.com

I'd love to welcome you.

# Alison Reid

# Thank you for reading Forbidden Hearts!

If you enjoyed this collection of irresistible alpha heroes, keep an eye out for more upcoming romance collections by Alison Reid, including:

**Alpha Kings** - *A Billionaire Alpha Male Romance Collection*

**Cautious Hearts** - *A Trust-After-Heartbreak Romance Collection*

**Dark & Dangerous** - *Brooding Heroes Romance Collection*

**Final Surrender** - *Alpha Heroes Yielding to Love Collection*

**Forever Mine** - *A Longing-for-Love Romance Collection*

**Guarded Hearts** - *A Surrender to Love Romance Collection*

**Hearts & Secrets** - *Small Town Romance Collection*

**Hearts in Peril** - *A Suspenseful Romance Collection*

**Hidden Truths** - *A Secret Identity Romance Collection*

**Lies & Hearts** - *A Lies, Secrets & Betrayal Romance Collection*

**Love After Regret** - *A Second-Chance Redemption Romance Collection*

**Misjudged Hearts** - *A Love After Judgement Romance Collection*

**Torn Between Hearts** - *A Love Triangle Romance Collection*

All of Alison Reid's books feature standalone stories, swoon-worthy heroes, and guaranteed happily-ever-afters.

# Books by Alison Reid

A Billionaire for Christmas

A Heart in Florence

After The Storm

Always You

Before I Fell

Before the Thaw

Beneath the Lies

Billionaire Bodyguard

Billionaire Rancher

Blueprints of the Heart

Branlow

Collide

Echoes of Deception

Falling for the Billionaire

Forever Yours

Heart of the Outback

Hearts on the Line

Hidden Gem

Kept Promises

Mended Hearts

Mistaken Hearts

New Year's Eve Kiss

Quiet Danger

Reckless Hearts

Reflections of Deception

Second Glance

Shadows of the Past

Shattered Dreams

Shattered Hope, Stolen Kisses

Still Yours

The Billionaire's Accidental Legacy

The Billionaire's Bargain

The Billionaire's Mistake

The Billionaire's Regret

The Billionaire's Secret Baby

The Billionaire's Unexpected Heir

The Blood Debt

The Playboy's Surrender

The Wrong Sister

Trust in Time

Undercover Billionaire

Until you Loved Me

Vows of Vengeance

Wife in Name Only

# Find all my books on Amazon:



# About the Author

Alison Reid writes contemporary and small-town romance filled with heart, passion, and second-chance love stories. Her novels feature strong heroines, irresistible heroes, and the happily-ever-afters readers adore.

Before turning her love of storytelling into a publishing career, Alison spent thirty-five years working as an engineer—proof that happily-ever-afters can be built as carefully as any blueprint. She began writing as a hobby during the COVID lockdowns and quickly discovered a passion she couldn't ignore.

Alison is happily married, has two grown children, and shares her home with two beautiful dogs who are convinced they deserve to be her main characters. When she's not writing, she enjoys reading, spending time with her family, and imagining new love stories. She hopes her books give readers a few hours of escape, joy, and swoon-worthy romance they won't soon forget.